Fiona Tomlinson

Deborah Challinor is a freelance writer
and historian living in New South
Wales. She is the author of many best-
sellers including *Isle of Tears* and the
trilogy *Kitty*, *Amber* and *Band of Gold*,
and several non-fiction titles including
Who'll Stop the Rain? and *Grey Ghosts*.

BOOKS BY THE SAME AUTHOR:

Children of War trilogy
  Tamar
  White Feathers
  Blue Smoke

Trilogy
  Kitty
  Amber
  Band of Gold

Isle of Tears

Grey Ghosts

Fire

Union Belle

Who'll Stop the Rain?

TAMAR

Deborah CHALLINOR

📖 HarperCollins*Publishers*

This novel is a work of fiction. Any references to historical events; to real
people, living or dead; or to real locales are intended only to give the fiction a
sense of reality and authenticity. Other names, places, characters and incidents
are either the product of the author's imagination or used fictitiously, and
their resemblance, if any, to real-life counterparts is entirely coincidental.

HarperCollins*Publishers*

First published in 2002
This edition published in 2012
by HarperCollins*Publishers (New Zealand) Limited*
PO Box 1, Shortland Street, Auckland 1140

Copyright © Deborah Challinor 2012

HarperCollins*Publishers*

31 View Road, Glenfield, Auckland 0627, New Zealand
Level 13, 201 Elizabeth Street, Sydney NSW 2000, Australia
A 53, Sector 57, Noida, UP, India
77–85 Fulham Palace Road, London W6 8JB, United Kingdom
2 Bloor Street East, 20th floor, Toronto, Ontario M4W 1A8, Canada
10 East 53rd Street, New York, NY 10022, USA

National Library of New Zealand Cataloguing-in-Publication Data

Challinor, Deborah.
Tamar / Deborah Challinor.
Originally published: 2002.
ISBN 978-1-86950-775-6
I.Title.
NZ823.3—dc 22

ISBN: 978 1 86950 775 6

Cover design by Priscilla Nielsen
Cover images by shutterstock.com
Typesetting by Springfield West

Printed by Griffin Press, Australia

50gsm Bulky News used by HarperCollins*Publishers* is a natural, recyclable product
made from wood grown in sustainable plantation forests. The manufacturing processes
conform to the environmental regulations in the country of origin, New Zealand.

This book is for my husband, Aaron Paul,
who paid for everything while I wrote it.

Part One

❧

Tamar
1879–1887

CHAPTER ONE

Plymouth, March 1879

Tamar Deane had read her dead sister's letter so many times the writing was almost illegible. Poor, dear Brigid, she thought, adjusting her perch on the tin trunk holding all her worldly possessions. Carefully folding the worn pages, she slipped them into a pocket of her cloak and concentrated on the chaos around her. She wished she knew what she was supposed to do next.

She was sitting on a windy quay at the Port of Plymouth waiting to board the ship *Rebecca Jane,* bound for Auckland, New Zealand. Professional outfitters dashed past, looking for customers who had forgotten to pick up goods ordered for the long trip, and hawkers loudly advertised their wares in the hope of tempting emigrants to make last-minute purchases.

'Marine soap,' warbled one toothless old crone carrying a tray around her scrawny neck. 'Pins an' needles, thread an' tape, best quality, pegs fer yer shipboard washin'!' She bent in front of Tamar and rasped into her face, 'Get yer purse out, missy. Support a poor ol' woman!'

Recoiling from the woman's sour breath, Tamar stood smartly. 'No, thank you, I don't need soap.'

'Come on, missy,' urged the hag, grasping a fold of Tamar's cloak and tugging tenaciously. 'Don't be a Shylock, I can see yer not short of a penny.'

'*No!*' blurted Tamar, alarmed now. 'Leave me alone!'

Suddenly the old crone's tray went tumbling, sending her scrabbling after the scattered contents on her bony hands and knees.

'God bugger ma bloody days! Can a body no' even emigrate wi'out being pawed at? Get out o' here, ye scraggy auld witch!'

Tamar jumped at the strident curse uttered only inches from her ear. Standing beside her was a petite woman, surprisingly small for the timbre of her voice, with a pronounced bust above a tiny waist and an abundance of glossy, deep red hair piled high on her head with a slightly silly hat balanced on top.

'Sodding wind,' the woman muttered as she hunched forward to light a cigarette inside the protection of a startling indigo coat worn over a bright orange dress. The tobacco finally caught and she straightened, inhaled mightily and shot a twin plume of smoke out through her small, upturned nose.

'That's better,' she said to Tamar. 'Used to smoke a pipe but it wasnae good for business. Changed to cigarettes. Much more elegant, d'ye no' think?'

Startled, but not wishing to seem impolite, Tamar nodded.

'Ma name's Myrna McTaggart, from Edinburgh. I saw ye in the barracks last night. Emigrating, are ye?' she asked, waving a finely manicured hand towards the *Rebecca Jane*.

'Yes, I am,' Tamar replied cautiously. 'I'm going to New Zealand.' She hesitated for a second, then added, 'I'm Tamar Deane, from Truro.'

'Aye, Cornwall — I thought so. Ye've the accent, but ye dinnae sound like *poor* Cornish. Why were ye staying in yon poxy barracks if ye've a cabin booked?'

'I've not got a cabin booked,' answered Tamar. 'I'm going steerage.'

'Have ye no money then?' persisted Myrna McTaggart. 'Ye *sound* like ye do.'

'No, I'm not wealthy. Our mam taught us to speak properly, that's all.'

Myrna McTaggart turned, clearly looking for Tamar's mother. 'Where's the rest of ye family, lassie?'

Tamar felt tears beginning to prickle her eyes. No, she thought, I will not cry. 'I have no family,' she replied bluntly. 'They died. I'm emigrating by myself.'

'No!' exclaimed Myrna McTaggart. 'Ye're just a bairn!'

'I am not! I'm seventeen years old!' Tamar replied in a defiant but dangerously wobbly voice. Then, to her dismay, defiance turned to misery and her bottom lip quivered. She covered her face with her hands.

The older woman immediately moved closer and rested a light hand on Tamar's arm. 'I'm sorry for prying, lassie,' she said. 'I didnae mean to upset ye.'

'You haven't,' lied Tamar. 'Only I'm not sure what will happen when I get to New Zealand. Or even what I'm supposed to do now.'

Myrna shook her head sympathetically and led Tamar back to her trunk. 'Sit down, lassie,' she said soothingly. 'Ye're upset. Tell me all about it.'

So Tamar, grateful for someone to talk to, did.

In the nine months since Brigid's letter had arrived in June of the previous year, Tamar had spent many long hours pondering her future. Her sister, older by eighteen months and suffering from a weak constitution, had emigrated to New Zealand in October

1877. She died during the voyage, but her letter had been forwarded from New Zealand with a covering note from a Mrs MacNeill, the ship's matron, expressing her condolences and advising that Brigid passed away peacefully. Tamar was convinced Brigid had died of tuberculosis, and had already seen what a miserable and agonising death that could be, but was grateful for Mrs MacNeill's kind words.

The letter arrived four days after her father died. Her mother had passed away three years earlier, giving birth to her third daughter, born prematurely and too frail to live. Mother and daughter had been buried together in the village churchyard.

After her da's death, which had not been entirely unexpected, Tamar had gone to see the Methodist preacher. He advised her to pray; if she wholeheartedly placed her faith in God, her future would be revealed, but if it was not, then she would do well to re-evaluate her commitment to her religion. Tamar left the preacher feeling angry, cheated and no more enlightened. The Lord, she felt, had done her very few favours lately.

Instead of praying, she had gone home and worked out how much money she could scrape together. The cottage was rented and the Deane family owned little of real value; her father's funeral had exhausted most of his meagre savings. The only items which might fetch a decent price were her mother's modest jewellery.

Gwen Teague had come from a well-off Penzance family, but when she declared her intention to marry Nolan Deane, a copper miner, her family had disowned her. She left with only her personal belongings and an angry sense of pride that prevented her ever contacting her family again. Her marriage to Nolan had been happy and satisfying, despite the fact that money was always scarce. She had loved him until the day she died. She had also cherished their two daughters and taught them fine dressmaking, and to read and write as well as manage their own finances, insurance against the possibility they may not find suitable husbands.

Now, critically appraising herself in the small mirror above the fireplace, Tamar saw a younger, seventeen-year-old version of her mother's striking features. Thick, wavy auburn hair past her shoulders, wide green eyes, a finely sculpted but not particularly small nose, and a generous, full-lipped mouth with one slightly crooked bottom tooth. Both sisters had inherited this imperfection from their father; their mam said it made them 'unique'. Gwen Deane had been an attractive woman, but her greatest attributes had been her determination and refusal to accept what she considered to be second best, something Tamar liked to believe had also been passed on to her.

She made herself a pot of tea and sat at the kitchen table. Remembering the plans her da had been making to follow Brigid to New Zealand, Tamar realised now he had known he would die soon. He had sent Brigid first, hoping she would reach New Zealand in time for her health to benefit. Nolan had then prepared Tamar to follow. As frightening as it sounded, emigrating on her own was still her best option. There was nothing left for her in Cornwall.

Two weeks later she moved to Truro and found employment as a junior seamstress in a small but profitable dressmaking business. Mrs Tregowan's shop was a tiny ground-floor establishment of two rooms in busy Boscawen Street, specialising in wedding and formal gowns. Mrs Tregowan was the proud owner of several expensive sewing machines imported from America from the Davis Sewing Machine Company, which allowed her staff to assemble gowns far more quickly than by traditional methods.

Tamar was responsible for measuring customers during their initial consultations, adding finishing touches to the garments and making the last, painstaking adjustments after final fittings. She enjoyed her work but laboured long hours and did not socialise.

However, the pay was adequate and Mrs Tregowan paid a small bonus whenever a particularly fine gown was completed on time.

After eight months Tamar had saved enough to emigrate. With the money she received for her mother's jewellery, she felt confident she would have enough. She handed in her notice in February and, with a good reference from Mrs Tregowan, began her journey to the Port of Plymouth. Four days in a crowded, airless and badly sprung coach had taken her to Torpoint, at the mouth of the Tamar River, after which she was named.

The seas had been rough during the crossing to Plymouth, but not as rough as the emigration barracks at the Plymouth docks. Tamar arrived late in the afternoon and was informed by a self-important emigration clerk that she was lucky she had a place; those who did not had to stay in even more loathsome accommodation.

Tamar had been appalled at the state of some of the emigrants. They were loud and unruly and many, adults as well as children, were crawling with vermin and smelled terrible. She had been raised in near poverty, but personal cleanliness had been impressed upon her from an early age. But it was more than how these unfamiliar people smelled; their behaviour itself was also disconcerting. The emigration agent who had interviewed her had discussed at length, in a discreet and almost apologetic manner, the requirement for emigrants to be of sound moral character. She could only assume the agent had not recruited these people.

She spent two nights sharing a dormitory with several single women, three married women and eight noisy, grimy children. Someone produced a jug of gin, and four of the women had proceeded to get messily drunk. The whole dormitory had been kept up until all hours by their singing and laughing and, after they finally fell into a drunken sleep, their snores, belches and farts. The second night had been little better and Tamar had risen early and come down to the dock as soon as possible. They were her peers, these poor, working-class, uneducated women, but she had been dismayed at their behaviour. She was also dismayed at her reaction, and reminded herself sharply of one of her mother's earliest lessons; that tolerance and acceptance were virtues to be nurtured.

'And so here I am,' said Tamar, her tears forgotten.

'What did ye have in mind when ye get to New Zealand? For a job, I mean,' asked Myrna.

Tamar pulled out a handkerchief and wiped a nose made runny by crying and the raw wind. 'I'm a good seamstress. My sister was too, and we planned to start a business. When we had enough money.'

'So will ye do that by yeself now?'

'I think so, if I can. It will be harder now, I expect.'

Myrna agreed. She narrowed her eyes and looked at Tamar appraisingly. 'Mmm, but ye're a pretty wee thing. Wi' that auburn hair and those big green eyes ye'll no' be on your own for long.'

Tamar went red. 'Thank you, Miss McTaggart. I am hoping I might meet someone in New Zealand.'

'Och, ma name's Myrna, lassie. And I've no doubt ye'll meet a good man, no doubt at all.'

Tamar nodded politely, then cleared her throat. 'There is one thing I would like to seek your advice about, Miss, ah, Myrna.'

Myrna raised her finely plucked eyebrows. 'And what might that be?'

'My passage was booked on the understanding I would be accompanied by my father. He had already died when I booked it. I lied to the agent. I'm not old enough to emigrate on my own.'

Myrna tapped her boot thoughtfully, her hands on her curvaceous hips. 'And ye must travel accompanied?'

'Yes.'

'Oh, well, that's easily fixed, lassie. Wait here a minute.'

Myrna elbowed her way through the busy crowd, returning several minutes later towing a small, inoffensive-looking man.

'Tamar, meet George Kellow from St Ives. One o' your lot. For a small fee, he's kindly agreed to be your uncle. Ye'll board wi' him and his family, then go your separate ways as soon as we're in the Channel. D'ye get ma drift?'

Tamar instantly felt better. Her dilemma *had* been easily fixed. She reached for her purse. 'How much do I owe you, Mr Kellow?'

'Och, I've already paid the wee gentleman,' replied Myrna. 'Dinnae worry yeself.' She pulled the lapels of her bright blue coat together over her ample bosom. 'Aye, well, it looks like we're boarding. I must be off and organise ma girls,' she said, inclining her head towards a group of young women standing by a vast pile of trunks and bags. 'I'll see ye on board, lassie. If there's anything ye need, be it even just a wee chat, ye'll come and see me, aye?' And off she swept, her head high and the tails of her extravagant coat flapping.

Tamar stared after her. What a strange woman, she reflected. Myrna looked to be in her forties, but very well preserved and attractive. Her clothes, although gaudy, were expertly made, and she wore several expensive-looking rings, although none on her wedding finger. She was clearly a woman of some income, but she was coarse-mouthed, somewhat raucous, and perhaps not terribly well bred. But quite likable, thought Tamar, and very kind. She slung her bag over her shoulder and bent to take hold of her trunk.

'I'll take that, Miss,' said Mr Kellow. 'Seeing as you're my niece.' He had an amused smile on his weathered face.

'Thank you,' she replied. 'How much did Miss McTaggart pay you?'

'Ten pounds.'

'*What?*'

'Ten pounds. 'Tis a criminal offence after all. But we've the six little ones an' not a lot of money.'

'So how is it you know Miss McTaggart?'

'Know her? I never seen her before!' Mr Kellow laughed at her startled expression. 'She just come up an' asked if I were wanting to make a bit of money. I were, so here I am. Come on, Miss, I'll introduce yer to your aunt.'

They dodged through the crowd until Mr Kellow stopped in front of a woman with five small children milling about her like ducklings, and a round-faced baby balanced on her hip. Mrs Kellow was even smaller than her husband, and just as weathered and harried looking.

'It's Tamar, isn't it?' asked Mr Kellow. 'Tamar, this is Mrs Kellow.'

Mrs Kellow nodded and said anxiously, 'George, we should board now, with the rest of the crowd. While there's a rush.' Tamar gathered she was not overjoyed at having a new niece, even if it was only for the next hour.

She hefted up her trunk and followed the Kellows up the gangway. At the top stood a man Tamar assumed was an emigration official. Stopping people as they boarded, he was checking their papers, ticking their names off against a list, then directing them on. She felt sick as she waited her turn.

Standing directly behind George Kellow, she heard him explaining that she was his niece. His face expressionless, the man held out his hand for Tamar's papers. 'Tamar Deane?' he asked. 'It says you're travelling with your father. Where is he?'

Nerves already stretched as tight as a bowstring, Tamar burst into tears. 'He *died*!' she sobbed.

The official watched her impassively for a moment, then turned back to George Kellow. 'Your wife's side?'

Nodding a little too enthusiastically, Mr Kellow added,

17

'Daughter of the wife's recently departed brother. Very sad it were.'

The man made some ticks on his list, and crossed one name off. 'On you go,' he said, not looking at them again. Tamar closed her eyes in relief and the Kellows relaxed visibly as they surged forward.

The deck was pandemonium, crowded with emigrants saying goodbye to friends and family and children running about shrieking with excitement or wailing in confusion, piles of luggage, ropes, provisions, boxes and bales, live chickens in crates and fresh dung from the ship's milking cows. All this was overlaid with the sharp smell of the sea and the reek of a slightly stale catch from the fishing boat moored at the next quay.

'Pay heed!' bellowed a seaman, standing on a large cask to get the passengers' attention. 'I am First Mate of the *Rebecca Jane*, bound for New Zealand. We expect the voyage to take three months, less if the wind favours us, and in the interests of shortening our running time we will not land at Cape Town. The Master will be aboard shortly and we will head into the sound in an hour. Move your trunks over to the afterhatch for the lumpers to take down, but take out what you need now because we'll not be opening the hold for another month. Take the rest of your belongings below. The Second Mates will show you where to go. Cabin passengers will be boarding shortly. All non-passengers ashore.'

Tamar turned to George Kellow and his wife, mouthed 'thank you', smiled at his wink, then dragged her trunk to the afterhatch, already surrounded by a mountain of scruffy-looking luggage. As she moved towards the main hatch there was a mad crush as people fought to get down the steep ladder first for the best berths. When it was Tamar's turn to descend into the creaking belly of the ship, she could barely make out her surroundings. As her eyes became accustomed to the gloom, she saw there were no best berths.

A man's voice called, 'Single women over here!'

Tamar moved towards what she assumed was the front of the

ship, where a young crewman held yet another list. He looked up and asked, 'Name?'

'Miss Tamar Deane,' she replied.

'Papers?' Tamar handed over her certificate of passage and confirmation of medical examination and the crewman ticked her name off.

'Through this door and you'll see the single women's quarters.' He pushed the door open with his foot and pointed. 'See? Bunks on your left, put your gear on one, you'll be taking your meals at the mid-ship tables back the way you've come. Matron'll have a word when everyone's settled.'

Tamar stepped into the cramped and stale-smelling cabin, closed the door behind her and looked about for a bunk. Remembering what Brigid had said in her letter about the incessant noise from married couples and families in the middle of the ship, she chose the berth furthest from the door. The bunks were built one above the other, extending from the hull into the centre of the cabin. She dropped her gear onto the bottom one, a very narrow space she could see she would have to get into feet first. There was a small shelf at the back but nowhere else to put her things, with only a small curtain at the front for privacy.

Wearily she pulled her thin blanket and a sheet out of her travel bag and spread them on the sad-looking mattress. She bent down to examine it closely, looking for wildlife and other unpleasant signs of past use, but could not see properly in the gloom. The four lanterns in the cabin did little to penetrate the murk.

'Don't *think* there's anythin' livin' in 'em, an' they smell like they've 'ad a good wash, but yer never can tell!'

Tamar jumped at the voice, hitting her head on the top bunk. Hearing a giggle, she turned and saw she had walked past three young women reclining in the bunks nearest the door.

'You gave me a fright!' she gasped.

'Sorry, luv,' said the speaker, a girl with heavy blonde hair tied back with a green ribbon. 'Thought you'd seen us on yer way in.'

'No, I didn't, I'm sorry. It's quite dark in here.'

'It is,' said the blonde girl. 'An' cramped. Could get stuffy after three months. I'm not lookin' forward ter it. I'm Polly Jakes.' Climbing out of her bunk, she indicated her companions. 'An' this 'ere's Sally Thomas and Jane Shilton.'

Tamar introduced herself. Polly, Sally and Jane were emigrating to New Zealand in search of a better life and, hopefully, husbands. Polly was petite, pretty and cheerful and pleasingly round. Sally was slender and dark while Jane was solid but fit-looking with wavy black hair. Tamar judged them to be in their early twenties and immediately envied their obvious comradeship.

'Phew,' said Jane, fanning her face with her hat. 'There's no air in 'ere already. Let's go up on deck, shall we, see what's happenin'? You comin', Tamar?'

Absurdly pleased to be invited, Tamar hung her bag on a nail at the back of her bunk and followed them back through the swarming, din-filled married quarters and up the ladder to the deck. Most of the equipment and provisions strewn about just half an hour before had gone. As they moved towards the bulwark closest to the dock they heard a commotion below; looking down, they saw a group of well-dressed people standing around an enormous pile of luggage, some of which was being hoisted onto the shoulders of various crew members. Cabin passengers, thought Tamar.

As a crewman lifted a particularly heavy-looking case, one of the women in the group shrieked, 'Careful with that, you clumsy fool! My best Wedgwood china is in that case. If I find any of it broken when we reach New Zealand, I will hold *you* personally responsible!'

The crewman looked at the woman, middle-aged and over-dressed in a bustled gown bedecked with braid, fringes and piping, topped off with an ornate lace cap, its long ribbons flying in the strong breeze. 'Of course, Ma'am,' he replied. 'I know 'ow yer valuables need ter be treated, Ma'am.'

He plodded up the steep gangway, balancing the crate expertly on his right shoulder. As he neared Tamar and her new friends, he said under his breath, 'They should be shoved up yer arse, Ma'am,' and winked at the girls.

Polly laughed out loud and Tamar held her hand over her face to conceal her smile, which she hastily wiped off as the party began to imperiously ascend. There appeared to be several families with children, as well as two or three single men. One of these was white-haired and distinguished-looking, while the other two were quite young, perhaps in their late twenties or early thirties. Each doffed their hat politely as they passed.

From somewhere above a bell rang, evidently a signal the ship was about to cast off as crewmen began to untie ropes holding the ship to the dock, while more trunks and provisions were raced up the gangway. Emigrants began to line the bulwarks for what, for most, would be the last view of their homeland; many wept openly and children cried loudly at their parents' distress. The *Rebecca Jane* shuddered as the tugboat towing her into Plymouth Sound moved away from the dock.

Tamar felt an aching sadness and bit her lip to stop herself crying again. She would miss Cornwall's harsh beauty, its wild coastlines and mists and rains, but most of all she would miss her family. But she knew she would never see them again in this life, so did it matter where she was? In a perverse way this made her feel better. She raised her head and let the sharp wind blow into her face and lift her hair.

'You all right, luv?' asked Sally.

'Yes, I'm fine. It's just that New Zealand's such a long way away.'

'I know, but think of them opportunities. A new country, new jobs. New men! They do say there's three fer every unattached girl!' She uttered the last comment with such enthusiasm Tamar had to smile.

They stayed on deck until the dock and Plymouth itself had receded into the distance. The wind picked up as the *Rebecca Jane* moved into the sound; her sails were unfurled as the tugboat detached itself, turned around in a lazy half-circle and began heading back into port.

CHAPTER TWO

The *Rebecca Jane* was seven days into her voyage. Mild sea-sickness had set in amongst her less robust passengers almost as soon as she reached open water, but Tamar herself was hardly afflicted; she quickly found her sea legs and as long as she went up on deck for fresh air, she felt fine.

She was sharing the single women's quarters with another eighteen young women, plus the ship's matron, Mrs Mary Joseph, a quiet, ineffectual-looking woman in her mid-forties. Her husband, a skilled carpenter, was accommodated in the men's quarters. Like most on board, they were emigrating to New Zealand to start a new life. Myrna McTaggart's four girls were also in the single women's quarters, but Myrna was not. Tamar had come to know the girls, Vivienne, Bronwyn, Jessica and Letitia, quite well over the past week. It was difficult not to, in such intimate and close quarters.

Tamar had remarked that, for sisters, they did not look at all alike, although they were all very pretty. The girls burst out laughing, then informed Tamar they were not sisters and Myrna was not their mother; she was their employer. Myrna ran a training school for domestic servants and had decided to move her business out to New Zealand where the demand for skilled domestics was high. The girls were her first trainees in the new colony. Myrna, they said, was a shrewd businesswoman and could afford to pay for a private cabin.

The diminutive but relentlessly cheerful Scotswoman, however, had so far elected to spend a considerable amount of her time in the single women's quarters, to Mrs Joseph's unvoiced but obvious disapproval. She privately thought Myrna vulgar with her flashy clothes and coarse language. Myrna seemed to get on with almost everyone, but confessed that at times she found the company of most of the cabin passengers dull and their attitude towards her standoffish. She thought the girls were much more fun.

Tamar agreed. She had barely had time to be lonely since the *Rebecca Jane* sailed from Plymouth. Although there were long hours when there was little to do, there was always someone to talk to. Most of the girls were young and eager to reach New Zealand, and never tired of talking about their plans and what, or who, they might find there. Tamar liked most of her cabin mates, although she was wary of a handful of fairly rough girls. Their ringleader, a big, aggressive English girl called Eliza, was rude, foul-mouthed and somewhat intimidating.

It had taken several days for the girls' daily routine to establish itself. Mrs Joseph had lectured them vigorously on where they were permitted to go on the ship. There was strictly no entering the single men's or crew's quarters under any circumstances, no access to the poop deck which was for the sole use of cabin passengers, and they were to avoid going through the family quarters at night; it would certainly not do for a married man to see a young woman in her night attire, or vice versa. There was a closet privy in the single women's quarters and this, for modesty's sake, was to be used rather than the other sanitary facilities. Bathing would be carried out regularly every second day, using buckets of sea water, and laundry was to be done on Fridays.

The girls had worked out a roster detailing who would collect and prepare the rations, which were prescribed by the ship's surgeon, Dr Adams, and handed out under supervision. The food was adequate some of the time but, in Tamar's opinion, frequently left a lot to be desired. On one occasion they received spoiled meat that had to be thrown overboard, but emigrants who had come from poverty more dire than Tamar's thought the food was lovely. Every few days a supply of preserved meat, with rice or potatoes, pickled cabbage or dried peas, mustard and flour was served out to those on mess duty. Women nursing babies were allocated a quantity of beer and small children received fresh milk from the ship's cows. Like the other steerage passengers, the single women cooked their meals in the community galley and ate at the large central tables in the middle of the ship. On occasion, however, if the family quarters were particularly noisome, they dined in their own compartment. Cabin passengers had their markedly superior meals cooked for them and served by stewards in their own area.

The family quarters, where most of the emigrants were housed, stank; its confined space was cramped, gloomy, airless and oppressive, particularly when the weather was too inclement to venture on deck. Dr Adams insisted the floors were thoroughly swabbed out with sea water and sprinkled with chloride of lime every second day, and bedding aired on deck at every opportunity, but the smell of unwashed people and human waste persisted. An official instruction stated that chamber pots were not to be used in sleeping and eating areas and the privies used instead, but many were too embarrassed, preferring to squat over their pots behind their bunk curtains. Whenever Tamar went through the family quarters to go up on deck for air, she held her nose to stop herself retching.

The atmosphere in the single women's quarters was not particularly refreshing either, but under the guidance of Mrs Joseph most of the girls made an effort to keep themselves and their area clean. The privy was sluiced with sea water and chloride of lime regularly, and the few small portholes above the bunks opened briefly whenever the weather permitted.

Initially, a handful of girls resented having to bathe as regularly as Mrs Joseph demanded and their body odour was beginning to disturb their roommates. Tall, big-boned, sour-faced Eliza, who came, ironically, from Bath, took particular offence at Mrs Joseph's efforts to get her to wash.

'I only 'ad a wash once a fortnight at 'ome, an' I aren't changing that fer the likes of you, yer snotty old cow,' she snapped one day, standing threateningly over the much smaller Mrs Joseph. 'Sod off an' kip somewhere else if yer don't like it!'

The blood drained from Mrs Joseph's face and her already thin lips compressed into a white line but, humiliated and intimidated, she had not responded.

The girls continued to make an effort not to breathe too deeply around Eliza for the next few days, but the denouement came mercifully soon. Sweeping into the single women's quarters one evening after dinner, Myrna stopped dead in the middle of the cabin, fanned her face theatrically and exclaimed loudly, 'God Almighty, what *is* that dreadful pong? There's no' a dead fish in here somewhere, is there?'

She prowled around the cabin, sniffing suspiciously at each of the girls, much to their mortification. When she came to Eliza lying in her bunk, she stopped. 'Och, it's *you*, lassie! Ye stink!'

Eliza uncoiled herself from her bed and stood up. 'Yer wot?' the big girl said menacingly.

'I said, ye *stink!*' repeated Myrna even more loudly, craning her neck to look into the much taller woman's face. 'Ye pong. Did ye mam no' tell ye to wash when ye have your courses? Ye smell like a heap o' dead whelks rotting on the shore!'

Everyone froze in horrified anticipation, waiting to see what Eliza would do. Tamar glanced at Mrs Joseph sitting motionless at her small work desk, mouth open and face crimson with embarrassment.

Eliza raised her hand.

'Dinnae even think about it, lassie,' said Myrna. Quick as lightning she grabbed Eliza's right ear with her long fingernails and pinched and twisted hard. Eliza yelped and bent her head down to Myrna's level in an attempt to ease the pressure.

'Let go, yer bitch,' she wailed.

'When ye agree to keep yeself clean,' replied Myrna calmly. 'Ye've no' a hope in hell o' getting yeself a laddie smelling the way ye do, not to mention the fact that ye're making life for the lassies here verra unpleasant. Well, are we agreed?'

When Eliza said nothing, Myrna gave her ear an extra, particularly brutal, wrench.

'*Ow!*' shrieked Eliza. '*Yes!* Yes, I'll wash!'

Myrna let go, stepped back and lowered her voice. 'Who raised ye, lassie?'

Eliza subsided onto her bunk, her eyes watering and her hand held protectively over the side of her head.

'Who taught ye about being a woman?' repeated Myrna.

'No one,' replied Eliza sulkily. 'Me mam died when I were little.'

'Thought as much,' remarked Myrna. She took Eliza's hand and pulled her gently but firmly to her feet. 'Ladies,' she announced to the stunned onlookers, 'we will be in ma cabin for an hour.' And, pushing Eliza in front of her, she stepped out through the cabin door.

'Bloody 'ell!' exclaimed Polly after the door swung shut. 'Never thought I'd see *that* 'appen!'

Everyone started talking at once, ignoring Mrs Joseph's pleas for decorum and a care for language.

'I feel sorry fer 'er, really,' said Jane. 'Not knowin' what ter do an' all that. Can't be nice.'

'Don't worry, Myrna will sort her out. She's very good at that sort of thing,' replied Letitia. She looked accusingly at the remaining handful of girls who, along with Eliza, had been refusing to wash regularly. 'At least we'll be able to breathe properly in here now, won't we?' she said pointedly. The smelly ones nodded rapidly.

Eliza came back an hour and a half later with red and swollen eyes, but smelling infinitely better. In fact, Tamar thought she detected a hint of lavender water as the big girl walked past. The girls raised their eyebrows at each other but nothing was said.

The smell below decks was always worse when the weather was rough. The first real bout of bad weather and serious *mal de mer* arrived just over a week out from Plymouth. Until then, as the ship sailed south past the coasts of France and Spain towards the Canary Islands, the weather had been fair and unusually calm.

Those passengers who had already experienced mild seasickness as soon as the *Rebecca Jane* had reached open water, but had recovered and gained their sea legs, were horrified to find that as the ocean swell grew, their seasickness returned tenfold. On the first day of really rough weather, the conversation below decks became steadily more muted and by mid-afternoon, many had retired to their bunks, feeling extremely ill. As their nausea increased, tempers frayed and established routines began to falter. In the cabins, most managed to confine themselves to vomiting into bowls and buckets, but below decks, there was no room for such elegant manoeuvres and the stricken simply threw up in their bunks or onto the floor.

In the single women's quarters, only Tamar and one of the other girls were not seasick. Nor was Myrna, who claimed she had never been ill a day in her life. Mrs Joseph took to her bunk as soon as the *Rebecca Jane* started to roll, her face grey and miserable-looking under the wilting lace of her house cap.

The first vicious storm struck the ship suddenly at three o'clock in the afternoon of the following day, forcing the Captain to forbid anyone venturing on deck. The seas rapidly became mountainous and huge waves crashed over the ship, sea water pouring through the hatches and drenching below decks. As much equipment as possible had to be lashed down and almost everyone was confined to their bunks, the rolling and pitching of the ship making it unsafe for the few who were not seasick to wander about. Many of the children and more than a few adults cried out in fear as the ship creaked, groaned and heaved around them, lamps swinging wildly in the gloom as mighty waves crashed against the hull.

Tamar spent much of the three-day storm tending to those too sick to help themselves. Initially she confined her ministrations to the girls in her cabin but on the first evening of the storm, Dr Adams asked for anyone able and willing to help him with his rounds. Myrna offered to take over from Tamar in the single women's quarters, so Tamar volunteered. She was appalled at what she saw when she stepped into the family quarters.

Almost all of the steerage passengers were ill, their retching moans barely audible above the sounds of the storm and the ominous groaning of the ship's timbers. The floor was awash with sea water, vomit, uneaten food and people's belongings. Several children and adults lay in this mess, too weak to drag themselves into their berths. The smell of human waste fouled the air, some of the ill unable to make use of their chamber pots, or using them instead to vomit into.

'My God,' Tamar exclaimed, one hand over her mouth and nose and the other tightly clutching a dripping beam above her as the ship rolled. 'This is awful! How could they all get this sick so quickly?'

Dr Adams shrugged. '*Mal de mer* always comes on rapidly. If you feel you're not up to it, then it's probably a good idea to go back to your compartment. It's Miss Deane, isn't it? I will understand.'

'No, no,' replied Tamar. 'It's just that they're all so *sick*.' As she said this, a woman thrust her head out of a bunk and vomited onto her skirt.

'I hope you've got plenty of clean clothes,' said Dr Adams. 'This is going to be a messy job.'

Tamar sighed as deeply as the stinking air allowed; she did not have a lot of clothes, but she could always wash anything that became soiled. She would have to.

'The cabin passengers are more or less sorted out,' Dr Adams said briskly. 'One or two of them aren't sick and they're graciously lending a hand with their fellow travellers, so they're relatively comfortable.' He looked about. 'Conditions down here are much worse.'

Tamar glanced sideways at the young doctor. He was obviously educated and from the privileged classes, but did not seem particularly sympathetic to his peers. How curious.

'We need to see what we can do for them, especially the infants and younger children because dehydration will affect them more. I expect most of the adults will be all right, but while they're lying in their beds vomiting, they'll be no use at all to their children.'

Adams squinted into the gloom and beckoned to a boy and an older woman sitting side by side at one of the long tables in the centre of the cabin. At his signal they waded carefully towards him through the five or six inches of slops, the woman holding up her skirts to reveal sagging, hand-knitted woollen stockings and tatty boots liberally coated with scum and sea water.

'This is Miss Deane,' said Adams, introducing Tamar to the pair who nodded politely. As the *Rebecca Jane* executed a particularly violent lurch they all clutched at something solid. 'And this is

Henry Jones and Mrs Annie Croft, both steerage passengers and both of whom, like you and I, Miss Deane, are not affected by seasickness. What we need first is more light. Henry, go up on deck and find a crewman, that is if they haven't all been swept overboard by now, taking care to make sure that doesn't happen to you. Ask for some extra oil lamps and candles. Mrs Croft, you have no young children of your own?'

'No, sir,' the older woman replied in a soft Irish lilt. 'Mine are all grown and can take care of themselves.'

'Please call me John, Mrs Croft, or Dr Adams. After all, we're standing in the same vomit.'

'Well then, Doctor, call me Annie,' said Mrs Croft.

Tamar also introduced herself, feeling out of her social depth. It was not usual to address a gentleman of Dr Adams' status by his first name, and neither was it usual for him to address women he was not well acquainted with by theirs, even if they were several classes below him.

Adams pushed up the sleeves of his coat in a businesslike manner. 'Well, we'd better get busy. Off you go, Henry, and be careful,' he said as the boy waded into the shadows. He turned back to the two women. 'First, we need to lift these people off the floor. Then Annie, if you start at the far end, Tamar and I will start at this end. We'll need to wash our hands between each examination. Are you aware of what to look for, Annie? Dry skin, fever, headache?'

'Yes, Doctor, I seen dehydration before in little ones,' Mrs Croft responded confidently.

'Make a mental note of which ones you think are suspect, and I'll come and look at them and we'll start giving them sugar and water.'

Between them they set about assisting those passengers on the floor back into their bunks. As Mrs Croft washed her hands then sloshed away into the murk towards the other end of the compartment, John Adams turned to Tamar and explained,

'What you need to do is put your hand to the child's brow. If it's abnormally hot or cool, that's a sign they're low in fluids, which happens when people vomit excessively. Also, if you pinch the skin on the backs of their hands and it doesn't smooth out straightaway, that's another sign.' He took Tamar's hand and held it up under a lamp while he pinched a small segment of her skin. 'See? Yours is quite elastic. You must be very healthy, and with a completely cast-iron stomach, I'd say, to be impervious to seasickness.'

Tamar wasn't sure whether she felt complimented or not. Without thinking she replied, 'I certainly need it to eat some of the food we've been getting, Dr Adams.'

'Please call me John. I don't stand on formality.'

'John, then.' Tamar suddenly realised it was the doctor's job to prescribe the passengers' diet. 'Oh, I do beg your pardon. I didn't mean to be rude about the food,' she said, embarrassed.

'Yes, well,' he muttered. 'Some of the food *is* a bit substandard. However, it's not my job to procure it, only to ensure everyone gets enough. The quality is up to the emigration company and, ultimately, the Captain. Unfortunately, it's not uncommon for some of the money allocated for provisions to go into private pockets. The voyage is gruelling enough for steerage passengers, without depriving them of food. Especially the children. I've spoken to the Captain, but as we won't be calling in to any ports, nothing can be done, I'm afraid.'

He handed Tamar a hard piece of strong-smelling soap and indicated a bucket of water sitting on the table, in which he began to scrub his own hands vigorously.

'I'm a great believer in the theories of Louis Pasteur, a French chemist who has discovered that many illnesses are caused by tiny things called bacteria — organisms that can be spread by physical contact.' Shaking the water from his hands he reached for a clean cloth. 'It's very important that we don't pass bacteria from one passenger to the next. As you know, everyone was examined before embarkation, but I fear some may have lied about their health. I would hate to start a shipboard epidemic.'

Tamar nodded and watched as John bent to examine a small patient. The doctor, who appeared to be in his late twenties, was not particularly tall, with piercingly blue eyes and fair hair that was already receding. Although not strictly handsome, his cheerful face was appealing and she decided that this, together with his forthright manner, made him rather likable.

'This one's all right,' he commented. 'Weak, but she's not showing signs of dehydration. Water with lime juice will suffice.'

Sloshing and mild swearing announced Henry's return, followed by a crewman carrying four burning oil lamps.

'No candles,' said the sailor. 'Cap'n don't allow 'em below decks on account of fires. These lamps should help, but don't let 'em spill.' He touched his cap to Tamar before he turned and headed back to the ladder.

'All right, Henry,' said John. 'Put a lamp on each table and take the other one and help Mrs Croft see what she's doing.'

John handed the remaining lamp to Tamar and they began to work their way around one end of the family quarters, feeling clammy foreheads for temperatures and asking those with the energy to respond how they felt.

John chatted as they went, asking Tamar what had made her decide to emigrate and what she planned to do in New Zealand. In response she briefly recounted her family tragedy and her subsequent realisation there was nothing left for her in Cornwall, and talked of her plans to work as a seamstress. John nodded in silent sympathy as she spoke.

'What about you?' she asked.

'Well,' he replied, not looking up from the child he was examining. 'I am a physician, but I have no desire to practise general medicine for the rest of my life. My real passion lies in reconstructive surgery. There have been some incredible advances in this field in the last twenty years, particularly since the American Civil War. I spent a year in America and I've seen the work being done, not only on war injuries but also on birth defects such as cleft palate. I firmly believe that if there's a chance a patient's quality of life can be improved by surgically enhancing their appearance, it should be done. Otherwise, who knows what talents and abilities may be lost to the world? This one's not looking too good,' he added, as he rolled a small child on to its side. 'We'll come back to him shortly.'

He moved on to the next bunk in which a woman and a four-year-old boy lay in each other's arms. As he carefully separated them, the woman clutched his hand feebly and croaked, 'Can yer look at me little 'un, sir? She were very poorly before.'

'Where is she?' asked John, looking into the bunk above and in those on either side.

'Down by me feet somewhere. I were cuddlin' 'er 'cos she were shiverin', but then I nodded orf and she's slipped down,' the woman muttered, closing her eyes with the effort of speaking.

John gently extracted the little boy from the bunk and handed him to Tamar, then reached in past the woman and felt around under the blanket. 'Oh, Christ,' he mouthed.

'What?' asked Tamar.

'I think I've found her,' he whispered grimly.

He leaned forward into the cramped cubicle with both hands, almost kneeling on the semiconscious woman's chest, then carefully withdrew a small, limp bundle. Signalling for Tamar's lamp, he pulled a swaddling blanket back from the grey face of a small baby. Her lifeless eyes were half open. 'She's been suffocated. Her mother probably rolled over onto her, God help them both.'

Tamar stared at the dead infant in horror, then down at the little sleeping boy in her arms. 'What will you tell the mother?'

'Nothing yet. She's not fully conscious, been seasick ever since the storm started, I expect.'

'Where's the father?' asked Tamar.

John shrugged, and covered the baby's face with the blanket. 'He won't be far away, but he's probably sick as well. I'll put off telling them as long as I can, but I will have to inform the Captain.' He picked a small wooden box off the floor, tipped the water out of it, placed the infant's body gently inside and laid the box on the table.

Tamar and John continued their ministrations, but their conversation was subdued and confined to the matter in hand. John found seven more small children whose conditions required medical assistance, and two adult women in the same state. After an hour, the four of them had been around the whole compartment. They were tired and emotionally drained, their clothes reeked of vomit, and their hands were red and chapped from washing. Telling the others to take the opportunity for a short rest, John left to prepare a sugar and water mixture for those who were badly dehydrated. Then, when the seriously ill in the family quarters had been attended to, the sick in the single women's and single men's accommodation were checked.

John Adams and his small team of helpers had very little sleep over the next two days and nights, kept busy administering fluids to the sick and preparing bland food for the few who could keep it down. To their relief, there were no further deaths. John decided there was little point in cleaning out any of the living quarters until the storm had abated and the passengers had stopped being sick. Many were awake but still incapable of moving from their bunks. Tamar snatched a few hours' sleep but, like Myrna, she was completely exhausted by the time the storm had begun to pass.

By the morning of the fourth day the foul weather receded, leaving the skies almost clear and the seas and the stomachs of many of the *Rebecca Jane's* passengers significantly calmer. There had been two deaths; that of the baby girl, and one of the ship's cows, which had been destroyed after breaking its hip, and would be butchered for food. As well, two men suffered broken bones caused by falls during the storm, and now resided in the men's hospital area. In the hold several ruined casks and crates of provisions which had come loose and broken open were discovered.

The tiny body of the suffocated infant was buried at sea that afternoon after a short service performed by the Captain. Her devastated parents and small brother huddled together for comfort, the woman inconsolable.

Tamar's cabin mates had also recovered, although no one had much of an appetite for the next few days. Routines were re-established and the living quarters rigorously cleaned out and bedding washed and dried in the blustery wind on deck. It took Tamar several days to catch up on her sleep, but she found she had made some new friends. Several women from the family quarters gave her small tokens of appreciation, and many of the children began to say hello and address her cheerily as Miss Deane whenever she went through the crowded compartment.

Tamar also found herself spending some of her time on deck with John Adams. As the ship's surgeon, he was expected to mingle with the steerage class on occasion and when his expertise as a physician was required. However, like Myrna, he did not altogether enjoy the company of his peers with their formal dining arrangements, their snobbery, their refusal to set foot on the main deck where the steerage passengers took their exercise, and their outrage when anyone but themselves or the Captain appeared on the poop deck. On the other hand, he did enjoy breaking rules, particularly social ones.

Tamar Deane was a mystery to John. She clearly had not come from a monied background, yet she was well-spoken, educated and intelligent, and conducted herself with a quiet dignity and resolution uncommon in one so young. He felt she was struggling with her new status as a young woman with no family, but suspected she would adapt soon enough and do well for herself in New Zealand.

Furthermore, he had been unable to help noticing Tamar's physical attractions, as well as her unassuming but friendly and astute manner. He found himself looking forward more and more to the time they spent together, and was beginning to wonder how she might feel about being the wife of a revolutionary, but altruistic and therefore probably not very wealthy, doctor.

April 1879

A week after the storm, the *Rebecca Jane* sailed out of the northeast trade winds and into the doldrums off the Ivory Coast. The wind deserted her sails, leaving them to hang limp and heavy as she meandered slowly towards the equator. Temperatures shot up, fraying tempers and turning below decks into a hot, airless furnace. Passengers spent as much time on deck as possible, and some of the single men volunteered to help with deck work as an antidote to the increasing boredom. John Adams was kept busy treating cases of sunstroke and sunburn.

The nights were especially arduous. The Captain gave orders for extended hours on deck so passengers could take advantage of the marginally cooler evening temperatures; men went about in their shirtsleeves, and women without shawls.

The passage through the doldrums became profoundly tedious, the monotony broken only by the daily routines of preparing meals, cleaning and, for the children, a shipboard school. Parents were relieved and grateful as it gave them a welcome break from their offspring, most of whom were fractious and bored. Several cases of wife-beating, and one of husband-beating, were reported to the Captain who declared the culprits would be incarcerated in irons if it happened again.

Myrna and Tamar had become firm friends. Tamar found the older woman a stabilising, if slightly eccentric, influence and she valued and enjoyed their time together. One afternoon found the women strolling the deck and enjoying a slight breeze. Myrna was wearing emerald green boots, a purple skirt with a small bustle, and a tight-fitting long-sleeved jacket in leaf-green silk. With her red hair piled up, she was vividly spectacular.

'Would ye fancy a pot o' tea in ma room, lassie?' she asked Tamar, who nodded. She had visited Myrna in her comfortably furnished cabin several times and had thoroughly enjoyed herself, although she had received withering looks from first-class passengers as she passed them in the narrow corridor. Tamar shuddered to think what the ladies had thought of Eliza.

There had been a marked improvement in Eliza's personal hygiene and behaviour since that embarrassing evening, but no one had been able to summon enough courage to ask her what had been said. When the women were settled in high-backed wing chairs on either side of the cabin window, Tamar asked what had happened.

'Well,' replied Myrna, prising her shoes off and massaging her liberated toes. 'Lovely shade these, but Christ, they hurt ma feet. Getting ruined by the sea water,' she observed, inspecting one elegantly small, water-marked ankle boot. 'But yon Eliza, first I persuaded her to tell me about what sort o' life she's had, which was no' an easy task. She didnae want to say much about that. She's no' had it easy, poor lassie. Her mam died when she was wee, leaving her and her da to bring up three bairns. The da sounded a hopeless case, always on the whisky and no' working regularly. And he was free wi' his fists and his personal charms as well, the bastard. He died recently, thank God for small mercies. Seeing the brothers and sister are auld enough to look after themselves, Eliza thought she'd try emigrating. She's no' a bad lassie, ye ken, just ignorant and scared. I had to tell her what to do when she was having her courses, poor thing didnae know. She wasnae using anything so no wonder she ponged. I gave her some o' ma own cloths, showed her how to fold them and pin them in, and talked to her about washing them and her body regularly, a chore though that is on this ruddy ship.'

Having washed her own sanitary cloths in a bucket of sea water recently, Tamar recalled how they had dried stiff and unyielding and were very uncomfortable to wear afterwards. The cloths were a common sight hanging up to dry in the single women's quarters where male eyes hardly ever ventured, but she had no idea what the women in the family quarters did with theirs. Wore them wet, she supposed. They could hardly hang them flapping gaily from the ship's bulwarks.

'Aye, and I taught her about what her courses mean, she didnae know even that. Och, I'm surprised the lassie hasnae had several bairns by now — she said she's lain with more than a few laddies. She's verra lucky her da didnae give her one.'

Tamar raised her eyebrows at these frank comments, but then Myrna never minced her words.

'Dinnae look at me like that,' said Myrna, pouring two cups of tea and adding three cubes of sugar to her own. She lit a cigarette and blew the smoke towards the ceiling. 'I know ye might have had a sheltered upbringing and ye're only seventeen, but I'll lay money on your mam having told ye all about that sort o' thing. Am I right?'

Tamar nodded. Her mother had explained the physical

and emotional differences between men and women, and the importance, in her mind, of settling with a man who would care for and honour his wife. She had referred, with a small private smile, to the loving and physically satisfying relationship she enjoyed with the girls' father, but pointed out that this did not always happen; often the best a wife could hope for was affection, respect and financial support.

'I suspect the lassie will be better behaved now,' continued Myrna. 'All she needed was a bit o' pride in herself. I pointed out that no one can make ye feel small or bad except yeself, and I think she kens that now. She's no' stupid, despite what comes out o' her mouth.'

Tamar agreed. Eliza was not lacking in intelligence, just decorum. The two women sipped their tea in comfortable silence for several minutes. Eventually, Myrna said, 'Tamar, we're becoming good friends, aye?'

Tamar nodded again.

'Well, then, lassie, there's something I need to tell ye, though ye might be a wee bit shocked to hear it. Biscuit?' she asked, offering a tin of shortbread. Tamar took one and waited for Myrna to continue.

'Ma girls have told ye I run a training establishment for domestic servants and they're coming out to New Zealand wi' me to start a business?'

'Yes, they said something about that when we left Plymouth.'

'Well, I'm becoming verra fond of ye, and I have no wish to lie to ye about what sort o' business I'm in. Lying isnae a good basis for a friendship, so I'll come right out wi' it. What I do is run a brothel.'

Tamar choked on her shortbread and coughed violently, spraying crumbs into her lap and spilling her tea. Myrna reached over and took the cup and saucer, patting her back firmly.

'Och, I can see it's come as a bit o' a shock,' she said unnecessarily.

Tamar nodded, her face bright red and tears streaming down her cheeks. Myrna sat back and waited patiently for her to compose herself.

'I needed to tell ye, lassie, ye'll have found out once we get to New Zealand anyway, and I dinnae want to lose ye as a friend,' she added quietly. Then, hesitantly, she asked, 'Are we still friends?'

Tamar looked at the colourful, vivacious little woman, and things fell into place; Myrna's money, her tough, capable way of dealing with people, and the attractive girls travelling with her. At the same time she saw Myrna's kindness and generosity and her compassionate attitude towards those in need. She thought her mother would probably have liked her, and surprised herself a little by saying, 'Yes, Myrna, we are still friends.'

'Well, I'm verra pleased,' replied Myrna, relaxing into her chair. 'Verra pleased indeed. Drink ye tea before it gets cold. I'd be happy to tell ye all about how the business operates if ye have an interest.'

'Well,' Tamar said after a second. 'If we are to be friends, I might as well know what it is you do.'

She did not say so, but she was intrigued by how a brothel was run. She knew there were such things of course, and had even worked on several gowns for prostitutes from the high-class brothels of Truro for Mrs Tregowan, but beyond that she knew very little about the profession, other than what she had seen on the streets.

'I dinnae work maself any more,' commented Myrna, reaching for another biscuit. 'I'm getting a bit long in the tooth and ma body isnae as youthful as it used to be. Aye, and I'm too fond o' ma food. Not that I dinnae still get offers, ye understand. But I've done ma time on ma back.'

Tamar said curiously, 'Do you mind me asking how old are you?'

'I'm fifty-one this year. Well, at least I think I am. I dinnae have a birth certificate.'

Tamar was astonished. She had thought Myrna was years younger. Her bright eyes, vibrant hair and clear, virtually unlined skin belied her real age. And when so many of the working-class women she had known in Cornwall had looked old before their time, she had assumed a life of prostitution would guarantee premature signs of ageing.

'You don't look it.'

'Well, thank ye, but I've made an effort to take care o' maself. It's despair and lack o' hope that makes a woman look old, ye ken, and I've never run out o' hope. O' course, I can afford to treat maself well. That helps.'

'How long have you been a …' Tamar's voice tailed off; she was not sure what to call Myrna and did not want to offend her.

'Whore? Prostitute? Harlot? Strumpet? In the trade, lassie, we call ourselves working girls, because that's what we do. We work for our money. By God, do we work sometimes. It's no' an easy profession, but there's some that's suited to it, and a lot more who are not. Maself, I started when I was sixteen years old, on the streets of Edinburgh. I met a man who set me up in ma own place and he was ma only customer, but he was too free wi' his fists, so I left him and went to work in a brothel. Och, it was a fine house, verra fine, and I made a lot o' money. I wasnae quite as cuddly then, although I had ma charms. Then I worked in France for a year or so, and the things I learned! When I had enough money, I set maself up in ma own house, first back in Edinburgh, then down in London, and I've been verra successful. For maself, the business side of it has the most appeal these days, so here I am, off to New Zealand to establish the finest house o' pleasure in the colony!'

'Where will you settle?' asked Tamar, fascinated.

'Auckland. It's no' the capital any more, but it's a busy town and I have enough money to set me and ma girls up in a nice place.'

'Will there just be Letitia, Vivienne, Bronwyn and Jessica?'

'To start wi', aye,' said Myrna. 'Ma girls have been wi' me for a wee while now, and they're all verra good at what they do. I expect I'll need to take on a few more when I get the business up and running. They cannae be just ordinary working girls though, ye ken. I provide a quality service so I'll be keeping ma eye open.'

Tamar said nothing for a minute and helped herself to another piece of shortbread, seeing she had spat most of the first one all over herself. She wanted to ask Myrna some more questions, much more personal ones about what prostitutes did, but felt too embarrassed, although she was comfortable asking about one issue.

'What happens if a working girl gets with child?'

'Och, there's plenty o' things ye can do to prevent it, but if it happens there are steps ye can take. There are herbal remedies. If a girl misses her courses she can take an infusion o' pennyroyal, or rue works as well. Some girls use lead, but I've seen two lassies die from that.'

'Do the herbal remedies always work?'

'Not always, no.'

'Then what?'

'Then I dinnae have a choice but to let the lassie go. I run a business, no' a nursery,' replied Myrna bluntly. 'I dinnae like to have to do it, but there's no real reason in ma line o' work why a lassie should get herself in the family way if she's taking care o' herself. If it happens, it's no' ma responsibility and all ma girls ken that.'

Tamar pondered this gravely, then asked a more general question. 'Will it be easy to set yourself up in Auckland?'

'Should be. I've the money, but there's a lot to be seen to. There's the premises, which need to be big and grand o' course, the furnishings, and suppliers o' food and drink — I'm considering a wee dining salon for ma customers. Not to mention suppliers o' all the other things we'll be needing. Costumes, good linen, cosmetics and the like, and tools o' the trade. A doctor to keep a regular eye on ma girls, one or two maids, a cook maybe. No doubt there'll be bribes for the constabulary, there usually are. I'll do ma own books, I dinnae trust anyone else. But I've done all this before, it just takes planning. And money, o' course.' Myrna scrutinised Tamar for a minute. 'I suppose you'd no' be interested in that sort o' a career yeself? Ye've the looks, and your manner is certainly appealing.'

Tamar smiled and shook her head. 'Thank you, no,' she replied. 'I don't think that's what my mam had in mind for me.'

'No, probably not,' said Myrna with a rueful laugh. 'I do see the hard edge ye need for that line o' work, though. But ye're right, I think ye're bound for better things. And as I said, it's no' an easy life. And besides, I've an idea yon wee doctor has taken a fancy to ye.'

'John Adams? Me?' said Tamar, genuinely surprised.

'Aye, him that moons over ye every minute ye spend together. Have ye no' noticed the way he's always looking at ye and contriving to talk to ye when ye're on deck?'

'Well, yes. But I thought he just liked my company. I like his. In fact I'm quite fond of him and his different ideas, but that's all. He's … I don't know … he's just John.'

'Oh dear,' murmured Myrna. 'Someone's going to be disappointed. Ye could do a lot worse for yeself, lassie.'

'Mam always said we'd know when we met the right man. She said we'd get this feeling, a sort of *knowing*, like she and my da had. She said there's no mistaking it. I want to have that when I meet the man I'm going to marry.'

'Aye, well, maybe your mam did have one o' those marriages, and a lucky woman she was if she did. But Tamar, it doesnae always work out like that,' Myrna replied gently. 'Sometimes ye settle for what's close enough. Ye're only seventeen and I ken ye dinnae think so, but ye're a naive wee thing. Och, no doubt that'll get knocked out o' ye in the next few years, New Zealand is still a rough colony, but dinnae pass up a good opportunity just because ye cannae settle for something less than your dreams. Otherwise ye could well still be dreaming when ye're auld and lonely and it's too late. Dinnae let that happen, lassie. It'd be such a waste.'

Tamar was silent.

'It's just a word o' advice. Look beyond what ye first see. And dinnae mistake lust for love — it's no' the same thing. Being lonely isnae a verra nice thing sometimes, especially for a woman. I ken that well.'

'I know,' Tamar responded sincerely. 'But as you say yourself, I'm only seventeen.'

'True. There's plenty o' time yet,' replied Myrna, helping herself to two more biscuits.

CHAPTER THREE

Days later, when it seemed the temperature could get no hotter and the wind was a mere memory, a strong breeze swept across the ship and snatched away several hats, tossing them overboard to bob lazily on the slow swell. The crew cheered; after weeks with almost nothing to fill her sails, the *Rebecca Jane* had finally been picked up by the strong southeast trades.

She made up for lost time sailing down the western coast of Africa. The weather was more often fine and when it did rain, the ship's tainted fresh water supply was replenished. There was delight in encountering sea life; luminous algae, dolphins and porpoises, whales and deep sea birds. Some passengers amused themselves by shooting at sharks and snaring albatrosses with a hook and line. The great sea birds were made into soup, although the sailors never touched it, believing the old superstition that albatrosses were the spirits of drowned sea captains. Small fish caught over the side also made a welcome change from preserved meat.

As the *Rebecca Jane* approached the Cape of Good Hope and turned east across the bottom of Africa, the weather became noticeably cooler. It was no longer pleasant to spend evenings on deck and as the ship neared the Roaring Forties, the harsh latitudes below the Cape, passengers were again largely confined below decks. A little more than halfway to New Zealand, the most arduous and challenging leg of their journey had begun.

Sharing a pot of tea at one of the long tables in the family quarters one evening, John Adams remarked to Tamar that in his view, the voyage thus far had been relatively free of medical problems. 'Accuse me of being immodest if you wish,' he said, 'but I think diligence is the key. That, and rigorous pre-embarkation medical examinations. I know of one ship's surgeon who lost almost forty passengers because they were not thoroughly checked before they sailed. We're also lucky we haven't stopped at any ports and picked up anything.' He poured himself another generous mug of tea. 'But I shouldn't speak too soon, we've a long way to go. We've five women expecting, two of whom will deliver before we reach Auckland. And there was that dreadful business with Mr and Mrs Mayhew.'

Mrs Mayhew was the woman who had accidentally smothered her infant daughter. Her grief-stricken husband had berated his wife, who was herself deranged with guilt and grief, to the extent that she hurled herself overboard. A rope had been thrown to her but she floated on her back, staring at the horrified passengers, until her clothes had become waterlogged and she sank beneath the surface. Mr Mayhew had been inconsolable and was confined to the men's hospital, withdrawn and refusing to eat or speak. The couple's four-year-old son had been taken under the wing of another family; if Mr Mayhew did not recover, the child would have to be fostered.

John went on, 'There's also the matter of the food. It's not getting any fresher, as I'm sure you've noticed.'

Tamar had noticed, and had stopped eating meat, dreading to think what state it would be in by the time they reached Auckland.

'I'm confident we have enough lime juice to prevent any of the nutrition-related diseases,' said John. 'But if we strike a bad batch of meat, food poisoning will become a serious risk. What a ghastly thought. It's bad enough having to inspect the privies now when everyone's more or less healthy.'

John had become accustomed to discussing his duties with Tamar; she was an interested and sympathetic listener and he valued her opinion. John would have talked to Tamar about anything, as long as he could sit and look at her. His growing infatuation had not gone unnoticed. One of the older cabin passengers had taken him aside and suggested his association with Tamar, a young single woman and a steerage passenger, was unseemly. John had thanked him for his advice, then ignored it. Following that, someone else stated loudly at dinner that in her opinion, any relationship between cabin and steerage passengers was to be strongly discouraged. Fortunately Myrna had been dining in the single women's quarters and had not heard the comments at first hand but John, unable to decide whether he was amused or angry, had recounted the conversation to her.

Her response had been predictable. 'Ignore the interfering auld bitch. It's no business o' hers what ye do.'

'I know. *That* doesn't bother me. It's Tamar herself. The more time I spend with her, the more time I *want* to spend with her, and it worries me that she might be concerned about the difference in our class.'

'Och no, laddie, she's no' that sort o' person. She's only seventeen and wi'out a family. She's feeling fragile and doesnae want to rush into anything. And nor should she, so dinnae push her.'

'She could do worse,' replied John, slightly petulantly.

'Aye, she kens that. Why d'ye no' leave it until we get to New Zealand? There's plenty o' time,' Myrna added, wondering whether Tamar could come to love the young doctor. But she doubted it, not with the high ideals Tamar had shared with her over the past weeks.

'But someone else will surely come along. I'll lose her!'

'Aye, and if they do, then ye wouldnae have had her anyway, would ye?' John said nothing and remained on deck in the cold wind for some time, staring moodily into the dark sea.

Thinking back to this conversation with Myrna, John reached across the table, picked up Tamar's hand and looked searchingly into her wide, green eyes. The moment was somewhat spoiled by the ship lurching violently and sending his half-full mug of tea into his lap. 'Bugger,' he said.

Tamar laughed. John's stomach flipped at her lovely smile and warm, bright eyes. 'Tamar,' he said, ignoring the hot tea soaking into his trousers. 'I need to tell you something.'

Tamar's smile remained but inside she flinched, resisting a childish urge to put her fingers in her ears. She was not prepared for, and did not want to hear, what John was about to say.

'You *are* aware of how much I think of you, aren't you?' he asked in a whisper, leaning forward so his words could not be heard by curious ears.

Tamar swallowed, choosing her words carefully. 'I know you like me, and you like to spend time with me,' she whispered back.

'Oh, it's more than that, Tamar. Much more. No, look at me,' he continued as she averted her eyes, blushing hotly in the dim light of the oil lamp. 'I know you're young and have plans, but I have hopes that one day you might think of me as more than a friend. I know you would like to marry, that you don't want to be alone, and, well, I can wait. You do want a husband and children, don't you?'

Tamar looked up miserably and blurted, 'Yes, but I want a husband I'm in *love* with!'

'And you can't love me, is that it?'

Beginning to cry now, Tamar replied, 'I don't know, John. I don't know *what* I can or can't do. I need you as a friend, can we please leave it at that for now?' She sniffed inelegantly, wiping her eyes on her sleeve.

John sighed and sat back, running his hand through his receding hair then rubbing his temples wearily.

'Well,' he said eventually, 'if that's all you want for the moment, then yes, of course, if you can't accept anything else right now. I will *always* be your friend. But how I feel about you will never change, whatever happens.'

Embarrassed and feeling awkward, he stood and walked away, leaving Tamar to gaze sightlessly at the worn table top, a tear running slowly down her cheek.

'Never mind, luv. You'll work it out,' said a woman's disembodied voice from behind her, and a wrinkled but clean handkerchief was pressed gently into her hand.

The next day it became clear John Adams had spoken too soon about several things. He apologised to Tamar and said that although he had meant every word, he had not intended to upset her. Tamar accepted his apology and reiterated, as kindly as she could, that she hoped their friendship could continue.

She was flattered by his attentions and sincerely fond of him but, for her, the compelling attraction she so hoped for was missing. She had no doubt she could have a contented life if she became his wife, but she wanted more; she wanted passion and romance, she wanted to experience the love her mam and da had shared.

As it turned out, any thoughts of passion were swept away when the first case of food poisoning was reported. By the time John had examined the patient, a child from steerage lying doubled up on her bunk, clutching her stomach, half a dozen others had fallen ill.

By the end of the day, severe diarrhoea and vomiting had struck almost all the steerage passengers and John had traced the source to a cask of spoiled pork. Fortunately, cabin passengers had not been affected, as they only ate fresh meat butchered on board.

Tamar, who had been avoiding meat, was again prevailed upon to help. To make matters worse, the outbreak of food poisoning coincided with their passage into the Roaring Forties, the vicious, prevailing westerly winds ever present between the latitudes of forty and fifty degrees south, and the task of helping the sick was made more arduous by the ship lurching and pitching. Many of those afflicted were unable to reach the privies and vomited and evacuated their bowels where they lay. Five children died, four of them under the age of two. After four days of violent vomiting and diarrhoea, one of the pregnant women went into labour prematurely, resulting in the death of her infant.

John and Tamar also became ill. Tamar retired to her bunk where she was nursed by Myrna and John, before he was forced to admit he was too ill to work.

Tamar spent three ghastly days curled up in her bunk, her battered body working to purge itself. She thought she was going to die, and several times prayed she would. After the first twelve hours she gave up staggering to the privy and, as she grew progressively weaker and began to lose control over her bowels, became resigned to soiling herself, weeping with pain and embarrassment.

'Och, lassie,' Myrna said matter-of-factly after one particularly messy accident. 'Dinnae worry about it. It's only shite and it'll wash out.'

John dragged himself from his own bed to monitor Tamar at regular intervals, insisting the privy and her bunk were doused repeatedly with chloride of lime and her bedclothes changed with fastidious frequency. Tamar thought it highly unlikely he would be quite so enamoured of her now he had seen her lying in a smelly puddle of her own watery diarrhoea, but she was wrong.

On the evening of the third day she fell into a deep sleep and did not wake until late the following afternoon, feeling parched and decrepit, but no longer sick. After a cup of tea, which she was moderately confident would stay in her stomach, she rose carefully, stripped off her dirty clothes and washed herself in a bucket of sea water. Gingerly though, because her stomach muscles were aching and her nether regions raw from the diarrhoea. Myrna helped her change her bedding and she went back to sleep. When she awoke again, she felt almost human and was welcomed back to the land of the living by her roommates, most of whom had fully recovered.

The funeral for the children who had died had been held while Tamar was ill, and Polly described how tragic it had been when the little shrouded bodies were consigned to the sea. The atmosphere onboard the *Rebecca Jane* was subdued, with the increasingly foul weather and rough seas doing little to improve the situation.

May 1879

By the time the food poisoning subsided, the *Rebecca Jane* had sailed down into the subantarctic region of the Indian Ocean. About a month out from New Zealand, she still had four thousand miles to sail. The weather was bitterly cold, the winds shrieking through the ship's ghostly rigging. Ice formed on the decks and on ropes and cables that had frozen solid. Sightings of huge, floating icebergs were not uncommon.

As conditions on deck were intolerable, life was again largely confined to the belly of the ship. The confinement was made worse by the gales forcing the *Rebecca Jane* over on a steep cant, making walking difficult and even dangerous; nothing stayed where it was put unless tightly secured. There were several nasty accidents with hot water and food in the galley, and three cases of broken bones. After ten or so weeks of shipboard life, some passengers were beginning to doubt the wisdom of their decision to emigrate, while others regretted loudly they had not secured passage on a ship fitted with steam engines.

The provisions for the steerage passengers were definitely past their best, and some were beginning to suffer from a lack of fresh food. John Adams increased the allocation of lime juice as generously as he could, and ordered extra food for children and nursing mothers, but little could be done to improve their health save a concerted effort to prevent another outbreak of food poisoning. John insisted all edible provisions be inspected frequently and thoroughly for spoilage, with any found suspect tipped overboard.

He also demanded three of the remaining pigs be slaughtered, roasted thoroughly and shared amongst the steerage passengers over several days. This made John unpopular with his fellow cabin passengers, the pigs having been intended for them, so he ate below decks for a week, tired of listening to their complaints. What the steerage passengers really needed, however, were fresh fruit and vegetables, and neither would be forthcoming until the ship berthed. John was distressed by the poor standard of nutrition but doubted anyone would die from it. And if the ship continued to make good time, he hoped they would reach their destination before anyone's health really began to deteriorate.

The final leg was tedious in the extreme. Entertainments were limited to impromptu concerts and games of cards and dice in the gloomy and fetid family quarters. Tempers continued to unravel, and the cramped conditions caused petty dislikes and irritations to develop into overt antagonisms and, at times, violence.

Tamar spent most of her time in the company of Polly, Myrna and her girls, and John Adams. John had not mentioned his desire for a more permanent relationship with Tamar again, but she often caught him watching her when he thought she wasn't looking. She felt uncomfortable but he seemed cheerful enough when they spent time together and did not seem to begrudge her discussing plans for the future which did not include him.

Tamar had formed a strong bond with her new friends. She was fascinated by Myrna's girls, and although fully aware of what they did for a living, she was surprised to discover their friendship was unaffected. She had always assumed women who sold their bodies would lack the morals, emotions and character traits most 'normal' women displayed. But Myrna's girls were cultured, elegantly groomed, well mannered and very well spoken.

All had been working as prostitutes for several years before they decided to emigrate, and had no illusions about their work. Talking to Tamar one day, Bronwyn described how they felt about themselves and their chosen profession.

'We've all come from working-class backgrounds, all poor, and none of us likely to rise above it by marrying the lad down the street and having ten little ones and getting old before our time. For us, the one thing we have is our looks.'

Tamar concurred; the girls were certainly attractive. Bronwyn was tall and willowy with luxuriant black hair, exotic dark eyes and a sensuous mouth. Letitia's hair was a rich brown with deep red highlights, and Vivienne's a pale rose gold. Both had lovely faces and spectacular figures. Jessica, younger-looking than her colleagues, was petite and slender, her straight blonde hair framing delicate and child-like features.

'So, we decided to use them,' continued Bronwyn. 'I started with Myrna first and the others came later. She taught us all to speak nicely and how to dress and what a customer needs and wants. There's more to it than just opening your legs. There were nine of us working for her in London, but some of the others wanted to go their own way and Myrna thought two of them wouldn't be suitable for New Zealand. Myrna runs a good house. She pays well and she banks what we earn so we've all got tidy sums put away. More than we'd ever have if we'd stayed at home, cooking, cleaning and washing nappies. Oh, we won't be doing this forever,' she added. 'We'll be too old in another ten years to make the money we're making now, but until then, we'll be doing all right. And afterwards, well, I might start my own business. Or I might get married.'

'You're all quite different, aren't you?' Tamar asked. 'Looking, I mean.'

'Yes, we are, and that's quite deliberate. I'm tall and dark for the men who want something a little foreign-looking, although I'm English born and bred, and Vivienne and Letitia both have the round hips and beautiful, big breasts. Jessie looks like she's only fourteen, but she's nearly twenty. She's for customers with a liking for young ones.'

Tamar pulled a face.

Bronwyn responded bluntly. 'Some men are like that. And Jessie's as tough as they come, in spite of how she looks.'

'I wouldn't have thought Myrna would have that sort of thing in her house.'

'As far as she's concerned it's better to provide the service than have some poor little girl having it forced on her. And Myrna's running a business. She has to cater for demand and no doubt men in New Zealand will be the same as men everywhere else.'

The two women were silent for a minute. Then Tamar asked hesitantly, 'But do you think you *will* get married?'

Bronwyn laughed, displaying even, white teeth. 'Will any decent man have me after all this whoring, you mean? I can't see why not. Not every man wants to marry a virgin, and we're not ordinary streetwalkers. I've already had offers. But we'll see, it's a way off yet. I would like a child though,' she added wistfully.

'So would I,' Tamar replied. 'Lots, in fact. But don't you feel … used, sleeping with so many different men?'

'No, I give them what they want and they go away happy. They give me money and I'm happy. It's better than doing it for nothing for the rest of my life. And I get to wear fine clothes, I eat well, Myrna looks after us and I meet interesting people. Gentlemen too, not great lumbering stupid oafs covered in dirt, although some of them can be a little difficult to handle. But that's part of the job. Myrna has strict rules about what is and isn't allowed.'

'And you never get tired of it?'

'Not really. Well, sometimes it can be a bit boring. Some of the customers aren't what they think they are between the sheets, and sometimes they moan on and on about their awful wives. But when that happens I just think about my bank account, because where else am I going to make this sort of money? Sometimes it is exhausting, when we've been busy all afternoon and half the night, but that's the same with all jobs. Didn't you get sick of sewing gowns sometimes?'

'Yes,' Tamar replied. 'And it was hard work!'

'Well, there you are then. Like any other job it has its ups and downs.' Bronwyn giggled at her own joke. 'I expect when I've had enough and it's time to get out, I'll know, but that hasn't happened yet.'

Polly had also taken a great interest in Myrna's girls. One day she asked Tamar outright what it was they did, not believing their elegant grooming and cultured manners were destined for domestic service. Tamar evaded the question but Polly persisted until Tamar suggested she ask Myrna. Surprisingly, Myrna had told her, but requested that she keep it to herself as she didn't want the entire ship knowing the nature of her and her girls' business. Not that she was ashamed, she explained, but because she felt it would cause all sorts of trouble.

After that, Polly spent a significant amount of her time talking with Letitia, Vivienne, Bronwyn and Jessica. Unable to keep the information to herself, she told Sally and Jane, who were rather uncomfortable with the news; they continued to be friendly with Myrna's girls, but kept themselves a little aloof. But the secret went no further, and the rest of the women remained ignorant of the girls' true profession.

About a week out from New Zealand the temperature increased and the weather improved as the *Rebecca Jane* sailed into the calmer and slightly warmer waters below Tasmania. Land-based sea birds became a common sight and now and then vegetation bobbed past the hull. The mood on board also began to lighten as the emigrants neared their destination. All were heartily sick of the voyage, weary of the ever-worsening food, the constant lack of privacy, of each other's company, the episodes of ill health, and the extremes of temperature they had endured over the past months.

Tamar longed for a decent soak in hot, clean water and yearned to put on freshly washed clothes not stiff with dried salt. She had run out of soap for her hair, which had been lank and greasy for weeks, the head and body lice infesting the ship were driving her mad, and her body craved fresh fruit and vegetables. She was deeply frustrated to learn they could be at sea for another two weeks. Yesterday, the Captain had advised the *Rebecca Jane* was about to begin her run north into the Tasman Sea and up the west coast of New Zealand, but land would probably not be sighted until they passed Cape Maria van Diemen at the northernmost tip. After that, it would be several days further before they finally arrived in Auckland.

In anticipation, and amidst an almost party-like atmosphere, the hold was opened and the emigrants began to prepare their belongings for disembarkation. To their horror, a number of trunks and boxes had been rotted by sea water leaking from above and were in various stages of mouldy disintegration. Rats had eaten every-thing they could find and made themselves cosy little homes. Even worse, some of the cabin passengers' luggage had been broken into and valuable items removed. There was an uproar and the Captain ordered a ship-wide search for the stolen belongings, although nothing was recovered and he was never able to establish whether it was his crew or light-fingered passengers who had committed the thefts.

With the weather now much improved, the passengers spent more of their time on deck, many positioning themselves along the bulwarks in the hope of being the first to see land. The children had reached a level of excitement nearing hysteria and were almost uncontrollable but now the end of the voyage was near, their behaviour was tolerated. Dances were held on deck in the evenings and there was a new feeling of optimism, goodwill and hope.

On the morning of 4 June the cry of '*Land!*' came from a sailor perched high in the rigging. The word spread quickly and within minutes the upper deck was swarming with people eager for their first glimpse of New Zealand. Some were disappointed, as all that was visible was a long, low line of white cloud on the eastern horizon, but for most the sight was heartening. Several days later, as the *Rebecca Jane* rounded the top of the North Island, the view was more rewarding; dark, forest-clad hills were clearly visible, with white-capped waves breaking on rugged shores. The emigrants were disappointed again as the ship's passage between the Three Kings Islands and Cape Reinga was shrouded in low cloud and winter fog, obscuring any view of the coast, but by afternoon the weather had lifted and the empty, white beaches of North Cape came into view.

The *Rebecca Jane* turned south and began the last three days of her voyage down the eastern coast of the North Island, sailing past the Bay of Islands and Whangarei Harbour on her right and

Great Barrier Island on her left, and finally into the Hauraki Gulf. By the time she slipped past the region's youngest volcano, the scrubby island of Rangitoto with its curious symmetrical crater, and on into the mouth of the Waitemata Harbour, the light had faded and the Captain gave the order to lower the anchor in the Rangitoto Channel. Grumbling, his passengers prepared to spend their last night at sea.

In the morning most were up, packed and on deck before the sun rose. It had begun to rain during the night, the weather was cold and windy and the harbour choppy, but the emigrants waited expectantly for the sun to rise. As it did, the shoreline of Mechanics Bay, so named for the first immigrant tradesmen known as 'mechanics' put ashore there, slowly revealed itself. Rain glistened on the dismal, grey buildings lining the waterfront and the churned-up mud road. A railway embankment rose above a sprawling brickyard and a blackened foundry and untidy stacks of timber lay everywhere. To the right on a small, partially excavated point sat the derelict remains of the demolished Britomart Barracks, once home to the 58th Regiment. On board the *Rebecca Jane* the emigrants, immigrants now they had finally arrived, were silent.

'Bloody 'ell,' said a man behind Tamar. 'Is this it? It's worse than 'ome!'

CHAPTER FOUR

June 1879

Had the sun been shining, the immigrants might have felt more enthusiastic about their new home. From their vantage point in the Waitemata Harbour, they would have been able to see the wooded, rural slopes of Parnell Rise overlooking Hobson and Judges Bays and the gentle hills of Remuera. To the southwest was Orakei Basin and, almost behind them, Mission Bay and St Heliers. Across the harbour was the Devonport peninsula, dominated by Mt Victoria and North Head.

As the sun rose higher, the Captain ordered the anchor lifted and the *Rebecca Jane* was towed to Queen's Wharf, where the immigrants were to disembark. The process was frustratingly slow and several hours passed before they were on solid ground, waiting impatiently for transport to Auckland's immigration barracks. While they waited, sheltering from the cold drizzle, they amused themselves by staggering about, their sea legs not yet adapted to the sudden lack of rolling motion. Most of the cabin passengers had already departed in hired coaches or had been collected by friends or family. As Tamar and Myrna stood under the inadequate shelter of a sunshade, Tamar spied John Adams striding purposefully towards her, hat in hand.

'Tamar,' he said, coming to a muddy stop and handing her a folded piece of paper. 'This is where I'll be staying,' he said, pointing at his note. 'Dr Basil Stokes is a friend of mine, and he's putting me up. As soon as you are settled, send me a note and I'll come and see you. Then when I've set myself up, you can come and visit me. I'll have my own rooms by then, and a house. Tamar?' he added, a pleading note creeping into his voice. He reached out and took her hand. 'Will you visit me?'

Myrna quickly turned away and busied herself lighting a cigarette.

Tamar nodded. 'As soon as I am settled somewhere permanent, John. I promise. Whatever happens, we'll always be friends.'

John gazed at her solemnly, suspecting he was on the verge of losing her. Tamar saw the sadness in his eyes and her heart ached for him. 'I promise there will always be a place for you in my life.'

Myrna raised her eyebrows and thought, what *are* you playing at, lassie? Tamar was passing up an offer most women would kill for. John Adams may not be the most handsome man in the world, but he was possibly the kindest and certainly the most loyal.

John leaned forward and kissed Tamar very gently on her cheek. 'I'm going now,' he said. 'Please keep in touch.'

'I will,' she replied as he walked away, ramming his hat aggressively on his damp head.

'Oh, dear, I hope I haven't upset him.'

'We'll see, lassie, we'll see,' Myrna muttered as she gazed after John.

The transport, a convoy of carts drawn by bedraggled-looking horses, finally arrived and the immigrants loaded their belongings and climbed in, chattering excitedly and pointing out interesting sights as they drove through the muddy streets. When they arrived at the immigration barracks many were relieved to see the building was better maintained than the barracks at Plymouth. They were asked to show their medical certificates to immigration officials as they filed in through the main entrance, given a perfunctory tour of their temporary accommodation and advised a lecture about their new country would be held in an hour's time in the dining hall.

Tamar had little sleep that night, excitement was high and most did not turn in until after midnight. Speculation was rife about employment opportunities and the next morning many of the men rose early, eager to explore the town and begin job hunting. By the end of the day none of those who returned had found work, but most remained positive.

The new immigrants were only permitted to stay at the barracks for a few days so finding other accommodation was a priority. Tamar, Polly, Jane and Sally decided they would relocate together to a boarding house and one of the immigration officials recommended a respectable establishment on Ponsonby Road. 'It's not cheap,' he warned. 'Best you find yourselves good jobs before you settle in too comfortably.'

'Oh, we will, Mister, don't yer worry yer 'ead about us!' Polly replied optimistically. 'This 'ere's the land of opportunity.'

Myrna and her girls had already left the previous day, Myrna having rented a house in Mt Eden while she went about the task of setting up her business. The farewell had been emotional but the women parted on an optimistic note, Myrna taking Tamar to one side to tell her she could help them if things did not go as well as they hoped.

As the girls climbed down from the carriage outside the boarding establishment on Ponsonby Road and waited for their luggage to be unloaded, they stared up at the house that would be their home for as long as they could afford it. It was a slightly shabby but still handsome two-storeyed wooden residence with verandahs along the front and a modest portico over the front door. Tamar and her friends looked at each other, eyebrows raised; none of them had ever been in such a big house before, let alone lived in one, but while they had a little money they intended to make the most of it.

'Well,' said Polly, her hands on her hips, a wide smile on her face and her fluffy blonde hair escaping from under her hat. 'This is a bit of all right, isn't it? I wish everyone back 'ome could see me now. Wouldn't they be *green*?'

She walked boldly up to the front door and banged the brass knocker. The girls heard footsteps hurrying up the hall inside, then the door opened halfway and a bespectacled, middle-aged face peered out.

'Yes?' asked the woman, her foot wedged firmly behind the half-opened door. 'Can I be of assistance?'

'We understand you've rooms fer lease ter single women,' said Polly brightly. 'We're new immigrants an' we've just arrived.'

The woman held her hand out through the gap in the door. 'Papers please.'

The girls handed over their documents and waited while the woman read them slowly and thoroughly.

'Well, then, good morning to you,' she said when she'd finished, evidently satisfied. 'Seamstresses and domestics, I see. I am Mrs Barriball. I apologise for my hesitation but one cannot be too careful,' she said, opening the door wide. She was dressed in a severe black grosgrain gown with a small collar and a white lace cap with black ribbons. 'Come in, please. Put your things in the hall and take a seat in the parlour,' she said, indicating a room off the wide hallway to the right. 'I will be with you shortly.' She hurried off, her skirts swishing, towards the back of the house.

Tamar dragged her trunk over the doorstep then led the way into the gloomy front room.

The parlour was dominated by a large fireplace inlaid with pressed tin and an intricate pattern of blue, green and white enamel tiles surrounded by an ornate wooden mantelpiece. On either side sat two over-stuffed wing chairs piled with cushions, flanked by occasional tables with lace doilies and a collection of china figurines. Vases filled with silk flowers and ostrich feathers were intermingled with framed photographs along the top of the mantelpiece, and on the polished wooden shelves above the fire. On the floor was a worn floral carpet with strategically placed rugs, and the walls were decorated with faded floral wallpaper. Everywhere the girls looked there were ornaments and potted plants. Arranged in front of the fire and facing it were two slightly aged-looking sofas draped with embroidered antimacassars, and behind them several more heavily laden side tables. On the walls hung two ornate mirrors and six or seven framed portraits of unsmiling, dreary-looking people. The curtains were heavy and draped so little sunlight could penetrate the room.

'God,' said Tamar, perching gingerly on the edge of one of the sofas. 'I'm glad I don't have to dust in here.'

'Well, we might yet, if we run out of money,' said Jane. 'Be good practice, though, fer domestic service.' Jane and Sally intended to go into service as soon as they could, while Tamar and Polly, also a seamstress, were looking for sewing positions.

'Now, ladies,' said Mrs Barriball as she swished back into the room. 'Sit down, please, while I avail you of the rules. Which,' she added, looking at them sternly over the top of her small spectacles, 'I expect to be adhered to. I run a respectable establishment and there is no place for slovenliness, low morals or unladylike behaviour.'

She seated herself in one of the chairs next to the fire and took a deep breath. 'First, there will be no gentleman callers. You may have lady friends to visit, whom you may entertain in the parlour, but no gentlemen. There is a strict curfew of nine thirty at night. Second, I expect a high standard of neatness and cleanliness. You will attend to your own rooms but I will supply you with clean linen on a regular basis. You will do your personal laundry in the laundry at the back of the house. There are chamber pots under your beds, but I would appreciate you availing yourselves of the privy off the laundry whenever possible. Breakfast is at six thirty in the morning and supper at seven thirty in the evening. You will have to provide your own luncheon. No cooking in your rooms, and no alcohol or tobacco.' Mrs Barriball paused briefly, then continued. 'You may not be here long as the job market is not what it used to be. I am not out to rob young women of their money, but I charge the going rate for a clean, wholesome, quality establishment, and I doubt any of you has independent means,' she said not unkindly, glancing at the girls' worn and plain clothes. 'But while you are here, I hope you enjoy your stay. Now, do you have any questions?'

No one did, so Mrs Barriball showed the girls to their individual rooms. Tamar's was upstairs at the front of the house, overlooking Ponsonby Road. The room was furnished with an iron bedstead, a wardrobe and a mirrored chest of drawers on which sat a large china ewer and bowl, and a straight-backed wooden chair in front of a small writing table, on which a *Bible* had been conspicuously placed. There was a large rug in the middle of the floor and several paintings on the walls. It was nowhere near as fussily decorated as the parlour, but it was comfortable. Tamar unpacked her belongings, then went to sit quietly on the verandah, her mind contemplating the events of the last few months and what the future might hold.

The following day the girls rose early, breakfasted, and walked to the end of Ponsonby Road. Mrs Barriball loudly disapproved their lack of chaperone but they politely ignored her. The unpaved road was dotted with puddles and piles of horse dung and before long they were hitching their skirts out of the mud.

'Me boots aren't going ter last long at this rate,' complained Sally. 'An' I've only got the one pair.'

At the end of Ponsonby Road they spent some of their precious money on a public carriage into the central commercial district around the wharves and lower Queen Street. They wandered about for most of the morning, gazing at the new brick and plaster commercial buildings interspersed with older, less grand wooden shops and premises. Occasionally they passed small groups of Maori sitting or standing in the street dressed in an eclectic range of European clothing. The girls were fascinated and a little unnerved as they had never seen dark-skinned people, especially not with exotically tattooed faces. Tamar noticed some of the women had tattooed chins, whereas the men with tattoos were marked all over their faces. They tried not to stare but their curiosity did not seem to bother the Maori, several of whom waved cheerfully.

'They're called *moko*,' whispered Sally. She pronounced the word to rhyme with cocoa. 'Mrs Barriball said.'

'What? Them brown people?' asked Polly.

'No. The patterns on their faces.'

'What do the patterns mean?' asked Tamar. 'They're all different.'

'Dunno. Why don't yer ask one of 'em?' suggested Polly.

'No!' replied Sally hastily. 'Mrs Barriball said if we seen any of 'em we're ter stay away. She says they're not civilised.'

The girls walked quickly off, glancing nervously behind them, much to the amusement of the Maori.

By midday the girls had been into almost every shop and marvelled over the fine clothes and goods they expected to be able to afford as soon as they found work. Hungry and with sore feet they frittered away more of their money on lunch at the rather splendid Albert Hotel, smiling graciously at the obviously wealthy women also lunching there, who glared at the girls when they laughed too loudly. Polly did not help matters by ostentatiously demonstrating her version of upper-class 'airs'.

After lunch they explored some of the smaller lanes off Queen Street but soon retreated as they encountered evidence of poverty and misery. They had noticed this on Queen Street as well — the stench of raw sewage, people with their hands out or drunk in public — but the pathetic peddlers selling nothing worth buying and the beggars and poorly dressed, underfed children running about in the cold without shoes or coats seemed more sordid and depressing in the smaller, darker alleys.

'Reminds me of 'ome,' Jane muttered. They were shocked and a little subdued. None of them had expected to see such blatant poverty in New Zealand; it was something they thought had been left thousands of miles behind them.

A week later, the girls were forced to admit New Zealand was not the land of limitless opportunity enthusiastically described by the emigration agents. Many emigrants had been attracted by cheap assisted passages, part of Julius Vogel's scheme to bring emigrants to the new colony, but by the time the girls had boarded the *Rebecca Jane* at Plymouth, the colony was saturated with debt. They had no way of knowing, but they had arrived on the eve of a long and severe economic depression.

In the following weeks Jane and Sally found employment as domestics and both moved out of Mrs Barriball's boarding house, but Tamar and Polly were unable to find positions. After three weeks, seriously regretting they had spent so much at Mrs Barriball's, they were forced to move to a less appealing boarding establishment in lower Shortland Street.

The narrow, streetfront house, in dire need of paint and repairs, accommodated ten single women and consisted of a series of tiny bedrooms leading off a dingy central hallway smelling of cabbage and boiled mutton. There was a large kitchen cum parlour at the far end of the hall, and a small shared bathroom. The privy was an offensive-smelling long drop across a small back yard where a sad and mangy little dog was kept. The accommodation was basic and the boarders provided and maintained their own linen, but it was almost clean and, more importantly, cheap. Polly missed the grand fireplace in Mrs Barriball's parlour, the vases with the ostrich feathers and the large comfortable bedrooms. She vowed to Tamar on their first night at Shortland Street that she would own a parlour like that herself one day.

The boarding house had a first floor where the landlady and her family lived. The tenants rarely saw them as they had their own entrance, the husband coming and going irregularly as he did shift work on the wharf. His wife, a harassed and angry-looking woman in her thirties, managed the boarding house and looked after their five small children. Tamar and Polly spent their days walking the central commercial area, knocking on doors and asking for work. They stood for hours in long queues of unemployed women, only to be told there was none. They were both running out of money, Polly especially, and were beginning to despair. Their path each morning took them past the ever-growing slum of Chancery Street with its cramped and decaying houses with broken windows and filthy back yards, and they wondered how long it would be before they were forced to live in such poverty.

Tamar knew that if she visited Myrna, her friend would offer to loan her money, if not make an outright gift, but she felt too embarrassed to do this; it was too close to begging, and an admission of failure. It would be even more humiliating to contact John Adams and might encourage him.

In the last week of July, almost two months after they arrived in Auckland, Tamar and Polly were walking up a wet and windy Queen Street when they saw a man place a notice in the window of the premises of Arthur C. Ellis, Draper. They glanced at each other, then rushed through the door. Inside, the interior was tastefully appointed in polished wood with gleaming brass fittings. An extensive range of fabrics, from the practical to the opulent, was artfully displayed around the walls. At the back was a wide wooden counter with a cash register and several bolts of cloth, and behind it stood the man who placed the notice. He sported muttonchop whiskers and an impressive moustache, and was in his shirt sleeves, wearing a bow tie with a dark grey waistcoat matching his trousers.

'Ladies,' he said, leaning forward with his hands on the polished counter. 'And what can I do for you on this not very fine day?'

'You have a notice in your window, sir, advertising employment. We'd like to apply,' said Tamar in a rush.

'Yes, I do,' the man replied genially. 'But I only have one position. For someone who knows fabrics and has experience cutting patterns. Preferably someone with a recommendation attesting to their skills and character.'

Polly, who did not have a reference, kept smiling but Tamar saw tears welling in her eyes. In an artificially cheerful voice Polly said, 'Well, that lets me out, dunnit? I'll wait outside fer yer, Tamar,' and turned and quickly left the shop.

'Oh dear,' said the man. 'I hate to see a pretty girl disappointed, but times are hard. So, I take it you have a recommendation?'

Tamar nodded and silently handed him Mrs Tregowan's reference.

'I'm Arthur C. Ellis,' said the man as he read. 'You are Tamar Deane, I gather? And you've had cutting experience?' When she said she had, Mr Ellis continued, 'We don't do garment cutting, but you need to know how it's done so you can measure the correct lengths. And you also need to know about fabrics so you can advise customers on the drape and fall of curtains and the like. Do you think you can do all that, and operate the register? I see you have your letters and numbers. I need a scrupulously honest shop girl.

I've two other assistants, a woman who does the sewing and a boy who works in the storeroom, but you'd be required to do a bit of sewing when we're pushed. Oh, and you need to be able to lift the bolts of cloth down onto the counter for cutting.'

'I'm sure I can do all that,' Tamar replied confidently.

'Your recommendation says you hail from Cornwall,' Mr Ellis observed.

'I do, sir. From just outside Truro.'

Mr Ellis raised his eyebrows. 'I thought so. I came out almost twenty years ago. Bodmin was my home town. It will be a treat to hear another Cornish voice in the shop. The job's yours, Miss Deane. We'll start with a six-week trial and if it works out you'll be taken on as permanent staff. Does that suit?'

Tamar smiled broadly and said yes before he could change his mind. Mr Ellis told her what her wages would be and her hours of work, and asked if she could start the following Monday. The hours were long with only Sundays off, and the pay unspectacular, but infinitely preferable to nothing. Tamar left the shop feeling as though she were floating six inches above the ground.

'I got it! I got it!' she exclaimed to Polly, who was waiting down the street.

'I thought yer might,' she replied. 'An' yer deserve it. I'm right pleased fer yer.' And she was. 'When yer've got a bit of money together yer should find yerself somewhere nicer to live an' all.'

'But what about you?' said Tamar, trying to contain her excitement in deference to Polly's continuing unemployment. 'We need to find *you* a job. I'm not moving anywhere until I know you're all right.'

'I'll be fine,' Polly replied resolutely. 'I know 'ow ter take care of meself.'

'I'll talk to Mr Ellis on Monday. He might know of something.'

As it happened, Mr Ellis knew of a manufacturer who was

offering outwork on a piece-rate basis. The money was a pittance but Polly, whose finances were almost totally depleted, took up the offer and sat in her room from morning to dusk, sewing 25-pound cloth bags. She was paid two shillings per gross and when she finished a batch, she carted them to the manufactory and collected cloth and thread for the next lot. At the end of each day her eyes, back and head ached, and her fingers were raw and blistered. She hated it but as she could now afford to pay for her room and board she persevered, telling Tamar she was quite happy to do it until something better came along.

Delivering a finished set of bags to the factory one day, Polly was told by a woman smoking a pipe and leaning against the wall that there were positions going for manufactory workers. Polly went straight in and joined the queue. There were five vacancies and Polly was selected to fill one. The pay was low, eight and a half shillings a week, but better than for sewing bags. Conditions in the factory were noisy, dirty and often dangerous and she would be required to work a seventy-two-hour week of six twelve-hour days. After she had been informed she had one of the positions she went outside, sat in the gutter and cried with relief.

Tamar was pleased her friend would be earning better wages but concerned about the conditions in which she would be working. Mr Ellis regularly held forth on the conditions factory workers had to put up with, and how something should be done about it. Tamar felt guilty about her own position, which was positively luxurious compared to Polly's, and tried to give her friend money whenever she had any extra, but it was always politely refused.

'I've got enough to keep me goin', luv, thanks,' Polly would always say. And she did. She was living hand to mouth, and the reality of owning a fine parlour with vases of ostrich feathers was as far away as it had ever been, but she was surviving. She made friends at the factory and, being a social person, the camaraderie during her days at work made the miserable conditions and poor pay almost tolerable. Most days, anyway.

At the end of Tamar's six-week trial, she was taken on as permanent staff and given a small increase; in appreciation of her efforts and her lovely way with the customers, Mr Ellis said. She could now afford to move to better lodgings and away from the endless stink of boiled cabbage. She talked it over with Polly, who could not afford to move, and Polly assured her she would be fine on her own and Tamar should start making moves to improve her position.

'After all,' she said, 'yer're not goin' ter attract that fine man who's goin' ter sweep yer off yer feet living in this poxy bloody dump!'

Tamar laughed, but she knew Polly was right. Within the week she found considerably more comfortable accommodation at a boarding house in Cook Street. As she loaded her trunk into the cab she had hired to move her things, Polly stood at the door and watched. When she was ready, Tamar hugged her and asked her to keep in touch; she could come into the shop or to Cook Street any time, and nothing would change.

Polly knew, however, that things inevitably *would* change, and she stood staring down Shortland Street for some time after Tamar had departed, as if Tamar might turn round and come back. After twenty minutes, Polly went inside and shut the door behind her.

September 1879

One Saturday morning Tamar was at work when the bell over the shop door chimed. She looked up to see Myrna McTaggart sweep into the shop, resplendent in violet-coloured taffeta, which accentuated her red hair, and a jaunty little matching hat with feathers. Myrna stopped dead.

'Tamar *Deane*,' she exclaimed. 'Where *have* ye been? Och, I'm a poet,' she added, and laughed.

Tamar hurried from behind the counter, her arms open wide. The two women hugged fiercely. 'It's so *good* to see you, Myrna. Where have *you* been?'

'Well,' the older woman replied, glancing keen-eyed about the shop. 'We were renting a wee house in Mt Eden while I was looking for a place to buy, but I've found one now. A verra lovely place in Dilworth Terrace in Parnell. We're in the middle o' making alterations and redecorating, and we'll be open for business in three or four weeks.'

'Parnell!' said Tamar, impressed. 'I didn't realise you had *that* much money!'

'I didnae quite have enough, but I made maself a suitable arrangement with a verra helpful gentleman.'

'Oh,' said Tamar, surprised. 'Do banks lend money for … your sort of business?'

'No, lassie, no' a bank, a moneylender, and they lend money for any sort o' business they think will be profitable,' laughed Myrna.

'So are you living there yet?'

'No, we cannae move in for a week or so; the tradesmen are still there and we havnae organised the furnishings. That's why I'm here. Mr Ellis was recommended as the best draper in town, so here I am. I didnae ken *ye* were working here, though.'

A discreet cough alerted them to Mr Ellis's presence.

'Mr Ellis, this is my good friend, Miss Myrna McTaggart. We came out on the ship together.' Mr Ellis stepped forward and gently took hold of Myrna's gloved hand.

'*Delighted* to meet you,' he said, with a wide smile.

'And yeself, Mr Ellis. Your premises are as elegant as I have been led to believe,' Myrna replied, favouring the draper with a dazzling smile of her own.

'And what can I hope to do for you, madam? A set of velvet curtains for your parlour perhaps? A length of damask for a pretty tablecloth?'

'Och, more than that, I should hope,' said Myrna. 'I'm looking to furnish ma new home in Parnell. I have eleven bedrooms, two parlours, a drawing room, a dining salon, a large kitchen and all the other amenities ye would expect. I require them all to be furnished to a verra high standard including drapes and lace curtains, bedspreads and linens and anything else I might need. D'ye think ye can be o' assistance?'

Mr Ellis's eyes lit up and his eyebrows almost flew off his forehead. 'Indeed, madam, indeed I can! Come this way if you please. Just this morning I received a new shipment of quality silk from the Orient, not to mention some lovely venise. And you'll be needing towelling as well, I expect.' He led Myrna away, his hand on her upper arm, on a tour of his vast collection of fabrics and accessories. Tamar smiled to herself; Mr Ellis was clearly in his element.

An hour and a half later Myrna had chosen the fabrics she wanted and had given Mr Ellis and his seamstress instructions. Mr Ellis promised to make her order a priority. As Myrna prepared to leave, she drew Tamar to one side. 'How is Polly? I havnae seen anything o' her at all.'

'I haven't seen her for some time,' replied Tamar, feeling very uncomfortable. 'I've been to her lodgings twice in the last month, but she hasn't been at home. She might have been at work at the factory, but I didn't like to go at night by myself. And I've sent three or four notes, but she hasn't responded.'

'Factory!' exclaimed Myrna. 'Ye mean she's slaving away in a sweatshop? And is she no' sharing accommodation with yeself?'

Tamar explained what had happened since they left the boarding house on Ponsonby Road.

'Och, well, I'd better go and find the lassie maself, then. This isnae always a safe town, ye ken. I'll let ye know when I track her down,' Myrna said. 'Well, I'll be away now. I'm off to pick out some furniture but I'll be back next week to see how yon Mr Ellis is getting on with ma drapes. I'll talk to ye then.' She kissed Tamar on the cheek and left the shop, the bell chiming behind her.

'What a *magnificent* woman,' said Mr Ellis, his eyes sparkling. '*Truly* magnificent. And wealthy too, I suspect. You don't happen to know how she came by her money, do you, Miss Deane?'

'No,' Tamar lied. 'But I think she has some sort of business.'

'And you did introduce her as *Miss* McTaggart? Not Mrs?'

'No, she isn't married, Mr Ellis. Well, not to my knowledge.'

'Well, well,' said Mr Ellis, thoughtfully twiddling the ends of his moustache.

'But I don't think she's looking for a husband at the moment,' Tamar added gently. Mr Ellis went pink.

CHAPTER FIVE

The following Monday Myrna hired a cab and went to the boarding house on Shortland Street. 'Good evening to ye, lassie,' said Myrna when the door was opened by a slightly grubby-looking young woman. 'I'm looking for Polly Jakes. Is she in?'

'No,' replied the girl sullenly. 'She'll be working.'

'At the factory? At this hour?' said Myrna, looking surprised.

'She don't work at t'factory. She's on t'streets.'

'*Working* the streets, do ye mean? Where?'

The surly girl nodded but volunteered nothing more.

'Oh, Christ,' said Myrna angrily as she dug in her purse for some money. 'Here. No doubt this will loosen your tongue.'

'Down t'hill by Customhouse Street. Queen's Wharf end.'

'How long has she been doing this?' demanded Myrna.

The girl shrugged indifferently.

'Well, thank ye *so* much for your help,' Myrna said sarcastically as the door was shut in her face.

Back in the waiting cab she ordered the cabbie to head towards Customhouse Street. As they arrived she asked him to drive slowly. Women stood on several street corners, their faces partially illuminated by the dim gas streetlights, with more hanging about the wharf gates. Leaning out of the cab window as they drove past, Myrna peered at them closely.

At the intersection of Customhouse and Commerce Streets, she asked the cabbie to stop; across the road stood someone who vaguely resembled Polly. The girl was looking in the direction of Quay Street at three drunken sailors attempting to hold each other up. Myrna crossed the road and walked up behind her.

'Polly Jakes! What the hell d'ye think ye're doing?'

When the girl turned, Myrna saw she had been mistaken. 'Sorry, lassie, I thought ye were someone else.'

'Myrna?' asked the girl in a doubtful voice.

Myrna saw it was indeed Polly. 'God bugger ma bloody days! What on earth have ye done to yeself?'

Polly was at least twenty pounds thinner and her shabby dress hung off scrawny, stooped shoulders. Her blonde hair was filthy and she had a large open sore at the corner of her mouth. Even in the dim light Myrna could see the pallor of her skin and deep shadows under her eyes. 'Ye look like shite, lassie! What's happened to ye?'

Polly stared back for so long Myrna thought the poor girl had been struck deaf. Then she sat in the dirt, put her face in her hands and wept. Myrna picked up her skirts and squatted beside her. 'Aye, ye've fallen on hard times, haven't ye?' she asked gently.

Polly continued to weep but managed to nod. Myrna handed her a handkerchief and waited patiently until the distraught girl gained some control of herself. 'I 'ated the factory so much,' she said when she had recovered a little. 'It were all right to start wiv', but it got worse. I were so tired an' the money were never enough. An' some of the other girls said this were a good way to make money, so I started about six weeks ago but I just aren't doing so well. There's too many 'ores around!' she wailed bitterly. 'I can't afford proper food an' I've gotten sick an' ugly!'

Myrna stroked Polly's bony back soothingly. 'It's all right,' she murmured. 'I ken what it's like. I've been there, remember? Though

I dinnae recall ever smelling quite as bad,' she added as she caught a whiff of Polly's body odour. 'Ye've lost yeself, haven't ye?'

Polly nodded miserably.

'Well, there's nothing for it, I'm taking ye home with me,' said Myrna, straightening up. 'We'll go back to yon boarding house and get your things. Get up now, a lady doesnae sit in the dirt.'

'I'm not a lady. Not any more,' mumbled Polly.

'Yes, ye are!' replied Myrna angrily. 'And dinnae forget that, lassie!'

She helped Polly up and led her to the cab. The cabbie jumped down, then recoiled when he saw the state of his extra passenger.

'Och, dinnae be stupid, man,' Myrna snapped testily. 'Ye'll no' catch anything!' Then, after the cabbie had reluctantly helped Polly into the cab, she added deliberately, 'Well, ye'll *probably* no' catch anything. Back to Shortland Street, and be quick about it.'

When they arrived, Myrna banged loudly on the front door. The same sour-faced girl answered. 'Aye, it's me again,' said Myrna. 'I've come to collect this lassie's things.'

The girl stood dumbly aside as Myrna barged past and led Polly into the hall. 'Which room?' Myrna asked.

'This one,' said Polly, pointing to a doorway halfway down.

Myrna opened the door and said, 'God Almighty, what a fleapit. Well, get your things together. What *is* that godawful stink?'

'Cabbage,' replied Polly, dropping her few tatty personal belongings into a carry bag, then she hesitated.

'There's one other thing I 'ave ter get. I won't be a minute.'

She headed down the dingy hallway, opened the back door and went outside. Myrna followed and watched while Polly untied a small, pathetic-looking black and white dog. She scooped him up and stuffed him into her bag, jamming his head down and quickly snapping the clasp shut. 'I'm ready,' she said as she straightened up, staggering slightly.

'Are ye all right?'

Polly nodded. 'Just dizzy. I'm a bit 'ungry.'

'Och, that's easily fixed. Are ye paid up in ye rent?'

'I owe a few weeks.'

As they re-entered the house Myrna dropped a pound note onto the kitchen table, then they went out through the front door and climbed into the cab. Myrna told the cabbie to go, and they turned and headed in the direction of Mt Eden.

Polly fell asleep, her mouth open and the mangy little dog curled on her lap; Myrna had to wake her when they arrived and help her up the short path. Jessica answered when Myrna rang the bell.

'Hello, you're back. Oooh, who's that?' Jessica asked in a shocked voice, pulling a disgusted face at the bedraggled figure next to Myrna. Polly fainted and dropped the dog. He whimpered and immediately hopped onto her unconscious form.

'Bugger. Help me get her up,' directed Myrna. 'Get the others.'

When Letitia, Vivienne and Bronwyn appeared they carefully picked Polly up and carried her into the parlour.

'Pooh,' said Letitia, holding her elegant nose and stepping back. 'She stinks.'

'Aye, she does,' replied Myrna, rubbing Polly's still hands. 'Can one o' ye prepare a tub?'

Polly came around by the time the water for her bath had been heated and poured into the tub. Myrna removed her dirty clothes, wrapped her in a blanket and propped her up on a sofa in the parlour with a generous glass of brandy. The dog crouched on her bare feet, refusing to move. Myrna's girls were firing questions at Polly and she looked as if she was going to cry again.

'Let her alone, will ye?' said Myrna crossly as she helped Polly into the bathroom. 'She's exhausted and no' well. Ye could be helpful and lend her some soap and hair rinse and find her something to wear after she's bathed.'

The little dog sat down in the middle of the parlour and started a terrible, heart-rending yowling.

'Oh, Christ, bring the bloody thing in as well,' muttered Myrna over her shoulder. Letitia and Bronwyn herded the dog down the hall with their feet and guided him into the bathroom. He spotted Polly lowering herself into the tub and launched himself in with a pathetic little splash.

Myrna was shocked at Polly's condition. She was very thin and her ribs and hip bones jutted out in an ugly, painful way. Her breasts had shrunk and her skin was mottled and bruised. 'God, lassie, how could ye let this happen?'

Polly shrugged, her eyes half closed. 'I got so tired at the factory an' I couldn't afford food,' she replied eventually. 'It were food or lodgin's, an' I didn't want ter sleep on the streets. It didn't get any better when I were street-walkin' an' I just lost control of it after that, especially when I got sick.'

'Ye poor wee thing,' crooned Myrna, rubbing chamomile rinse into Polly's hair, pouring a generous dollop over the dog as well.

'Was it bad?' she asked after a while. 'The men, I mean?'

Polly nodded. 'It weren't what I thought it would be like. Yer know, from what Bronwyn an' the girls told me.'

'Och, lassie, it's a completely different kettle o' fish when ye're on the streets,' said Myrna. 'The customers dinnae have the money, nor the manners. Were ye hurt?'

'I got belted a few times. I thought it were me own fault 'cos I were no good.'

Myrna shook her head. 'No, lassie. There's some men who need that. And they're no' necessarily the piddly spenders either. It's no' your fault.'

She looked down at the little dog crouching unhappily at the end of the tub, his ugly head and skinny shoulders poking out of the water. He was a terrier of some sort, but looked suspiciously as if he had an assortment of breeds in him. 'Is this your wee mongrel?' she asked.

'Well, 'e is now. 'E were at the boardin' 'ouse when we got there. 'E never got fed properly so I'd give 'im some of me food. I think 'e likes me.'

'Clearly,' replied Myrna dryly.

'Can I keep 'im?' Polly asked. 'I'll look after 'im an' make sure 'e's clean.'

'Is he important to ye?'

Polly nodded.

'Aye, well, ye can keep him. But the first time he makes a mess inside the house he's by his wee self, all right? What's his name?'

'Cabbage,' said Polly, smiling for the first time that night.

Myrna helped her finish bathing then assisted her out of the tub, wrapped her in several large towels and sat her on a wooden chair. Then she got on her knees next to the tub and scrubbed the little dog vigorously. Now considerably cleaner, he was lifted out of the bath and rubbed until his short fur stuck up, then examined for ticks. Myrna found six or seven and pulled them off, bursting their blood-engorged bodies with her long fingernails. She rinsed her hands and walked over to stand behind Polly. 'Ye've got headlice,' she observed.

Myrna combed out Polly's wet hair for the next hour, slowly and painstakingly removing every nit and egg. Polly almost nodded off again.

When Myrna had finished she asked, 'Have ye anything else wrong? No infections o' any sort?'

'Yer mean the sore on me mouth?'

'No, lassie, that's probably from no' enough good food. I mean your fanny.'

'I don't think so.'

'Well, that's a relief. And a surprise. I'll get John Adams to come and have a look at ye tomorrow, just to be sure. I think ye should have a feed now then go to bed. Ye can talk to the girls tomorrow when ye've had a decent rest.'

Polly was put into bed in a borrowed nightdress and given soup and bread and a cup of tea, but she fell asleep before she could drink the tea. The little dog was also sound asleep, curled up on Polly's feet, snoring softly and emitting an occasional gentle fart.

Myrna stood and watched Polly's sleeping form. 'Ye poor little bugger,' she said quietly.

Polly slept solidly for almost twelve hours and woke in the early afternoon, feeling better. She ate an enormous lunch then went back to sleep. John Adams had been summoned and arrived that evening. He examined Polly and pronounced she was very run down but her physical condition would no doubt improve after a few weeks of wholesome food. He added she showed no sign of syphilis or anything of a similar nature, and recommended rest and a proprietary tonic to keep her calm and help rebuild her strength. Sitting in the parlour later sipping a brandy, he asked Myrna what would happen to Polly.

'She'll stay with me, I suppose. I cannae put her out on the street again and leave her to fend for herself.'

John nodded. 'Will she work for you?'

'I cannae say,' replied Myrna, placing her tea cup on a side table and lighting a cigarette.

Myrna did not drink alcohol. She had in her younger days and got herself into such serious trouble she'd sworn off it. In her opinion, for some people at least, drink was the Devil's right hand and to be avoided at all costs; her own father had been a drinker and she had watched him die of it at an early age.

'I havnae said anything,' she continued. 'She's no' the sort o' lassie I usually have working for me. She's a wee bit rough around the edges, bless her heart, and she'd need a bit o' polishing.'

John nodded but kept quiet. He knew what Myrna's line of work was, but he wasn't particularly offended; she looked after her girls, unlike some.

'Have you seen Tamar?' He always asked. He had been deeply disappointed when Tamar had not contacted him, but had resigned himself to the fact she was not ready or willing to marry. He refused to admit she might never be ready or willing to marry him.

'Aye, I have, now that ye mention it,' replied Myrna carefully, noting how the young doctor's face was suddenly full of hope. 'She's working in a draper's in Queen Street. I saw her when I went to organise the furnishings for ma new house. She's looking verra well.'

'Really?' he said, trying unsuccessfully not to convey his delight. 'Queen Street, you say? I've been meaning to get new curtains.'

Myrna nodded and deliberately changed the subject by asking how his practice was coming along, knowing how much he liked to talk about his work. He now had his own house and rooms at the bottom of Parnell Rise and was building up a reasonable clientele, mostly wealthy people whom he visited at their residences, and described with enthusiasm how he was also beginning to establish a good relationship with some of the less fortunate folk in the area. These patients were rarely charged for his services; if he charged a fee they would not come to his clinic, too embarrassed to admit they could not pay.

'They're poverty-stricken. Living in squalid, dirty little shacks with not enough food, children sick all the time, the women constantly pregnant. Some of them have only been in New Zealand a short time. They can't get jobs, or only the sort that almost kills them. It's a disgrace, encouraging people to emigrate without having honest work for them and refusing them assistance of any sort. A disgrace,' he repeated vehemently, knocking back the last of his drink. 'And the Maori people I see are hardly better off. But

83

I'm sure you're sick of hearing me hold forth on this subject, Myrna. I seem to bend your ear with it every time we meet.'

'Och, no, laddie. At least someone's concerned for the poor beggars. And ye're right, it is a disgrace.'

'Yes, well,' replied John, standing up and reaching for his hat. 'I must go. I need an early night. I have a young girl with a dreadful harelip I'm repairing in the morning. I'm going to try closing the defect and moving some extra tissue into the area if I can. Her parents are more terrified than she is.'

'Another one o' your charity cases?' enquired Myrna, her eyebrows raised. 'Ye'll no' make any money, John, if ye keep fixing folk for free.'

'Yes, she is, and yes, I will make money. I charge my wealthy clients exorbitantly. There's a method to my madness, Myrna, don't worry.'

As he let himself out of the front door Myrna thought, oh, I'm sure there is, laddie, I'm sure there is.

The next day Polly declared she felt almost human, if a little unsteady on her feet. Cabbage clearly felt more comfortable with his new surroundings although he followed Polly everywhere, even to the privy. Myrna and three of the girls had gone to the new house in Parnell to supervise the placing of the new furniture, while Vivienne stayed behind to keep an eye on Polly.

By early afternoon Myrna had returned and was having tea with Polly in the kitchen. When she casually asked what her plans were, Polly thought for a moment, her eyes fixed on the sugar bowl in front of her.

'Well, I were thinkin',' she said slowly. 'Do yer think I could … well, can I work fer yer? Like Letitia an' the others? It weren't the work I minded when I were on the streets, it were the fact I couldn't make enough money and I were so lonely. It would be different workin' fer *you*. I think I can be really good at it,' she added hopefully, glancing up at last.

Myrna looked at the girl. She certainly looked better now she'd had some sleep, a good bath and a few decent meals. She was still too thin and sickly looking, and in Myrna's experience men did not like skinny women, but that could be fixed. She shouldn't put too much back on, Myrna reflected, just enough to bring her round breasts back and fill out her hips and buttocks. Her cheekbones were beautifully defined although her face was a little gaunt, but no doubt the youth would come back into it when she filled out again; Polly was a very pretty girl and her hair, when it regained its condition, would be lovely. However, there was the small problem of Polly's common accent and unrefined manners.

Myrna thought for a minute, wondering how to put it without offending the girl. 'Well, lassie, ye know I run a high-class establishment. Ma girls will be the finest this town has seen. I've put a lot o' work into them, grooming and teaching them how to speak and behave like ladies.'

Polly sat up straight, clasped her hands demurely in her lap, and said in a very cultured voice, 'Oh yes, Miss McTaggart, the ladies who grace your fine establishment *would* have to be lovely, if only so that their beauty would not be eclipsed by your own. If I was fortunate enough to become one of your employees, I am more than confident my own personal graces and charms would be the equal of theirs with very little effort. Would you care for more tea, Miss McTaggart?'

Myrna's mouth had fallen open. She shut it with an audible click, then laughed out loud. 'Where on this earth did ye learn to do that?'

'Oh, I've always been good wiv' voices. I used to 'ave me mam in fits when I were little,' replied Polly, reverting to her normal accent. Then she did a perfect imitation of Tamar, followed by a very creditable rendition of John Adams.

Myrna clapped her hands in delight. 'Aye, ye do have a gift,' she said. 'But can ye keep it up?'

'Well, of course,' said Polly in her new accent, 'if that is what is required.'

'And there'll be more to it than that, lassie. Ye'll need to learn how to dress properly, how to have intelligent and charming conversations wi' the customers, and what it is a man likes between the sheets. And there's the other matter too — good at it ye may be, but ye'll still be a whore. That doesnae worry ye?'

A shadow passed across Polly's pale face. 'Myrna, I'm already a whore.'

'All right, lassie. I'll take ye on. The house willnae be opening for a few more weeks, so there'll be time enough, I suppose.'

Polly jumped up, almost scaring the life out of Cabbage who was messily eating a bun on the kitchen floor, and hugged Myrna.

'Thank you! I won't let you down, I promise!' She snatched the dog up and swung him around as he stubbornly hung on to the bun. 'Rich, Cabbage, we'll be rich! I can have my parlour with the ostrich feathers and you can have as many buns and as much roast lamb as you like! And a little silk coat in the winter.'

God Almighty, thought Myrna. That poor wee dog.

The following day Myrna went to see Tamar and find out how her order for soft furnishings was coming along. Mr Ellis confirmed her goods would be ready by the middle of the following week. Would she like him to come to her new home and fit the new drapes? No she would not, she would do that herself. After Mr Ellis had retreated in a mild sulk, Myrna told Tamar she had found Polly, who was safe and in one piece. She also told her of Polly's decision to work in Myrna's house.

'Is that a good idea?' asked Tamar, looking concerned.

Myrna described exactly what Polly had been doing when she found her.

'I see,' said Tamar. 'So she might as well then?'

'Aye, she might as well,' Myrna agreed. 'Ye havnae had a wee visitor?'

'John, you mean?' Tamar replied, blushing slightly. 'Yes, he was in yesterday morning. He came to say hello then he was off to do some surgery. Did you tell him I was here?'

Myrna nodded. 'That isnae a problem, is it?'

'Not at all, it was lovely to see him. He looks well and he seems happy.'

I know what would make him happier, Myrna thought.

The women parted, Myrna having extracted a promise that Tamar would come to the Mt Eden house on Sunday evening for supper.

As Myrna left the shop, a tall, fashionably dressed gentleman held the door for her. Looking back through the big glass window, Myrna observed him wander around the interior before stopping in front of several bolts of white lace. By the time Tamar emerged from the back of the shop, Myrna had gone on her way. 'Can I help you, sir?' Tamar asked.

When the man looked up and smiled at her, her heart lurched. His eyes, so deeply brown they were almost black, matched heavy ebony hair. A five o'clock shadow was evident on his chin and upper lip, even though it was not yet midday, and contrasted with his pale skin. His nose was strong and straight and he had regular white teeth in a smile that tilted the corners of his mouth attractively. Elegantly dressed, he wore high black leather riding boots, snugly fitting beige trousers, a dark brown waistcoat over a white shirt, and a well-cut black top coat of good quality broadcloth.

'Yes, please,' he replied, removing his black top hat. 'I'm looking for some lace. My wife is about to have our first child and she wants some suitable decoration for the crib.'

'Well, sir,' said Tamar, recovering quickly from her disappointment at the man's mention of a wife, but nonetheless bewildered by her fleeting, irrational response. 'We have some lovely Brussels lace, and some very fine examples from Ireland. Is this the type of thing you're looking for?' she asked, indicating one of the laces.

He looked doubtful. 'Well, I don't know anything about this sort of thing but Anna has her heart set on something pretty for the baby. What would you put on a baby's crib?'

'I'd probably choose a border of the Brussels lace on a gathered swathe of white satin or silk, if it's a ruffled effect Mrs, ah — I'm sorry, sir, I didn't catch your name.'

'Montgomery,' he replied. 'Peter Montgomery.'

'If Mrs Montgomery wants something really pretty, that's what I'd recommend.'

'Well, whatever you think best. Can you have it made up? I'm coming back into town next week and I'll pick it up then. The baby is not due for another two weeks or so, so I expect there will be plenty of time.' Peter Montgomery favoured Tamar with another of his devastating smiles. 'Do you have children of your own, Mrs ...'

'Miss,' replied Tamar. 'Miss Deane. No, I am not married, Mr Montgomery.'

'Well, you should be, Miss Deane. Someone is going to be a very lucky man.'

Tamar blushed. 'Thank you,' she said quietly, not daring to look at his face, then realised she would have to. 'Brussels lace is rather expensive, Mr Montgomery. Would you like a quote?'

'No, whatever it costs is acceptable,' he replied expansively, producing a card and placing it on the counter. 'These are my details. I'm sure you'll do a lovely job. Next week, then? Probably Thursday, I expect. Until then, Miss Deane,' he said. He returned his hat to his head and left the shop as Tamar stared after him.

Tamar went to supper at Myrna's the following Sunday and had a thoroughly enjoyable evening catching up with her friends, although she was aghast at Polly's physical condition.

'Don't look at me like that,' Polly countered. 'You should have seen me a week ago. I've put on pounds!'

'What's happened to your voice?' Tamar asked, incredulous.

'My voice? Oh, this is my posh accent. I'm a lady now,' replied Polly, giggling.

Coincidentally and, he insisted, completely on the spur of the moment, John Adams also called in and stayed for a brandy. He and Tamar chatted for some time. John could not stop talking about the operation he had performed on the little girl with the harelip. He was extremely pleased with the result, although it would be some time before the swelling went down and the final effect would be obvious.

'It will be marvellous, if it works as well as I think it should. Before, her upper gum and teeth were exposed up to her nostrils and she really did look odd. She was teased by the other children to the point where she wouldn't go outside. Now, she'll look fairly normal and if it heals well, the scar may not even be very noticeable in a few years. And it will heal well, if her parents take the appropriate care. She needs complete rest and to keep her face immobile while the wound mends. After that, she should be fine. Some decent food wouldn't go amiss either, but I've taken care of that.'

Typical John, thought Myrna. He won't make a penny out of this, which was one of the reasons she was so fond of him. At the end of the evening John offered to take Tamar back to her lodgings in his new phaeton, and was thrilled when she accepted.

'Do you think they'll get together?' Bronwyn asked Myrna after the couple had been farewelled.

'No' unless yon lassie gets her feet on the ground about love in the real world. But she's no' stupid. She'll work it out one day.'

All through the following week Tamar looked forward to Peter Montgomery's return. The days seemed to crawl by. To her confusion and discomfort, whenever she recalled his smile, or the black hair on the back of his pale hands, she felt her cheeks flush and a ripple of excitement run through her. In a way she was appalled. The man's wife was about to give birth to their first child, but she could not help what she was feeling.

On the appointed day she waited eagerly all morning, feeling nervous and telling herself she was being silly. When he did not appear, she felt first a sour disappointment, then considerable annoyance with herself, doing her best to put him out of her mind.

He came in two days later, just before closing time. 'Mr Montgomery,' she said as calmly as she could as he came through the door. 'One moment, I'll fetch your crib set.'

She rushed out the back to fetch the brown paper package containing the beautifully finished bedding. Behind her Peter Montgomery opened his mouth to say something, but Tamar disappeared through the door before he could.

'Here it is!' she said when she returned. 'I hope Mrs Montgomery likes it.'

'Unlikely,' he snapped. 'She died on Tuesday.'

Tamar thought she had misheard him. 'Pardon me?'

'I *said*, she died on Tuesday,' Montgomery repeated angrily. 'The baby came early and there were complications. They both died.'

'Oh, I'm *so* sorry, Mr Montgomery,' Tamar exclaimed, raising her hands to her face.

'So I don't want this,' he continued bitterly, indicating the package on the counter. 'I'll pay for it but you can do with it what you want. I never want to see it again.'

He withdrew some money from his pocket and flung it angrily

onto the counter. The coins bounced across the other side and landed on the wooden floor. Peter Montgomery turned and left the shop, leaving Tamar standing behind the counter in open-mouthed shock.

When Mr Ellis learned what had happened, he had a temporary lapse of his usual business prudence and mailed Mr Montgomery's money back to him.

Several days later, a large arrangement of exotic flowers arrived by messenger for Tamar. A note with it said:

Dear Miss Deane
Please accept my Sincerest Apologies for the way in which I behaved towards you. I am appalled by my actions. The Darkness which has fallen upon me in my hour of grief is obscuring all I see and do. Please consider these blooms a token of my deep Regret regarding the unseemly manner in which I conducted myself. I beg that my inexcusable behaviour has not poisoned your opinion of me.
Yours Most Sincerely,
Peter Montgomery

Perplexed, Tamar placed the flowers in a bucket of water and folded the note carefully. She would show it to Myrna and ask her what she made of it.

CHAPTER SIX

As it happened, Tamar was unable to visit Myrna until the following week, on the eve of the move to the house in Dilworth Terrace. When Tamar arrived, she found the hall and parlour filled with trunks and boxes. The girls were running about excitedly, stuffing items into already overflowing cases. Cabbage darted about, his yapping adding to the confusion. Myrna, an island of calm, sat in an armchair smoking a cigarette amidst more boxes in the parlour. She looked up when Tamar came in.

'Hello, lassie. Come to give us a hand?'

'Yes, I have,' said Tamar, perching herself on a trunk and absently holding out her hand for Cabbage to sniff. Since he had settled in, the dog had become very proprietorial and went to some lengths to investigate anyone he considered a stranger. As Tamar had only visited once before, in his opinion she fell into this category.

'What's left to do?' she asked, looking around.

'No' a lot, really,' replied Myrna, standing up. 'Just the linen. Ye can help us wi' that if ye like, then come for a ride to the new place. There's one big load to take over tonight, but we'll come back here to sleep and take what's left tomorrow. Have ye met Sven yet?' she asked.

Tamar shook her head.

'He's a new immigrant I hired yesterday, Scandinavian or some such thing. Cannae speak a word o' English. *Sven!*' she yelled into the hall.

Almost immediately a very tall, massively built man emerged from the kitchen.

'Madam?' he enquired in a deep, rumbling voice.

'Well, he's no' *completely* wi'out English,' amended Myrna. 'Sven, this is ma good friend, Miss Tamar Deane.'

Sven bowed his head and held out his hand to Tamar. Looking up she shook it and said, 'It's very nice to meet you, Sven.'

'Sven's going to be ma security manager, driver, and man about the house, aren't ye, laddie?'

The big man nodded and smiled, although it was obvious he hadn't fully understood. He was not handsome, but his sheer size demanded attention. At least six foot four, he was well-muscled with a broad chest and bulging arms. His fair, close-cropped head looked oddly balanced on his massive neck, his pale eyes close together above a big, shapeless nose and wide mouth. His large ears stuck out and the lamplight from the hallway shone through them, making them glow pink. He looked menacing, but when he smiled, his countenance was transformed into gentle benevolence.

'Can ye start loading these onto the cart?' Myrna asked, pointing first at the trunks and boxes in the hall then outside towards the horse and wagonette on the street. Sven picked up the largest trunk, shouldered it effortlessly and manoeuvred it sideways through the front door and down the path.

'I think he'll be a verra handy laddie,' Myrna said, looking after him. 'Ye never know when ye might need someone wi' muscles the size o' his,' she added, turning back to Tamar. 'Anyway, lassie, ye've a look on your face like yon wee doggie when he thinks we havnae noticed him pinching a sausage. What's on your mind?'

Tamar handed Myrna Peter Montgomery's note and told her

about his visit to the shop after his wife and child had died.

'I dinnae know the man,' said Myrna after she read the note. 'But o' course he could well move in different circles. I'll ask John.'

'No, don't do that,' said Tamar quickly.

Myrna looked at her shrewdly. 'Och, it's like that, is it? The man's only just become a widower, lassie. He'll still be in mourning.'

'I don't mean anything like that,' lied Tamar guiltily. 'I don't want to hurt John's feelings. But what do you think the note means?'

'I think it means this Peter Montgomery is keeping his options open.'

'Oh no,' insisted Tamar vigorously. 'He was distraught with grief. Heartbroken. I'm sure he didn't know what he was saying.'

'Well, if he was distraught, then God only knows what he meant by this,' Myrna sniffed, handing the note back to Tamar. 'Ye'll have to wait and see.'

Tamar stuffed the note into her bag and followed Myrna into the parlour where the girls were packing linen into cases.

An hour later the wagonette was loaded up and they were ready to go. Sven drove with Jessica beside him and the others went with Myrna in her new landau, squashed together with the top down so they could enjoy the mild evening. By the time they reached Parnell, the sky was the colour of Indian ink and a full, yellow moon had risen. On Dilworth Terrace, Myrna pulled into a gate and stopped at the bottom of a driveway which went up the side of a tall, shadowed house.

Tamar stared in awe at the gracious, moonlit building. A large, two-storeyed wooden structure, its front door was close to the street but afforded privacy by a camellia hedge and a wrought-iron fence and gate. A short path led to a wide verandah with a finely turned wooden balustrade, which extended along the front of the house and down both sides. The heavy front door was flanked by stained-glass panes and surmounted by a glass arch fashioned to resemble sunrays. The second storey had a balcony, also extending around the house but not quite as wide as the verandah below. Both were decorated with intricate wooden fretwork. Many of the sash windows on both floors were almost full-length and almost every room had a set of French doors opening onto the balcony or verandah. At the very top of the house was a large octagonal belvedere, its windows providing views in all directions.

The girls unfolded themselves from the landau and waited for Myrna to unlock the front door and light several incandescent gas lamps on the foyer walls. As Sven took the wagonette up the drive and began to unload, Myrna ushered Tamar inside and smiled when she heard her draw in a sharp breath.

'It hasnae turned out bad, has it?'

Tamar was speechless. The walls of the spacious foyer were a deep maroon, and the high ceiling with its ornate plaster centrepiece a rich off-white colour. In front of them a wide, carpeted staircase led up to the second floor. To the right of the finely turned bottom newel post stood an erotic but tasteful marble sculpture of a naked woman. Myrna led Tamar into a room to the left of the foyer. 'This is the salon where customers will be entertained and choose which lady they wish to spend time with.'

It was a large and beautifully decorated corner room, slightly masculine in style but very elegant. There were rich embossed velvet drapes caught at each window, and heavy cream lace curtains. Five deep, plush sofas were arranged in a horseshoe around the large fireplace, with strategically placed side tables and foot stools. Several walnut sideboards stood against the walls, with an expansive mahogany drinks cabinet positioned to one side. The wallpaper was a small, discreet floral and two Venetian mirrors and several semi-erotic paintings hung above the sideboards.

Luxurious carpets covered the polished wooden floor and the

lighting was provided by gas lamps in brass wall brackets and a splendid triple-shaded brass pendant in the centre of the ceiling. After admiring the room, Tamar followed Myrna out past an ornate *étagère* against the wall in the foyer and into another equally elegant room.

'This is the dining room,' said Myrna, indicating the gleaming mahogany dining suite. The room featured another large fireplace and the windows were again draped with heavy curtains. 'For the customers, should they feel a wee bit peckish.' Leaving the dining room, she showed Tamar into the next room down the hall.

'In here's ma office where I'll be keeping ma business books.' In the office was an elegant walnut secretary and a matching sideboard, a sofa and several wing chairs with side tables. A patterned rug covered most of the floor. It was a stylish but businesslike room. Tamar made appropriate noises of approval and they carried on down towards the rear of the house.

'And this is the side entrance. For customers who dinnae want to be seen coming in the front way.' Myrna unlocked a smaller wood and stained-glass door opening onto the verandah. Like the front door, this one was flanked by a pair of cane stands. Sven was methodically piling the trunks and boxes from the wagonette, and began carrying them inside as Myrna opened the door.

On the opposite side of the hall was an indoor privy for customers. Myrna went into the small room and pulled the chain on the high cistern. The privy flushed with a clanking whoosh. 'Height o' luxury and convenience. Cost a pretty penny, too.'

Tamar, who had never seen a flush privy, could not resist pulling the chain herself and smiled delightedly as the water swirled magically away down the bowl.

Through a set of semi-glazed double doors halfway down the hall was the kitchen. It was fitted with a massive Orion coal stove with two ovens, and had several general work surfaces, a spacious pantry and a big table in the middle. Across the hall was the girls' off-duty parlour, furnished comfortably but not as grandly as the salon. Behind the kitchen at the back of the house was a generous laundry with several tubs, a large copper and a hand-operated wringer for linen. Opposite the laundry was a small bedroom for the maid Myrna was planning to employ, and outside off the back porch was another small room which Sven would occupy, as well as an old-fashioned non-flushing privy.

'Now for upstairs. I think ye'll like the girls' rooms,' said Myrna proudly. Mounting the stairs they could hear the others calling to each other and laughing. All eight bedrooms had access to the balcony encircling the house, their interior doors opening onto a large space around the stairwell. Several sofas and a sideboard stood against the landing walls, with vases for fresh flowers. Also on this floor was a bathroom and a separate flush privy. Myrna explained she preferred the girls did not keep chamber pots in their rooms. 'Doesnae do for the customers to kick over a pot full o' piss in the middle o' things.'

Tamar opened a large double cupboard on the landing and saw it was half-filled with fine new linen.

'We'll put the rest in tomorrow. There's a hell o' a lot o' it,' said Myrna. 'Mind you, we'll be needing it if we're going to change the sheets between every customer. It's no' pleasant for a gentleman to be reminded o' those before him.'

Polly darted out of a bedroom, grabbed Tamar's hand and pulled her inside. 'Isn't it lovely?' she exclaimed, indicating her new room. It was indeed a charming boudoir, decorated with yards of lace, chiffon and silk. The walls were a pale lilac complemented by green and violet floral rugs on a polished floor. There was a large wrought-iron bed covered with pillows and an embroidered satin bedspread, a night stand on either side, a chest of drawers topped with a fine lace runner, a lady's dressing table with mirror and small upholstered chair, and a big double-doored, mirrored wardrobe in one corner. The glazed French doors were artfully draped with brocade curtains and heavy lace. The effect was very pretty, feminine and opulent.

'It's beautiful,' agreed Tamar with a twinge of jealousy. 'It really is.' She turned to see Myrna standing at the door. 'You've done a lovely job of all this,' she said admiringly.

Myrna nodded her thanks. 'Well, I let ma girls choose the colours they wanted, and took it from there. The more feminine the better, I said to them. A man likes to feel he's in a lady's boudoir. Makes it more titillating. Would ye like to see ma private salon then, lassie?' she asked.

Tamar nodded and followed Myrna up a steep and narrow flight of stairs to the belvedere room. Of considerable size, it was octagonal and had windows facing in all directions and a narrow set of French doors opening onto a balconette looking over St George's Bay. Myrna opened the doors; the velvety breeze brought Tamar the salt from the ocean and she could hear waves faintly washing against the shore.

'The sea reminds me o' Scotland. It has a verra soothing effect,' said Myrna as they both looked out towards the water. 'What d'ye think?' she asked, turning back into the room.

The expansive bed was of polished mahogany and covered with a heavy taupe damask bedspread with matching tasselled pillows and bolsters. Several oriental silk carpets with red accents covered the floors, and a sofa and two wing chairs, upholstered in the same fabric as the bedspread, were arranged facing the French doors. The walls were papered a deep, blood red and Myrna's bedroom furniture was plain and dark but extremely elegant. There were none of the frills and bows which adorned the girls' rooms below. It was a sophisticated room, clearly belonging to a woman.

'How on earth did you manage to find a house like this?' asked

Tamar eventually, sitting herself on the sofa and stretching her legs in front of her.

'Och, I looked around but I couldnae really see anything that suited. I'd verra nearly settled on a place on Parnell Rise but it wasnae quite right. Overpriced, too. And then I was advised this one was going at a reasonable cost — probably because it wasnae finished upstairs, and no' decorated inside. The man who built it, an Australian by the name o' Willoughby, ran out o' money before he could finish and went back to Australia in a bit o' a hurry. He was a land speculator and went broke when the banks called in their loans. Been empty ever since. It was ideal for ma purposes, I could oversee the design o' the girls' rooms, and it's in a good spot — no' right in town but no' too far away.'

'It must have set you back, all this.'

'Aye, it has. The decorating hasnae been cheap and the garden out the back has to be developed, but I think I'll soon get ma money back. We'll be opening next week. I've been asking around, discreetly o' course, and there isnae another house as fine as this in Auckland.'

Tamar spent several hours helping Myrna's girls unpack their things and rearrange their furniture. They were in a high state of excitement and Myrna had to yell at them when it came time to turn off the lamps, lock the door and go back to Mt Eden for their last night in the rented house.

Tamar only went to the house on Dilworth Terrace once after that, for dinner the evening before it opened; once customers started coming Tamar would be unable to visit without risking association with Myrna's business. John Adams was there and everyone sat around the big table in the dining room and ate off Myrna's fine china dinner service with her equally fine silver cutlery.

Tamar had received a surprise when she knocked on the door and none other than Eliza opened it. Her tall frame was still gaunt, but she looked happy and her customary sneer had been replaced by a wide smile that made her, if not pretty, then at least personable. Her hair was clean and tied back under a house cap and there was no sign of her earlier personal hygiene problems.

When Eliza ushered Tamar into the salon, Myrna said from her position on one of the sofas, 'Good evening to ye, Tamar. And what d'ye think of ma new maid?'

Eliza blushed as everyone cheered, John and the girls a little rowdy and pink-faced as they had already had several drinks. Sven sat quietly, his large body parked gingerly on the edge of a sofa as if frightened he would break it, not understanding most of what was being said but keeping his eyes on Eliza.

By the end of the evening, John was decidedly unsteady on his feet and had to be driven home by Sven. Myrna sent the girls to bed for a decent night's sleep before their first day of business, while she and Tamar sat talking in the salon for another hour. Myrna did most of this, focusing on her plans for the business. She had sent Sven, attired in a decent suit and hat, around most of the gentlemen's clubs in Auckland with money to bribe the waiters to discreetly leave her business cards in places where they would be seen by prospective customers.

Patronage was by appointment only and she had already received almost a dozen requests for appointments over the following week. She knew by experience that after the first few weeks, word of the quality service she provided would spread and business would pick up even more. She was still in the market for two or three more girls but had decided to wait until she had a better indication of the level of demand; no sense in over-extending, she said to Tamar.

She was also pleased to have Eliza working for her. The girl had knocked on the back door several days ago asking if Myrna had any positions. Myrna was preparing to let her down gently, then realised it was domestic work she was after. Eliza laughed and said she was well aware she was not in the same league as Myrna's girls but she could make beds, wash linen and clean a house as well as anybody. She could also cook, although she would need some practice if anything fancy was required.

Myrna gave her the job, suspecting a position of responsibility and trust could be just the thing to bring out the best in Eliza. When she asked how she had heard about the new business, Eliza replied there was word on the street that a fine new house was about to open with beautiful young ladies catering for wealthy gentlemen. The street girls were not overly bothered as their clientele were not big spenders, but they were well aware of where Myrna's house was and the type of service she was offering.

Eventually, Myrna said to Tamar, 'Have ye heard from that Peter Montgomery then?'

Tamar went red. 'Yes, I have … yesterday I received an invitation to lunch with him at the Thames Hotel. I'm not sure whether to go or not.'

'D'ye want to?'

'Well, yes. I *do* feel attracted to him, I can't deny it. I think he's a special person, he's different, and I feel so sad for him.'

Oh, aye, thought Myrna, the man's special all right. So special, here he is seeking the company of a woman he barely knows not four weeks after his wife has been put in the ground. She made a mental note to ask around her ever-widening circle of contacts about Peter Montgomery; she did not want Tamar involved with someone who may not be suitable. Then she sighed. No doubt she could interfere as much as she pleased but, knowing Tamar, there would be little she could do if the girl decided to form an attachment.

'Just be careful, lassie,' she said. 'Will ye go by yeself? It doesnae bother ye being seen wi'out a chaperone?'

'No, it doesn't. I *am* a working woman, I'll be eighteen soon, and I walk to and from work by myself every day so why shouldn't I have lunch with a gentleman at a reputable establishment? It will all be in public view,' Tamar said stubbornly.

'Aye, it will at that,' Myrna agreed reluctantly, a faint worm of apprehension squirming in her stomach. She had mothered girls for most of her adult life and she was having a hard time trying not to mother this one.

On the following Friday Tamar went to work in her one good outfit, a two-piece skirt and bodice in bronze sateen. It was without a train as the muddy streets of Auckland made clothes with exaggerated hems impractical, and had no bustle as they had recently gone out of fashion. The skirt had once had room for padding at the back, but Tamar had altered the length so she could wear it unpadded. Her salary had not extended to new clothes and she was making do with what she had.

Mr Ellis, used to seeing her wearing a practical mid-grey ensemble, told her she looked charming and asked what the occasion was. When Tamar told him she was meeting a gentleman for lunch, he raised his eyebrows but gave her an extra half hour.

At exactly midday Peter Montgomery arrived with a small posy of flowers, which he presented with exaggerated gallantry to Tamar.

They walked to the rather grand Thames Hotel on the corner of Customhouse and Queen Streets, Tamar's hand resting proudly on Peter's arm. When they reached the hotel they were shown to a table for two in the fashionable dining room. Peter pulled Tamar's chair out for her when they sat down and, to her relief, ordered for them both. This was her first meal in such a genteel establishment and the combination of this and being alone with Peter Montgomery made her feel odd and more than a little nervous.

Peter selected the pressed tongue, followed by pigeon pie and vegetables in aspic, with a light trifle for pudding. He also ordered a bottle of burgundy and a brandy for himself while they waited. Tamar opted for a glass of lemonade. She could think of very little to say and did not want to mention Peter's bereavement, so she sat in silence. From across the table he watched her, absently swirling his brandy around the bottom of the heavy glass.

Finally, to Tamar's acute embarrassment, he said exactly what she had been thinking. 'Miss Deane, I expect you're wondering what I'm doing inviting a young lady to lunch so soon after my wife's death.'

Tamar nodded, forcing herself to look him in the eye.

'When I came into your shop to pay for the things for the baby, I was extremely upset and terribly rude and I apologise again. It was unforgivable.'

Out of politeness Tamar began to voice her denial, but Peter held his hand up. 'I know I was. You were shocked, I could see that, and you were only trying to be sensitive of my feelings. You are a very compassionate young lady.'

'Thank you, Mr Montgomery.'

'Do I gather from your charming accent that you're from Cornwall?'

When Tamar nodded, Peter took another sip of his drink. 'I am an Englishman and have not been in New Zealand long myself, and I do not have many friends. I have acquaintances at the Northern Club where I stay when I'm in Auckland, but no one with whom I can share my grief. Afterwards I thought back on your kind words and felt appalled at the way I had treated the one person who had shown me kindness and sympathy. My wife was similarly a kind woman and I sorely miss her. We were so looking forward to the birth of our child. It was to be the first of many. Of course, there won't be any at all now,' he added bitterly.

'But you reminded me of my dear wife, and I could not let myself pass up the opportunity to ask if I may enjoy your acquaintance under slightly happier circumstances. I am not yet over my grief, it has only been a matter of weeks, but I thought that while I'm in town on business you may allow me to spend a little time in your company.'

Tamar felt both flattered and terribly sorry for him; he obviously missed his wife very much and longed for female company. He was a handsome, vital-looking man but his face lacked the spirit and sense of life that had so moved her when he first came into the shop. His desperate loneliness was almost palpable.

She smiled. 'I would be delighted to spend some time with you, Mr Montgomery. If we can arrange a suitable time, I'm sure we could walk through the park.'

'Miss Deane, thank you,' he replied. 'You have no idea what this means to me. Would you think me too forward if I suggested this Sunday? I'm going home on Monday afternoon after my business is concluded and I would feel so much better if I could see you again before I leave.'

At that point, their entrée arrived. Peter asked for the burgundy to be delivered to their table and they ate in silence. Tamar took very small bites, terrified in case she spilled food or committed some other dreadful *faux pas*. The wine came and Peter poured himself a glass. Tamar did not particularly like red wine, but she accepted what Peter offered as she did not want to offend him or appear gauche. She forced herself not to pull a face after her first sip.

Peter began to talk about his house and the block of land he owned at Huia, southeast of the Waitakere Ranges. He had originally purchased the block two years earlier for the impressive stands of *kauri* covering its hills, and since then had harvested a considerable number of the huge and ancient trees and sent them to the local mills for processing. Once sold, he used the money to purchase and run cattle and sheep.

He had built his house some miles inland from the small settlement of Huia, and consequently neither he nor his wife had had much to do with the other settlers. He had plans, however, to purchase more land and build a grander house closer to the settlement to benefit his commercial endeavours as well as his social life. He came into Auckland regularly on business and would be continuing to do so for the foreseeable future.

Their main course arrived and, between bites of pigeon pie and sips from his second glass of burgundy, Peter asked Tamar about her life. She was surprised to find how easy it was to describe her family history, her desire to have her own dressmaking business and how she would like a family. When he asked how old she was she told him she was eighteen, although it would not in fact be her birthday for another month. Peter informed her he was twenty-nine years old and had been married for three years before his wife died.

By the time they were served their pudding, most of which Tamar had to leave because she had eaten too much, she felt she knew Peter a little better. His manner had relaxed, no doubt due to the wine he'd consumed with his lunch and the port he was finishing with now, and she found him charming, interesting and just as attractive as she had thought when they first met.

After lunch Peter escorted her back to work, lifted her hand to his lips and kissed it, leaving with a promise to call the following Sunday afternoon, when they would stroll through the park. Through the glass of the shop window, Tamar watched him stride purposefully down the street until he turned a corner and she could no longer see him. She had been confused by his kiss, even if it had only been on the back of her hand. Surely it wasn't appropriate behaviour for a man who had so recently lost his wife? She should have pulled her hand away, she reflected, and hoped Mr Ellis had not seen. But Peter Montgomery was so *compelling*, and the way he looked at her with his mesmerising black eyes made her shiver. There was something about him — a lot, if she was honest — she was very attracted to, whether he was a widower of only four weeks or not. Still, it was only an infatuation, and the poor man, alone now without his small family, deserved some kindness and understanding. As a woman, it was her duty to provide it. Platonically of course, she told herself. Yes, she would offer him friendship and if, over the course of a year or two, their relationship developed into something more meaningful, well, she would think about that when it happened.

CHAPTER SEVEN

January 1880

By the end of the year Tamar had spent considerably more time with Peter Montgomery. He returned to Auckland on several occasions after their luncheon in September. They now used each other's first names and strolled comfortably arm in arm when they walked out together. They went picnicking at Shelly Beach in Ponsonby and yachting from St Mary's Bay, listened to a brass band in the Domain, and went by coach to visit the beautiful Ellerslie Gardens. They went to dinner at the nicer hotels and Peter took Tamar to her first opera at the Theatre Royal.

Tamar was enchanted. The Theatre Royal seated 1600 patrons and was lavishly decorated with an intricately painted curtain and tints of gold, salmon and lavender decorating the proscenium arch. The patrons were just as splendid in their glittering formal clothes, feathers and jewellery.

During one of Peter's earlier visits he had taken Tamar to a seamstress to be fitted for a new gown. At the time she had been unsure whether she should accept such a gift from a man who was still in mourning, but Peter insisted his feelings would be irreparably hurt if she declined. At his suggestion she chose a length of fashionable Louis velveteen in a deep mauve that highlighted her auburn hair. It was made into a slim-fitting, tight-waisted evening dress that showed off her shapely figure and finished with ruched three-quarter sleeves draped with black lace. Together with the black evening gloves and violet evening slippers Peter also insisted on buying, she wore the gown for the first time to the Theatre Royal.

Just before Christmas, which Peter was unable to spend with Tamar because of business commitments, he presented her with a large amethyst in a heavy gold filigree setting on a gold chain and a pair of matching earrings. Shocked at the intimacy and expense of the gift, Tamar tried to decline. Oblivious to her arguments about his state of mourning, Peter begged her to accept, insisting his heart would be broken if she did not. She need not wear the jewellery, but to know she had accepted it would ease his loneliness. Unable to bear the haunting sadness in Peter's eyes, Tamar accepted, but put the jewels in her dressing table. Perhaps, after a suitable length of time, she might feel more comfortable wearing them.

She missed Peter during the Christmas festivities but spent some of the holiday with Myrna. She felt odd celebrating Christmas at the height of the balmy New Zealand summer, although the vibrant red blossoms of the *pohutukawa* trees gave Auckland a festive air. But it was not the same without snow, or the bitter winter cold she was used to. Christmas without a big open fire felt strange and left her feeling somehow bereft, although she noticed almost everyone celebrated in the same manner in which they had at home. Christmas puddings abounded and wreaths of holly decorated many front doors. Where their owners had obtained the holly, Tamar had no idea, but it looked pretty, and gave her a brief pang of homesickness.

In the second week of January, Peter called for her and when they were sitting on a bench admiring the flowers in Albert Park, he produced a wide gold ring set with pearls and a sizable Ceylonese sapphire, and asked her to marry him.

Tamar was so startled she gasped and dropped her sunshade. She had been aware of Peter's growing affection, and in her most fervent imaginings had allowed herself to consider a proposal from him one day, but certainly not at this early stage! She was even more shocked at her own excitement.

'Peter, it's a beautiful ring, and I'm so very flattered,' she breathed. 'But it's less than five months since Anna died. Surely you must mourn for at least a year?'

'I *am* in mourning,' said Peter earnestly, placing the ring in its box on the bench between them and turning to face her. 'I mourn every day. And it's eating me away — I can't live with the loneliness. Surely I'm not meant to die of a withered, broken heart at my age? Not when I've met you and I know I love you and we could be so happy together.' He took hold of the black mourning band around his upper left arm and tore it off. 'I wasn't meant to live by myself. I loved Anna, but she's gone. Why must I continue to suffer?'

Tamar was stunned by the emotion in his voice. 'But it would only be another seven months. That's not long if we are to spend our lives together.'

'Seven months! Seven months *is* a lifetime,' he said dramatically. 'Please say yes, Tamar! If you reject me, I don't know what I'll do — I'll have to go back to England at the very least. I won't be able to stay here without you. I couldn't watch you marry someone else.'

'Oh, Peter,' sighed Tamar. 'I don't want to marry anyone else. It's just that this is so *soon*. It's *unseemly*.'

Peter took his hat off and brushed an imaginary speck from the brim. 'It's now or never, Tamar,' he said, looking up at her, a heavy lock of his dark hair falling over one eye. 'I can't wait. I love you too much, and I need you.'

Had Myrna been sharing their park bench, she might have jammed Peter's hat back on his handsome head and told him to take his amateur theatrics somewhere else. Then she might have turned to Tamar and told her she was being manipulated by a man obviously used to having his own way, and to be very careful.

Tamar, eighteen years old, without a family and with her head filled with visions of this wonderful, generous, *passionate* man sailing out of her life, panicked.

'Please, Peter, give me a day or two,' she pleaded, her hand on his arm where the mourning band had been. She wanted to marry him, and could not contemplate the idea of losing him now he had declared his love. 'I love you too, but we have to do the right thing. What will people say?'

'*Damn* what people say, Tamar! We don't need anyone else!'

In his words Tamar heard an echo of her mother and father's romance. They had done what they wanted and married against everyone else's wishes — and their marriage had been wonderful.

'Can we meet on Friday?' she asked. 'That's only two days away. Will you still be in town?' When Peter nodded she quickly added, 'Can I have until then to decide? I do want to marry you, but I want it to be perfect. I don't want people whispering behind our backs. Please?'

Peter took a deep breath as if about to speak, and stood up; for one terrifying moment Tamar thought he was going to walk off. Instead he held out his hand to her and said, 'All right then, Friday it is. I can wait until then. I want you to be happy, Tamar. I want that more than anything else. But will you wear my ring today? On the other hand if you like, until you say yes, but please accept it. It will give me hope.'

He opened the ring box, took out the sapphire and placed it gently on a finger of Tamar's right hand. 'Until Friday,' he repeated.

'So, have ye said yes?' asked Myrna.

They were sitting in the Bellbird Tea and Coffee Palace on the corner of Victoria and Queen Streets. Myrna had come into town to visit a seamstress about costumes for her girls, and Tamar had joined her for lunch. Peter's ring caught the sun and sparkled as she stirred her tea.

'Not quite. I said I'd like time to think. But I've made up my mind. I'm going to say yes.'

Myrna sat back, looked at her young friend and lit a cigarette, much to the loudly voiced indignation of two matrons at the next table; it was acceptable for ladies to smoke tobacco in private, but indulging in public was still seen as rather 'modern'.

Myrna glared at the more imperious of the pair, who was trying to stare her down. 'If ye dinnae like it, sit somewhere else,' she snapped. Deeply offended, the two woman rose amid the rustle of voluminous skirts, snatched up their purses and left the premises.

'Are ye sure ye ken what ye're doing?' Myrna asked as she turned back to Tamar. 'It's a verra big thing, marriage. It's no' a decision to be taken lightly.'

'I *am* sure,' Tamar replied a little crossly. 'I told you what my mam said about the feeling when a woman meets the man who's really right for her. Well, that's what I feel whenever I think of Peter and every time I'm with him. He's exciting and interesting and he loves me. And I love him.'

'Exciting, is he? Dinnae confuse lust wi' love, lassie. Anyone can have the first, thank God because ma business depends on it, but the second is harder to find and a hell o' a lot harder to hang on to.'

'Lust has nothing to do with it!' exclaimed Tamar indignantly. 'He's never even touched me except to hold my hand and kiss my cheek! And he does love me. He's said so and he bought me that expensive gown and the lovely jewellery. And he's so lonely. He said he needs a woman to share his life with and he wants it to be me. Why are you being so nasty, Myrna? What's wrong?'

'I'm sorry, Tamar,' said Myrna, sighing. 'I havnae even met the man and I'm judging him. It's just so soon after his first poor wee wife.'

'He's lonely and doesn't want to be by himself. What's so wrong with that?'

'Well, verra little, I suppose, providing ye feel happy about it yeself. Will ye be going to live wi' him? Where did ye say he lives? Huia, is it?'

'Yes.'

'That's a long way, lassie. Several days' travel at least. I dinnae even think there's a decent road yet. That doesnae bother ye?'

'No. His house is not too far from the town and he's thinking of building closer. And I expect there will be little ones soon,' said Tamar coyly.

'What? Ye're no' *pregnant*, are ye?' exclaimed Myrna loudly, causing heads to turn in their direction.

'No, I am *not* bloody well pregnant!' hissed Tamar. 'Don't judge everyone else's behaviour by your own!'

There was a horrible silence. Tamar looked at the older woman's anguished face and immediately regretted her words. She leaned forward wearily and put her face in her hands. 'I'm so sorry,' she said in a muffled voice. 'I didn't mean that. It's just that I don't want to lose him and I really wanted you to be happy for me. You're the closest thing I have to a mam now, and it matters to me what you think. Please forgive me. I don't want to fall out with you.'

Myrna looked at Tamar's bent head. She flicked her cigarette butt through the open window and leaned forward. 'I dinnae want that either, lassie. If ye're sure about this Peter Montgomery, then ye have ma blessing and I wish ye both the verra best.'

Her unease was still strong, but she had not been able to discover anything about Peter, except that he was a farmer and a businessman who stayed at the Northern Club when he was in

Auckland and liked his drink, which was not particularly out of the ordinary. But because she did not want to upset Tamar, she pushed her doubts to the back of her mind and made herself sound enthusiastic. 'Have ye a date in mind?'

Tamar wiped her eyes and smiled, vastly relieved Myrna had given her blessing. 'No, not a firm date, but Peter said he would like it to be as soon as possible. I think the beginning of July. By then it will be ten months since his wife died. I'd rather wait the full year, but I don't think he'll agree.'

Myrna raised her eyebrows. 'And ye'll be having a big church wedding?'

'Well, yes, a church, but not a big one. Just a few friends. You will come, won't you?'

'I wouldnae miss it for the world, lassie.'

When Peter called for Tamar on Friday evening she told him she would accept his proposal, provided they waited until the beginning of July. He swept her into his arms and kissed her full on the lips, leaving her breathless and embarrassed in case someone had seen. Then he moved the sapphire ring from her right hand to her left. 'You'll never regret your decision, Tamar my love,' he said. 'And July is acceptable to me, but only just! I'll do everything in my power to make you happy, I promise. We'll build a beautiful new house and have dozens of little Montgomerys to fill it!'

His enthusiasm was infectious and any doubts Tamar may have retained about the haste in which they were to marry were banished.

They decided they would marry in St Paul's Anglican Church at the bottom of Princes Street. Tamar was a Methodist, but as she had not set foot inside a church since her father's death, she wasn't bothered as long it was a church, and she was wearing white. Or ivory, as it turned out, as the white fabrics Tamar sampled did not complement her complexion or the colour of her hair. Peter promised her the most spectacular wedding gown Auckland had ever seen.

The following day he returned to Huia but not before he had taken Tamar to the dressmaker who made her evening gown and told the woman to spare no expense with Tamar's wedding outfit.

Mr Ellis was unhappy when Tamar told him her news, but cheered up when Tamar asked him to give her away and promised to seat him next to Myrna at the wedding breakfast.

Peter told Tamar to begin the wedding arrangements, and not entirely sure how to go about it, she enlisted Myrna's help. Myrna's girls were thrilled and could not stop talking about the forthcoming event, and frequently came into town to have lunch with Tamar and discuss her plans.

Each trip to the dressmaker was an event to be discussed in detail, the girls deeply envious of Tamar's wedding gown. It was lustrous heavy ivory satin, fitted and full-skirted with a swathe of lightweight gold dupion silk attached to the waist at the back to form a scalloped train extending several feet beyond the hem of the gown itself. The fitted bodice was also embroidered with gold thread. The neckline was modest and, together with the tight full-length sleeves, was draped with ivory organza. A long veil of exquisitely fine ivory net attached to a small circlet of silk orange blossoms completed the ensemble.

Tamar also had a small trousseau made, consisting of a night-dress for her wedding night, some new underclothes, a riding outfit, two day dresses and an afternoon dress with the appropriate accessories. She felt guilty charging it to Peter's account, especially the extravagant wedding gown, but he insisted she have whatever she wanted. Tamar had invited Polly to be her bridesmaid and decided on a bronze-coloured silk gown for her, with an organza overskirt and fitted sleeves.

By mid-June, the preparations had all been made. A two-tiered cake decorated with gold and bronze trim had been ordered, a private room at the Thames Hotel reserved for the wedding breakfast, the menu selected, and the guests invited. Myrna and her girls, including Eliza, were coming, and Jane and Sally, who had been thrilled with their invitations. Peter had also invited several friends from the Northern Club, one of whom was to be his best man, plus several business acquaintances and their wives.

After much deliberation, Tamar also decided to invite John Adams. He had been devastated when Myrna gently broke the news that Tamar had a serious suitor.

Deciding that having her as a friend was better than not having her at all, he accepted. Besides, he was curious to meet Peter Montgomery.

Myrna had been introduced to Peter two weeks before the wedding at a dinner one evening at the Waitemata Hotel. Polly, as Tamar's best friend and bridesmaid, also came along. After watching Peter Montgomery while they sat in the lounge and had a drink before their meal, Myrna had to admit the man was very attractive in a dark sort of way. And he was certainly charming and entertaining, although he was tossing back the brandies a little too quickly for her liking.

Tamar and Myrna had decided it would probably not be wise to tell Peter she ran a brothel, so they reverted to the subterfuge about the training establishment for domestic servants.

'You must be doing very well, Miss McTaggart. That's a lovely gown you're wearing. The cut is very becoming and I've always liked brocade, its subtle sheen is so flattering to a woman's skin,' commented Peter, sipping his fourth brandy and eyeing Myrna's elegant rust-coloured gown. She had dressed conservatively, forgoing her usual peacock colours.

Myrna raised her eyebrows in surprise. 'Aye, Mr Montgomery, I'm doing verra well, thank ye.' She was startled at his appreciation of her outfit; most men did not know one fabric from another, but this man seemed to have a well-honed appreciation of what became a woman. That, in her opinion, made him either homosexual or a practised ladies' man. He was probably not the former as he had already fathered a child, and she strongly hoped he was not the latter, for Tamar's sake.

'There is considerable demand for trained domestics, as I'm sure ye will be aware, Mr Montgomery. Do ye have a lassie yeself? To look after your house, I mean?' she enquired innocently.

Peter either missed or ignored the innuendo. 'Not any more. My first wife had a housegirl to help her when she was expecting but I let her go after … she was no longer needed.'

There was an embarrassed silence at the reference to Peter's recently deceased first wife.

'I shouldn't think I'll *need* help,' said Tamar quickly. 'I'm used to housework and I looked after my own family for three years after mam died.'

'No, my dear,' said Peter, patting her hand. 'I'll get someone in. There are plenty of native women who will jump at the chance to earn a few pennies. They're not the most fastidious of house-keepers, but you can train them quite well if you get one with a few brains.'

Tamar was a little disconcerted. She'd never heard Peter speak of Maori before. Clearly he did not view the native New Zealanders in a particularly positive or complimentary light. She herself had not formed an opinion as she'd had very little association with them, except for those she had seen on the streets.

'No, really,' he carried on, emptying his glass with a gulp. 'Some are quite clever. I've been dealing with a few regarding the shipping of my timber, and there's one or two who have successful operations running clippers up and down the coast, although I suspect there aren't many left. The business of coastal trading has been taken over almost entirely by Europeans, and quite rightly too. We have a much better understanding of the principles of commerce. Anyway, ladies, shall we go in to dine?'

They followed a waiter to their table and were seated. As they ordered, Peter requested a bottle of best claret and their meal was enjoyable. They chatted as they ate, Peter describing his ideas for his land at Huia, the grand new home he was planning to build for Tamar, and his views on political issues of the day. He was witty and intelligent, but above all attentive to Tamar. Myrna conceded he was obviously besotted with her, and Tamar with him. She seemed content to sit back and let Peter do the talking, following his every movement with her eyes and laughing at his witty comments. And the more he drank, the more amusing he became until Tamar, Myrna and Polly were beset with laughter. Oh, he's a charmer all right, thought Myrna, wiping her eyes on her napkin.

After the main course, Peter ordered another bottle of wine and then excused himself briefly.

'Well?' said Tamar. 'What do you think?'

'He's very handsome,' replied Polly. 'I'd marry him. And he's rich too. He must be, all the things he's bought for you and the cost of the wedding. I think you've fallen well and truly on your feet.'

'Yes, I think I have. But the money doesn't matter. I'd be happy living with him in a little cottage.'

'Ye dinnae think he's overly fond o' his drink?' asked Myrna, aware she was being critical but unable to stop herself.

'A little, perhaps,' Tamar agreed. 'Lots of men drink, and it never causes him any problems. And he's so charming and funny.'

'Och, well, let's hope it stays that way,' said Myrna, more to herself than to anyone else. She had observed the unfortunate effect alcohol could have on some men, how it could make them angry and violent and bitter. She hoped Peter Montgomery would not turn out to be one of them.

July 1880

The afternoon of the first day of July was bright with winter sun, the breeze a little brisk but not unpleasant. Seated in the front two pews of St Paul's, the wedding guests waited expectantly for Tamar to begin her walk down the aisle with Mr Ellis.

As the church organ wheezed out the opening bars of the wedding march, the guests turned to admire the bride. Tamar looked truly glorious in her ivory and gold gown and there was a collective sigh from the women in the congregation. Peter, resplendent in a formal black frock coat and matching trousers, a brocade waistcoat in bronze, and a high-necked cream shirt with cravat, beamed proudly as he watched her walk towards him on Mr Ellis's arm.

The ceremony was short and simple, and the guests and the newly married Mr and Mrs Peter Montgomery were outside the church in less than thirty minutes. Tamar hurled her bouquet of cream roses exuberantly into the air. Eliza, already a head taller than the other women, caught it easily, smiling widely as she hugged the flowers to her flat chest.

After the photographer fussed about arranging everyone for formal photographs, the party made their way to the Thames Hotel for the wedding breakfast. Tamar and Peter followed in an elegant hired brougham pulled by a pair of matching chestnut horses. Sitting proudly in the carriage holding her new husband's hand and feeling absurdly joyous and blessed, Tamar reflected that the only other thing she could have wished for was the presence of her family.

The reception was a thoroughly pleasant affair. Peter and his best man made speeches, both toasting the bride's beauty, and Myrna wished the couple happiness and prosperity. True to form, Peter had ordered more than enough alcohol and by the time the meal was over, the guests were conversing loudly and laughing uproariously at every remotely witty utterance. Myrna's girls were on their best behaviour and Tamar thanked God none of Peter's friends from the Northern Club appeared to have been past customers. Mr Ellis became quite drunk and made a fool of himself over Myrna, who rebuffed him politely but firmly. John Adams, who had maintained a resolutely pleasant smile and an enthusiastic demeanour, excused himself early. Myrna watched him go, sad for his disguised but, to her at least, still discernible hurt. She noticed Tamar looking after him with a fleeting expression of sorrow.

Later in the evening, when their guests had finally departed, Peter led Tamar into the private lounge for a nightcap before they retired to the suite he had booked for their wedding night. He ordered port but she opted for tea as she was feeling decidedly lightheaded.

'Tired, my dear?' he asked as they sat opposite one another in the lounge. A small table between them held Peter's bottle of port and his half-smoked cigar. His face was ruddy and his eyes sparkled.

'A little,' replied Tamar.

In truth she was both tired and nervous thinking about what awaited her in their wedding chamber. For some months she had been battling with an insistent and disturbing physical urge she had never experienced before. She suspected it was not at all seemly, but felt a desperate need to lie naked with Peter, to allow him to rub his virile body against hers and feel the two of them joined together, physically and emotionally. She wanted to be taken and owned by him, and left exhausted but fulfilled by his caresses and his love.

But she was still nervous. She had a reasonable idea of what was entailed regarding the physical act, but couldn't imagine the details. She knew what went where, but how on earth did it fit? What if it *wouldn't* fit? How mortifying! And would it hurt her? Would she bleed? Myrna told her making love would come naturally once she became used to it, and not to worry, but she *was* worried. Peter had been married. What if his new wife was too inexperienced and he spurned her?

She started as Peter asked, 'What are you thinking about, my lovely? Has your wedding day been what you envisioned?'

'Oh, yes, it was beautiful. Perfect,' she replied truthfully. 'More than I could have ever asked for.'

Peter poured himself another generous measure of port. 'I said I would give you anything you desire, and I meant it. Here's to our marriage and our life together, my beautiful new wife,' he said, raising his glass and emptying it. Then, waggling his eyebrows playfully, he asked, 'And is my beautiful new wife ready to retire to our wedding suite?'

Tamar nodded, feeling herself blush hotly.

'Well then, Mrs Montgomery,' he said, getting unsteadily to his feet and offering his arm. 'Let us retire.'

As Tamar rose from her chair, he turned back to the small table and picked up the bottle. 'No sense wasting good port,' he said.

Walking arm in arm, they went upstairs to their suite. When they unlocked the door, they saw the cover had been turned down and a small posy of bright flowers placed on each pillow.

'Oh, that's a nice touch,' said Tamar, nevertheless embarrassed that the staff of the Thames Hotel knew this was the bed upon which she would be deflowered.

'Yes, isn't it,' replied Peter distractedly, removing his coat and throwing it over the back of a chair. He sat on the bed and wrestled his boots off. 'God, I'm dying for a pee. Where's the privy?'

Tamar pointed through a door into the bathroom. Peter went in and she listened in embarrassment to him urinating for what seemed at least five minutes.

He pulled the chain and came back out. 'That's better,' he said. 'I like those flush privies. We must get one in our new house, don't you think?'

Tamar nodded. She was not sure what to do or say next. Peter solved the problem by taking her hand and sitting her on the bed. He leaned forward and kissed her lips, his tongue tasting of port.

'Are you nervous?' he asked, reaching for the bottle on the night stand and pouring himself a measure.

Tamar nodded again, hesitated, then took his hand. 'You'll have to show me what to do,' she said shyly, unable to look him in the eye.

'My darling, I will treat you with the care and respect you deserve. Don't you worry,' he crooned, sipping his drink and closing his eyes. He opened them again a second later and hurriedly put the glass down. 'God, the room's spinning. Perhaps I've overindulged a little. Why don't you prepare yourself, dearest, and I'll lie down while I'm waiting,' he suggested, lying back on the bed with his arm over his eyes.

Tamar went into the bathroom, shutting the door behind her. She unpacked her new nightdress and draped it over the side of the tub and sat on the privy seat to remove her shoes and stockings. She undressed slowly, removing her veil and carefully rolling it up and placing it on the washstand. Then she shrugged out of her wedding gown, folding it equally carefully and draping it over a chair, followed by her princess petticoat, her corset and finally, her combination chemise and drawers.

Until she'd had her wedding outfit made, she'd been resigned to climbing into a pair of drawers, a short chemise, her corset, a separate camisole over that followed by a long, full petticoat tied about the waist. The layers were murder in the summer heat, but the dressmaker had shown her patterns for the new combinations and advised they were all the rage amongst fashionable women, so she'd had several sets made for her trousseau. Tamar giggled; why on earth was she thinking about underwear on her wedding night?

She observed herself in the bathroom mirror. She knew she was shapely and pleasingly proportioned, and she hoped Peter would think so too. A ripple of anticipation ran through her body and goosebumps rose on the smooth, white skin of her rounded buttocks. She slipped the delicate nightdress on over her head, brushed her hair until it shone, then paused for one last look. The long-sleeved, loose-fitting gown was of pale rose organdy with a lily-of-the-valley design embroidered across the bodice and on the sleeves. In the light of the bathroom's gas lamp, its colour imparted a soft and alluring glow to Tamar's skin and hair.

She took a deep breath, opened the bathroom door, and walked slowly across to the bed. When she saw Peter was deeply asleep, snoring slightly with his mouth open, she didn't know whether to laugh or cry. Instead, she climbed in next to him, kissed his brow and rolled over and went to sleep herself.

Chapter Eight

The following morning Peter Montgomery and his new wife boarded the train from Auckland to New Lynn. Tamar sat uncomfortably. She was sore between her legs and her sanitary cloth was chafing. She had bled after Peter made love to her that morning, and was not sure how long it would continue so had taken the precaution of using a cloth. The lovemaking had not been quite what she had expected.

She had woken in their hotel room early, feeling thirsty. She yanked on the bell pull to summon a maid, and when a discreet knock came a few minutes later she asked for a pot of tea. When it arrived Tamar poured a cup for herself and one for Peter. As she moved about the room he woke up.

'Oh, Christ, my head,' he moaned, his eyes shut tightly.

'Do you want some tea?'

He nodded, swore, then clutched his skull. Tamar placed his tea on the night stand while he slowly sat up and swung his legs over the side of the bed, still dressed in his wedding shirt and trousers. He stood cautiously, extracted a small silver flask from his bag on the luggage stand, then shuffled back and poured something into his tea cup.

'Whisky. Just a drop. I've a ghastly headache, but it will go in a few minutes. It's the best cure for a hangover, works every time.' He drank his tea in one long draught, poured himself another and added more whisky. 'God, that's better,' he muttered after a minute. 'I really am sorry, Tamar, falling asleep like that. I assume we didn't … '

When Tamar shook her head, he said, 'Christ, I'm sorry. Not much of a wedding night, was it? Will you forgive me?'

Tamar smiled. 'Of course,' she said, reaching over and tentatively touching his messy hair. 'I fell asleep too. We had a long day.'

As the whisky began to filter into Peter's bloodstream and his headache receded, they rang for room service and asked for breakfast to be delivered. After they had eaten Peter had a quick bath and a shave, emerging from the bathroom wearing only a towel around his waist, little runnels of bath water leaving tracks through the dark hair on his chest and legs. Tamar had removed her nightdress and sat on the side of the bed, preparing to change into her day clothes. He stared at her naked body.

'You are as beautiful as I imagined,' he breathed, moving to stand in front of her. 'Truly beautiful.' He removed the towel and let it fall on the floor. Tamar was confronted with his large, purple, erect penis bobbing six inches from her face.

God in heaven, she thought, and closed her eyes.

Peter joined her on the unmade bed, pushing her gently back and lying next to her. He kissed her face, then her round breasts, their small, pale nipples erect in the cool morning air, and rubbed his hand across her flat stomach and hips and down her thighs, then back up over her pubic hair. 'Are you ready?' he asked, his voice thick with passion.

Tamar had no idea whether she was ready or not, but felt that it would be gauche of her to say no, so she said nothing. Peter rose to his knees, pushed her legs open and said, 'My God, what a lovely pink vulva you have. Like a luscious little fruit.' Tamar

124

felt her face turn crimson. 'Mine now,' he had added, positioning himself between Tamar's thighs and settling onto her. Propping himself up on one elbow, he used his hand to guide his engorged penis into her vagina. It went in a short way and then stuck.

'Ow!' Tamar exclaimed out loud before she could stop herself.

'Sorry, my darling. Do you need a little help?' Peter moved to one side, raised his hand to his mouth and spat onto his fingers. Rubbing his saliva over the opening of Tamar's vagina and the head of his penis, he repositioned himself and drove into her. Tamar felt a sharp, burning pain and bit her lip to stop herself crying out.

As Peter lay still for a second, she felt extremely, roundly full and wondered how on earth his penis was able to fit inside her. As he started to move again, the pain subsided a little and she felt able to accommodate him better. With one hand resting on his upper back she placed the other against his chest in the hope she might discourage him from pushing too hard. She couldn't and he did, thrusting faster and saying her name over and over, his face buried in her hair.

After what seemed like hours but was only a few short minutes, his thrusting grew more urgent and powerful and she felt his body stiffen and his buttocks clench tightly. He lifted his head and she saw his eyes were screwed shut and his teeth bared. With one final thrust that shoved her body up the bed and banged her head against the headboard, he let out a strangled, grunting cry and went rigid, then collapsed slowly on top of her, panting and sweating and apparently unconscious.

Tamar wondered if he was all right. Perhaps he had hurt himself. He'd certainly hurt her, but then she was aware some pain would be involved at first and had not expected any less. In fact, the process had been less traumatic than she'd anticipated. She was sore and feeling battered, but the sharp pain had already gone. Peter groaned and moved off her, rolling onto his back and opening his eyes. As he moved, Tamar felt a trickle of something warm dribbling out of her and stinging the bruised flesh between her legs. She wondered vaguely if she was now pregnant.

'I'm sorry, darling,' Peter murmured eventually. 'I couldn't hold myself back. Next time it will be better, I promise.' As he rolled over and lay his head on her breast, she wrapped her arms around him, feeling strangely as if she was cuddling and soothing a child.

When they got up to dress, Tamar saw the sheet had been stained with a mixture of Peter's semen and her blood. Mortified, she insisted on scrubbing the bloody patch, then folded the sheet across the bottom of the bed, hoping the chambermaid would not notice. Peter told her she was being silly — this was the wedding suite and the staff saw messes on the linen all the time.

Now, as the train neared its destination, Tamar wondered if there would be a repeat performance tonight. She hoped not as she was sore and tired, but knew that if Peter wanted to, she would oblige him. And it had not been completely unpleasant. Nothing like the vision of intense sensual ecstasy she'd nurtured in her imagination, but she had enjoyed the physical closeness and the sensation of experiencing Peter's passion, even if her ardour had not matched his.

The coach trip from New Lynn to Titirangi was slow and bumpy and they did not arrive until after dark. They spent a moderately comfortable night in the town's one hotel, Peter grumbling because it was dry but cheering up when they made love again. They rose early the next morning to continue their journey. Again their physical union had not been especially fulfilling, but Tamar had enjoyed the intimacy and consoled herself with the expectation that their lovemaking would improve with time.

The last leg of their journey was tedious and uncomfortable, and they were obliged to share the coach with a couple with several small children. The children were tired, bored and irritating and their parents seemed to have little to say to each other. The woman was pregnant and the coach kept having to stop so she could relieve herself in the bushes. The road was unpaved and the heavy rains had caused washouts in several places; these could only be crossed when the coach was empty, the passengers walking behind, trying not to tread in the mud or slip in leaf mould fallen from the dense, overhanging bush.

Closer to Huia the scenery became more impressive as the solid dark green of the forest was relieved by stands of giant *kauri*, their trunks, some up to forty feet in girth, soaring straight and uninterrupted for eighty or so feet until thick branches formed an ancient canopy. Whenever the coach stopped, the cool weight of the forest was like a living thing, the smell from the lush undergrowth damp and dark and the silence broken only by the ringing calls of bellbirds and *tui*. Tamar was enchanted but Peter was out of sorts, irritated by the whingeing children and eager to reach their destination.

They arrived at Huia at eight o'clock in the evening. The tiny town had a general store run by a man who was also the local Justice of the Peace, a one-storeyed hotel with basic accommodation, a stable and forge with a workshop and a public office. Rather than continue in the dark to Peter's property several hours further into the bush, they stayed the night at the pub.

In the morning they collected Peter's horse and cart from the stables, loaded their luggage, picked up some supplies from the store and headed off. They followed the tramway leading down from the sawmill, where the great kauri logs were dragged by bullock teams to be processed, and up into the hills before turning onto a smaller track, which they followed for an hour. Crossing several shallow streams, they climbed a steep hill through dense bush, the horse slipping and sliding on the muddy, rutted track, and came out on a ridge with panoramic views of the bush below, broken here and there by a patchwork of scrubby paddocks. Eventually they came to a gate.

Peter halted the horse and pointed down one side of the ridge. 'There it is, Mrs Montgomery. Our land and your new home. The fence line is the boundary, but you can't see it where it runs into the bush.'

The house sat on a flat piece of land overlooking a small valley surrounded by bush-clad hills. Peter's block was not huge but it encompassed several acres of forest and open paddock; in Cornwall, he would have been considered a moderately wealthy estate owner. As he flicked the reins, the horse started off down the hill towards the house.

It was bigger than a cottage and a substantial home compared to others she had glimpsed on the way, which seemed little more than shacks, but nothing like the grand houses in Auckland. Tamar was charmed regardless. There was a verandah running along the front of the single-storeyed wooden building and around one side, with the front door and a set of French doors opening onto it. The bare winter branches of a climbing rose grew up the verandah posts and in front of the house was a large circular garden containing early daffodils, snowdrops, bright blue lobelia and cheerful pansies.

Peter helped her off the cart, led her onto the verandah and opened the front door. She giggled as he swept her up and carried her over the threshold and deposited her in what was clearly the parlour. While he went to unload the cart and let the horse into a paddock, Tamar wandered around her new home.

The parlour was spacious but cosy with whitewashed walls and comfortable furniture. Two armchairs and a well-used sofa were arranged in front of the generous fireplace, and a kauri dining table and eight chairs stood in one corner. The floor was of unpolished wood, with several brightly coloured rugs. The large windows and French doors let plenty of light into the room but Tamar could see their heavy curtains would keep out the cold when drawn.

The kitchen was basic but adequate, she thought, with a wood-burning range and a hot plate set into the fireplace with six or seven heavy black hooks holding kitchen utensils above it, and a bread oven built into the brick chimney. There was a bench along one wall under the window, a butter churn, a large wooden work table, a sideboard against another wall for china and plenty of shelves. Through the window Tamar could see a small meat safe and cool store on the shady back porch, and beyond that a hand pump. She assumed it drew water from the stream in the valley below.

Opposite the kitchen was a furnished but unused-looking bedroom. Out the back door off the porch was the laundry with a small fireplace for heating the copper, and behind that another small room, empty except for a bed. Some distance from the house was the privy, a long-drop in a small wooden building of its own.

Tamar retraced her steps to explore the larger of the bedrooms. It too had a fireplace and was furnished with a double bed, a wardrobe, a ladies' dressing table and a large set of drawers. The house was cold, dusty and rather untidy, but the cosily arranged curtains and touches of lace and patchwork showed it had been well-tended by Peter's first wife.

Feeling a little unnerved at the deceased woman's linger-ing presence, Tamar left the house and wandered into a small orchard of young fruit trees growing around a neglected vegetable garden. Several cows and four or five scruffy chickens grazed in a small fenced-off paddock. Behind the orchard under an older, more established tree was a small cemetery, with two graves. The headstones read:

Anna Maria Montgomery
Beloved Wife of Peter
1855–1879

and

Constance Sophia Montgomery
1879

Tamar knelt on the grass and closed her eyes, feeling desperately sad for the pathetically small grave in which the baby had been buried, and the pain she imagined Peter had felt when he had laid them to rest. She vowed she would do all she could to be the loving and comforting wife Peter so obviously yearned for.

Tamar unpacked, then made some tea and went to join Peter, who was having a lunchtime port on the verandah. There was a pair of old wicker chairs and a small table there, and they sat in silence, looking over the valley.

'It can get bloody cold here at this time of year,' Peter commented eventually. 'I'll get some firewood in. The water freezes in the pump some mornings. Still, it's cosy enough inside. And there are plenty of preserves in the kitchen. Anna usually did all that over the summer.' He fell silent.

Tamar said gently, 'I saw the graves. Do you still miss them?'

'Well,' he replied, 'I have you now. And I never knew the child, she died almost as soon as she was born. But it will be different when we have our own. Anna was by herself when it happened, but I'll make sure you have someone with you when the time comes. When I next go to Huia I'll arrange for one of the Maori women to come out, to help you in the house. And then, by the time you *are* expecting, you'll be comfortable with her. Do we want her to live in or not? I don't fancy the idea of one of them under our roof night and day. What do you think?'

Tamar didn't particularly want a housegirl and had not given it much thought. If she had to have one, she would rather meet the woman before she decided on what the accommodation arrangements would be. In truth, she wanted to have a go at managing the house herself. She'd been perfectly capable running her da's house, and couldn't see why she shouldn't be able to do so here, although Peter had warned her he sometimes conducted his business at home, which meant having people to dinner on occasion. Also, when he hired gangs to work on his block, they needed feeding three times a day. Still, she couldn't see any real problem.

The following week was happy and satisfying, although Tamar was kept busy and began to wonder whether some help might not be a good idea. She rose early in the quiet, dark mornings to light the kerosene lamps and start the wood fire in the kitchen for cooking and to heat water. She made bread every second morning before she prepared their breakfast, which was always porridge, Peter's favourite; he was adamant he was unable to do a day's work without it. After he had gone she washed the dishes in a basin with water heated on the stove, cleaned the oven and hot plate and scrubbed the kitchen table until it was spotless. Then she meticulously swept the kitchen floor with a *manuka* broom, otherwise the house would be overrun with rats and mice. When she had emptied the chamber pot she had her wash, using the large bowl and ewer, then made the bed and swept out the rest of the house. If Peter was coming home for lunch she would begin preparing it at about eleven in the morning, clean up again after he had gone, then repeat the performance at around four in the afternoon for dinner.

After lunch she worked in the garden planting or harvesting

vegetables and fruit for preserving. Although the vegetable garden had run to seed it was still well-stocked with rhubarb, turnips, carrots, winter cabbages, potatoes, parsnips, silver beet and *kumara*. Tamar spent much of her time weeding and re-planting, and planning the new vegetables she would add when spring arrived.

Every second day she did the household washing. This involved carrying water from the pump to half-fill the copper in the laundry, waiting for it to heat, adding washing soap, then sloshing the clothes and linen around for what seemed like hours until they were clean. She then moved them piece by piece into a tin tub and rinsed them with cold fresh water, then wrung them all out by hand, struggling with the bed sheets until she had removed as much water as she could. The first time she'd hung the laundry on the clothesline it broke, causing her to swear loudly, and she had to do it all again; after that she made sure not to overload the thin ropes. Anything delicate was soaked and handwashed very gently and laid outside in the sun to dry, or hung in front of the stove or the fire in the parlour. When the washing had dried she ironed it, including the linen, with a box iron she discovered in the laundry.

In the evenings, she sat with Peter in the parlour and sewed or read by the light of the fire and kerosene lamps. They went to bed early, and often made love. Tamar was becoming accustomed to their physical intimacy and was no longer sore or nervous. She was beginning to respond to Peter's advances, enjoying the way he touched her body and taking pleasure in exploring his. There was still no wild ecstasy, but his passionate appreciation was obvious, and enhanced her own excitement. Having had no other lover, she did not know whether he was skilful, but found his attentions stimulating in a way that was new to her and made her feel needed and wanted. She loved being with him, still could not stop looking at him constantly whenever they were together, and delighted in keeping house for him. She was, she supposed, very happy with her lot, although she did feel lonely when she was by herself.

As they lay together one evening, Tamar's head resting on Peter's furry, slightly sweaty chest, she decided it was time to broach the subject of a housegirl. 'I dropped the washing in the mud again today,' she said.

'Did you?' replied Peter sleepily.

'Yes, and I think I *would* like someone to help me around the house. Some days I only just manage to get everything done, and it would be nice to have some time to myself.'

Peter nodded, 'And in a few weeks I'll be getting a gang over to help with the next stand of *kauri* and you'll be even busier feeding them. Shall I see if I can find someone when I go into town tomorrow?'

Tamar smiled in agreement and snuggled down under the covers, grateful once again for Peter's concern and generosity.

The next morning as she prepared breakfast, he came into the kitchen and leaned against the heavy wooden table, silently watching her. She finally stopped and turned to him, raising her eyebrows.

'There's a trunk of Anna's things in the spare bedroom. Clothes and bits and pieces,' he said, looking moodily out the window. 'I don't particularly want to see them again. Would you mind going through them? Put the decent things in a bag and I'll take them into town. The storekeeper might be able to sell them. You might want to keep the baby things though.'

'If that's what you want, then yes,' she replied. 'I'll do it while you're away.'

Peter nodded, his good humour apparently restored. 'Right, then. What's for breakfast. Porridge?' he asked hopefully.

Half an hour later, Tamar waved him off from the front verandah, then threw herself into her morning chores. When she had finished she went into the spare bedroom and found the trunk, square, dusty and a little sad-looking. She did not particularly relish the idea of rummaging through Anna's things, but he'd asked her to do it, so she would.

Kneeling in front of the trunk, she opened it slowly. On top was a collection of new baby clothes. Lifting each item out piece by piece, Tamar saw there were five tiny white gowns in lawn, muslin and fine linen, and several knitted jackets. The little garments were intricately embroidered, several with pin tucking and a broderie anglaise trim. Four tiny bonnets were flattened together under half a dozen small woollen blankets and other baby bedding, and a handful of knitted booties with satin ribbons lay next to a pile of folded napkins. Tamar was poignantly reminded of the lace and satin Peter had ordered for his new baby less than a year ago.

She fetched a sheet on which to lay the garments to keep them clean. Looking at the array of baby finery spread in front of her, she felt desperately sad and her throat ached with her need to cry; for her husband, for baby Constance who had barely lived, and for Anna who had died bringing her into the world.

Turning back to the trunk, she lifted out one of Anna's dresses. Under that were other well-made articles of clothing, several hats, two pairs of boots, and a few personal things including a silver-backed hair brush and mirror. At the very bottom was a heavy woollen riding coat with a hood and several deep pockets. As Tamar lifted the garment she felt the crackle of a slim package; taking it out she saw it was an envelope addressed to someone in England. It was sealed but had no postmark. Knowing she shouldn't, she opened it. It was dated September 12, 1879, written in a small, elegant hand and signed by Anna Montgomery.

Guiltily, Tamar read:

My Dearest Mama,

I hope this letter finds you well. I am feeling very well myself, although I am large with Child now and expect to be delivered three weeks hence. I am almost fully prepared except for some items for the Child's crib which Peter has ordered from Auckland. A Midwife has been visiting and will attend the Birth. I am sorry you will not be with me when our Baby arrives, but that cannot be helped. Perhaps we will be able to come Home to visit when our finances have improved.

We still owe the Bank a lot of money, and we have ceased any spending not absolutely necessary, but Peter has been working very hard, and has spent a lot of time improving the condition of the land and felling timber. He has taken a marked turn for the better since I confronted him, as you suggested. I have told him I can no longer tolerate his behaviour when he has been drinking, and that if he raises his hand in anger against me again, I will withdraw all of my attentions from him, even after the Child is born. When I told him, he wept and threw himself on the floor at my feet, saying he does not understand what is happening to him and that if he were just able to make a little more money and was not so worried about the arrival of our Child, he would not feel so pressured about our debts and would not have such a need to drink.

I have asked him to cease drinking altogether and he says he has. I believe this is the only way to avoid the trouble which always comes when he drinks — his violence, his anger and his awful melancholy. When he does not drink, he is a loving man and very easy to love in return. I fear that if he continues to drink he will only get worse. He was always controlled when he drank when we first met, but in the years since we moved out to our Block, his behaviour has progressively worsened and he cannot seem to stop once he starts.

However, all is well at the moment and Peter is as loving and attentive as he used to be. I have high hopes for our future and

he has promised to improve his ways and I trust he will. He is so
desperately looking forward to our Child and dearly wants it to
be a Boy but says that if it is a Girl as lovely as me, he will be just
as happy.

Tamar read on but barely took in Anna's description of her garden
and the clothes she had made for her baby.

She folded the letter back into the envelope and slid it into the
pocket of her skirt. She was severely shaken, her heart pounding
violently; was this the same man she had married? Peter had never
shown any sign of anger or violence, although she had to admit he
could be a little short-tempered. And he had *never* been physically
abusive. But a small, insidious voice inside her head asked, but how
long have you known him? You spent less than a month all told
in his company before you married, and only a few weeks since.
How well do you *really* know him?

Tamar told the voice to shut up. Obviously Peter was drinking
again, but the worst that had happened had been him falling asleep
on their wedding night, and she had been grateful at the time.
But, her discomfort growing, she realised she had no idea of the
state of Peter's finances. What about the clothes and jewellery he'd
bought for her? And the cost of their wedding? Tamar twisted
the sapphire engagement ring on her finger nervously. How much
had it cost?

As she stuffed Anna's clothes into several sacks and rolled up
the baby things to be stored, she felt confused and worried. But as
the afternoon wore on she began to talk herself into an explanation
that made sense of what she had read. Although Peter had loved
her dearly, Anna had obviously not understood the strain he'd been
under due to his finances and the imminent birth of their child.
Perhaps she'd been in some sort of emotional state herself, due to
the changes Tamar knew women experienced during pregnancy,

and had directed her anxiety towards her husband. Her behaviour may have even driven him to striking her. By the time Tamar began preparing the evening meal, she was convinced that whatever had happened between Peter and Anna had been the result of an inability on Anna's part to cope with her physical condition. It also occurred to her Anna may have been lying or exaggerating to her mother.

On the other hand, the matter of Peter's finances still niggled. She would talk to him about that, introducing the subject casually, but she would not mention his drinking. She was not Anna, after all. Not pregnant, and not unable or unwilling to understand the fears and pressures of a man struggling to make ends meet while he turned rugged bush into productive farmland.

Peter was not home by eight that evening. Tamar left his dinner in a pot on the stove to keep warm. When he had still not arrived by ten she became concerned and decided to wait up for him. It had started raining heavily and she worried that his horse might have slipped on the rough track; he could be lying somewhere hurt.

An hour later, she heard a noise outside and ran to open the front door. Through the rain she saw Peter in the murky dark, drenched to the skin and his trousers and coat covered with mud, picking himself off the ground and swearing while his horse skittered nervously. He looked up and saw her.

'Sort this bloody horse out! Fucking bastard just threw me,' he said angrily as he stepped onto the verandah and handed her the reins. As he went inside Tamar smelled alcohol on his breath and his clothes. She stepped into the heavy rain and stroked the horse's head gently, speaking soothingly until he settled down. When she removed the saddle and blanket she saw the animal had been sweating heavily and had several long, shallow cuts on his right shoulder.

She led the horse down to the paddock, slipping and sliding

on the sodden grass, then returned to the house, dripping wet. Inside, she towelled her hair dry, sponged her wet clothes as best she could and went to join Peter in front of the parlour fire. He was sitting in one of the armchairs, a glass of whisky in his hand, staring fixedly into the flames.

She sat opposite, picked up her sewing and asked casually, 'Did your business go to your satisfaction?'

Peter nodded but did not look up.

Tamar tried again. 'So you got everything sorted then?'

'Timber fellers'll be here Wednesday week, pack of thieving bastards.'

'How do you mean?' Tamar asked, alarmed that Peter had been robbed.

'I *mean*, they're charging me an arm and a leg. I'd do it myself but the job's too bloody big.' He was slurring his words. She had a sudden unwelcome vision of the behaviour Anna had described.

'Were you in the hotel tonight?' she asked hesitantly.

He nodded. 'And all afternoon.' He looked up and snapped, 'Well, there's nowhere else to do business.'

Tamar bent her head to her sewing for a few minutes, then asked, 'Can we afford to pay the timber-felling gang?'

Peter rearranged himself in his chair and took a leisurely sip of his drink. Had Tamar been watching, the expression on his face would have reminded her of the sleek bush rat she caught in the light of her lamp on the way out to the privy one night, sharp black eyes darting about as if it couldn't make up its mind which way to jump.

'Of course I can afford it,' he replied casually. 'Why wouldn't I?'

'I just wondered, that's all. I thought you might be a bit short of cash after our wedding.'

'No,' he lied. He had asked for the bills to be sent to him by post and had collected them from the Huia post office that morning.

He had already decided his creditors could wait.

'That reminds me,' he said over his shoulder, as he rummaged in his coat pocket. 'There's a letter for you, from that rich friend of yours, that McTaggart woman.' He withdrew an envelope and handed it to her.

Tamar was itching to open it but put it aside to read later. Peter sat down and poured himself another hefty whisky. Tamar stitched in silence as he drank rapidly. As he was pouring himself a third, she was unable to keep her mouth shut. 'You don't think you might have had enough to drink already?' she asked.

'What?'

Tamar looked at her husband, suddenly nervous. 'The whisky. You don't want a headache tomorrow.'

Peter narrowed his eyes, all trace of good humour gone. 'You don't think I can handle my drink?' he snapped.

'Oh, I know you can! I know how you hate feeling sick, that's all.'

Tamar panicked, wishing to God she'd kept her silence. Were Anna's words true after all? She sat back in fright as Peter made his way unsteadily towards her, but relaxed slightly when he knelt and placed his hands on her knees. 'Put your sewing down,' he said gently.

She did, encouraged by the change in his voice.

'I know I drink sometimes but it's nothing to worry about,' he continued in a reasonable tone. 'It's never caused a problem, has it? Every decent, hardworking man has a right to the odd tipple after a day's work. Why is it bothering you?'

'It's not bothering me,' lied Tamar.

'Good. Then let's go to bed. I've been thinking about you all day and I've missed you,' Peter said, running his hands sensuously up her thighs and caressing her hips. Then he stopped and asked jokingly, 'What's this in your pocket? Not a love letter from an admirer?'

Tamar's heart jumped into her throat. 'No, of course it isn't.'

'Well, what is it then? Let me see it.' He fumbled for the pocket opening and dug his hand into the folds of Tamar's skirt. Yanking the envelope out he read the address then slowly looked up at her, his eyes glinting dangerously. 'What are you doing with one of Anna's letters?' he asked in a flat voice.

'I … I found it when I was going through her things,' stammered Tamar.

Peter tore the letter out of its envelope and quickly scanned it. 'Christ, is *this* what's upset you? Anna's lies about me?' he said as he got to his feet and strode over to the fire, thrusting the letter into the flames. He whirled around to face her. 'She wasn't well. Had all sorts of strange ideas about what was going on and now you have too, all because you couldn't keep your nose out of someone else's business!' He splashed himself another whisky and continued angrily. 'What I do and what I drink is my business, and I'll damn well do as I please.' His voice rose. 'I'm *sick* of women telling me how to behave and interfering with every fucking thing I do. If you really loved me, you'd support me, not criticise and moan every time I take a drink. You're as bad as Anna and I won't tolerate it in my own house! Do you hear me? I won't fucking *have* it!'

He was yelling now, enraged, spit flying and his face red. Tamar cowered in her chair as he loomed over her, aggressive and frightening, whisky slopping out of his glass.

'You're all the same, you bloody women! I've given you a nice house, clothes, everything a woman could want, and still, *still* you're ungrateful! You're not making any effort at *all* to understand how hard it is for me. Christ! Why is nothing I do ever good enough for you? No wonder I have to bloody drink!'

Tamar was appalled, not only by Peter's behaviour but also by his wild accusations. She had never complained about her situation, and he'd never given any indication he was unhappy in any way.

This abrupt transformation in his personality was terrifying.

'Well?' he demanded, clearly expecting some sort of response.

She felt too frightened to say anything but knew he would continue berating her until she did. 'In … in the letter …,' she stammered. 'In the letter, Anna said she asked you to stop drinking. Did you?'

Peter snorted derisively. 'For a couple of months, but I don't know why. Nothing changed. And that's because my drinking wasn't the problem, *Anna* was. And then she bloody well died,' he said in disgust.

Tamar thought it was probably pointless, and unwise given his mood, to ask him if he would consider leaving off drinking again. Instead, to placate him, she said, 'I really *do* understand how hard it's been for you, Peter, losing her and the child. I know it must still grieve you terribly.'

'Yes, it does,' he replied bitterly. Then, his temper having apparently subsided as quickly as it had flared, he waved his hand dismissively. 'I need to think. Go to bed.'

Tamar took the opportunity to escape and went into their bedroom, closing the door behind her softly so as not to give Peter any reason to yell at her. She lit the kerosene lamp, changed into her nightdress, climbed into bed and rolled on to her side. Then she cried.

She cried because she did not understand what had just happened, because she could not work out what she had done to displease Peter and make him so angry, and because she had no idea what to do. Perhaps the fault lay with her. Perhaps she was not doing enough to make him happy. All she could do was carry on loving him and taking care of him, but she would try harder.

But most of all she cried because she had left Myrna's letter, full of familiarity and comfort, in the parlour and was too scared to go back and get it.

CHAPTER NINE

August 1880

Tamar awoke to find herself alone in bed. She got up, peed in the chamber pot and went into the parlour.

Peter was asleep in the armchair, his face pale and puffy, the empty whisky bottle on the small table beside him. He had vomited on the floor and down his shirt. There was a large damp patch on the front of his trousers and she smelled urine as she bent over him. When she moved to straighten up, a heavy hand fell on the back of her neck. 'Tamar?'

She twisted hurriedly away, wary.

Peter opened bloodshot eyes and blinked heavily. 'Tamar, please help me. I feel so *ill*,' he said weakly.

'You fell asleep in your chair,' she said from a safe distance. Even from there she could smell his revolting breath.

'Help me, please. I have to be sick.'

Tamar ran into the kitchen and grabbed a bowl. She hurried back into the parlour, placed it on his knees and held his head while he threw up. Not much came out except watery bile smelling of whisky. He continued to retch violently.

Finally he stopped and sat back, a long string of spit on his chin. She fetched him a towel. 'Christ Almighty,' he said, his arms limp at his sides. 'How much did I drink yesterday?' Tamar shrugged. 'I'm so sorry, please forgive me. Oh God, I have to go to bed. My head's splitting.'

He rose to stand, swayed, then found his balance. Holding on to the chair he turned and shuffled towards the bedroom, clutching his head. Tamar followed, helped him out of his filthy clothes and pulled the covers over him. Then she picked up her own clothes and took them into the parlour, gently shutting the door behind her. She dressed, cleaned up the mess on the parlour floor and went about her morning chores, keeping herself busy so she would not think about the night before.

At midday, as she was taking fresh bread out of the oven, Peter came into the kitchen. He had brushed his hair, dressed in a clean shirt and trousers, and looked utterly miserable and full of remorse. 'It *is* a problem, isn't it?' he said.

Tamar, slicing a loaf of the hot bread at the end of the table, did not look up.

'I just can't seem to stop once I start. I don't know what comes over me. I hope I didn't say anything to upset you last night.'

She lifted her head. 'Can you not remember?'

'I remember being in the hotel yesterday afternoon, falling off that sodding horse somewhere, then waking up this morning. Why? What else happened?' he asked, a note of panic in his voice.

Tamar put several slices of bread on a plate and placed them in front of him with a dish of newly churned butter. He pushed the butter away but pulled off a piece of the bread and ate it. When it was clear it was going to stay down, he ate a bigger piece.

'You were upset. And angry,' replied Tamar. 'You accused me of interfering with your drinking.'

'Why? Were you upset with me?' He obviously had no memory of Anna's letter.

'Yes, I was a little. You seemed to undergo a complete change of personality.'

'Did I?' said Peter, with such a startled look Tamar wondered if he really couldn't remember. She finished slicing the loaf.

'How's your head now?' she asked.

'A lot better than it was earlier. Are you still angry at me?'

Tamar said nothing.

'I *do* remember you asking me to give up my drinking,' he said.

She hadn't; he was obviously remembering something Anna had said, but Tamar chose not to correct him.

He continued. 'I think you're right, it doesn't agree with me. I promise you I *will* stop drinking, from now on. I swear it, Tamar, on the Bible.'

He looked so forlorn, vulnerable and sincere that Tamar felt her heart melt. Eager to encourage the return of his usual frame of mind, she wordlessly nodded her acceptance, both of his vow to stop drinking and his overt need for her approval. She moved next to his chair, and let him wrap his arms around her waist and rest his head against her stomach as she stroked his hair. It was then she remembered Peter had gone into Huia for two reasons.

'Did you find a housegirl?' she asked as she sat and buttered a piece of bread. The issue of Peter's drinking was not forgotten, but she let it rest.

'Yes! I did, a Maori girl. Not sure how old she is but she looked fairly clean and she can speak English. She has to see her family first, but she'll be here Monday. She comes from the settlement near Te Henga on the coast, but she was in Huia yesterday and the storekeeper said she was looking for work so I made her an offer. I've forgotten her name.'

'How much will you pay her?'

'As little as possible,' said Peter with his mouth full of bread. 'They don't need much — a bit of tobacco, some booze, they don't care. You'll have to keep her in line though. They can get a bit uppity. Give them European clothes and they think they're the same as us.'

Tamar frowned. She'd wait and see, she decided. If Peter was unable to keep his word about not drinking, a domestic who thought she was above her station would be the least of her worries.

The following Monday Tamar was weeding the flower garden when she looked up to see a figure on horseback riding down the track. As the horse neared, she saw the rider was a woman. Tamar stood and waited for her to approach.

'Good morning,' Tamar said cautiously, removing her gardening gloves.

'Good morning,' replied the girl, expertly reining her horse to a halt. 'Excuse me, but are you Mrs Montgomery?'

'Yes, I am. You must be the girl my husband employed last week.'

'I am Riria. I have come to be your housemaid.'

Tamar was immediately struck by how extraordinarily beautiful, brown and wild-looking the girl was, sitting bareback on her chestnut horse with her head held high. Her skin was a milky coffee colour, and thick, dark brown hair fell loosely down her back past her narrow waist. Her eyes were brown, huge and almond-shaped, set under dark, naturally arched brows and above wide cheekbones. Her nose was flat and her lips full. Tamar was startled to see both lips were defined by a thin, black tattooed line which merged into a neat motif on her chin.

A *moko*, she thought, remembering Sally's word for the tattoos on the Maori they had seen in Auckland.

The girl was wearing a plain brown European-styled dress with a high neck and long sleeves. It was patched in several places but clean and appeared to have been painstakingly maintained.

Her boots, which looked like those usually worn by men but in a smaller size, were visible as she sat astride the horse, the skirt of her dress hitched above her knees. She looked a solid girl but not at all overweight, with full round calves and strong thighs. Her shoulders were wide for a woman and her breasts sat high, evidently without the benefit of undergarments, Tamar noticed. Almost as eye-opening as the *moko* was the small black Tyrolese hat she wore, complete with a white-tipped black feather.

Riria swung her leg over her horse and slid to the ground; on her feet she was not as tall as Tamar had first thought, but at around five foot five neither was she short. She struggled out of the small pack she was carrying on her back then bobbed an awkward curtsy towards Tamar.

'Oh, don't do that,' Tamar said, embarrassed. 'You don't have to curtsy to *me*.' She held out her hand instead. Riria reached out and shook it, smiling for the first time. Her teeth were even and very white.

'Bring your horse around the back,' said Tamar, leading the way. 'We'll put him in the horse paddock, then you can come inside and have a look.'

'The horse is *wahine*,' replied Riria.

'Pardon?'

'*Wahine*. It means woman. Female.'

'Oh,' said Tamar. 'Well, we'll put *her* in the horse paddock, then.'

After the horse had been attended to, Tamar took Riria into the house. She felt awkward about offering her a cup of tea; she had never had a domestic servant and was unsure of the protocol she should be observing. Then she remembered how thirsty she'd been after her own trip from Huia, and put the kettle on the stove regardless.

While she waited for the water to boil, she showed the girl around the house and explained what needed to be done. Riria, who had worked for a European woman before, said she was familiar with the work that would be required.

As they sat to drink their tea at the kitchen table, Riria announced, 'I have brought my possessions with me. Mr Montgomery said he did not know if I am to live here or not. He said you would make that decision, Mrs Montgomery.'

Tamar noticed the other girl's English was very good, if a little formal, but wished she would not call her Mrs Montgomery. She felt it forced her into a role she suspected she would not enjoy. To her surprise, she had taken an instant liking to the girl with her quiet dignity, and sensed they were closer to being equals than they were to the roles of lady of the house and domestic servant.

'Well, why don't you stay here for a few nights and we'll see how it goes? It's a long way for you to come up from Huia every day.'

'Thank you. I will do that, Mrs Montgomery.'

'Please don't call me Mrs Montgomery. My name is Tamar.'

'Yes, Tamar,' replied Riria. 'And you may call me Riria, rather than *Miss* Riria.'

Tamar looked at the other girl for a startled second then burst out laughing, realising with delight she may have found the company she had been longing for after all. Curious, she asked Riria about her family and her people.

Riria was seventeen and had been born at Kainui near Te Henga, where most of her family still lived. Her people were *tangata whenua*, people of the land, and were known as Te Kawerau a Maki. They were descended from Tahuhunui, who had captained the ancestral *waka* Moekakara to Aotearoa many generations ago.

She had two older sisters, both of whom had their own families, and one younger brother. As Riria's family were of high rank, the tribe's elders had selected a husband for her when she was eleven but she had defied them, insisting she was too young to marry, and had run off when she was fifteen to work for a European family at Karekare. She had since mended the rift with her parents, but only just; they were unhappy with her doing the housework of white folk.

Riria, however, wanted to learn how Europeans lived, believing one day there would be a place for Maori alongside *Pakeha*, as she called white-skinned Europeans. She could already read and write English, but wanted to become familiar with European customs. But she was still not ready to settle down, convinced the world had more to offer than a husband and babies. Tamar sensed a kindred spirit, although she herself was only a year older and already married. But not pregnant. Her period had arrived several days ago.

By the time Riria had moved her belongings into the little room off the back porch, been given a guided tour of the garden and orchard, and helped Tamar prepare the evening meal, Peter had arrived home. He nodded to Riria but ignored her after that, telling Tamar to sit with him in the parlour while the dinner was cooking.

'You can't be too friendly,' he said after they sat down and Tamar had brought him a cup of tea. 'It's just not done. They need to be kept in their place. Oh, it's fine for *some* Europeans to have relationships with them, the poor and the riffraff and what have you, but not for us. There are certain standards and we must keep them. Mind you, if they're dying out as it's said, we won't have to worry about them soon.'

'Shush!' said Tamar, horrified Riria would overhear him. 'She's a nice young girl. I think she'll be very good.'

'Is she? Good,' he said absently as he flicked through a copy of last week's *Auckland Weekly News*.

Tamar took the opportunity to reread Myrna's letter once more. Everything was fine, Myrna had written. Her business was flourishing, and Polly had taken to her new profession like a duck to water. Sven and Eliza seemed to have developed a relationship of some sort, although Sven was so shy Myrna wondered if he would ever make any progress with his courtship. John Adams was doing very well, raking in money from his rich patients then spending it all treating his poor ones for nothing. Tamar was missed by all, and everyone hoped she was settling happily into marriage. Tamar was amused to note the letter was written in such a way that it gave no indication of Myrna's real business. Tamar still did not think Peter would approve.

As the weeks passed and winter progressed, Tamar settled comfortably if not always happily into her new life.

She saw no evidence Peter was drinking and on the two occasions he went into Huia, he came home sober. He did not, however, seem to be relaxed. His moods fluctuated alarmingly between a passionate and intense love for her and boisterous enthusiasm for their life on the land, to deep depression and a bitter conviction that his life had somehow been blighted by the actions of others and was doomed to failure. Some days he worked himself to the point of exhaustion but often paced the floor at night, unable to sleep and wanting Tamar to stay awake with him until he could.

He was also becoming short-tempered and irrational. Tamar tried to soothe and placate him whenever she could, but was often left emotionally exhausted from attempting to guess what mood he would come home in. One evening he overheard Riria calling Tamar by her first name and yelled at the girl, insisting his wife be addressed as Mrs Montgomery. Tamar suspected he was jealous of the friendly relationship developing between the two women and felt left out, so she and Riria, who seemed to have a very wise head on her shoulders, kept their conversation to a minimum when Peter was about.

But whenever Tamar decided to confront Peter about his unpleasant and gloomy behaviour, he seemed to sense her displeasure and revert to his normal, charming self in a matter of minutes. It was tiring for Tamar, but he was so appealing when he was in a good mood, she found herself quickly forgetting the less pleasant aspects of his behaviour.

It had been decided Riria would live in the house from Sunday night to Thursday night, but she would go to her sister's home at Pararaha near the coast on Fridays when the weather allowed, returning on Sunday afternoon. The weather had degenerated to the point that travel in the bush had become arduous; the rains were frequent, rendering the tracks slippery and dangerous, the air was cold and the mists that rolled off the Waitakere Ranges disorienting. However, some days were fine and clear, if cold. On one such occasion, when Riria had gone to her sister's, Peter announced he was going into town to see about the shipment of his latest batch of timber, but would be home for dinner.

He arrived back around midnight, drunk, foulmouthed and belligerent, with a badly swollen eye and his wallet missing, telling Tamar he'd been robbed and beaten by a pair of thugs behind the Huia hotel. As before, he drank himself unconscious and spent the night slouched in a chair in the parlour. Tamar went to bed early and left him to it. This time he shat as well as wet himself.

The next day he was profoundly remorseful and apologetic, begging Tamar's forgiveness and swearing never to touch a drop again. She accepted his apologies and tried to feel sympathetic, but her trust was beginning to erode. She still loved him desperately and believed he had the strength to overcome his dependence on alcohol, but she dreaded his trips into town. She could no longer be sure what sort of state he would be in when he returned.

The term 'alcoholism' was relatively new and was discussed more and more frequently in the newspapers, particularly by the prohibitionists, and Tamar was appalled to think her husband could be afflicted. Based on what she had seen herself, alcoholism was something that happened to unfortunates from the lower classes, not to an educated gentleman with means.

In a fit of temperance-inspired zeal Peter decided to stay away from town; he would send Riria in with the cart to collect supplies. Tamar was pleased and relieved, convinced that if he stayed out of the hotel in Huia, he would be able to avoid temptation. His mood improved and he went out happily to work and more often than not came home relaxed. On one awful day, Tamar thought she could smell alcohol on his breath and confronted him. He denied it, saying he'd accidentally eaten *tutu* berries and had swallowed kerosene to make himself vomit, adding that he felt very hurt that she doubted him. She dropped the subject at once, dismayed by her own suspicions.

The atmosphere improved and Tamar and Riria got on with the job of looking after the house and preparing for spring. They cleared and replanted the vegetable garden and put in more fruit trees and cane fruits. They made soap and candles, stored in a tin with a tight lid away from mice, churned butter and cheese and made savoury powders from herbs with a pestle and mortar, and took an inventory of the preserves already in the cupboards. They whitewashed throughout the house, scoured the wooden floors with fine sand and cleaned the windows until the glass was spotless.

As the weather improved, they went into the bush and gathered plants and barks for medicinal purposes. Riria had a huge store of knowledge about herbal medicines. They collected *pukatea* bark to be steeped in water and applied to running sores, *manuka* leaves for infusions to stop coughs, *koromiko* for diarrhoea and *kawakawa* for toothache. Riria also pointed out the *kareao* vine — made into an infusion and swallowed in large enough quantities, it would bring on a miscarriage, as well as *kohekoke* leaves used to dry up the milk of women who had lost their infants.

Tamar had not yet fallen pregnant. She was surprised, and

beginning to wonder if there was something wrong. When she tentatively brought the subject up with Riria, she had laughed.

'Why do you want to have babies so quickly?' she asked. 'There is plenty of time. You will be sorry when they come. Always crying and puking and doing *tiko* all the time. And your belly will stretch and so will your *tara*. When your husband goes to put his *tehe* into you, it will be like a stick in a bucket!'

Tamar, who was used to Riria dropping Maori words into her conversation, had a fair idea of what she was talking about and giggled. But she was concerned all the same. She wanted to give Peter a child, hoping it would help him feel more settled, and make up for the little one he had lost. However, she was also worried about the dangers of giving birth in the middle of the bush with only Riria and her female neighbours to help. But if it happened then so be it, she thought. After all, now she was a married woman she had a duty to produce and raise children.

Several more chatty, cheerful letters had arrived from Myrna, all asking when Tamar was coming to visit. She approached Peter one unseasonably cold and miserable September night as they sat in front of the parlour fire.

'Now that you mention it,' he said thoughtfully, 'we *could* go for a few days. I need to settle a contract for shipping the *kauri* we milled. It won't make us any money mouldering away in the bush. I could do with a few days in Auckland.'

Tamar was pleased he sounded so cheerful about the prospect, as he had been growing morose again. She immediately wrote to tell Myrna they would be in Auckland within two weeks. Peter wrote to a business associate, asking that meetings be arranged to discuss the shipment of the timber, and they sent Riria off the next day to send the letters from Huia.

Tamar was highly excited at the prospect of seeing Auckland and her friends again; she had been away for three months but it felt much longer. However, she wanted Riria to accompany them but was worried Peter would not allow it. Surprisingly, when she plucked up the courage to ask, he agreed, although reluctantly. He had mellowed slightly towards the girl since she had been living with them, although he still tried to discourage their friendship.

'I suppose she can come,' he grumbled. 'But we must make it clear she's our servant and your maid, nothing more. And for God's sake, find her something decent to wear. That brown rag of hers is falling apart. Can't you give her something of yours? What about that dreadful grey thing you used to wear when you were working?'

'No, it would be too small. I haven't really got anything suitable,' Tamar replied, looking up at Peter with large, manipulative eyes. He contemplated her for several seconds, then sighed.

'Send her into town for some fabric then and make her something. But nothing too fancy! We don't want her getting airs.'

Tamar jumped up and kissed him. 'No, just something simple but smart,' she replied happily and ran out to tell Riria.

Riria was intrigued with the idea of going to Auckland but, to Tamar's surprise, failed to appreciate the prospect of a new outfit. 'What do I want with a new dress? What is wrong with this one?' Riria asked, holding out the skirt of her brown frock, patched in four places and almost worn through in several more. 'It is clean and in one piece.'

'Yes, it's clean. But don't you want a nice, smart new one?'

'What for?'

Tamar opened her mouth and then closed it again, it dawning on her that Riria did not value clothes as she herself did. Then, with a very unpleasant jolt, she realised that until she met Peter, she had not particularly valued them either. Now she had gowns she hadn't even worn. Had she changed that much in such a short time?

'Will you feel ashamed to be seen with me wearing such a patched and worn dress?' asked Riria, astute as always.

Tamar had the grace to blush. She considered lying and saying Peter had ordered it, but decided she owed Riria more than that. 'Yes,' she answered. 'If you want a new one, I'll give you the money for the fabric and make it up for you. You decide.'

Riria looked at Tamar for a full minute then said, 'If it is such an important thing to you, then I will have a new dress.' She shook her head slowly. 'You *Pakeha* women are *porangi*.'

In the end, Riria selected a pale blue fabric which Tamar made into a skirt and a long-sleeved bodice jacket that buttoned up the back with a high neck and a small lace collar. She refused, however, to wear a corset, saying she had no interest in having her innards pushed up through her mouth.

Again they endured the tedious journey from Huia by coach, worse this time because the roads were even muddier, staying overnight at New Lynn then boarding the train to Auckland. Riria was fascinated by the urban scenery as they drew closer to the city, asking repeatedly about every large building until Peter told her to be quiet. On arrival they walked to the Waitemata Hotel, across from the railway station, a porter hurrying behind with their bags.

Tamar and Peter were shown to their room while Riria was taken to the staff quarters at the back of the hotel. She made a striking and rather formidable figure striding down the hallway, her head held high in her little black hat. Her hair, which she refused to tie up, bounced gently behind her, and her new dress accentuated her shapely figure. Several of the staff stopped to stare, the men in veiled appreciation and the woman in disapproval of her *moko* and what appeared to be her refusal to be intimidated. Riria stared back, sweeping past them imperiously.

Upstairs, Tamar took her time unpacking. She had brought a day dress, her afternoon dress and her mauve evening gown. She had looked everywhere for her amethyst pendant and earrings but had been unable to find them, wondering where on earth she'd put them and hoping they hadn't been lost; Peter would be hurt and very annoyed. She sat down at a small desk and wrote a note to Myrna, advising her they had arrived, took it down to the reception desk and asked that it be delivered to Myrna's address. Peter had gone to his club but would be back later, and Tamar hoped Myrna would join them for dinner.

She ran herself a hot bath in the luxuriously large tub in the bathroom adjoining their room and lounged decadently in it for over an hour, adding steaming hot water at her leisure. At home they had to be content with crouching in a tin tub in front of the kitchen range if they wanted more than a perfunctory wash. This bath was so deep she could stretch out and only her head and toes broke the water. She made the most of it before she got out, pulled the plug and wrapped herself in several large fluffy towels. As she was putting on her robe, a knock came at the door. It was Riria with a return note from Myrna saying she'd be delighted to meet them at the Waitemata for dinner that evening, but she would arrive a little earlier to take tea with Tamar and catch up on what had been happening. As it was now almost four, Tamar decided to make herself respectable.

Riria laid out her afternoon dress, a salmon-coloured silk, while Tamar sat at the dresser and did her hair. She normally wore it parted in the middle and pulled back in a chignon fixed with hair pins, but tomorrow night when they went to dinner with Peter's business associates, she would ask Riria to help her put it up.

Struggling into her corset, she grunted and groaned as Riria tugged on the laces. She didn't bother to wear one at home; it was uncomfortable and as she had a naturally small waist, she had no real need. But she was in Auckland now and this is what ladies wore in Auckland, so she forced herself into it, wishing she owned one of the new styles that fastened more conveniently in the front. Riria, who thought such garments were absurd, gave the laces an extra hard yank, forcing a small fart out of an unprepared Tamar. Both women dissolved into hysterical giggles and collapsed onto the bed.

Eventually they got themselves under control and when Tamar finished dressing they went downstairs to wait for Myrna in the private lounge, although Riria received a very disapproving look from the waiter who scuttled to attend them. Tamar chose to ignore him but Riria scowled ferociously back and said something guttural in Maori, causing him to retreat rapidly as soon as he had taken their order.

'What did you say?' asked Tamar, bemused.

'The first four ingredients from your scone recipe. I expect he thought I was cursing him,' replied Riria, smirking.

Tamar giggled. Riria *could* be intimidating at times, especially when she was annoyed; handsome and strong, she radiated a sense of power not seen in many women. Her coffee-coloured skin, untamed hair and facial tattoo contributed to the effect, but her regal bearing and quiet but assertive manner seemed to unsettle people most. Tamar was also aware of an air of sexuality, something subtly wild and natural, and she was sure this had an effect on the men Riria encountered. No doubt women were also aware of this at some level, and perhaps resented her for it.

Myrna arrived half an hour later, looking glamorous and beautifully groomed as usual. She and Tamar hugged, and Tamar introduced Riria.

'Good afternoon, Miss McTaggart,' Riria responded.

'Myrna, dear, ma name is Myrna. Och, and what a lovely wee thing ye are, too!' exclaimed Myrna in her rich Scots accent. Wee was not a word Tamar would have chosen to describe Riria, but Myrna called everything that appealed to her 'wee'.

'Yes,' Tamar replied. 'Riria is my friend and helper around the house. Peter employed her for me.'

'Oh, yes, and how is the charming Mr Montgomery?' asked

Myrna a little sarcastically, looking about her as if expecting to see him hovering somewhere in the recesses of the lounge, perhaps near the small bar tucked discreetly into one corner.

'He's fine, thank you. He's at his club,' said Tamar, and burst into tears.

'Oh dear,' said Myrna, not sounding surprised at all and moving to sit closer to Tamar. 'It's no' taken him long, has it? He's ground ye down already.'

'He's … oh, I don't know where to start. I feel so disloyal talking about him.' Tamar sniffed loudly, then blew her nose and sat up straight. 'He drinks too much,' she blurted. 'And he has terrible moods, Myrna. I don't know what on earth to do about it.'

'He hasnae harmed ye, lassie, has he?' asked Myrna. She felt vindicated in terms of her earlier intuitions, but the petty victory was overshadowed by her concern that Tamar had enmeshed herself in an unpleasant and possibly dangerous situation. 'Does he strike ye?' she asked Tamar, then turned towards Riria who was studiously examining her hands. 'Does he?' she repeated sharply.

Tamar said quickly, 'No, no, he's never touched me in anger.' She considered telling Myrna about Anna's letter, but thought better of it.

Myrna shook her head angrily, still looking at Riria. 'And do you know anything about this, lassie?' she asked. Riria looked steadily back, her mouth firmly closed, saying nothing. It was obvious to Myrna she knew something. 'Come on, girl, out wi' it.'

Riria's eyes flitted towards Tamar, across to Myrna, then back to Tamar again.

'Riria?' said Tamar nervously, a sick feeling nibbling at the pit of her stomach. 'Riria, what do you know?'

'He keeps a supply of *wihiki* in the forest. I have seen where he hides it,' she admitted reluctantly. Privately she thought Peter Montgomery was a *poaka*, a pig, and didn't deserve Tamar, but she had no wish to disillusion her friend.

Tamar gasped. 'He told me he'd stopped drinking! He *promised* me! How could I be so blind?'

'Because ye wanted to be, lassie,' Myrna replied, sighing. 'And men who like the drink will promise ye *anything* as long as ye get off their backs about it. And women,' she added, remembering her own past behaviour. 'But forget about what's done, what are ye going to do about it?'

'Nothing. I can't.'

'And why not? Ye can leave him. Ye've no bairns on the way?'

'No, but I can't. He's my husband. I love him, Myrna! Don't you see that?'

Myrna rolled her eyes. She did see it, and had seen it many times before; good women who wasted their lives on men who cared more for the bottle than their own families, completely unwilling or unable to overcome their addictions. She sighed again. Why couldn't Peter Montgomery just fall off his horse and break his miserable neck? That would suit everybody.

'And what's your opinion?' she asked Riria.

'It is Tamar's decision. As long as I am employed there, I will be her friend. She must do what her *manawa*, her heart, tells her to do.'

'Aye, lassie, I expect she will and all,' agreed Myrna resignedly.

'I don't want to talk about Peter,' Tamar said suddenly, a forced note of gaiety in her voice. 'It was my decision to marry him and things are not always bad. Let's talk about something else, shall we?'

Myrna, happy for once to move away from the topic of Peter Montgomery's myriad character defects, launched into a gossipy and amusing monologue about what was happening in Auckland, who was doing what to whom and what people were saying about it, and how her own business was doing. She stopped when Tamar inclined her head discreetly towards Riria and raised her eyebrows. 'Ye've not said?'

Tamar shook her head.

'Oh, well, *I* might as well, then. After all, it's no' a secret.' Myrna turned to Riria and began. 'Ye see, lassie, I run a …'

'House of sex,' Riria finished for her.

There was a second's silence.

'How did you know that?' asked Tamar, surprised.

'The boy who brought the message back. He said to me it was from the Scottish lady at the whorehouse on Dilworth Terrace.'

'Oh,' said Tamar. Then, 'Are you shocked?'

'No. Why should I be? It is better that men buy what they need from a woman who is willing to sell it, than take it from a woman who is not willing.'

'Quite right,' said Myrna. 'A lassie who understands business as well as human nature. I like that. Do ye no' have such a thing as rape amongst your people then?'

'Yes, we do,' replied Riria, frowning slightly. 'We have *utu* as well.'

'*Utu*?'

'Revenge,' said Riria.

CHAPTER TEN

Peter failed to appear and Myrna and Tamar sat down to dinner without him.

'Ma girls couldnae make it. They're working, but they'll come into town tomorrow and we'll have morning tea together. We dinnae open for business until two in the afternoon. The girls need their rest. They're dying to see ye.'

Tamar nodded, her mouth full. She was looking forward to seeing the girls, especially Polly. She swallowed and asked, 'How *is* Polly?'

'Well,' said Myrna slowly. 'She's certainly popular wi' the customers, and verra good at her job, but I'm no' sure about what's going on in that head o' hers.'

'How do you mean?'

'She seems happy enough, but she takes it all a wee bit seriously. I cannae put ma finger on it. It's almost as if she has this *need* to take as much money as she can off the men. Good for business, but no' that healthy for her. I wonder if something awful didnae happen when she was on the streets and she hasnae told us. She seems to have gone a wee bit hard. Oh, I ken working girls have to be hard in many ways, but I mean hard *inside*. Brittle. Like something might break. But, on the other hand, she laughs and jokes wi' the girls same as she used to. And as I said, she's popular wi' the customers.'

'Have you talked to her about it?'

'I've tried. She says everything's fine.'

'Perhaps it's just the way she chooses to handle the job.'

'Perhaps,' agreed Myrna, not sounding convinced.

Peter still hadn't returned by the time Myrna left, so Tamar went back to their room and prepared for bed. She had a quick wash, brushed her hair out then braided it for sleep, changed into her nightdress and got into bed with a book. She could not concentrate on the pages in front of her; she was concerned about his lateness and was beginning to feel hurt, angry and humiliated. If, as Riria had alleged, he *was* still drinking, chances are he would come in drunk, having been at his club since mid-afternoon. How could she not have noticed? Or *had* she been aware but chosen not to acknowledge it, even to herself? And if he had been drinking, what sort of mood would Peter be in tonight?

She did not have to wait long to find out. He knocked on the door half an hour later and when Tamar let him in, it was immediately obvious he was drunk. But, to Tamar's relief, not aggressively so. But she had come to know how he could turn in an instant, and she was wary. His face was flushed and his eyes bright. He removed a flask of whisky from his coat and placed it on the nightstand, flopped onto the bed and lit a cigarette.

'Sorry I missed dinner,' he said, blowing a perfect smoke ring. 'I was catching up with some of the fellows from the club.'

'Have you eaten? Shall I order something to be brought up?' asked Tamar hopefully, thinking a meal might help to sober him.

'No, but you can take the lid off that whisky and pour me one.'

Tamar felt a sudden, brittle flash of anger; Peter was not stupid and knew she would be disappointed and concerned by his drinking. He was playing some sort of masochistic little game, pretending nothing was wrong, and trying to involve her in the charade. If she poured him a drink, she would be condoning his behaviour. 'No,' she said defiantly. 'You promised.'

He lay on the bed and smiled lazily at the ceiling. 'That's funny,' he said conversationally. 'I could have sworn you said no then, but I'll give you the benefit of the doubt and assume it was some other bitch whining through the wall next door. I *said*, get me a drink.'

Oh God, thought Tamar in sudden fear. She turned and headed for the door; slinking down the hall in her nightdress would be preferable to facing Peter in one of his drunken rages. But before she could open it he was behind her, his weight jamming the door shut. 'And where do you think *you're* off to, my sweet little flower?' he said, still in a very pleasant tone of voice.

You bastard, thought Tamar, you absolute bastard. She turned to face him. 'Nowhere,' she said dully, knowing she was beaten. 'Sit down and I'll get your drink.' Perhaps if he drank enough he would pass out, as he had on other occasions.

He didn't. He drank his first glass straight off, finished his cigarette, poured himself another and sat down in an armchair. 'Come and be nice to me, my beautiful Tamar,' he said, patting his knee. 'Come and warm me up.'

Tamar moved over to stand in front of him. This was new, wanting sex when he was drunk. New and distasteful. He smelled faintly like an animal beneath the whisky fumes, sweaty and pungent. She started to lower herself onto his lap but he turned her around and pushed her down to kneel on the floor. Pulling the ribbon out of her hair he unwound her long braid then with his left hand tightly gripping a fistful of her hair, he undid the buttons on his trousers with the other until his erection rose through the opening in his underpants. Tamar, suddenly realising what he wanted, turned her head away. She felt sick. Peter twisted her head back again, guiding her face down to his crotch. His penis smelled of urine and she grimaced.

'Open your mouth,' he ordered. 'Be nice.'

When she didn't, he tugged her hair viciously.

'Ow!' she cried, tears springing to her eyes.

'Well, be nice then,' he repeated in an incongruously reasonable voice.

Tamar did as she was told, taking his penis between her lips.

'Suck it.'

She did, cautiously, and Peter began to move in and out of her mouth, thrusting further and further each time. Tamar started to choke, gagging every time he touched the back of her throat. Her eyes watered and she began to salivate.

'Put your lips over your teeth. They're too sharp,' he muttered, hunching forwards and placing his free hand firmly on the back of her neck so her head was trapped in his lap. She shut her eyes and concentrated on not throwing up. Saliva poured out of her mouth and down her chin and her jaw muscles were aching. She tasted blood. Just when she thought she must vomit, he stopped and withdrew. He moved her head away, stood and pulled her up off the floor. 'On the bed,' he directed. 'I'm ready.'

He took Tamar's arm, steered her towards the bed and pushed her roughly back. Then he tugged her nightdress up to her armpits and stood back to push his trousers and underpants down. They tangled around his ankles as he stepped forward. Cursing, he sat on the bed and removed them completely, then turned and positioned himself between Tamar's legs. She lay still, unresponsive and strangely detached. Peter didn't seem to notice as he inserted his penis and began to thrust. She was dry and it hurt but eventually he penetrated her fully. Tamar still did not move and lay motionless until he had finished. Drunk as he was, it took him some time.

He rested for a minute, then got off her. 'I'm going downstairs for a drink,' he said, pulling his trousers and boots back on. He did not look at her. 'I'll be back later.'

When he'd gone, Tamar got up slowly, rinsed out her mouth repeatedly and wiped between her legs with a towel, then climbed into bed. She did not sleep for a long time. She did not cry either.

'Why is your *ngutu* swollen?' asked Riria, pointing to Tamar's bruised upper lip. They were walking up Queen Street, on their way to meet Myrna and her girls for morning tea.

'I bumped it last night,' lied Tamar.

Riria snorted. 'You mean someone bumped it for you!' she replied, not fooled for a second.

Tamar was too ashamed to divulge what had really happened, so she said nothing. When she had awoken, Peter had been asleep beside her. Surprised she had not heard him come in, and moving very cautiously so she would not wake him, she had crept out of bed and padded silently into the bathroom, locking the door behind. As she was sitting on the privy waiting for her bath to run, there had been a knock on the bathroom door.

'Tamar? Tamar, please let me in. I'm so sorry!'

Sorry my arse, she thought. That was one of Myrna's new sayings and she rather liked it.

'I have to use the privy!' came Peter's muffled voice through the wooden door.

'Use the one down the hall,' she replied wearily. There was silence for a minute, then she heard the door to their room open then shut again. The water in the tub was almost scalding but she welcomed it, wincing as the heat stung her bruised vulva. She slid under the water, closing her eyes to its soothing embrace. She stayed there until she heard Peter at the bathroom door again. Go away, she thought.

'Please come out. I need to talk to you!' he called plaintively.

Tamar ignored him. When she finally emerged from the bathroom, he was lying curled on the bed, weeping. He begged her forgiveness and promised it would never happen again; it had only happened because he had gone to his club and had been coerced into taking a drink by friends whom he had not seen for months. To refuse would have been extremely rude. His tone of voice implied that even he knew it was a pathetic excuse.

'And will you be coerced into taking another drink at your meetings today? And tonight at dinner?' Tamar asked acidly.

'No! I *swear* it!' he replied vehemently, sitting up slowly, holding his head. 'I wouldn't even go if I could get out of it, but I can't. Please believe me!'

Tamar didn't know whether she did or not, although Peter looked extremely sick and certainly very sorry for himself.

'When is your first meeting today?'

'Midday.'

'Why don't you sleep until then?' Tamar suggested. 'Riria and I are meeting Myrna this morning and then we're sightseeing. We'll be back later this afternoon.'

Riria knocked on the door, come to help Tamar dress, which they did in silence. Peter lay in the bed with the covers pulled up to his ears, asleep. Riria tilted her head at his motionless form and raised her eyebrows. Tamar shook her head, then turned to the mirror to adjust her hat and pull on her gloves. They said nothing until they were on the street, and then the only comment Tamar made was that Peter had come in drunk. Riria knew her well enough by now not to push her.

Morning tea seemed to lift Tamar's spirits. Myrna's girls were fascinated by Riria, asking to touch the fine raised ridges of her *moko* and whether it had hurt when she'd had it done.

Riria made a face and nodded. 'Of course. But it is a badge of honour. I wear it with pride. My *moko* announces to the world who I am. It is a visual manifestation of my *whakapapa*, my heritage.'

Although Myrna's girls were full of questions for Tamar about life in the bush, they did not bring up the subject of her marriage. Perhaps Myrna had said something. If so, Tamar was grateful. She did not feel like telling them what had been happening, but neither did she want to lie to them. Polly seemed her normal exuberant self, and Tamar could not see what it was that had concerned Myrna.

Later, Riria and Tamar hired a cab and spent a pleasant after-noon touring Auckland, Tamar pointing out the sights including the gardens in the Auckland Domain, J. Partington's spectacular windmill off Symonds Street and St Paul's Church where she and Peter had been married. Riria was amused by the sight of people crowding into horse trams and trotting about in dog-carts or the fancy, dainty little two-person phaetons.

'What is wrong with riding a horse if you want to go some-where? Or walking?' she asked Tamar.

'People with money don't walk anywhere,' replied Tamar. 'Especially the ladies.'

'Eh? Why not?' said Riria.

'Because that's the way it is.'

Riria snorted and shook her head but continued to gaze avidly about her. When they returned to the hotel so Tamar could ready herself for dinner, Peter was also in, having just returned from his meetings, which had evidently been successful. Tamar saw no indication he been drinking. He had met with someone, he said, who would collect and ship his timber, and would also be at dinner that evening. A Maori, Peter said, sounding faintly amused. 'It will be interesting to see if he has any table manners. Mind you, he seems to have some education, speaks English well, so you never know.'

Tamar thought his comment hypocritical coming from a man who had done to her what Peter had the night before, but she refrained from saying so. He seemed to have cheered up since morning, and had stopped the pathetic whining and grovelling she was beginning to find almost more disturbing and disappointing than his drunken behaviour; she did not want to do or say anything that might cause his mood to deteriorate.

As usual, they would go on as if nothing had happened. He had sworn to abstain from drinking yet again, and she had accepted his apologies, both pretending it would be all right; Peter because he truly believed it and Tamar because she was too weary to say otherwise. There was no question of leaving him. The current law decreed that a divorce could only be obtained by a husband, and only on the grounds of his wife's adultery.

Tamar took her time getting dressed, Riria assisting while Peter absented himself to the private lounge. First Riria laced her into her corset then lifted the mauve velveteen evening gown over her head and fastened the many hooks and buttons at the back. Next, Tamar sat at the dressing table while Riria gathered up her heavy auburn hair and arranged it in a high, slightly dishevelled style that fell about her face in gentle waves. Riria stepped back, critically assessed her handiwork, and made a few small adjustments, rearranging a strand here and fixing a hairpin there.

'It's beautiful, thank you, Riria,' said Tamar, pleased at the image of the lovely and sophisticated young woman who looked back at her from the mirror, relieved her swollen lip had gone down. Her throat and ears were bare but there was nothing she could do about that, except hope Peter didn't notice she wasn't wearing her amethysts.

The house on Princes Street was grand, as were most residences backing onto Albert Park; clearly, Peter's business associate was successful and wealthy. They were ushered by an English-accented butler into a spacious, elegantly decorated formal parlour where seven or eight people were already seated. Tamar was introduced to their host, Frank Coulthard, a robust looking man in his early fifties, and his pretty wife Abigail, who appeared considerably younger. The Coulthards in turn introduced Tamar to the other dinner guests.

'We're waiting on three or four more guests to arrive,' explained Frank Coulthard. 'Te Kanene whom you met this afternoon, and his nephew, Kepa, may dine with us also, and the Becks. You know Thomas and Julia Beck already, I believe?'

Peter nodded. Thomas Beck was also in the timber business, although he ran a much larger operation. As he and Tamar seated themselves they were offered a sherry. Peter declined, to Tamar's relief, but she accepted a small half glass and settled back to admire the Coulthards' fine furnishings. As opulent as Myrna's house, she observed, but without the sensuous and titillating touches. The other dinner guests were also spectacular, the ladies in particular. There was an abundance of silk, satin, fine lace and feathers, and their husbands' wealth was reflected in the jewellery they wore. Tamar touched her own bare throat self-consciously.

The Becks arrived shortly, followed almost immediately by two Maori, the room falling silent as they were announced. The first, Te Kanene, was a tall thin man, possibly in his early fifties; Tamar could not tell from his brown, weathered face. He was tattooed over his forehead and across his nose and cheeks, but his chin and taut jawline were unmarked. His dark, wiry hair was almost entirely grey and cut short in a European style, although a long, slender piece of polished greenstone hung from his pierced left ear. His prominent nose was hooked, and his slightly bulging eyes were sharp, shrewd and black, like those of a bird. A predatory bird, Tamar reflected, as the man seemed to take the measure of everyone in the room. He was attired in stylish evening wear. Altogether he cut a fine figure, a curious and slightly mesmerising combination of gentility with more than a hint of suppressed cunning and savagery.

It was, however, the younger man who caused Tamar to swallow her sherry the wrong way and choke painfully. Peter patted her absently on the back as she leaned forward to hurriedly put her drink down. Recovering, she regained her composure but could not prevent herself from staring. Kepa was quite possibly the most beautiful man she had ever seen. She remembered her manners and lowered her eyes, but not before his image seared itself into her mind and her very soul.

'Right, then,' announced Frank Coulthard jovially. 'We're all here now so shall we go in to dinner?' He offered his arm to his wife and led his guests into the dining salon, a smaller but equally elegant room off the wide hall.

They were seated at a huge oval dining table and chatted amongst themselves while they waited. There was an ornate silver epergne holding a low but extensive floral arrangement in the centre of the table, flanked by two pairs of silver candlesticks and five or six small fluted silver dishes containing relishes and sauces, and a bewildering array of cutlery. Tamar was seated with Thomas Beck on one side and a short, corpulent man whose name she had forgotten on the other. Peter sat opposite between Te Kanene and one of the female guests, and Kepa was seated further down on Peter's right. When Tamar looked over at the young Maori he was staring openly back at her. She blushed and quickly looked away.

Te Kanene, missing nothing, leaned back in his chair and motioned to his nephew. '*E tama! Kaue e tiromakutu. He whakatoi!*' he hissed. Kepa, well aware that staring was indeed rude, lowered his eyes briefly.

First came tiny mussel fritters, then a huge tray on which rested a rack of lamb surrounded by roasted potatoes and yams, followed by several dishes of minted peas, squash and tiny carrots, and a basket of warm, fresh bread rolls. Several bottles of wine were also brought to the table. Again, Tamar was pleased to see Peter place his hand over his unused wine glass and indicate he would prefer water.

She felt a little out of place surrounded by people she did not know and who were obviously much more at ease with the social situation, but she managed not to scatter her peas across the fine damask tablecloth and kept a surreptitious eye on which piece of cutlery Thomas Beck used with which dish. She noted Te Kanene's table manners were considerably more polished than her own. Peter seemed quite at home but she wished he had warned her the evening would be so formal. He seemed to forget she didn't come from the same social stratum and was not yet practised at the level of etiquette required at such occasions.

She was therefore horrified when she stuck her fork into a slightly under-cooked yam and it shot off her plate and disappeared under the gracefully arching leaves of the floral arrangement. Oh God. Should she retrieve it and put it back on her plate, or ignore it? She looked around and saw Kepa smiling directly at her, clearly amused. She felt a terrible urge to laugh and bit her lip hard to stop herself.

She was saved, however, by Thomas Beck, who speared the yam deftly with his fork, popped it into his mouth and said chattily, 'I'm particularly partial to yams myself. Thank you so much for putting it to one side for me, Mrs Montgomery.'

'You are welcome, Mr Beck. They *are* very tasty, are they not?'

'Indeed,' he replied, smiling broadly. 'You, my dear, are simply stunning. I am surprised your husband has not introduced you to Auckland society before now.'

'Thank you, Mr Beck. We have not long been married, and we spend much of our time on Peter's block in the Waitakeres. Perhaps you know it?'

'No, never been out your way, we're further up near Kumeu, but I know Peter. Quite well, in fact. Everything going well now, is it?' he asked.

'Yes, it is, thank you,' she replied, not quite sure what he was implying.

Thomas Beck elaborated. 'The financial side of his business, I mean. I see the loan as an investment really, although I am aware of course that what he's already borrowed from the bank will have to be repaid first. But I hear that's a good little block of land. If Peter's plans for its development come to fruition, I should see my money doubled, I expect.'

Loan? Bank? What plans? Tamar was mystified and beginning to feel slightly foolish. 'Yes, yes,' she replied vaguely. 'I expect you will. I hope so, anyway.' What had Peter been up to now?

Across the table, Kepa was talking to Abigail Coulthard. Tamar watched him out of the corner of her eye and was again struck by how extraordinarily attractive he was. Not conventionally hand-some, but somehow wild and very, very alive. He wore his black shoulder-length hair tied back in a short, tightly plaited queue and his left ear was pierced with a small greenstone stud. His nose was well defined but straight and quite narrow, although its lines suggested he may come to resemble Te Kanene as he grew older. His lips were full and curved, almost arrogant, and his dark eyes rimmed with long, thick black lashes most women would kill for. A small, fine scar running from his hairline into his left eyebrow did not detract from his appearance. He was not tattooed and was clean-shaven, and seemed to have very little facial hair, although he was clearly beyond boyhood. He was darker than Riria, his rich skin colour accentuated by the white shirt and pale gold waistcoat he was wearing. When he smiled his teeth were strong and white in his dark face.

'I say, this is a nice drop,' said Harold McLeod, the rotund man sitting next to Tamar, holding up his glass of red wine and squinting at it. 'You can't beat a good Frog burgundy. Whoops, I hope no one here's a Good Templar? Or French?'

'I'm neither,' said Frank Coulthard. 'I suspect being a Prohibitionist would be no fun at all, so I don't mind if my soul is damned by the indulgence of my sensual appetites. If drinking wine like this is a sin, then I'm going straight to hell, I'm afraid.'

James Wallace, a man in his late thirties sitting on Abigail Coulthard's right, announced, 'I read somewhere the other day that the Prohibitionists are saying the fight for temperance is one of class more than anything else. You know, the humble working man against "the luxuries and appetites, the financial greed and moral inertia of the well-to-do", I think the wording was.'

'That's silly,' said his wife Mary, from the other end of the table.

'That's us, isn't it?' added Julia Beck, sounding faintly bemused.

'It's those poor natives I feel sorry for,' said Ena McLeod patronisingly. She was as round and as tactless as her husband. Tamar winced and glanced at Te Kanene. Mrs McLeod barged on regardless. 'You see them lying drunk in the street, it's disgusting. Even the women. They don't seem able to control themselves. It must be dreadful to have a such a debilitating character defect.'

There was a brief, embarrassed silence and Peter avoided Tamar's eye.

Kepa spoke up. 'But who is selling it to them? That is the question that should be asked.'

'Oh, unscrupulous *Pakeha* traders. As usual,' replied Frank Coulthard. 'They trade it in exchange for land, and it wouldn't surprise me if it's officially condoned. Covertly, of course, but I suspect the Native Land Courts. Either that or the poor buggers are plied with alcohol until they don't know what they're doing, pardon my language ladies, then when they awake the following day, they find they've signed away their tribal lands for next to nothing. Or they get into debt and lose it anyway. *That* is what is dreadful, Mrs McLeod, not the occasional intoxicated Maori in the street. And there are plenty of European drunks rolling around in the gutters as well. Mind you, I understand in the Hawke's Bay and on the East Coast there are just as many sly grog shops run by Maoris as there are by *Pakeha*.'

'That is true,' agreed Te Kanene benignly, cutting into a slice of pink lamb.

'You hail from there, do you not?' asked Abigail Coulthard.

Te Kanene nodded. 'Our *iwi* is Ngati Kahungunu and our ancestral lands reach from Wairoa to Wairarapa.'

'Te Kanene is in coastal shipping,' explained Frank Coulthard, deftly changing the subject. 'And a bit of overseas trade as well, I believe. I understand your people have been in the business for decades. What is it you haul?'

'Timber and gum, and anything else that will go on a clipper, a schooner or a scow,' replied Te Kanene. 'Many types of cargo. From sheep and wool to cattle and foodstuffs, passengers and their household goods. It will be a scow that will transport Mr Montgomery's timber from Paratutae in a week or so.'

'So how many vessels do you have?' asked Harold McLeod curiously.

'Seven,' answered Te Kanene, a measure of undisguised pride in his voice.

'And it's a family business?'

'Yes. I am training my *iramutu*, my nephew Kepa here, to take over the management. I am becoming too old to spend my days at sea and I wish to have my feet on firm ground in my advancing years. He is grown enough and I will pass the responsibility to him soon. He has a good head for business.'

Abigail Coulthard said, 'Frank tells me your wife often accompanies you on your voyages. She must be a remarkable woman.'

'She does, yes, and she is,' responded Te Kanene. 'Although she too is growing tired. She would like to spend more time with her *mokopuna*, so it will suit both of us.'

Julia Beck turned to her right. 'And will *your* wife accompany *you*, Kepa?'

The young Maori man looked her steadily in the eye. 'I do not have a wife.'

'No? Surely you must be quite a catch for some young maiden?' she replied, ignoring her husband's stern look of disapproval.

'Perhaps,' said Kepa. 'But I am not ready for marriage. I have not yet met the woman I wish to spend my life with.'

'We have tried to marry him off,' interjected Te Kanene. 'But it seems he has his own ideas about what a wife should be. But he is only twenty and is young. There is time.'

Peter, who had noticed Kepa gazing openly at Tamar, was uncomfortable with talk of the young Maori's marital status. 'So which ports do you trade from, apart from the Manukau?' he asked abruptly, deliberately changing the subject.

'Those on the East Coast and the Hawke's Bay,' answered Te Kanene quickly, observing Peter's irritation. 'Sometimes we come up north as far as Moehau, or the Coromandel as you call it, and the Waitemata, and now and then to Paratutae or Whatipu or Kaipara on the West Coast for the timber trade. But we generally ply from the ports of Auckland and Tauranga to Dunedin, and more often between Te Kaha and Oamaru. I have also taken clippers to the Americas and to England in the past, although I am unsure at this time if we will continue to venture so far afield. That will be up to Kepa.'

Peter said, 'I thought most of the coastal shipping was in

European hands now. You still seem to have a fairly robust business. How is that?'

'We change with the times, despite the fact we still use sail and not steam. You may be aware Maori coastal traders are denied access to steam-powered vessels.' Te Kanene said this in the blandest of tones but did not drop his gaze. 'We also have considerable capital. It has therefore not been easy for other traders to put us out of business, although it has been tried. So, unlike other Maori ventures, our line has remained solvent and successful. Of course, the coming of the railway may change that.'

After dessert, the women were escorted by Abigail Coulthard to the parlour for tea, coffee or cocoa, while the men retired with her husband to the drawing room for port and cigars.

The women discussed fashions, the theatre, children, interior decorating and, incongruously, the latest attempts to discourage prostitution and rescue the city's fallen women from their immoral and slavish profession. There was already one refuge for such unfortunates in the city, financed by Auckland's social and financial elite, but the problem was still rife. Tamar wondered briefly if Myrna's ears were burning, but she doubted it; she knew Myrna's views on what she termed 'interfering do-gooders,' and they were not generous, although she believed the refuges were a good idea for street girls who either needed a rest or wanted to get out of the business.

'I do think we should be sympathetic of the poor creatures,' Mary Wallace announced fervently. 'They are victims of social injustice and poverty. We have an unfair economic system and these women are suffering because of it. It is an abomination.'

The other women in the room looked at her in mild surprise.

'I had not realised you were one of these new feminists, Mary dear,' commented Ena McLeod, straining the seams on her already protesting evening gown by reaching for the sugar bowl. 'How fascinating.'

'I am not a feminist. I simply feel we should concentrate less on punishing the poor wretches and direct our energy more towards their rehabilitation. They should not be blamed for what has befallen them.'

'That is of course true,' responded Julia Beck wryly. 'If men were not so keen to pay for the services of these women, there would not be a problem, would there?'

'Oh, but it's only the poorer sorts who have to pay for that sort of thing in any case,' insisted Ena McLeod. 'Gentlemen never do.'

There was an incredulous silence. Julia Beck snorted indelicately. I must tell Myrna, thought Tamar. Her business will be ruined.

'Yes, well,' said Abigail Coulthard, and changed the subject to that of the City Council's plans for a new design competition to upgrade Albert Park.

Tamar tried to pay attention but her mind kept wandering back to the young Maori, Kepa. What was it about him? Why did she find him so hypnotic? She felt confused, guilty and rather shocked. Tamar had not formed the same derogatory opinion of the race Peter had, but still, to be so physically attracted to a native man was disturbing. One heard about European men who fell in love with Maori women and sometimes even married them, but for a white woman to have those sorts of feelings towards a Maori man was indecent. The idea of what those physical stirrings might lead to conjured an image of herself Tamar had never considered or even suspected. The vision was frightening, but uncomfortably exciting.

It was another hour before the party broke up and the Coulthards' guests congregated noisily in the foyer as they readied themselves to leave. As Tamar collected Peter's hat and gloves from the sideboard, she found herself standing next to Kepa. Before she was aware of what was happening, he had discreetly taken her arm and was leaning towards her. At his touch, her stomach felt as it used to when she was a child swinging as high as she dared on the rope hanging from the tree outside the family cottage.

'I must see you again,' was all he said before he turned away, leaving Tamar standing with her mouth hanging unbecomingly open and her face burning.

Yes, she thought fervently. You must.

Chapter Eleven

October *1880*

The return trip to Huia was uneventful. Tamar had decided not to question Peter about her conversation with Thomas Beck. So far he had been true to his word about avoiding alcohol and was in high spirits, a state of affairs she did not want to compromise.

They had been home a week and he had gone into town to supervise the loading of his timber. The *kauri* logs had been carted to Huia from where they would be barged to Paratutae then loaded onto one of Te Kanene's scows. Peter had departed yesterday afternoon but did not expect to be back until the following day.

Riria had also gone into town for supplies but would be back later in the afternoon. Having just relieved the two house cows of their milk, Tamar struggled to close the heavy paddock gate. She lifted the unattached end and was hefting it closed when it slipped, tilted wildly and knocked over one of the pails.

'Damn!' Her hands fumbled as she hoisted the gate and attempted to swing it upright and back on its hinges. It slipped from her grasp and crashed to the ground.

'You bloody bastard!' she yelled and gave the empty milk pail a hard kick; it sailed into the paddock, frightening the cows. Tamar felt a rumbling in her bowel and farted vigorously, venting her anger in the most satisfying manner she could think of.

'Can I be of assistance, Mrs Montgomery?' said a voice behind her.

She whirled around in fright and almost fainted from embarrassment; Kepa was standing behind her, not even bothering to conceal his broad grin.

'Do you normally address your gate with such eloquence?' he asked in an amused voice. 'What a novel idea. I must try it myself.'

Tamar was mortified. First I choke in front of him, she thought, then I fling yams across the dining table, and now he's caught me farting like a draughthorse. To hide her red face she bent to retrieve the gate.

'Let me,' said Kepa, hurrying to assist. 'I'm sorry I startled you. I knocked but no one came to the door.'

'I didn't hear you ride up,' replied Tamar.

'No. I left my horse at the front of the house.'

Tamar stood and watched as he expertly hefted the gate back onto its hinges. 'My husband is not here,' she said. 'He's meeting your uncle's scow out on the coast.'

'I know. I've just come from there.'

'Oh.' Tamar retrieved the remaining milk pail, struck anew by his beautiful face. Remembering her manners she asked, 'Would you care for tea?'

Kepa nodded and followed her inside.

'If you'd like to wait in the parlour,' said Tamar, ushering him into the warm, dark room and opening one of the curtains. 'I've been heating it. It was cold first thing this morning. That is, if you're feeling the cold. You might not, of course.'

She was aware she was prattling, but didn't want him standing over her in the kitchen watching her fumble with the tea things. A heavy quilt was draped over a drying frame in front of the fire, so she moved it out of the way and indicated a chair. Why couldn't she have tidied up properly this morning?

Kepa sat down and looked around. 'This is a very cosy house,' he commented. 'You must have worked hard to make it so comfortable and inviting.'

'Peter's first wife, Anna, did most of this,' said Tamar awkwardly.

'Ah yes, I heard he had been tragically widowed. Last year, was it?'

'Yes … I'll make the tea,' she said and fled from the room.

In the kitchen she cursed herself for putting on her oldest dress that morning and not bothering to do her hair properly.

Why was he here? Part of her wished he was not, but another was intrigued. What on earth was she doing receiving him when she was alone? He had said he wanted to see her again, but she never thought he'd actually come. When the water boiled she gathered the tea things on a tray, carried it into the parlour and placed it on the small table. She sat in the chair opposite but, nervous and ill at ease, stood up and added several more small logs to the fire.

'Sit down, please, Tamar.'

She sat abruptly and repeated, 'Peter isn't home. Oh, I said that, didn't I?' She felt silly.

'I did not come to see your husband, I came to see you.'

'Why?' she blurted.

'Because I had to,' he replied bluntly. 'Because since I met you I have not been able to stop thinking about you. Your face, your hair, your body, your shy and funny manner have all enchanted me. You *know* what I am saying because you feel it too. I saw it then and I see it now,' he continued boldly.

Tamar could not believe what she was hearing; his words were straight from a romance novel. Except in those, the heroine was not usually dressed in a drab grey house dress and wearing clogs and woollen stockings. And she was not usually someone else's wife.

In a voice shot with panic and confusion she said, 'But I'm married, Kepa! It isn't right!'

Reaching over, he gently grasped her slim wrist. 'What you feel in here is always right,' he said, pointing at his abdomen.

Tamar started in shock; he had seen into her very core and knew the turmoil she was experiencing. Her stomach felt as if it were plummeting and her heart thudded wildly. This, she suddenly thought, this is what Mam told me about. Oh, but it *isn't* right because he's the wrong man!

Kepa let go of her wrist and sat back, the firelight casting soft shadows on his face. 'It is your choice. I will leave if you ask me. But if I do, I believe you will regret it.'

Tamar put one hand over her face. What was happening? How could he say these things? He was frightening her. She had a husband; their relationship had its troubles, but it was solid and safe. No, she corrected herself, it wasn't safe, but it was predictable. She had a future and some security. How could she toss that away in a moment of lust? And yes, that *is* what this is, she realised with a jolt. Lust. For a young Maori who made her heart and blood race, who could ruin her completely. She would not shame herself and succumb to this humiliating and conscienceless betrayal by her own body.

She stood to ask him to leave but found herself sitting in his lap. Gently, he lifted his hand and smoothed errant strands of auburn hair behind her ear. 'Are you sure?' he murmured.

She nodded wordlessly, too shocked at what she was doing to speak, her face against his, feeling the smoothness of his jaw, so unlike Peter's.

'Then let me feel your beauty,' he said, sitting her up and placing his hand on her face. He moved his fingers lightly over her skin, feeling every contour and hollow, her wide eyelids and the flare of her nostrils, her parted lips and the long lines of her pale throat.

'*Te ngeru*,' he said. 'You have the face of a cat. Wide with big eyes, and so soft. And you have the character of *te ngeru*. Fast, clever and sensuous, but you do not allow it to be seen. You act like *te kiore iti*, the mouse. It does not suit you. You need to flex your claws.'

He pulled the pins holding her untidy chignon and let her hair fall, reached down and removed her ugly work shoes, then lifted her to her feet. He put his arms around her and rested his chin briefly on top of her head, then lowered his lips and kissed her, gently at first, then passionately. Tamar responded in kind as his hands roamed her back and over her arms and face, then tentatively across her breasts. She shivered violently, embarrassed her nipples had risen. Kepa reached for the buttons on her bodice and began slowly undoing them, then stood back and slid the sleeves gently off her shoulders and extracted her arms, as if undressing a small child. He grasped the hem of her camisole and lifted it over her head, exposing her round white breasts with their small, erect nipples. He bent his head and kissed and then slowly licked and sucked them; Tamar's knees went weak as she rested her hands on his head. Her eyes closed and she let out a small moan as his lips and teeth created sensations that darted from her breasts to the twitching flesh between her legs.

Kepa suddenly stepped back. Dragging the quilt off the drying frame, he spread it on the floor in front of the fire, manoeuvred Tamar onto it, then knelt in front of her. Unhooking her skirt, he slid it together with her petticoat down her legs, followed by her drawers, and helped her step out of the pile of clothes. Standing naked except for her stockings and garters, she shook uncontrollably.

Making an odd, small grunting noise, Kepa rested his head against her flat belly. She jumped as she felt his tongue on her goose-pimpled flesh, probing first her navel then lapping across her pelvis to her right hip while his left hand caressed the other.

Then his hands moved down and he fumbled with her garters and slid her stockings off. When she was completely nude he guided her backwards until she subsided into one of the chairs near the fire. She sat with her knees chastely together and her hands in her lap, her body humming like a tight wire.

Kepa began to undress. First he removed his rough coat and serge work shirt, then his boots, socks and moleskin trousers. Tamar marvelled at his fluid grace. Whenever Peter took his clothes off, he hopped around the bedroom like a demented rabbit. Her eyes widened when Kepa finally stood before her naked.

His lean, muscled body was in prime condition, the muscles on his chest, abdomen and arms rigidly defined. His long legs were shapely and when he turned to kick his clothes away from the hearth, she saw his smooth brown buttocks were round and firm. His body, like his face, was almost hairless, with only a thin line starting at his navel and widening as it merged with his tight, wiry pubic hair. His penis stood stiffly upright and his testicles were raised.

As he moved to kneel in front of her she closed her eyes, keenly anticipating his entry. She felt a driving, frantic need to be joined with him, to have him fill her and take possession of her body. She felt his hands parting her thighs, but instead of his penis nudging her vagina she became suddenly aware of something warm and soft caressing her vulva. She opened her eyes and looked down. Kepa had his head between her legs.

'Stop!' she squawked, horrified. 'What are you doing?'

He sat back and laughed. 'I am tasting you. This is where the essence of your womanhood lives, and I wish to know and experience it.'

'But … '

'You need not be concerned,' he replied, amused. 'Your scent is intoxicating. It is, what is the *Pakeha* word? An aphrodisiac? I was aware of it the first time we met and it has lingered in my nostrils and my mind. Please, Tamar, let your claws come out.'

Tamar was uncomfortable with this frank admission of Kepa's sexual awareness, but made no move to stop him when he lowered his head again. The sensation was extremely pleasurable and like nothing she had ever experienced. At his insistent licking and probing, she felt her body respond and her hips began to rock in time with his caresses, an odd but heavily voluptuous tingling beginning to focus itself around a tiny, highly sensitive area of her vulva.

Kepa, sensing the beginning of her climax, pulled back and took her hands. He pulled her down onto the quilt and stretched himself out on his back, indicating wordlessly for her to mount him. Amazed at her own boldness, she settled herself onto his thighs. He grasped her hips and moved her up his body so she was positioned above his rearing penis, then settled her slowly onto it. She was unable to stop herself gasping as she felt his flesh penetrate hers. He slid into her immediately and as he did she pushed down to meet him, her hands squarely on his chest. As he gazed up at her she turned her face away, unable to meet the savage passion in his eyes.

'No, little cat,' he said quietly. 'Look at me. I want to see who you really are. Let yourself go.'

She turned back and their eyes locked as they moved together. Again, the sensation of tingling began to grow in her, stronger this time, inevitable and all-consuming. She wanted to tear her eyes away from Kepa's incandescent gaze but she couldn't; she felt utterly connected to him, physically, mentally and emotionally. As her orgasm neared, her face began to burn and she moaned involuntarily, bearing down on his penis more and more insistently. At last the tingle gave way to an excruciatingly pleasurable sensation and she came, crying out loudly and throwing her head back, her spine contorting with ecstasy. She shuddered several times, then flopped forward onto Kepa's chest, her hair sticking to her damp face and her body twitching. He stroked her back and buttocks soothingly while she lay on him, panting shallowly.

'*Taku whaiaipo*,' he murmured, then began to thrust into her again, his own orgasm approaching. Tamar pressed against his broad chest and wrapped her arms around his head, her face in his sweet, male-smelling hair. She raised her pelvis so he could move in and out of her faster and more fluidly, and closed her eyes. He climaxed ferociously, his fingers digging into her buttocks and his body jerking compulsively beneath her for some minutes before he relaxed and loosened his grip.

They lay together for an hour, warm in the heat of the fire and their intimacy, then made love again. This time Kepa positioned Tamar on her knees and took her from behind. She giggled as his thrusting shunted her across the floor, wondering what state her knees would be in tomorrow. As they lay together again, she said, 'This is what they were talking about.'

'Who?'

'Some friends of mine. They said lovemaking could be like this.'

'I did not think *Pakeha* women discussed such things.'

'These ones do.'

Kepa grunted, amused. Then he said, 'I cannot be with you.'

'I know,' Tamar replied. The idea was unthinkable. She could not divorce Peter, and she could not marry a Maori, even one as wealthy and educated as Kepa.

'I feel it in here,' he continued, his hand near his heart. 'My *manawa* tells me we are meant to be together, but I do not think it can be. My family would not allow me to marry a *Pakeha*.'

Tamar raised her eyebrows in surprise. Kepa did not seem the sort of person who would allow himself to be controlled by anyone, including his family.

He shook his head at her expression. 'No, it is not that. I am not influenced by how I appear in the eyes of others. My people were once strong and proud, but as a race we are dying. We are losing our lands, our health and our very spirit. To keep our integrity we must not continue to weaken our blood. My wife must be full-blooded Maori. I could not champion the cause of my people with confidence and authority if it were otherwise. And I must. That is what I was born to do.'

'Yes, I understand,' replied Tamar quietly. 'I don't belong in your world.'

'No,' Kepa agreed bluntly. 'But the world is changing, this country is changing. Our time will come but until then, you must live your life and I must live mine.'

Strangely, she was not upset. She knew that when he left, he would not be coming back. Kepa had given her something precious, a new physical and emotional awareness of herself. That was enough.

They dressed and Tamar prepared lunch, which they ate sitting on the quilt in front of the fire, their legs crossed like children. Kepa talked about his childhood on the East Coast, his plans for the future, and his family's plans for his future, which, he stated wryly, were not the same thing. His father, Te Roroa, was a powerful chief, and wanted his son to follow in the footsteps of Te Kooti, who had vexed and eluded the colonial troops on the East Coast during the land wars.

'Do you know of Te Kooti?' Kepa asked.

'I've heard he's a prophet and warrior who has visions, and who went about murdering innocent settlers about ten years ago. And some of his own people.'

Kepa laughed. 'You should never listen to gossip. It is almost always born of fear or ignorance. Te Kooti is an influential and powerful man. And yes, he does have the blood of both warriors and innocent people on his hands, but which successful military leader does not?'

'Is he one of your people?'

'No. He is Rongowhakaata, and lives in the King Country. I believe he has had his day.'

Tamar looked at him curiously. 'I thought you said you admired him?'

'No, I said he is powerful and influential. I have admiration for him, and his *Ringatu* religion has benefits for Maori, but I have not yet decided if I will support him as my father does. Our struggle for independence will last a lot longer than Te Kooti, although I would not be surprised if his religion endures.'

Kepa was convinced the battle against Maori repression could not be won by tribal dignitaries on muddy rural *marae* waving sticks at each other and bemoaning their plight. He and his uncle believed the only solution was to acquire financial means, education and political power, and play by *Pakeha* rules. Hence he was committed to seeing his family's shipping line prosper, with the financial rewards used to further their cause.

'Why don't you give the money to your people?' asked Tamar.

'They do not know how to make it work for them yet. Wealth is not the answer, but it is a means to an end,' he replied, helping himself to another piece of bread.

Tamar talked of her life in Cornwall, and her life now. Feeling a little disloyal, but relieved at being able to voice her thoughts, she described Peter's destructive drinking, leaving out the less savoury aspects. She told Kepa they were in serious debt but Peter had chosen to keep this from her, and confided she was beginning to suspect he had pawned her jewellery.

She spoke of how her initial, naive, love for Peter had become somewhat frayed but she was still committed to their marriage. She also said she did not know why she had consented to Kepa's lovemaking, but did not regret it. He listened without comment, accepting and uncritical. 'You will need to be strong,' he said when she had finished.

'Perhaps, but I chose this for myself, and I *will* live with it. He is not a bad man. And I believe he loves me in his own way.'

Kepa nodded. 'I expect he does. When did you say he will be arriving back?'

'Not until tomorrow.'

'So you are alone here?'

'No, my companion Riria should be back very soon,' said Tamar, glancing at the clock on the mantelpiece.

'I will go,' Kepa said, getting up from the floor. 'I would not like to compromise you, even in the eyes of your servant.'

'She isn't my servant. She helps me and she is my friend.'

'Either way, I think it is not a good idea for me to be seen here.' He pulled his boots on and reached for his coat. Then he went to Tamar and held her tightly to his chest, stroking her hair.

'You are a very special, beautiful woman. I will remember this time always. I had to come to you. I had to have this.'

Tamar smiled. 'I'm glad you did. So did I.'

'I do not know when I will see you again, but I will,' he added.

As he bent and kissed her they heard the sound of a horse and cart outside. Tamar returned the quilt to the drying frame as she heard Riria step onto the verandah and call out, then followed Kepa as he opened the front door and went outside.

'Riria,' she said uneasily, hoping her face would not betray her. 'This is Kepa, Te Kanene's nephew. Remember I told you we met in Auckland? He stopped by to visit and stayed for lunch.'

At a glance Riria took in Tamar's flushed face and tousled, loose hair. She looked Kepa up and down. '*Tena koe*,' she said stonily.

Kepa nodded. '*Tena koe.*'

'Oh, your hat,' exclaimed Tamar, 'I'll get it for you,' she said and ducked inside.

Riria stood with her hands on her hips, her eyes narrowed. 'Visiting, is it?' she said to Kepa in Maori.

'*Ae.*'

'Then I hope you intend to take responsibility for this *visit*,' Riria replied pointedly as Tamar came back out, Kepa's hat in her hand.

'I will,' he responded in an equally sharp tone. He bowed to Tamar. 'Thank you so much for a delightful morning, Mrs Montgomery. Please tell your husband I called.'

Unlikely, thought both Tamar and Riria as they watched him climb onto his horse.

'Good day to you,' he said as he turned and headed up the drive.

As he rode out of the gate Tamar asked, 'Do you know Kepa?'

'No. What was he doing here?'

'Visiting.' Tamar felt her face redden.

'He is an attractive man,' said Riria.

'Yes, he is,' agreed Tamar as she went over to the cart and began to help Riria unload it.

Nothing else was said.

Peter came home the following day in a black mood, convinced Te Kanene had swindled him. 'Bloody Maoris,' he complained. 'They're worse than Jews when it comes to doing business.'

Te Kanene had refused to take a note for the amount owed and had insisted on cash payment. Peter viewed this as extortion and had said so. Te Kanene had responded by pointing out that the timber could be shipped under his terms, or left to rot on the barge in the Manukau Harbour. As his was the only ship fitted for transporting timber in the area at the time, Peter had little choice.

Tamar, who was suffering from severe guilt, made an effort to commiserate and cheer him up. She prepared his favourite meal and served it at the dining table in the parlour with candles and a vase of freshly cut flowers from her garden, and responded enthusiastically when he made love to her that night. Instead of his face, however, it was Kepa's dark skin and mesmerising eyes she saw. Although Peter was an affectionate lover, the difference between the two men was like serge and satin, Tamar thought wistfully.

She began to suspect she might be pregnant about four weeks later, and was certain by the end of November when she missed her period for the second time. Her breasts had become extremely tender and she was feeling sick in the late mornings and often had to lie down. She was horrified and became more and more miserable and withdrawn. Riria finally confronted her about it.

'How far gone are you?' she asked one day as Tamar lay on her bed with a cool, damp cloth across her aching forehead.

Tamar reacted without surprise. 'When did you know?' she replied in a dull voice.

'A month ago. Your smell changed.'

God, thought Tamar. Maoris and their bloody noses.

'Whose is it?' asked Riria bluntly.

Tamar looked at her friend mutely as a tear rolled down her temple and into her hair. She didn't trust herself to speak.

'You lay with Kepa.' It was not a question. 'Did you also lie with your husband before or soon after?' Riria never referred to Peter by his Christian name; her opinion of him did not allow for such intimacies.

'After.'

'Then it could be his.'

'Yes, but I won't know until it's *born*, will I?' cried Tamar miserably. 'What am I going to do?'

Riria was tempted to say that this is what happened when people from different races had impetuous sexual liaisons, but the anguished look on Tamar's face made her hold her tongue.

'Kepa's skin is not that dark, and your husband is not fair,' she said, but she knew it was a fatuous thing to say. The *Pakeha*'s hair may be almost black, but his skin was as white as parchment. 'Perhaps you will miscarry. It happens often. You could make it happen,' she added.

Tamar shook her head. 'No, I couldn't do that. What if it *is* Peter's?' She moaned and rolled onto her side and covered her face with her hands, knowing she was behaving pathetically.

'Have you told him yet?'

'Who?'

'*Your husband!*' said Riria a little crossly. 'Come on, *e hine!* Take control of yourself! If you will not rid yourself of the child then you have no choice but to bear it.'

She knelt at the bedside and pulled Tamar's hands away from her face. More gently, she said, 'Tamar. If the child is your husband's, then well and good; if it is not, then you must decide what to do. I do not believe your husband will accept it, and it will be very hard to raise a half-Maori child by yourself. You will be shunned by your own people, and perhaps by mine as well. You must consider giving it away, as a *whangai*. But until then, no matter who its papa is, you must be strong and healthy so it grows properly. You cannot lie around doing this *Pakeha* ladies' thing of swooning. Stand up and be strong! *Kia kaha, e hine!* Do not forget who you are; I will be here to help you.'

Tamar sat up and rubbed her face. Riria was right; she had made her bed, and it was time for her to lie in it.

'I'll tell Peter tonight,' she said eventually. 'And you're right, there is nothing I can do about it now.'

Peter was beside himself with delight when she advised him of her condition. He was so thrilled he went into Huia the next day and got drunk to celebrate.

Tamar, too immersed in her own misery, hardly even noticed.

Chapter Twelve

The following months were not happy ones. Tamar had her nineteenth birthday in November, and she and Peter passed an uneventful Christmas and New Year. Myrna had invited them to Auckland for the festive season but Tamar could not face the combination of oppressive summer heat and arduous travel.

By February her pregnancy was more than obvious and she was beginning to feel ungainly. She was starting to waddle when she walked and her back ached if she stood for too long. As well, she was compelled to make endless trips to the privy as the growing baby pressed on her bladder, and she wished her mam was alive to explain to her what to expect. Riria, however, made up for it with knowledge gained from assisting members of her family. She kept a constant eye on Tamar, refusing to let her do heavy work but insisting she keep active and eat and sleep well.

Peter was drinking heavily again, blaming the stress of the impending birth. He was convinced Anna's fate could befall Tamar and, giving up all pretence, drank regularly in the evenings. Once every week or so he would drink himself into unconsciousness, particularly if he had gone into Huia. Several times he did not return until the following day, sick and remorseful.

Tamar despaired. Peter was completely unpredictable. She lived in a state of anxiety, wondering if he would put the lid on the bottle and come to bed in a relatively benign state, or continue drinking until he had driven himself into a violent rage. Sometimes the Peter she had fallen in love with emerged from the depressed, bad-tempered and insecure creature he had become, and she felt almost able to relax. But it never lasted and he seemed to be getting worse.

One evening in March, he came home from town, drunk as usual, and in a particularly foul temper. He would not talk to her for at least an hour and when he finally did, he questioned her insistently about who had been to the house, and when. Tamar was immediately wary, a small black spider of fear creeping up her spine.

'Why?' she asked nervously.

'Because I want to *know*. Don't be obtuse.'

Tamar recounted the few visits she'd had from neighbouring women in the area, but did not mention Kepa.

'No,' said Peter angrily. 'I mean *last* year. In the months before Christmas. Who came then?'

'Before Christmas? No one as far as I can recall,' lied Tamar. 'Except for the work gangs, of course, but you were here then. Why?'

Peter ignored her. 'What about when I went to Paratutae to load the timber?'

'No. No one.'

Peter was silent for a few minutes. Then he asked, 'Are you sure?'

'Of course I'm sure,' Tamar snapped, agitated and alarmed. 'I get so few visitors I'm sure I'd remember when and who they were.'

'I'll ask Riria.'

'Do that,' replied Tamar as she went into the bedroom and closed the door. She changed into her nightdress and climbed into bed, worried Peter would come in and question her again.

But within twenty minutes she was asleep and did not hear him open the bedroom door, look in at her for some time, then close it again quietly.

Peter walked silently down the short hall and out the back door, stepped down off the porch and relieved himself on the grass. When he had finished he stood for some minutes in front of Riria's small room. He listened for a minute then opened the door gently.

He crept in with exaggerated care, closed the door quietly and waited for his eyes to become accustomed to the darkness. The room was quite bare, containing only a bed, a washstand and a rail across one corner holding Riria's one spare dress, her winter coat and her backpack. The curtains were open, a bright bar of moonlight falling cross her bed.

He observed with pleasure her long hair spilling across the mattress and the inviting shape of her body under the thin cover. Squatting beside the bed, he carefully placed his hand over Riria's mouth. She woke immediately and attempted to sit up but he pushed her back.

'I want to talk to you,' he said quietly, his face close to hers. Her eyes were big with fear and the whites glinted. He felt her jaws begin to clench. 'Bite me and I'll hit you so hard you won't know what's happened.'

Riria relaxed her jaws. She knew she was strong but he was much stronger, and she could tell from his breath he had been drinking. She had seen his drunken rages many times and did not want to provoke him.

'I want you to tell me something,' he breathed in her face. 'And if you lie, I'll make you very, very sorry, do you understand?'

Riria nodded. Peter removed his hand.

'Has that black bastard Kepa Te Roroa been sniffing around?'

'Who is Kepa Te Roroa?' asked Riria.

Slightly appeased, he said crudely, 'Maori bastard, about six feet tall, long black hair, tight trousers with a cock the size of a bull's.'

This described most of the men Riria knew, but she thought it unwise to say so. She shook her head. 'I have seen no one like that. Not here.' Riria lied easily, her eyes never leaving Peter's.

He stood up and looked down at her. 'If I find out you're lying, I'll kill you.'

Riria believed him. The look of anger in his eyes was replaced by one of anticipation as his eyes wandered over the outline of her body. He sat on the edge of her bed. 'I think it's time you started giving me my money's worth, my beautiful brown girl,' Peter said slyly, inching the cover off her. Underneath she was naked, as he had hoped.

She grasped the blanket and spat, 'Fuck off.'

Peter laughed. 'Oh, you know how to swear in English. How charming.'

Riria slapped him hard across his face. He slapped her back, equally hard.

'I like that,' he said, leering drunkenly. 'I like a bit of spirit. Tamar's a sweet wife, but she has no passion. She did once but I don't think she likes me much any more. And she doesn't understand me. I thought at the beginning she might, because Anna never could. Still, she can have babies and I'm sure she'll be a fine mother. But while she's doing that, there are things I need, and I want you to give them to me. Let go of the blanket.'

As Riria reared up to slap him again, he pushed her down with his forearm across her throat so she could not breathe and grabbed a fistful of her hair.

'Now,' he said menacingly, his face inches from hers. 'You can be nice to me, or I can tell Tamar you threw yourself at me. She'll be heartbroken. I know what great friends you are and it would be awful if you had to leave, wouldn't it?' He lessened the pressure on her neck. 'And anyway, what does it matter? I know what you Maoris are like. What's one more man? And I'm an Englishman, that should be a treat for you.'

Riria had no intention of telling him that if he raped her he would be stealing her virginity. And he did rape her. Brutally and quickly. She lay limp as he humped and grunted on top of her, her gazed fixed on the black branches of the tree outside her window. He was heavy and, in her eyes, obscenely hairy, and stank of sweat and alcohol. When he lifted her legs and pushed them to her chest to accommodate himself better, she winced in pain as his long penis thrust roughly inside her. She felt humiliated, lying folded almost in half like a bird trussed for a *hangi*. He did not take long, groaning his way to a jerking climax after four or five minutes. She remained still as he rolled off her, sat up and pulled his trousers back on, then left in silence.

She lay unmoving for the next thirty minutes until she was sure he would not return. Opening her door she let herself out into the moonlight, naked and shivering, and walked quickly to the water pump. She washed herself for the next twenty minutes, scrubbing frantically to remove the stink of him. Off her face where he had kissed her, her breasts where he had slobbered, but most vigorously between her legs, sore and slick with his semen. Then she leaned forward and vomited violently onto the grass.

July 1881

Tamar's labour pains began early one morning. Mistakenly thinking she needed to move her bowels, she sat for some time on the privy before she realised what was happening. When she called out, Riria came to help her inside.

Peter was away on the coast but expected home later that afternoon. Riria offered to ride into Huia for the midwife but Tamar, terrified of being left alone, begged her to stay. 'You've helped deliver babies. Please don't leave me, Riria,' she pleaded. 'What if something goes wrong and I'm by myself?'

'Nothing will go wrong,' replied Riria. 'You are fit and young. Women your age can have their babies in a field if they need to. Maori women can, anyway.'

As the morning progressed, Riria sat with Tamar while she rested between contractions, and walked her around when they came, explaining that lying down slowed the process. The bedroom had been prepared with several sheets on top of sacks spread across the quilt, and a pile of fresh towels folded at the end of the bed. There were smelling salts and some brandy on hand, and a large pot of water boiling on the range, but there was little else Riria could do until it was time for the baby to be born.

At two in the afternoon, when Tamar's waters had broken with a gush and her contractions were fiercely regular and four or five minutes apart, Riria helped her into the bedroom and into a nightdress. As she lay on the bed with her back propped against a pile of pillows, Riria washed her hands and asked Tamar to part her legs.

'I need to see whether you are opening up enough. The baby could come soon or in a few hours but you need to be ready when it does. If it does not look like you will be, I will have to get the midwife.'

She carefully inserted her fingers into Tamar's vagina, a look of concentration on her face. 'I think the gap is opening,' she said eventually. 'And the baby's head is in the right place. It should be soon.'

The next two hours were the most physically painful Tamar had experienced. The baby was large and she was not and she feared it would become stuck and they would both die. Her contractions and the horrendous, grinding pain were increasing but nothing felt as if it was moving.

At around three in the afternoon they heard the front door open and a minute later Peter looked into the bedroom. 'Oh my God,' he said, his face blanching.

Riria went to the door. 'Go away,' she said, pushing him out. 'The baby is almost here.' She locked the door after him.

They heard him rummaging around in the sideboard, looking for something to drink. They glanced at each other, a silent message passing between them; he would be blind drunk by the time the baby arrived.

After another long, sweaty, painful sixty minutes in which Tamar decided she didn't care whether she lived or died, Riria announced she could see the baby's head. 'Can you get onto your knees?' she asked.

Tamar nodded and Riria helped her kneel so she was facing the bed rails. Riria went behind and knelt down. 'You have to push now,' she urged.

Tamar took a deep breath and, her knuckles white around the bed rails, pushed as hard as she could. She cried out as she felt a monstrous tearing sensation, as if the opening of her vagina had torn all the way to her anus, then a disconcerting feeling of something giving way very quickly.

'The head is out,' Riria said behind her. 'You must keep pushing.'

Tamar grunted again and pushed the baby out. Riria placed her hands deftly under the bloody, slimy little bundle.

'Jesus bloody Christ,' swore Tamar, panting heavily and beginning to cry, her red, sweaty face collapsed against the pillows. Behind her, Riria bit and tied the umbilical cord as the baby opened its tiny mouth and let out a lusty cry.

Tamar turned and subsided onto her back. 'What is it?'

'A *tama*, a boy,' replied Riria, passing the infant to Tamar who placed him on her bare and wobbly but considerably flatter belly. They both scrutinised him for a minute.

'What colour do you think he is?' asked Tamar nervously. 'Is he white?'

It was hard to tell. The baby, still streaked with blood and covered with greasy, white *vernix caseosa*, had an abundance of black hair. He was the creased, purple colour of many newborns, his skin colour not yet obvious. 'Wait for a while. This purple colour will fade,' replied Riria.

Peter rapped urgently on the door and when Riria opened it, he asked hopefully, 'Is everything all right? Has she had it? Is it a boy?'

Riria stepped back to avoid his whisky-laden breath. 'Yes. We have not finished. Stay out,' she replied tersely, shutting the door in his face and re-locking it.

She returned to the bed, dipped a cloth into a basin of warm water and began to sponge the blood and muck off the infant as Tamar lay him on the mattress beside her. He whimpered and when he was clean and wrapped in a soft blanket, Riria placed him in Tamar's arms. 'He needs to go on your teat,' she said.

Tamar undid the buttons at the neck of her nightgown and opened it to expose her breasts. She held the baby against one and lifted it so he could grasp the nipple. He tried to suckle but nothing happened. 'There's nothing,' said Tamar, surprised.

'It will come. Keep him there.'

Tamar looked tenderly at the infant, his lips puckered around her nipple and his eyes screwed tightly shut. She smiled, her face and body relaxing as he suckled vigorously. 'He's strong,' she said, looking up at Riria who was also smiling.

Then her face contorted as she was racked by another contraction. 'Oh God, what's that?'

'The *whenua*, the afterbirth. Push again when it hurts like that.'

Tamar held the baby for another few minutes then lay him

beside her. She leaned back and bent her knees to assist the expulsion of the afterbirth while Riria firmly massaged her lower belly. The shiny, bloody sac slipped wetly out and lay between her legs, the purple-coloured umbilical cord trailing from it. Riria picked it up, wrapped it in a cloth and put it to one side.

'What are you doing?' asked Tamar, a look of distaste on her face.

'It must be buried to mark his *papakainga*, his home.'

Peter knocked loudly on the bedroom door again but they ignored him.

The baby, who had been in the world for almost an hour now, slept and did not stir when Tamar opened his blanket. Both women stared silently at the tiny body. The purple tinge to his face, limbs and body was fading. He was dark, far too dark-skinned to be mistaken for a European child. 'What am I going to do?' whispered Tamar.

'I do not know,' replied Riria, remembering Peter's insistent questioning on the night he assaulted her. 'We must not let him in,' she said, inclining her head towards the door.

'We'll have to or he'll know something's wrong.'

At that moment a loud crash shook the bedroom door, then another. They heard Peter yelling from the other side, 'Let me in! I want to see him!'

There was another crash, the flimsy lock splintered and the door flew open. The noise woke the baby and he started to wail. Tamar and Riria froze as Peter strode over to the bed, a glass of whisky slopping in his hand. He looked down at the infant then asked, 'Why is he so dark? Christ, he looks like … '

He stopped, an expression of sickly realisation stealing across his face. He looked first at Tamar then at Riria. Then, very quietly, he said, 'It isn't mine.'

Tamar's look of stricken terror told him all he needed to know. Peter carefully placed his glass on the dressing table and walked out of the room. He returned almost immediately, his rifle in one hand.

'Whose is it?' he asked in the same, quiet, measured voice. He raised the rifle. When the two terrified women maintained their silence, he sighed heavily and rubbed his hand across his flushed, bristled face. 'You're a pair of lying whores,' he said conversationally, his eyes glittering dangerously. 'I knew that bastard had been here.'

Tamar moaned with terror and clutched the baby to her breasts, her hand protectively over his delicate skull.

Peter waved the barrel of the rifle at Riria. 'What did I say I would do if you lied to me?'

'You said you would kill me,' replied Riria, her voice steady but her eyes wide with fear.

'That's right. So get outside and start running.'

Riria looked from Peter to Tamar. 'Mrs Montgomery needs help,' she said. 'She cannot be left alone.'

'*I'll* look after Mrs Montgomery. Now get outside, you scheming Maori *bitch*.'

Riria walked slowly into the parlour. Peter followed close behind, jabbing between her shoulderblades with his rifle until she moved out onto the verandah. 'Start running.'

She turned, stood as tall as she could and looked him in the eye. 'My family will hunt you down.'

'They'll never know. I'll bury you in the bush and they'll never find you.' He sighed again, as if what he was about to do was an arduous but necessary chore. 'I just can't have this. People lying to me and making me look a fool. Now off you go, go on.'

Riria stared at him then turned and stepped off the verandah and began to walk towards the gate, her head high. Her bowel spasmed as she heard the click of the rifle being loaded, and she cursed herself for not attacking the *Pakeha* when his rifle was empty. She began to pray as she walked, her back crawling where she imagined the bullet would enter. As she reached the end of the driveway she began to hope he would not fire.

He did, and missed. Riria darted through the gate, snatched up her long skirts and ran towards the bush. Peter reloaded, aimed and fired again. He saw a spray of bright blood splash up from Riria's head as she went down and her body rolled limply into the bracken. He grunted and leaned unsteadily against the verandah post for several minutes watching where she had fallen, her pale blue dress visible and unmoving. When he was satisfied she was not going to get up, he went inside into the bedroom.

Tamar was lying curled on her side, the baby folded protectively in her arms. He was whimpering weakly. Peter casually propped the rifle against the fireplace, took a quick gulp from his whisky glass on the dressing table, then strode over and snatched the infant. Tamar screamed and tried to get up but he shoved her violently down.

'He *is* lovely, isn't he! Congratulations, Mrs Montgomery! I'll just put him in his crib, shall I? He looks tired,' said Peter brightly. He sounded completely mad.

Tamar shrieked, 'Don't touch him!' She swung her legs over the side of the bed, feeling faint and nauseous and aware blood was seeping from between her legs. As Peter lowered the baby into the crib she tried to stand, but sank to her knees, retching.

'Damn, Tamar, you *are* being messy today. And you're normally so fastidious! Except for whose cock you let up you, of course,' Peter commented. With a thoughtful expression, he picked up a pillow, held it inches above the baby's face, and looked over his shoulder to observe Tamar's response.

Tamar screamed and pulled herself up by the rails at the foot of the bed. She lunged towards the crib but Peter shoved her away, hard. She flew backwards, twisting as she fell, and crashed into the fireplace, her head hitting the solid iron fender. She twitched once, then lay still.

Peter stared at her inert body and the blood pooling beneath her face, then closed his eyes, a tortured expression suddenly distorting his features. I've killed her, he thought. My lovely Tamar, now she's gone, too. He started weeping. 'I wouldn't have hurt him,' he sobbed. 'But you hurt *me*.' He covered his face with his hands. 'Why? *Why* does everyone have to leave me? I can't deal with any more *loss*!'

He turned to the baby, silent and eerily observant now in his crib, bent down, tucked the cover gently around the child, and kissed his small, dark, wrinkled forehead. 'I wanted lots of children,' he whispered.

Then he picked up his rifle, grabbed the brandy Riria had set aside for Tamar, and slowly walked onto the verandah where he set the bottle carefully on the rail. He came back inside for a chair, which jammed obstinately in the doorway, but he forced it through. Then he collected his whisky glass from the bedroom and took that outside as well, deliberately not looking at Tamar's motionless form. Still crying, he settled himself into his chair and poured a drink, the rifle propped beside him.

It was almost dark. When she regained consciousness she carefully explored her head and discovered a long, shallow groove across the top of her skull where the flesh was torn and some of her hair was missing. She had a splitting headache and her face and chest were covered in congealed blood. She kept passing in and out of consciousness but had managed to stay awake for some time now, as she watched the moon rising over the tree tops.

She lay still, ignoring the bracken tickling her skin and the insects wandering casually over her. From where she lay she could see Peter on the verandah, the rifle next to him and an almost empty bottle resting in his lap. He was talking to himself, sobbing now and again and occasionally shrieking Tamar's name in rage and despair. She watched him raise the bottle to his lips and drain the contents, then stand and hurl it viciously against the side of the house. He almost fell over but righted himself against the wall and staggered inside.

Riria could hear him thrashing about, the sound of splintering furniture and breaking glass discordant in the still dusk.

When he came out again he had his hat on. Climbing laboriously onto his horse, he headed up the drive, out the gate and down the track in the direction of Huia. Riria heard him muttering to himself as he went past. He did not even glance at where she lay, but she suspected that even if he had, he would have been too drunk to notice if she were dead or alive. Still, she lay there for some time before she dared to get up.

Standing slowly, her hands over the wound on her head, she took a few steps then sat down hard in the middle of the track, feeling dizzy and sick. She breathed deeply and rested for a minute before she got to her feet again. This time her legs supported her and she walked slowly along the drive, stepped onto the verandah and went inside.

There was silence, with a single lamp diffusing the shadowy darkness. From the parlour she saw Tamar's body lying on the bedroom floor, her head on the hearth of the dying fire. Riria darted forward, then clutched the doorpost as dizziness washed over her again. When the bright, painful stars had receded, she stepped into the bedroom and knelt by Tamar, two fingers on her throat feeling for a pulse; it was there, but very weak and irregular. Riria could see an ugly, deep gash on her friend's face through which white bone glimmered. She shook Tamar but there was no response so she stood and looked around for the baby.

A sharp little squeaking noise made her leap almost out of her skin. Stepping over to the crib she saw the infant lying placidly, one tiny arm upraised and his hand open like a miniature starfish. Closing her eyes in profound relief, she picked him up and held him against her cheek. He was very cold and his small face almost blue, but his lips pursed and his tongue poked out as if looking for something to suckle. Riria placed him on the floor nearer the fire, then rolled Tamar onto her back and said her name loudly; again there was no response so she shook her hard. Tamar's eyes opened blearily, one bloodshot and both blackly bruised.

She mumbled something incoherent then squinted painfully. 'Oh God!' she cried, clutching at Riria's skirt. 'I thought he'd killed you! And he smothered the baby!' she wailed, her eyes darting about in panic.

'No, no, he did not smother him,' replied Riria, placing the baby in Tamar's lap and helping her to sit. 'The *Pakeha* has gone, but we must hurry. He thinks he has killed us but if he returns and finds he has not, he will try again.'

Tamar burst into relieved but dangerously hysterical tears, rocking over the small form pressed against her belly. Then, frowning, she lifted her hand and touched her temple. 'What happened to my face?'

'It has been cut.' Riria did not say how deep and gaping the awful wound was and that the bone was clearly visible. 'I will clean it for you.'

'You've got blood all over you,' said Tamar confusedly. 'Is it mine?'

'No. I was shot, but I am all right.'

Riria got up off the floor and soaked the corner of a towel in the basin of water, cold now and slightly bloody. She wiped away as much dried and congealed blood from Tamar's wound as she could, then tore a sheet into strips to use as bandages. When she had pulled Tamar's hair back and wrapped the injured side of her face, she said again, 'We must hurry. We have to leave.'

'Leave? Where will we go?'

'To my *kainga* at Kainui. We cannot stay here. If your husband comes back he will find us. I think he is *porangi*, he has lost control of his mind.'

Tamar put her hands to face. 'I can't, I feel sick. My head hurts.'

'You *must*. Can you get up?'

Riria took the baby from Tamar as she rose shakily to her feet. She held on to Riria's arm, leaned over and retched hollowly. 'I smell,' she said distractedly, wiping her face on her already filthy nightdress. 'And I'm cold.'

Riria went to the wardrobe and pulled out several pairs of Peter's work trousers, two shirts and two heavy work jackets.

'We will wear these, to keep warm. We cannot travel fast, it will take us several days to reach Kainui.' She opened one of the dressing-table drawers and extracted a pile of folded towels. Handing them to Tamar she said briskly, 'Put on the trousers and fold one of these between your legs. You will bleed for a few days.'

Tamar took off her nightdress, clamped a towel between her thighs and changed into Peter's trousers and shirt. The trousers felt odd against her skin and were too big, but they were warm. Riria also donned a pair of trousers, a shirt and a jacket, then went to the basin and washed as much blood as she could from her own hair.

'Dress the baby,' she ordered, then went to fetch her backpack and heavy coat.

Tamar, moving sluggishly, unwrapped the baby and dressed him in a haphazardly folded cloth nappy and as many clothes as would go on him, then folded the blanket around him and placed him gently on the bed. He lay there blinking, then opened his mouth and cried. Tamar picked him up then sat down gingerly and put him on her breast. She watched dazedly as Riria came back and began stuffing items into her pack.

'We will take the baby's clothes, the cloths for your bleeding, some food and water and a billy. You will have to leave everything else.'

Tamar shrugged vacantly. Recalling Peter's expression of cold hatred as he had knocked her down, she felt her own anger beginning to ignite, although it felt muffled and somehow far away. She said dully, 'There's nothing here for me any more. I'm ready.'

They hurried through to the back of the house and Tamar waited while Riria caught their horses in the dark and saddled Tamar's; she would be unable to ride without a saddle. She helped Tamar onto her mount and handed her the swaddled infant. A wave of dizziness swept over Tamar and she almost dropped him.

Riria stood and thought, then ran back into the house, emerging a minute later with a bed sheet, which she fashioned into a sling. She motioned for Tamar to hand the baby back to her in exchange for the sheet. 'Tie it around your middle and over your shoulder.'

Tamar did as she was told and when Riria handed the baby back she saw how she could place him inside the folds of the sheet against her chest and still have her hands free. Riria mounted her own horse and they rode in single file through the gate where they turned right onto the track up into the black, bush-clad foothills of the Waitakere Ranges.

Tamar did not look back.

CHAPTER THIRTEEN

Their journey to Kainui on the west coast took three nights and almost three full days. Tamar soon became feverish, her skin flushed and damp. She was still bleeding heavily and Riria had to wash her sanitary towels several times. The baby seemed content to sleep, wake, cry and be fed, then sleep again. Tamar's milk had come in but Riria worried that if she developed an infection, the baby would be harmed by nursing from her. However, they had nothing else to feed him with and he could not go without.

The gash on Tamar's head was causing her fever. Riria had first inspected the discharge from between her legs but the blood was clean and not foul-smelling, so she assumed that was not the source of the problem. She was deeply relieved as she had seen several women die from such complications after childbirth. The wound on Tamar's head, however, was a different matter.

The first time Riria had unwrapped the bandage the edges had not closed over the bone and were puffy and red. By the evening of their first day, a thick greenish pus oozed from it. She gently pressed the area to expel as much as she could, Tamar yelping with pain, but knew she had not cleared it all. Before she applied a clean bandage, she made an infusion of *pukatea* bark in the billy over a small fire. She soaked a fresh strip of cloth in the dark liquid, then tied it around Tamar's head and face, hoping the curative properties might help clear the infection.

Tamar was unable to eat by the second day and barely able to sit on her horse, so Riria slung the baby around her own chest. It rained heavily throughout the day and the rough track was slippery and dangerous. By late afternoon Tamar was delirious and Riria stopped for the night. She made a small bivouac, lit a fire and prepared a basic meal.

When the sun disappeared, she lay next to Tamar and put her arms around her to keep her warm, the baby between them. Wary of squashing or suffocating him, Riria stayed awake throughout the night, holding him to Tamar's breasts whenever he woke and cried. Riria was comforted by the night sounds of the forest although Tamar tossed and muttered, sweat soaking her clothes. She was beginning to smell unpleasant. At times she tried to tear her clothes off, and at others she shivered uncontrollably. She had not spoken coherently for some time and Riria was concerned she would die in the night.

Just after the sun rose, Riria slipped and slid down to a nearby stream with the billy and brought back cold water. She dribbled some into Tamar's mouth and used the rest to sponge her burning body.

Soon they were ready to go again but it was obvious Tamar was unable to ride. Riria spent the next hour making a litter out of branches and large *nikau* fronds. She tied the rough contraption securely together with slender supplejack vines and attached it to the saddle of Tamar's horse.

When she had rolled Tamar's limp body onto the litter and tucked her heavy winter coat around her, she unbridled her own horse, whacked him on the rump and sent him galloping down the track to find his way home. She estimated they were five or six hours away from Kainui, and hoped they would get there in time. Slinging the baby around her middle, she mounted Tamar's horse and headed off.

The heavy rain returned, stinging Riria's scalp as it pelted into her open wound whenever the track left the shelter of the trees. Her hat, she remembered regretfully, had been left behind; she wound her long hair and fixed it on top of her head with twigs. She stopped repeatedly to check Tamar, who was still burning with fever, muttering and asking for the baby, her mother and Myrna. Riria laid him on her chest so he could feed, but she suspected Tamar was unaware.

Riria sat on the wet ground with her head in her hands. She was in pain, exhausted and shaken by the events of the past few days. She was a strong and capable young woman, emotionally and physically, but she had been utterly terrified, convinced she was going to die. If that pig of a *Pakeha* had not been so drunk, he would have killed her with his first shot.

Over the past year she had watched him slowly losing his battle with alcohol. He had come to her room drunk half a dozen times since that first night, but had only raped her again on the two occasions he had been able to maintain an erection. She had not told Tamar as she hadn't wanted to distress her during her final months of pregnancy. Because she hadn't wanted to leave Tamar on her own with him either, she had stayed, assuming he would direct his physical needs towards his wife again after the baby arrived. She held no hope of improvement in his behaviour. She had seen the horrendous destruction wreaked by alcohol in some of her own people, the slow and insidious erosion of morals, responsibility and hope, and had no reason to suspect it would be any different for *Pakeha*.

As she tied the sleeping baby against her chest, she heard the sound of voices coming from further down the track. She stood very still, straining to hear, but when she realised the voices were speaking in Maori, she relaxed a little and waited.

When the travellers came into sight she saw her father, several younger men, and a woman of middle age. They were armed and looking warily about them as they came.

'Father!' she cried out, waving frantically. 'Father, it is me, Riria!'

Her father, Te Hau, slid off his horse and hurried towards her. 'Are you all right?' he asked anxiously. 'Your horse came home without you. We thought something had happened.'

'It has,' replied Riria. 'But I am safe.'

'That is good. Whose baby is that? Surely it is not *yours*?' he said in alarm. 'And what is wrong with your head? I see blood.'

Riria lifted her hand to her scalp. 'I was shot.'

'*Shot*! By whom?' replied Te Hau, outraged.

'It is a very long tale. I will tell you later. I think my friend is dying.'

Riria led her father to where Tamar lay, barely conscious and moaning feebly. 'This is the *Pakeha* woman I was working for. The baby is hers.'

'Where is her husband?'

'Gone,' replied Riria caustically. 'He almost killed us.'

Te Hau's eyes opened wide in rage. '*Where is he?*' he demanded.

'Father! I will tell you later! We must help Tamar.'

Te Hau motioned to the woman in his party. She hitched the skirts of her European dress over her knees, dismounted and hurried over. Squatting beside the litter she asked Riria, 'What is wrong with her?'

'A fever. I think her blood is poisoned.'

The woman, named Atawhai and the healer for her community, pressed her fingers against Tamar's jaw under her ears, in her armpits and around her groin. Tamar's sanitary towel was leaking and blood had seeped into the crotch of her trousers. Atawhai also noticed her swollen, milk-filled breasts. 'When was her baby born?' she asked.

'Three days ago,' replied Riria. 'I think the wound on her head is infected.'

Atawhai quickly unwound the bandage on Tamar's head, sniffed, then wrinkled her nose in distaste. 'Yes, this is the source of the poison. How long has she been like this?'

'Two nights and days. I did not know what to do for her.'

'You have done well to get her this far, child,' Atawhai replied. 'We must take her to the village, or she will die soon. There are some things we can do that might save her.'

She stood and clicked her fingers at two of the young men waiting silently on the track. They dismounted and came over to her, rifles slung over their shoulders, their feet slapping in the mud.

'She needs to be taken to the village. If we make the horse run she will fall off so you will carry her.'

The men took off their weapons and laid them on the litter next to Tamar, then bent and picked her up effortlessly and started off down the track in a slow, smooth, synchronised jog, the litter bouncing gently between them.

The rest of the party followed behind, leading the riderless horses. An hour later they came out of the bush onto cultivated land near the coast, and were soon walking through the large gardens which surrounded Kainui. As they rode through the high, intricately carved gateway in the *punga* fence encircling the settlement, a group of adults followed by a tail of curious, large-eyed, raggedly dressed children came to meet them. Riria handed the baby, bawling at the top of his lungs, to an old woman standing at the front of the group, dismounted and stretched her legs and back wearily.

'He is hungry,' she said to the woman, nodding at Tamar, still on the litter on the ground. 'He needs to feed.'

The woman carried the baby over to Tamar's prostrate and silent form and placed the infant at her breast. Riria squatted down as well and took Tamar's hot, damp hand. 'It will be all right now,' she said quietly, though she doubted Tamar could hear her. 'We are safe.'

Atawhai squatted next to her. 'She is very sick,' she said. 'She may die. Are you prepared for that?'

Riria moved her head in a barely discernible nod, and looked pointedly away.

Tamar and the baby were carried to a small wooden building some distance behind the big carved and decorated *wharenui*, or meeting house, that dominated the village. Inside, she was laid on a low platform topped with a thin mattress stuffed with *raupo* and raw wool, as Atawhai issued orders to the women who had followed them. The baby was removed from Tamar's breast, much to his indignation, and handed to a young woman whose own breasts were swollen with milk; mollified, he fastened his small mouth to her large brown nipple and shut up instantly.

Tamar's filthy clothes were removed and a basin of water placed on the compacted earth floor. As Atawhai began to sponge Tamar's body, she shook her head. The *Pakeha* girl was far too thin, her pale limbs scrawny and limp. Her pubic hair and thighs were caked with filth, and she smelled dreadful. But like Riria, Atawhai did not think the girl carried an infection inside her, which was remarkable given the circumstances.

She removed the bandage from Tamar's face and head and gave the wound a thorough wash and examination. If this girl survives, Atawhai thought sadly, she will no longer be known for her beauty.

The deep gash started an inch below Tamar's hairline on the right side of her forehead, travelled down towards her right jaw, dissecting her eyebrow and nicking her swollen upper eyelid, then bit into her upper cheekbone before it stopped several inches from the base of her right earlobe. Atawhai hoped the infection had not set into the bone; if that happened, there would be little hope. As it was, she doubted the girl would be alive tomorrow.

She removed as much infected matter from the wound as she could, thankful her patient was still unconscious, and gave the order for several medicinal infusions and a poultice to be prepared. When they arrived in a series of small bowls, she bathed the wound with a dark, sharp-smelling liquid then applied a greenish grey paste to the bone and around the puffy edges, before wrapping a clean cloth around Tamar's head and across the right side of her face. Riria then lifted Tamar's head and torso so Atawhai could pour small amounts of another infusion into her mouth; much of it spilled down her chin and neck but enough went in to satisfy Atawhai. She also massaged Tamar's swollen breasts and expressed some of the milk to ease the pressure.

'We will give her *kohekohe* to dry her off,' she said, thinking out loud. The young woman sitting on the floor nursing Tamar's baby nodded placidly, her munificent breasts sufficiently productive to feed her own infant plus another.

When Atawhai had finished, she covered Tamar with several blankets and sat back on her heels. The coming night would be the test of this girl's spirit. If the fever broke and the girl survived until morning, she would probably live. If not, then they would have to bury her in their own *urupa*, high on the hill overlooking the sea.

Riria rose early the next morning and walked from her family *whare* to the village privies, moving slowly as she was stiff and sore. Atawhai had cleaned her scalp wound the previous evening, saying it should heal well and her hair would probably grow over the scar, and that she was lucky to still have her brains inside her head. Riria was not bothered by the thought of a scar, but she had been worried her hair might not grow back; she was not vain about many things, but she was proud of her long, thick tresses.

As she sat on the privy enjoying the first bowel movement she'd had in days, she yawned until her jaw cracked. She had been up late talking to her father and the village elders, although her deep, personal shame would not allow her to mention the sexual assaults. Her father had been incensed and was all for taking a *taua*, or war party, to hunt this Montgomery *Pakeha* down and claim *utu*, but she had asked him to wait until Tamar's future became clear.

Riria knew from experience that when her proud and impetuous father calmed down, he would see the man was not worth a death sentence from a *Pakeha* court. In a white man's court, in the case of a Maori killing a *Pakeha*, no circumstance would be accepted as mitigating; her father would be sentenced to death without a moment's hesitation. Furthermore, Riria had her own plans for Mr *Pakeha* pig Montgomery, but she kept these to herself.

The issue of the baby's parentage had caused some consternation. The elders knew Te Kanene and were aware of Kepa's status amongst his people.

'That boy is too handsome for his own good,' Te Hau said. He was sitting cross-legged next to the central fire in the *wharenui*. 'This is a stupid and foolish action he has taken. It has already almost cost the lives of three people, including my precious daughter Riria, and it will go on causing trouble. He has thought with his penis, that boy, instead of with his head.'

The elders had muttered in agreement. To be sexually active was one thing, but to impregnate a woman, and a *Pakeha* one at that, was definitely another, and much more serious. The woman herself was not important, although Te Hau's daughter seemed to have formed a friendship with her, but the resulting child was; he was the grandson of a powerful chief and must be raised as such, by his own people.

Riria looked from face to face through the flickering flames and the spiral of fragrant smoke twisting lazily up through the chimney opening, searching for any indication of what the elders might be thinking. 'She will want to keep her baby,' she said boldly.

'She cannot,' Te Hau snapped. 'She does not know how he should be brought up. Because of who he is, there will be many things he will need to learn. He must go to his own people. I hear Te Kanene is expected at Tinopai in the Kaipara Harbour in a day or two. I will send a message. He can have the responsibility of it. It is not our decision to make.'

'She will be heartbroken.'

'She will probably be dead by tomorrow so it will not matter,' Te Hau replied bluntly.

Then, at the anguished expression on Riria's face, Te Hau's own tattooed features softened. 'Daughter, you know the child must be raised by his own family. We cannot do it and neither can his birth mother. *If* she recovers, she must go back to her own people and forget her son. She must consider him dead. That is the way it must be.'

Riria knew he was right but could not prevent herself from imagining Tamar's utter despair. 'Where is Kepa?' she asked suddenly.

'Ingarangi, so we hear,' one of the elders replied. 'On business for Te Kanene. He went six months ago and is not due back until year's end. And probably just as well.'

England, Riria thought disgustedly. Does he have no sense of honour? He said he would take responsibility for his actions but he has run away! She frowned angrily as she got to her feet and bid the men around the fire a terse good night. They stared after her retreating back in silence.

'Your daughter has a mind of her own, Te Hau,' one of them commented. 'And she should think before she speaks.'

'I know,' Te Hau replied resignedly. 'She does think before she speaks. That is what worries me.'

This morning, as Riria trudged towards the small *whare*, she recalled with a surge of anger her father's decision about Tamar's baby. It occurred to her the poor little thing still had no name. But her father had been right about several things — the baby's future as well as Tamar's frailty. As she approached the hut she felt increasingly nervous. She had asked Atawhai to wake her if Tamar's condition worsened, but would not be surprised if the older woman had left her to sleep.

Pushing the door gently open, she went inside. Atawhai was sitting on a low stool next to the platform. For a horrible, heart-stopping moment Riria thought her dear friend was dead, then saw her slow, shallow breathing and heaved a sigh of relief. 'How is she?'

Atawhai looked at her for a full minute before she replied. 'She is alive but the fever has not broken. She must be stronger than she looks. She might survive.'

Riria knelt and gazed at Tamar's deathly pale face. The flesh around her eyes was not as dark as it had been, and was turning the sickly yellow of healing tissue.

'She still needs to be bathed with cool water to reduce her heat, and she is due for another drink of the infusion soon,' Atawhai continued. 'Perhaps you could do that? I must eat.'

Riria nodded and went to fetch a basin of fresh water and some cloths. When she returned Atawhai left the *whare*. Riria bathed Tamar, prattling on about nothing in particular in the hope she might somehow hear and be comforted. When she held Tamar's head up to administer the infusion, she was momentarily heartened to see her throat involuntarily swallow. She was no longer rambling but was no more conscious than she had been yesterday. This worried Riria; the tossing and turning and yelling out had at least shown her friend's mind had still been active.

217

Now, she looked like a corpse, still and white as if her spirit had already flown.

As the day wore on Riria visited Tamar regularly, spelling Atawhai so she could rest or prepare more medicines. The baby was brought into the hut several times but seemed content to be carried or nursed by the girl who had suckled him the night before. When placed on Tamar's chest he wailed, perhaps aware his mother was hovering between life and death. Or perhaps just wanting the touch of someone who did not radiate such an aura of illness, reflected Riria sadly. At least he was in safe, caring hands.

Over the next five days Tamar's condition slowly improved. Atawhai declared her past the point where she was likely to die. She did not recognise anyone and her mind seemed to be engaged in a monumental battle in a dark and private place, but she was mending physically and the wound on her face was beginning to heal. Atawhai, however, was worried about her mental state.

'She still has a touch of the fever but not enough to confuse her mind. She seems to be in a state of shock. She lost a lot of blood after she gave birth but the flow is decreasing. It should cease altogether soon. You say she was terrorised?'

Riria nodded. 'I think so. I was not in the house when it happened but she thought her husband had murdered both myself and the baby.'

'Was she making sense when you found her?'

'Not really. She was dazed.'

Atawhai thought for a minute, her arms folded across her drooping breasts. 'Mmm,' she muttered finally. 'Then we will just have to wait and see. Her recovery may be long and difficult if her mind has been affected.'

Two days later Tamar's fever broke completely and she slept for almost twenty-four hours, apparently undisturbed by whatever had haunted her earlier. On the afternoon of the eighth day she opened her eyes, still a little puffy but no longer full of fear, and looked about her. 'Where is my baby?' she asked in a rough, cracking voice. 'Riria?'

'I will get her. You are safe now, child,' Atawhai replied in Maori. She could not speak English fluently herself but the intent of Tamar's questions had been clear. She hurried out of the hut.

When she returned with Riria, Tamar was trying to sit up. Atawhai gently but firmly pushed her down and said, 'You must rest. You are still very ill.' Tamar looked at her uncomprehendingly.

Riria grasped Tamar's white hands in her own strong brown ones and rubbed them gently. 'I am so glad you have returned to us,' she said in English.

'Where is he?' asked Tamar, a strident note of panic in her voice. 'The baby?'

Riria and Atawhai looked at each other. 'He is safe,' replied Riria. He was, but he was no longer at the village. She would tell Tamar when her friend felt a little stronger, if she could put her off for that long.

'I will get something to help you sleep again,' said Atawhai and went out. She returned almost immediately with a brown glass bottle. Pouring a little of the contents into a cracked but dainty teacup she signalled for Riria to prop Tamar up so she could drink.

'What is it?'

'Opium,' replied Atawhai. 'It will help the girl relax.'

Tamar drank the liquid and sank back onto the mattress. In a few short minutes her eyelids were drooping heavily and she drifted back to sleep.

When she awoke six or seven hours later, she again demanded to see her baby. I will have to tell her, thought Riria grimly when she had been summoned by a small boy who told her the skinny *Pakeha* lady was awake and could she come to the *whare* quickly.

Inside, Riria knelt beside Tamar's bed. Again she took her

friend's hands in her own. 'Tamar,' she began hesitantly. 'I have something to tell you.'

'He died, didn't he?' interjected Tamar, the light in her eyes fading.

'*No*!' replied Riria quickly. 'He is alive.'

Tamar closed her eyes in relief.

'But he is not here any more. He has gone.'

Tamar looked blankly at her. 'Gone? Where?'

'With Te Kanene. Father sent a message and he came and picked him up five days ago. He is taking him back to the East Coast so he can be raised by his own people. He is safe, Tamar, but he has been taken from you.'

Riria shut her own eyes and felt her heart clench as Tamar let loose an eerie wail of such agonising pain and despair it could be heard in the cool, still moonlit night, across the village and as far away as the gently lapping waves on the nearby beach.

The following day Atawhai allowed Tamar to sit and eat her first solid meal in almost two weeks, a plate of stew with a chunk of bread. Tamar ate some but had to leave most of it. She was extremely thin, her knees and elbows and the bones of her ribs and hips protruding alarmingly. Atawhai was also dosing her regularly with a tonic she said would help to restore her strength and vigour, and had suggested she start going for short walks. Riria accompanied her, holding her elbow in case she felt faint or lost her balance. Tamar was very weak, but by the end of the day she could manage almost fifty yards on her own. The men of the village stared at her curiously but the women gave her sympathetic looks, aware she had lost her child. Assorted scruffy children tagged along behind her, fascinated by anything new or different, and Riria shooed them away, whacking one or two on the bum when they would not heed her.

Tamar spent the next week recuperating. She was rapidly gaining strength, Atawhai stuffing her so full of food she gained back at least half of the weight she'd lost. Riria, however, was worried about her state of mind. Tamar wept often and was deeply mourning the loss of her child. One day as they sat on a hill overlooking the sea, watching the men of the village land their canoes on the curved, white beach, she broached the subject of Tamar's future. 'You could stay here,' she suggested.

Tamar pulled a twig off a bush next to her and absently began to strip the leaves. 'I don't belong,' she said. 'I can't do anything useful and I'd just be another mouth to feed.'

'You could learn,' replied Riria hopefully, but she knew in her heart Tamar would never fit in properly.

'No. I have to go back.'

'To the house?' said Riria in disbelief.

'No! I'll never go back there.'

Riria relaxed. She had not thought her friend would be so stupid or self-destructive, but wondered if her experiences had affected her mind to the point where she no longer cared about her own welfare. They sat in silence for a few minutes.

'I am sad my marriage is over,' Tamar said eventually. 'But I don't believe it was ever what I thought it was, or wanted it to be. I think I'm sad for my lost dreams, for what I wanted and imagined, not for what I had. But the sadness is just as real.' She picked another twig and added flatly, 'I think I'll go to Myrna's. I could work for her.'

Riria turned and looked at her friend, shocked. 'No! You are not a whore!' There was no easy way she could articulate her next thought, so she said it bluntly. 'And not with your face looking like that.'

Tamar said nothing. Riria was not telling her anything she didn't already know. Her face was badly scarred. She had examined the wound in a hand mirror several days ago and had been appalled. It was healing well but the infection had distorted the flesh to the point where her right eyebrow was completely misaligned where it had grown back, the scar above it thickly puckered and a reddish purple colour. Her right eyelid was pushed down by a knot of scar tissue so her eye looked permanently half shut. The cut on her cheek had healed more evenly and would probably fade to a discreet white scar, apart from the area over the bone just below her eye, which was raised and a little puckered, but her eye, brow and temple would remain disfigured forever.

'I suppose not,' she said with a laugh that was half bitter and half sad. 'Nobody would pay to look at a face like this.'

'But you are still beautiful, Tamar,' replied Riria adamantly. 'You are beautiful inside and you always will be, if you do not allow this thing that has happened to steal your spirit. You may marry again and have more children. You can have a good life if you choose.'

'I've slept with two men already and given birth to an illegitimate, half-caste child. Who would want me after that?'

'Perhaps nobody, if you insist on telling everyone. This is your business, Tamar, nobody else's. It is not tattooed across your face like a *moko*. Your pain is, but not your secrets.'

Tamar smiled. Riria was always so practical.

'You were unfortunate to marry someone sad and weak, but he will reap what he has sown and you are wiser now.'

Tamar sighed. 'I think I should leave soon, Riria,' she said, taking a deep breath and tossing her loose hair back off her face. 'I'm almost recovered and you're right — I need to get back to my life and whatever it has in store for me. But I will never marry again, I know that.'

Two days later, Tamar was ready to leave. She had no appropriate clothes of her own so the village women had donated an old skirt, bodice and coat, and a well-used black straw hat. She fashioned herself a veil from a scrap of cherished but generously offered chiffon, which she attached to the rim of the hat to cover the right side of her face. She was oddly attired but at least it was in women's clothing. Te Hau had offered the use of his horse and cart and, at his daughter's insistence, provided some money. Riria would accompany her back across the ranges, taking the furthest route possible from Huia as far as Henderson, where Tamar would catch the train to Auckland.

As Tamar stood by the cart, Atawhai held out her arms. Tamar stepped into them, taking comfort from this skilled old woman who had worked so hard to keep her alive. She felt herself beginning to cry. She seemed powerless to stop her frequent tears, but Atawhai told her they were good, a sign her heart was beginning to heal. 'You must weep, child,' she said. 'The tears will wash out the pain. If you hold on to them, the hurt will fester inside and never leave.'

Tamar also hugged the girl who had nursed her baby, today with her own fat brown infant perched on her wide hip, and the other women who had helped her. Finally she was ready to leave and climbed up next to Riria. As they drove through the village gate she turned and waved, wondering if she would ever come back.

The trip to Henderson took several days as the tracks through the ranges were difficult because of the recent rain. On several occasions they had to get off and push the cart out of the mud. However, they arrived safely, if a little dirty, purchased a ticket and sat at the railway station waiting for the train.

As the locomotive approached, belching clouds of smoke and steam, Riria turned to Tamar. 'I have something for you,' she said, and reached under the collar of her dress and extracted a greenstone pendant on a thin leather thong. She lifted it over her head and offered it to Tamar. The pendant was two inches long and half an inch wide and of a particularly flawless dark and pure jade. '*Pounamu*, so you will not forget me.'

Tamar took the pendant and put it on. She was crying again. 'Oh, Riria. I'll *never* forget you. How could I?'

She leaned forward and embraced her fiercely and they clung together as the train came into the station and pulled to a noisy halt. The guard jumped down and told the handful of waiting passengers they should board immediately.

With a final hug Tamar turned away from Riria and climbed onto the train. She appeared at a carriage window a few seconds later, opened it and stuck her head out. 'We'll see each other again, I know we will,' she yelled over the noise.

Riria nodded silently and waved as the train slowly began to pull out. She remained alone on the platform until the train had travelled out of sight, then walked back to her father's horse and cart and drove out of the small settlement.

But instead of taking the road that would lead her back over the Waitakere Ranges to Kainui, she turned and started off in the direction of Huia, a grim and resolute expression on her proud, brown face.

Tamar arrived in Auckland at five in the afternoon. She hired a cab and gave the driver the address of Myrna's house on Dilworth Terrace. People had stared at her on the train, at her strange, patched clothes and her disfigured face, but she ignored them. No one spoke to her but she was not bothered by their reticence; she was in no mood to make polite conversation.

As the cab pulled up outside Myrna's, the cabbie opened the hatch in the roof and called down, 'Are yer sure this is where yer want ter go, Missus? This is a brothel.'

'I am aware of that, and I don't care if it's the gate to Hell itself. Let me out please.'

The cabbie hopped down and opened the door for her, staring

pointedly at her face as he did so. 'Nasty scar yer've got there, Missus,' he observed.

'Yes,' replied Tamar as she handed him his fare. 'Thank you so much for being so polite as to mention it.'

'I were only saying,' grumped the cabbie as he swung himself back onto his seat and clattered off.

Tamar watched him go, then turned and walked up the path to the front door, rang the bell and waited. She could hear footsteps hurrying down the hall inside and braced herself to confront whomever would open the door.

It was Eliza. She looked Tamar quickly up and down and said, 'Go away. We don't give ter beggars,' and shut the door in her face.

Tamar took her hat off and rang again. Eliza answered immediately. 'Look, piss orf, I said!' she snapped. 'Go on! Bugger orf!'

'Eliza, it's me. Tamar Deane.'

Eliza stared for a second then raised her hands to her mouth and screamed. She turned and ran inside, leaving the front door wide open. 'Miss Myrna! Miss Myrna, come quick! It's Tamar and somethin' terrible's 'appened ter her face!'

Myrna appeared immediately from her office and hurried towards the door. When she saw Tamar she stopped dead then lunged forward again, her arms out, as recognition dawned on her. 'Oh ma *God*! Ye poor wee lassie, what's happened te ye?'

'I've come home,' said Tamar, as she burst into tears yet again.

CHAPTER FOURTEEN

July 1881

Tamar sat in Myrna's garden, a woollen rug over her knees, the weak winter sun failing to keep the chill from her bones. She wondered if she would ever feel warm again. Cabbage lay quietly at her feet, as if sensing she needed company but not entertainment.

The spot where she'd placed her chair was protected from the breeze by a trellis covered with rampant honeysuckle, but she had a peaceful view of the shrubs and flowerbeds Myrna had planted. The garden would be beautiful in another twelve months, a quiet haven from the comings and goings inside the house.

Tamar heard the faint clatter of a horse's hooves along Dilworth Terrace and tensed, wondering whether the horse was being ridden by someone looking for her, relaxing only when the horse continued down the street.

Myrna emerged from the house followed by Eliza carrying a laden tea tray. She pulled a garden chair next to Tamar and sat down, lighting a cigarette, while Eliza poured two cups of steaming hot tea. After Eliza had gone, Myrna asked, 'How are ye feeling this morning, lassie?'

Tamar did not reply immediately, her gaze captured by the sight of a small mauve butterfly flitting from leaf to leaf on the honeysuckle. Cabbage took a half-hearted snap at it but missed, his head flopping limply back onto his outstretched paws. Somewhere a lone bee buzzed lazily.

'Tired,' she said eventually. 'Very tired.'

'Aye, it's a ghastly experience ye've had,' responded Myrna. Her heart ached for this pale young girl with the grotesque scar on her face and an even more ragged one on her soul. 'Ye slept well?'

'Not really. I dreamt he came after me.'

'Peter?' Myrna was not surprised; Tamar's fear and pain hung about her like heavy, black fog. 'I dinnae think he will. He's no' the guts.'

Tamar did not respond and they sat together in silence. Myrna was extremely upset, cursing herself over whether she could or should have done more to prevent Tamar's disastrous marriage. She'd almost had a heart attack when Tamar appeared on her doorstep, skinny as a garden rake and her face horribly disfigured. In her private parlour, Tamar collapsed on the sofa, looking dumbly at Myrna, her face distorted by pain and despair and unable to speak. The girls had hovered, visibly bewildered and stunned, but Myrna sent them back to work with a flap of her hand and shut the door.

Tamar had eventually stammered something about a lost baby and Peter trying to kill her, but her sobbing rendered her almost incoherent. Together Myrna and Eliza helped her up to Myrna's room and put her to bed with a large glass of brandy to calm her. Clearly exhausted, she had not woken until this morning when, considerably more composed, she told Myrna what had happened.

Myrna had known all was not right with Tamar's marriage, had in fact always suspected Peter would turn out to be trouble, but she had not been fully aware of the extent of his alcohol dependence and how inextricably enmeshed Tamar had become in his misery.

Now she wondered who this man was who had seduced her and ultimately caused her such pain. 'D'ye love this Kepa?'

Tamar shrugged. 'I don't know if you'd call it love, I'm not sure I know what the word means any more. But I know I felt safer and more alive with him than I have at any other time in my life. I *had* to be with him. He was what my mam said he would be, the man who would come along and turn me inside out.'

'D'ye have a future wi' him?'

'No,' replied Tamar bluntly.

'Is that what's grieving ye so badly?'

Tamar inhaled deeply then let her breath out very slowly before she said, honestly, 'No, it isn't. I think that's partly why I did it.'

'Aye, well, ye cannae be blamed for following your heart. Or the rest o' your body, if it comes to that. Is it what Peter did to ye, then?'

'No, Peter's sick, I understand that. I hurt him badly and yes, I *am* worried he'll come after me. But it's the child, my baby. I can't even remember what he looks like!' Tamar's voice cracked with emotion. 'I only had him for a few hours and I didn't even name him. I was going to call him Nolan, after my da.' She looked up at Myrna. 'I feel so *stripped* of him. I'll never see him again, and that hurts my very *soul*.'

She put both hands over her mouth and half cried out, half sobbed. Myrna reached out and touched her gently. 'Aye, losing a bairn is perhaps the hardest thing a woman has to face,' she commiserated gently.

Tamar wiped her nose inelegantly on the back of her hand. 'I'll never have the chance to tell him not to eat snails or say it's all right when he wets his pants. I'll never tuck him into bed or make him a birthday cake or get jealous when he grows up and falls in love with some woman who isn't me.' She lapsed into silence. Myrna waited patiently, knowing there was more to come. 'I've been such a fool. A stubborn, arrogant, childish fool.'

Myrna shook her head. 'No, ye havnae, lassie. Ye made a mistake, that's all.'

'*No*, I did *not* make a mistake,' Tamar snapped. Anger surged through her, directed mostly at herself. 'I did it deliberately. Marrying Peter, sleeping with Kepa, *all* of it! I knew what I was doing but I wouldn't let myself see what was happening to Peter, and I wouldn't let myself see what was happening to *me*. Who am I, Myrna? I don't know any more. How could I have done this?'

'Well,' answered Myrna carefully, 'ye're certainly no' the wee lassie I met on the *Rebecca Jane*.'

'No, I'm not. I feel so dreadful, so *detached*, as if this is all happening to someone else. What's *wrong* with me?'

'Och, it'll be the shock. In time ye'll marry again and have more bairns, I'm sure.'

'No, Riria said that, but I don't think so,' said Tamar, shaking her head sadly. 'I would have died if she hadn't been there. And it was my fault she was almost killed too. God, how could I have been so blind and *stupid*!' she spat vehemently.

Privately, Myrna had wondered the same thing. But, alarmed at the ire in Tamar's voice, she said instead, 'Well, maybe ye've grown up a little. I'd be verra surprised if ye hadnae, after all that.'

'And what if Peter comes for me? I never want to see him again.'

'Is he likely to, d'ye think?'

'No doubt he hates me, but that could be the very thing to bring him here. He was very vindictive and angry during those last few months.'

'Well, we'll worry about that *if* it happens and no' before.'

Myrna poured them both more tea and changed the subject. 'I sent a message to John Adams last night. He can take a look at your face when he gets here.'

'Oh Lord, I hurt him terribly as well, didn't I?' Tamar groaned. 'My mam would turn in her grave if she knew how selfish I've been.'

Myrna suddenly leaned over and roughly grasped Tamar's elbow. The cup of tea balanced on her knees sloshed over into its saucer. 'Look, lassie,' Myrna said, 'I ken ye've been badly hurt and ye've lost your bairn, but I cannae *abide* self-pity. Ye made a mistake, now *learn* from it! Put it behind ye and look ahead. It will all have been for nothing if ye spend the rest o' your life feeling sorry for yeself. If *I'd* gone around dragging ma arse every time I made a mistake, I'd've worn it off by now! And clearly I havnae,' she added tersely, pointing at her ample buttocks.

Startled, Tamar could do nothing but stare at her friend.

'I mean it,' continued Myrna. 'Pull yeself together, lassie, or ye'll be doomed. Ye've your whole life, ye're only nineteen, so *make* something o' yeself. That's what ye started out to do, so *do* it! Dinnae let any o' this stop ye!'

She glared at Tamar who dropped her eyes and fiddled with the teaspoon in her flooded saucer. She's right, Tamar thought. I have to put my life into some sort of order. But it's so much easier to flounder pathetically in pain and self-pity and blame. So black and seductive and soothing, so much less frightening than facing tomorrow. And so gutless. Shifting uncomfortably, she pulled at the waistband of the dress Bronwyn had lent her; she'd not yet recovered her figure and her stomach was soft and extended. God, she cursed silently — I'm a physical and mental ruin. But, despite her misery, she knew she had choices; she could rebuild her life, or she could give up now. She grimaced inwardly. The acceptance of this realisation, this knowledge that she could take control of her life angered her because now she knew it, she could not un-know it. The knowledge gave her a splinter of hope.

She looked slowly around her; at Myrna, at odiferous little Cabbage, at the trees behind the house, and the shrubs and scattered winter flowers in the new garden. 'If those are yellow,' she said finally, her voice unsteady as she pointed to a bed of leafless rose bushes, 'they'll look lovely in that vase in the salon. Can I stay here, Myrna?'

'That's ma girl,' said Myrna, smiling broadly and thinking, thank Christ for that; she's made a decision. 'O' course ye can. And when John comes, ye'll hold your head up and greet him like the long lost friend he is.'

Tamar nodded and closed her eyes. For the first time in months she felt she was regaining some control. She would stay with Myrna and heal physically and mentally, and when she was strong, well, she would worry about tomorrow when tomorrow came.

John arrived in the early afternoon, just before Myrna opened for business. He was appalled by Tamar's condition. He examined her scarred face in silence, his lips compressed and white with fury. When he had finished, he said, 'You've been very lucky, Tamar. The scar indicates the infection was very deep. You could have died.'

He sat down abruptly and repeated angrily, 'You could have *died*, Tamar! Why did you not get away from him before it came to this? How could you let this happen to yourself? God Al*mighty*.'

Myrna said harshly, 'That's enough, John! She feels bad enough as it is wi'out *you* carping on.'

Tamar thought of a thousand things she could say to justify why she had stayed with Peter, why she tolerated, excused and even condoned his drinking and his behaviour, but now they sounded like weak, pathetic excuses. She felt deeply ashamed; the truth was she had stayed because she thought she would be better off, and had been willing to trade her self-respect for a warped and shallow illusion of security. In her own way she had been just as sick as Peter, and the realisation shocked her. Taking a deep breath, she decided it would be best if she told John everything. 'I also had a child,' she said quietly.

John stared at her, then opened his mouth to say something.

Tamar held up her hand. 'No, let me finish. I gave birth to him just over two weeks ago, but …'

'A child! Where is it?' exclaimed John, unable to help himself.

'He's been taken home to his people.'

'What?' said John, completely confused.

'If you'll just shut up for a minute, I'll explain!' snapped Tamar. 'His father is a Maori.'

There was a dreadful silence as John absorbed Tamar's words. 'A Maori?' he parroted stupidly.

'Yes, a *Maori*,' Tamar reiterated sharply. 'From the East Coast. A coastal trader. I met him, we had a liaison and I had his child.'

John looked at her briefly, then lowered his eyes in embarrassment. 'I see.'

'No, you *don't*,' insisted Tamar, stamping her foot. 'He *moved* me, John. It's as simple as that, and I'll never regret it,' she added defiantly.

John nodded towards Tamar's face. 'Did Peter do that when he found out?'

'Yes, after the baby was born and it was obvious he wasn't the father. He was drunk. We had to flee to my housegirl Riria's village.'

'Your marriage is over, then?'

'It is as far as I'm concerned.'

'What are you going to do?'

'I'm staying here for the foreseeable future. After that, I don't know.'

'Will you look for the child?'

'No, she will *not*,' interjected Myrna. 'She'll leave him to be raised by his own folk, where he belongs.'

John looked to Tamar for confirmation and she nodded. He stood and walked over to her again and lifted her damaged eyelid gently with his thumb. He squinted and pursed his lips thoughtfully as he manipulated her ragged eyebrow, then stood back and contemplated her. 'I could fix that,' he said after a minute. 'Or at least make it tidier.'

'My face?' asked Tamar.

'Yes. I could remove some of the scar tissue in a month or so when it's settled down, then realign and restitch the wound so it isn't so obvious. You'd need ether, I'd have to knock you right out. That can be dangerous,' he warned.

Tamar shrugged as if the prospect wasn't a concern.

'Right then,' he continued, very businesslike now. 'And you're otherwise healthy? No problems associated with the baby?'

'I'm still bleeding a little but I gather that's normal. My milk dried up. The woman who looked after me was very competent. I had a fever but she fixed that too.'

'Yes, Maori know what they're doing with their plants and herbs. You were lucky she was there.' He coughed discreetly. 'And, ah, the father of the child?'

'In England, apparently. I'm not expecting to see him again,' Tamar added.

Myrna interrupted, 'The lassie needs to rest and recover, John, as I'm sure ye ken.'

'Quite, quite,' said John hurriedly. He stood up and gathered his hat and gloves. 'I'll see myself out.'

As he reached the parlour door he turned and looked again at Tamar. Although one side of her face was disfigured, she was still strikingly attractive. The scar was something that had been temporarily applied to her features, something he could remedy with a scalpel and needle. But had her experiences scarred more than her face? He glanced at her waistline, for the moment shapeless from carrying the child of a man who had not been her husband. While John realised he didn't care what colour or race the child's father had been, he did care about what had made Tamar break her marriage vows and commit adultery. Clearly life with the

233

mentally unstable Peter Montgomery had been hell, but he had a distinct feeling that in itself was not the reason she had taken another man to her bed. With a stab of grief, he saw she was no longer the woman he thought she was. Perhaps she never had been. Although he tried never to judge others, he realised with a feeling of acute sadness and loss that he *had* judged Tamar, and found her wanting; he still loved her, but he was no longer *in* love with her.

With dismay, Myrna saw all of this reflected in John's homely, open face.

'And Peter Montgomery?' he asked from the doorway, pulling on his gloves. 'Where is he now?'

'I don't know,' replied Tamar. 'And I don't care, as long as he stays away from me.'

Riria knew where Peter Montgomery was.

After she had seen Tamar onto the train she headed south on one of the lesser-used bush tracks towards the Manukau Harbour, stopping for the night outside Titirangi where she left the cart, then continued on the following day until she reached Big Muddy Creek. Then, turning inland, she rode through the bush until she arrived at the outskirts of Huia, almost blinded as she rode directly into the setting sun. She settled down for the night in the dark, damp security of the forest. She was in no hurry.

The following morning she rose with the sun, had a rudimentary wash in a nearby stream, and watered her horse before she headed into the hills towards Peter Montgomery's house. Not wanting to be seen, she picked her way through the bush, stopping frequently to listen for any indication of other travellers.

When she eventually reached the turnoff to Peter's house Riria led her horse some way into the bush and tethered him to a tree. She would walk from here; she had no intention of accidentally meeting the *Pakeha* pig on the rough, narrow track.

Reaching into her backpack she pulled out a short cloth *tatua*, then removed her dress, drawers, socks and boots, stuffed them into her pack and wrapped the *tatua* around her waist. It was a warrior's garment, and covered her from her belly to her upper thighs. Now almost nude, she shivered slightly in the cool morning air. Her skin prickled with goose bumps but her long hair helped keep her warm as she withdrew a well-sharpened knife from her pack and tucked it carefully into her waistband.

It was approaching midday by the time she reached the house and concealed herself in the ferns opposite the front gate, almost exactly where she had lain when she had been shot. She fancied she could still smell her own blood in the damp earth.

There were no signs of life in or around the house and the curtains were drawn, although she saw the *Pakeha*'s black horse grazing in a paddock. She decided to wait until the sun was overhead before she ventured down to have a look around. Without his horse he would not be far away.

She lay inanimate for over an hour, watching and waiting. Then, just as she was contemplating moving, the sound of a gunshot reverberated up the small valley, rudely fracturing the silence. Riria jumped, then ducked her head and froze. Where had the shot come from? Inside the house perhaps, but she could not be sure. She remained motionless for another fifteen minutes, but the shot was not repeated.

I could lie here in these ferns forever, she thought angrily, exasperated by her fear. Very slowly she raised herself from the undergrowth and began to move stealthily back into the shadows of the forest, keeping as low as possible. When she was out of sight of the house she moved quickly through the trees parallel to the track for about a hundred yards, ran silently across the open space and into the bush following the fence line down the hill on the eastern side of the house. She emerged from the trees towards the rear of the building. Keeping within the cover of the bush, she squatted on her heels and listened.

When she was sure there was no movement from within the house she withdrew the knife from her *tatua* and slid sinuously through the fence and ran lightly through the long grass to the back of the house. She waited there, her naked back pressed hard against the rough external wall of her old room, listening for some minutes, then very slowly extended her head around the corner of the house and took a quick look at the porch. It was empty and the back door was open.

Despite the cool air her hands were slick with sweat and she could feel it beginning to trickle in her armpits. Riria took a deep, noiseless breath and stepped onto the porch, wincing as a board creaked. She quickly lifted her foot, but still nothing moved inside the house.

As she stepped into the gloomy hall she became aware of a low moaning coming from the parlour. It sounded like an animal in pain but she stayed where she was, wary of some sort of trick. Very slowly she began to move again, the muscles in her strong calves and thighs quivering with tension. When she reached the doorway to the parlour she crouched down and peered into the darkened room.

The coppery smell of fresh blood mixed with stale cigarette smoke and spilt alcohol was overwhelming. As her eyes became accustomed to the gloom she was able to make out a crumpled shape on the floor. The moaning sound came again, louder this time.

Suddenly the shape on the floor moved and Riria saw it was Peter Montgomery. She leapt back and held her knife ready as he laboriously rolled over. Her eyes widened when she saw the pistol lying under the chair.

The upper portion of his left jaw, cheek and temple had been blown almost completely away, exposing the ragged remnants of several teeth and his tongue, and, higher up, something glistened wetly in the weak light. His left eye was pulverised, and his right eye stared fixedly at Riria. He mumbled indistinctly, bubbles of blood forming on his lips.

Riria approached him extremely warily, aware she was experiencing several conflicting emotions. The first was anger that he had already done to himself what she had come back to do and had robbed her of *utu*. The second was nauseating pity — at his inability to face the demons in his life and his even more obvious inability to shoot himself cleanly in the head. '*Hakawa!*' she spat. 'Only a gutless fool takes his own life.'

Peter held out a shaking, blood-spattered hand towards her. 'End it,' his eye seemed to beg.

In anger she kicked out at his arm and jumped away from him. '*Kao!*' she shrieked, all of her pain, humiliation, fear and hatred coming out in the one short word. '*No!* Lie there and die, *Pakeha* pig! Like I had to lie there. Like you left Tamar to die!'

Peter's one good eye closed and he drew in a ragged, liquid breath.

Riria untied the *tatua* from her hips, threw it onto the floor and began a wordless, wild war dance, or *ngeri*. She bent her knees and stamped her foot and slapped her full, high breasts and flat belly. She bulged and rolled her eyes grotesquely, then turned and displayed her buttocks. Her long hair flew as she whirled and hissed and bared her teeth and stood defiantly with knees bent, completely still except for her arms held rigidly out in front of her, palms flat and facing the floor, her hands quivering violently.

His bloody and shattered head lolling, Peter's single eye stared straight at Riria as she straightened up and looked down at him, panting.

She saw he had begun to weep, a tear rolling slowly down the undamaged side of his face. Remorse, or just fear she would not finish him off? If she walked out of the house now he could take hours to die, alone and in agonising pain.

Riria's vicious and insulting *ngeri* had acted as a conduit for her enormous rage and humiliation, and left her now with a vague sadness for this sick, ruined man. She felt emotionally purged and clean, knowing the weight of his sins would follow him wherever he was about to go, while she had been set free. She squatted beside him and picked up her knife and then the pistol, one in each hand, and raised her eyebrows. He nodded at the gun then closed his eyes in gratitude as she cocked it, placed it against the back of his head and fired.

'May your God go with you,' she said in English as Peter's body spasmed once, then relaxed as he died.

Riria watched the pool of blood around his head grow rapidly wider for a minute until his heart stopped pumping, then said a short *karakia* in Maori to help his spirit on its way. She lay the pistol on the floor, then picked up her *tatua* and her knife and went out to the water pump. Some of Peter's blood had splattered her and she was anxious to wash it off as quickly as possible, worried the blood from such an unhappy man may somehow taint her own spirit.

When she felt clean she retied her *tatua*, took one last glance around her, then headed back into the forest.

She could go home now.

CHAPTER FIFTEEN

August 1881

A little less than a fortnight later, Eliza informed Tamar there was a policemen and another man at the door wanting to speak to her.

'Bring them into the parlour please, Eliza,' Tamar replied apprehensively. 'I'll be there in a minute. And can you get Myrna?'

While Eliza ushered the visitors in, Tamar checked her hair in the mirror and took a deep breath. 'I have done nothing wrong,' she reassured her reflection, her heart hammering.

The two men rose from the sofa as she entered the parlour. One was dressed in the uniform of the New Zealand Constabulary Force but the other, an older man, was wearing civilian clothes. Myrna was already seated and was busy pouring tea.

'Mrs Peter Montgomery, of Huia?' enquired the older man. He had a full moustache, fashionable mutton-chop whiskers and shrewd, blue eyes.

When Tamar nodded he continued. 'I am Detective Archie Childs of the Auckland Police. This is Sergeant David. I'm afraid we have some rather tragic news for you, Mrs Montgomery. It is with regret that I must inform you your husband Peter Montgomery was found dead at your home in Huia five days ago.'

Tamar blinked and waited for a surge of grief, or regret, but she felt nothing. She cleared her throat, feeling she should say something. 'How did he die?'

'He suffered a gunshot wound. Or several,' replied Detective Childs. 'We are not entirely sure what happened but he died around two weeks ago. His body was discovered by one of your neighbours, who alerted the local constabulary.'

There was a short silence while Detective Childs observed the newly widowed Mrs Montgomery. He saw she was not at all distressed; either that or she had extremely good control of her emotions. 'May I ask when you last saw your husband?'

'Around a month ago, if I remember rightly, I have been ill and my memory is not serving me well.'

'I'm sorry to hear that, Mrs Montgomery. Please forgive me for raising such a personal matter but I understand you were recently delivered of a child? Your neighbour's wife advised Sergeant David you were expecting an arrival in June or July.'

Tamar glanced at Myrna who nodded.

'Yes,' Tamar replied. 'The child died, soon after birth.'

'My condolences.' Detective Childs used a small pair of silver tongs to drop two cubes of sugar into his tea, looking thoughtful as he stirred. He looked directly at Tamar. 'That's a dreadful scar, Mrs Montgomery. How did you receive it?'

Tamar said without hesitation, 'My husband assaulted me.'

'And this was a recent assault?' asked the detective. 'Around the time your child was born perhaps? And would that also have been the last time you saw your husband?'

Tamar nodded, confirming what the detective had already surmised.

'Was Mr Montgomery a violent man?'

'He could be.'

'We've talked to some of the locals and they implied Mr Montgomery was prone to excessive alcohol consumption, and his behaviour when intoxicated was aggressive and unpredictable. He does not seem to have been a popular man.'

Tamar said nothing.

'It must have been frightening, living with a man with such unpredictable behaviour. Frightening enough for someone to want that behaviour to stop permanently, do you think?'

'Was he murdered?' asked Tamar, in genuine surprise and shock.

'He appears to have been shot twice. Once through the side of his face, possibly by way of the mouth ...'

'*Suicide*?' interrupted Myrna.

'Perhaps,' replied Sergeant David. 'But he was also shot in the back of the head.'

'Yes,' continued Detective Childs. 'The perplexing thing is that Sergeant David found the pistol behind Mr Montgomery's body. It was positioned so far away in fact it seems unlikely he could have shot himself with it.'

'What are ye saying?' demanded Myrna.

'It appears Mr Montgomery may have attempted to kill himself, failed, and was finished off by someone else,' said the detective slowly, his eyes on Tamar. 'Either that or he was shot twice by someone who missed the first time.'

'Do you think *I* did it?' asked Tamar bluntly.

'I am obliged to talk to everyone who was in contact with Mr Montgomery before he died,' replied Detective Childs, his voice giving no hint of his personal views. 'Why don't you tell me what happened the last time *you* saw him, Mrs Montgomery?'

Myrna said quickly, 'Hold ye horses, does she need legal representation?'

'Of course not. I am merely attempting to put the pieces together, Miss McTaggart.'

Tamar told him the truth. 'I was delivered of my baby at home.

My domestic servant assisted me. My husband was drunk when he saw the infant and became enraged. He was convinced the child was not his.' At this, Detective Childs' eyebrows lifted but Tamar ignored him. 'He assaulted my servant and myself, causing the wound to my face, and we were forced to flee. We went over the Waitakere Ranges to my servant's home at Kainui. The child died on the way and I became ill with fever. I stayed at Kainui for twelve or so days, then I came here.'

'So you were not in the vicinity of your home a fortnight ago?'

'No. I was here by then. Or on my way here.'

'Can anyone vouch for your whereabouts around that time?'

'You can ask the people at Kainui, or the guard on the train I boarded at Henderson. And of course everyone here knows when I arrived. Miss McTaggart can confirm the date.'

'I'm sure,' said the detective, glancing at Myrna whom he suspected would say whatever suited her. He was well aware he was sitting in the private parlour of Auckland's most elegant brothel, and what an astute and formidable woman its madam, Myrna McTaggart, was.

'And your servant accompanied you from Kainui to Henderson?'

'Yes, that's right,' replied Tamar. 'How did you know? And how did you know where to find me?'

'We've already talked to Riria Te Hau. Her version of events was the same as yours, although she neglected to mention the infant died on the way to Kainui. Her people have confirmed she returned from Henderson after seeing you onto the train. So we are left with a deceased person who may or may not have been murdered, and no one able to shed any light on what might have happened. As he had been dead for some days by the time his body was discovered, we are unable to establish his exact time of death. I am afraid we may have to regard this as an unsolved suspicious death.'

The detective paused, then added, 'You do not seem to be overly perturbed by your husband's demise, Mrs Montgomery. Can I assume your marriage was an unhappy one?'

'Yes, you can. I truly hope my husband did not suffer, but I can't in all honesty say I will grieve for him.'

'There will be the matter of his estate; will you be expecting to benefit?'

'I doubt it,' replied Tamar.

So did Detective Childs. He had already talked to Peter Montgomery's bank, his lawyer and several of his business associates, and it was clear the man had been indebted up to his eyebrows. He rose and collected his hat and gloves. 'Thank you very much for your time, Mrs Montgomery and Miss McTaggart, and again I apologise for being the bearer of bad news.'

After Eliza saw the policemen out, Myrna turned to Tamar with her hands on her hips. 'Well, fancy that! Ye didnae do it, did ye?'

'No, I did *not*!' Tamar shot back, indignant.

'More's the pity. Still, at least someone did.'

Outside as Detective Childs and Sergeant David climbed into their cab, the sergeant asked, 'Do you think she did it?'

'No, I don't. And if she did I don't know if I'd blame her. By all accounts Peter Montgomery was a prize bastard and from what we've been told, anyone could have done the deed. I'd love to know who fathered that baby, though. And where it is now. No, she's better off without him, I'd say. Pity about her face. She'd be a fine-looking woman without that scar.' He looked up at Myrna's house. 'She should find herself more salubrious lodgings, if she wants to keep her reputation.'

'I don't know,' said Sergeant David wistfully. 'It looked quite nice to me. I liked that statue at the bottom of the stairs.'

Childs looked at him and shook his head.

The following day Tamar received a note from Peter's lawyer offering his condolences and requesting her presence at his rooms in Victoria Street the following afternoon.

Myrna volunteered to go with her and the next day Sven drove them into town in the landau. Tamar was wearing a hastily acquired black mourning gown, hat and gloves, all purchased with money provided by Myrna, and had arranged her hat so the veil concealed much of her face in the traditional fashion of widowhood. Tamar felt very little grief for Peter's passing but the veil covered her scar nicely.

The lawyer, Mr Mahoney, was small, dapper, concerned and sincere. 'Thank you so much for coming in, Mrs Montgomery,' he said to Tamar after she and Myrna had been seated in his office and served with tea. 'I learned of your whereabouts from Detective Childs. I hope my intrusion at this difficult and trying time has not inconvenienced you.' He fussed with some papers on his desk before he continued. 'I understand how bereft you must feel, but there are certain issues regarding Mr Montgomery's unfortunate and untimely demise that I am compelled to impart to you in my capacity as your late husband's lawyer.' He looked embarrassed and cleared his throat. 'Mrs Montgomery, are you aware of the state of your late husband's financial affairs?'

Tamar lifted her veil slightly, took a sip of tea, put her cup down and shook her head. 'No, Mr Mahoney, I am not. Mr Montgomery did not consider it necessary to share that information with me.'

'Ah. I see,' said Mr Mahoney. 'Then in that case it is my duty to do so.' He pressed his hands together as if praying, his fingertips against his lips, and lowered his eyes before he continued. 'I am afraid I have to tell you he died owing a considerable sum.'

He looked up to gauge Tamar's reaction and glimpsed her large eyes looking unwaveringly at him through the dark net of her veil. 'It appears he was a gambler, Mrs Montgomery.'

Myrna rolled her eyes in disgust.

'I know he played the occasional game of cards.'

'I mean he was a *serious* gambler. He lost a lot of money at the gaming tables. So much, in fact,' continued Mr Mahoney apologetically, as if Peter's financial incompetence was his fault, 'he had to borrow a considerable sum against the property at Huia and another large sum from a business associate, Mr Thomas Beck.'

Tamar thought back to her cryptic conversation with Thomas Beck at the Coulthards' dinner party. Where she met Kepa. 'I've met Mr Beck. A very pleasant man,' she replied.

'Indeed. I provided the legal services for the loan from Mr Beck, and I was aware of the monies owed to the bank. When Detective Childs advised me of Mr Montgomery's tragic demise, I accessed his bank accounts and, unfortunately, there is very little left. Nothing in his personal account and very little in his business account. There is no easy way to say this, Mrs Montgomery, but the bank will foreclose on the property at Huia and sell it to recoup the money loaned to Mr Montgomery, and the balance will go to Mr Beck to repay his loan. Based on current land values, there will be an outstanding amount owing to Mr Beck of around seven thousand pounds. And there are several outstanding accounts at various businesses, which brings the total amount owed to almost nine thousand pounds.' Mr Mahoney could not bring himself to tell Mrs Montgomery one of the outstanding accounts was for her wedding dress and trousseau. He reluctantly added, 'Mr Montgomery made no provision for your financial welfare. There was an insurance policy but this was cancelled in December and the money withdrawn. I'm sorry.'

That *bloody* bastard, thought Myrna.

Tamar was stunned. 'I don't have nine thousand pounds.'

Mr Mahoney felt desperately sorry for her. He had advised strongly against Peter taking on such a massive level of debt but to no avail. 'There may be ways in which you could raise the money. I may be of some help — I would waive my fee, of course.'

'That willnae be necessary,' Myrna said quickly. 'I have considerable financial means o' ma own, Mr Mahoney, and I will be assisting Mrs Montgomery out o' these dire financial straits in which her late husband has so thoughtfully left her.'

'Myrna, no,' said Tamar, shaking her head. 'I'll come up with it one way or another. I can talk to the bank.'

'Ye'll do no such *thing*. How can ye? Ye'll be saddled wi' debt for the rest of your days. Use that brain o' yours, lassie, and get off your high horse. Ye've been dropped in it, so ye have, so let me help ye out o' it.'

Bravo, thought Mr Mahoney. He had heard Myrna McTaggart, madam of the finest brothel in Auckland, was doing very well for herself. He was intrigued to see the gossip was true — the fiery little Scotswoman was not only a successful and very acute businesswoman but generous as well. He wondered if she was happy with her current lawyer.

'Mr Mahoney, will ye be so kind as to furnish me wi' an itemised list o' the monies owed. Down to the last penny. Mrs Montgomery and I will go to the bank to discuss the sale o' the land at Huia and the repayment o' her husband's loans. When the outstanding debt is finalised, I will pay it. Through you. I dinnae wish the entire town to ken where the money is coming from, d'ye understand?'

'Of course, Miss McTaggart. And will the money be in the form of a loan?'

'No. In the form o' a gift, Mr Mahoney.'

'You are a very generous woman, Miss McTaggart.'

'To those who matter to me. I would appreciate that list o' debts as soon as possible, delivered to ma place o' business. Ye ken where that is?'

'I do indeed. I will have it prepared and delivered before noon tomorrow.'

On the way to Peter's bank, Tamar turned to Myrna and said, 'Thank you, Myrna. Again. But you have to let me repay the money somehow.'

The older woman smiled. 'Och, but ye *will* pay it back, lassie, but no' in cash. Ye'll be learning to take care o' the financial side o' ma business. I believe it's time I slowed down and put ma feet up. I'm no' getting any younger, and I need a hand now the house is doing so well. But we must get John to have another look at your face. I cannae have ye representing ma business looking like Frankenstein's monster.'

Tamar was not insulted; she knew she looked odd. But she was reluctant to approach John in case he was unable to do anything about improving her scar. This, she knew, was a resurrection of an old behaviour; hiding from what she didn't want to confront. Damn, she thought, I'll *have* to face up to it. Then she smiled. *Face* up to it. That was quite funny, really. 'I know,' she said. 'I'll send a note and ask him to come tomorrow if he's not too busy.'

The visit with the bank manager was successful. He was solicitous and full of concern for Tamar's financial position, although clearly anxious to recoup the loan he had advanced to Peter. He agreed to arrange the sale of the land at Huia as soon as possible — he thought it would not be difficult as the land still encompassed many fine *kauri* stands — and confirmed he would start the process immediately. He also offered his condolences, which Tamar accepted graciously, but when he suggested his bank may be able to lend her money to pay the balance of Peter's debts, she declined.

'Thank you, but I will honour those myself,' she had replied, wondering if she was the only person in the North Island of New Zealand who had not known Peter owed money all over the place.

That afternoon she wrote John Adams a short note asking him to call, and had Sven deliver it to his clinic. A reply came back immediately; he would attend Tamar the following morning.

She felt nervous as she sat in the parlour waiting for him. On a slightly irrational level she suspected her scar was God's punishment for her adultery; she deserved to be disfigured and should carry the mark of her sins for the rest of her days. The pragmatic side of her character, growing stronger every day, told her not to be so silly; the scar was the result of her face coming into contact with an iron fender and if the disfigurement could be improved, then it should. Although John had already said he could do something about it, she worried the scar may be irreparable. Then she worried about the extent of her vanity, remembering how her susceptibility to flattery, and her naive and unrealistic vision of life, had gotten her into this situation. To stop the incessant chatter in her head, she made tea and sliced some cake for John for when he arrived.

Half an hour later he did, out of breath and full of apologies. 'An emergency,' he said, flinging his gloves and hat onto the sideboard and collapsing onto the sofa. 'On the wharf. A winch line broke and took out the eye of one of the wharf-hands. He refused to go to the hospital, insisting he'd rather come and see me. I couldn't save the eyeball, it had been ruptured, but I think the socket should heal cleanly enough for a prosthesis. Is that cake for me? Good, I'm starving. I haven't had breakfast.'

Finally, after two quick cups of tea, John examined Tamar's face. He prodded gently and pulled the scarred tissue this way and that as he considered the best approach. 'Have you got a hand mirror?' he asked Myrna. Eliza was despatched to find one. When it arrived

John gave it to Tamar to hold in front of her face.

'What I can do,' he said, indicating the worst of the scarring, 'is to excise this lumpy bit and suture the edges evenly together to minimise the disruption to your brow. And I'll line your eyebrow back up so it will match the other one. I'll have a go at excising this bit of scar from your eyelid as well so you can open your eye properly, although that might be a bit trickier. And I might as well nip out this lumpy bit on your cheek while I'm at it. It won't be perfect, you'll still have a noticeable scar, but that should fade to a white line, and your face won't look crooked and dragged down any more. How does that sound?'

Tamar thought it sounded wonderful.

Myrna asked, 'And ye said she'll be needing … what did ye say?'

'Ether. Yes, I couldn't do it while she's awake.' He turned to Tamar. 'You'll see the scalpel and the needle and won't be able to relax. Your facial muscles must be completely at rest, or the layers of tissue and muscle under the skin won't line up properly when I suture them. Anyway, it will be very painful. Best you're asleep, I think.'

Tamar nodded in wholehearted agreement.

John continued, helping himself to a fourth slice of cake. 'I've talked to Basil Stokes, my colleague,' he said, with his mouth full. 'He's agreed to manage the ether while I'm operating. But I should tell you that using ether has its own problems. Not enough and the patient can wake up, too much and the opposite can happen.'

'Ye mean it could kill her?' said Myrna in alarm.

'Well, technically, yes. But we won't be needing huge doses. After all, we're not taking her leg off.'

Sometimes Tamar hated John's relentlessly cheerful attitude towards his work.

'But I trust Basil,' John went on. 'He's a fine physician, and this procedure will need someone who knows what he's doing. So, when would you like to do it?' he asked, looking at Tamar.

'Ah,' she said, dithering nervously. 'I'm not sure.'

'Then I'll decide for you. The sooner we do it the better, while the tissues around the scar are still pliable. They'll stiffen eventually, which will make the procedure more complicated and possibly less successful. Friday afternoon suit you?'

'*This* Friday?' asked Tamar. It was Wednesday now.

John nodded. 'I have a clinic in the morning but I can be here at one. We'll perform the procedure in your private room, then we can avoid moving you afterwards. And it's clean here, although we'll have to cleanse your room thoroughly before we start. Can Eliza do that, Myrna?'

'Aye.'

'Right then, Friday it is. Tamar, I want you to rest, drink gallons of fluids but no alcohol, and don't go out. I don't want you to run the risk of catching a cold.'

Tamar nodded.

'Until Friday then, ladies,' said John, gathering up his things. 'I must rush, I have an advanced case of haemorrhoids to look at, in the backside of a rather important local personage. I've told him to stop eating dried apricots, but has he heeded my learned advice? No, and now he has excruciatingly painful piles the size of a bunch of table grapes. Still, it's money, isn't it?'

'And that reminds me, John,' said Tamar. 'How much will this procedure cost?'

John waved his hand dismissively. 'Nothing. You're my friend and I never charge my friends for my services.'

Tamar's eyes filled with tears as he left. 'He's such a good man,' she said eventually.

'Aye, lassie, he is.'

Friday was a bitterly cold August day. Nervous and unable to sleep, Tamar rose early and busied herself lighting fires and opening doors to allow the heat to disperse throughout the rooms. Myrna had offered Tamar her private quarters at the top of the house for the surgery and her recuperation. Her own small room was at the back of the house on the ground floor, where she would be disturbed by Eliza and Sven as they worked.

John and Basil Stokes arrived at the appointed time and went upstairs to lay out their surgical equipment, while Tamar sat nervously in the kitchen. The girls sat with her, hushed and serious-looking. Polly, in a voice that was almost a whisper, said, 'We'll be praying for you, Tamar.'

Myrna bustled in, took one look at the long faces and clapped her hands loudly, giving everyone a fright. 'Right!' she said. 'Enough o' this doom and gloom. She's having her scar repaired, no' her head removed. Bronwyn, ye and Letitia have customers at two o'clock. Had ye no' better start getting ready for them? Come on, the rest o' ye, out o' here.'

'But we're worried about Tamar,' complained Jessica.

'Och, but sitting around behaving like she's already died isnae going to help her! John assures me there's nothing to worry about, so out ye go.'

When the girls had left, Myrna sat next to Tamar and took her hand. 'Are ye a wee bit frightened, lassie?' she asked kindly.

Tamar shook her head. 'I trust John implicitly. I'm a bit nervous about the ether, but no, I feel quite calm. If God intended me to die young I'm sure that would have happened back at Huia.'

'Oh, we're talking to God again now, are we?'

'Let's just say I'm considering a penny each way.'

Myrna laughed. 'I dinnae blame ye, lassie.'

They heard a polite cough and turned to see Basil Stokes standing at the kitchen door. He was tall and thin with a long face, slightly protruding teeth and fine, pale hands. 'We're ready for you now, Miss Deane,' he said hesitantly.

He led the way upstairs to Myrna's room and ushered them both in. John, standing next to an array of surgical instruments laid out on a cloth-covered nightstand, turned and smiled. 'Ah, Tamar, could you change into your nightdress now, please? Will you be staying, Myrna?'

'Aye, just until she's asleep.'

'Righto,' said John cheerfully. 'We'll let Tamar get ready.'

He and Basil left the bedroom while Tamar undressed. Myrna's bed had been moved to one side and a narrow table set up in the middle of the room and covered with several plain white sheets. The carpets had been rolled back and a strong smell of cleaning fluid permeated the air.

'Eliza's done a good job,' prattled Tamar nervously as she slipped her nightdress over her head. 'We could eat off that floor.'

'I'm no' that hungry, maself,' replied Myrna.

John knocked discreetly and called out, 'Ready?'

'Aye,' Myrna called, and John and Basil came back in. They helped Tamar onto the table and covered her with a sheet, then John took a crisp white cloth and tucked it snugly around her hairline so her face alone was exposed.

John's surgical instruments were positioned to one side of the table, while Basil had set up his equipment on the other. He settled his skinny frame into a straight-backed chair and picked up the portable ether inhaler. It was an odd-looking contraption and Myrna eyed it doubtfully. 'Oh, aye, and how does that work?' she asked.

'*Well*,' said Basil, his long face suddenly alive with enthusiasm. 'First I employ this reservoir bag at the side, which is filled with nitrous oxide, which puts the patient to sleep. The ether goes into this chamber here, which can be rotated around the inhaler, this mask part which goes over the patient's mouth and nose. And by rotating the chamber, different amounts of ether can be administered as required. The ether is what *keeps* the patient unconscious. It's a marvellous invention; it makes the delivery of the correct amount much more reliable.'

'Really,' said Myrna, winking at Tamar.

John tied a small cloth mask over his own mouth and nose.

'He's no' knocking *you* out as well, is he?' asked Myrna.

'Well, hardly,' replied John through his mask, too preoccupied to notice she was joking. 'This is to help prevent any bacteria I might be carrying on my breath from coming into contact with the patient while I'm operating. It's a relatively new idea but you can't be too careful with open wounds.'

'Aye, well, if ye say so,' replied Myrna doubtfully.

John signalled to Basil he was ready to begin. As Basil carefully placed the mask over Tamar's mouth and nose, she grasped Myrna's hand tightly, her eyes widening in last-minute panic.

'There, there, lassie,' crooned Myrna. 'I willnae let anything happen to ye.'

Basil manipulated the reservoir bag into position, and as Tamar breathed in her one good eyelid began to droop. She struggled briefly against the nitrous oxide filling her lungs, then dropped rapidly into unconsciousness. Basil quickly lifted her eyelids to check she was properly out, then began to administer the ether.

Myrna was a little disconcerted at the speed with which Tamar had gone under. 'Is she all right?'

'Oh, yes,' replied John. 'Basil?'

'She's fine. I'll be taking her pulse every minute or so. If she goes blue around the lips I'll ease off with the ether, and if she stirs I'll give her more. Simple.'

'I bloody well hope so,' said Myrna. 'Tell me when ye've finished. I'll be downstairs in ma office. I dinnae think I can watch this.'

John waited until Myrna had gone before he tilted Tamar's head and made the first incision above her right brow. A line of bright red blood welled up and ran down into the cloth wrapped around her hair. John began excising the scar, cutting deftly as he went. 'Pulse?' he asked after a minute.

'Fine,' replied Basil.

They worked in silence for the next forty minutes, oblivious to noise from the street or the floors below. As John cut out each thick ridge of scar tissue, he sutured the edges of the wound with fine catgut threaded through a slim, curved needle. Basil removed the mask from Tamar's mouth and nose from time to time to minimise the possibility of her facial skin being pulled out of shape while John stitched. As he carefully removed the scar from the delicate skin of Tamar's eyelid, he broke into a heavy sweat and beads of moisture ran down his face. Basil leaned over and mopped up the worst of it. 'Nervous, John?'

'A little. I've done this before, but never on someone I've cared so much about. I'd hate to cock it up.'

'Is this the girl you were hoping to marry?'

'Yes, but I'm not so sure now.'

'Really? Why not?'

'Well, for a start, I don't think she wants to marry me. She's changed, I don't think she's the girl I used to know any more. Pass me that sponge, will you? I still care very deeply for her, but perhaps we were always destined to be nothing more than good friends. She's very dear to me, though. Very dear,' he added softly.

Basil grunted again, knowing his friend well enough not to poke his nose in where it wasn't wanted.

John worked silently for a further ten minutes, tied off his last suture, blotted the few remaining drops of blood oozing from the fresh wounds, then stepped back to admire his work. 'What do you think?'

Basil squinted at Tamar's face for a moment. 'It's a vast improvement. Just her eyebrow being aligned again helps. And if the new scar on her eyelid doesn't thicken up too much, she should regain full use of it.' He looked up at his friend. 'Are you happy with it?'

John nodded. 'She's young and her skin is still elastic. Providing she keeps her face still while the new scars are healing, the result should be pretty good.'

He removed the bloodied cloth from Tamar's hair and positioned several layers of fine cotton padding over the new wounds. Folding a strip to form a pad he gently placed this over Tamar's right eye to keep it closed, then re-wrapped her head in strips of white muslin until most of the right side of her face was bandaged. 'Can you stay with her while she wakes?' he asked. 'I'll go and let Myrna know we've finished.'

Basil nodded and took Tamar's pulse again. He had not administered ether for the last ten or twelve minutes and her eyelid was beginning to flutter. She shouldn't take long to come around, he thought. She would have a headache when she did, though; ether affected most people that way.

He looked up as Myrna and John entered the room, followed by three of the gorgeous young women he'd noticed earlier.

'Is she awake yet?' asked Myrna.

'Not quite. I'd say another ten minutes before Miss Deane is fully back with us,' replied Basil, feeling shy in front of the women and completely unable to stop himself from gazing down Bronwyn's inviting cleavage as she leaned over Tamar. 'John's done a marvellous job. Some of his best work.'

'Can I sit with her?' asked Myrna. 'Perhaps ye can clean yeself up and go and have a cup o' tea. Or something stronger if ye fancy it.'

'Thank you but no, I'll stay until Miss Deane is completely awake. But could I trouble you for a bowl of hot water and a towel? I'd like to wash my hands.'

'O' course. Eliza?'

As Eliza left to fetch the water, Myrna turned to John. 'And it went well?'

'Yes, I'm expecting a good result. I think she'll be pleased.'

'Pleased enough for her spirits to be lifted?'

'I hope so. The scars should be barely noticeable. She's not to bend or lift anything for the next week, or laugh or cry. Or yawn. Anything that will move her facial muscles, in fact. I'll drop in every day to change the dressings and keep an eye out for infection, and in eight or nine days I'll take the sutures out. She'll have a whopping headache for the rest of today, but that should have gone by late tonight. Give her some laudanum if she's in too much pain. Her face will hurt a bit but it shouldn't be too bad if she keeps still. And she can only eat soft food. I don't want her chewing at all if possible. I'm sure Eliza can come up with something suitable.'

As Tamar moaned weakly and moved her head, Basil leaned forward and chafed her cold left hand vigorously between his own.

'Miss Deane?' he called. 'Miss Deane, can you hear me?'

Tamar nodded slowly and licked her dry lips. As she opened her left eye Myrna stepped forward and took her other hand. 'It's all right, lassie. John's done a fine job and all's well. How d'ye feel?'

Tamar licked her lips again and croaked, 'I'm thirsty.'

As Myrna helped Tamar to slowly sit and sip from a glass of water, John and Basil cleaned and packed away their equipment. By the time they had finished Tamar was almost completely awake. They helped her off the table and over to Myrna's bed.

She lay back with her bandaged head against the pillows and the cover pulled up to her throat. Myrna had closed most of the curtains, making the room warm, cosy and dim.

'Polly, can ye sit with Tamar while I see John and Mr Stokes out?'

Polly dragged a chair over to the bed, pulling a face as it

screeched painfully across the polished wooden floor. 'Ooh, sorry, Tamar,' she said.

'It's all right, I'm not made of glass. Just a bit of a headache.'

'Does it hurt? Your face?' asked Polly.

'No. It feels numb at the moment.'

'Well, I suppose that's good then.'

'*I* think so,' said Tamar, trying not to smile. 'John?'

'I'm here,' he said from the door.

'Thank you. For this, and for everything. And you, Mr Stokes. Thank you for *your* help.'

'Think nothing of it, Miss Deane. It was an honour,' said Basil.

John said, 'Try to get some sleep now. I'll see you again tomorrow.'

He walked over to the bed and kissed Tamar's forehead gently, before he and Basil took their leave.

CHAPTER SIXTEEN

Nine days later Tamar sat nervously on the sofa as John removed her bandages. As the last one was unwound and the single remaining cotton pad peeled off, she picked up the hand mirror but held it in her lap. John and Myrna both carefully looked out the window. No one moved. The clock on the mantel ticked loudly.

'Shall we leave ye, lassie?' Myrna asked.

Tamar said, 'No, it's all right.' She took an audible breath and raised the mirror to her face. Saying nothing, she stared silently at her reflected image.

John held his breath.

Tamar said flatly, 'It's revolting.'

'Och, no, lassie, it's a *huge* improvement!'

Tamar lowered the mirror and smiled. 'Not my face, my *hair*! I haven't washed it in nearly two weeks and it's *disgusting*!'

John laughed. 'I'm glad to see you've got your sense of humour back. You're going to need it while I'm removing these sutures. And when I have you'll really be able to see the improvement.'

'I don't care, as long as they're out, they're itching like hell and my face has been still for so long I feel like a china doll.'

As Tamar lay back, John took out a tiny pair of sharp, curved scissors. 'Swelling's gone down a lot,' he remarked as he sat on a footstool next to the sofa. 'Now, this might sting, so try not to jump.'

Tamar lay perfectly still while John skilfully snipped and removed the dried, black stitches and dropped them into a small bowl. When he had removed the last one, he sponged away a few small spots of blood and helped Tamar up. 'There we are,' he said cheerfully. 'You can look in the mirror again.'

Tamar did. A wide smile stole across her face. She glanced up at Myrna and John, both of whom were also smiling, then looked back into the mirror and admired her new face. Or rather, her reconstructed old face. Gone was the thick ridge of scar that had grossly separated her right eyebrow and pushed down the eyelid underneath. In its place was a thin pink line, a little puffy and scabby, but the improvement was immense. The heavy scar under her eye had been replaced by a thinner suture line, already much less noticeable.

'Will it get any better?' she asked. 'Will the pink colour fade?'

'Yes,' said John, 'after about a year. All that will be left will be a few, thin white marks. Now, can you open your eyes as widely as possible?'

Tamar obliged and sat there looking like an owl while John manipulated her right eyelid.

'Now close your eyes, then open them again normally.'

Tamar's newly repaired eyelid slid up easily, only a very slight, almost undetectable droop indicating the presence of scar tissue.

'I just look as if I'm a bit sleepy,' she said delightedly into the mirror. 'And look at my eyebrows! I think they're more symmetrical than they were before!'

'Good, now ye can pluck them. Ye look like ye've two hairy caterpillars on your face.'

Tamar threw back her head and laughed, relishing the feeling of her cheek muscles stretching after so many days of immobility.

She jumped up and moved to John who was standing by the fire, smiling at her response.

As she embraced him she said, 'I can't thank you enough, John.'

As he began to speak she put her fingers to his lips.

'No listen, please,' she beseeched. 'I need to say this.' She took one of his hands in both of hers. 'I'd resigned myself to spending the rest of my life with the marks of Peter's anger on my face for all the world to see, and for a while I was convinced I deserved it. But then I realised I didn't. Not then, and certainly not now. I know I made a mistake. Several, in fact, but I refuse to go on paying for them. Those marks are gone now, thanks to you, and I feel clean again, inside and out. And that means I can start again.'

There was a loud honking noise as Myrna blew her nose into a handkerchief and wiped her eyes. Struggling to contain her emotions, she said briskly, 'Well, as that seems to be sorted, can I assume we can all get on wi' our lives? Ye've a lot o' bookwork to be learning, lassie.'

'Yes, but first,' said Tamar emphatically, 'I'm going upstairs to have a long bath and wash my hair.'

September 1881

Tamar took to the commercial machinations of Myrna's business like a duck to water. She'd always been competent with numbers, but until now had never had a chance to test her ability.

There was much more to Myrna's book-keeping than Tamar had realised. First, of course, there were the transactions regarding money coming into the business via the customers. Myrna kept meticulous records of who had visited when and what fee they had paid, but pointed out to Tamar such information was to remain strictly confidential, for obvious reasons. Tamar was highly amused to see fat little Harold McLeod, whom she had met at the Coulthards' dinner party, was a regular customer, and wondered which lucky girl serviced him. She also noted Thomas Beck had been once or twice, but did not find this quite so amusing as she had liked his pretty wife, Julia.

As well as money coming in, Myrna's books also detailed money going out, and it was a considerable sum. The girls were paid well, as were Eliza and Sven and other part-time staff. Eliza had originally been in charge of the laundry when the house had first opened but the amount of linen to be laundered became overwhelming and Myrna hired another servant just to manage that alone. There were also costs associated with the 'tools of trade', including imported French condoms, the girls' cosmetics, their costumes and food and drink, both for those living at the house and for the customers. Then there was repayment of the funds Myrna had borrowed to set up the business, as well as money paid out to ensure various officials turned a blind eye to the goings-on at Dilworth Terrace, although several of those not comfortable with accepting bribes opted for discreet complimentary visits.

Myrna also gave generously to several charities, but in strict anonymity. Tamar was surprised to see one of these was the Auckland refuge for 'fallen women'. When she asked Myrna why she donated so much, Myrna replied that she firmly believed that in order to attract money, one also had to give it away; and she gave to the women's refuge because she felt a deep empathy for the poor wretches. 'I've been in the gutter maself, ye ken,' she explained.

Going through the accounts and receipts for the girls' costumes one day, it occurred to Tamar that she could save Myrna a considerable amount of money if she made the girls' clothes herself.

'I can design and cut and sew as well as any dressmaker,' she said eagerly when she raised the idea with Myrna. 'And you wouldn't have to pay me. I could do them much cheaper than the woman who's making them now, and the girls wouldn't have to traipse into town for their fittings. And I'd really enjoy it. I haven't done any sewing for ages. All I'd need would be a decent sewing machine and a good source of fabrics. I'm sure Mr Ellis could be of help.'

Myrna was heartened to see Tamar's enthusiasm; her mood and general outlook had improved dramatically since her surgery, but Myrna still worried that with too much time on her hands she'd fret over her lost child. She suspected dressmaking, which she knew Tamar loved, would be therapeutic and constructive. 'Aye, well,' she replied. 'We could certainly do wi' cutting corners in terms o' overheads. It's a good idea, lassie, if ye're happy to do it.'

'I'd love to, and I just happen to have an advertisement for the latest in treadle sewing machines,' Tamar said innocently, whipping a square of newsprint cut from the *Auckland Weekly News* out of her pocket and thrusting it under Myrna's nose. 'The Home Shuttle American lock-stitch model. Jacob Joseph & Co in Wellington import them from Australia. The cost is three pounds seven and six, which is a lot, but listen to what it can do!' She took a deep breath and read enthusiastically from the advertisement. 'It can hem, fell, bind cord, braid, seam, tuck, ruffle, hemstitch, gather, or gather and sew on at the same time, and it sews silk, linen, woollen and cotton goods with silk, linen or cotton thread, and it comes with bobbins, an oilcan, screwdriver, five needles ...'

'Yes!' cried Myrna in exasperation. 'For God's sake, *yes*, ye can order one! Today, if it will shut ye up.'

Tamar beamed and hugged Myrna, then ran off to write to Jacob Joseph & Co immediately. Tomorrow, she would go into town to talk to Mr Ellis about fabrics and trimmings.

The next morning, however, Tamar received an unexpected

visitor. Getting ready to go out, she was carefully applying a smear of cosmetic cream to her scar. The last of the scabs had healed, leaving her with a thin pink line, but she was still a little self-conscious. She expected that by the time it faded to white she would have become used to it, but until then she would disguise it whenever she left the house.

Eliza knocked and poked her head around Tamar's door.

'There's a man 'ere ter see yer, Miss Tamar.' For some reason, Tamar had been 'Miss' to Eliza ever since her return to Auckland.

'A man?' replied Tamar curiously, turning away from her mirror. 'Who?'

Eliza shrugged. 'One of them Maoris.'

Tamar's heart pumped a massive, irregular beat as she stared at Eliza. '*What?*'

'Said 'is name's Tee Kar-ninny or somethin' like that.'

'Oh.' Tamar's hopes and heart rate plummeted, and she chided herself for being so foolish as to think it might have been anyone else.

'Do yer know 'im, or shall I send 'im on 'is way?'

'Did he say what he wants?' Tamar was flustered.

Eliza shook her head. 'Just that 'e needs ter see yer, if yer're available.'

'Tell him I'll be there in five minutes. Can you ask Myrna if I can use her office, please?'

'Do yer want Miss Myrna ter be there?'

'No, but can you tell her it's Kepa's uncle?'

'Oh,' said Eliza, intrigued. The girls all knew about Tamar's illegitimate son and the man who had fathered him, and the presence of his uncle was exciting news. She hurried down the hall to usher in Te Kanene, whom she had left standing on the front verandah, and to find Myrna.

Tamar sat angrily in front of her dressing table, looking through

263

her reflection into the silvered depths. Te Kanene? What on earth could he want? She screwed the lid back onto the pot of cosmetic cream, distractedly tucked a strand of hair behind her ear and stood up.

'Te Kanene,' she said coldly as she entered Myrna's office. The tattooed, imperious-looking Maori stood at the window, the sun behind him. When he stepped forward Tamar did not offer him her hand. Instead, she sat in a wing chair and indicated he should sit opposite her.

'Mrs Montgomery,' he began as he lowered himself onto the plush upholstery.

'Miss *Deane.*'

'As you wish,' replied Te Kanene.

Without preamble Tamar said, 'Where is my child?'

'He is safe,' said Te Kanene. He appeared to be contemplating something as he picked a loose thread off his immaculate trousers and flicked it onto the carpet. The late-winter sun streaming through the window glinted on the small gold hoop he wore in his ear. No greenstone today, observed Tamar irrelevantly.

Te Kanene looked up at her, his gaze steady. 'Miss Deane, I have matters of some importance I wish to discuss. I believe they would be better discussed in a civil manner. I appreciate your anger but ...'

'No, you do *not*,' Tamar shot back. 'He was not your child. How *could* you understand?'

Te Kanene drew in a composed breath and let it slowly out. 'I did not say I *understand* your anger, Miss Deane. I said I appreciate it.'

Tamar did not respond.

'May I continue?' he asked reasonably.

Tamar nodded, struggling to keep a firm grip on her emotions. He was right — there was no need for her to behave aggressively. 'Please go on.'

'I wish to discuss the child, but first I have been asked to pass

264

something on to you. From my nephew.' He withdrew a small, cloth-wrapped package from the inside pocket of his coat and passed it to Tamar.

She stared at it, making no move to open it. 'I had not expected any communication.'

'No,' said Te Kanene, his tone suggesting he would have preferred it that way himself.

Tamar began to unwrap the package. Cocooned inside the short length of fabric was a tiny flax *kete*, or bag, in which was nestled another small bundle. Unwrapping this, Tamar found another package which fitted easily into her palm. She felt as if she was playing a child's party game. Removing the final layer, she saw her amethyst pendant and earrings, with a folded piece of notepaper.

She opened the note slowly, feeling her heart lodge solidly in her throat, and read the date — January 1881. Her eyes caressed the large, flowing handwriting covering the page.

Tamar,

I do not know when or where this will find you. I am at Ahuriri (Napier) waiting for my ship to be provisioned and fitted for a voyage to Ingarangi. I will be away for a long time — possibly a year. I have been told you are with child. I assume it is mine.

You know I cannot be with you at this time. I regret that. You must do what you think best. Te Kanene may be able to help you.

Take care of yourself, Tamar. I have not, and will not, forget our time together. I will see you again.

He had signed the note *Arohanui, K,* followed by a short postscript:

I believe these are your missing pieces of jewellery. I saw them displayed in the window of a pawnshop in Auckland, so I am returning them to you.

Tamar read the note again, more slowly, this time, then looked at Te Kanene.

'Did you know he knew I was expecting a child?'

'Yes. He told me before he left for England.'

Tamar lifted a hand and absentmindedly massaged the scar on her brow.

Te Kanene commented, 'May I say your face is much improved.'

'How do you know about that?' asked Tamar in surprise. Then she remembered. 'Oh. When you came to Kainui?'

'Yes, but you were still sick. You did not know me.'

'You came to the village to take my baby?'

'Te Hau, Riria's father, summoned me. Riria was against my taking the child.'

Tamar was once again flooded with feelings of gratitude and affection for Riria. She realised she missed her friend very much.

She said suddenly, 'Did you know my husband is dead? Perhaps murdered?'

Te Kanene examined the blunt but beautifully manicured fingernails on his right hand for several seconds. 'Yes. I had heard something.'

'Who killed him?'

He shrugged elegantly but said nothing.

'Was it you?' pressed Tamar.

'No.'

Tamar believed him. If it had not been Te Kanene, she thought, and Kepa was in England, then it could have only been one other person. 'Riria,' she said quietly.

'You must try and understand the concept of *utu*,' said Te Kanene impassively.

'Are you telling me it *was* Riria?' said Tamar, looking at him sharply.

'I was not there, so I cannot say,' he replied, although Te Hau

266

had in fact informed him of exactly what his headstrong daughter had done to the *Pakeha*. 'But if she did, she would have had her own reasons. *Utu* is not taken lightly. Do you care by whose hand he died?'

'I suppose not,' replied Tamar. 'Where is my child?'

Te Kanene gazed at her, as if contemplating how much he should tell her, then seemed to come to some sort of decision. 'He is living at Maungakakari, our family's village in Hawke's Bay, just north of Napier. He is being cared for by my *tamahine*, Kepa's sister. She and her husband have no children of their own.'

'And he is safe and healthy?'

Te Kanene nodded. 'Yes, he is well. We have named him Kahurangi-o-te-po.'

'What does that mean?'

'Roughly translated it means blue cloak of the night sky.'

Tamar considered the name then nodded in approval.

She hesitated before she asked, 'Who does he look like?'

'His father, but he has green eyes. Like yours,' replied Te Kanene. 'You do understand why I had to take him?' he added, his voice almost gentle.

Tamar sighed. 'No, not really. I only know that when I discovered he had been taken from me I almost gave up. I could have raised him. A baby needs his mother.'

'No, a baby needs *a* mother,' corrected Te Kanene, comfortably secure in the customs and traditions his people had lived with for generations. 'Not necessarily the woman who gave birth to him. Where would you have gone with him? You could not have returned to Auckland with an illegitimate half-caste child to raise.' He paused and reached into his coat again. 'May I smoke?' When Tamar nodded he drew out a pipe, forcefully tamped in a wad of tobacco and lit it before continuing. 'And Kahurangi-o-te-po is no ordinary child. He is the first son of the first son of my brother Te Roroa, a powerful chief. He has to be raised in a certain way.'

'I could have gone to Hawke's Bay with him.'

'No,' said Te Kanene bluntly. 'You are too *Pakeha*. And there is Kepa.'

'What about Kepa?'

'He has work to do. He cannot afford to be distracted by such trifling issues as lust and love. And he would have been, with you there.'

'How can you be so sure?'

Te Kanene made a wry face. 'Because, Miss Deane, I know my *iramutu* well. I would have to be blind and deaf not to know how he feels about you. And if he *is* to marry, then he must marry a woman of his own race.'

'You *sent* him to England, didn't you?'

'Yes,' Te Kanene replied shamelessly. 'For his own good. And yours, although I do not expect you to thank me.'

'No, I certainly won't,' replied Tamar angrily. 'I think you're a crafty, selfish, interfering old buzzard.' Tamar had never seen a buzzard but she imagined that if she did, it would look and behave exactly like Te Kanene.

He nodded his head and smiled slightly, as if she had complimented him. 'You will see one day that I have made the right decision. For everyone.'

Tamar was interrupted by a knock on the office door. Myrna poked her head into the room and asked, 'Everything all right, is it?'

Tamar stood. 'Yes,' she said. 'Myrna, this is Kepa's uncle, Te Kanene. Te Kanene, this is my good friend Miss Myrna McTaggart.'

Te Kanene rose and bowed low over Myrna's outstretched hand. 'Good morning, Miss McTaggart,' he said. 'I am very pleased to meet you.'

'And I you,' replied Myrna politely. 'Can I get ye anything?'

'No, thank you, Miss McTaggart. I have almost finished my business here.'

Myrna looked over Te Kanene's shoulder at Tamar and raised her eyebrows. Tamar mouthed, 'It's all right,' and Myrna responded with an almost imperceptible nod.

'I'll leave ye to it then,' she said and left the room.

'I would like to be kept informed of my son's progress. You cannot deny me that.'

'No,' he agreed. 'I will not keep news of his health and welfare from you. Do I assume correctly you will be living here for some time?'

'Yes, for the foreseeable future.'

'Then, as his guardian, I will send word at regular intervals. But I will ask you not to contact him during these early years. It will only confuse him. He is better off where he is, a slightly pale, green-eyed Maori child living amongst Maori, than a brown-skinned child living amongst *Pakeha*.' When Tamar looked at him doubtfully, he added, 'I know what I am talking about. You have not been in Aotearoa long enough to appreciate what I mean. When he gets older he will be told. He can make his choices then, when he is mature enough to manage the consequences. But I suspect he will always be more his father's son than yours.'

Tamar knew that if her son were to be raised a Maori, this would indeed be the case, and the thought hurt her badly. But, her heart aching with a sense of loss that was almost physical, she suspected Te Kanene was right.

She asked sadly, 'Will he get the best of care?'

'Of course.'

'I want to meet him when he is older. And I want to contribute towards his upkeep,' Tamar added. 'I am his mother and I will not allow that to be forgotten or ignored. He also has Cornish blood in his veins. He has a heritage other than yours.'

'There is no need for you to give money, if that is what you mean. My family has more than enough.'

'And so will I, eventually,' replied Tamar with a blossoming sense of dignity. She didn't know if what she had just said was true, but the idea suddenly appealed to her very much. 'If you choose not to use it now, I will have it placed in a trust fund for his education. I insist that he receive the very best.'

'Oh, he will, there is no doubt. This child will carry on the work of his father, and his father before him.'

'Good,' said Tamar. 'I'm glad we agree.'

Te Kanene nodded. 'I think, Miss Deane, we agree on more than you care to admit. We are both committed to this child's welfare. You are his natural mother, and you are right — that cannot be forgotten. And so we will work together for his benefit.'

Tamar sighed, partly in relief and partly in annoyance. Intuitively she knew he would be a powerful, if perhaps not always loyal, ally.

Te Kanene rose. 'I will leave now,' he said. 'I feel we have come to an understanding.'

'Yes, Te Kanene, we have. For now,' replied Tamar, standing herself and escorting him to the front door. As she opened it he turned and took her hand, a formal handshake, nothing intimate, his piercing eyes looking directly into hers. Tamar could clearly see Kepa in him.

'You are a strong woman, Tamar Deane,' he said. 'I see it, my nephew sees it, and your son will also see it one day. You must make that strength work for you.'

He let go of her hand and descended the steps. As he turned at the gate and walked off down the street, Tamar stood looking after him, long after he had disappeared.

CHAPTER SEVENTEEN

February 1882

'Stand still, will you, Polly?' said Tamar through a mouthful of dressmaking pins.

'But it's so *hot*,' complained Polly, the breeze from the lace fan she was flapping in front of her face barely touching the sweat trickling down her neck. The French doors were wide open but the mid-morning air was heavy. 'I wish it would rain.'

It was an abnormally hot, humid Auckland day and Tamar was putting the final touches to a new gown. The bustle had disappeared completely from fashion and this new dress had tight three-quarter-length sleeves and a fitting bodice above a flaring, princess-line skirt. Unlike most gowns of the day, however, this one was made from fine, slightly transparent pale green muslin, which accentuated Polly's shapely figure and offered a hint of the pleasures beneath. Fashionable evening gowns were already cut low in the bodice but this one was exceptionally daring, the neckline not quite covering Polly's upthrust breasts and nipples. The dress was saved from vulgarity by a swathe of semi-opaque gauze draped around the neckline, but if one looked hard enough Polly's large brown nipples were still visible, which was of course the intention.

When Tamar had begun sewing the girls' costumes last year,

Myrna had stipulated they should be alluring and a little risqué, but not whorish. The idea was to tempt the customers, not excite them beyond the point of no return before they even got upstairs.

Tamar sat back on her heels and wiped the sweat from her own brow. The faint scent of honeysuckle wafted in through the open doors on a slight breeze that died almost before it reached her. She opened the collar of her dress and blew down her cleavage but found scant relief.

Just before Christmas she had decided she'd had enough of wearing widow's weeds and, flouting convention, had made herself several fashionable, prettily coloured dresses, wearing them well before her year of mourning was officially over. As she now lived and worked at a brothel, she hardly thought it would make any difference to what people thought of her.

'I've got a headache,' moaned Polly. 'I need some of my medicine.'

Tamar frowned. Polly had been needing a lot of her 'medicine' lately. 'Well, have some then,' she replied, 'if it will make you stand still. You're supposed to be wearing this dress tonight.'

'I *know*,' snapped Polly. She stepped off the low stool, went to her dressing table and pulled open a small drawer. Selecting a flat, brown glass bottle she removed the cork and took an unmeasured swig. And then another. And then one more.

'Just for luck,' she said. As she replaced the cork she noticed the bottle was almost empty. 'Bugger, I'll have to get some more. I'll go up the street later.'

'To the pharmacy?' asked Tamar. When Polly nodded she said, 'I'll come with you — I need to get one or two things myself.'

Tamar was worried about Polly. Since before Christmas, her friend had become progressively sadder and more lethargic; rarely now did anyone see the happy, carefree Polly, except for when she was working. Between two in the afternoon and one the following morning when the house was open for business, she was vivacious, sparkling, witty and very popular with the customers. She was in demand and very busy, sometimes accommodating five or more men in one day, and none had ever complained they were not getting their money's worth.

Tamar and Myrna both sensed that, for some reason, Polly was frantically throwing herself into her work, but neither had been able to find out why. Myrna had talked to her several times but she insisted she was fine and merely anxious to build up her nest egg; she still talked, though less frequently, about owning a parlour with ostrich feathers in a vase on the mantelpiece, and a special chair by the fire for Cabbage.

Myrna had not been satisfied with Polly's explanation. She confided to Tamar that even though Polly was popular, she might have to insist she stand down from working if she continued to show signs of being, as Myrna put it, 'no' quite right in the head'.

And on occasion, Polly was quite obviously that. The girls had made a habit of meeting around the kitchen table on Sunday afternoons, the only day they did not work, to talk about anything they needed to air, usually their customers. They started drinking tea or coffee but as the afternoon wore on they would often open the gin or sherry. The tone was usually lighthearted and occasionally hilarious, but several Sundays ago something disconcerting had occurred.

On this particular Sunday Polly started drinking early but instead of being lifted by the alcohol, she seemed to withdraw into herself, barely smiling whenever one of the girls told a particularly amusing anecdote that would have the others almost crying with laughter.

The girls delighted in entertaining each other with stories of their various customers. Myrna knew it was irreverent, and unkind to the men, but they would never know and she firmly believed it helped her girls banish or at least contain any unpleasant feelings they might harbour about their profession; to mock the men they serviced helped them regain their sense of power. So she encouraged it and laughed with them, sometimes even contributing amusing stories from her own past.

'What I hate,' said Vivienne, 'is when they won't hurry up and do the business. I put such a lot of effort into them before they hop on, so I won't have to lie there forever, but this one customer, Mr Reece — the one with the really hairy back and the awful breath?'

The other girls, who did indeed know Mr Reece, groaned in sympathy.

'Well, last time I had him he just would *not* finish. But the closer he got to it the heavier he breathed on me and it was *revolting*. It was so foul I had to keep on throwing my head from side to side to get away from it. I think he thought I was writhing in passion. And I couldn't help it but I started saying no, no, no! And he started saying yes, yes, yes! And he seemed to like it so I went *no, no, no* and he went *yes, yes, yes*, and we started to sound like a train pulling out of the railway station. I had a terrible time not going Whoooo*oooh*!'

The girls, all except Polly, were giggling madly by this time.

'I had Perry Thompson last night,' said Bronwyn. Perry Thompson was a customer in his mid-thirties, single, financially well off and rather handsome. He was not unpopular, but he had a rather inflated opinion of his appeal to the opposite sex and an unfortunate misconception regarding his sexual prowess. At every intimate encounter with the girls — and they *had* compared notes — he would disrobe, flourish his penis proudly and say, 'How's *that*?' in a triumphant tone. The girls would all make appropriate noises of appreciation and anticipation and Perry Thompson, secure in his conviction that he was about to provide a truly memorable treat, would throw himself enthusiastically into the sexual act and go away very pleased with himself.

'I quite like Perry,' said Letitia. 'I feel a bit silly going *ooh* and *aah* every time he drops his trousers, but he's harmless. And he thinks he's giving us something special, so that's nice.'

'Unlike that Gareth Hunt,' added Jessica. 'He's an odd one.' She turned to Myrna. 'I really don't like him, he scares me.'

'What is it ye dinnae like?' asked Myrna, concerned. Gareth Hunt was a new but frequent customer and she had not yet had the opportunity to form her own opinion of his character, something she always liked to do.

'I can't quite put my finger on it,' replied Jessica. 'He seems so ... angry. I usually feel comfortable with the customers, but not with him. Sometimes I get the feeling he'd like to beat the shit out of me.'

Several of the other girls nodded in agreement.

'He's no' violent though?' asked Myrna.

'No, he's rough, but not violent,' said Jessica. 'But I'm sure he could be. He doesn't like to cuddle. It's all *get your clothes off, get on the bed, open your legs* with him. All I can say is I'm glad I'm not his wife.'

'He's married?' asked Letitia in mild surprise.

Jessica nodded. 'He said something about a wife last time I was with him. It wasn't very nice either.' She shrugged and sipped her sherry. 'I don't know. Some men are just like that, I suppose.'

'They all are,' said Polly, gazing into her gin as if it held some great secret.

'Aggressive and nasty?' said Bronwyn in surprise. 'Not in my experience. Sad perhaps, and lonely. Or just randy. Well, the ones we see anyway, but not nasty.'

'Tamar's was a real bastard,' said Polly vehemently. 'Look what he did to her.'

'Aye, but he was verra ill, although I agree that's no' an excuse,' replied Myrna. She looked at Polly closely, observing her face was flushed and her eyes half closed. Too much gin, or something else?

'I'm glad he's dead,' replied Polly angrily. 'Aren't you, Tamar?'

Tamar thought for a minute. 'I don't really care. Not any more.'

Polly sat very still, the knuckles of the hand holding her glass white with tension.

'Well, I bloody do,' she said finally. 'And that Gareth Hunt's cut from the same cloth. What gives him the right to treat women the way he does?' she asked, looking around angrily. 'I know we're whores, but we're still people, aren't we?'

There was a brief, uncomfortable silence.

'Of course ye are, lassie,' said Myrna. 'And if ye dinnae like the way a customer's treating ye, say so and I'll have a word. I'll ban the man if I have to. Why, has someone had a go at ye?'

'*No!*' snapped Polly. 'Oh God, what's the point?'

She drained her glass, pushed her chair violently back from the table and rushed from the room, leaving the girls staring after her.

'What was that all about?' asked Letitia eventually.

'I dinnae ken, but the lassie's no' happy, is she?' said Myrna.

Tamar had agreed then and she agreed now. She finished pinning the hem of Polly's gown, wiped the sweat from her face again and looked up at her friend. 'That should do it. You can take it off. Shall we go out soon?'

Polly nodded as she let the dress drop to the floor and stepped out of it. Tamar went to stand in front of the open doors, holding her arms up to catch the faint breeze, keeping her back turned while Polly changed into street clothes.

'Shall we go to that new pharmacy on Parnell Road?' she asked over her shoulder. 'He has some lovely imported perfumes in the most beautiful crystal bottles.' She turned around to see Polly dressed and sitting on her bed, frowning. 'What? Would you rather go somewhere else?'

'No,' said Polly furtively. 'No, the new one's fine,' she added.

'All right then,' Tamar replied, slightly mystified. 'I'll meet you downstairs, shall I? I need to get changed.'

Polly nodded as Tamar went downstairs to her own bedroom. There, she selected a dress suitable for the street, changed and quickly put on walking shoes. Standing in front of her dressing-table mirror she turned sideways and ran her hand over her stomach, flat and taut again. And so it should be, she reflected — she'd given birth to her son over eight months ago now. Her breasts had remained fuller, however; Myrna said having a baby had matured her figure, and perhaps it had.

She felt a brief but sharp pain in the region of her heart, as she always did when she thought of her son. Te Kanene had been true to his word and had sent two letters describing the child's health and progress. The second letter, received several weeks ago, had been accompanied by a photograph. The image of a young Maori woman holding a very chubby, contented-looking baby was reasonably clear. The smiling woman's features were a more feminine version of Kepa's, and to Tamar's delight the infant did indeed look like his father.

When she had first taken the photograph out of the envelope, she had experienced a vicious pang of jealousy, bordering on nausea, at the thought of her son being nurtured by another woman. A note on the back of the photograph declared; *'My tamahine, Mereana, holding Kahurangi-o-te-po. You will not be able to see this, but his eyes are the same colour as yours.'* Tamar had been surprised that Te Kanene had provided this detail; for someone who had judged her unsuitable to raise her own son, he was treating her with a compassion she found incongruous and confusing.

She leaned towards the mirror and lifted her heavy fringe from her damp brow, inspecting the scar, which was indeed fading to a thin white line. Recently, she'd come to the realisation that she couldn't care less about it. She was alive, and that was enough.

She picked up her hat and gloves and went out into the hallway, wishing gloves were not so *de rigueur*. Her palms were damp with sweat, making the process of tugging on the thin, clinging fabric a chore. 'Ready?' she asked as Polly hurried down the carpeted stairs, her long georgette skirt swishing as she moved.

Polly nodded as she stood in front of the mirrored *étagère* in the foyer and tied the ribbons on her velvet-trimmed straw hat. Turning around she said, 'Yes. Let's go.'

The two women walked up Dilworth Terrace towards the intersection with York Street that would take them onto Parnell Road. To their left, through the pines growing on the slope hugging the shore, they could see the sea stretching into the hazy distance and Rangitoto Island squatting on the horizon. The street was still unpaved and the mud of winter had dried to hard, uneven furrows that frequently twisted the ankles of inattentive pedestrians. Tamar and Polly kept to the extreme edges where patches of grass were flourishing. Before long Polly had opened her fan and was flapping vigorously at her face again. 'It's too hot,' she grumbled. 'I'm sure it wasn't this hot last summer.'

Tamar couldn't remember whether it had been or not. 'It will pass,' she said. 'And then we'll all be moaning because it's too cold.'

'I won't,' replied Polly. 'I miss the cold.'

They walked in silence until they reached Parnell Road. The pharmacy was situated just up the hill from John's surgery. They sat for a while outside the shop in the shade of a verandah to catch their breath and recover from their walk. Several cabs went past, the horses sweating freely and their hooves kicking up small puffs of dust from the street. A gentleman passing on horseback raised his hat and nodded politely.

'Shall we go in?' asked Polly.

Tamar nodded and Polly followed her inside where the temperature was noticeably cooler. The lighting was soft, shining off a gleaming brass rail bordering a long glass-topped counter and polished mahogany woodwork. The shop interior was lined almost to the ceiling with shelves, labelled drawers and glass-fronted cabinets displaying an extensive selection of patent medicines, proprietary lines, cosmetics, perfumes and toiletries. At the rear was a dispensing counter, again of solid mahogany, backed by a large mirror in which the pharmacist could look to see who was in his shop when he had his back turned. The real pharmaceuticals, the raw powders, herbs, solutions and chemicals, were stored in glass bottles and jars in a small dispensary beyond the work bench. On the counter sat a range of goods for sale, including bottles of colourful pastilles for sore throats, and cachous — the small, perfumed sweets so popular with considerate smokers who worried their breath might offend. Tamar sniffed appreciatively, loving the rich combination of floral and chemical smells.

A young apprentice, smartly suited with a starched collar and tie and sporting a weedy ginger moustache, asked if he could be of assistance.

'Yes,' said Polly quickly. 'I'd like the chemist to make up four bottles of my usual, please. Decoction of Opium. For Miss Polly Jakes.'

'Four?' asked the assistant, his carroty eyebrows raised.

'Yes, thank you, four. I'm travelling shortly and do not know when I shall be able to replenish my stocks.'

Tamar looked at Polly in surprise. Travelling? Where?

'If madam could wait just one moment, please,' said the apprentice. 'I shall advise Mr Hillman of your request.'

He disappeared out to the dispensary. The bell over the door tinkled as a man and a woman entered the shop.

'Are you going somewhere?' whispered Tamar.

'No,' replied Polly. 'But if I get a couple of bottles at once, that saves me having to traipse up here every time I run out.'

'But it's a lie.'

Polly shrugged. 'Does it matter?'

The ginger-moustached apprentice reappeared with an older man whom Tamar recognised as Mr Hillman. 'Now,' he said. 'Which of you two ladies is wanting the Decoction of Opium?'

'I am,' replied Polly.

'Well,' he said, shaking his head slowly. 'I don't normally dispense that much at once.'

Polly favoured him with one of her most charming smiles. 'Well, you see, Mr Hillman, I'm going abroad shortly and I am concerned I will run out of my medicine before I reach my destination. I suffer grievously much of the time and the thought of having nothing to soothe my pain quite terrifies me.'

Mr Hillman asked, 'And where are you travelling to, Mrs … '

'Miss Jakes,' replied Polly chattily. 'I'm going back to England. My mother is unwell.'

Tamar, torn between embarrassment and astonishment at the glibness of Polly's deceit, looked away.

'You've patronised my shop before, have you not?' enquired Mr Hillman politely.

'Oh, yes. It's quite the best pharmacy in the area.'

'And I've prepared this for you several times, haven't I?'

Polly nodded and smiled ingenuously again. Mr Hillman looked at her, a slight frown on his face. As he opened his mouth to speak, Polly interjected. 'You will of course remember why I need my medicine? I have the misfortune to be chronically plagued by health problems peculiar to females.'

Mr Hillman shut his mouth.

Polly continued loudly. 'My monthly is very painful and prolonged. I just don't think I could cope without my medicine.

Shall I remind you of my symptoms? Will that be of help to you?'

The other couple in the shop, clearly listening, hurriedly turned their backs. Mr Hillman seemed lost for words. His young apprentice was bright red, his fair skin blushing hotly.

'No, no,' the chemist countered quickly, clearly mortified at the possibility that Polly might start describing the very personal details of her medical problems. 'No, I quite understand. Four bottles you need? One moment please.'

He hurried into his dispensary while the apprentice darted off to serve the new arrivals, a look of intense relief on his still-flushed face.

When Mr Hillman returned with four glass bottles containing Polly's medication, he took her money and said quickly, 'I'm sure this will do the trick, Miss Jakes. And I wish you well on your voyage and hope your mother regains her health.' He expertly wrapped the bottles in brown paper tied with pink string, and sealed the package with red wax.

'Thank you so much,' replied Polly graciously as he handed the parcel over the counter. 'Good day to you.'

Outside the shop, Tamar looked at her friend in dismay. 'You weren't like this when I first met you, Polly. You were as honest as the day is long. You've not been happy for ages, have you? Why not?' She pushed harder. 'Is it what you're doing at Myrna's?'

Polly was silent for a moment, looking away. Then she shrugged and said, 'I don't know. Most days now when I try to look forward, all I can see is emptiness. No future, no ostrich feathers, nothing. The only time I feel alive is when I'm working.' She lifted her parcel. 'Otherwise, this is the only thing that helps.'

Tamar had no idea what to say, although it was clear something was very wrong.

'I felt a little like that after I had Kahurangi. I know it helped me to talk about it with Riria. And Myrna. Perhaps you should talk about it, too. What's bothering you, I mean.'

'But that's the problem,' Polly replied in a flat voice. 'I don't *know* what's bothering me.'

Tamar thought back to something Myrna had said. 'Was it something that happened when you were working on the streets? Before Myrna found you?'

Polly averted her eyes from Tamar's gaze, shrugged again and said, 'I don't know. Let's go home now, shall we?'

But not before Tamar had seen the burst of panic and fear on her friend's pale face. She opened her mouth to say something, then thought better of it; now was not the time or the place. 'Come on then,' she said, and held out her elbow. Polly took it and they walked arm in arm back towards Dilworth Terrace.

Tamar knocked quietly on Myrna's bedroom door.

Eliza was worried. She said Myrna had not been down yet today, which was unusual, so she'd taken up a breakfast tray, knocked and left it outside the door several hours ago, thinking that perhaps Myrna was catching up on her sleep. She was normally in her office by nine o'clock and it was now almost twelve. Tamar knocked again, louder this time. 'Myrna? Are you awake?'

Silence. The breakfast had not been touched, the porridge congealed and the pot of tea stone cold.

'*Myrna*! Are you in there?'

Still no response. Tamar gently opened the door and looked inside. The drapes were drawn and she could see very little.

'Myrna?' she asked again as she went in. 'Are you awake?' There was a strange, coppery smell in the room.

'Tamar? Is that you, lassie?'

Myrna's voice was completely bereft of its normal volume and enthusiasm. Tamar approached the bed, a knot of unease forming in her stomach. In the gloom she could vaguely see Myrna lying on her back with the covers pulled up to her chin. 'Open the drapes, will ye? I'm no' feeling ma best.'

Tamar opened two sets of the heavy curtains, inviting the bright Auckland sunlight to flood the room. She had turned and was halfway back to the bed when she suddenly stopped. 'What's that on the floor?' she asked, shocked motionless.

Myrna turned her head laboriously and looked over the side of the bed. The oriental rug on the floor was stained with splatters of something red, spreading from under the bedclothes and dripping slowly down the mahogany of the bed base.

'Oh Christ,' said Myrna wearily and lay her head back on the pillows. 'Ye'd best get John.'

Tamar stepped over the mess on the carpet and carefully peeled back Myrna's blankets. The older woman lay in a soggy pool of dark blood, her sheets and nightdress saturated. 'My God, Myrna, what's happened? Have you cut yourself?' said Tamar, horrified.

'No, I think it's coming from ma insides. I cannae move. I'm in too much pain.'

Tamar ran to the door and screamed down the narrow stairs, '*Eliza*! Come quickly! *Anyone*!'

There was the sound of running feet and Letitia and Bronwyn appeared at the foot of the stairs. 'What? What?' cried Letitia, her eyes round.

'Myrna's bleeding! Get John! *Now*! Tell Sven to take you in the cart. Go on, *now*!'

Letitia disappeared and Tamar heard her running down the grand staircase, yelling for Sven at the top of her voice. Bronwyn came slowly into the room. When she saw Myrna she gasped and covered her eyes.

'Don't be pathetic, Bronwyn,' snapped Tamar. '*Help* me.'

Bronwyn reluctantly approached the bed, stepping gingerly

around the blood on the floor. 'What's happened? What's wrong with her?'

'Ye can speak to me, lassie. I'm no' dead,' said Myrna weakly, although she was deathly pale and her eyelids were fluttering.

'I think she's bleeding internally,' said Tamar over her shoulder. 'Help me get some cushions under her bottom.' She slid the pillows from under Myrna's head while Bronwyn snatched several cushions from the sofa. 'Now, when I lift her hips, get the pillows under her so her bottom half is higher than her top half. It might slow the bleeding.'

As Bronwyn did as she was told, they could hear a commotion outside. She ran to the window. 'Sven. He's not got the cart, he's riding bareback.'

'Is she all right?'

Tamar looked up to see Letitia, Eliza and the other girls crowded into the doorway of Myrna's room. 'No, I don't think so, but John will be here soon. Has anyone got smelling salts? I think she's fainting.'

As Eliza went for the salts, the girls moved hesitantly forward.

'I don't think we should crowd her,' said Tamar. 'Can everyone wait downstairs for a minute?'

'I want to see her,' said Jessica, big tears swimming in her eyes.

Tamar hesitated for a brief second then said, 'All right then, but only for a minute.' What if Myrna were to die and she'd stopped them all from saying goodbye? She pushed away the impossible thought of losing Myrna and bent down to the bed. 'Myrna? Can you hear me?'

'O' course I can hear ye. It's no' ma ears bleeding.'

Tamar smiled. The girls all filed past and touched Myrna's hand. Vivienne, realising she'd stepped in the blood on the floor, burst into anguished tears. 'Don't go, Myrna,' she sobbed. 'Please.'

'Come on, out now. We can't be upsetting her,' said Tamar,

shooing the shocked and distressed girls out of the room. 'Send John straight up.'

Tamar dragged up a chair and held Myrna's hand while they waited, smoothing strands of errant henna-dyed hair from her clammy brow. Tamar felt frightened and sick, and kept her mouth closed until she could trust her own voice. When she could, she bent closer to Myrna and asked gently, 'How do you feel?'

'Weak,' replied Myrna, addressing the ceiling. 'Verra tired. And ma innards feel like I've just produced a bairn. I havnae, though, have I?' Tamar shook her head. 'I didnae think so,' continued Myrna, a hint of a smile on her bleached lips. 'I've no' been wi' a man for years.' She grimaced in pain, swore and closed her eyes.

They sat in silence until they heard the clatter of horses outside. Tamar went to the window. 'John's here.' Seconds later she heard him running up the stairs, and went to the bedroom door to meet him.

He hurried in but stopped in his tracks when he saw Tamar. 'Bloody hell,' he exclaimed, staring at the front of her dress.

Tamar glanced down at herself; her skirt was smeared with Myrna's blood and her arms were streaked with it up to her elbows. 'It's Myrna,' she said, stepping out of his way. 'She's had a massive bleed.'

John dropped his bag, crossed to the bed and drew the covers back. 'Christ. Get me some warm water and some clean towels. And a new set of sheets,' he added without turning around.

When Tamar had gone he asked, 'Myrna? Can you hear me? When did the bleeding start?'

'This morning some time. I woke wi' a bad pain in ma belly and decided to stay in bed for a while. When I woke again I was bleeding everywhere. I couldnae get up and I couldnae yell out.' She grasped John's hand and looked him in the eye. Her own eyes, now that her girls were out of the room, were wide with fear. 'I thought I was going to die here, John. By maself.'

He nodded, the distress in her voice telling clearly of her fright. 'Have you had heavy bleeding before?'

Myrna nodded. 'Ma courses have been getting worse and worse. I've been expecting them to stop, but they havnae.'

'Are they still regular?'

'Och, no. They arrive whenever they feel like it.'

'How old are you, Myrna?'

'Fifty-five this year.'

John nodded and rubbed his hand over his high, shiny forehead. 'Well, we'll clean you up and have a look then, shall we? If you don't mind.'

Myrna smiled. 'Why should I? Ye'd hardly be the first to look up there.'

John laughed out loud. Then, more serious, he asked, 'Are you still in pain?'

'A little.'

'Well, that probably means a lot, knowing you. I'll give you some laudanum to take the edge off it.'

As he poured a draught of the opiate and held it to Myrna's lips, Tamar returned with two large bowls of water, followed by Eliza carrying a stack of fresh, white cloths and towels with a pair of snowy sheets folded on top of them.

'Och, no, Tamar! No' the *good* linen,' said Myrna crossly. 'It'll be ruined.'

No one took any notice. John set to work dipping the cloths into the warm water while Tamar peeled Myrna's nightdress off her thighs and stomach.

As John gently sponged Myrna's legs and lower abdomen he motioned to Eliza to unfold a clean sheet. 'When I roll her over I want you to pull the stained sheet from underneath her, then spread out the clean one.'

Myrna groaned as John helped her to roll to one side. Tamar bit her lip. She was finding it almost unbearable to see her friend in such pain.

'Right,' said John. 'It looks as if most of the bleeding has stopped. I'm going to examine you now, Myrna. Do you want Tamar and Eliza to leave or do you want to be chaperoned?'

'I couldnae care less, laddie. Dinnae be silly.'

Tamar asked Eliza to take away the soiled sheets and cloths, sat next to the bed and took Myrna's hand.

As John began his examination he said nothing, except to ask whether he was causing any pain. When he had finished some minutes later he rinsed his hands, dried them on a towel and perched himself on the end of the bed, a worried expression on his face.

'I'm not sure what it is, Myrna. I'm sorry but I just can't tell. This really isn't my field. You've lost a lot of blood, however. Are you supposed to be menstruating now?'

'I'm no' really sure any more.'

'I'll talk to some of my colleagues. They might have a better idea.' He coughed dryly into his hand. 'Tamar, could you get me something to drink, please?'

'Tea or brandy?'

'Brandy, thanks. Downstairs. I'll need to talk to you shortly.'

When Tamar had gone, John frowned. 'I didn't want to say this in front of her, but I think this is serious.'

Myrna sighed. 'Aye, I ken that, laddie. I have the cancer, no?'

'You might. This sort of extreme, irregular bleeding can be one of the symptoms.' He paused for a second and chewed on his bottom lip. 'And if you do, as far as I'm aware there is no cure.'

'I ken that as well. I've suspected for some time, but it's never been as bad as this. Ma mam died o' it, ye see.'

John nodded but said nothing.

'Well, laddie, if it is the cancer, how long will I have?'

John looked at Myrna. It saddened him beyond words to be discussing life expectancy with someone he had grown so fond of. 'I really don't know. Have you lost weight lately?'

'Unfortunately, no. I'm as fat as ever.'

'Is the pain constant?

'No, usually only when I'm bleeding.'

'Well, then, if it *is* cancer, it could be quite a while.'

'A year?'

'Perhaps.'

'Then bugger it, John. I'm no' going to waste it lying around in ma bed!'

'No, there's no need to do that, but you will have to take it easy, whatever this turns out to be. Perhaps you could hand some of your work over to someone else.'

'Aye, I've already started. I'm teaching Tamar to do the books, keep the place running, that sort o' thing. She's verra bright and capable, ye ken.'

'Oh, I know that.' He looked at her hard. 'You *have* known for a while, haven't you? Why didn't you say something earlier?'

'Would there have been much point?'

'I suppose not, but I could have given you something to ease the pain.'

'Aye, well, ye can give me that now. And I'd rather ye didnae tell Tamar.'

'That's your business. But I am going to talk to her about your care and how you need to cut down on your work. If you can make things easier by not driving yourself so hard, then I think it's worth it, don't you?'

'I'm no' sure if I agree with ye, laddie. I'd rather go doing something useful than finish ma life as an invalid.'

'Somehow I don't think you'd make a good invalid. Unlike some of my patients, who seem to dedicate their life to it,' said John. He began to pack his things into his doctor's bag. 'I've a colleague, a gynaecologist who's had a lot of experience with these sorts of problems. Hugh Templeton, his name is. If I bring him around, will you talk to him?'

'Cannae do any harm.'

'I'll arrange that as soon as I can.' He straightened up. 'There's nothing I can say except stay in bed until your strength comes back. Use the chamber pot, don't go downstairs. Eat lots of red meat and vegetables. Take the laudanum for pain. If you bleed like this again, send for me straightaway. I'll drop in on you regularly anyway. I'll send someone up to sit with you while I'm talking to Tamar.'

'Aye, fine, although I'm so tired I could sleep for a week.'

'It's the loss of blood. That washed-out feeling will go away in a day or two.'

As he turned to go, Myrna said, 'John? Thank ye. Again. I dinnae ken where we'd be wi'out ye sometimes.'

John smiled. 'Just look after yourself, all right?' He crossed the room and closed the bedroom door softly. In the dim light on the landing outside Myrna's room, his normally cheerful face was grim and grey.

CHAPTER EIGHTEEN

John brought Hugh Templeton to visit Myrna several days later. Templeton, a distinguished and learned man in his late fifties experienced in treating medical problems peculiar to women, examined her extensively and detected what he thought was a moderately large tumour in her womb.

After the examination he sat with Myrna and John and discussed her prognosis.

'I'm afraid, Miss McTaggart,' he said solemnly, 'I have to advise there is very little hope of recovery.'

Myrna nodded but said nothing. She looked resigned. Her face had regained some of its colour and character but she was still pale.

'I could operate and remove your womb ... '

At this Myrna shook her head stubbornly.

Templeton continued. 'But that procedure has many risks. It is also likely the cancer has already spread — the glands under your armpits and in your groin are considerably swollen, indicating the possible, if not probable, existence of cancer in those areas. I'm sorry.'

Nobody said anything for a minute.

'So,' said Myrna eventually. 'What can I expect?'

'There is no doubt you will experience more heavy bleeding.

There will be pain but we should be able to control that. You will weaken. You may lose control of some of your bodily functions, depending on wherever else the cancer has taken hold.'

'Will I lose ma mind?'

'Only if the cancer moves to your brain.' He didn't say he doubted she'd live long enough for that to happen.

'So I'm going to die in screaming agony in a bedful o' ma own shite. And when will this be? Next week?'

'No, no,' said Templeton, totally unflustered by Myrna's graphic language. 'It could be months, even a year. And no, you are unlikely to die in agony, although there will be pain. I have described the worst possible outcome.'

Myrna thought for a minute then asked, 'Could ma past line o' work have contributed to this?'

Templeton shrugged. 'I don't know. The patients I normally see do not usually have your colourful history,' he said diplomatically. 'I'd say it is more likely to be something to do with your mother having had it. The disease of cancer is not yet well understood.'

Myrna turned to John. 'As soon as I have ma strength back I'm moving ma things downstairs and Tamar can have this room. I'm no' peeing in yon pot any longer than I have to. Sven can help me move.'

As Hugh Templeton rose to leave, she thanked him for his opinion.

'Not at all, Miss McTaggart. If you wish to see me again, please send word.'

Halfway down the big staircase Templeton asked John, 'Is she always so resolutely cheerful and positive?'

'Never seen her anything but.'

'Mmm. That might change near the end, I'm afraid. It will be difficult for her. And you. You don't feel you're too involved?'

'Yes, I do,' replied John as they reached the bottom of the

staircase. 'But I'm keeping it that way. Thanks for coming, Hugh. I really appreciate it. Can you send your account to me?'

Templeton put on his top hat and gloves and checked his appearance in the *étagère* mirror. 'There won't be an account. I've always wanted to meet the famous Myrna McTaggart. I only wish it might have been under more pleasant circumstances.'

As if it knew its secret had been disclosed, the cancer took hold with frightening violence and tore through Myrna's body in the following weeks.

She began to lose weight rapidly and the level of pain she had been experiencing increased markedly. None who knew her well believed she would see the year out. True to form, however, she forbade anyone to mope and made a massive effort to get up every day, dress in one of her brightest, most flamboyant gowns and, with her hair styled in its usual cascade of red, riotous curls, spend at least part of the evening talking to customers in the salon. Her make-up was applied with a heavier hand to disguise the pallor of her skin, and Tamar had to make several new gowns to accommodate her shrinking figure, but she successfully managed to create the outward illusion of health.

But to the girls and to John, it was obvious she was preparing herself and tidying up her affairs. One day she spent almost three hours locked in her office with her lawyer and a representative from her bank.

She also spent more time with Tamar, teaching her everything she would need to know to run the brothel. Tamar absorbed the information like a sponge, especially when Myrna explained that the same principles could be applied to almost any business venture involving service, trade or commerce. By the end of May, Tamar was running the house single-handedly, and was becoming comfortable with the witty, intelligent and charming manner the role of madam required.

At the start of June, Myrna's health took a rapid turn for the worse. John again called in Hugh Templeton but neither could offer any hope. Laudanum was no longer enough to control her chronic discomfort so Templeton prescribed morphine, which she used regularly throughout the day and whenever the vicious pains woke her at night.

One wet, miserable morning, Tamar was woken early by the sound of tapping on her bedroom door. It was still dark; her bare feet cold on the wooden floor of Myrna's old room, she stumbled to light a lamp. She'd argued with Myrna about moving into the upstairs bedroom, but Myrna had been adamant, saying she'd be 'far and away' more comfortable downstairs.

'Come in,' she called when the lamp had flared.

Eliza poked her worried-looking face around the door. 'Miss Myrna wants ter see yer. I think it's urgent.'

Tamar glanced at the carriage clock on the tallboy. Four fifteen. She'd been asleep less than three hours. 'Does she need something?' she asked, noticing Eliza still wore her maid's uniform. 'Have you not been to bed yet?'

'No. I'm fair worried about Miss Myrna.'

Tamar lifted her warm robe from a chair, jammed her feet into a pair of quilted satin house slippers, and followed Eliza to the ground floor. Eliza knocked on Myrna's door and went straight in.

Tamar's old bedroom now smelled like a sickroom. There was a faintly unpleasant odour, not quite masked by the sachets of dried lavender placed strategically around the room.

'Come in, lassie,' said Myrna. 'Light a lamp. I cannae see ye.' Her voice was weary and husky with pain.

Eliza lit a wall sconce then left, closing the door softly.

'What is it?' asked Tamar gently as she moved a straight-backed

293

wooden chair over to the bed. 'Are you in pain?'

Myrna nodded and took a deep, ragged breath. 'I've had enough, Tamar.'

'I know. It's been very hard for you,' Tamar replied compassionately, stroking Myrna's thin arm, the bones rudely evident under her nightdress. Her friend was looking old, the disease scoring deep lines of pain in her tired face. Once pleasingly round, her belly was distorted by the tumour growing in her womb while the rest of her flesh fell away.

Myrna tried to sit up but failed. Instead, she turned and looked Tamar directly in the eye. 'No, I mean I've had *enough*. I dinnae want to do this any more.'

Tamar sat still, rigid with alarm and fear as she realised what Myrna was trying to tell her.

Seeing her expression, Myrna said, 'Aye, lassie. I'm going to finish it. I've thought about this for some time now, and it's *ma* choice. Look at me. I've grown ugly and I'm in constant pain. I cannae bear it. I'm no earthly use to anyone like this, least o' all maself.'

Tamar stared up at the shadows on the ceiling. She made no sound but her face crumpled as tears began to course down her cheeks. 'We need you here,' she said finally, knowing she sounded childlike but unable to stop herself.

'No. Ye know what to do now, and so do the girls. I want to go. I've had ma life and I'd no' change a minute. But I *will*nae be reduced to a stinking pile of skinny, diseased old bones! This is *ma* life and I'm choosing to end it.'

Tamar wiped her face and breathed in deeply. 'Now?' she whispered, wanting to clap her hands over her ears so she would not have to hear the answer.

'Aye. Now.'

Tamar struggled to find the words to beg Myrna to change her mind, to tell her she was desperately frightened of being alone again.

Instead she said, 'I love you.' The declaration came out sounding strangled as Tamar struggled to swallow the profound grief blossoming painfully in her chest and throat. She felt as if she'd swallowed broken glass. 'What do you need me to do?'

Myrna pointed to the nightstand with its array of medicine bottles. 'The morphine, lassie. I want ye to stay with me until I'm gone, if ye will. I dinnae want to go alone.'

Tamar nodded and bit her lip.

'Help me to sit up a wee bit then, will ye?'

When Tamar had rearranged her pillows and helped her into a semi-sitting position, Myrna reached for the bottle of morphine syrup and poured the thick liquid into a cut-glass tumbler. She drank it, then poured another and drank that, gagging slightly. She drank the third more slowly, then lay back, her eyelids closing slowly.

Tamar looked on in helpless despair. After a minute or two, she asked tentatively, 'Myrna?'

'Aye, I'm still here, love.'

Tamar walked around to the other side of the bed and got in beside Myrna. She tucked the blankets around them both, gathered Myrna's wasted body in her arms and laid the older woman's head against her chest. 'Comfortable?' she murmured.

'Mmm.'

They lay in silence. Outside it was still dark and wet but Tamar could hear an optimistic rooster crowing in someone's back yard. Myrna's breathing slowed. 'I've tidied everything up,' she mumbled indistinctly.

'I know,' replied Tamar. She felt strangely detached from what was happening, as if the only real task she would ever have was to comfort this woman, this friend, this constant giver of comfort and strength and hope, as she died.

Minutes passed. Myrna's breathing slowed further and her body relaxed as the morphine flooded through her. Tamar adjusted her position slightly.

'Tamar?'

'Mmm?'

'I love ye too, ye ken.'

Tamar leaned down and kissed her friend's brow. The deep lines of pain were dissolving. 'I know.'

There was no answer. Tamar waited for a few long minutes then pressed her fingers against the side of Myrna's still throat. There was no pulse.

Myrna had gone.

A surprisingly large number of people came to Myrna's funeral, given her profession. Many of her business associates and friends were there, all of the members of her household, a considerable number of patrons and a small selection of Auckland's better-known society figures. In donating generously to local charities, Myrna had won respect and friends in the process, despite the nature of her business.

Myrna's lawyer called late the following day. Tamar had suspended all work for a week as a gesture of respect for Myrna. All the girls had been badly shaken, with Polly in particular only coming out of her room on the day of the funeral, having spent the previous three lying on her bed, cuddling Cabbage and crying or gulping her 'medicine' and staring at the wall.

The lawyer, Mr Bonnington, came quickly to the point. Hitching the knees of his smartly tailored trousers as he sat in Myrna's office, he accepted a cup of tea but put it to one side. He opened his briefcase and withdrew a thin, folded sheaf of papers.

'Miss Deane,' he said. 'Are you aware of the arrangements Miss

McTaggart made before she passed away? Regarding her business affairs and her estate?'

'No, Mr Bonnington,' said Tamar. 'Why would I be?'

Mr Bonnington blinked owlishly behind his pince-nez. 'Perhaps I should acquaint you with Miss McTaggart's will.'

'Is that necessary?'

'Yes.' Mr Bonnington removed his spectacles, polished the thick lenses with a handkerchief, placed them back on the end of his nose, cleared his throat and began to read:

> *On the occasion of my death, I, Myrna Moira McTaggart, bequeath my estate to the named beneficiaries as per the following instructions:*
>
> *To Letitia McBurney, Bronwyn Doyle, Polly Jakes, Vivienne Bowden and Jessica Villiers I leave the sum of two thousand pounds each to be deposited into their personal bank accounts.*
>
> *To Eliza Andrews and Sven Langstrom I leave one thousand pounds each to be paid to them directly.*
>
> *To Dr John Adams, of Parnell Rise, I leave three thousand pounds to be paid directly to him to assist in financing his charitable medical treatment of patients who are unable to pay for their own care.*
>
> *To the Auckland Refuge for Fallen Women I leave the sum of five thousand pounds to be managed directly and strictly for the benefit of the women in the care of that institution (instructions for disbursement attached).*

Here Mr Bonnington finally took a large sip of tea before he continued.

> *Finally, I leave the remainder of my estate, including my house on Dilworth Terrace and all of its chattels, my business, my finances, and my personal possessions to Tamar Branwyn Deane, to do with as she chooses.*

Mr Bonnington folded the single sheet of paper. 'The will was signed by Miss McTaggart on 6 May 1882.'

Tamar fiddled with the cuffs of her day dress. This morning she had worn something pretty in honour of Myrna's preference for bright colours; she didn't think Myrna would have wanted her to go about in the 'dreary weeds o' the recently bereaved'. She didn't know what to say to Mr Bonnington. Hot, uncomfortable tears stung the backs of her eyelids. She blinked and cleared her throat. 'I was not aware Myrna had done this.'

'No, clearly not. Miss McTaggart had accrued a considerable sum of money. You are now a wealthy woman, Miss Deane. After the disbursement of the amounts earmarked in the will for the other beneficiaries, you will inherit approximately seventy thousand pounds. There are no further monies owed on this address, so you will also own a freehold business and premises.'

Tamar looked out the window. Most of the leaves had fallen from the deciduous trees outside. Perhaps they're in mourning for Myrna as well, she reflected sadly. 'I'm not sure what to do with it. The business, I mean.'

'Whatever you like, I should imagine,' replied Mr Bonnington. 'Keep it, close it or sell it. Miss McTaggart made it quite clear that it should be your choice.'

Tamar poured herself a second cup of tea. Her throat was dry and she didn't feel well. 'Do the others know?'

'No. I will be informing them when I have finished speaking with you. I trust they are all available?'

'Yes, no one's working at the moment. When will they receive their disbursements?'

'I will be arranging that tomorrow morning. They should be able to access their monies within a week.'

Tamar wondered if the girls would decide to stay. She didn't cherish the thought of rattling around in this big house all by herself. But on the other hand, did she want to own and run a brothel? She had never pictured herself as a madam. 'I'll have to talk to them about what they want to do,' she said out loud.

Mr Bonnington waited, but when it became clear Tamar was not going to add anything, he asked, 'If there are no more questions, Miss Deane, I wonder if you could be so kind as to gather the other beneficiaries?'

'Of course,' replied Tamar absently. 'John isn't here, though. Does that matter?'

'No, I will call in at Dr Adams' surgery later today.'

Tamar yanked on the bell pull to summon Eliza, and asked her to call everyone to the parlour, including Sven.

Eliza replied, 'Yes, Miss Tamar,' and hurried off, an anxious look on her tear-blotched face.

Mr Bonnington looked around the parlour, somewhat surprised at the nervous glances he was getting; he was more used to optimistic anticipation, if not overt greed, when reading the will of a recently departed relative.

But then Myrna McTaggart had not been a relative, she had been their employer.

'I have asked that you be gathered here this morning,' he announced formally, 'so that I may read the will of the late Miss Myrna McTaggart.'

He read the short document aloud, then looked up to gauge the response. No one said anything. One of the pretty blonde girls was crying and the manservant had his mouth hanging open. Mr Bonnington looked to Tamar for guidance.

From the sofa she said in a quiet voice, 'Well, then? What are we all going to do? Keep the business going, or go our separate ways? You've all enough money now to do what you like, so it's up to you.'

Letitia, Jessica, Vivienne and Bronwyn all looked at her. Polly was staring out the window, Cabbage curled in her lap.

Letitia said, 'We talked about this last night, Tamar. We want to stay here and keep working.'

Mr Bonnington coughed politely. 'I will be on my way now, Miss Deane, if there are no further questions. The future of this establishment is your concern, so I will leave you to discuss it. Should you wish to continue the business, I would be more than happy to remain your legal representative.'

'Yes,' replied Tamar. 'Thank you. I will be in touch.'

Mr Bonnington waited for the maid to escort him to the front door, but as she seemed busy exchanging meaningful stares with the Swede, he saw himself out.

When he had gone, Bronwyn continued, 'But we want you to be the madam, Tamar. You know how to run this business better than we do. Would you be happy to stay?'

Where on earth else would I go, thought Tamar. A vision of her own little dressmaking business appeared briefly in her mind, but it was a fleeting image, and a lonely one.

'Yes,' she replied with little hesitation, knowing she would never have said anything else. 'We'll carry on, if that's what everyone wants. It won't be the same without Myrna, but we'll be all right.'

The girls smiled in relief.

'And what about you two?' asked Tamar, turning to face Eliza and Sven. 'Will you stay on?'

They had been an unofficial couple for many months now but had made no moves in the direction of marriage. The hopeful look on Sven's plain but normally impassive face, however, indicated that Myrna's unexpected gift may have changed things.

In his halting but much improved English, he replied, 'I believe yes, that I think we are to stay.' He stood up and wiped his large hands on his trousers. His face began to turn red as he turned to

Tamar and announced, 'Miss Tamar, I wish to ask of you to have the hand of Eliza Andrews in betrothal.'

'Oh,' said Tamar in surprise and embarrassment, blushing herself. 'Why are you asking me?'

'You now are the lady of the house,' he said, his face flaming. Across from him Eliza raised her hands to her own face and giggled nervously. 'It is your permission I am needing, I think,' Sven continued. 'We had not the money for a wedding before, now we have so I need the permission also.'

Tamar turned to Eliza. 'Is this what you want?' When Eliza nodded, Tamar said, 'Well, yes, then. Of course!'

Later that afternoon Tamar went looking for Eliza. She found her in the kitchen, baking. 'Can I talk to you for a minute, Eliza?'

Eliza looked up from the table she was working at, wiped her floury hands on her apron and raised her eyebrows. 'Miss?'

God, I hate it when she calls me that, Tamar thought. 'Well,' she started, not quite sure what to say. 'It's about your engagement.'

As Eliza's long face grew suddenly wary, Tamar suddenly understood the English girl did not completely trust her. 'No, there's no problem,' Tamar said quickly. 'I wondered if you might want to have this.' She slid the pearl and sapphire ring Peter had given her off her finger and held it out to Eliza, her palm flat. 'It was my engagement ring,' she added, unnecessarily.

Eliza stared at it.

'Please don't be insulted,' Tamar continued. 'It doesn't really mean much to me any more. I'll understand if you don't want it, of course. I just thought I'd ask. It's been paid for,' she added, and allowed herself a small smile.

Eliza smiled back. 'It's lovely, Miss Tamar. And it were very nice of yer ter think of me. I'll 'ave ter ask Sven though. I don't know 'ow 'e'll feel about it.' She took the ring and slipped it into her apron pocket.

'Of course. You could sell it and use the money to buy something else. Whatever suits you.'

Eliza looked at Tamar thoughtfully. 'Does it mean so little ter yer now? The ring and everythin' it meant?'

Tamar gazed back, took a deep breath and nodded. 'Yes. I have a new life now, Eliza. I need to look forwards, not backwards.'

Eliza nodded herself. 'I 'ope me own marriage don't turn out like yours did, Miss Tamar, if yer don't mind me saying. But Sven's a good man, so I don't think it will.'

'No, I don't think it will either. I wish you the very best of luck.'
And she did.

CHAPTER NINETEEN

December 1882

Myrna, gone now for six months, was sorely missed. But life, as it nearly always does, went on. The house reopened for business and continued to profit under Tamar's management, Eliza and Sven were married in October, Letitia turned down a marriage proposal from a customer and summer arrived.

The only one not to have come to terms with Myrna's death was Polly. Her moods worsened and in November Tamar was forced to insist she stop working; customers had complained Polly was falling asleep at the very point when she should have been most awake, which, everyone agreed, was bad for business.

When Tamar told her, Polly had merely shrugged and gone up to her room.

Talking to John Adams several days later, Tamar said, 'I don't know what's wrong, it's as if she's completely given up. Before, when she was still enthusiastic about her work, it wasn't too bad. She was moody, yes, and not that easy to get on with, but since Myrna went, she seems to have lost all hope.'

'And she's drinking over half a bottle of Decoction of Opium a day? Well, if that's the case, I'd say she's well and truly addicted. That's not good at all, not in those amounts,' said John, frowning.

'I told her that months ago. I don't think she cares.'

'Addiction to opium-based preparations isn't that unusual. You'd be surprised the people who get into trouble with it. It's high time some sort of control was applied to its distribution, although I suspect I'm wasting my breath. While there are opium dens on every damned street corner, not much can be done to discourage people from using the drug.'

Tamar was fascinated. 'Dens on every corner?'

'No. I exaggerate. But they are around. There's one on Upper Queen Street and it's rumoured there's another down by the wharves.'

'Mmm, I wonder,' muttered Tamar. 'Polly's disappeared several times at night, and not come back until early morning, according to Eliza. I wonder if that's where she's been going?'

'Well, they say the cravings get worse until the poor victim is utterly consumed by his or her need. Perhaps her medicine isn't enough any more and she's advanced to the pure form of the drug. That can be fatal. Why don't you ask her?'

Tamar hesitated, then said, 'I don't want to. If I do, and she says she's not going to an opium den, then I might be told something I really don't want to know.'

'Such as?'

'Such as she's working the streets again.'

'Oh, surely not? Not after working here?' John was aghast.

'Well, she's been going somewhere. And if she *is* back on the streets, I'll have to ask her to leave, and I don't know if I can do that, John. She's my friend. I really think she needs help.'

'Yes, it's a difficult situation. Do you want me to talk to her?'

'You can try.'

'Well, is she in now?'

'In her room, I think. You know which one it is, don't you?'

John nodded as he stood up. 'Well, I'll try. But if she tells me something in confidence it will have to stay that way.'

'As long as she's safe, John. That's all I'm worried about.'

Tamar followed him up the stairs, leaving him on the first floor while she went up to her own room. She opened a window facing out onto the harbour and let the salt-smelling breeze waft in. She loved the view and only drew her drapes at night, not wanting to shut out the sight of the ocean, even if it wasn't the wild, hungry sea that had battered the coasts of her beloved Cornwall.

As she sat down on a sofa and picked up some sewing, there was a knock at the door. 'Come in,' she called, looking up as John entered. He'd been into this room many times before and Tamar could see no reason he should not continue to do so, propriety be damned. 'That was quick.'

'She told me to bugger off. I knocked and when she didn't answer I opened the door and went in. She was on the bed. I thought she was asleep but then I heard her muttering. She's not in a very good state.'

'I know that,' Tamar replied exasperatedly. 'That's why I've talked to you about it.' For someone so intelligent, John could be very obtuse sometimes.

He continued. 'So I shook her gently, and she rolled over, opened one eye, and said "It's you." When I asked if there was something wrong she said, "No. Bugger off," closed her eyes again and put her hands over her ears. I notice she's lost a lot of weight.'

'So what do you think I should do?'

'If she won't talk to anyone then there's not much you *can* do. Physically, she looks reasonably healthy although she's probably run down. It's her mind, I'd say. Something's obviously not right.'

'No,' said Tamar, getting up and going to the window again. The breeze lifted her hair off her face, exposing the faint line of her scar. 'I can't lock her in her room, and I'm not going to evict her while she's ill. I'd not ask her to leave anyway, this is her home. If she's not going to work she can have Eliza's old room. I'll have to get someone to replace her, I suppose.'

'She'll be a liability, Tamar, if she doesn't recover her health.'

'Yes, John, I know that. I was a liability once, remember? And Myrna took me in.'

'That doesn't mean you have to do the same.'

'Doesn't it? She looked after us, and she left me everything.'

'Yes, and you've got this place running very smoothly and profitably, but is this what you really want, Tamar? Running a whorehouse? You could sell up — someone might buy it as a going concern, and if not, then I'm sure everyone has enough put away to manage quite comfortably. Even Sven and Eliza.'

They'd had this conversation several times since Myrna had died.

Tamar rolled her eyes. 'You just don't understand, do you? I *owe* this to Myrna. This is why she left it all to me. So the others would be taken care of.'

John blew out his cheeks in frustration. 'Are you sure she didn't leave it all to you because she wanted *you* to be taken care of? Didn't she say in her will you could do whatever you wanted with the place? It was *you* she was worried about, Tamar, especially after what that bastard Montgomery did to you. The others can take care of themselves.'

'So can I!'

'Yes, but there are better ways to do it. You're wealthy now, you can afford to do just about anything you like. And New Zealand is a growing country — the depression will be over soon and there'll be plenty of things to invest your money in. You could even have your own business. A more socially acceptable one, I mean.'

'Oh, I know *that*!' she snapped, sitting back down with an angry rustle of taffeta. 'But what's money if I have no one to share it with? No one to talk to and no one to laugh with? If I sell this place and everyone disappears in different directions, I'll be alone, John. I *have* no one else.'

'You have me.'

'Not any more. I know how you feel about what I did, John. I'm not blind. Or stupid.'

He felt himself going red. He thought he'd successfully kept his feelings to himself, but obviously not.

'But we're still friends,' he said. 'Friends take care of each other.'

'Yes, yes, it's all very well you saying that now, but what about when you marry? And you will, John, I know. You need a wife, and you want one. It's obvious.'

'Is it?' he asked, slightly taken back.

'Yes. You'll have your work and you'll start your own family. Where will I fit in? You're being unrealistic.'

She was right and he couldn't think of anything to say that wouldn't sound trite. They sat in silence, Tamar looking out the window and John staring at his boots.

Eventually Tamar cleared her throat and said, 'I miss her terribly.'

'I know. So do I.' Then, as if Myrna had not even been mentioned, he said, 'What if you marry again? You're only, what? Twenty?'

'I'm not living my life based on what ifs. I've already done that once and it didn't work out.'

He couldn't respond to that, either. Silence again. He watched Tamar, deep in thought.

'I think I'll send Sven after Polly the next time she goes out,' she said after a few minutes. 'Then at least I'll know where she's going.'

It was clear their discussion about Tamar's future was over. 'Yes, I suppose,' he replied. 'She'll be extremely angry if she spots him.'

'John, these days Polly doesn't know when someone's in the same room half the time. She won't see him.'

They went downstairs. Tamar collected John's hat and gloves

307

from the parlour and saw him to the side door. As they waited for
Sven to bring his horse around, John had an idea. 'What was the
name of that girl who used to work for you at Huia?'

'Riria?'

'Weren't you quite fond of her?'

'Very.'

'Well, why don't you invite her to visit? She could keep you
company for a while. Perhaps you could even look at starting a little
business of some sort together. Something in the dressmaking line.
Or a drapery of your own? She could work for you.'

Tamar sighed and thought, oh John, stop trying to organise my
life. He'd never met Riria. If he had, he'd know that suggesting she
might like to work behind a counter was ludicrous. She smiled.
'Yes, I could write to her, I suppose.'

As she waved John off, she realised the idea was very appealing.

On the evening of the day Tamar sent her letter to Riria, Polly
slipped out of the house. Sven followed her.

'So?' asked Tamar when he had returned several hours later.

'A place on Customhouse Street.'

'Not on the streets?'

'No, Miss. She went inside.'

'Mmm.' Tamar looked at him for a minute. 'A brothel?'

'I do not believe so, Miss. I ask a man who came out after Miss
Polly enter. He say it was a den. He whisper it.'

Oh God, thought Tamar desperately. How the hell am I going
to sort this out?

She confronted Polly the following afternoon. Polly, her face
drawn and white with dark pouches under her dull eyes, denied
it. Then, when she realised she'd been seen, she confessed. They
argued bitterly, both angry at first, then both crying, and Tamar

told Polly that if she visited the opium den once more, she would have to leave. She suspected Polly knew she didn't mean it, but it was the only threat she had left. She left Polly lying on her unmade bed, having forced her to promise she would not go to the place on Customhouse Street again, and she would talk to John about her problem.

Two nights later, just before one in the morning, Polly went out again. This time Tamar followed her, intending to drag her out of the place herself if she had to. She waited for an hour, then asked Sven to get the landau and drive her to Customhouse Street.

By the time they arrived the street was almost deserted, save for a few drunken sailors and one or two tatty-looking whores hanging about under the dim street lamps. Sven stopped outside the place he had seen Polly go into, got off his seat and stuck his big head through the landau window, its retractable top up against the night. 'This is the place, Miss Tamar. Are you wanting me to enter?'

Tamar shook her head. 'No, Sven. I'll go in.'

Sven was appalled. 'Miss! It is a den of vice! Not for someone like you to visit!'

'I can take care of myself. Please open the door.'

Unwillingly, Sven stood back and helped Tamar out. As she looked about she lifted her dark shawl over her hair and secured it at her throat; she doubted she would be recognised, but there was no need to advertise her presence here.

In front of her, just off the street, was a narrow, dingy-looking wooden building jammed between what appeared to be two tall warehouses. A door opened and a man came out, staggered several yards, then bent over at the waist and vomited splashily onto the ground.

As she moved towards the door, Sven put a restraining hand on her arm. 'I will accompany you,' he insisted.

'No you *won't*, Sven. Wait in the landau, please. I won't be long.'

His brow creased in disapproval but he stood back as Tamar opened the door and went inside. Somewhere an invisible bell tinkled.

The door opened onto a narrow, poorly lit hall. Tamar stood for a minute to let her eyes become accustomed to the gloom. As she blinked, a heavy curtain at the end of the hall twitched and a small, slender woman stepped through. Tamar blinked again. She'd never encountered a Chinese woman before, although she'd seen one or two men on the streets.

'Madam?' asked the woman in a clear, sing-song voice. She was dressed in a long robe that fell straight down her slim body. Embroidered with flowers, dragons and other fantastic beasts, the robe was made of heavy silk with satin at the high collar and wide cuffs. The woman's shining black hair was pulled tightly back and fell in a long queue down her back. Her face, alien and exotically beautiful, was devoid of emotion as she stood silently.

'Good evening,' said Tamar. 'I'm looking for someone. I think she might be here.'

The woman made no movement or sound.

'Her name is Polly Jakes,' Tamar continued, uncomfortable with the other woman's lack of response. 'Thin, with fair hair. I understand she's been here before.'

The woman remained silent for a further minute then, in the same sing-song voice, said, 'We do not have names here.'

'I'm sure she's here. It's very important that I find her. She's not well.'

The woman considered, then, with a flick of her long plait, held the curtain open and gestured for Tamar to step through. The room beyond was moderately sized, windowless and filled with heavy, lazily moving blue smoke. Tamar coughed and waved her hand in front of her face. In the centre of the room two groups of red-eyed men sat around gaming tables playing cards. No one looked up.

'Where is she?' Tamar asked.

The Chinese woman crossed the room and went into a second narrow hall along which were several doors, all closed. The dark passage smelled of exotic spices and of something else, an essence heavy and sweet. At the end of the hall was another curtain. Tamar moved it aside and peered into the room beyond.

Polly sprawled lifelessly on a low couch, one arm resting limply on the floor, her head thrown back at an uncomfortable angle and her eyes closed.

She wasn't alone. As Tamar looked around the small room, lit only by two candles burning on a low table, she became aware of at least four other people. Three were European — a woman and two men, all asleep or unconscious on the floor — while the fourth was an elderly Chinese man. Sitting cross-legged on a cushion in front of the table, his small, slippered feet poking out from beneath his robe, he was drawing smoke up through a slender pipe, holding it deliberately in his lungs, then slowly letting it out again. His lizard-like eyes flicked towards Tamar for a moment, then resumed staring at the wall.

Here was the source of the sweet smell, coming from what she assumed was an opium pipe. It wasn't unpleasant, but it was very strong and slightly nauseating. She went over to Polly, bent down and felt for a pulse in her neck. It was there, consistent but very slow.

Tamar turned to the Chinese man and said, 'Help me get her up, please, if you would. I'm taking her home.'

He stared at her, his ancient face with its long wispy beard and equally insubstantial moustache expressionless. Shadows from the candles turned his features into a burnished skull. 'No,' he said.

'I beg your pardon?' said Tamar, nonplussed.

'I said no,' replied the man in clear, perfect English. 'She is where she needs and wants to be. Do not disturb her.'

'Rubbish!' exploded Tamar. 'She does *not* need to be in a place like this, drugged senseless!'

The man took another long, languid draw on his pipe, expelled the fragrant smoke and said, 'Are you sure of that? Here, she can escape. Here, her mind can be free of whatever is walking so closely behind her.'

'What on earth do you mean?' said Tamar.

He regarded her for a minute. The room was utterly silent except for the faint sounds of deep, slow breathing. 'Have you yourself not been haunted by some shame, some fear, some grief so monstrous it has consumed your mind?'

Tamar was shocked rigid. Yes, she had. How had this wizened, yellow little man known?

'For this one,' he continued, pointing steadily at Polly with a clawlike finger sporting an incredibly long, curved nail, 'There is nowhere else for her to go. Her fear has eaten her. The opiate is her only release. Do not take that from her.'

Tamar turned back to Polly's motionless form. She looked at peace. Insensibility had somehow stolen the lines of despair and misery from her face.

Fumbling through her pocketbook Tamar extracted several pound notes, folded them and attached a small silver money clip and held them out to him. 'Will you make sure she gets a cab when she wakes? She won't be safe on the streets the way she is.'

The money disappeared into the depths of the old man's robe. He nodded, took another slow draw on his opium pipe and deliberately turned away.

Outside it was still dark and Tamar told Sven to take her home.

'Miss Polly is all right?' he asked.

'As right as she'll ever be,' replied Tamar, and climbed into the landau.

The following morning, when Polly had still not returned, Tamar panicked and had Sven take her back to Customhouse Street. She banged for some time on the door of the building, which looked even more ramshackle and squalid, until it was finally opened by the Oriental woman. She looked much more ordinary in the light of day, and scowled at Tamar.

'Where is she?' Tamar demanded.

'Who?'

You obtuse cow, Tamar thought. 'The fair girl. From last night. You know who I mean.'

'Not here.'

'Then where's the old man?'

Haughtily, the other woman replied, 'My great-grandfather sleeps during the day. He cannot be disturbed.'

God, how old *was* he? 'When did she leave?'

'One quarter hour ago,' said the woman, and pointed vaguely down the road in the direction of Queen Street.

Tamar spun around and hurried back to the landau. 'About fifteen minutes ago,' she said as she stepped up into the carriage, its roof down now that the sun was up. 'She can't be far away. Go onto Queen Street.'

Sven pulled the horse around and whipped it into a trot. On Queen Street he turned left and started up the hill.

They spotted Polly quite quickly, on the opposite side of the road standing on the new footpath outside the towering facade of Thornton, Smith and Firth's Wharf Mill building. She was swaying slightly and apparently mesmerised by the passing traffic, although she seemed oblivious to everything else. Pedestrians, giving her a wide berth, ostentatiously ignored her.

'Oh God,' said Tamar. 'There she is. Stop!'

Sven yanked hard on the horse's head and Tamar had the door of the landau open before it had come to a complete halt. '*Polly!*' she yelled as she got out, ignoring the curious glances of passers-by. '*Polly!*'

Across the street, Polly did not seem to have heard. She remained where she was, still gazing intently at the traffic. Then, without warning, she stepped straight out into it.

Although Tamar saw everything in excruciating detail, it happened very quickly. An oncoming cab swerved, the horrified cabbie wrenching his horse savagely to the right in an effort to avoid the woman in front of him. The horse reared, its hooves slashing the air, then plunged down just as Polly walked beneath it. One hoof struck her on the side of her head and she dropped like a stone.

'*Polly!*' shrieked Tamar as she dashed across the dusty street. Around her, traffic was coming to a halt as curious pedestrians gathered around the body lying in the road. As Polly struggled to sit up, Tamar bent down and peered into her friend's blood-streaked face.

'Bloody hell, that hurt,' Polly mumbled as her hand moved slowly up to the pulpy mess above her ear. 'What happened?'

'It's all right, Polly, you've had an accident.'

'Have I really?' replied Polly in an interested tone. Then, as her eyes rolled up into her head, she fell back onto the road, unconscious.

Tamar yelled, 'Sven, bring the landau. We'll take her to John.'

Sven sprinted back to the carriage, leapt onto the driver's seat and urged the horses across the street, ignoring the curses of other drivers as he cut them off.

Once Polly was safely inside, stretched out on one of the seats, Sven spun the horses around and they clattered off in the direction of Parnell Rise.

CHAPTER TWENTY

John took one look at Polly's unconscious body and climbed into the landau. 'She needs to be in the hospital,' he said. 'She's out cold and her pulse is much too slow. You say she spoke before she passed out?'

'Yes, probably the most lucid thing she's said for weeks. She will be all right, won't she?'

They steadied themselves as Sven gave the horses an urgent flick with his whip and headed off for Auckland Domain and the hospital. John held Polly's head in his lap. 'I don't know, the brain can swell terribly after such a blow and it's hard to say what the result might be.' He looked up at Tamar. 'She may not survive. And conditions at the hospital are pretty dire. It might be new but it's badly administered.'

Polly was admitted to the hospital and, after she showed no sign of regaining consciousness by late afternoon, the matron sent Tamar home with a promise that if anything happened, she would be sent for.

On the way back Tamar began to cry helplessly. John comforted her as best he could, but by the time they arrived she was insisting she was to blame because she had left Polly at the mercy of a thieving Chinaman.

'What thieving Chinaman?' asked John, as he gave Tamar a draught to calm her nerves.

'I gave a disgusting old Celestial at the opium den money for Polly so she could get herself home safely. I shouldn't have trusted him.'

John fumbled in his pocket, then withdrew a bundle of pound notes folded with a silver money clip. 'Is this it? The sister gave it to me after they undressed Polly.'

'Oh,' said Tamar in a small voice. 'I thought the old bastard had kept it.'

'Obviously she *chose* not to hail a cab. It wasn't your fault, Tamar.'

Privately, John believed that after spending the night smoking herself silly, Polly would have been completely disoriented. Still, he felt deeply sad for the poor girl. Unlike her friends, she'd been unable to weather the hard times and tragedies they'd encountered since arriving in New Zealand. But, really, not an inordinate or unexpected number of tragedies, John reflected.

Six days later Tamar received a message advising Polly had regained consciousness, but when she arrived at the hospital it was shockingly clear the old Polly had gone forever.

She was sitting in a narrow bed, her hair tied back from her gaunt face under a thick bandage, her right eye still black. She was propped up against the wall but leaning to one side, her small hands resting palms up on the blanket. She was dribbling slightly and her eyes were open but utterly vacant.

Tamar asked hesitantly, 'Polly?'

'She can't hear you. Well, at least we don't think she can.'

Tamar turned to see a nurse hurrying down the ward carrying a pile of dirty linen. The nurse stopped at the end of Polly's bed, dropped her load onto the floor and tapped her head. 'Her mind's gone. Can't hear or see. Well, there's no visible signs, put it like that. Are you family?'

'No,' answered Tamar. 'A friend. She has no family.'

'The doctor will be doing his rounds shortly, if you want to talk to him. You can wait with her, if you like.'

Tamar nodded her thanks as the nurse picked up her linen and continued on her busy way. Unable to locate a chair, she perched herself at the end of Polly's lumpy mattress and waited. The ward was austere and rather crowded, but at least it appeared moderately clean; Tamar had heard the men's wards were filthy.

She watched Polly carefully, a painful lump in her throat. She called her name gently, touched her hand and used the blanket to wipe the dribble from the corner of her mouth, but there was no response. Polly was so motionless she reminded Tamar of a large rag doll. 'Polly, it's Tamar,' she whispered, desperate to see even a flutter of her friend's eyelids.

'Wasting your time there, I'm afraid.'

Tamar jumped to her feet. 'Are you the doctor?' she asked.

'Yes,' said a small, well-dressed man with a harried expression and a clipboard under his arm. 'Yes, I'm Doctor Hastings. And you are ...'

'Tamar Deane. A close friend of Miss Jakes.'

'Well, Miss Deane,' said Hastings. 'I'm afraid the prognosis is not good, she will probably remain like this forever, if she survives. It's a miracle she has so far. Such a blow to the head would have killed most people. The staff say she is a prostitute,' he added irrelevantly.

Tamar was silent for a moment, then replied dismissively, 'Yes, she is. Does she know what's going on?'

'Who can tell?' he replied, extracting a watch from his waistcoat pocket and ostentatiously checking the time.

Tamar was beginning to lose her temper. 'Well, *you* should. You're supposed to be looking after her.'

Dr Hastings sighed. 'Miss Deane, as far as I'm aware, and I've

317

had *considerable* experience with injuries like this, she is a vegetable. The only physical reaction we're seeing at all is a fit of violent sweating accompanied by involuntary shaking every five or six hours. She will in all likelihood remain this way until she dies, which could be quite soon. It will be a mercy. Oh, and she can swallow, but that's about it.'

The opium, thought Tamar; she still needs the opium. 'Does she have to stay here?'

'I'm afraid that would be impossible. We're dreadfully under-staffed at the moment and she's taking up a bed that could be used by someone else with a more positive prognosis. Does she have means, do you know?'

Tamar nodded.

'Really?' said the doctor, clearly surprised. 'Then I suggest you engage a private nurse as she will need constant attention. Now, if you don't mind, I must continue my rounds. I'm sorry I can't be more positive.'

Tamar sat with Polly for a while longer then said goodbye, promising that her next visit would be to take her home. As she left the ward the nurse she had talked to earlier handed her a piece of paper with a name and an address. 'Lottie Atkin is a friend of mine,' she said. 'She's a nurse who retired to care for her husband. He died recently, and she might be interested in looking after your friend. Go and see her, see what she says. She might be just the person you need.'

'Thank you very much,' replied Tamar, surprised and grateful.

'You're welcome. We're here to help,' said the nurse.

'Yes, well, somebody should mention that to Doctor Hastings.'

The woman giggled. 'I'd love to, dearie, but I can't afford to lose my job. And it's not his fault. We're fighting a losing battle.'

Tamar called on Mrs Lottie Atkin that afternoon, and came away with an arrangement that suited everybody. Mrs Atkin, although a liberal-minded and worldly woman, had no intention of relocating to a brothel, so it was decided Polly would be transferred to Mrs Atkin's home the following day. There, for a generous fee, she would have her own room and constant professional care. It was understood, due to Polly's serious physical condition, the arrangement would probably not be long term. It was also understood Mrs Atkin would administer regular draughts of Decoction of Opium. As a nurse she had seen opium addiction and was aware that if the poor girl did indeed have any mind left, she would be in utter torment; she was unlikely to survive very long, and Mrs Atkin believed it her duty to make Polly's remaining time as comfortable as possible. The only slight problem was Mrs Atkin's refusal to have Cabbage living in her house.

'It'll be enough keeping the poor girl clean as it is, without a smelly little dog jumping all over her all day. No, I can't allow it, I'm sorry,' she said adamantly.

'Can he visit? Polly is very attached to him and I'm sure it will do her good,' Tamar replied.

Mrs Atkin pulled a face. 'If he must. But he's not to go near the bed, and he must have a bath beforehand. They're filthy animals, dogs.'

'You have a pig in your back yard, I notice.'

'Aye, but I don't invite him in to the parlour for tea and scones now, do I?'

Sven, John and Tamar collected Polly from the hospital the following day. After she had been settled, John had a long talk with Mrs Atkin and pronounced her very able indeed. Tamar felt a little less guilty about leaving Polly in the care of a stranger, and said so on the way back to Dilworth Terrace.

'What was the alternative?' said John. 'Were *you* going to look after her twenty-four hours a day? She'll be well cared for, fed and kept clean, and Mrs Atkin said she would read to her every day. And

319

she'll still be getting her damned opium. You and the girls will visit?'

'Of course.'

'Then she'll be as fine as she can be, given the circumstances.' John didn't want to say that in his professional opinion Polly's battered and damaged body would more than likely fail within the next six months.

'I hope so,' said Tamar. 'I really hope so.'

When they arrived back at the house, Eliza met them at the side entrance. She looked nervously from Tamar to John, handed Tamar a card and said, 'There is a gentleman to see yer, Miss Tamar. In yer office.'

Tamar read the name on the calling card, and when she looked up her face was white.

John took her elbow. 'What is it? Not more bad news?'

'No. At least, I don't think so.' Tamar took a deep breath and said quietly, 'It's Kepa.' She looked at John steadily. 'The father of my son.'

'What's *he* doing here?'

'How should I know? And don't speak to me like that, please.'

'I'm sorry,' said John, only moderately contrite and aware of an unpleasant sensation of jealousy growing in the pit of his stomach. 'I thought you'd seen the last of him.'

Yes, so did I, thought Tamar. Her heart was racing and she felt weak and in need of a chair. Kepa, after all this time! 'Do you want to meet him?' she asked John, not at all sure she wanted to introduce them.

John, pretending nonchalance, removed his hat and gloves. 'I suppose so, seeing as I'm here,' he replied.

He followed Tamar inside, frowning in disapproval as she took off her hat and checked her appearance in the *étagère* mirror. Unaware she was holding her breath, she opened the door to her office.

Kepa stood looking at a painting above the fireplace, and turned towards the door as she entered. His hair had grown longer, but otherwise he was exactly as Tamar remembered him. No, she thought after a moment's reflection, perhaps his beautiful, strong, dark face had matured a little. They scrutinised each other in silence.

John, feeling foolish and childishly excluded, coughed into his fist.

Tamar started. 'I'm sorry, I'm forgetting my manners,' she said. 'John, this is Kepa Te Roroa. Kepa, this is my good friend, Dr John Adams.'

The two men stepped towards each other and shook hands briefly. No one sat down. There was an awkward silence. If John had been a cat the fur on his back would have been bristling, and he was doing a poor job of keeping the dislike off his face. Tamar felt uncomfortable standing between the two men, and wished John would relax. 'Let's sit down, shall we?' she said in a voice she hoped would not betray her own nervousness.

Kepa nodded, sank gracefully into a chair and absently pushed his dark hair off his forehead. He seemed at ease and completely unperturbed by John's hostility.

Watching the young Maori warily, John was aware of what Tamar had seen in him; he was extremely handsome with an athletic build and definite charisma. In a fit of pique, John decided to leave. 'I'm terribly sorry, Tamar, but I've remembered I'm supposed to be somewhere else. You must excuse me. Very nice to have met you, Mr Te Roroa.' He bowed slightly and walked out.

When the door had closed, Kepa observed in an amused tone, 'I do not believe your friend was pleased to meet me.' Then, more intimately, he added, 'I have missed you, Tamar.'

As he stood and moved forward to take her in his arms, she placed both hands on his chest and pushed him away.

'No,' she said.

They talked for over three hours. Tamar told him what had happened to her after his son had been born, how she had felt in the weeks after the child had been taken away, and of her flight to Auckland. He listened sympathetically, obviously moved when she spoke of her pain and her fear. Then, when she could finally bring herself to ask when he had returned from England, and he replied that it had been a year ago, she almost slapped him. 'And what have you been doing since?' she asked, her voice as controlled as she could manage.

'I was home for a week before sailing to the United States of America. Boston, Philadelphia, Washington, all along the eastern seaboard.'

Relieved, Tamar closed her eyes for a moment, grateful not to hear he had been back for twelve months and had not bothered to contact her. 'Whose idea was that?' she asked, knowing the answer.

'Te Kanene's,' Kepa replied. 'But it was a worthwhile experience. Interesting people, the Americans. And we brought back a very profitable cargo. We only arrived yesterday.'

'So you have not been home?'

'No. I have missed you, Tamar. I have thought of you often.'

She glanced up at him, then quickly away again.

'But I will understand if you do not want me in your life,' he continued. 'I realise how much trouble our last meeting caused.' He hesitated for a second. 'Do you miss him still? Our son?'

'Of course I miss him! What mother would *not* miss her child?' Tamar said angrily.

'And you have not seen him since he was born?'

Tamar shook her head.

'I have,' Kepa said. 'But not for the past year. I am looking forward to seeing him again. He was almost six months old when I left. My *tuahine* Mereana is raising him.'

'Yes, I know. Te Kanene sends me letters.'

'Does he?' Kepa raised his eyebrows. 'How uncharacteristic. My uncle is a shrewd and often merciless man.'

'I had noticed,' Tamar replied dryly. 'He took my son away from me.'

'He is my son too, and I believe my uncle did what he thought was best for everyone.'

But mostly his nephew, Tamar thought bitterly.

'Kahurangi is a lovely child. When you meet him you will know what I mean.' Tamar noted Kepa said 'when'.

'Will you have much to do with him when you go home?' asked Tamar. 'I assume you're staying, this time?'

'For now, anyway. And yes, I will have plenty of involvement with him, although he will still live with my sister. When he is old enough he will be told who I am.'

'And when will that be?'

'Soon. Perhaps when I get home. He will be talking by now.'

'Won't that confuse him, that he's not living with his real father?'

'No. Why should it? It happens all the time with my people. Everyone shares in a child's upbringing. Why should it matter whose house he sleeps in?'

Tamar looked away. It wasn't the way she'd raise a child. She looked back and found Kepa staring intently at her. 'Are you happy doing this, Tamar?' he asked.

'Running a brothel, you mean?' she answered bluntly.

'Yes. It is not something I imagined you would do.'

'No, I never imagined it, either. My friend Myrna left me the business when she died. Carrying on seemed the easiest thing to do.'

'Do you have plans for anything other than this?' Kepa asked, waving his hand vaguely at her desk.

'I won't be doing this forever, if that's what you mean.'

Kepa sat forward in his chair. 'Do your plans include me?'

'That's up to you, isn't it?' Tamar retorted, more aggressively than she intended.

'No, it is up to you. I still do not believe society is ready to accept us, but socially I have less to lose than you. And we are the *matua* of Kahurangi-o-te-po, whether others are happy about that or not.' He leaned even further towards Tamar and took hold of her wrist. 'And, Tamar, I still burn for you. That has not changed.'

She ignored his last comment by responding to the first. 'Kepa, I am the widow of a chronic alcoholic and hopelessly indebted gambler, I have given birth to an illegitimate, half-caste child, and I am the madam of a whorehouse. Do you think I'm worried about what people might think of me?'

Now he ignored her. 'I mean it, Tamar. I want you.'

Tamar didn't know what to say, feeling silly with her arm outstretched and Kepa holding her wrist. She moved to pull it back but he gripped more firmly, as if he did not mean to let go until she gave him a response.

What she wanted to say was, yes, I still burn for you, Kepa, but she could not permit herself to utter the words. This was wrong. She could not be with him. She would not be treated like one of her employees, a woman for some man to pick up and put down as he chose. But it was true, she *did* burn for him. And with that thought, her eyes brimmed with tears; for her predicament, for her own aching heart, for the shambolic state of her life. She stood, her voice unsteady as her tears threatened to spill. 'I think you should go.'

His answer was to take her in his arms. He lowered his mouth and began to kiss her, gently at first, then with more urgency. She kissed him back, as she knew she would, angry at herself, and at him, but unwilling to stop. She could feel his erection poking eagerly against her stomach. 'Yes?' he whispered.

Taking her silence as confirmation, he gathered her long skirt and petticoats above her waist, then lifted her easily onto the desk. Stepping back he released himself from his trousers, parted Tamar's thighs, then undid the ties securing her underdrawers and pulled them off her.

She gasped as he entered her. It did not take long, for him or for her, and she bit his neck hard to prevent herself crying out. When they stopped moving, a pile of papers balanced on the edge of the desk cascaded onto the floor.

Tamar started laughing, and then the tears came. She rested her head against his chest, weeping quietly, taking comfort from his strength and the soothing stroke of his hands on her back.

Riria's letter arrived on the last day of 1882, confirming her arrival in the first week of the new year. Tamar sent Sven to meet the train every day, but Riria, as independent as ever, knocked on the front door at the start of the second week of January, complete with travel bag and another little black hat to replace the one she left at Huia eighteen months ago.

Tamar went running down the hall to meet her, and the two women clung together in delight. Stepping back, Tamar said, 'You look wonderful! You haven't changed at all!'

And she hadn't. Riria's thick, lustrous brown hair still cascaded down her back and her beautiful, tattooed face was as strong and intelligent as ever. Smiling widely, she replied, 'You have, Tamar. You seem much happier. And what has happened to your face?'

Tamar touched the scar on her brow. 'My friend John, the doctor, fixed it last year.'

Riria raised her arched eyebrows. 'Then he must be a *takuta* of considerable skill. The mark has almost gone!'

Tamar was not at all interested in talking about her scar. 'Come in and tell me about everything you've been doing.'

At that moment Sven appeared, bowed towards Riria, said, 'Madam,' and reached for her luggage. She batted his hand out of the way and picked up her bag. 'I will do that,' she said crossly. Sven stepped back in surprise. Tamar smiled and shook her head at Sven, who shrugged and retreated down the hall.

Tamar took Riria upstairs and showed her into Polly's old bedroom. Riria dropped her bag on the floor, bounced on the bed once or twice and said, 'This is a very beautiful room. It is for me to sleep in?'

'It belonged to one of the girls who worked here, but she had an accident a month or so ago and isn't here any more.' She didn't elaborate. 'It's yours if you don't mind what the room was once used for.'

'Whoring?' asked Riria.

'Whatever you want to call it.'

'I do not mind,' answered Riria, looking about the pretty boudoir. 'As long as I am not expected to do the same.'

Tamar was mortified: did Riria think she had invited her here to work for her? She opened her mouth to protest, then saw Riria's smile. Tamar put her hand to her heart. 'I thought you were serious!'

'I think not!' replied Riria, laughing. 'Not after …' The smile slipped from her face.

With a sickening flash of comprehension, Tamar knew what her friend had been about to say. Her hands flew to her face. 'Oh, no! Please tell me no!'

Riria said nothing, her eyes filling with tears.

'Oh God, it was Peter! I'm so sorry, Riria. Why didn't you tell me?' She hurried over to her friend and embraced her. They rocked gently together, each remembering the terrifying months. Riria was first to pull back. 'It is in the past now,' she said quietly.

'You didn't …,' began Tamar, pointing at Riria's stomach.

'No. I could not have tolerated that.'

Tamar exhaled in relief. She felt sick, and dreadfully guilty. 'He's dead,' she said, as if this piece of information might somehow help, forgetting Riria already knew.

'Yes. A *pirihimana* came to Kainui to talk to me. About you, and what happened after I last saw you.'

Tamar remembered her conversation with Te Kanene. 'Riria,' she asked softly. 'Was it you?' She had to know.

The two women looked at each other steadily, both knowing the answer to this question would change their relationship forever. The silence seemed to expand to fill the room. Riria went over to the window, gazing through the heavy lace curtains at nothing. 'Yes,' she said eventually, and turned to face Tamar. 'He was going to die anyway, *e tuakana*. But if he had not, I would still have done it.'

Tamar expected to feel revulsion. She expected to feel horror and disgust at this wild and enigmatic young woman's confession. Instead she felt an intense sense of justice, which frightened her, and a vague sadness. She held out her hand. 'Let's go and have some tea, shall we?'

Riria smiled.

'I can't get over how beautiful she is. You know, for a darkie,' said Bronwyn.

Letitia nodded in agreement. 'In spite of that tattoo.'

'It's a crying shame she *isn't* working here,' Vivienne added. 'She'd make a fortune. She's exactly the sort of woman lots of Englishmen would fancy a romp with. Beautiful, buxom and brown. And there's definitely something *untamed* about her, don't you think? Pass the sherry, Bron.'

'I don't know,' said Bronwyn as she handed over the cut-crystal decanter. 'She frightens me a bit. She's still a Maori, even if Tamar insists on treating her as if she isn't.'

'I think you're jealous,' said Jessica matter-of-factly. 'Because Tamar likes her and because she's got better tits than you.'

'She has not! How do you know?'

'Because I saw her in the bath. They're beautiful — big and round with huge dark nipples. And she's younger than you.'

'Jessica, do you have to be such a bitch?' asked Vivienne.

'Yes,' the petite blonde girl replied.

'I didn't say I didn't like her, I said she frightens me a little, that's all,' said Bronwyn, pointedly ignoring Jessica. 'Especially since she got that old Maori man in to exorcise Polly's room. Spirits being attracted to misery and fear, my arse.'

'Well, don't let Tamar hear you saying anything against her. They've been through a lot together and I don't think she'd appreciate it,' observed Vivienne. 'Where are they, anyway? I thought we were supposed to be having dinner at seven? And where's John?'

As it was Sunday night and the girls were not working, Tamar had invited John for dinner so he could meet Riria. The girls were having a pre-dinner drink while they waited for him to arrive.

Eliza hurried past the parlour to answer the side door, and Vivienne said, 'Speak of the devil,' as they heard her welcoming John. He breezed into the parlour, flung his hat and gloves in the general direction of the sideboard and flopped down on the sofa.

'Sorry I'm late,' he said, helping himself to a large brandy. 'A patient. Usual story.' He looked around. 'Where's Tamar? I need to ask her something. And when are we eating? I'm starving.'

The girls were constantly amazed at the amount John ate and were forever teasing him. They had an easy relationship and treated him like a brother. John had come to know them very well over the past three years as he looked after their health and shared with them both the happy and less appealing aspects of their lives, and they valued his friendship and support. They joked with him about which one he was going to marry, although they all knew such a thing would never happen. He had never taken advantage of them, and they appreciated and respected him for that. They had all experienced physicians who preferred to be paid for their services in kind. To them, John was trustworthy, safe and reliable, qualities they did not readily associate with men, and they loved him for it.

In answer to his questions, Tamar swept into the room wearing a pale lavender tea gown in dupion silk with a moderately revealing neckline, above which her breasts rose becomingly. The bustle was coming back into fashion again, and her gown was contoured accordingly. Her auburn hair, swept up and falling in soft waves on either side of her face, was caught at the back with a purple silk flower. 'Oh, hello, John. You're here.'

'You're looking lovely as usual, my dear,' he said as he rose and kissed her cheek. 'And I have a favour to ask.'

'Yes, of course,' replied Tamar. 'But first I want you to meet Riria.' She stepped aside as the Maori girl appeared in the doorway. 'Riria, please meet Dr John Adams. John, this is my friend, Miss Riria Te Hau.'

Tamar and Riria had been shopping and Tamar had insisted on buying Riria several outfits. Tonight she was dressed in a simple cream satin gown, its lustre complementing her coffee-coloured skin and the cut emphasising her full bust, firm waist and generous hips. Her hair was loose, as usual, and she wore a white camellia tucked behind one ear. In the light of the incandescent lamps her big, dark eyes glittered and the voluptuous line of her full lips was accentuated.

John stared at her for several seconds, his mouth open, before he remembered his manners and stepped forward.

'Miss Te *Hau*,' he gushed, bowing low over her hand. 'I'm *delighted* to meet you.'

Tamar watched as Riria looked John up and down. He had closed his mouth now, but still looked like a stunned puppy. As the silence lengthened, Tamar thought, oh no, she's going to say something mean.

She didn't. What she said was, 'I am delighted to meet you, *Takuta* Adams. You must be a very skilled man to have repaired Tamar's face so artfully.'

Tamar let her breath out and smiled.

John went pink. 'Thank you, Miss Te Hau. How kind of you to say so.'

'You must tell me more about what you do.'

'I'd love to!' replied John enthusiastically, clearly thrilled with the opportunity to expound at length on his beloved work to such a captivating audience. 'Perhaps over dinner?'

As the girls pulled faces, Tamar interjected quickly, 'No, John, not while we're eating. Afterwards, perhaps. Shall we go into the dining salon? I believe Eliza is ready to serve.'

As everyone stood, John exclaimed suddenly, 'Bloody hell!' He looked around in embarrassment. 'I beg your pardon, ladies, but I've just remembered. I brought a guest, Tamar. He's waiting outside. I wanted to check with you before I invited him in. May I?'

'Of course, John. Go and get him. He must be wondering what on earth's happened to you.'

'Won't be a minute,' John replied, and hared off down the hall while the others seated themselves in the dining salon.

I do believe Riria has addled his mind, reflected Tamar, as she waited in the foyer for him to return.

The door opened and John came back in, followed by a tall man in his early thirties. He removed his hat and stood looking about him. His hair was a very light brown and a heavy lock flopped

330

untidily over his forehead above intelligent, lively, medium-blue eyes. His nose was neither big nor small, and his mouth looked kind and revealed good, even teeth when he smiled, transforming his face from pleasant to moderately handsome. He was broad across the shoulders and chest with a trim waist and long, well-muscled legs, and he was dressed for dinner. Cabbage, who had been loitering under the stairs, dashed jealously out and began to raise his leg against the man's boot.

'Bugger off, you horrible little animal,' said John, aiming a gentle kick at Cabbage's skinny rump. 'Tamar, I'd like to introduce my friend, Andrew Murdoch. Andrew's from Scotland — he runs a few sheep in the Hawke's Bay.'

CHAPTER TWENTY-ONE

A ndrew visited Tamar every time he travelled to Auckland on business, and even when he did not have business, although it took Tamar almost a year to realise this. He brought her hothouse flowers, imported chocolates and small gifts. Nothing too expensive or personal, just tokens of his appreciation of their time together, he said. After the first twelve months Tamar had to admit she was coming to value his company.

Andrew was in Auckland when Polly died in her sleep in August of 1883. He was extremely supportive when Tamar broke down at the cemetery. Overcome by a flood of grief and private guilt at her relief Polly was finally at peace, Tamar had to be taken home, Cabbage cuddled tightly against her chest and her head on Andrew's shoulder. Privately John was delighted to see something more than friendship developing between his two friends.

John himself had a fair bit to be pleased about, having fallen hopelessly and irretrievably in love with Riria. For ten months he used every flimsy excuse to visit her, and was delighted to find she had a natural gift for healing and was genuinely interested in his work. By July she was accompanying him to his weekly clinic for Maori patients who lived on the outskirts of Auckland, none of whom paid for his services with money. He rarely, however, found himself short of *kumara*, potatoes, pork or chickens. Riria extended her stay several times and in November, John asked her to marry him. To everyone's surprise, she accepted.

'Your mother and father won't like him,' Tamar said when Riria broke the news.

'They are not marrying him,' replied Riria, with characteristic logic. 'I know what I want and I believe I have found it in John.'

'I always assumed you'd end up with one of those big, handsome men from your own people.'

'Someone like Kepa?'

'Well, yes,' Tamar replied, slightly embarrassed. 'Someone more like him.'

'John loves me, he has a kind heart and he is intelligent. I do not care how short he is or that his head is smooth and shiny. He will treat me with respect and I will be safe with him. That is all I want. Will you make my wedding gown?'

'Of course I will,' Tamar replied, very happy for her friend.

They were married in March of 1884 at Kainui. Tamar and Andrew stayed at the village for several nights, a very new experience for Andrew, who was especially nonplussed when he and Tamar were offered sleeping accommodation together. Tamar explained that Maori had a different attitude towards courting couples, but when a certain light began to develop in Andrew's eyes she informed him she was not yet ready to subscribe to it, although she felt hypocritical saying so, given her history.

The wedding was an important occasion for Riria's people, and the guests numbered in the hundreds. Riria introduced Tamar to her many relatives, but Tamar lost track by the time she'd met the ninth or tenth *whaea*. 'Are they *all* your aunties?' she asked.

John grossly insulted Riria's father, Te Hau, by offering to pay for the wedding. He stalked off, flinging his cloak over his shoulders and muttering about discourteous *Pakeha*, until his wife sat him down and accused him of being a prideful man too stubborn and arrogant to bother trying to comprehend the way other people lived. Te Hau sulked for several hours, then took John to one side, thanked him for his offer, advised him all the necessary preparations had been made for the wedding but that if John wanted to make some sort of contribution, there was a particularly fine, although very expensive, stallion in the next village that would make a suitable addition to Te Hau's stable. John, desperate to make a favourable impression, agreed instantly.

Te Hau, who had been determined not to like this pale little *Pakeha*, decided the man might not be completely useless. He stuck out his hand and grunted. John took it and nodded back. It was a start.

On the day of the wedding the village hummed with activity. Numerous *hangi* had to be put down to cook the vegetables, pork and chickens, there was *kanga pirau* or rotten corn to be readied, bread to be baked and endless pots of tea to be brewed. Kainui was a dry village so officially there would be no alcohol, although Riria assumed there would be the usual group of uncles and the odd auntie having a sly drink behind the tall fence.

At three in the afternoon everyone crowded into the *wharenui* for the wedding ceremony, which was short, with only a few *karakia*. A prayer was also said in English to honour the handful of *Pakeha*. Riria wore a traditional *korowai* trimmed with kiwi feathers over a cream gown, decorated with subtle embroidery. Her long hair was caught up with an exquisitely carved greenstone comb, and long, matching earrings dangled almost to her shoulders. John himself looked rather resplendent in a new morning suit and striped silk tie.

During the ceremony, when Andrew took Tamar's hand and said to her, 'They look very happy, don't they?' Tamar pretended she hadn't heard. She suspected Andrew may be considering asking her to marry him, and she felt ambivalent about the idea.

The wedding feast was memorable. The bride and groom, Riria's immediate family, and Tamar and Andrew sat at a long table set up on the open space of the *marae* outside the *wharenui*, while everyone else sat on wooden benches or on the ground to eat. Several ancient relatives were ensconced in ornate wing chairs in deference to their age and status, their dusty brown feet resting on footstools.

After the eating there were speeches, most in Maori, which Tamar and Andrew could not understand, but which caused great hilarity. John must have picked up the gist of some of the speakers as he went pink several times. Tamar wondered if she would ever get used to the way Maori spoke about sex so casually and openly. Then came what Tamar assumed were different family groups who sang and danced, the women with their graceful hand and *poi* movements and the men stamping and chanting behind them, followed by the giving of *koha*, money or gifts, to the newlyweds and the bride's family.

Tamar and Andrew left Kainui the following day, although Riria and John would not be returning to Auckland for another week. Andrew went home and Tamar resumed the business of managing the brothel.

A new girl had been hired to replace Polly and seemed to be settling in well. Minette claimed to be French, although she confessed to Tamar her real name was Minnie Hodge and her Australian-born mother had been a prostitute servicing the gold fields of Otago. As far as her mother could recall, her father had been a genuine Frenchman, an itinerant goldminer. But she was very pretty, with an exotic air, enhanced by long reddish-gold hair and her version of a French accent, and she was very popular with the customers.

Eliza, having had her first child, a happy fat baby with his father's almost white hair, had reduced her hours and taken on more of a supervisory role, managing the two young girls who came in daily to do the housework. She still cooked, however, and was often in the kitchen with the baby balanced comfortably on her hip or nestled in a basket on the floor. She was pregnant again but refused to stop work, saying she would go daft sitting around with nothing to do.

Money from the business was still accruing steadily in the bank, and Tamar had no idea what to do with it. Auckland was growing rapidly, despite the deepening depression as prices for New Zealand agricultural products continued to fall. Some businesses failed, and many small farmers were forced off their land. Andrew never mentioned the state of his own finances, however, and Tamar assumed he had commercial interests keeping him afloat. She knew some farmers were benefiting from the new frozen meat export trade and thought he may be one of them.

As 1884 turned into 1885, Tamar found herself relying more and more on Andrew for companionship and sometimes advice regarding her business. He had a very shrewd head and was politically astute, and she valued his opinions. In 1882 there had been moves to repeal the Contagious Diseases Act, implemented thirteen years earlier ostensibly to control the 'red plague' of venereal disease, but in effect only serving to establish a system by which whores were licensed. Andrew assured Tamar the politicians would be unlikely to take the suggestion of repeal further. In fact, he thought the Act would possibly be made compulsory. Tamar was relieved to hear this; if the Act was repealed, there would be no legislation to enforce prostitutes to accept compulsory treatment for venereal diseases, which would bring the trade into even more disrepute, and this could seriously affect her business. She had enough bother with delegations from social purity, temperance and Pietist church groups banging on the front door at annoyingly regular intervals. She was never rude to them but always made it tersely clear her house was disease-free and run under the strictest of sanitary conditions.

By the end of 1884 Andrew made his intentions towards Tamar more than obvious: he wanted to marry her and take her to live in the Hawke's Bay. While not surprised, as they had been courting for two years, she was still not confident about saying yes. There were so many things Andrew did not know about her and she was convinced his family — his sister and brother-in-law who lived with him — would not accept a retired madam as a sister-in-law. He admitted it could be a slight problem.

'Aye, Jeannie is a wee bit self-righteous, but I'm sure that once she gets to know you she'll realise what a good woman you are. And I don't think Lachlan will give a toss either way. And besides, I will be taking you home as my wife, and that will be that. Jeannie can mope about with a face like a pickled egg and talk to God about it as much as she likes, but that's the way it will be.'

Tamar remained unconvinced. She had no difficulty with moving to some godforsaken part of the colony to be a sheep-farmer's wife; the idea of spending the rest of her life with Andrew Murdoch was becoming more appealing, but she could not marry a man who did not know about her past. She'd told him about her disastrous marriage to Peter, her flight from him and his subsequent death, but had never mentioned Kepa or their son. She feared that if she did, she would never see Andrew again, and she'd come to realise she desperately wanted to keep him in her life.

She had seen Kepa twice more, but they had not slept together; she had refused. He brought news and more photographs of Kahurangi, which Tamar kept carefully hidden. The child was three and a half now and, according to Kepa, healthy, happy and bright. It occurred to Tamar that if she married Andrew and moved to the Hawke's Bay, she would be in a much better position to see her son, but how could she do that without Andrew finding out? She could not entertain the idea of deceiving him. The possibility of a life with Kepa had never been a reality, so she had no compunction about taking another man as a husband. And Kepa understood that too, perhaps better than she did herself, although she still kept a very special place for him in her heart. She would never forget their precious time together and what she had once felt for him. What she still felt for him, if she were rigorously honest with herself.

All through 1885 Tamar continued to decline Andrew's offers of marriage, using her responsibility to her girls and Myrna's memory as an excuse. Andrew, however, refused to give up, believing that if he waited long enough, she would say yes.

And in 1886, she did. Three things happened that had considerable bearing on her change of heart. The first was that Letitia finally agreed to marry her beau, the customer who had been persistently asking her to be his wife since 1882. At the same time, Bronwyn left to start her own business. She'd spent enough years on her back, she said, and wanted a rest so she'd invested her considerable nest egg in a restaurant and bar in Queen Street. She apologised to Tamar when she also revealed Eliza was considering taking up her offer to cook there.

Tamar had also observed how happy John and Riria were, and wondered wistfully what it would like to have children with a man she loved, children she would keep. John and Riria's first child, Simon, had been born the year before, and they doted on him. Riria was pregnant again and John's practice was doing extremely well, despite some of his more affluent European customers withdrawing their patronage when he had taken a Maori wife, and they were more than comfortable in the house on Parnell

338

Rise. He had adapted to Riria's culture, and she to his, and they lived a life that successfully accommodated both, even if John did sometimes lose track of which of Riria's relatives were sleeping on his parlour floor.

The third thing that happened was an event that literally shook New Zealand. In the early hours of 10 June, Mt Tarawera, near Rotorua, erupted violently, belching huge clouds of hot ash, rocks and scalding mud thousands of feet into the air. Tamar was woken by the noise at three in the morning, and stood at her high window looking southeast at the lightning flashes zigzagging across the glowing, crimson sky, praying the conflagration was not originating from the Hawke's Bay where Andrew lived. If she had believed in hell, she might have been convinced the whole country itself had been transported to its gates.

In the weeks following the eruption, John attended several Rotorua Maori who had been caught in mudslides and ash falls and received terrible burns, brought to Auckland by relatives in the hope they could be saved. They had all perished, however, and Tamar had been profoundly moved by John's stories of their distress at having their ancestral lands so utterly devastated and their remorse at whatever they had done to make their Gods deliver such retribution. It brought home to her the fragility of human life. Was she being a fool for refusing to accept the chance of happiness Andrew was offering? She was beginning to suspect she was.

One evening in July she told him she would marry him. As he gazed at her silently, tears in his eyes, her heart plummeted; he's changed his mind, she thought. I've made him wait too long. 'Are you withdrawing your proposal?' she asked.

'Oh, Tamar, of *course* I'm not. I'm just speechless because you've finally agreed,' he said, taking both of her hands and laughing delightedly. 'I was sure that if I waited long enough you would say yes. Oh God, you've made me so happy! And I promise, I *promise*, I'll make you happy too.' He leaned forward and kissed her. 'When? Next month?'

Tamar didn't hear. 'Andrew,' she began. 'I need to tell you something first.'

'Anything, my love.'

Tamar prayed she wasn't going to hurt him too much, and ruin everything.

'I've never told you why I had to leave Peter, why he was so angry with me and tried to kill me.'

Andrew looked at her expectantly.

She took a deep breath and plunged onwards, her words falling over themselves. 'I committed an adulterous act with a Maori, which resulted in a child. If you want to withdraw your proposal, I'll understand,' she added quickly, not daring to look him in the eye.

Andrew was silent for several seconds. Then he said, very carefully, 'I already know.'

'*How*?' asked Tamar incredulously.

'John told me, just after you and I met.'

Tamar was speechless.

'I don't mind,' Andrew continued quickly. 'I've thought about it for a long time, and I don't mind. After all, it's in the past, isn't it?'

'Well, *I* bloody well mind! I'll kill him the next time I see him,' declared Tamar, absolutely incensed. 'Talking about my private affairs! How *rude*! What if it had turned you away from me?'

'Tamar,' said Andrew gently but persistently, 'I asked you whether it's in the past. I need an answer.'

'Of course it's in the past! I've seen the child's father perhaps three times since he was born. We have no relationship to speak of.' Then something occurred to her. 'Did you think I wouldn't marry you because there was someone else?'

Andrew nodded.

That bloody John, she thought. She leaned forward and placed her head on Andrew's solid shoulder. 'No, Andrew, there isn't anyone else. You've been my only companion since I met you.' She could feel his deep sigh of relief. 'I'm sorry if you thought otherwise.'

'No, no I didn't,' he lied.

'I was very young then, and unhappy.'

'Tamar, it's your business, not mine. I won't mention it again if you don't want me to. You *were* young, in a strange country and married to a very unpleasant man.'

Tamar sat up. 'No, please don't make excuses. I know what I did, but I've come to terms with it. I'm not a silly young girl any more.'

'You're not exactly old, though, are you?' Andrew said, looking fondly at her beautiful, clear, unlined face. 'You're only twenty-four. I'm thirty-five. How will you feel when you have to push me around in my bathchair?'

'Oh, don't be silly!'

'Just one question, though, if you don't mind.'

She raised her eyebrows.

'The father of your child comes from Hawke's Bay. Is that going to have an impact on us?'

She didn't have to think hard about her answer. 'None at all. Although I would like to see my son. If I can.'

The wedding was planned for the following January. Tamar told the girls she would be selling the house and winding down the business by Christmas. Bronwyn and Letitia were leaving anyway, Sven would go with Eliza and work in the bar of Bronwyn's restaurant, Vivienne was going to try to get work in another house, and Jessica was considering buying a small commercial business, a bakery or fruit shop. Minette left a week after Tamar's announcement, taking her regular customers with her to set up on her own. Tamar wished her well and gave her a generous bonus to help her on her way.

The house and most of its contents were sold in October via a property agent to a wealthy Englishman who was coming out in the New Year. The purchaser undoubtedly had no idea of his new home's past history, but he'd got it for a bargain so Tamar decided that was his problem, and the land agent, who'd earned himself a healthy commission, agreed. Tamar suggested she put the proceeds from the sale into Andrew's business but he declined, saying she should hold on to the money, along with her savings and the amount she had been bequeathed by Myrna. 'You might want to do something with it yourself one day,' he'd said.

'But it's a small fortune,' Tamar had replied. 'And I *don't* need it. You might as well make use of it. I realise farmers haven't been doing well over the last few years.'

But he'd waved her offer away, insisting it was her money.

They were married in a civil ceremony in Albert Park on 21 January 1887, with just a few friends present, then crossed the harbour to Devonport on the paddle steamer *Victoria* for a wedding breakfast at the Esplanade Hotel. Andrew's sister declined to attend, which did not bode well for them all living happily together when Andrew took his new bride home.

Tamar wanted a wedding completely unlike her first. She wore a gown of bronze and black striped silk with long, tight sleeves, a high Chinese collar, and a fitting bodice embellished with black piping. The skirt was split at the front and caught at each side with a black silk rose, revealing an underskirt of pale ecru brocade with black piping stitched in a complex pattern around the hem. From behind, the dress was a mass of fine pleats from the waist down, forming a short train. In her hair Tamar wore a silk rose to match her dress. Underneath her gown her corset was done up so snugly she almost fainted getting into the landau for the ride to Queen's Wharf. When the wedding party arrived at the Esplanade Hotel, she and Riria, heavily pregnant, retired to the ladies' room so she could let her corset out.

When Tamar could breathe properly again, Riria asked to see her wedding ring. Tamar removed her black lace glove, slid the heavy ring off her finger and passed it over. A wide gold band, it had a raised pattern of intricate Celtic knotwork around its circumference.

'Andrew had it made for me. I think it's beautiful,' she said as Riria examined it.

'Yes, the pattern is similar to some Maori motifs.' She looked searchingly at Tamar. 'And you think you will be happy with Andrew?'

'Yes, I do.'

'What is different this time?'

Tamar sat on a velvet upholstered chair, slipped her new shoes off and rubbed her sore feet. God, I'm getting more like Myrna every day, she reflected wryly, and was struck by a sharp pang of regret and sadness at Myrna's absence; she would have liked Andrew.

'He respects me. I believe he wants to share his life with me, all of it. He wants us to be partners, and I think we will be. Yes,' she added thoughtfully, almost to herself, 'I think I've finally made the right choice.'

As it turned out, however, it became evident Andrew had not shared everything about himself with Tamar. The day after their wedding, Tamar packed up her things and arranged to have everything she would not need for the trip to Napier sent ahead by coach. She and Andrew stayed in Auckland for another two days then, after a tearful farewell on the wharf, they boarded the steamer to Napier.

The trip was pleasant and uneventful, except that Cabbage, whom Tamar could not leave behind, was sick all the way. The weather was fine and the brisk ocean breeze a welcome respite from the summer heat. The steamship docked at the Port of Napier on the hot, still morning of 3 February and the minute Tamar disembarked, she was assaulted by a revolting reek.

'What's that dreadful smell?' she asked, wrinkling her nose in distaste.

'Stagnant water, open drains and other rubbish. The drainage isn't the best because a lot of the land's so low-lying.' He looked at her screwed-up face and laughed. 'The borough council's reclaiming the swampy areas, or forcing the owners to raise the land themselves, but money's tight and it's a big endeavour. Still, we should be able to come into town in a few years' time and not feel sick.'

'How far away is your home?' Tamar asked, hoping it was situated well beyond the reaches of this appalling smell. It was worse than Auckland.

'Don't worry, it's well out of town.' Andrew shaded his eyes with his hand and looked about the busy docks. 'I'm looking for Lachlan. I wired him to come and meet us with the wagon. There he is. *Lachie!*' he bellowed, waving his hat madly.

Lachlan turned out to be a stocky, dark-haired man of medium height with a cheerful, ruggedly handsome face, a ready smile and a mild Scottish accent.

'Andy!' he cried as he jumped down from the wagon. 'Good to see ye, mon. And this must be the new Mrs Murdoch!' He took Tamar's hand gently and bowed low. 'I can see now why ye refused to give up, Andy,' he added mysteriously.

'Tamar,' said Andrew formally. 'I'd like you to meet my brother-in-law, Lachlan McRae. Lachlan, this is Tamar.'

Tamar smiled and said hello, warming immediately to this genial young man.

Andrew looked around and said, 'No Jeannie?'

'Aye, well, ye know what she's like when she gets a bee in her bonnet.'

Andrew shrugged and bent to lift the luggage into the back of the wagon.

The trip to Kenmore, Andrew's farm, took almost five hours. Lachlan drove, pointing out various landmarks as they went through the town. Finally leaving it behind, they followed a rough gravel road into the rolling countryside. The further they travelled from civilisation, the wilder the land became, especially on the hills. Some of it was in pasture but the greater amount was still untouched bush.

After several hours they stopped for lunch, prepared and packed by a begrudging Jeannie, and Tamar went for a short walk to relieve herself behind a tall stand of mature *karaka*, making sure she held her long skirts well out of the way while Cabbage stood guard. When she'd finished she sat for a minute on a fallen log, listening contentedly to the heavy, warm silence and contemplating the possibilities her new life might bring. Several yards away a rabbit stuck its head up above a bush and watched her curiously. She could not understand why Andrew hated rabbits — they were so appealing. As far as he was concerned, the only good rabbit was a dead one. Then Cabbage barked and it bounced away in fright, its white bottom flashing.

On the other side of the trees, out of Tamar's earshot, Andrew was complaining about Jeannie.

'I swear to you Lachie, I'll not put up with any more of this nonsense. Our parents raised us to be tolerant, and tolerant she is not, not over this. I know running a brothel isn't socially acceptable, but it's just a business like any other. God, man, you know that — you patronised enough of them in your single days. It doesn't mean Tamar's immoral or a bad person.'

345

'Ye don't have to convince me, I can see she's a fine woman. It's our Jeannie you'll have to get around.'

'I won't have her upsetting Tamar. She doesn't deserve it.'

Unaware she was being discussed, Tamar tried to imagine her new home. She assumed it would not be too small as she and Andrew would be sharing it with Jeannie and Lachlan, and he had never implied there wouldn't be enough room to raise a family, but neither did she expect it to be particularly large. Andrew obviously had *some* money, and had been more than generous with it, but she had seen no indication he was particularly wealthy. He dressed well, but so did most businessmen with a pound or two. She must think of a way to get him to take advantage of her nest egg, although she did not want to insult him. Perhaps they could become business partners, an arrangement that might make it easier for him. She smiled softly as it suddenly occurred to her she had learned to trust again.

As the afternoon grew hotter and they drew closer to Kenmore, Andrew pointed out three or four homesteads nestled in the hills. One was quite grand while the others were less splendid but nevertheless still substantial and impressive.

'Our neighbours,' he said. 'If you can call them that. Some of the stations are so big you can ride for hours in several directions and not see another sign of life.'

Tamar quite liked the idea. 'How many acres do you have?'

'Oh, a few,' he replied vaguely.

In another hour, after which Tamar was sure her nose was beginning to burn even though she'd kept her wide-brimmed straw hat on all day, Lachlan turned off the main road onto a narrower but well-maintained track. It stretched out in front of them through a stand of tall English trees, then disappeared around a bend. Tamar was relieved to be out of the relentless afternoon sun and under the cool shade. As they rounded the bend, she was enchanted as a grand two-storeyed, balconied home surrounded by beautifully groomed lawns and gardens came into view.

'Lord, that's a lovely house,' commented Tamar. 'Whose is it?'

'Actually, it's ours,' Andrew answered cautiously. 'This is Kenmore.'

'*This* is Kenmore? This great mansion? Andrew Murdoch, you ... *bugger*!' exclaimed Tamar angrily, then whacked her new husband on the arm. Lachlan wisely kept his mouth shut as he pulled the wagon up in front of the wide portico over the front door. 'You lied to me! You said you didn't have a lot of money!'

'No,' Andrew replied, ducking as she hit him again. 'You assumed that. I never said it.'

'You've bloody well tricked me!' she swore indignantly. She felt foolish at having offered him what was probably an insignificant amount of money compared to what he obviously already had.

'No, I haven't. I didn't think it was important. You never seemed particularly interested in money, so I thought there'd be no point mentioning mine. Does it matter?' he asked, trying not to laugh.

'Excuse me,' said a cool voice from above. 'Lachlan, Andrew, I'm glad to see you're home safely.'

Tamar looked up to see a woman in her late twenties standing at the top of the steps, and hoped her swearing had not been overheard. Judging by the expression on the woman's face, it had. Tamar and Andrew both stepped down from the wagon as the woman came down to meet them.

'I'm Jeannie McRae,' she said, her voice icy. 'Obviously you're Tamar.'

'Yes. I'm very pleased to meet you, Jeannie,' Tamar replied untruthfully. 'I'm sorry, but your brother appears to have deceived me. You must excuse me.' She swept up the steps and into the house, then came out again a second later with as much dignity as she could muster. 'Lachlan, could you show me to my bedroom, please? I need to lie down.'

'Of course,' he said, and led her into the house.

'What does she mean, deceived her?' Jeannie asked her brother, who was staring after his new wife.

'I think she thought we weren't terribly well-off.' He turned to her. 'Which puts an end to your gold-digger theory.'

'I never said she was a gold-digger.'

'No, but you implied it.'

'Well, what do you expect? She's a brothel-owner.'

'She *was* a brothel-owner, Jeannie. And she didn't start the business, she just managed it. *And* she has thousands of her own in the bank. What would she want with my money?'

'Well, nothing, I suppose, if she has her own,' Jeannie grudgingly admitted. 'But she might be using you to gain respectability. Have you thought of *that*?'

Andrew sighed. 'Jeannie, Tamar has more respect from social and business quarters in Auckland than I might ever have. She was a superb businesswoman and donated a lot of money to charity. Her house was truly grand. She moved in some quite lofty circles, and so did the woman who left her the business. Don't be such a snob. This isn't Balmoral and you're not the Queen.'

'Then all I can say, Andrew, is that she's going to take a lot of getting used to.'

'And so are you, if you keep behaving like this. I've made my choice, and there's no more to be said about it,' retorted Andrew, and set off to find Tamar.

She was in an upstairs bedroom, stretched out on a chaise by an open window, staring at the ornate plaster centrepiece in the middle of the ceiling. Andrew came and sat at her feet. 'Are you not feeling well?' he asked, concerned.

Tamar transferred her gaze from the ceiling to his worried face, sat up and put her feet on the ground. 'No, I'm fine. But Andrew, I feel so foolish. You could have told me.'

'I'm sorry, darling, I just didn't think it mattered.'

'Well, no, it doesn't, but you could have said *something*.' She picked up her straw hat and fanned herself with it. Looking him directly in the eye, she added, 'I think you'd better tell me anything else I might need to know. I thought we'd agreed there were to be no secrets between us.'

'And there won't be, I promise. What is it you want to know?'

'Well, I'm not sure. I don't want to pry,' she answered primly.

Andrew smiled, leaned forward and kissed Tamar on her red nose. 'You're a funny woman, Tamar Murdoch.'

Before dinner Andrew showed Tamar the surveyors' maps of the Murdoch sheep station. The block was huge — 14,577 acres of flat and hilly land supporting 19,000 sheep, mostly Romneys, some English Leicesters, a few Cheviots imported from the Scottish Highlands, and a handful of Corriedales he was trialling. Andrew and Jeannie's parents, James and Adele Murdoch, had emigrated in 1850 from Scotland, where their families had been landowners for more than two hundred years. Andrew had been born in 1851, followed by two more children, one in 1853 and another the following year, who had both died, then Jeannie had arrived in 1858. A fifth child born after Jeannie had also died.

In 1855 James Murdoch had purchased 9000 acres in the Tutaekuri River area and, seven years later, an adjacent block of 5577 acres. The current homestead was the third house, the first two having stood on exactly the same spot. The first had burned down in 1857, and the second had been razed in 1870 to make way for a much grander home once the family's financial situation began to consolidate. James himself had died in 1879, followed

349

quickly by his wife in 1880, neither having lived to see their two surviving children marry. Jeannie had met Lachlan in 1882 and married him two years later. At Andrew's invitation Lachlan had come to live at Kenmore to be with his new wife and to help Andrew to run the station.

Two full-time shepherds and their families also lived on the station, and an extra nine or ten men came out for the shearing season. Although Andrew used the latest shearing equipment and the new hollow-top shearing tables, shearing 19,000 sheep was a long, arduous and expensive job and he was looking forward to someone inventing a machine that would do the job in half the time. He'd read recently that someone in Australia was working on a prototype fuelled by wood and sheep dags, of all things.

Most of his profits, he told Tamar, came from wool exports, although in 1882 he'd been one of the first to export frozen sheep and lamb carcasses when the new refrigerated ships were introduced. The deepening depression had indeed had an impact on his profits, but there was plenty of money in the bank and, due to the scale of his operations, he was still doing very well. Andrew also explained that although title to the land had been transferred to him when his father had died, as it had been assumed Jeannie would marry, he'd regularly shared the profits with her and ensured the land would go to both his and her children on their deaths.

Later, resisting the urge to wear her most flamboyant outfit, Tamar dressed for dinner in a stylish, pale grey satin gown and pulled her hair back in a simple style, fastened with two clips decorated with jet beads. At the dinner table, she commented on Jeannie's gown, which was an attractive deep burgundy. She wondered if Andrew's sister had made a special effort to impress her.

'Is the fabric in your gown crepe de Chine, Jeannie?' she asked conversationally. 'It's a lovely shade. And it's bespoke, isn't it? Your seamstress should be complimented.'

'Oh,' Jeannie replied, momentarily flustered. 'Yes, it is bespoke. A woman in Napier does my sewing. My special outfits anyway.' She stopped and her hand flew to her mouth.

Ah, I knew she'd dressed deliberately, thought Tamar. Andrew and Lachlan glanced at each other, aware that something had passed between the women but completely mystified as to what. They put their heads down and concentrated on their food.

'You sew then, Tamar?' asked Jeannie.

'Yes, I'm a trained cutter and seamstress and I did quite a lot of sewing in Auckland.' She did not elaborate.

'I'm not a very good seamstress myself,' Jeannie replied. 'I can crochet, tat, knit and embroider, but I'm hopeless with garments, I have to admit. Nobody will wear anything I make.'

'Perhaps I can help you, if you'd like,' volunteered Tamar. She knew Jeannie did not like her, but there was no point in feuding, especially if they were going to live together. 'I can't cook, and this meal is wonderful. Perhaps you could teach me to cook in exchange.'

Andrew looked shocked; he hadn't realised Tamar couldn't cook. But then he smiled as he caught on.

Jeannie nodded. 'No doubt we can work something out that suits us both.'

Tamar wondered if her new sister-in-law was referring to the domestic arrangements, or to their relationship.

Sitting in bed later, Tamar said to Andrew, 'She doesn't like me.'

'Och, give her time. She can't not like you forever. Who could?' he asked, sliding next to her under the cool linen sheets. 'I think she was surprised you didn't polish off the decanter of sherry before dinner and burst into bawdy songs after the pudding. She's had a sheltered life.'

'She doesn't seem naive to me.'

'No, she isn't naive, but she hasn't seen as much of the world as you.'

'No, I suppose not,' Tamar agreed.

Andrew leaned over and kissed her and she let herself succumb to the lovemaking she'd decided she was more than happy to become accustomed to.

The following day, Andrew gave Tamar a guided tour of the house, which was indeed splendid, and the equally beautiful gardens, then took her riding.

Tamar hadn't been on a horse for years and felt particularly unsafe balanced precariously on a side-saddle wondering when, not if, she was going to fall. She had ridden in Cornwall, but only shaggy little pit ponies. She did not end up on the ground, but did get into a terrible tangle with her skirts, her single stirrup, her crop, and the reins. And her hat blew away. Andrew laughed.

'You're going to have to get the hang of it, my dear. People do a lot of riding around here. There are some places you still can't take a wagon safely — especially between homesteads. Well, not if you want to get there before midnight. And I'm planning on doing a lot of socialising.'

After that she practised surreptitiously in one of the back paddocks, but still felt uncomfortable. The horse Andrew had given her was not particularly flighty, but had a tendency to take the bit between his teeth when he galloped.

The following week Andrew announced he wanted to have a dinner party to introduce Tamar to his friends, and decided she and Jeannie should deliver invitations to some of their closer neighbours by hand. Or rather by horseback.

'Perhaps you could get to know each other a little better on the way!' he suggested cheerfully. Both women gave him dirty, sideways looks. He was aware they had come to some sort of truce, but was still conscious of a barrier between them.

On the appointed day, Andrew and Lachlan set out early to check the station's western boundaries, leaving Tamar and Jeannie to themselves. They were standing together in the yard waiting for Rathbone, Kenmore's elderly gardener-cum-stablehand, to bring the horses around. The father of one of the shepherds, Rathbone was a dour little Irishman. He never said much to anyone, unless asked to discuss some aspect of the gardens. He lived for his herbaceous borders.

He silently held Jeannie's horse as she mounted, then led Tamar's over to the mounting block. She clambered on, then got straight off again.

'Look, I'm sorry, Jeannie, I just can't ride in this skirt. It's absurd. Rathbone, please put a proper saddle on my horse,' she said, and went inside. She emerged fifteen minutes later, wearing a pair of Andrew's work trousers and one of his shirts, carrying a shoulder bag in which she'd stuffed her visiting clothes. Rathbone, holding Tamar's re-saddled horse, took one look at the trousers and averted his eyes, utterly scandalised. Andrew's trousers were rather tight on her curvaceous bottom, leaving little to the imagination. Jeannie took a brief look, then turned her horse in the opposite direction and concentrated on looking between its ears. Even Tamar's horse shied.

'Hold him still, please, Rathbone,' she said as she stepped onto the mounting block. 'I can't get on if he's jumping all over the place.'

Rathbone gripped the horse's bridle, staring determinedly at his boots.

As Tamar placed her left foot in the stirrup and energetically swung her right leg over the horse's back, a low, soft, ripping noise could be heard. Tamar froze, becoming suddenly aware of a light breeze playing over her buttocks.

She got slowly down again, careful to keep her backside facing away from Rathbone, who had frozen in his tracks. 'Jeannie?' Tamar asked quietly. 'Did you make these trousers?'

As she looked at her sister-in-law, she was appalled to see she was crying, her hands over her face and her shoulders shaking uncontrollably.

Tamar thought, oh God, this must be the last straw. 'Jeannie, I'm so sorry. I'll get changed straightaway. The last thing I want to do is embarrass you.'

Jeannie removed her hands from her face, threw her head back, and brayed with hysterical laughter. Tamar stood stunned. 'That,' said Jeannie, 'was the funniest thing I've ever seen.'

Years later when she looked back, Tamar recognised the incident for what it was — the starting point of their lifelong friendship.

Part Two

❧

Joseph

1887–1902

Chapter Twenty-two

August 1887

Tamar had been living at Kenmore for almost eight months when Andrew took her into Napier to select new bedroom furniture, insisting Tamar should have something more feminine.

They were walking down Munroe Street when they passed a Maori woman leading a small boy. Tamar glanced at the well-dressed pair briefly, then stopped when something suddenly registered deep within her. The child had green eyes. She turned and saw them standing in the dusty street, staring back at her.

Her heart leapt wildly as she walked towards them. The woman stared directly at Tamar, an odd and not altogether friendly look on her strangely familiar face.

'Excuse me,' Tamar said, her pulse still racing. 'May I ask the name of your child?'

The woman hesitated, unable to ignore the striking resemblance between the boy and this *Pakeha* woman, then replied reluctantly in excellent English, 'He is Kahurangi-o-te-po Kepa.' She rolled her eyes as the child yanked energetically on her hand, adding, 'He is also known as Joseph.'

Tamar squatted in front of the child, 'Hello, little man,' she said softly, then looked up at her husband, her eyes swimming in tears.

'I think I've found him, Andrew.'

The boy, suddenly shy, hid his face in the woman's skirts.

Tamar said to her, 'My name is Tamar Murdoch. Are you Mereana?'

'Yes.' The woman hesitated again while she extricated the boy from her skirts, smoothing his hair gently as he leaned against her thigh, all the while keeping his small hand tightly within hers. 'Have you come to take him back?' she asked, her eyes reflecting fear and the beginnings of a deep sadness.

Tamar looked at the distress on the other woman's face, and the bewilderment on that of the little boy. She swallowed the painful lump in her throat and stood up. 'No.' She blinked hard and turned to Andrew. 'May I have one of your cards?'

She waited while he found a business card and handed it to her.

'May I give this to Mereana?' she asked quietly. Both women watched as half-formed shadows of fear, then resignation, chased each other across his face before he nodded.

Tamar turned back to the Maori woman. 'This is my husband, Andrew Murdoch. We live at Kenmore Station. Can you please give this to Kepa? There are things we need to discuss.'

Mereana nodded. '*Haere mai, tama iti,*' she murmured to the child, then glanced at Tamar. 'I will tell Kepa we met.' She gave a small smile that failed to reach her eyes. 'Good morning to you both.'

Tamar watched as they walked away. The little boy turned around and stared curiously, then they rounded a corner and were lost from view. Tamar took Andrew's hand and gave it a reassuring squeeze before they walked on, both lost in their own thoughts.

Later, taking tea in their hotel, they talked about what had happened.

'Do you think Kepa will contact you?'

Tamar shrugged. 'I don't know, I haven't seen him for several years. He's written once or twice, about the child, but nothing else.'

'He looks like you.'

'Kahurangi? I thought he looked like his father.'

'He has your eyes and nose.'

'Well, that's a relief. I understand Kepa comes from a long line of very beaky people.'

Andrew laughed, then added more seriously, 'But you want to see Kepa?'

'I don't honestly know. I want to see my son, very much, and if I have to go through Kepa to do it, I will.'

Andrew had heard this note of stubborn determination before. 'What will you do if he doesn't contact you?'

'I haven't really thought about it. Today has come as a shock to me; remember I haven't seen my son since he was born.'

Andrew leaned forward and took her hand. 'Of course, my love, I understand. It must have been very strange, seeing him walking down the street.'

Tamar poured herself a second cup of tea and sat staring at the pretty, patterned teapot for several minutes. 'It hurt me, Andrew. In my heart. All those years and somebody else has been bringing him up. He doesn't even know who I am.'

'Perhaps not, but that woman did. She didn't seem too happy.'

'Mereana is Kepa's sister and has mothered him since he was born. How would you feel if you suddenly bumped into your foster child's real mother?'

'Frightened, probably. Worried I was going to lose my child.'

'Exactly. So what am I going to do? I want a relationship with my son, desperately, but I don't want to hurt anyone.'

Andrew was silent for a minute. 'Would it make a difference, do you think, if we had children of our own?'

'Not to me. I'm sorry, Andrew, but he will always be my first-born.'

359

'There are no signs of that happening yet?' Andrew asked hopefully.

'A child? We've only been married a matter of months, Andrew. Give it time.'

'Aye, but we've been … very active … I rather thought … ' He tailed off.

Tamar smiled. 'These things happen when they happen. Sometimes it can take ages, and at other times it happens just like that, and at the most inopportune time.'

She of all people should know.

Tamar received a message from Kepa a week later. She showed it to Andrew who, although not altogether happy about it, agreed he should come to Kenmore.

'Might as well get it over with' was all he said.

Tamar, aware her husband was uncomfortable with the idea, asked Andrew to be at home when Kepa came. He was, and was cheered by the fact Kepa brought a woman with him who turned out to be his wife.

Tamar, on the other hand, felt a stab of jealousy. Parehuia and Kepa had been married for a year. She was very attractive, Tamar couldn't help noticing. As for Kepa, he had the same disturbing effect on her he had always had. Tamar wondered when his magnetism would no longer have any power over her, and hoped it would be soon; she felt guilty and confused at still having such feelings.

Feeling slightly flustered she welcomed the couple into the parlour and disappeared to make tea. Over refreshments, Kepa described their son's progress.

'He has a European name, Joseph, as well as his Maori name. Te Kanene thought it would allow him to mix with both Maori and

Pakeha with greater ease. Do you like Joseph as a name?'

'Yes, I do. Who chose it?'

'I did,' said Kepa. 'When he was two years old. Our family prefers his traditional name, however.'

'And which does he prefer?'

'He likes Joseph. He will not answer to anything else now, *whakatete* boy.'

'Then I shall call him Joseph,' declared Tamar.

Her son, it seemed, had recently begun his formal education at a native school and was doing very well. 'He speaks Maori fluently,' said Kepa proudly. 'He has always spoken some English and is improving every day. His English reading is going very well too, I understand. I have hopes he may attend Te Aute College when he is old enough.'

Tamar was pleased to hear this. Te Aute was a prestigious school near Napier established for furthering the education of promising Maori boys. If her son was bright enough to do well there, he would be assured of a good start in life.

'Who will pay for his education?' she asked.

'Primary schooling is free as you know, and the trust fund you set up after he was born will provide more than enough for his further education. Unless you had something else in mind?'

'No, not at all. That's exactly what I intended.'

'Good,' said Kepa, brushing crumbs off his trousers and resting his strong hands on his knees. 'No doubt you would like to become acquainted with our son? That is really what I came to talk about.'

Parehuia's full lips compressed slightly at Kepa's intimate reference to the child who would forever connect him to this *Pakeha* woman. She knew Tamar had been her husband's first love, and was even more conscious of how he still felt about her, although she knew he thought he'd kept this hidden. But Kepa was married to her now, under European law no less, and as long as he did nothing about his feelings for Tamar, no one would be harmed. Parehuia knew she could satisfy Kepa as a lover and companion, and the child they were expecting would help keep him from straying.

Tamar cleared her throat nervously. 'Does he know I'm his real mother?'

To her surprise, Kepa replied, 'Yes. I told him years ago I am his natural father and his real mother is a *Pakeha* woman living somewhere else. Then, after Mereana told me what had happened, I sat down with him and explained who you are.'

'And what did he say?' asked Tamar, careful not to sound too eager.

'Well, it was dinner time and he asked if he could have something more to eat.'

'Oh.'

'But afterwards he wanted to know if he would now have three mothers. He already has Mereana, then when Parehuia and I married she became a sort of stepmother. And now he will have you. I think he is a little confused, but then he is only six years old. However, he asked to meet you. He said he thought you were a very pretty lady.'

Tamar smiled.

Kepa continued, 'Mereana has not said anything but I suspect she fears you will claim your son. She is upset, as she loves the boy very much. Do you want him back?'

Tamar had thought about nothing else for the past week, during which her maternal desires had battled fiercely with her conscience.

Andrew awaited his wife's answer with interest. Tamar had not discussed the issue of reclaiming the child, and because they were so open with each other he took that to be an indication she was not seriously considering the possibility. But he was aware her son's sudden reappearance in her life had caused her considerable emotional chaos.

Tamar fiddled with her sleeve while she thought about what she wanted to say. Finding her son had been almost as traumatic as losing him, but she had to voice her decision, for her own sake as much as everyone else's. She took a deep breath. 'Yes, I want to claim him, Kepa, but I'm not going to. Mereana has been his mother, she cares for him as she would her own son, and I don't want to hurt either of them by insisting he live with me. However, now I have seen him I have no intention of losing contact. What I would like is an arrangement where I spend some time with him each month. He will remain with Mereana until he is of an age to decide himself, but I would like to share in decisions regarding his upbringing, and I will continue putting money into the trust fund for him.'

Kepa smiled in relieved approval. He had not been looking forward to telling Mereana she was about to lose Joseph, and Te Kanene, who had considerable influence over *whanau* affairs, was steadfastly insisting the child would be better off in a Maori community. Kepa's father, Te Roroa, was extremely fond of his little *mokopuna*, and would have bitterly resisted any attempt to take him away. And he himself would have been devastated; his son was precious to him and he made a point of spending as much time with him as possible. He would have missed him dreadfully, despite the impending birth of a new child.

Parehuia also smiled, in admiration more than anything else. She knew her sister-in-law would have been shattered to lose Joseph. What this *Pakeha* woman was about to do was noble and compassionate, and demonstrated she was more than just a pretty face above a shapely body. This pleased Parehuia. Somehow it made the fact Kepa had fallen in love with Tamar considerably easier to live with.

Andrew was quietly pleased: he could see Tamar had put everything that had been on her mind in order. He'd had his own doubts about raising his wife's illegitimate part-Maori child, especially when that child's handsome and virile father would probably visit regularly. Andrew had real and considerable respect for the Maori race, but he suspected he could well have found such a situation intolerable. The sooner he and Tamar started their own family, the better.

Tamar herself was experiencing a relieved sense of having done the right thing, but she could not help thinking about what it would have been like having her son grow up with her. Still, she would see him regularly and share in his life as much as she could, and that would have to do for now, providing the arrangement worked out as planned.

It did. Mereana was so grateful Tamar had chosen not to reclaim Joseph she went out of her way to make his visits successful. Kepa had said Tamar could be trusted, and Mereana soon found this to be true. At first she had been concerned that Tamar might try to tempt Joseph with promises of a privileged *Pakeha* life, but there was never any evidence of that.

With her own money Tamar purchased a small but comfortable cottage in Napier to be used whenever she and Andrew, or Jeannie and Lachlan, came into town, and when she was spending time with her son. Mereana would deliver the boy to the cottage, stay for tea with Tamar, then leave them together. When it was time for him to return home, either Mereana or, more rarely, Kepa would collect him, or on occasion Tamar and Andrew would take him back to his village.

Tamar looked forward to her visits with Joseph immensely. The first time he had been a little over-awed and Tamar had invited Mereana to stay overnight, but then Joseph had decided he was too big for that and insisted he would be fine by himself. After two or three visits he was considerably more at ease, and they found they got on very well, although they received some sideways looks when they were out together. There had initially been a question about what Joseph would call Tamar, and she had been especially pleased when, after learning that Cornish children often called their mothers 'Mam', Joseph decided that's what he would call her.

Tamar helped him with his English reading and he attempted to teach her to speak Maori, which she picked up relatively easily, although Joseph insisted she never quite got the accent right. Tamar also taught him about the Cornish side of his heritage, his family tree, what Cornwall was like, and what sort of people his grandparents and aunt had been. As well, she talked openly about her relationship with his father, and what had happened after he had been born. He was a delightful child, very bright, inquisitive, sometimes cheeky and at others quite introspective. Tamar soon realised he thought deeply about many things, and she went to considerable lengths not to fob off his endless questions with fatuous answers.

A year after his visits began, Tamar told him he would have a new half-brother or -sister the following year.

'Just like Huriana is your half-sister,' she explained. Huriana was Kepa and Parehuia's child, born some months earlier.

Joseph thought for a minute then asked, 'So, if Huriana is my half-sister, and this new baby is to be my half-sister or -brother, what relationship will they have to each other?'

Tamar thought, he looks so like his father. His beautiful father. She shook her head slightly as if to dislodge the traitorous thought. 'I really don't know, Joseph,' she answered. 'Where do you get these difficult questions?'

Joseph shrugged. 'Is Uncle Andrew pleased about your baby?'

'Oh yes, he's delighted. It's his baby too.'

'I know that,' replied Joseph. 'I know all about that sort of thing.'

'Oh? Do you really?' asked Tamar, intrigued.

'Of course. Our *kuri* had puppies. They came out of her *tara* and I made *Mama* tell me how they got in there.'

'Is that right?' said Tamar, trying very hard not to smile. Lucky Mereana.

'Yes, except *Mama* said it takes longer to make babies than it does to make puppies. When will your baby be here?'

'Oh, around February, I expect.'

Joseph's small face creased into a frown. 'Huriana smells.'

'Most babies do.'

'Did I?'

Tamar leaned forward and kissed his cheek. 'I don't know, little man. I didn't have you long enough to find out.'

Joseph looked thoughtful. 'Did you feel *pouri* when I was taken away?'

'Sad? Yes, very. I thought I'd lost you forever.'

'Was it the same when *Papa* went away?'

'When he went away where?' Tamar replied, wondering what her son was getting at.

'After he made me,' said Joseph, as if Tamar were being deliberately obtuse. '*Mama* says there has to be a *mama* and a *papa* to make a baby, and *Papa* made me, but then he went away and you were by yourself. Did you feel sad?'

Tamar thought, how do you explain something like this to a little boy? 'It was a very difficult time, Joseph.'

He ploughed relentlessly on. 'And why weren't you and *Papa* married?'

'I already had a husband.'

'No, after that one died!' said Joseph in exasperation.

'Oh Joseph!' exclaimed Tamar, becoming cross. There was a limit to how frank she was prepared to be, even with her son. 'Ask me in ten years' time. You're too young to understand!'

'*Papa* said to Uncle Te Kanene he is very fond of *Mama* Parehuia, but it is you he thinks about when he is having a *whawha tupere*.'

'A what?'

Joseph, his face a portrait of childish innocence, made a pulling gesture near the base of his belly.

'Joseph!' Tamar was horrified.

'He did, Mam! I heard him!'

'Well, I think that's enough of that sort of talk!'

The boy responded enthusiastically, 'Uncle said that too! And he said *Papa* would do well to remember what happened last time he had ideas like that!'

Tamar had had enough of this conversation, which she was finding more than a little disturbing. Not the sex — she was, after all, a retired madam, although she felt Joseph was too young to have knowledge of such issues — but the fact she still featured so predominately in Kepa's sexual desires. How many other people had her son blurted this out to? 'Have you mentioned this to anyone else, Joseph?'

'No,' he answered truthfully.

'Good,' said Tamar, immensely relieved. 'Let's get you something to eat then, shall we?'

January 1888

'What will you do about Joseph when the baby comes?'

'How do you mean?'

Andrew and Tamar were relaxing in their bedroom at Kenmore. Summer was at its sweltering peak and Tamar was stretched out on the chaise next to an open window, dressed in a light cotton dress and with her feet bare. Such was the size of her stomach these days she was forced to recline on her side supported by a pillow;

resting flat on her back made her legs go numb and she had great difficulty getting to her feet.

'Well, you won't be able to travel into town to visit him, will you?'

'Why not?'

Andrew looked a little shocked. 'There'll be the confinement after the child arrives, then you can't travel backwards and forwards with a tiny infant.'

'Maori women do it all the time.'

'Not with my heir, they don't. I think you should wait until he's not quite so new before you start trotting him all over the countryside.'

'You're convinced it will be a boy, aren't you?'

'Aye, and don't change the subject. Why not have Joseph here? Just for a while, anyway.'

'Yes, I suppose I could. I want him to get to know our baby. He'll be a half-brother to the child after all.'

'Och, I understand that, Tamar. I just don't think it's necessary for you to travel for a while.' He leaned forward and kissed her gently on the tip of her nose. 'Humour me, darling, please. Or I'll be forced to put my foot down.'

He was serious and Tamar knew it. 'Yes, you're probably right. We'll sort something out, then, shall we?'

She kissed him back and he hugged her as tightly as her swollen belly would allow.

'Good. And it's time we talked about getting some help in the house, too.'

Tamar raised her eyebrows. 'Have you talked to Jeannie about that? She takes a lot of pride in what she does.'

'She won't have to give it up. She'll just be doing less of the physical work. And she'll have someone to order around. She'll enjoy that.'

'Andrew, that's unkind.'

'Perhaps, but I know my sister. And there will be a lot of extra work with laundry and what have you.'

'Yes, I suppose there will be, especially if there are more babies after this one. Talk to Jeannie. If she's happy about it, then so am I.'

Jeannie was not averse to the idea of employing a housekeeper, providing she retained overall control of the household. Secretly she was thrilled; she was longing for Tamar and Andrew's baby to be born and intended spending as much time with the infant as she could. She'd been knitting and crocheting and embroidering for months. Her union with Lachlan remained childless, and to alleviate her disappointment she planned to lavish attention on her new niece or nephew.

Five women were interviewed for the position. Two were atrocious, two would have done, but the fifth and final applicant was judged eminently suitable by both Tamar and Jeannie. Her name was Mrs Nora Muldoon, she had excellent references, and appeared to be what was commonly referred to as a 'treasure'. She could cook, clean house, had experience supervising staff, and was accustomed to managing children. Fifty-two years old and widowed for the past ten, Nora Muldoon was an unusual-looking woman, short and wide across the middle with a receding hairline and a face that for some reason only moved on one side on the rare occasion she smiled. She had one grown son, seeking his fortune somewhere or other in New Zealand, but had not remarried because she didn't believe she would find a man of her dearly beloved but sadly departed Harry's calibre; and anyway, she couldn't be bothered.

Mrs Muldoon had been employed at Kenmore for just two weeks when she came across Tamar doubled over in the parlour one morning, her face turning an alarming maroon colour. Mrs Muldoon knew immediately what she was seeing.

She hurried over and patted Tamar on her hunched shoulder.

'Coming early, is it? You sit there, Mrs Murdoch, and I'll send Mr Murdoch to fetch the midwife. Don't fret now, giving birth is as easy as pie if you can manage to relax, even with your first.'

Tamar wasn't in the mood to divulge this would be her second child.

Andrew was enjoying his pipe in the sunshine when Mrs Muldoon found him. Tamar could hear his exclamation from where she was sitting in the parlour, and he rushed in a moment later.

'My God, Tamar. Why didn't you say something at breakfast?' he asked, crouching in front of her.

'This wasn't happening at breakfast,' said Tamar through gritted teeth. 'It's just come on. I think you'd better go for Mrs Platt. Now.'

Mrs Platt was the midwife. Normally an unflappable man, Andrew leapt up, took three steps backwards, turned in a full circle until he was facing Tamar again, then waved his arms ineffectually. 'Where's my hat?'

'Oh, sod your hat,' said Tamar. 'Mrs Muldoon, fetch Lachie and ask him to go with my husband. And can you get Jeannie, please? She can help me upstairs.'

Mrs Muldoon nodded and left the room.

Andrew looked desperately worried. 'Will you be all right? We'll be gone a good hour and a half.'

'Of course I will. I know what to expect, and Jeannie and Mrs Muldoon are here. I'll be fine, Andrew. Now, can you go away please. I'm rather busy.'

Andrew kissed Tamar on the cheek and hurried out. Tamar could hear him yelling to Lachie as he clattered down the hall.

Between them Jeannie and Mrs Muldoon assisted Tamar upstairs where she changed into a cotton nightgown and settled into bed. She got up fifteen minutes later and started pacing the room, finding the contractions easier to manage if she was moving around. Mrs Muldoon left to fetch clean sheets and cloths, and to start the copper boiling for hot water.

'Nervous?' asked Jeannie, who was.

'No,' said Tamar, who wasn't.

Mrs Platt arrived two hours later, examined Tamar and pronounced her progress 'just dandy'.

James Andrew Murdoch was born at a quarter past four that afternoon. His parents were delighted beyond words, although his mother was extremely tired; 'wee' James had turned out to be not so wee, and Tamar felt as if she had been run over by a team of bullocks. Gathering her new, tightly swaddled baby in her arms, she looked down into his creased little face.

'Hello, little man,' she said, in love with him already.

CHAPTER TWENTY-THREE

June 1893

Joseph, settled comfortably against a *tukutuku* panel in Maungakakari's richly decorated *wharenui*, was dying to pick his nose. He knew, however, that the moment his finger strayed anywhere near his nostrils, his great-uncle Te Kanene would clip him across the head and tell him to get outside and blow his nose, which would be very embarrassing. Almost twelve years old now, he balked at the thought of public humiliation and sniffed vigorously instead, drawing a sharp look from the hawk-eyed, bat-eared old man.

Joseph yawned until his jaw cracked. He had spent the past two days at Kenmore visiting his mam and his new half-sister, and had risen early to ride back. Very proud of the two-year-old colt his father had given him as a mark of his approaching manhood, he refused to admit he was exhausted and his balls hurt from riding bareback. It had been worth it; his new half-sister, Keely Jean Murdoch, was very appealing with her bright blue eyes and thick auburn hair.

He had a sackful of half-brothers and -sisters. His father and stepmother Parehuia now had another child, a boy named Haimona, and his foster parents had also produced two children.

Keely was his mother's fourth child (counting himself), as after James had come Thomas Kevan in 1890. James and Thomas were still too young to be interesting. Joseph preferred the boys from his village, friends his own age, but he was very fond of them. He had been visiting Kenmore for several years and was comfortable there, despite differences between life on the wealthy sheep station and Maungakakari.

Tonight the elders were hosting a *hui* from the greater Hawke's Bay area. Joseph was old enough to sit in the *wharenui* and listen to the old men, but his attention was wandering; whatever was up his nose was driving him to distraction. He waited until the speaker had finished, then quietly moved towards the door.

Te Kanene watched him leave. The boy was growing up. Already tall, he looked very much like his father at a young age, although paler of skin and his eyes had retained the deep green inherited from his mother. Te Kanene worried about him. A perceptive and intelligent child, he was beginning to develop a mind of his own. His father had one too, Te Kanene reflected sourly, of which Joseph himself was at least one result.

Maori boys were encouraged to grow up quickly on the East Coast, and Te Kanene could see a time fast approaching when Joseph would no longer be content playing childish games with his friends. Joesph was a keen and able student but had become bored with his lessons. He now spoke, read and wrote both English and Maori effortlessly, knew his arithmetic backwards, had an interest in European history, and couldn't care less about geography. But it was more than that; Te Kanene sensed a restlessness, something that flowed deeper in his veins than the desire to hurry up and be a man. Whatever it was, Te Kanene suspected it had come from his parents. Such a combination of intellect, physical attractiveness and stubborn independence could be a good thing, or it could be a disaster, especially in a boy not dark enough to be Maori, but nowhere near the right shade to be *Pakeha*.

Te Kanene tried to turn his attention back to the white-haired elder gesticulating with his walking stick and expounding at length on the sitting of the first Maori Parliament at Waitapu, but found his mind drifting back to the boy. Joseph was enrolled at Te Aute College next year, and hopefully his studies would keep him out of trouble, but until then something would have to be done with him. Of course, his father had been sent to sea, but at an older age and, unfortunately, too late to prevent him from committing his ill-advised and far-reaching indiscretion with Joseph's mother.

Te Kanene nodded almost imperceptibly. Perhaps that was the answer; he could send the boy away for the next six months on one of the family's trading vessels. Up and down the coast, and possibly across to Sydney. That should keep him occupied, or at least limit the strife he could get himself into. He would have to be under the watchful eye of someone who could be trusted, but Te Kanene had just such a person in mind.

He sighed inwardly; he was getting too old for this. His older brother Te Roroa headed the *whanau*, but had delegated the tricky business of running the family to Te Kanene. Over the years he had also built up the shipping business — now managed by Kepa — to a point where it would continue to earn the family a comfortable income. Perhaps it was time for him to step down. Then he could see out the rest of his days in peace, sitting on the sunny verandah of his new European-styled house in the village, worrying about nothing more than what his wife would place in front of him on the dinner table. He was in his early sixties now and had to admit, even if only to himself, the prospect of retirement was attractive.

Outside, having energetically cleared his nostrils, Joseph breathed in the cool, fresh air and, with it, the delicious smell of hot pork. He spied his friends Wi and Ihaka loitering near the

374

newly opened *hangi* pit, waiting to carry the baskets of meat and vegetables into the *wharekai*, and hurried over to join them. You never knew when a stray *kumara* might fall out. He was given a job immediately, and followed the others towards the dining hall, a basket balanced on his shoulder and the smell of freshly cooked meat wafting pleasantly about his face.

A group of elderly women sat in the porch of the *wharekai*, blankets around their shoulders and woven mats beneath them to keep them off the cold ground. Four were *kuia* from Maungakakari and the other three were *manuhiri*, visitors. One was a truly ancient woman Joseph had seen before, at another village. She was a healer of considerable skill and rumoured to have the gift of divination. No one knew exactly how old Te Whaea was and her frightening reputation had long been employed by exasperated parents when their children would not behave.

Joseph was staring at the old woman, half in fear and half in fascination, when she suddenly looked straight at him. He averted his eyes, but tripped and almost fell. The women cackled with glee and Joseph felt himself going red. Ihaka elbowed him in the back and laughed. 'She will get you!' he taunted as he dumped his basket on a table inside the *wharekai*. 'Te Whaea will come for you tonight and steal you away!'

'Oh, shut up!' said Joseph, feeling foolish.

He plonked his own basket next to Ihaka's. Sometimes his friend really got on his nerves; he never knew when to stop. Of all those who teased him when he decided to only answer to the name Joseph, Ihaka had gone on about it the most. They had even come to blows when Joseph finally lost his temper after Ihaka accused him of denying his Maori heritage. They came out of that with bloody noses and didn't talk to each other for days, something that hurt Joseph far more than his injuries. He and Ihaka were best friends and he couldn't understand why his European name upset the other boy. Eventually Te Kanene took Joseph aside and pointed out that because Ihaka's skin was very dark he would always be excluded from *Pakeha* society. Joseph was more likely to be accepted, and Ihaka was frightened he would lose his friend. Since then Joseph had been more tolerant of Ihaka's teasing.

Joseph shrugged and added offhandedly, 'She is only an old woman. None of what they say is true.'

'Oh, yes it is,' shot back Wi, looking shocked. 'She can look into a person's eyes and see what will happen to them!'

'That is only a children's story,' replied Joseph, sounding more confident than he felt.

'It is true! My grandmother swears it!'

'Then I will ask Te Whaea to divine our futures,' said Ihaka, and without waiting for a response he hurried out of the dining hall.

Joseph glanced at Wi, who looked nervously back, and they followed Ihaka into the late-afternoon sunshine. They found him squatting in front of the old women. As they approached he rose, with a mischievous grin. 'I have asked her, Joseph. She will tell your future first.'

Te Whaea beckoned to Joseph to sit. He moved reluctantly towards her, feeling apprehensive. Almost twelve years of hearing tales of ghosts and fairies and angry gods had made him as superstitious as anyone else in his village, despite his claims to the contrary.

Close up, Te Whaea looked even older. Her face was wrinkled like the pebbled bed of a river, and the *moko* patterning her lips and bristled chin had faded and spread with age. One eye was sunken and watery, the other blinded by a milky membrane. There was not a single tooth left in her head and her white hair hung over her bony shoulders. She also smelled, and Joseph involuntarily leaned back as she bent towards him and stared into his face. As she scrutinised him, he grew increasingly uncomfortable. What was she looking at? What was she looking *for*? Without preamble she opened her gummy mouth and spoke. 'You are not full Maori,' she declared in a voice like wind in dry reeds.

There was a moment's silence, then Ihaka exclaimed, '*Ea*! Everyone knows his mother is *Pakeha*. Look at his green eyes and light skin. This is not magic!'

One of the old women reached out with her walking stick and struck Ihaka's bare shins. 'Do not be cheeky, boy!' she reprimanded. 'Have respect for your elders!'

Ihaka sat down hurriedly, but Te Whaea appeared not to have heard, her single functioning eye still gazing at Joseph. She thrust a gnarled forefinger at his face and spoke again. 'You will live between two worlds, but you will come to a crossroads. Choose your path wisely, or you may lose yourself forever. But you have many things to do before that.' She hawked and spat onto the ground, closed her eyes briefly, then opened them again. 'When the wars come, to lands and shores and seas far away, you will fight first for the *Pakeha* queen, and then the *Pakeha* king. There will be untold carnage and the world will weep.'

Pakeha king? Joseph had no idea what she was talking about. He looked uneasily at his friends, an uncomfortable frisson of fear wriggling down his spine, but turned back when the old woman spoke again.

'Your blood will spill onto the soil of another people, but you will honour the *mana* of your ancestors.' She sat utterly still for a moment, then shook her head sharply before adding almost casually, 'One of your brothers will die in battle. I do not see your ultimate fate. That is all.'

Joseph realised Te Whaea had finished and got dazedly to his feet. As he did, the old woman scratched her skinny rump through her dusty black skirt, glanced disparagingly at Wi and Ihaka and rasped, 'Next.'

Both boys stood quickly and began to back away. 'I have changed my mind,' muttered Ihaka.

'So have I,' agreed Wi. 'Thank you,' he added politely before he turned and ran off, followed closely by Ihaka who had, temporarily at least, lost his bravado. Joseph forced himself to walk after them, refusing to let anyone see how shaken he was by Te Whaea's words, even though he hadn't understood most of what she had said.

As they went, the *kuia* who had wielded the walking stick turned to Te Whaea and asked curiously, 'Did you see his fate, grand-mother?'

Te Whaea said nothing for several moments, then nodded and replied, '*Ae*, I did.' Then she shut her toothless mouth tightly and said no more.

August 1893

Joseph went to sea a month after his twelfth birthday. He thought it a wonderful idea and his father agreed it could do him no harm, but Tamar was not so enthusiastic. She felt he was too young, but eventually conceded he had to do something to fill in the time before he went to Te Aute, and an introduction to seamanship was as good as anything. The sea was in his blood, after all.

He sailed on the *Whiri*, a swift and handsome schooner and the pride of the family's fleet. The *Whiri* had been built eight years before in the northern milling town of Aratapu by James Barbour, a renowned shipbuilder; Barbour himself had selected the timber from the bush. The keel came from a *kauri* log over a hundred feet long, the planking and spars were heart *kauri*, and the framing best quality *puriri*. It was generally agreed the *Whiri* was one of the finest schooners built in New Zealand. She had originally been engaged in transporting timber but Te Kanene had ordered her hold modified and now she could ship almost anything.

Joseph's first visit to the *Whiri* had been on a wet and windy day in July, just after she arrived at the Port of Napier for minor repairs after encountering a cyclone in the Tasman. He had been introduced to Cassius Heke, captain of the *Whiri* and the man who would be charged with his welfare while he was at sea.

Cassius Heke was a huge man, a full-blooded Maori with chocolate-dark skin, a wide flat nose and permanently bloodshot eyes. When Joseph climbed out of the dinghy and scrambled up the rope ladder onto the schooner's deck, his first sight was of Heke's ugly face leaning towards him and a heavily muscled arm outstretched to help him over the bulwark. He took the offered hand and was almost flung across the deck by the man's strength. As he steadied himself with as much dignity as he could muster, he noted Te Kanene and his father both declined Heke's offer and negotiated the bulwark on their own. His father's amused wink suggested that he too had once been tossed across the deck by the big man.

Te Kanene stepped forward and touched foreheads with Heke. Kepa flicked the sea spray off his coat and swept his damp hair off his face before he too leaned forward to *hongi* the captain and introduce his son. 'Cass, this is my son Joseph.' He turned to Joseph. 'This is Captain Cassius Heke, boy, the best captain navigating southern waters.'

When Joseph stepped into the *hongi* he couldn't decide whether the enormous seaman was scowling ferociously for a particular reason, or if he always looked like that. Then Heke's face broke into a wide, gap-toothed smile that changed his countenance completely, and Joseph decided he must have been born with perpetually bellicose-looking features. He was so tall Joseph had to stand on his toes for the traditional greeting. Heke stuck out a large callused hand, took Joseph's in a crushing grip, and said in moderately good English, 'Welcome to *Whiri*, boy. She a good ship, but you got to remember who she named after. Treat her good and she behave, treat her bad and she do the same to you.'

Joseph nodded solemnly. Whiri was one of the youngest in the Maori pantheon of gods, usually depicted as a red or black lizard. He embodied all things playful or naughty, and was notorious for perpetrating unwelcome tricks. The schooner *Whiri* was painted black below her water line and deep red above, with a stylised lizard as a figurehead and an intricate Maori pattern carved across her bow. In full sail with her double masts, huge expanses of white canvas sail and long, lethal-looking jib boom she was a magnificent sight, the envy of many coastal traders. Joseph gazed around the tidy deck with mounting anticipation of the adventures to come.

'Boy?'

'Pardon?' replied Joseph, snatched rudely from his florid imaginings.

'I said sit down. Captain Heke wants to ask you some questions,' said Te Kanene irritably. It vexed him greatly when Joseph went off into one of his dreams; inattention could be a dangerous thing.

Joseph and Kepa sat on a coil of thick rope while Te Kanene leaned against the foremast. Picking up a heavy, long-handled axe, Cass turned to several rounds of wood lying on the deck and delivered a mighty blow to the closest, grunting in satisfaction when it split neatly in two. He was wearing a sleeveless woollen vest and worn trousers held up almost under his armpits with a piece of string, and Joseph observed his bulging arm and chest muscles with awe. The light rain had stopped and Cass paused to remove a grubby handkerchief from his back pocket and mop his face.

'You think you up to this, boy?' he asked Joseph.

'I believe so, *e koro*,' said Joseph. 'I have heard a lot about it from my father and uncle.' This was true. 'I think I know what to expect.' This wasn't.

'Is that right?' replied Cass in a kind voice. He had talked to Te Kanene and Kepa several times about taking the boy on and it had been made very clear that Joseph was to be treated no differently from the rest of the crew. The boy would be on board to learn the seaman's craft, but his family's primary motive was to toughen him and give him a taste of real life before he went to what Cass privately viewed as that milksop Maori boys' college outside Napier. Cass didn't approve of books and pretty clothes and the teaching of European manners; he believed life taught the greatest lessons, especially when that life was not always smooth or easy.

Cass smiled to himself. The boy looked a fine lad, even if he did have more than a drop of *Pakeha* blood; if his job was to teach the boy to look after himself, then that's what he would do. A Ngati Koata from D'Urville Island, he owed nothing to Te Kanene's family except respect, and that he was more than willing to give. For the past fifteen years they had paid him generously to captain their most valued ships, because he was the best. He might not look or behave like a conventional sea captain but he knew the waters around New Zealand and Australia intimately, and the crews he signed on — usually Maori but occasionally from other parts of the world — were always experienced and competent. The *Whiri* was his responsibility; now this boy would be too, and he didn't mind, providing the boy was able to pull his own weight.

'You get seasick?' he asked Joseph conversationally.

'No, *e koro*. Well, not so far.' Joseph didn't want to say he had never been more than a mile offshore.

'Say to me Captain, eh, or Cass. Not *e koro*. I wish to speak my English better. Only speak Maori when we have to, eh?'

Joseph nodded. He was happy conversing in either tongue.

Cass said, 'The work is hard and you got to be hard too. No puking soon as the swell comes, no moaning about sore hands, no being feared of the rigging, and no crying to go home.'

Joseph opened his mouth in protest, mortified to think anyone might consider him likely to behave in such a manner. 'Of course not!' he countered angrily. 'A man would not do any of those things!'

'Oh, you a man, eh?' said Cass, amused. 'Well, I tell you something, Joseph — the sea can be a bloody bitch, and so can *Whiri*. You learn, but you learn hard. You got to have the guts for it, boy.'

At this, he picked up his axe and resumed chopping. Joseph watched while he struggled to think of a suitable reply. With his eyes following the axe's powerful arc as it swept down over Cass's shoulder, he saw the exact moment when it embedded itself in Cass's lower leg with a solid, sickening thwump.

The captain let out a bloodcurdling scream, staggered backwards and spun around, the axe's long handle protruding at a ghastly angle from his shin.

Joseph's gorge rose as he visualised the axe head smashing through muscle and bone, and before he could stop himself he let out a small cry of horror. Next to him Kepa sat motionless, and Te Kanene seemed frozen in his position against the mast.

Joseph leapt to his feet, his boots skidding as he lunged towards Cass. 'Stand still!' he yelled. 'Don't move! I'll pull it out!'

Cass collapsed heavily to the deck moaning with pain, the axe handle jerking violently as he writhed. Without thinking Joseph stepped forward, planted one foot between Cass's legs, the other on the man's knee, grasped the handle and yanked as hard as he could.

Behind him Joseph could hear the sound of choking. He turned to see Kepa doubled over, his face in his hands and his shoulders jerking spasmodically. 'It is out now,' Joseph assured him in a shaky voice, wanting to sit down before his legs betrayed him. 'Father?'

Kepa dropped his hands to his knees and raised his head. He was convulsed with laughter, tears of mirth running down his cheeks.

Joseph stared at him, then turned back to Cass. The captain was sitting up, both legs stretched in front of him, giggling and leaning forward to inspect the new hole in his trouser leg. 'Eh?' said Joseph in confusion as Cass glanced up, all evidence of his previous agony gone.

'You done all right, boy, you got guts,' Cass said, still giggling like a loon. 'You be fine.'

He grasped both trouser legs and pulled them halfway up, revealing a well-muscled and scarred calf on the right, and an extremely battered wooden leg complete with its own boot on the left.

'This my demonstration leg, eh,' he said, and fell backwards again, hands over his eyes, overtaken by another fit of giggles.

'That was a good one,' said Kepa, wiping his eyes and struggling to contain his laughter. 'You get better every time.'

Even Te Kanene was allowing himself a smile. The expression looked out of place on his customarily dour face. 'He does that to all his crew before he signs them on,' he said to Joseph dryly. 'He says it takes the measure of a man, and he is usually right. Some men have been known to vomit.'

Joseph experienced a twinge of anger as he realised he had been tricked, then felt it subside almost immediately as he saw in his mind's eye how horrified he must have looked. With a sheepish grin stealing across his face, he asked, 'Did he fool you, Father?'

Kepa nodded. 'He fools everyone, boy.'

'Did *you* vomit?'

'Certainly not,' said Kepa.

This elicited renewed giggles from Cass. 'No, but for a Maori you went very white, eh? You was one very pale Ngati Kahungunu.'

He was pleased. He didn't perform the 'demonstration' so much to gauge a new crew member's squeamishness, but to find out if the man could laugh at himself. Crewing a fast and temperamental schooner was a matter of dedicated teamwork, and a man who couldn't laugh at himself would never fit in. He got laboriously to his feet and wiped his big hands on the seat of his trousers. 'You be all right,' he said again. 'Welcome to *Whiri*.'

Joseph's first voyage was a short run from Napier to Auckland, around the top of the North Island to Kaipara to pick up timber, then back to Auckland. When the *Whiri* sailed into rough weather on her second day, Joseph spent six windy, cold and very uncomfortable hours hanging over the stern rail behind the wheelhouse heaving his roiling guts out. He had started off near the bow but moved when the crew complained the contents of his stomach were ending up all over the deck. After those miserable first hours he gained his sea legs, accepting the crew's teasing in the light-hearted vein it was intended.

He soon adapted to life at sea and his duties as ship's boy. He tied his shoulder-length hair back, abandoned footwear in favour of bare feet, which made climbing the rigging much easier, and tacked his trousers up to stop the constant flapping of wet fabric around his ankles.

The crew numbered eight, including Joseph and Cass. They were all Maori — a mate, three able seamen and an ordinary seaman — except for the cook, a taciturn Irishman named O'Leary. His speciality was a tasty and filling boil-up, made from pork bones and watercress or *puha*, together with incongruously delicate bread rolls baked every second day in the small galley oven. On longer journeys when fresh green vegetables ran low, they would be substituted with potatoes and *kumara*, or succulent yams if the *Whiri* was sailing through the Pacific Islands. Fresh meat was always plentiful on the shorter journeys, and the crew often brought their own contributions of preserved mutton bird and other fowl.

They ate heartily but even so, Joseph noticed his waistband was loose by the end of his first week. He wasn't surprised; he had never worked so hard in his life. He was on duty for eight hours, then had a meal and as much sleep as he could manage, woke to another meal and a further eight hours of scrubbing the decks, privy and sleeping areas, checking the cargo and hauling the thick ropes of the standing and running riggings for up to an hour at a time. By the end of the third day his hands were blistered and bleeding and his knees, inner thighs and buttocks raw from the chafing of his salt-soaked canvas trousers. His muscles and bones ached and the skin on his face was red and sore with wind and sunburn.

He was exhausted, in considerable pain and missed his friends and family, but uttered not a single word of complaint. Instead, he made sure he was out of his berth on time at the start of every shift, did everything he was asked, and volunteered for extra work on the rare occasions he had a few spare minutes. His crewmates were hard men, tough, resilient and given to occasional, if somewhat harsh, practical jokes, and Joseph won their respect and admiration. The mate, a wiry, wild-looking man named John Hohapeta with missing front teeth and a heavy *moko* covering his thighs and buttocks, gave him a jar of evil-smelling grease to heal and harden his battered palms, and a salve for his chafed skin. The rest of the crew showed him how to work the ropes in a way that minimised damage to his hands, and never gave him jobs beyond his size. And although he teased Joseph about his 'poor colleen's hands', O'Leary took it upon himself to stuff him with as much extra food as possible, because he was 'still fekkin' growin', to be sure.'

By the time Joseph realised he would probably not die from his physical exertions and fatigue, he was beginning to enjoy his new life. He began to feel comfortable within the camaraderie, and was mesmerised by the crew's tales of strange, far off places. And the allure of the ocean herself was having a profound effect; at home, he had only been up the coast as far as Gisborne, and inland to Taupo, but now he became aware of endless new lands to be visited and explored.

Cass was pleased with Joseph. He had never doubted the boy would be up to the task, but now he would be able to report to Kepa when the *Whiri* returned to Napier that his son had both mental and physical stamina, and was more than capable of looking after himself on board ship. He had yet to be tried on shore. In fact, that had been the only point of contention; Joseph had wanted to go ashore in Auckland and Cass had denied him, pointing out they were only calling into port long enough to pick up a cargo for Kaipara and he would be needed to help load it. In truth, none of the crew would be available to chaperone Joseph, and Cass was sure Kepa wouldn't want his son running about the Auckland waterfront by himself. Joseph shut up after that, but not before Cass glimpsed a look of determination on his young face.

CHAPTER TWENTY-FOUR

It took until December for Joseph to convince Cass he would be safe ashore. He had been home to Maungakakari twice since August and his family had expressed delight at his growth and obvious good health, although Tamar was unimpressed by the calluses on his palms and the wide pink scar on the back of one hand caused by the careless use of a sharp knife. During these short visits Joseph argued vehemently with his father about shore leave, pointing out that if he was old enough to sail with an experienced crew, then surely he was capable of going ashore in a strange town without too many problems. After all, there were gangs of children younger than himself living on the streets, and nobody worried about them. Kepa didn't quite follow his logic but eventually agreed his son should be permitted ashore the next time it was appropriate, provided Cass approved, and at least one of the crew was with him.

The opportunity arose when the *Whiri* called in at Wellington on the way back from Dunedin. With the schooner berthed at Queen's Wharf, the crew had an evening's shore leave while they waited for a cargo to arrive from Australia.

Cass and O'Leary stayed on board, while Joseph went into town with the rest of the crew. John Hohapeta and one of the able bodied seamen, Noho Reti, were charged with his care.

John, Noho and Joseph parted company from the others and headed for a favourite tavern of coastal traders, a nefarious premise in Willis Street named the Blue Lady. According to John, a drink at the Blue Lady was an essential part of Joseph's education.

Inside, the dimly lit bar was crowded, the reek of sweat, tobacco and fish from the fishmonger's next door almost as overpowering as the noise. John and Noho elbowed their way expertly to the bar, Joseph close behind.

'What do you want to drink?' asked Noho. Neither he nor John spoke English well and preferred Maori while not in the presence of their captain.

Joseph had no idea what to ask for. He shrugged apologetically.

John and Noho exchanged glances. 'Better give him beer,' said John, the more responsible of the two.

'One beer, two rum,' barked Noho to the man behind the bar.

As they waited, Joseph looked around. The room was packed: every table and booth was taken and people stood three deep at the bar. Most were seamen, although clearly not all were from New Zealand. Joseph saw several men whose skins were black, their white teeth shining unnervingly in the gloom, sailors speaking rapidly in strange languages, and what had to be an American Indian, a copper-skinned man at least six and a half feet tall whose long hair was braided and entwined with small blue feathers.

Noho elbowed him in the back, handed him a large mug of foaming beer, and pointed at a table whose occupants were rising from their stools. 'Get over there and grab that table, boy,' he said.

Joseph wove his way across the room and sat down at the newly vacated table. John and Noho joined him a moment later, both emptying their mugs before Joseph had barely begun to sip his own drink.

John got up for refills while Noho looked on with amusement at Joseph's beer moustache. 'Nice, eh?' he said, pointing at Joseph's still brimming mug.

'Mmm,' replied Joseph. His nose was tickling from the bubbles in the ale and he was stifling the urge to sneeze his head off. Not wanting to appear un-seamanly, he raised the mug to his lips and emptied it in one long, belly-bloating draught. For a terrible moment he was sure he would vomit, then, with considerable relief, emitted the loudest, longest burp he had ever manufactured. 'God,' he muttered in English, wiping his mouth with the back of his hand.

'Good boy,' said Noho approvingly. 'More?'

Joseph nodded as the older man returned to the bar. John sat down in his place. 'You should be careful how much you drink, eh?' he warned, emptying his own refill in a single draught and looking longingly back at the bar. 'Might get us a flagon.' And he was up and off again.

In less than two hours, John and Noho had almost finished the flagon. Joseph had consumed four large mugs of beer and was feeling light-headed, although very pleased with himself. A sensation of warmth and contentment had spread from his stomach to the rest of his body and he had the sure feeling all was right in his world. He had proved he was a seaman, was inordinately proud of the fact he was developing a man's body, and he had two marvellous friends in John and Noho, who were looking after him so well. No, he thought to himself, things couldn't be much better.

When the second flagon of rum arrived, Joseph poured several generous tots into his mug.

John enquired solicitously, 'Is that wise, boy?' He and Noho, both somewhat the worse for wear, eyed each other and burst out laughing. Joseph smiled too, but he wasn't sure why. The rum burned its way into his gut and he felt his face flushing with the heat.

'Who are those ladies?' he asked, pointing towards a cluster of gaudily dressed women near the bar.

'They are not ladies,' replied John. 'They work here.'

'They look like ladies to me,' replied Joseph.

Noho snorted into his rum. 'They are whores, boy. You know what a whore is?'

'Yes,' said Joseph, 'a woman who exchanges her physical favours for money.'

'That is one way of putting it, I suppose,' said Noho. 'Ever had a woman?'

'No,' said Joseph, his face going even redder.

'Noho, I do not believe Cass would approve,' interjected John. The twinkle of amusement in his bloodshot eyes belied his serious tone.

'Cass is not here,' replied Noho. 'The boy will do it one day. Might as well be now, while we are here to watch out for him.'

'Do what?' asked Joseph. His head was beginning to spin.

'*Onioni*,' Noho said, adding emphasis by crudely thrusting his hips backwards and forwards, bumping the table and spilling everybody's drinks.

'Oh,' said Joseph. He felt weak all of a sudden. He had been sexually aware for some time, and was well versed in the ways of procreation, as far as it applied to dogs, pigs and horses: he was hazy on the details of how men and women did it, but had pieced together snippets of information with Wi and Ihaka. One thing he had no doubts at all about, however, was the reaction of his body on the rare occasions he had inadvertently seen naked female bodies. Even the sight of young mothers in his village nursing babies at their full breasts had aroused him, a response which left him feeling shamed but squirming with guilty excitement.

The thought that he might be about to have his first real sexual experience quickened his pulse, and he took another long swallow of his rum.

'Do any of those women take your eye?' asked Noho.

Joseph nodded. One definitely did; a young-looking *Pakeha* girl with long dark hair wearing a bright green dress. He pointed at her and almost died of embarrassment when she turned around suddenly and caught him.

He whipped his arm down, stared hard at his mug and muttered, 'The one in green.'

Noho nodded, stood up and beckoned. The girl rose and he crossed the floor to meet her: they stood in the centre of the crowded room with heads bowed, talking. Eventually the girl nodded and accompanied Noho back to his seat.

As she came to a halt in front of Joseph and smiled, he eyed her surreptitiously up and down, determined not to demonstrate his nervousness.

She was not tall; about five foot three and a good inch shorter than Joseph. She looked no older than sixteen, but her breasts filled out the front of her cheap dress and her hips, below a small waist, were wide and well padded. Her face was pretty but not beautiful, with bright, youthful features. She was also drunk.

She perched herself on Joseph's knee and helped herself to his drink. 'What's yer name?' she asked in a sweet voice.

'Joseph.'

'Mine's Emerald. Pleased to meet yer, Mr Joseph,' she giggled, wriggling about on his lap.

This close, Joseph could smell her. Sweat, alcohol and something more; a heavy, heady musk that made his heart thump and his penis grow rapidly in his trousers. He moved slightly in embarrassment but it was too late; she had felt his erection and was pressing her buttocks against him suggestively. 'Happy ter see me, are yer?'

Joseph glanced at his friends for an indication of what he was supposed to do next. Drunkenly amused, they raised their mugs to him in a silent, conspiratorial and altogether unhelpful toast. His cock was behaving with a mind of its own and he wasn't at all sure what to do about it.

Emerald laughed at his obvious discomfort, which made him wince; she was squashing his balls. He placed his hands around her waist and moved her so his thighs took the weight of her ample bottom, rather than his genitals. More comfortable now but still very conscious of his erection, he sat there, wondering what to do.

Just as his silence was becoming embarrassing, she spoke into his ear, clearly under the impression she was whispering. She wasn't, and Joseph pulled his head back smartly. 'You're a pretty one, aren't yer? Want ter go upstairs?'

Joseph shook his head, reached for his drink and took a very large swig. He was in an unfortunate predicament; if he stood, everyone would see the extent of his physical arousal, but he couldn't sit here and miss his opportunity with this warm, soft and inviting girl. Emerald's closeness was pleasantly suffocating, and his senses were reeling. He made a decision. 'We will go upstairs,' he said.

Emerald nodded and got unsteadily to her feet, ineffectually attempting to smooth the crush of wrinkles from her skirt, making her breasts wobble. Joseph bit his lip. When Emerald held out her hand, he took it.

They crossed the room and went through a door which opened into a dank-smelling anteroom at the bottom of a steep, narrow staircase. There was very little light and Emerald paused at the base of the stairs to light a candle in a wax-encrusted holder.

She handed it to Joseph. 'You can carry this, luvvie. Follow me.'

Joseph did. The steps were wooden and very rickety, and initially he concentrated on where he was placing his feet. Then he glanced up, and his focus changed immediately: Emerald had grasped the back of her skirt and with every slow step she took, she slid it higher up her legs, revealing black high-heeled ankle boots that had seen much better days, red silk stockings caught above her knees with black lace garters, and the backs of a pair of well-muscled, smooth white thighs.

Joseph's breath caught in his throat and he felt his erection, wilted slightly after the short journey across the tavern, spring rigidly to attention. With an excruciating thrill that jolted him from head to toe he realised Emerald was not wearing underdrawers, and by the time she reached the landing at the top of the stairs, her full and luscious backside was revealed in all its inviting, candle-lit glory.

Joseph grew harder with each step, until he feared even the slight rubbing of his trousers against his engorged penis would be his undoing. They were standing on a narrow landing with five doors. Emerald dropped her skirt and pulled a key from her bodice, then bent to the keyhole of the door directly in front of them. After fumbling and dropping the key twice, she unlocked it and beckoned coyly to Joseph to follow.

Inside, she moved around the dingy little room lighting the gas brackets on the walls. There was a single bed in the centre with its head against one wall, a straight-backed wooden chair and a dressing screen, and a small table in one corner with a bowl and a cracked ewer.

'Sit down,' she ordered, indicating the chair. Joseph did so gratefully. His head was spinning and he was starting to feel sick.

Emerald sat on the bed and belched resonantly, patting her chest apologetically. 'Dearie me,' she said, and felt under the pillows. Withdrawing a half-full bottle of gin she plucked out the cork with her long fingernails and took several deep swallows before offering it to Joseph, who declined, correctly judging himself too unsteady to get up off his chair unaided.

Emerald put the bottle down and led him to the bed.

'Sit there,' she cooed.

She began to slowly disrobe, an inviting smile on her face and her eyes slightly unfocused. Off came her dress, tossed vaguely towards the chair. This was followed by much sinuous and erotic wriggling as she removed her corset, then slid her chemise up over her hips and breasts and drew it over her head. The moment was only slightly spoiled when the undergarment caught inelegantly on her nose and became stuck for a moment, but Joseph barely noticed, mesmerised by her heavy white breasts and the triangle of dark fur above the juncture of her shapely legs, still clad in their stockings and boots. He dared not breathe.

Emerald ran her hands slowly down her body in self-admiration. 'Pretty, ain't I?' she murmured.

Joseph nodded. She was *very* pretty.

She moved closer to the bed and, standing less than a foot away, raised one leg and placed a booted foot on his knee.

Joseph gasped involuntarily. Her vulva was only inches from his face, open, pink and moist. In spite of his intoxicated state, it was altogether too much for him; losing what little control he had managed to maintain thus far he began to convulse as his orgasm gripped him. Doubling over he thrust his hands into his lap as waves of painful pleasure swept through him.

Emerald waited patiently, taking triumphant delight in the knowledge she had the power to make men do this. Or boys, in this case.

As Joseph's spasms subsided, she stepped back from the bed, reeling slightly. She was suddenly very weary; this boy was her seventh customer, and she was tired, very drunk and getting sore.

Joseph glanced up at her, his luminous green eyes brimming with apology and humiliation. 'Sorry,' he muttered. He looked miserable.

'Don't be, luvvie,' she replied. 'Feeling sick, are yer?'

When Joseph nodded she got onto the bed next to him, pulled him down beside her and drew a blanket over both of them. 'Lie with me, sweetie, have a sleep. You'll feel better in the morning. I ain't workin' no more tonight, I've had a right gutsful.'

She rested his head against her breasts and closed her eyes. Within minutes they were both asleep and snoring gently.

John and Noho were by now almost paralytically drunk. When Noho vomited onto the floor between his knees, they both decided they'd probably had enough and staggered outside, holding each other up and singing tuneless snatches of half-remembered songs.

Weaving along Willis Street and down the hill towards Queen's Wharf, they completely forgot their young charge, lying asleep in the arms of a whore.

Cass was livid. 'What you mean, left him behind!' he bellowed at the two sorry-looking seamen standing unsteadily in front of him.

Despite their inebriation, John and Noho were horrified when they realised what they had done. Cass had been on deck, perched on a box splicing ropes by the light of a kerosene lamp, waiting patiently for Joseph's return. The sight of him sitting there as they wobbled up the gangway had reminded them all too suddenly they were supposed to be looking after the boy.

'Where is he?' demanded Cass angrily.

'Blue Lady,' Noho mumbled, hanging his head in shame.

'By hisself?'

There was no response.

'John,' said Cass threateningly.

John muttered, 'No. With a whore.'

Cass swung his massive arm and hit John hard across the side of the head. The other man fell to his knees, then staggered upright again, making no move to hit back.

'Only a young one,' he said, as if this would make a difference. 'We sorry, Cass. We was drinking rum, eh.'

'Bloody useless bastards!' spat Cass. 'I trusted you! Get below. Go on, fuck off!'

John and Noho shuffled towards the cabin door and their bunks, knowing the best thing they could do was remove themselves from his sight until Cass calmed down.

Cass remained on deck, pacing in an agitated circle while he thought about what he should do. The repercussions could be disastrous; Te Kanene would have his balls. He snatched up his splicing knife and hurried down the gangway, his false leg — the footless wooden peg he customarily wore while aboard *Whiri* — thudding hollowly as he went.

He would have to find the boy and bring him back.

Cass knew the way to the Blue Lady like the back of his hand and it took him less than twenty minutes to get there. People in his path stepped smartly aside as they saw his face set in a particularly grim scowl and his huge fists clenched.

At the Blue Lady he barged his way up to the bar.

'Seen a boy?' he demanded.

The barman, who knew Cass well, nodded. 'This tall?' he asked, holding his hand at shoulder height. 'Long black hair, green eyes, pale fella?'

Cass nodded.

'Seen him earlier,' said the barman. 'Ask them girls over there,' he added, pointing towards the table still occupied by several whores.

Cass marched over, the table falling silent as he approached. Looming over the women he found out what he wanted to know and headed through the door at the rear of the room, ducking his head to avoid hitting the low lintel.

He clomped up the stairs, briefly contemplated the five closed doors in front of him, and started on the far left. That room was empty but the next was not. Inside, on the bed, were a naked male figure and a semi-clothed woman, their features shadowed in the dim light.

Cass grasped the man roughly on the shoulder, realising it wasn't Joseph even before he saw the face. The woman squealed in alarm as the man exclaimed angrily, 'Fuck off! I were 'ere first!'

Cass snorted in disgust. 'Seen a boy?' he asked.

'No, yer dirty pervert, sling yer 'ook,' the man retorted, rolling back onto the woman.

The room next door was also occupied. Cass pushed the door open and walked across to the bed. In it, enveloped in the arms of a very well-developed young girl, was Joseph. They were both asleep.

He reached down and yanked off the blanket. Joseph didn't stir but Emerald opened her eyes groggily and mumbled, 'Who the fuck are you?' her voice not at all sweet.

'I'm here for the boy. What you done to him?'

'Nothing, he's asleep,' Emerald protested.

'Get up,' Cass growled.

Ignoring her nakedness he took hold of her arm, pulled her roughly off the bed and propelled her towards the chair, vaguely intrigued to see she was still wearing boots and stockings. As she sat down heavily he retrieved her chemise from the floor and threw it at her. 'Put it on,' he ordered.

When she had covered herself he stood in front of her, his huge bulk forcing her to crane her neck upwards to see his face. 'What happened?' he demanded.

'What do yer think happened?'

'Don't be smart, girlie. Answer me.'

She shrugged. 'We didn't do nothing. It were over before he started. He's a boy,' she added, as if this explained everything.

397

Cass searched his vocabulary for the correct English words and failed. Making a circle with the thumb and forefinger of his left hand, he poked his right forefinger through it repeatedly. 'None of this?' he asked.

'Nah,' said Emerald, shaking her head. 'Not even close.'

'What about this?' Cass asked, pointing to his own backside.

Emerald was deeply affronted. 'What do yer think I am? I got standards!'

It was Cass's turn to shrug. Opening his mouth and waggling his tongue in a suggestive manner, he raised his eyebrows enquiringly.

'None of that either,' Emerald replied. 'That's only for me special customers.' She swept her hair back off her face and adjusted the straps of her chemise. 'Who cares anyway? He's only a ship's boy. Very pretty, and well developed for a young 'un, but still a kid.'

'Who cares is not your business,' said Cass dismissively, moving back to the bed. He bent over and shook Joseph; the boy was still sound asleep. Cass slapped him none too lightly across a cheek and barked in his ear, 'Get up, boy!'

Joseph stirred and rolled onto his back, moaning, his eyes half open. 'I feel sick,' he said groggily to no one in particular.

Cass dragged him roughly to his feet. 'You been very dumb, boy,' he muttered as he pushed Joseph around the bed and towards the door.

'Hey!' said Emerald. 'What about me money? I ain't been paid!'

Cass rummaged in a pocket and withdrew a crumpled one pound note, tossing it in Emerald's general direction as he and Joseph went through the door.

'A pound!' she exclaimed indignantly. 'I'm worth more than a bloody *pound*!'

'Then get in that tavern and work for it. You done nothing for this boy,' replied Cass, shutting the door in her face.

He managed to get Joseph, still only semi-conscious, down the stairs and outside through the back door. In the alleyway behind the tavern, he had to stop and wait while Joseph vomited noisily. After that the boy couldn't seem to find his feet, and Cass wondered how much those two drunken fools had let him drink.

Seeing no other alternative, he picked Joseph up, slung him over his shoulder and made his way back through the dark Wellington streets.

In the morning Joseph awoke with a pounding headache, a mouth that tasted utterly foul, and no memory of how he got back to the *Whiri*. As he lay gazing at the ceiling of his sleeping compartment, wondering whether he was going to be sick, the door opened and Cass stuck his head in.

'Food on the table, boy,' he said gruffly, and withdrew.

Joseph snatched his blanket over his mouth and nose as the smell of fried meat wafted in. He shut his eyes again: he could remember going to the tavern, drinking beer and rum, and talking to a girl in a green dress, but beyond that his mind was disturbingly blank. He sat up gingerly, wincing as his head hammered, and looked around for his trousers; they were draped over the end of his bunk, and they stank. Joseph tossed them into a corner and got out a clean pair. What on earth had he done last night?

The greasy odour of food assaulted him again as he stepped out into the main cabin. The crew, busy eating breakfast, glanced up and grunted greetings, but the atmosphere was subdued, and he saw John had a fresh bruise across his cheekbone.

Joseph sat down and reached for a piece of bread, chewed it without enthusiasm and gagged slightly as he swallowed. The pitcher of water was much more appealing, and he helped himself.

The others ate in silence until one by one they rose from the table and went up on deck, leaving Cass and Joseph alone. The silence grew while O'Leary emerged to clear the table of food and plates, then retreated again to his galley.

Eventually, Cass said, 'Well?'

Joseph's response was an oily and ominous burp. He clapped his hand over his mouth and turned away from the table.

'Oh, for God's sake, boy, go and get rid of it!' said Cass crossly.

Joseph lurched up from the table and hurried across the cabin to the privy. Inside, he leaned over the hole in the wooden seat and vomited until he feared his eyes would burst. He briefly considered lying on the floor and going back to sleep but the privy's smell was too much and he reluctantly went back to face Cass. He barely had his bum on the bench before Cass started.

'You a disgrace, boy, you know that?'

Joseph nodded. Clearly he was *in* disgrace: he wasn't sure why but he certainly was not going to anger Cass further by asking.

'You know what you done?'

Joseph shook his head, certain Cass would tell him anyway.

He did. 'You shamed yourself drinking too much alcohol, and you lay with a common slut. Your family have your guts for garters if they find out. Have you no *mana*, boy?'

'Everyone else was doing it,' replied Joesph, his truculent tone belying his genuine bewilderment.

Cass slammed his hand on the table, making Joseph jump. 'You *not* everyone else, Joseph! You the son of Kepa, son of Te Roroa, nephew of Te Kanene. This behaviour becomes you not at all!'

Joseph couldn't think of anything to say, and sat in miserable silence, staring at the tabletop.

Cass continued, but in a slightly more conciliatory tone. 'Do you know about *wharetangata*, boy?'

Joseph thought for a minute but had to admit, 'No, not really.'

Cass threw up his hands and rolled his eyes theatrically. 'Bloody shit, I knew it,' he swore passionately. 'It be the same thing everywhere. Fathers not teaching sons the right things, mothers not teaching daughters. Too many *Pakeha* ways coming in and our traditions forgotten.' He pointed at Joseph. 'This is what is happening, boy — the children growing up not knowing how to behave, going off to schools learning *Pakeha* nonsense and missing out on what they really need to learn!'

He was angry mostly at Kepa; for not educating his son about the concepts he needed to keep himself strong and pure, and for giving him permission to go ashore without that knowledge. He was also angry at Te Kanene; the old man had, after all, made such a long and loud fuss when Kepa had gone off and impregnated Joseph's mother. Speaking in Maori now because he did not have the English words he needed to express himself clearly, he took a deep breath and tried to explain.

'*Wharetangata* embodies the sacred value of your loins, boy. From there comes the seed that perpetuates your line and builds on the *mana* of your ancestors. It is your duty to honour your family line, to respect it and to keep it pure. There are several aspects to this. The first is a matter of hygiene — you must not defile your body by having sexual contact with a woman who is dirty. This is a filthy thing to do to yourself, and at the very least it invites disease. I have seen many a man suffering an inflamed and festering penis from going with these women, boy, and it is not a pretty sight. The second is, it is beneath your status to sleep with such a woman. A woman who dishonours herself by allowing any man to use her does not have self-respect and is not worthy of your attentions. Remember who you are, boy. *Always* remember that.'

Joseph was giving Cass his utmost attention, but his face betrayed his anxiety; he had no idea if he had had sexual relations with the girl in the green dress or not.

Cass kept a straight face; the boy's horrified look as he realised the possible repercussions of his actions was a sight to behold. He was tempted to prolong Joseph's discomfort, but could not bring himself to be so harsh.

'According to the girl you did not have sexual contact. I think you will be safe, from disease at least.'

Joseph closed his eyes in relief.

'But that might not have been the worst of it. A sore penis is one thing, but what of the possibility of starting a child, had you thought of that? A child you might never have known existed, a child with the blood of your father and his father and all your ancestors running through its veins, left in the doubtful care of a dirty and dishonoured woman. What would become of such a child? It would never find its way back to its own people and would grow up empty of spirit, unless you claimed it. But how could you claim it, boy, if you did not know of its existence? Because of *wharetangata*, it is *imperative* that you be responsible for any issue from your loins. To father a child and not claim it is to bring great dishonour on yourself, boy. Children have always been the hope of our people, and they always will be.'

Joseph nodded, speechless with gratitude to discover he hadn't done any of these dreadful things.

'Becoming a man by lying with a woman is something to be joyously celebrated by your whole family, not a furtive, emotionless deed to be done in the dark with some soulless, disease-ridden female who does not even know your name. That is not the action of a man, that is the behaviour of an animal. Be grateful you did not do such a thing.'

'I am,' Joseph replied fervently.

'There is still the matter of the alcohol,' added Cass harshly. 'There is also great shame in being so weak you drink too much and lose control of your body and fall down and vomit all over yourself. You were a pig last night and you smell like one this morning. I am *very* disappointed with you, Joseph. I had hoped for more honourable behaviour from you.'

Joseph's eyes stung with tears. This was the worst thing of all — Cass's obvious and deep disapproval. 'I am sorry to have disappointed you, *e koro*,' he said. 'It will not happen again.'

'No, you are right, it will not,' agreed Cass. 'You will not be granted shore leave again.'

'Will you tell my father?' asked Joseph.

'Do you think I should?'

Joseph replied, 'I think that is up to you. But I also think that if he is to be told, then I should be the one to tell him. It was my error and I will take responsibility for it.'

Cass drummed his fingers on the table. Privately, he was pleased at Joseph's willingness to take responsibility for his actions — and it went some way towards restoring his faith in the boy.

'I will think on it,' he replied. 'Perhaps that should be your choice, not mine.'

Joseph nodded and rose from the table; what he wanted most was to go back to his bunk and sleep off his headache, but he knew there was work to be done. He was deeply ashamed of his actions and vowed never to put himself in the same position again. He also felt considerable anger towards his father for not telling him of his responsibilities as a man. Had Kepa not raised the subject because of what had happened with Joseph's mother?

Or had Joseph been too busy running about being half Maori and half *Pakeha* to take heed of the lessons and traditions taught by the wider family he had grown up with? The thought that the ease with which he had been living in both worlds might have caused him harm stopped him in his tracks.

Thinking Joseph was going to be sick again, Cass looked hurriedly about for a receptacle.

'No,' said Joseph, reading his mind. 'I am fine. I had a thought.'

'A good one?'

'An important one.'

Cass nodded and watched him for a minute, his face creased in thought. Reverting to English, he asked, 'Boy, you really want to go to that fancy school?'

'No,' Joseph answered truthfully.

'Well, why you going, then, eh?'

Joseph shrugged. 'Because my father and Te Kanene both want me to, I suppose, and so does my mother.'

'You be better off sailing on *Whiri* with me for a couple of years,' said Cass.

'I know, but are *you* going to try and persuade them?'

'No,' replied Cass, knowing such a suggestion was absurd. Suddenly, he got up and began to mince across the cabin floor, helping himself to imaginary snuff, smiling vacuously and waving to invisible friends in a wickedly accurate rendition of some of the more effeminate Englishmen he had encountered. 'You turn into one of these, boy. All lace and velvet and empty head!'

Joseph laughed, then clutched his temples. 'Ow,' he said.

Cass laughed as well. 'Go up on deck, boy. See if the wind blow your sore head away, if she don't blow it off.'

CHAPTER TWENTY-FIVE

Joseph's apprenticeship came to an end in February of 1894, two weeks before he was due to enter Te Aute College. It was with genuine regret that he said a reluctant goodbye to the crew. He would miss Cass most of all, with his lifetime of knowledge and his irrepressible sense of humour. But it was time to embark upon the next phase of his own life, and he knew the next three years at Te Aute would be tempered with memories of his time aboard the *Whiri*.

For Joseph, Te Aute was not a particularly pleasant experience. He enjoyed the mental stimulation of his lessons, which included Latin, physiology, geometry and algebra, and the physical demands of the sporting curriculum, but not the rigid structure nor the compulsory attendance at Sunday morning services. Many of the boys were older, and most were full Maori, but he soon found a 'crowd' with whom he felt at ease. During his time there he met many notable students, including Te Rangi Hiroa, who would follow in the footsteps of an earlier graduate, Apirana Ngata, and become a founding member of the Young Maori Party. He did not envy them the illustrious destiny for which they were being groomed.

Joseph dedicated much of his first year at Te Aute to pulling against the reins. He disliked being told what to do and where to go, and he detested the European style of schooling. Maori traditions were maintained but, in Joseph's view, only so far as to ensure students were not too abruptly alienated from their heritage: as far as he was concerned, Te Aute existed to transform Maori boys into middle-class *Pakeha*. He worked hard to prevent this happening to him, which confused his friends who knew he was half European. He appreciated the enrichment of his academic knowledge, and the easy comradeship he developed with his fellow students, but was relieved to pass through the school gates for the last time at the end of 1896, having decided the world of academia and politics was not for him.

Instead, to the chagrin of Te Kanene and his father, he chose to work on the land. He considered returning to sea, but as he already had a rudimentary knowledge of seamanship and coastal trading, decided he would do better to learn something new.

After a stay at Maungakakari, followed by several days at Kenmore over New Year with Tamar, who was pregnant again, he took casual work on local sheep stations, learning to muster and shear, and to shoot and ride as if he had been born to both. He quickly grew to love the harshness and solitary beauty of the outdoor life almost as much as he had loved the sea, and once and for all put the possibility of a career involving books and letters out of his head.

It was while he was working on a station southwest of Napier that he received, on the first day of May, a telegram from Andrew Murdoch advising his mother had been delivered of her child but the infant was unlikely to survive.

When Joseph arrived at Kenmore several days later, he was tired and filthy from riding day and night without rest. Andrew, the lines of grief etched on his face, met Joseph at the front door and told him quietly what had happened.

April 1897

'*God bugger my bloody days!*' Tamar screamed, straining until her face turned scarlet and the veins in her temples bulged.

'Now, now, Mrs Murdoch, that's no way to talk!'

The midwife, who had taken over from Mrs Platt a year ago, frowned at Tamar who lay on the bed, legs wide apart. She was covered with sweat and stray strands of her hair stuck to her damp face. 'For God's sake, Mrs McSherry, I'm having a baby. I think I can swear if I feel the need, don't you!'

Mrs McSherry didn't think so, but who was she to comment on the behaviour of rich folk? That was the trouble with this colony — people behaved in any manner they chose, not at all like they did in England.

'Now then,' she continued, as if Tamar hadn't uttered a word. 'Push again. Hard, now.' She prayed this delivery would not prove difficult: the local doctor was currently en route to a station up in the hills. She'd given Tamar raspberry-leaf and nutmeg tea in the first stages of labour to settle her nerves, and those of the unborn baby, but the woman was swearing like a trooper. Most unseemly.

Tamar gave another mighty push and grunted as the baby's head crowned. 'Christ Almighty,' she groaned.

'Really, Mrs Murdoch, you should know what to expect by now! This isn't your first delivery, after all.'

No, thought Tamar as she gritted her teeth, but it's definitely going to be my last.

John Adams had advised her not to fall pregnant again after Ian had arrived the previous year, but accidents happened, as she well knew. But they had both been pleased at the news, although

Andrew had been concerned for Tamar's health; after Ian, John had stated quite bluntly that in his view she was getting a bit long in the tooth to expect complication-free childbirth. Now, lying flat on her back straining to push out her sixth child, she had to agree.

'Another push, Mrs Murdoch. We're nearly there.'

Tamar heaved mightily and the baby's head popped out accompanied by a gush of blood. When Mrs McSherry cleared the muck away from the tiny face she became alarmed; the infant was very blue and the umbilical cord seemed to be wrapped around its neck.

'You're going to have push even harder this time, all the way out if you can,' she said. 'Come on now, push!'

Eyes squeezed shut, teeth bared and hands gripping the bedhead behind her, Tamar strained again, feeling her insides were about to tear away from the rest of her. Nothing budged.

'And again!' urged Mrs McSherry, her voice rising. '*Now!*'

Tamar summoned what remained of her strength, took a huge breath and gave a massive shove. '*Jesus fucking Christ!*' she screamed, unable to hear her own curse because her ears were blocked with the enormous pressure of bearing down.

Mrs McSherry leaned forward as the baby suddenly slid out. She quickly removed the umbilical cord from around its neck, cleared out its mouth, tipped the tiny body upside down and briskly slapped the wrinkled little buttocks. The baby was a girl and Mrs Murdoch blew her cheeks out in relief as the infant took a small breath and began to mewl weakly.

'Mam?' asked a small, worried voice from the bedroom door. 'Mam? Are you all right?'

Mrs McSherry turned to see a little boy peering around the door. 'Get away with you, boy,' she snapped.

'And get your da in here. Now.'

A minute later, Andrew hurried in. 'Tamar?' he asked apprehensively.

'Yes, I'm fine, it's all right,' Tamar reassured as she lay back, utterly exhausted.

Mrs McSherry finished cutting the umbilical cord, tied it off, wrapped the infant tightly and placed her in Tamar's arms.

'I believe your wife is fair, Mr Murdoch. I'm not so sure about the wee girl. You'd do well to call for the doctor. He's over to the Sinclairs at Toihi Station, I believe.'

Andrew kissed his wife's damp forehead and gently pulled the blanket back from his daughter's face: the child was very blue and she breathed shallowly and irregularly. He nodded, then left the midwife to clean up the bloody sheets and make Tamar comfortable while he hurried downstairs to send for the doctor, hoping like hell he could get to Kenmore soon.

Dr Logan bent over the child, moving one finger slowly backwards and forwards in front of her face, then palpated her tiny limbs, lifting then lowering them gently. Tamar and Andrew waited in silence.

'She's not responding very well,' he said as he straightened up. 'I'm not sure if she has any visual acuity, but I suspect not. I believe she may have sustained considerable damage during the prolonged labour. She's very weak.' He turned to Tamar. 'Have you named her yet?'

'Yes, Brigid, after my sister. Brigid Ann Murdoch.'

'Mmm. Well, all I can say is it might be a good idea to prepare yourselves. I can't say anything more, I'm afraid.' He thought for a second. 'She's nursing properly?'

'She's taking a little. I try her every hour.'

'Well,' said the doctor, repacking his bag and snapping it shut

409

with a loud click. 'I suggest you keep on with that, and keep her warm and comfortable. I really can't suggest anything more, I'm afraid.' He'd seen this many times — newborns too weak or damaged to hold on to the slim chance at life they'd been given.

At the door he turned and said again, 'I'm sorry,' leaving Tamar and Andrew in little doubt regarding their daughter's prognosis.

Through eyes flooded with tears Tamar looked at her husband. Andrew's face was white. 'Oh, Andrew,' she said. 'It's so unfair.'

He sat down beside her and plumped the pillows behind them, putting his arm around Tamar's shoulders and drawing her head against his chest. 'I know it is, my darling.'

'What shall we tell the children?'

'All they need to know is that she's very sick. We'll deal with anything else *if* it happens.'

Tamar did not share his optimism. She had been holding Brigid almost constantly since the birth, and knew there was something very wrong. The poor little mite was barely conscious most of the time and almost totally unresponsive. They sat together for several minutes, leaning on each other for support and strength.

'Do you want to bring them in? They haven't even seen her yet.'

'Aye,' said Andrew, heaving himself wearily off the bed. He carefully lifted the baby out of her crib and nestled her into Tamar's arms, stooping to place a gentle kiss on the child's tiny, screwed-up face. 'Shall I send Jeannie up, too?'

Tamar nodded slowly but did not take her eyes off her daughter; her need to gaze at her newest child for as long as she could, to breathe in her baby scent and memorise her features and the silky feel of her exquisitely soft skin, was overwhelming.

She glanced up as the bedroom door opened, and her eyes filled with tears as a troop of children filed in. First was eight-year-old James, brown-haired, already tall, earnest and independent. Behind him came Thomas, a year younger, fair-haired, gentle and sensitive, followed by their younger sister, Keely. Auburn-haired like her mother, she was already showing signs of the grace and poise she would develop as a young woman, although now, dressed in a calf-length cotton smock and pinafore, long stockings and high laced boots, her hair in ringlets and her bottom lip wobbling, she looked all of her five years. Ian, the baby, was wriggling in the arms of the long-suffering Mrs Muldoon.

'Children,' said Tamar gently, 'come and see your new sister.'

They shuffled over to the bed and carefully leaned over the small bundle in Tamar's arms.

'Why is it all blue?' asked James after a minute.

'*She*, James,' replied Andrew softly. 'And her name is Brigid.'

'She's a funny colour because she's not very well,' Tamar answered. 'Now, who wants to hold her first?'

'*Me!*' shouted James and Keely at the same time.

James turned and pushed his little sister away. 'No, *me*! I'm the oldest.'

Keely shoved him back. 'And *I'm* the girl. Boys don't play with babies!' At the thought of not being first to hold the new baby, her face crumpled and large tears appeared, hovering on her long eyelashes.

Andrew suppressed a smile. Keely insisted on doing every-thing her brothers did, but had no compunction whatsoever in demanding what she believed were her feminine rights, when it suited.

'No, I think Thomas can hold her first, seeing he's the only one who isn't arguing,' he said.

Thomas' face lit up and he extended his arms stiffly, as if expecting to be handed a heavy bag of potatoes. Andrew lifted him next to Tamar and she passed him the small bundle, making sure his arm supported the baby's head. He looked down at the little face, a look of wonder on his own. 'Why is she so small?'

'Well,' said Andrew, 'she had to be that little to live inside your mam.'

'My turn now,' interrupted Keely, clambering onto the high bed and insinuating herself between Tamar and Thomas.

'Da!' wailed James. 'It was *my* turn next.'

'Hold your horses,' Andrew said softly. 'You'll have your turn in a minute. We need to be very gentle with her.'

There was a light tap on the door and Jeannie looked in.

'Jeannie,' said Andrew. 'Come in. We're just about to talk to the children and we thought you should be here too. Is Erin about?'

Erin was Jeannie and Lachlan's six-year-old daughter, usually inseparable from Keely, but for once the two were not together.

'No, she's in the garden,' Jeannie replied, frowning as she contemplated the new baby. 'I think she realises something's not right. She's quite upset. I'll fetch her in soon.'

Andrew nodded, then turned to Tamar and raised his eyebrows.

'I'll do it,' she said heavily. She patted the bed beside her, inviting James to snuggle up. When he had settled himself she spoke, her voice low and soothing. 'I said before that Brigid is very sick.' Three little heads nodded solemnly. 'Well, that means God might want to have Brigid with him in Heaven. She's so special she's already just about an angel, and we can probably only have her for a very short time.' Her voice broke. 'Do you understand what I'm saying?'

Keely burst into tears, James looked away and Thomas bit his lip, his own eyes brimming. His voice wavering he asked, 'Is she going to die? Like Cabbage?'

Cabbage, stiff and grumpy with arthritis and his dark patches almost completely grey, had died last year. Andrew had made a small casket and the children had buried their beloved pet in the family cemetery and erected a cross painted with 'Cabbage'. The writing had worn off but Keely still put wildflowers on the grave from time to time.

'Well, sort of like Cabbage,' Andrew replied. He looked at his sister helplessly.

She rescued him. 'But Cabbage went to dog Heaven. *If* Brigid goes to Heaven, she'll be the prettiest, happiest, most special angel with her own little throne right next to God.'

Thomas digested this. 'If God wants her soon, will she always be a baby or will she grow up in Heaven?'

Bloody hell, thought Andrew. 'I don't know. But nobody knows what will happen to Brigid yet, except for God himself. She might be allowed to stay here after all.'

But she wasn't. Brigid Ann Murdoch died in her sleep two weeks later and was buried in the family cemetery, not far from Cabbage.

John Adams, who had been notified by wire, had been en route to Napier when Brigid died. He and Riria arrived the day after the funeral. Tamar and Andrew waited on the front steps to meet them, surrounded by their surviving children. As John jumped from the driver's seat, his wife stepped down behind him.

'Riria!' cried Tamar, hurrying down the steps, her arms held wide.

The two women embraced fiercely. Under the portico, John and Andrew shook hands and patted each other on the shoulder — as close as they could come to an embrace, despite their close friendship.

'You lost her,' said John, reading the other man's face. Tamar's quiet sobbing confirmed his fears. 'I'm so sorry, Andrew.'

'There was nothing that could be done, she was too weak. Tamar took it hard but I think she's starting to come to terms with it now.'

'And you?'

Andrew struggled to control his voice. 'We still have four healthy children — others haven't been so lucky. There won't be any more, though.' He leaned forward and kissed Riria's cheek as the women joined them.

'Very wise,' said John quietly before he embraced Tamar. 'I'm so sorry,' he said. 'How are you feeling?'

She wiped her eyes with a lace-edged handkerchief, and then her nose. 'A lot better now, thank you, John. It was very difficult when she died.'

John nodded in sympathy; he and Riria had lost a child several years ago.

Jeannie appeared at the top of the steps. 'Hello, John, Riria,' she said. 'Mrs Muldoon is preparing tea, if you'd like some.'

Inside, James, Thomas, Keely and Erin were sitting at the bottom of the stairs, all wearing black mourning sashes and armbands. Keely skipped over to John. 'Hello, Uncle John. Our sister died. She's an angel now. Have you got a present for me?'

'That's rude, asking for presents,' said James, coming forward to shake John's hand like a miniature adult and offering his cheek to Riria for a kiss.

'Well, let's see,' said John, patting his pockets exaggeratedly. 'I might have. Yes, here we are,' he said, withdrawing four small packets from inside his coat.

'Ooh, goody,' said Keely. 'Lemon drops.'

'Thank you, Uncle John,' said James and Thomas in unison, pocketing theirs for later.

'Thank you, Mr Adams,' said Erin, shy as always.

Mrs Muldoon came bustling down the hall, shooing the children out the front door. 'Out you go and play while your parents talk to Dr and Mrs Adams. Go on, off with you,' she said. 'Tea is served in the parlour, Mrs Murdoch.'

Tamar led the way into the parlour, a large, warm room with autumn sun streaming through the French doors. She poured tea for herself and for Riria, while John and Andrew helped themselves to brandy.

'You've left the children at home?' Andrew asked Riria.

'No. They have gone home to Kainui to be with my parents for a month. We sent them last week before we left to come here.'

John and Riria had three children of their own ranging in age from twelve to eight; a boy named Simon, the eldest, then Rose aged ten, then another boy, David.

Jeannie joined them and helped herself to tea and a slice of cake.

'Ian's fine, still asleep. I've just checked on him.'

'Thank you, Jeannie,' Tamar said gratefully. She was more than happy for her sister-in-law to be closely involved in the care of her youngest son; Jeannie loved children but Erin's birth in 1891 had been accompanied by severe complications that almost killed her and left her incapable of further pregnancies. She and Lachie had resigned themselves to Erin being their only child, and doted on her, but Tamar willingly shared her own children as often as she could.

'Is that Madeira cake?' asked John, leaning forward and slicing himself a slab the size of a doorstep. 'My favourite.'

Tamar almost smiled, pleased to see he hadn't changed, although he had finally grown fatter. She and Andrew saw John and Riria twice a year at most, and she cherished their time together. Then, with a stab of pain, she remembered what had brought them together this time.

She had been to Brigid's grave twice today. The grave itself was so small and final-looking, and the thought of her tiny daughter lying beneath the heavy soil in her small white casket made her chest ache. But strangely, the pain was not the same as it had been when she lost Joseph. Somehow, it had been worse knowing he was alive somewhere but unable to see or hold him. This time she knew her child had gone forever, and the agony was slightly more bearable. Most New Zealand mothers experienced the death of at least one child, and she had been offered the support of several local women who had been through similar bereavements, which had been comforting.

She looked up to see Riria watching her closely. 'Are you really all right?' her friend asked.

Tamar nodded, although the lines of sorrow etched on her pale face betrayed the depths of her pain. 'I will be, Riria. I have Andrew and the children, you and John are here now, and Joseph's coming soon. Yes, I will be, eventually.'

Joseph steadied himself as he walked down the wide hallway to meet his mother. She darted out of the kitchen at the sound of his footsteps on the wooden floor, and hurried into his arms, weeping.

He was easily taller than her now, and he sent an impassioned glance towards Andrew over her head; he adored his mother, and it hurt him terribly to see her in such pain.

'We lost her, Joseph. We lost our little girl,' she sobbed into his shoulder as he held her.

'I know, Mam.' He didn't know what else to say. 'I came as fast as I could.'

Tamar nodded and pulled back. 'I know you did, my love.'

Joseph said nothing. Instead, he put his arm around his mother and gave her shoulder a gentle squeeze as she blew her nose.

Andrew cleared his throat and said, 'John and Riria are here. They arrived yesterday.'

'I'd better say hello, then,' said Joseph.

'And when you've had a rest and something to eat, I'll take you up to see Brigid,' added Tamar.

Joseph had met John and Riria when he had been staying at Kenmore. He had taken to Riria immediately, but felt ill at ease with John. In fact, he had been slightly rude the first time they met. Joseph had only been ten, distrustful and slightly in awe of the balding *Pakeha takuta*, until Andrew had taken him aside and bluntly catalogued the charity John had given, and was still giving, to many of the Maori people of Auckland. Joseph revised his opinion, and began to notice things about his mother's friend he rather liked; the man's compassion, his integrity and honesty, and, most of all, his constant good humour. They now got on very well, although they never saw each other often enough to consider their relationship a true friendship. Joseph liked John and Riria's children, too; they were bright and happy.

After several cups of tea and three large sandwiches, Tamar took Joseph to visit Brigid's grave.

Arm in arm they walked up the gentle hill behind the house, and opened the gate in the wrought-iron fence enclosing the small cemetery. His half-sister's grave was pathetically small, and Joseph felt his eyes prickle with tears as he gazed at the flowers piled over the little hump of fresh soil. There was no headstone, but no doubt there would be soon.

'I'm so sorry, Mam,' he said, taking Tamar's hand.

Tamar nodded but said nothing; her tears were still very close, and she didn't trust herself to speak. Joseph closed his eyes and began to murmur a *karakia*. As Joseph concluded his prayer, there came the gentle laughter of a fantail. They both turned and spied the small bird, perched with its black and yellow tail splayed, on a low branch of a nearby tree.

'Ah,' said Joseph. '*Te piwakawaka*. A good sign.'

'Why?' asked Tamar.

'He arrives to accompany the souls of the recently dead to the underworld. Brigid is beginning her journey, and she will not be alone. Can you not feel her?'

Holding herself perfectly motionless, Tamar strained with every nerve of her being to feel even a whisper of her daughter's spiritual presence. As a gentle breeze lifted her hair about her face, a small smile played on her lips. 'Yes.'

Tamar remained with her eyes closed for some minutes until

the fantail launched itself into the air and swooped past her, one small wing almost touching her shoulder. They watched in silence as the bird flew away.

'She's gone now, hasn't she?' Tamar said.

Joseph nodded. He gently took his mother's hand, and they walked back to the house.

CHAPTER TWENTY-SIX

October 1899

N ame and age, lad?'

'Joseph Deane, sir. Twenty-three, sir.' A lie.

The interviewing officer, the Hawke's Bay district commander of the New Zealand Volunteer Force, squinted warily at the young man. He'd seen him once or twice on training exercises but had never met him.

'Race?'

'European.'

The commander tapped his pencil lightly against the side of his nose. If this boy was a twenty-three-year-old European, then he was a monkey's uncle. There were express instructions from the British Colonial Office to exclude native troops. Apparently, it was a 'white man's war'. But Dick Seddon didn't seem to have a problem with it, and volunteers *had* been called for, so why shouldn't this boy go to South Africa and fight for the Queen? He looked fit, more than met the height requirement of five feet six inches, and seemed keen. 'Can you ride and shoot?'

'Of course, sir. I am proficient in both.'

An educated one, too. Where the hell were they coming from, these literate, well-spoken Maoris? 'You'll have to pass tests.'

The young man nodded.

The commander made up his mind. 'Righto then, lad. Sign here. There's a contingent of two hundred leaving in three weeks. Report to the railway station by ten in the morning next Monday to catch the train to Wellington. There'll be provision to have your horse transported. I assume you have your own mount?'

Joseph nodded and signed the piece of paper the commander thrust across the table at him, deliberately substituting Kepa with Deane as his surname.

He had not discussed his decision to volunteer with anyone. His father would not be pleased, he knew, and both of his mothers, Mereana and Tamar, would hit the roof, but it was his decision. He would have to break the news to them as soon as possible, although he wasn't looking forward to it. He had lied about his age — he had only recently turned nineteen but was big and mature-looking for his years — and he knew the commander could have looked up his records, and checked his ethnicity, but he hadn't, which Joseph took as tacit approval. And if the commander of the district's Volunteer Forces approved, then his parents would have to as well.

Outside, Joseph stopped to compare notes with a handful of other young men who were also volunteering, then untied his horse from the hitching rail, swung into the saddle and trotted down Dickens Street, his head high. He felt elated at the prospect of going overseas to fight, but nervous as well, which he took to be a healthy sign. Te Kanene, who had fought alongside Te Kooti in the early 1870s, and the fearsome Titokowaru in Taranaki before that, said that any man who claimed to be unafraid of battle was either a fool, a liar, or simpleminded.

'You have what!' exclaimed Kepa, whirling about to face his son.

'I've volunteered to go to South Africa. To fight for Queen Wikitoria.'

Kepa shook his head slowly and sat down. 'You *stupid* boy. It is not our war and *she* is not our queen.'

Joseph stared straight ahead, refusing to catch his father's eye. He would not be dissuaded.

'Why?' his father demanded. 'Eh? *Why?*'

Joseph remained silent.

'Is it because all your sheep drover friends are doing it? Speak up, boy! If you are old enough to fight someone else's war, you are old enough to explain your reasons.'

'Because I want to. Because all my *tupuna* were *toa*, and now it is my turn to become a warrior. It is my right,' Joseph shot back.

Kepa was unconvinced. 'Not everyone has to be a warrior to prove himself. I have not been to war, and I have plenty of *mana*.'

Yes, thought Joseph, but you sailed all over the world doing all sorts of illegal, adventurous and dangerous things. And that never did you any harm.

'I forbid it,' said Kepa.

'It's too late. I've signed,' Joseph replied stubbornly.

'You are not old enough.'

'I lied.'

Kepa glared at his son. Although he had fathered three children, this boy was his first-born and he cherished him dearly. 'I suppose you said you are *Pakeha?*'

Joseph nodded.

Kepa snorted in disgust. 'Let them fight their own wars. This argument in South Africa about who owns the goldmines has nothing to do with you.'

'Perhaps not, but where else am I going to find a war?'

There are plenty here still to fight, thought Kepa, although the weapons are words and laws, not guns and bayonets. He should never have condoned his son joining the Volunteers, although the boy had done *that* behind everyone's backs as well. He had definitely inherited his mother's obstinate independence, there was no doubt about that.

'Have you told Mereana?'

'Not yet.'

There was a short silence as Kepa caught the pleading look in his son's eyes. 'Do not look at *me!*' he exclaimed. 'I am not telling her!'

He and Joseph had both been on the receiving end of Mereana's volatile temper, and they knew she would not be at all happy about her foster son's latest escapade. No doubt she would blame *him*, Kepa reflected sourly. 'You had better go and tell her before she hears from someone else. You know that will only make it worse.'

Joseph nodded, picked up his hat and turned to leave his father's house.

'When do you leave?'

'Monday. On the train. We are to be equipped and trained in Wellington.'

Kepa looked at his beautiful, vital, intelligent and headstrong son and felt his heart ache with love, pride and fear. 'We will talk before you go,' he said gently.

Joseph smiled. It was all right.

'So have you given your approval?' asked Tamar as she handed Kepa a cup of tea.

They were in the parlour at Kenmore. He had brought Parehuia with him, and she sat on the sofa looking regal, calm and as stylish as usual in a smartly tailored European riding outfit. Andrew had stayed long enough to greet them, but left to visit a neighbour to negotiate the cost of a boundary fence. These days he preferred to leave Kepa and Tamar to discuss matters concerning their son.

'I had no choice,' Kepa replied. 'He had already volunteered by the time he informed me. You know what he is like. He will be here tomorrow to talk to you himself, but I thought we should warn you.'

'Yes, well, it has come as a shock, I must admit,' said Tamar. 'Will he be in any danger?'

'Yes,' replied Kepa flatly. 'I cannot see Kruger and Steyn backing down. The Boers won the first war in 1881, and that will encourage them to fight for their independence even more resolutely this time. Do you not read the papers?'

'Yes, but I'm Cornish, remember, and I have about as much respect for English authority as you do, Kepa. But I suppose I'll have to keep up with the papers now, if Joseph is going to be over there.'

Kepa nodded glumly. 'The press is full of it. The whole of New Zealand seems to be delighted at Seddon's offer of contingents. *Pakeha* New Zealand, anyway. Approval of his offer was roundly supported in the House, with only one dissenting vote in the Legislative Council.'

Tamar was silent as she busied herself cutting a tea cake into slices.

Kepa watched her. She had aged well, he thought. At thirty-seven and the mother of five children, she was still slender and beautiful, and still dangerously attractive. This, however, was not something he acknowledged to anyone but himself, although he suspected Tamar was aware of his feelings. He also suspected the attraction remained mutual. But he had a wife of his own now, a fine woman whom he respected and cared for deeply and who had borne him two beautiful children. Their relationship now pivoted around their son, although to Kepa's surprise he found he liked and respected Andrew; the two of them got on well whenever they met. If Andrew had any misgivings about his wife having contact with the father of her illegitimate son, he hid them well.

'It's not what I had in mind for him, going off to fight in a war,' said Tamar with a slight frown.

'I had hoped to see him make something of himself, perhaps even move into the political arena,' said Kepa. 'Te Aute educated him for that, and he certainly has the ability. The boy is a born leader. But no, he has to go trotting off all over the most godforsaken stations this part of the country has to offer, sleeping in sheep muck. It annoys me, Tamar. He could be doing so much more.'

'I rather gained the impression he was enjoying the life,' replied Tamar.

'Oh, yes, he loves it. But that is not the point.'

'Isn't it?' asked Tamar. 'He is only nineteen. Why force him into something he doesn't want to do?'

Kepa appeared not to hear. 'I had thought it was time to bring him into the family business. Stupid boy.'

Tamar smiled wryly. 'I seem to remember you gallivanting around the world when you were younger.'

'That was different, I was older. I thought Te Aute would have fostered the boy's brains, not dulled them,' Kepa muttered crossly.

Tamar rolled her eyes. 'We sent him there to further his education and broaden his mind. Well, now it has been broadened, and so have his horizons. The whole world is out there, and he wants to see it.'

'Yes, but why did he have to pick a *Pakeha* war!' complained Kepa, fidgeting with his teaspoon.

Tamar laughed out loud. Kepa was too used to getting his own way. 'I don't want him going either, but he is, so we should support him. Stop complaining and make the best of it.'

Parehuia smirked behind her teacup. She liked it when Tamar

told her husband off. She loved him dearly but he was getting to be more like his manipulative old uncle every day.

Tamar continued. 'We'll all go to the railway station to see him off on Monday. And perhaps we'll go to Wellington as well.'

Joseph and his cohorts were given an enthusiastic and spectacular farewell by the people of Napier on the morning of their departure for Wellington. It seemed as though the whole town turned out to wave them goodbye, with a carnival atmosphere at the railway station as throngs of people, many clutching small Union Jacks, swarmed alongside the train.

The horses had been settled into high-sided, open-topped boxes directly behind the engine while the troops rode in carriages further back. Joseph and his mates leaned out of windows, accepting last-minute embraces and packages from friends and family. Tamar noticed several groups of Maori — so much for their sons being banned from fighting under the British flag, she thought.

A piercing whistle sounded and the engine let out a huge belch of steam and smoke and began to move slowly forward as station workers ran about shooing people away from the tracks. The crowd cheered madly as the long line of carriages moved out. Tamar's children were caught up in the excitement, screaming and yelling and flapping their little paper flags. They had little understanding of what it meant, and were making the most of the trip into town and the break from their lessons.

'They will not all return,' commented Kepa gloomily, hanging tightly onto his own two children to prevent them running off.

'No,' agreed Parehuia. 'Perhaps not. But Joseph can take care of himself. You have seen to that.'

'*Ae*,' replied Kepa, although his voice was heavy and he did not sound as if he believed her. 'I know.'

The trip to Wellington was long with several stops to pick up water and more volunteers, and to stretch the horses in their cramped boxes. The train crossed the North Island at Palmerston North and continued south down the west coast to Wellington. The men and animals were then transported to Campbell's farm at Karori where a training camp had been established, to meet up with the rest of the First Contingent.

Over the following fortnight recruits from throughout New Zealand arrived to be outfitted, provided with a mount if they had not supplied their own, and issued with Martini Enfield .303 rifles. With the Government ill-prepared to supply much of their equipment, the fledgling Regular Army was pushed to the limit to ensure every soldier had what he needed, including heavy khaki overcoats and military clothing scrounged off the territorial Volunteer units. The Union Steamship Company was equipping the *Waiwera* to transport the men and their horses to South Africa, victuallers nationwide prepared food and shipped it down to Wellington, and saddlers and canvas workers toiled to supply equipment for the brave volunteers. The race to get the First Contingent ready for embarkation was a national effort, with every donation and contribution reported in the papers.

Major Alfred Robin, a competent and experienced Regular Army officer, was given command of the contingent, and another ten officers were selected in time to familiarise themselves with the two hundred and four men in the first contingent. Joseph was in Number 1 Company, drawn mainly from the North Island, while the men of Number 2 Company came from the South Island.

Joseph and his new mates spent their evenings talking about what awaited them in South Africa, and discussing the humiliating fate of those who had been sent home because their equestrian skills were not up to standard.

There was some concern amongst the recruits that the crisis

would be over by the time they got to South Africa, but when news came through that war had broken out between Britain and the Transvaal and Orange Free State Boers on 11 October, many breathed a sigh of relief. How disappointing it would have been to have to turn around and come straight back without even seeing a weapon presented in anger. Especially after the public and private send-offs most had attended, strutting about in their new uniforms, heads high and backs straight, modestly accepting the compliments and best wishes of everyone they encountered.

On 21 October the First New Zealand Contingent was ready to sail. Tamar and Andrew travelled to Wellington to see the ship off, although this time they left the children in the capable hands of Jeannie and Mrs Muldoon. There was great excitement in Wellington, and a huge, cheering crowd had congregated at Jervois Quay to watch the troops of the First Contingent march down Glenbervie Cutting from Karori to the docks. The harbour was afloat with small boats preparing to follow the *Waiwera* out as far as they could, and bands on board several steamers played rousing, patriotic music. Premier Seddon made a long and fervent speech, which was greeted with much cheering and shouts of 'Bravo, New Zealand', followed by Robert Stout who made the mistake of saying he hoped the war would be over by the time the New Zealanders got to South Africa. There were loud cries of 'No!' from the crowd, and Andrew shook his head in amazement.

'I don't think some of these people know what it really means,' he said in Tamar's ear. 'Those Boers know what they're doing and they're not afraid to fight. Look at what happened at Majuba Hill. The British were slaughtered.'

Tamar nodded, although she didn't know what had happened at Majuba Hill, or even where it was. She really must read the papers more often. Next to her a woman in a plain brown dress and an old-fashioned bonnet was wringing her hands anxiously. 'Oh, I 'ope 'e'll be safe,' she muttered to no one in particular. 'That's our Donald,' she said, nudging Tamar and pointing at an obscure face in the line of young men boarding the *Waiwera*. 'Me only son. D'you 'ave a lad going?'

'Yes,' Tamar replied. 'I do, although I haven't spotted him yet.'

'God keep 'em safe. My Jack'll be 'eartbroken if our Donald don't come 'ome,' the woman added miserably. Seddon's words of victory and glory had obviously been of little comfort.

As the troops boarded the ship, they disappeared into its belly only to reappear minutes later along the rails, some of them climbing into the rigging for a better view. Hundreds of horses had also been taken on board, and their glossy, muscled haunches could be seen lined up in a long row of wooden stalls in the middle of the deck, rolled canvas shades ready to be let down as protection against inclement weather. As the ship began to pull away, a band struck up an energetic version of 'Rule Britannia' and the crowd erupted into wild cheering.

Tamar and Andrew watched until the *Waiwera* was heading out of the harbour, escorted by dozens of small boats as far as the heads.

'Well, that's it, I suppose, until the next contingent.'

'Will there be another one?' asked Tamar, taking Andrew's hand as they were jostled by the crowd.

'I expect so, unless the thing blows over, but I doubt it somehow. I'd say this could be the first of many.' Feeling Tamar's tension, he stopped and affectionately tucked a stray strand of hair under her hat. 'Don't worry. He'll come home. He knows what he's doing.'

Tamar nodded. She'd told Kepa the same thing, but it had been different when she had said it — Joseph had only been leaving for Wellington. Now he was on his way to South Africa.

As soon as the *Waiwera* had sailed out past the heads, word was passed that the troops could relax and settle themselves in. Rumour had it there was a race on with the first of the Australian contingents to see who would be the first antipodean troops to land at Cape Town in support of the Empire.

The New Zealanders reached South Africa on 23 November. The weather had been kind, although many had become seasick, particularly when the *Waiwera* dipped into the southern latitudes after passing the southern tip of Australia. A dozen horses died during the trip, their corpses winched overboard and consigned to the sea. To fill in time, the contingent practised pistol shooting and bayonet charges on deck, although this proved to be somewhat dangerous when one soldier bayoneted himself in his right thigh after a particularly violent lurch of the ship. When the weather prevented access to the deck, the men stayed below cleaning their equipment, sleeping and telling each other how much the Boers would regret New Zealand's offer of assistance to the Empire when they finally got to South Africa.

When they arrived at Cape Town, a flat, dusty settlement backed by Table Mountain shimmering in the heat, they had only a few days to exercise their horses, regain their land legs and pick up extra equipment. Almost immediately, they were sent to join Major-General Sir John French's Cavalry Division, which was blocking and harassing the Boer force occupying Colesburg in the north.

Joseph and his mates felt self-conscious riding into Slingersfontein, the British camp outside Colesburg, wearing their slightly rag-tag khaki uniforms, their badges and equipment hurriedly dyed or painted brown, but soon found their presence was more than appreciated. The British had discovered that conducting a war using traditional infantry tactics on open ground against a mounted enemy who could and did disappear into the terrain at will was less than productive, if not foolhardy. The New Zealanders, who fought like infantrymen on the ground but used their horses to enhance mobility, were welcome reinforcements.

The terrain suited the New Zealanders. The temperature was similar to home, and the Drakensberg Mountains, temporary base of the Boer forces, were not dissimilar to some of the country Joseph had ridden over in Hawke's Bay. The high, grassy veldt was another matter, but most of the New Zealanders, many of whom were more than comfortable moving about rough country on horseback, felt at ease.

Joseph was involved in the New Zealanders' first major action at Jasfontein Farm outside Colesburg on 18 December. As part of a mounted reconnaissance patrol, Number 1 Company was moving through a series of small hills, or *kopjes*, when they were fired on by a concealed Boer party. Joseph had his head down fiddling with a stirrup buckle and got the fright of his life when he suddenly realised the flat, cracking noises were bullets whizzing past his head. The company was ordered to spread out and return fire, but the Boers countered with heavy artillery and the word came to withdraw. In the mad dash across 800 yards of open ground, the man next to Joseph went down, tumbling almost gracefully out of his saddle. Joseph pulled his own horse up viciously and cantered back to him, oblivious to the bullets kicking up small puffs of dust around him.

'*Bradford*!' he bellowed, leaning so far over he almost fell off himself. '*George*! Can you hear me?'

Private George Bradford said nothing, on his back in the dirt, his spread legs revealing a gaping wound in his groin. Joseph felt sick. As he went to dismount, another rider skidded to a halt near him, Sergeant Bob Thornton.

'*Deane*!' he shouted over the din. 'Leave him! He's dead, man! Get out of here!'

Joseph stared at Bradford, not entirely convinced the man *was* dead, until a bullet pinged off the metal water bottle attached to the side of his saddle. He whirled around, booted his horse and followed the rest of his company as they retreated beyond the range of the Boer artillery.

Bradford's horse came in soon after, with its rider's bandolier still tied around its neck. Of Private Bradford, there was no sign. When a search party returned later to the scene of the skirmish, there was nothing but a large patch of dried blood on the ground. They discovered weeks later Bradford had not been killed outright, but had been picked up by the Boers and taken to one of their field hospitals where he was treated for ten days before he finally died of his wounds.

Bradford's wounding and disappearance sobered Number 1 Company. Until then, the war had been an adventure; now, a mate had died and many of the young New Zealand troops suddenly realised they might not all be going home. Perversely, this increased the bravado of some, while others became subdued.

As Joseph and members of his section sat around a camp fire that evening, they talked about Bradford's disappearance in hushed tones. Joseph felt guilty because he had not stopped to check; the wounded man might still have been alive.

'Well, he can't have crawled far, not with his balls blown to buggery,' declared Barry Price crudely as he tipped tea leaves into a large billy.

'I didn't say his balls were blown off,' replied Joseph, even though he suspected they might have been. 'I just said he had a groin wound.'

'Have you seen what one of them bullets can do?' asked Price. 'Blow the shit out of you.'

'So where is he then?' asked Jimmy Malone, a second-generation Irishman from Waipukurau and the section's corporal.

Price shrugged. 'Maybe the ghosts got him.'

'What ghosts?' asked Albert Baker nervously. Albert, like Joseph, had lied about his age when he volunteered and was only eighteen but, unlike Joseph, he was naive and somewhat gullible.

'Them that lives in the Drakensberg Mountains. Ghosts of dead Boers. A darkie was telling me mate, Davey White in Number 2 Company, about them. They come down and take dead bodies back into the hills.'

In the semi-dark Joseph saw Price surreptitiously elbow Malone and wink as Albert Baker's eyes widened.

'Shut up, you jokers,' interrupted Sergeant Thornton. 'You're talking bollocks. There are no ghosts, lad,' he said to Albert. 'They're pulling your tit.'

Thornton had served with the New Zealand Armed Constabulary in the 1870s and had fought against the legendary Te Kooti. He'd seen what talk of ghosts and spirits had done to Maori troops in his unit. He wasn't having that here, load of cobblers that it was. Privately, he was of the opinion that either the Boers had picked Bradford up, or an animal had dragged the corpse away, but he wasn't going to say that, not with young Baker's eyes already popping out of his head. Who the hell had let boys like him into the contingent? 'He might be in a Boer hospital,' he added, picking his teeth with a twig. 'You never know.'

Price leaned to the left and let out a loud, resonant fart that reverberated almost musically against the log he was sitting on.

Albert Baker, fear forgotten, giggled madly. That boy really has had a sheltered life, thought Thornton, shaking his head. He turned to Joseph. 'Forget about it, Deane. There's nothing you could have done, except get your own head blown off. I saw him — he was either dead or very close to it. It was your first man down. You'll get used to it,' he added philosophically.

Joseph nodded, but he wasn't at all sure that he would.

Chapter Twenty-seven

October 1900

Joseph forced himself to wait until his tea had brewed before he allowed himself to open his letter. It was only the fourth he had received since he'd been in South Africa; the mail system was woeful and letters from home went astray with disappointing regularity. Mug in hand, he settled down to catch up on the news from Kenmore.

> *My Dearest Son,*   *July 1900*
>
> *I hope this letter finds you well — Andrew sends his regards, as do the children. Did you receive my last parcel? Mrs Muldoon made the fruit cake, Jeannie the shortbread, and Keely knitted the socks. When I suggested they might be a little long, she said you could always give them to your horse to wear if it gets really cold.*
>
> *The children all miss you, but Keely most of all, I suspect. Rathbone caught her knocking the blooms off his prize dahlias the other day, and said she was very rude to him when he told her to stop. Andrew is of the opinion she will grow out of this rather unpleasant behaviour, but she is eight now and there is no sign of it yet. She can be a delightful child, but I fear we have spoiled her, and are now paying the price.*

It turned out that the dahlia episode was a result of being banned from playing with the other children. Evidently they are sick of Keely insisting on being the Queen and ordering them to be killed in battle so she can put flowers on their graves. James tells me this is not on, because everyone knows British soldiers hardly ever die. It is worse for poor little Ian — because he is the youngest, he is nearly always relegated to being the 'dirty Boer', and has to die at least twice a day.

We had one of our dinner parties at Kenmore last week, and I am afraid that some of Andrew's opinions did not sit well with several of our guests. He does not approve of the Fifth Contingent being sent so closely on the heels of the earlier New Zealand contingents, and said so quite bluntly, adding that New Zealanders should not be quite so quick or willing to dance to the Empire's tune. Well, several people were scandalised — it was rather amusing, really. It is not the war he objects to, so much as New Zealand's lack of autonomy in matters pertaining to it.

Nevertheless, we have all been very busy raising money for the Patriotic Fund. We had a floral fête in Napier, with a parade of floats and children dressed up as little soldiers and nurses and Zealandias and Britannias. Unfortunately, there was also an effigy of President Kruger, and when somebody set fire to it the children appeared absolutely delighted. I am not sure if this level of enthusiasm is quite healthy.

We have also been busy preparing food and comfort packages and sending them off via the New Zealand Express Company. We read in the papers that you are moving around a lot, so we hope that they are finding you.

People are doing all sorts of things for the Fund. There are several women's groups going about the country dressed in uniforms similar to the outfits worn by the New Zealand contingents, performing military exercises and riding decorated bicycles in formation to raise money. There was a photograph in the Weekly Press recently of one such group, the Dannevirke Huia Khaki Contingent, and I must say they did look a little odd. Andrew and I had quite a giggle, until we read how much money they had raised.

Another rather startling phenomenon is the rise in the number of School Cadets, there are literally thousands, and we hear it is the same with the Volunteers. Thomas and James are both members of the Cadets, although their training is a little irregular from what I can see. They dash about being little soldiers with wooden guns, although both have their own rifles for rabbit shooting, but their father will not allow them to take them to school. I should imagine that most of the school boys around here have their own guns. I am not sure I am happy with my boys being trained as soldiers at such a young age — it is bad enough having you away fighting in South Africa — but Cadets is part of the school curriculum, so I do not expect there is much I can do about it.

But, my dear, enough about us. How are you? Are you getting enough rest and plenty to eat? Were you at New Zealand Hill, or involved in the relief of Kimberley and Mafeking? The newspapers were full of stories about the exploits of the New Zealanders, and there were parades and even half-holidays in some towns after Mafeking. We have received three of your letters, but they were dated months before they arrived.

Is there any news yet of when you might expect to come home? With the latest contingents arriving in South Africa, I was hoping the First may be relieved. There are rumours, of course, but we know nothing for certain.

We received news last week that John has also volunteered for South Africa. He will serve as a doctor but does not yet know which contingent he might be attached to. Riria is not very pleased, but he is adamant he can be of some use to the New Zealand troops, and no doubt he is right.

Well, that is all from me at the moment. We all miss you very much, Joseph. Your father rides out every three weeks or so to chat about how you are getting on and to ask whether I have news of you.

Please take care, my dear, and know that you are constantly in our thoughts and our hearts.

All my love to you, your loving mam.

Joseph folded Tamar's letter carefully and tucked it away inside his shirt. 'One of my mam's friends has volunteered to serve over here,' he said. 'John Adams. He's a doctor and he does reconstructive surgery.'

'That'll come in handy,' said Jimmy Malone as he threaded a thin strip of rag down the barrel of his rifle and pulled it slowly out through the other end. 'Plenty of bits to sew back on.'

The New Zealanders considered themselves well and truly blooded — they had lost men to disease, battle and capture. In February the First Contingent had ridden with French's Cavalry Division into the Orange Free State, relieved Kimberley, defeated the Boers at Paardeberg, then gone on to end the siege of Ladysmith. The long, hard march to Kimberley had been gruelling for the men but had taken an even worse toll on their horses. As the animals died from exhaustion their corpses were left where they dropped. This angered the New Zealanders, many of whom had brought their own horses and were very attached to them, and their loss affected morale. They blamed the British for not allowing the animals to acclimatise after they had arrived in South Africa, and for pushing the mounted units so hard. Joseph's own horse had been shot from under him and he was now riding a remount captured from the Boers. Mounts provided by the British were considered inferior and avoided whenever possible.

Joseph's contingent had also been part of the force that marched into Bloemfontein, capital of the Orange Free State, before its annexation by the British eight weeks later. In May, the first three contingents amalgamated to form the New Zealand Regiment commanded by Alfred Robin, now a Lieutenant-Colonel, and had subsequently taken part in the British advance through the Transvaal. The besieged town of Mafeking, defended by Colonel Robert Baden-Powell, was relieved en route, and both Johannesburg and Pretoria were taken from the Boers in the early weeks of June.

The battles, particularly in the earlier months, had been true baptisms of fire, but the New Zealanders were quickly becoming battle-hardened and developing a reputation for toughness, resilience and ability. These manly virtues were trumpeted, exaggerated and repeated endlessly in the newspapers at home to such an extent that Joseph laughed out loud one day as he was reading a copy of the *Auckland Weekly News* sent to Albert Baker by his mother. Mrs Baker had helpfully underlined all the bits describing how brave, cool and collected the New Zealanders were under fire.

Joseph had been amused, but he'd also felt moderately angry. It was a pity the papers were printing nothing about what most New Zealanders in South Africa believed was the general incompetence of many of the British commanders. In Joseph's opinion the enlisted men weren't too bad, but they were treated poorly by their superiors and the result was a marked lack of enthusiasm for fighting and considerable tension amongst the British ranks. At times the New Zealanders had also suffered from British incompetence. At Ottoshoop in August, the British commander Major-General Paget had launched an ill-considered attack against a strong Boer position. New Zealanders, Australians and the British yeomanry had been pinned down by heavy fire for a whole day; the wounded had to be left where they lay, the Red Cross flag was ignored and medical officers shot as they ran about trying to tend the fallen. That night, the Boers launched their own attack on the weakened

Imperial troops. They were repelled and eventually disappeared into the night, but by then the New Zealanders had lost ten men, including five officers, with sixteen men wounded.

Malone glanced at Joseph, then went back to squinting down the barrel of his rifle. 'No offence,' he said, 'but how is it your mam has doctors for friends, you being a Maori?'

'My mother is *Pakeha*.'

'Ah. That'll explain why you're not very dark-skinned.'

Joseph left it at that. There was no need to tell everyone everything about himself. In fact, none of the men in his section shared much about their private lives. Names, hometowns, occupations, that was enough. What mattered was what they did now. Here, a man's value was judged by his ability to stay alive and how much he could be depended upon. Joseph had done his share of picking mates off the ground by their webbing and dragging them out of harm's way. Nobody commented on the fact that he was clearly not a full-blooded European.

Malone half-heartedly waved at the flies settling on his face. 'Well, I hope your mam's friend is good at holding out a bucket and cleaning up shite — there's more men sick here than wounded. We had another three go down during the night.'

Joseph nodded, unsurprised. The day before, Barry Price had been carted off on a stretcher suffering from the dreaded enteric fever. He'd been pasty-faced and complaining of being too hot for a day or so, but had refused to see a medical officer. He prided himself on being as 'hard as nails', but the matter had been taken out of his hands when he'd collapsed at breakfast yesterday morning.

Sitting on a box outside the section's tents, he'd raised his rump to deliver one of his monumental farts, but instead of the usual trumpeting blast, there was an explosive, watery sound and a revolting stench. With an incredulous look on his unshaven face, he'd declared, 'Fuck! I've shit meself!'

Then he'd risen, caught a full whiff of his own stink, belched violently, doubled over and vomited onto the ground.

'Oh, bloody *hell*,' Malone had exclaimed, skipping quickly out of the way to avoid being splattered, his hand held protectively over his mug of tea.

Price had collapsed onto his side in the dirt, his hands clutched to his stomach, and emitted another noisy torrent of diarrhoea.

'Oh, shit.' This from Joseph. 'Get a medical officer, someone.'

Sergeant Thornton slowly sauntered off towards the MO's tent, as if this sort of thing happened all the time. And it did; there were more men in hospital with enteric fever than there were with battle wounds. When a medical officer arrived, dressed in his shirtsleeves with his braces hanging down and shaving soap still on his ears, he didn't even bother to examine Price.

'Bugger. Another one,' he'd muttered to no one in particular. Then he had asked of Thornton, 'Has everyone else had the same food and water as this man?'

When the sergeant nodded, the MO swore again. 'Right, chuck it all out, it's probably contaminated.'

Joseph and the rest of the section had looked at each other nervously, wondering who would be next.

Price was now on his way to a hospital, a journey of several days by bullock wagon, his personal possessions sent with him in case he didn't come back, and his horse allocated to someone else. Joseph wondered if they would see him again.

On 25 October the Transvaal was annexed by the British, and the Empire's newspapers smugly speculated the war was virtually over. Field Marshal Lord Roberts had been replaced by his chief of staff, General Lord Kitchener, and the First New Zealand Contingent was preparing to return home after eleven months of continuous

service. Forty or so men left Pretoria bound for New Zealand at the end of the month, followed in December by the remaining members of the contingent who did not want to stay in South Africa.

Joseph, Jimmy Malone and Sergeant Thornton all opted to continue fighting and transferred to the Fourth Contingent, the Rough Riders. Albert Baker, who had never quite adjusted to being a soldier, went home, as did the remaining four from the original section. Barry Price had died in hospital five days after he had fallen ill, and another soldier had been severely wounded and sent back to New Zealand in June.

The Fourth and Fifth Contingents had originally been sent from New Zealand to Beira, the capital of Portuguese East Africa, and had arrived between late April and mid-May. It had been intended that both contingents would travel by train to Rhodesia, but rail congestion kept them confined to camps where malaria and dysentery caused more casualties than battle ever could have. The troops left Beira a month later and marched hundreds of gruelling miles to Bulawayo in Southern Rhodesia. In August both contingents travelled by rail to Mafeking, where they joined the second brigade of the Rhodesian Field Force.

Joseph and his mates connected with the Fourth Contingent when the column arrived in southwestern Transvaal in December. Despite the British annexation of Orange Free State and the Transvaal, Kruger, Steyn and other Boer leaders had sworn to carry on their battle against the Imperial forces. They were backed by thousands of well-armed Boers in the field, and a civilian network that doggedly supported them. The style of warfare had changed from conventional military tactics to clandestine guerrilla warfare in which Boer commandos launched sudden, devastating attacks, only to disappear just as rapidly afterwards. They were fast, elusive and effective, and the British found the new style of fighting extremely frustrating.

Kitchener retaliated by forming columns of highly mobile mounted riflemen to actively hunt and eradicate the Boer commandos, destroy property and crops, capture supplies and drive off stock, and round up Boer women and children for internment in what soon came to be known as concentration camps. Kitchener's strategy received much support in the Empire's newspapers, but many of the New Zealand troops — in demand for these operations because they were efficient horsemen and reasonable shots — found the work distasteful, and were not slow to say so.

Privately, the British attitude towards Boer civilians shocked Joseph. He understood the best way to stop the commandos was to deprive them of their civilian support, but he could not agree with the herding of women and children, as if they were no different from farm animals. He was reminded of the stories Te Kanene had told him about Maori being cleared from their lands after the wars of the 1860s, rounded up and relocated onto small reservations that would never be able to sustain them. His uncle had talked about the long, trudging lines of frightened people, their eyes full of mistrust and anger, their faces masks of despair and bitterness.

Joseph could see all of that in the Afrikaner civilians, and he could see hatred as well. He thought how ironic it was that he was inflicting the same fate on the Boers as had befallen his own people, and for the same reason — greed for land. In both cases, the British had been the protagonists. For the past twelve months, Joseph had been able to justify his motives for fighting. Nothing to do with land or goldmines or loyalty to the British Empire, his reasons were based on the inherent right of a man to become a warrior, to prove himself, to experience victory and earn *mana*. But there was no *mana* in terrorising women and children, burning down homes and crops, and destroying people's livelihoods. Yesterday a woman spat at him, and he'd been unable to look her in the eye.

When the remaining members of the First Contingent joined up

441

with the Rough Riders, Joseph and Jimmy Malone were erecting their tent when Joseph heard his name called. Turning around, he saw a uniformed figure standing behind him. When he finally recognised who it was, he leapt forward to shake the other man's hand.

'Dr Adams!'

Joseph was shocked. Normally, the doctor was in rude health; today, he was as white as a ghost, shiny with sweat, and extremely thin. John caught Joseph eyeing his baggy trousers and the way the collar on his khaki jacket gaped.

'Good to see you, Joseph,' he said, shaking the younger man's hand enthusiastically. 'I'm here with the Fourth, but only temporarily. God only knows where I'll be tomorrow, or even tonight for that matter. And I'm *Captain* Adams, for the duration, but please call me John.'

'I'm not allowed,' Joseph replied. 'You're an officer.' John noticed how the boy's rather formal pronunciation was relaxing. Must be the influence of his scruffy bloody mates, he thought. Actually, he was rather enjoying the loose, casual attitudes of many of the New Zealanders he was working with. They were rough and rude and often had foul mouths, but they were easygoing and as honest as anyone else in this godforsaken place, providing they were treated fairly. Their lack of respect for their superiors, and particularly for the British officers, was refreshing and something he shared. He didn't mind the casual way the men spoke to him, and thought the other officers shouldn't be bothered by it either.

'You don't look well, Captain Adams, if you don't mind me saying,' commented Joseph.

John got out a large, dirty handkerchief and wiped his brow. 'It's John, and no, I'm not, really. When we were stuck at Beira almost everyone had dysentery and malaria and of course I picked the bloody things up as well. It's not too bad now, but the malaria recurs on and off. And I don't think my stomach will ever be the same, but perhaps that isn't such a bad thing — I was putting on too much weight.' He didn't add he was often forced to spend hours in the latrine, doubled over in agony until his bowels cleared. He changed the subject. 'But you're looking well, Joseph. Army life must suit you. Oh, and your mother sends her love. I've a letter for you in my tent. I'll dig it out for you later, unless you want it now?'

Joseph shook his head. 'Just when you have a minute, thanks. I got one from her the other day.' John looked as if he was going to keel over at any minute. 'Are you sure I can't get you anything? Water or something?'

'No, I'll be right. It's just a touch of fever and it goes away pretty promptly.' He looked at his watch, hanging loosely around his bony wrist. 'Damn, I've a meeting with the other medics. About the flies in the latrines. Should be exciting,' he said dryly. 'I'll drop in later and catch you up with the news from home. And I'll bring that letter.'

Joseph nodded and watched as John walked away. He walked slowly as if he was in pain. Joseph thought he looked closer to sixty than fifty. He'd obviously been very sick and Joseph wondered why he didn't pack it in and go home. He probably could, as he'd volunteered and wasn't a member of the regular New Zealand Army or the Volunteers.

After the evening meal was over and Joseph had been to check his horse had been fed and watered, he returned to his tent to find John and Jimmy Malone sitting outside sharing a large bottle of brandy only vaguely camouflaged by a canvas bag. Drinking in the lines wasn't allowed, but it happened. Pulling up a box, Joseph accepted a drink. He'd rarely drunk alcohol before South Africa, mainly because of the dreadful experience at the Blue Lady all those years ago, but he'd had his share of morning-after headaches since he'd volunteered. John Adams looked a little better, now the sun had gone down. It must be hell having a raging fever in the heat of the day.

In little over an hour the bottle was empty. Joseph was feeling fuzzy-headed and Jimmy Malone had a silly grin plastered across his face. John was almost asleep on his box, his head lolling then jerking upright at regular intervals. He'd informed Joseph and his mate that his capacity to drink had diminished drastically after his illness, and now he was proving it. Getting drunk was unwise, but they were relatively safe here and at least he'd get a decent night's sleep. He missed Riria desperately, and his children, but he refused to succumb to whatever parasites had taken up residence in his body. His job was to patch soldiers up or, if they were really ill, arrange for them to be sent to a hospital, and home if necessary, but he was buggered if he was going to lie down and be carted off himself.

He looked up as he became gradually aware of someone standing in front of him — khaki riding breeches tucked into a pair of long, brown riding boots polished to an extremely high gloss. A riding whip was being tapped slowly against the left one.

With exaggerated care he finally said, 'Major Walbridge. Good evening.' Joseph and Malone were busy studying the ground between their boots.

'Captain Adams,' said Walbridge briskly. 'Everything all right?'

Major Walbridge was British, a cavalry officer, and not at all popular. He made unwise decisions in the field, wouldn't take advice from anyone, including his noncommissioned officers, disapproved strongly of colonials, and insisted he be saluted at all times. The New Zealand and Australian enlisted men took turns walking past him in camp and saluting him so he would have to continually salute back in the hope that his arm would eventually drop off and he would be invalided back to England.

John made an effort to sit up straighter. 'Yes, thank you, Major. Just catching up with old friends.'

444

'Is that alcohol I can smell?' asked Walbridge, leaning forward, his nose twitching like an over-sized rabbit.

'No, I don't think so,' replied John earnestly, squinting to bring the two images he could see of Walbridge back to one.

At that moment Malone's wooden box broke under his weight, pitching him backwards into the tent behind him. All three distinctly heard him say 'Fuck' as his head hit the tent pole with a loud crack. This was followed by giggling, which rose until it resembled the strange, hooting barks of a hyena.

'What's the matter with him?' asked Walbridge.

'Bad case of sunstroke,' replied John without missing a beat. 'I'm thinking seriously of hospitalising him.'

Walbridge's mouth puckered in distaste. 'Hmm, well, you'd better do it soon then, hadn't you?'

He remained standing in front of John and Joseph, as if waiting for something else untoward to happen. Eventually he said, 'Well, goodnight then, Captain Adams,' but made no move to go.

John suddenly realised what was required and saluted so hard he almost knocked himself off his box. Joseph followed suit.

'G'night, Major Walbridge,' said John, except it came out sounding like Walbitch.

The major disappeared from sight between the rows of tents.

'What a bastard,' said John. 'And on that note, my boy, I'd better be heading back to my own tent. Good to catch up with you.'

'And you, John,' replied Joseph.

They both stood unsteadily and shook hands. John looked around cagily, took two wobbly steps forward, said, 'You look a lot like your father, you know, but you've definitely got your mother's eyes,' then wandered off.

Joseph never saw him alive again.

Chapter Twenty-eight

Early the following morning, John was woken by someone shaking his shoulder. 'What?' he mumbled, not bothering to open his eyes. He didn't feel well, although his fever seemed to have departed, thank God.

'Wake up, John,' said the voice, urgent now. 'Get your gear together right away. You're coming with us. Mellor's orders.'

John opened his eyes. 'Oh, it's you, Dick,' he muttered and sat up slowly, feeling bilious and painfully aware of his pounding head. He blinked blearily at his friend. 'Are there wounded?'

'No,' replied Dick Raynor, a lieutenant with the New Zealand mounted infantry. 'But Mellor wants to see you.'

John sighed and disentangled himself from his grubby blanket. God, his tent smelled like a distillery. 'Just give me a minute,' he mumbled.

He staggered out of his tent five minutes later, splashed water over his face and head and pulled up his braces. The sun wasn't even over the mountains, but the camp was bustling. Something was obviously in the wind. He headed off for Major Mellor's tent.

Major Mellor oversaw the medical care of several British regiments as well as a number of the New Zealand and Australian units. He was a surgeon with the regular British army, but John considered him good at his job and generally not a bad sort. He'd decided not all British army officers were twits, but those who were certainly let the team down, and unfortunately they were often the ones with the most responsibility.

'Good morning, Adams,' said Mellor, standing behind his desk. For some reason he hardly ever sat down: John suspected haemorrhoids. As usual, the major looked wide awake, smartly turned out and cheerful, despite the early hour. 'Indulge in a spot of liquid refreshment last night?'

John nodded gingerly, mindful of his sore head.

'Well, a man's entitled to his relaxation,' Mellor said. 'Some of your boys are coming with us after General De la Rey. Apparently he's at Rustenburg. You and a couple of the other medical officers will be going with them, under the command of Lieutenant-Colonel Kendall.'

Mellor looked John in the eye, the expression on his face as empathic as his rank allowed. Lieutenant-Colonel Kendall was an odious, incompetent fool.

John nodded. He had come to South Africa to provide New Zealand troops with medical care, and he wasn't particularly bothered about which contingent; he'd been with the Fourth and Fifth for the last seven months, now it looked as if he'd be with the Second and Third.

Mellor moved papers from one side of his desk to the other. 'Good-oh. You'll be leaving in an hour. And have a decent breakfast, you look like a dog's backside. How's the malaria — causing you much trouble?'

'The odd recurrence of fever, Major, that's all. Annoying but not life-threatening. I'll be on my way, then. No doubt I'll see you again, sir.'

'Yes, I'm sure you will,' agreed Mellor with a half-hearted salute. 'Good luck.'

'Thank you, Major.' John returned an equally limp salute and went outside.

He'd have time to write a quick letter to Riria, then gather his things and stow them in one of the medical wagons. As usual, he would be travelling on horseback, unless a patient in one of the wagons needed attention. It was not necessarily the trauma of their wounds that killed the men, but often the protracted journey to the nearest military hospital. The journey could take days in crippling heat infested with the ever-present flies, infecting wounds and spreading disease. The luckier ones were wounded near the railway on which the Red Cross hospital train shuttled between Pretoria and Cape Town; while they ran the risk of Boer attacks, at least the journey was quicker.

John had worked for a fortnight in Bloemfontein General Hospital, assisting with rudimentary reconstructive surgery, and after only twenty-four hours he'd already decided that if *he* were ever wounded, he'd rather take his chances on the veldt where at least the air was clean. The hospital had been appallingly overcrowded with triple the patients it was equipped to handle, many of them victims of the enteric epidemic. The staff were overworked and exhausted, the wards had been seething with body lice and filthy, despite the efforts of the orderlies, and there had been a serious water shortage. He'd also been to the huge No. 4 General Hospital at Mooi River Camp in Natal. The entire facility was under canvas, with staff forced to live in gumboots when it rained because of the mud, but at least the conditions were less crowded, and more hygienic because the air was able to circulate more freely.

As the Third mounted and headed out onto the veldt, John sought out Dick Raynor and, as was his custom, gave him the letter for Riria. He never let himself dwell on the idea he might not come home from South Africa, but before every major operation he felt an overwhelming compulsion to write and tell her how very much he loved her.

It was Raynor who told Joseph, months later, what happened.

The trek to Rustenburg was long, hot and arduous. John treated sunstroke, diarrhoea, saddle sores exacerbated by sweat and made septic by filth, and extracted several rotten teeth. Progress slowed as the condition of the horses deteriorated and their riders were forced to dismount, and by the time they arrived men and animals were profoundly fatigued. There was to be no rest, however, and over the following weeks there were numerous skirmishes between the British and De la Rey's men, but De la Rey himself, and his equally infamous cohort, General Christiaan De Wet, remained elusive.

In March, John found himself riding at the tail end of a column of New Zealanders just below the border between Cape Colony and Orange Free State. His stomach had still not settled and since December he had suffered a further recurrence of malaria. He was tired and homesick, and had had a gutsful of chasing Boers across the harsh South African veldt. Months ago he had come to the conclusion the British should get out of South Africa, but he knew his opinions would serve no purpose, except perhaps to have him court-martialled. Some of the New Zealanders and Australians might agree, and possibly even some of the British enlisted men, but as far as the British commanders were concerned, John knew his words would fall on deaf ears. They still spoke loftily of military might, of glory, and of essential acquisitions for the Empire, ignoring the bitter, exhausted mutterings of their men and, at times, the outright rebelliousness of the colonials they commanded.

But here they were, a column of around a hundred and thirty British and New Zealand troops, on yet another cloudless morning with the sun already murderously hot, plodding towards the blue mountains in search of Boer guerrillas. There was very little talk amongst the tired troops, only the clanking of their equipment, the occasional horse snort and the dull, unsynchronised *clop* of hundreds of hooves hitting the hard, baked ground.

John was nearly asleep, hoping for his own sake the rest of the column was alert. Evidently they were, for as the first Boer bullet ricocheted off a rock fifty yards in front of him, he heard Lieutenant Turner bellow '*Take cover*' as the men ahead of him whirled their mounts and scattered. John's horse bolted without being asked, carrying him behind the shelter of a long, low outcrop of rock. John slid to the ground and crouched low, his heart thudding and blood pounding in his ears, and peered through a gap in the rocks.

They had been approaching a high *kopje* and the bullets seemed to be originating from there. John wondered why the scouts riding ahead had not alerted the rest of the column. Perhaps they were still trotting along half a mile in front, chatting blithely to each other, the Boers having let them pass in order to snare the bigger prize. Or perhaps they were lying dead on the far side of the *kopje*.

The men had recovered their wits and were spreading themselves out behind the rocks to return fire, the British on the left and the New Zealanders on the right. Together with the two medical wagons, their mounts had been moved quickly out of range, and were held in check. The horses had been trained to stand steady during rifle and artillery fire, but occasionally one would bolt and panic the rest, causing complete pandemonium.

Lieutenant Turner and the other New Zealand officers were barking orders and moving the men into better firing positions behind the shelter of one end of the rocks, while their British colleagues did the same behind the other. The barrier afforded by the outcrop was low, but as long as no one stood up straight, they would be relatively safe. However, when John glanced to either side and then behind, he saw there was nowhere for the troops to go. If they went forwards or to the left or right they would be mown down, and if they went backwards, they would expose themselves to snipers. In front of the rocks was a stretch of open, stony ground about five hundred yards across to the base of the *kopje*, and on it lay two bodies — men who had not moved fast enough. John squinted but could not tell whether they were alive or dead. He could, however, see at least two of the Boer positions on the *kopje* — one halfway up the hill and another nearer the top. They appeared to have selected their firing positions carefully, suggesting this was no hit-and-run raiding party.

In the middle of the troops pinned behind the rocks crouched the senior officers. Lieutenant-Colonel Kendall, and a New Zealander major, John Anscombe, were arguing, both waving their arms and yelling, although their voices could barely be heard above the din of the rifle fire. John crawled on his hands and knees towards them; he had to do something about the fallen men on the off-chance they were still alive, and he would not be able to drag them back himself. As he approached the senior officers, he could hear angry words.

'What's happening?' he asked Raynor, who was sitting against the rocks with his revolver on his upraised knees. He looked stunned.

'They're bloody *arguing*, for Christ's sake!' Raynor exclaimed incredulously. 'Kendall wants us to charge the bloody *hill*! God only knows how many bloody Boers are up there! We'll be annihilated!'

John stared at him in dismay, then turned to watch. The Lieutenant-Colonel had gone red in the face and there was a scum of white foam collecting at the corners of his mouth; John wondered if the man was about to have a fit. Anscombe was shaking his head violently, his teeth almost bared in his anger. Both men were on their knees, looking incongruously child-like as they faced each other, faces inches apart. Suddenly Anscombe threw up his hands and pulled away. He turned to Raynor and spat through gritted teeth, 'We're going over. Get the men ready.'

'It'll be murder!' replied Raynor, forgetting he was talking to a senior officer.

'Yes, it will, but the bastard's convinced we can take the hill,' said Anscombe, his face white with rage. 'Get them ready.'

Appalled, John could see in his mind's eye the dead and dying spread over the ground between the rocks and the base of the *kopje*. 'Haven't we got another column northeast of here?' he asked, then pointed back towards the horses and wagons. 'Couldn't someone back there be sent to fetch them?'

Raynor shook his head. 'The column's more than a hundred bloody miles away. Two riders have gone, but we could all be dead by the time they get here. *And* we're pinned down. We can't get to our horses now, either.'

'Why don't we just wait until it gets dark?'

Raynor shrugged and indicated his head towards the Lieutenant-Colonel, who was now arguing with one of his own officers. 'Ask him,' he said as he crawled away to break the news to his men.

John sat back on his heels. There were three medical officers with the column, and a handful of enlisted men who had volunteered as stretcher bearers; the medical wagons were well behind them, safely out of the way but unreachable. The dread that had been growing in the pit of his stomach threatened to engulf him as he scuttled behind the rocks to find Beale and Carter, the two British MOs. They would have to be ready.

They thought they were, but in the end there was little anyone could have done. The first wave of thirty men ran straight into a solid wall of bullets. A quarter fell while the rest managed to scramble back behind the safety of the outcrop, some wounded and all disoriented. Kendall bellowed at them to go back out, but his order was ignored. Incensed and screaming at his officers to ready the troops for a second charge, the Lieutenant-Colonel threatened the column with court martial and kicked wildly at the men near him. John suddenly realised the man was mad with fear and watched in horrified fascination as Kendall slowly stood to his full height and raised his arm to give the order to charge. No one moved to stop him.

Kendall was shot instantly, crumpling to the ground clutching the left side of his chest, dark blood spurting through his fingers. John scrambled over but it was obvious he had been mortally wounded. He placed his hand over the hole in the man's chest and applied as much pressure as he was able, but could do nothing more as Kendall's life pumped out of his body and soaked into the dusty ground. After a minute John took his hand away and moved back, thinking how peculiar it was that natural justice was delivered in such strange but sometimes logical ways.

The second charge had been aborted the minute Kendall had hit the ground. The Boers on the *kopje* stopped firing. John went into a huddle with Carter and Beale as they considered how best to retrieve the wounded, whose cries of pain and confusion could be clearly heard. After a brief discussion it was decided a heavy fusillade would be laid down to cover the medical officers and volunteers as they tried to reach the wounded. The Red Cross flag had been raised, but there were few illusions about what protection it might afford. John was to take the right-hand section while the two British medics would take the middle and left-hand sections.

As instructions were relayed down the line of men behind the rocks and they reloaded and positioned their rifles, Major Anscombe asked John if he was ready.

'No,' John replied. 'But then I'll never be ready for this sort of thing.' He took his watch off and handed it to Anscombe. 'If anything happens, can you make sure my eldest boy gets this? Raynor has a letter for my wife.' He shook his head glumly. 'She'll be so annoyed with me if I get myself killed.'

'Then don't,' Anscombe said gruffly. 'Straight out, pick up the live ones, and straight back in. The dead can wait. And if gets rough, turn around and come back. No point losing more men.'

John nodded and swallowed. His mouth was bone dry, his heart beat wildly, and his anus was clamped shut; although terrified, he had no intention of shitting himself. He looked at Beale and Carter, who appeared as frightened as he was, and raised his eyebrows. When they nodded, Anscombe passed the message down the line to Jarvis, the British major now in command, who looked at his watch, counted down, then gave the order to fire.

The near-silence exploded as almost a hundred troops simultaneously fired up at the *kopje*. Although the Boers responded instantly, their aim was hampered by the intensity of the British fusillade. John immediately scrambled over the rocks and sprinted for the nearest body. He could hear nothing over the incredible noise but sensed two of the volunteers close behind. The first man he reached was dead, shot through the neck, and he hurried on to the next, moving erratically in the vain hope he might be able to dodge the Boer bullets. The next man was alive and John signalled for him to be picked up and taken back.

Out of the corner of his eye he could see Carter and Beale and their quartet of volunteers dashing madly from body to body. He almost laughed; they looked absurd, like deranged ants scurrying across a vast tablecloth snatching up crumbs.

The next man was also still breathing, although the pulpy, bloody mass extruding from the side of his head suggested he wouldn't be for much longer. John left him. As he bent to inspect a man lying only a few feet further out, the prone body jerked as it was riddled with bullets. There was no new explosion of blood and John was briefly thankful the man was already dead.

It was when he was turning back towards the shelter of the rocks that he was hit. He felt no pain but was aware of being propelled forward, as if he'd been violently shoved by a giant, invisible hand. He landed face first, bounced slightly, then lay still with his arms outstretched and his head skewed uncomfortably to the right. He couldn't tell exactly where his legs were, but for some reason that didn't seem to be important. And he couldn't hear anything, only a heavy, ringing silence. Had it been a bullet, or an artillery shell? He hadn't seen a big gun on the hill. And why could he smell oranges?

He blinked. There was grit in his left eye and a good handful of it in his mouth as well. He saw a pair of brown boots going past his head, then a blur of faded khaki as someone seemed to float to the ground only feet away. More silence, and now everything was fading to a fuzzy grey. There was still no pain.

John felt his pulse dropping far too quickly. He knew he should get up, but he was too tired. He closed his eyes and muttered, 'Oh Riria, I'm so sorry.'

A single tear ran across the ridge of his nose and plopped into the dust. Then, as he began to sink into blackness, he sighed once, and let himself go.

'For fuck's sake!' roared Anscombe as he watched John go down. It was not his usual habit to swear in front of his men, but fuck it. His revolver clicked on an empty chamber and he flung it viciously towards the *kopje*.

'God, what a *cock*-up,' he spat at Raynor. 'We get five back but lose three more. I'd *kill* that bastard Kendall if he wasn't dead already!'

Raynor said nothing; he was too stunned. Was John still alive? Captain Beale obviously wasn't; the top of his head seemed to be missing. John lay motionless and Raynor's eyes were riveted to the pool of blood beneath him; it was no longer spreading. He shook his head, blinked back tears and tried to get a grip on himself.

'So what do we do now?' he asked, his voice thick and painful in his throat.

'I don't know,' said Anscombe wearily, rubbing his dirty face with even dirtier hands. 'I'll go and talk to Jarvis. Tell the men to sit tight and not waste their bullets.'

He moved off and Raynor passed the word along the line, although most had stopped firing when the last volunteer staggered back in. Then he sat and stared at nothing in particular while he waited for Anscombe to return. The attempt to rescue the wounded had been a disaster. And they were still pinned down.

Anscombe came back. 'We're waiting until dark, then we're retreating. At least Jarvis seems to have a brain. Have half the men stand down and the other half remain at their posts.'

The men settled in, making themselves as comfortable as they could behind the protection of the rocks. Most broke open their dry rations or lit cigarettes, but there was not much water. Captain Carter tended the wounded as best he could. The afternoon heat increased, the air still and hazy and the raw sun blazing down; everyone kept their hats on despite the sweat pouring down their dusty faces.

In less than an hour, the vultures came. Their huge wings flapping lazily, they circled low above the flat ground between the *kopje* and the rocks and the troops could see the bright blue of their long, bare necks. These were Cape vultures, the second largest in Africa; they fed on the carcasses of large mammals.

As one bird swooped down and landed on the body of a dead trooper, several men cried out in disgust and fired. Word was passed immediately that ammunition was not to be wasted, and the men had to satisfy themselves with hurling rocks and curses. The big, ugly birds went away eventually, but there was little doubt they'd be back.

The day dragged on, the Boers apparently in no hurry to move. The troops wondered what would happen when the sun went down. It was unlikely they could slip away unnoticed as the Boers would surely be waiting. Would there be another furious fire fight in which more of them would die? None of them believed they would not get away; there were too many of them for that, but not enough to keep charging the *kopje* until every Boer had been killed. And what would be the point? What value was there in taking one rock-strewn, scrub-covered hill in the middle of bloody nowhere? No, it made more sense to sit it out and wait for night, even if that meant lolling for hours in the stinking sun, listening to flies buzzing around dead mates and letting the anger and frustration build until it could be harnessed and directed at either the Boers on the hill, or the next lot they came across.

Gradually, the air started to cool as the sun slid down the sky. It would take time for the heavy black night to roll over the land, and the troopers were anxious to minimise any activity that might suggest they were preparing to move, but did what they could. Each walking wounded was allocated a man to help them and crude litters were fashioned from belts, shirts and jackets for those unable to help themselves. One man died during the afternoon, which made the load lighter.

The dead would have to be left where they were. As soon as the Boers departed, and they would probably be gone one way or another before the sun rose too high tomorrow, a party would collect the bodies so they could be afforded a decent Christian burial back at the camp.

As the rich purple shadows of early evening lengthened and

merged into blackness, the troops were ready.

By now they'd all had nervous pees, quietly gathered their things, fastened down anything that might make a noise, carefully folded rags into the mouths of the wounded to prevent them from crying out, and checked and reloaded their rifles. One by one they began to move silently from the rocks, walking slowly with their shoulders hunched, expecting to hear Boer fire at any second. The wounded went first followed by the bulk of the enlisted men, then the officers, all moving quietly and trying not to stumble.

Only minutes after the last man had crept away from the shelter of the rocks, the darkness relinquished a handful of small four-legged shadows that moved stealthily towards the bodies left behind. They made thick snuffling noises and carried the foul stink of the carrion that sustained them. Soon, the snuffling turned into the sound of something heavy being dragged, then the gentle, almost liquid noises of tearing and chewing.

When the evacuating column reached their horses, they finally dared breathe normally. Some offered up silent prayers of thanks, while others leaned against their mounts and swore in muffled relief. They had no way of knowing the Boers had themselves used the cover of darkness to evacuate the *kopje* an hour earlier, and were now miles away. They had numbered less than two dozen, and would have been unable to maintain anything more than a very minor skirmish with the British, come daylight.

When the sun rose, the retrieval party was already on its way back to collect the bodies of the fallen troopers. Dick Raynor lead the small group, and his orders were to circle the hill from a safe distance to ascertain whether the Boers were still there or not, and if they weren't, then the bodies were to be picked up and brought back to join the main column. It would be an unpleasant job as the dead men had already been lying in the full sun for at least half a day, and decomposition set in quickly in the intense heat. There was a pile of heavy shrouds in their wagon, but Raynor expected no one would be riding down wind on the long trip back to camp.

When they reached the *kopje*, it was clear the Boers had gone. Raynor signalled to his men to close in, but as they approached the area in front of the rocks, every man pulled up his mount and stared, slack-jawed and uncomprehending.

On the ground were a handful of dark, glistening, buzzing mounds. Raynor was unable to grasp what he was seeing until he suddenly realised the shimmering black carpets were alive. He cried out in horror and millions of blowflies rose up, hovering in the air with a sickening, teeth-rattling drone. Where they had been lay a strew of human bones, mostly stripped white but blemished here and there by shreds of dark, drying flesh.

Raynor leaned over and vomited onto the dirt, splattering his horse's front legs. Behind him he could hear several of his men doing the same, then someone asking him what should they do.

He wiped his mouth on his sleeve and, unable to take his eyes off the horror in front of him, snapped, 'How the hell should *I* know? What do *you* suggest?' He was heartily sick of this war and desperately wanted to go home to his gentle wife and his safe, undemanding public servant's job.

'We could collect 'em all up, sir, and sort 'em out later.' Private Biddle had a cast iron stomach, and sensibilities to match.

Raynor hesitated, retching behind his hand at the thought, then agreed. 'Fetch the shrouds. We'll have to jumble the lot all in together — one of the MOs can organise them when we get back.' Then he remembered there was only one medical officer left. The other two were here.

He got off his horse and cautiously approached the mess on the ground. The stink was faint but it was there, the meagre flesh left on the dismembered skeletons fetid already. He got his handkerchief out and held it over his nose and mouth, then turned to help the men lay a large shroud next to the bones.

When nobody moved, he said through his handkerchief, 'Come on, gather them up!'

Biddle said cheerily, 'Aye, they won't pick 'emselves up, will they?'

Raynor gave him a dirty look, motioned towards the scattered bones and snapped, 'Get on with it.' He himself stood back, unable to even contemplate touching the remains.

When all of the bones, buttons, watches and other items had been collected and placed on the shroud, someone pointed out that there weren't enough skulls.

'*What*?' snapped Raynor. Was there no end to this hideousness?

'There should be eight of 'em, sir,' replied one of his men uneasily. 'Two went down when we first got ambushed, then eight in the first wave, five got brought back in, then three more went down. That makes eight. There's only seven 'ere, sir.'

Raynor closed his eyes.

'Filthy, scavenging bloody animals,' muttered Biddle, offended at last.

All of this Dick Raynor recounted to Joseph when their paths crossed many weeks later. Private Deane seemed to fold the information into himself, whether to examine it later in private, or to leave it there forever, Raynor could not tell.

He said, 'John talked of you and your mother often, so I thought you would like to hear what happened. Perhaps you could relate the … more palatable bits to Mrs Adams. I've already sent John's letter to her, and there will be the official notification. Major Anscombe is writing to her as well, I believe.'

Joseph nodded. 'Yes, John was one of my mother's very good friends. Has been for years.' He looked the other man in the eye. 'He didn't have to volunteer. He did it because he thought he could help.'

'I know,' agreed Raynor, looking at his hands. 'And he could have gone home whenever he wanted to.'

There seemed to be nothing else to say. Joseph thanked Raynor and watched him walk away. He wondered if Riria knew yet. And what about his mother? How would she take the news? Would she, as he had done, squash the anger and the hurt down inside herself, or would she sob and rant and rail and lash out at someone in her grief? Either way, he would not be there to help her.

Kenmore, April 1901

'For what we are about to receive, may the Lord make us truly grateful.'

Andrew reached across the table for the large meat dish. He lifted the lid and sniffed. 'Whew!' he said theatrically. 'What's that smell?' He narrowed his twinkling eyes and scrutinised each of the children until he came to Thomas. 'It's *you*! It's your oxters!'

Thomas sniffed his armpits. 'No it isn't!' he retaliated indignantly.

'Oxters! Oxters! Stinky, stinky *oxters*!' taunted James, giggling.

'They're *not* stinky!' wailed Thomas, his face crumpling into tears.

Whoops, thought Tamar, he's in one of his sensitive moods. 'Leave him be, Andrew, and you be quiet, James. You're upsetting him.'

'Well, he shouldn't be such a sook,' complained James, helping himself to minted peas.

Andrew patted Thomas's thin shoulder. 'I'm sorry, son. It's not you, it's Mrs Muldoon's mutton stew.'

'Andrew, don't be silly,' rebuked Tamar, trying to keep the smile off her face. 'Mrs Muldoon makes a lovely stew.'

Andrew winked at Thomas, who brightened at his father's attention.

'Da,' said Ian, five now and recently graduated to eating at the dining table. 'Why's it called a oxter?'

'*An* oxter,' Tamar corrected.

'I don't know,' replied Andrew. 'I suppose it's a Scottish word. *My* da used to say it all the time. Did yours, Lachie?'

Lachie nodded.

'Why? Did *he* have stinky oxters?' Ian asked.

'That's enough,' said Tamar. 'We don't discuss personal hygiene at the dinner table.'

As she reached for the potatoes, Mrs Muldoon came quietly into the room. 'Mr Murdoch,' she murmured. 'May I have a word, please?'

'Of course,' said Andrew, buttering a slice of bread.

'A private word, if you don't mind.'

'Oh. Certainly.' Andrew and Tamar glanced at each other as Andrew followed Mrs Muldoon into the hall, where she stopped abruptly and said in a loud whisper, 'There's a Post Office boy at the door. With a telegraph.'

With a sudden sinking feeling, it hit him. 'Oh God, it must be Joseph!'

He hurried to the front door, where a boy of about thirteen stood miserably under the portico, cap in one hand and a folded piece of paper in the other. As he handed it over he mumbled, 'Telegraph, sir. Arrived at Napier Post Office this morning,' and turned away, not wanting to be involved in someone else's grief.

'Hold on,' said Andrew gruffly as he fished in his pocket and presented a handful of coins. What a rotten job for such a young lad.

'Thank you, sir,' said the boy as he stuffed the money into his pocket and ran down the steps.

Andrew opened the telegraph, dreading what he would read. It was bad, very bad, but not the news he had been expecting.

> *Tamar and Andrew,*
> *John reported killed in South Africa. Need your help. Please telephone.*
> *Riria.*

Andrew looked up at Mrs Muldoon who was standing at a discreet distance. 'You'd better get Tamar,' he said dully, then moved slowly over to the stairs and sank onto the bottom one, the telegraph fluttering from his hand. He bent his head in grief, willing himself not to weep.

'Andrew? What is it?' Tamar asked as she hurried into the foyer. Glimpsing the pain on her husband's face, she cried out in disbelief, 'No, not *Joseph!*'

Andrew shook his head. 'No, dear,' he said. 'It's John. He's been reported killed.'

Tamar snatched up the telegraph and read it for herself. 'There must have been a mistake,' she said eventually.

Andrew took her in his arms. 'No, darling. It's from Riria. She would have been informed officially.'

Tamar looked up at him in bewilderment. 'But I don't *want* him to be dead,' she said childishly.

'I know,' he murmured tenderly as she started to cry. He hugged her to him, feeling her intense physical and emotional pain as her chest heaved and her shoulders shook. Weeping himself now, he smoothed her hair and rocked her gently, the wretched telegraph discarded on the floor.

Andrew rode into town the following morning to telephone Riria. He went straight to the Post Office and asked for a connection to be put through to Riria's number, then went outside to wait for the Postmaster to tell him his party was on the other end.

The connection was poor and he could barely hear Riria, but he gathered she and the children would be boarding a steamer for Napier the next day. He attempted to express how he felt about John's death, but gave up in the end and just said he was terribly sorry.

Riria arrived six days later. With her were Simon, sixteen now, darkly handsome and looking uncannily like his mother; Rose, who at fourteen was surprisingly fair although with Riria's striking features; and twelve-year-old David. John had always joked he was vastly relieved his children took after Riria, and not himself.

Riria was clearly not herself. She was upset and agitated, but in Tamar's opinion not behaving like a newly bereaved widow. She wondered if her dear friend was suffering from some sort of emotional disturbance in response to the shocking and unexpected news. Her suspicions were confirmed later that afternoon when Riria made a very odd request. 'If you do not mind,' she said conversationally, 'I would like to leave the children here when I go to Port Chalmers.'

Andrew and Tamar glanced quickly at each other.

Uneasy, Tamar enquired, 'Dunedin?'

'Yes, I will be going to meet the next troopship. John will be on that one, or the one after.'

There was a painful silence.

'Riria,' said Andrew gently. 'John won't be coming back.'

'The telegraph and the letter from Major Anscombe were both misinformed. He is still alive.'

No one knew what to say. Riria didn't seem to notice their discomfort. 'I have consulted a *tohunga*,' she continued. 'He has told me he has seen John alive. I would know in here if he had been killed,' she added adamantly, tapping her breast. 'He is not dead. I know it.'

Andrew moved over to the cabinet where the drinks were kept. He poured a small brandy and handed it to Riria. 'Drink this, dear,' he said compassionately. 'It will help settle your nerves.'

'There is nothing wrong with my nerves and there is nothing wrong with my mind,' she responded firmly. 'I know exactly what I am talking about. John will be coming home.'

The Second and Third Contingents were expected home any day now, having been relieved by the arrival of the Sixth Contingent in March. Riria fully expected John would be with them.

She left for Dunedin two days later, boarding the train to Wellington then travelling by steamer to Christchurch, then Port Chalmers, in time to meet the troopship. When she returned two weeks later, she was unperturbed by the fact John had not been on board the SS *Tongariro*. She departed for Auckland with her children, but not before asking Tamar and Andrew if she could bring them to Kenmore again when the next troopship came home.

Out of kindness and worry for her state of mind they agreed, not at all sure they were doing the right thing. They had seen the telegraph from the New Zealand Government, and Major John Anscombe's personal letter, and were both convinced John had indeed been killed, although they were having a great deal of trouble coming to terms with his loss themselves. John had been very special, and what they would do about Riria, they had no idea.

CHAPTER TWENTY-NINE

May 1901

After more than eighteen months of war, Joseph decided he'd had enough and requested permission to return home with the Fourth and Fifth Contingents in June. To his slightly guilty relief, his request was granted. Sergeant Bob Thornton had remained with the Fourth, Jimmy Malone had been sent home just after Christmas with his left arm amputated at the shoulder, and Joseph, assigned to work with a British mounted unit, had seen nobody he knew for months.

The war had meandered depressingly on, neither side willing to capitulate and the British stubbornly pouring more men and arms into the conflict. The Fourth and Fifth had been split between different British units — the Fifth serving most of its time with the Kimberley Flying Column — and the enforced separation quickly eroded the New Zealanders' morale. As always, decent horses were at a premium. Over two hundred animals had died or been removed from service in April alone, and there were never enough replacements. While on the move the men slept in the open, suffering from extreme heat, or numbing cold and heavy rain, depending on the season. Food was often scarce, sickness was still rife, and the New Zealand contingent had been depleted by the voluntary transfer of 170 men to permanent positions within the South African Police or Railways Departments, operating under British military command.

At home, public enthusiasm for the war was beginning to waver; there seemed to be no end in sight and no one appeared to be winning. Letters questioning the wisdom of New Zealand's continued involvement began to appear in the newspapers, and cartoonists had a field day, although the official line still maintained New Zealand's full support for the Empire. Despite waning public ardour, when the Government raised a new contingent in February 1901, almost six hundred men volunteered. The Seventh Contingent was farewelled on 6 April by a crowd noticeably less enthusiastic than its predecessors, the troops packed uncomfortably on board the *Gulf of Taranto*, a small chartered ship. Aware of the public change of heart, and mindful of the next election, Seddon stated no further contingents would be raised unless expressly requested by the British authorities.

Joseph had been deeply affected by John Adams' death. Raised within a warrior culture, he had no problem accepting people were killed in war, but he could not reconcile the doctor's fate with the fact he had died rescuing men wounded as the result of a British commander's incompetence. The more time Joseph spent in South Africa, the more he came to believe the war was injust. There were lurid rumours of what had happened to the bodies of the men killed at the base of that miserable *kopje* in March. The story of the missing skull had assumed legendary proportions, some insisting body parts had been dragged off by wild animals, while others swore black Africans had stolen the bones for sinister and barbaric witchcraft rituals. Although Joseph could see the rumours for what they were — speculation and ghost stories — he was nevertheless upset. A man's head was *tapu*, or sacred, and it was essential it be interred with the rest of his remains. His dreams were beset with visions of John Adams' headless spirit wandering the earth — incomplete, lost and in endless purgatory.

Late in April Joseph witnessed the execution of three Boer soldiers, discovered hiding in a barn. They had been wearing British uniforms and, as a result, were sentenced to death, a policy introduced after British forces suffered heavy losses when ambushed by Boers wearing captured khaki. The trio had been lined up in front of a wall, their hands tied in front of them and with the indignity of their appropriated trousers removed. All three had stared unflinchingly at their captors until, silent and impassive, they had been blindfolded, then shot. They died like men, and when Joseph glanced at the faces of his cohorts, he saw many shared his shame. Although not involved in the execution, he had felt sickeningly *whakama* at having been there.

The following week, prior to his return to New Zealand, he was assigned temporary guard duty at a Boer concentration camp in Pretoria. By mid-1901 more than ninety thousand Boer civilians and their African servants and farmworkers had been incarcerated. Camp Irene, where Joseph was detailed, was one of the largest and most notorious. It was overcrowded and unsanitary, with death from disease and starvation common. Henry Campbell-Bannerman, leader of the British Liberal Party, had been campaigning to have the harsh treatment of Boer civilians moderated. There were moves afoot to improve conditions in the camps and cease future imprisonment of Boer women and children, but when Joseph entered Camp Irene he was appalled at the conditions in which the prisoners were living. The compound was criss-crossed with stinking, open drains holding raw sewage, the accommodation and utility buildings filthy, dark and poorly ventilated. Everywhere he looked he saw skinny, dull-eyed, listless children in dirty rags, and equally emaciated women, their faces lined with anger and a hopeless despair.

He was assigned for the next two weeks as one of two guards in the hospital ward, and shook his head in disbelief the first time he entered the extensive, dormitory-like building. It was packed with rows of stretchers no more than six inches apart, the whole ward reeking of illness. Fat black flies crawled over everything, the patients too weak to wave them away.

Initially he had scoffed at the idea that this roomful of sick and dispirited women and children, most of whom looked as if they could barely sit up let alone attempt an escape, needed to be guarded. But a visiting British medical officer had been stabbed by a patient who had concealed a knife beneath her skirt, and the entire ward was now judged too dangerous to be left unsupervised. Sister Abercrombie, one of the four British nurses at Camp Irene, rolled her eyes when she imparted this information to Joseph, as if she too thought the situation absurd, but added under her breath that in her view the British officer overseeing the camp shouldn't be in charge of a chicken farm.

She bustled ahead of him, her floor-length grey uniform and slightly grubby white apron swishing as she walked. At the end of the long ward she lifted aside a blanket tacked to a door frame and stepped into an annexed area.

'This is where you will be accommodated,' she said, opening a door to a small room. 'Rather basic, but I can get you some soap and water if you want to scrub it down. We keep the rest of the ward as clean as we can but, without adequate supplies, we're fighting a losing battle.'

Inside the narrow room was a low cot with two blankets folded at the end, a single wooden chair and a small shelf in one corner.

'It's nurses' accommodation, but we keep one or two rooms spare. It's mixed because we haven't the space for propriety. As you're assigned to guarding the ward, you're accommodated here, like the other fellow you'll be working with, but the other guards have their own building. You'll be eating with them, and using their privies,' she added. 'Oh, and there are a couple of Boer women in this annex. They work as nurse aids in the ward so they're permitted to sleep here, as they're often on call.'

As she said this, another door opened and a young woman emerged. She stood around five foot six inches tall and was unhealthily thin. Her dirty blonde hair was pulled harshly back under the distinctive pleated bonnet most Boer women wore, and she was dressed in a drab, patched dress. As she glanced up, Joseph was startled to see she was attractive despite her thinness, with huge, almost luminous pale blue eyes, a small upturned nose and a mouth that would have been sensuous had it not been set in a frown. She shot him a hostile look as she brushed roughly past and disappeared into the ward.

'*That* is Lina Van der Hoeven, one of the nurse aids. You'll get a lot of that, I'm afraid,' commented Sister Abercrombie matter-of-factly. 'Most of them are very bitter. And, to be honest, I can't say I blame them — rounded up and herded into camps, their homes destroyed, and some of them have lost husbands and sons — but who am I to comment on the wisdom of the powers that be?'

'So you don't consider the British should be in South Africa?' Joseph asked, a little surprised at this woman's rather cynical commentary.

'I'm a nurse, Private Deane, not a politician,' she answered, a little grimly. 'I go where I'm needed — I don't have any say in *why* I'm needed.'

Joseph considered her reply, then changed tack. 'If these women are all as bitter as you say, then how do you get anyone to cooperate?'

'They don't, sometimes, but women have a knack of making the best of things. They know we nurses are here to help, and they do as much as they can to help themselves. Lina, for example, lost her husband last year and her baby daughter five months ago. She has two other children under six, poor little mites, but she helps in the ward as much as she can. She works her fingers to the bone, because it helps to take her mind off everything else. She may be bitter, but I've never had cause to complain about her.'

'Why don't the British let these women and children go?'

'Don't be naive,' the sister replied, smiling. 'You know the answer to that as well as I do. If we did, they'd go straight back to their land, rebuild everything, plant new crops, and start supplying and supporting their menfolk as soon as they could. Wouldn't you?'

'I expect so,' said Joseph.

'Well, there you are, then. So they need to be kept out of the way. Except that thousands have died in these camps, which I imagine has only made their men more intent on fighting to the death.' She sighed and looked at the watch pinned to the front of her uniform. 'You'll have to excuse me, I've work to do. We had more deaths during the night, two children, and I need to certify them before the women prepare the bodies for burial. Welcome to Camp Irene.'

Joseph was assigned to work with another soldier named Gabriel Lightfoot, an Aboriginal tracker with an Australian mounted unit, who was also waiting to go home.

They were sitting outside the hospital ward enjoying a cigarette before starting their first shift together, Joseph on a wooden box and Gabriel Lightfoot cross-legged on the ground.

After examining Gabriel's heavy brow, wide flat nose, dark skin and dirty bare feet, Joseph said, 'I thought Blackfellows weren't allowed to serve in the Australian military?'

The Aborigine looked back at Joseph, then scratched his backside contemplatively and grinned widely. His teeth were a startling white in his dark face. 'And I thought Maoris weren't supposed to be in the New Zealand military, mate,' he said in a thick Australian accent.

Joseph laughed out loud. 'I'm only part Maori.'

'And I'm only part Aborigine. Yolgnu, from Arnhemland. Me mother's a Blackfeller and me father, well, Christ knows who he was, except he was white.'

Joseph grinned again and stuck out his hand. 'Other way round for me. My mother's white and my father's Maori. Ngati Kahungunu from the East Coast of the North Island.'

Gabriel spat on his palm and energetically returned the handshake with another grin. They sat in silence for a minute. Then, as he painstakingly rolled tobacco into a coarse paper and licked the edge to stick it down, Joseph asked casually, 'What do you think of this place?'

'It's a fucking disgrace, mate. All them high fences and frightened kids and the stink of them dunnies. Reminds me of home.'

Joseph lit his cigarette, inhaled then let the smoke drift back out through his nose. 'That bad, is it? At home, I mean,' he asked with genuine interest.

'In some places, yeah,' Gabriel replied.

Thinking back on the experiences of his own people, Joseph asked, 'Does it bother you?'

Gabriel had his head down rolling his own smoke. He lit it and said, 'Nah, not really. *My* people are part of the land. We been there forever, and that won't change. Ya can't kill the land.'

'So why volunteer?' asked Joseph, curious. 'You don't owe the British anything. Or didn't you volunteer?'

'Oh yeah, I volunteered all right. Don't know why, really. Something to do, I suppose. There's no other way a feller like me's likely to see the world. What about you?'

'We all volunteered. In some ways I'm glad I did, but I'm sorry as well. It's not what I thought it was going to be.'

'And what was that?' Gabriel enquired cynically.

'More like the way my people used to go to war, armies lining up against each other, rules of battle, honour. All I've been doing here is chasing bloody Boers all over the countryside, and when I haven't been doing that, I've been frightening defenceless women and children and slaughtering cattle and chickens.'

Gabriel snorted in amusement, licked his thumb and index finger and pinched out his half-smoked cigarette, carefully putting it in his shirt pocket. Tobacco was scarce. 'And I've spent the last two bloody years telling people what direction they should be pointing in.' He laughed. 'Most of them British couldn't find their own arse with both hands.' He stood up and stretched mightily until his spine cracked. 'Looking forward to going home. Haven't seen me mother for a couple of years.'

'Do you have a wife?'

'Not likely, I'm only eighteen — plenty of time for that later.'

Joseph was startled; he'd assumed Gabriel was in his twenties. 'You must have been young when you signed up then,' he said, slightly awed.

'Sixteen, mate.'

'I was nineteen.'

'And I was bloody bored. Come on, time to start work.'

Joseph and Gabriel did six hour shifts, then had six hours off, during which they were spelled by two other guards who, like them, sat at the doors at each end of the ward, trying not to hear the piteous groaning of sick, frightened children. As many of the patients had enteric fever, there were frequent embarrassing noises accompanied by equally embarrassing smells. It was tedious and stultifying work, and no one except the camp commander expected any trouble.

By the end of the second day, Joseph was beginning to wish he'd volunteered to spend the last few weeks of his active service out on the veldt. Gabriel didn't seem bothered, shunning his wooden chair and sitting motionless for hours in a trance-like state on the floor, staring at nothing. Joseph envied his ability to disconnect mentally. Sister Abercrombie lent Joseph dog-eared copies of Thomas Hardy's *Tess of the d'Urbervilles* and Emily Brontë's *Wuthering Heights*, which he regarded as 'women's books', but read from cover to cover anyway, and a handful of penny dreadfuls sent from England. He'd consumed the lot by the end of his fourth shift and was bored again in no time.

He then turned his attention to entertaining the children. They were wary at first, eyeing his khaki uniform and the rifle propped casually against his chair, but began to thaw when he started his bird whistles, carefully enunciating the Maori name of each bird as he mimicked their sound. Even Gabriel took notice, nodding in appreciation. Joseph whistled until his lips and cheeks ached, furiously trying to think of some other way to entertain them before he lost the ability to smile. Cat's cradle was next, and had the advantage of taking ages to show each child how to successfully manipulate the length of twine.

Joseph also tried to engage Lina Van der Hoeven in conversation but she refused to be drawn, although he noticed her smiling when he'd been whistling earlier. She's a moody one, all right, Joseph reflected after his third attempt had been rejected.

Mealtimes were the highlight of Joseph's day. The food for camp staff was certainly nothing to write home about, but it was better than the field rations he'd been subsisting on for the past year. The meat was tough, but at least it had been alive relatively recently, and the vegetables were reasonably fresh, if overcooked. In the field, fresh fruit and vegetables had been a rare luxury.

After dinner one night towards the end of his first week at Camp Irene, Joseph stuffed his pockets with hard buns and fruit, as had become his habit, and went back to his room, planning to retire early for a decent sleep before he was woken in the small hours for his next shift. Lying on his rickety cot, boots and jacket off, he had the door open to let out the ever-present musty smell. As he munched his way through a bun and then a pear, he heard footsteps, raising his eyes when they stopped outside his door.

Lina Van der Hoeven was standing in the doorway, watching him. There was a hungry, furtive look in her huge eyes as they followed the pear core when he placed it on the floor.

'Hello,' Joseph said, sitting up and wondering what she wanted.

'Good evening,' she replied. She looked nervous. 'May I please enter?' she added, her English heavily accented.

'Of course,' Joseph responded, shifting up the cot so she wouldn't have to sit too close to him. He was somewhat startled when she stepped in and deliberately closed the door.

She sat on the foot of the cot and looked at him. There was an embarrassing silence that Joseph interrupted by getting up and lighting a candle. As he returned, he was surprised to see she had removed her bonnet. Her straight blonde hair, freshly washed and shining, was loose about her shoulders, framing her face becomingly. The candlelight accentuated the startling allure of her wide eyes and Joseph thought he glimpsed, deep within them, an unnerving combination of despair, hate and expectation.

He was even more shocked when she undid the buttons of her plain blouse, slipped it off, then lifted her short chemise over her head. Naked from the waist up, she leaned back on the cot, provocatively displaying her breasts as she stared unsmilingly but directly into his eyes.

Joseph was torn between sudden embarrassment and excitement, although his rapidly growing erection suggested the latter was overtaking the former. But there was an air of desperation about this woman, and a distinct sense of unwillingness that made him uneasy; he suspected whatever was being offered would have a price and involve little dignity.

He picked up Lina's clothes and handed them back. 'Get dressed,' he said impassively, and sat on the floor with his back to the wall, facing her.

'British *bastard*!' she spat as she roughly pulled her chemise and blouse on. 'You think you are too good to bed a Boer woman?'

'No,' said Joseph. 'I think you're too good to bed me. And I'm a New Zealand Maori, not British. Why are you doing this?'

'It does not matter. I made a mistake,' she said bitterly as she rose, snatched up her bonnet and stepped towards the door.

'Yes it does,' Joseph replied, jumping to his feet and intercepting her. 'You came here for something, but it wasn't me. What was it?'

Lina looked at him with such vitriol he stepped back. 'Food!' she hissed. 'Food for my starving children. I have seen you stuffing your face like a king for the past four nights while my children's stomachs growl. They are dying and you are wasting good food!' She pointed angrily at the abandoned pear core on the floor.

Joseph was mortified. 'Why didn't you ask for something?'

'Because I am a Boer woman,' replied Lina haughtily, 'and I do not ask the British for *anything*! I will trade, but I will not beg.'

'And you were willing to trade your body for stale buns?'

'Your leavings are better than the rubbish fed to us.'

Joseph shook his head and said, 'I had no idea.'

'Go and look in the prisoners' dining halls if you want to see what our children are expected to survive on! It is not even enough to make their bowels move once a week!'

Feeling suddenly tired and profoundly sick of the whole stinking mess this war had become, Joseph said wearily, 'I am sorry. For insulting you regarding your offer, and for being unaware of your children's need for food. I will bring you as much food as I can — I'll leave it under the blanket on my cot and you can help yourself.'

Lina stared silently at Joseph for some time, as if debating whether to trust him or not, then finally said softly, 'Thank you, Private Deane. Your kindness will be appreciated.'

Joseph nodded and held the door open. As she brushed past him he said quietly, 'I was tempted, Mrs Van der Hoeven. Very tempted.'

Lina glanced over her shoulder and allowed him a small smile as he closed the door after her.

Over the following five days, Joseph scrounged food for Lina and her children and left it in his room. It was always gone by the time he came off shift. With interested amusement, Gabriel watched him sneaking fruit into his pockets and, once, stuffing almost a whole loaf of bread down his trousers, but he said nothing.

On 8 June Joseph was scheduled to board a train at Pretoria bound for Cape Town, to connect with a troopship on 12 June. Two nights before he left Camp Irene, Lina came to his room and this time gave herself freely to him.

Joseph had enjoyed intimate associations with a handful of girls since the fiasco with the charming Emerald almost a decade ago, but had deliberately avoided Durban's whores during his furloughs. Many of them had been appealing but, with Cass Heke's admonitions still clear in his mind, he had left them to the attentions of those with less personal discipline. Observing a good number of them only days later complaining of excruciating urinary tract infections, Joseph had congratulated himself on the wisdom of his decision.

Lina Van der Hoeven, however, was not a girl. At thirty-one she was ten years older than Joseph, and it showed in her lovemaking; with her, Joseph was transported to heights of physical pleasure he had so far only glimpsed. She was passionate and exquisitely responsive, and demonstrated no inhibitions whatsoever when it came to demanding what she wanted. Despite his delight in her, however, Joseph felt a sadness; in the generosity of her passion he sensed a lingering grief for her lost husband.

Afterwards, they lay together in companionable silence, Lina's head on his shoulder, until she murmured, 'Do you think I am a whore?'

Joseph looked at her in shock. 'What did you say?'

'A whore. I barely know you and we have slept together.'

He rolled over and studied her face in the moonlight shafting through the small, high window. 'No, I don't. A whore would ask for money, not food for her starving children.'

Lina shook her head and smiled sadly. 'You have a lot to learn, Joseph Deane.'

He turned onto his back and pulled her against him. 'Lina?' he asked tentatively. 'What do you want most in the world?'

She didn't hesitate. 'To have my husband and my baby alive.'

'Did you love your husband?'

'Yes, Piet was a fine man, and he died fighting for the things he believed in. I loved him very much.'

Joseph thought for a moment. 'After that, then, what would you most want?'

Again no hesitation. 'To get my children and myself out of this stinking prison so I can carry on the fight. It is not over yet and there is work to be done. I have learned a lot here about nursing, and there is much I could do to help our men.'

'What would you do with the children?'

'I have family who have not been imprisoned. They would take them.'

'What if I could help you escape?'

'From this camp?' she asked, her eyebrows raised sceptically. 'How? You would be shot for treason if you were discovered!'

'*If*, yes, but I think I know a way to avoid that. I can find out when the late-evening shifts for the perimeter guards start and end, and I know for a fact that they're pretty casual about getting to their posts on time. If I could open the wires, you could wriggle through with the children and be miles away by the time anyone noticed you'd gone.'

Lina reached up and gently stroked Joseph's cheek. 'Why would you do that for us?' she asked.

'Because it's wrong to lock up children. Despite what you think, Lina, I *have* learned a lot in South Africa, and I don't like much of what I've seen. I'm going home in a few days and I can't just leave it like this.'

'You could die,' she reminded him.

'So could you.'

'Yes, but my children and I have nothing to lose. You do.'

'Could you live with yourself if the children were hurt or killed?'

'It would be easier than watching them die here.'

Joseph, his heart racing now the idea had been voiced, said, 'It would have to be tomorrow night.'

'We will be ready.'

Chapter Thirty

Joseph sat through his last day in the hospital ward, anxiously awaiting the end of his shift and trying not to look at Lina as she went about her duties in case anyone suspected a connection between them.

He had confirmed the time the guards would be changing over on the stretch of perimeter fence behind the hospital ward, and knew who they would be — two British troopers who were habitually late. But Lina would still only have ten minutes to get herself and her children through the fence and away into the darkness. In that time Joseph would also have to loosen and bend the fence wires, then replace them so there was no evidence of an escape.

Off duty now, he had packed his kit ready to leave the following day, and was lying on his cot waiting for darkness, his stomach churning and his mouth dry. If they were caught, the best he could hope for would be ten years in a military prison; Lina would probably be shot. He checked his pocket watch; the guards would change at ten o'clock and it was eight thirty now.

At nine forty-five he heard a discreet tap, the signal that Lina and the children were ready. He waited until the tap came again then opened his door. Lina was standing in the corridor, a dark shawl over her hair and carrying a small backpack. The children were dressed in every item of clothing they owned; the nights were growing cold and Lina had no idea how long they would have to sleep in the open. Their eyes were huge and they clung to their mother's skirts, but Lina appeared calm.

'Ready?' she whispered.

Joseph nodded. They moved quietly down the hall to the outside door. Joseph stopped, opened it and cautiously stuck his head out, looking in both directions. The hospital ward was situated at the rear of the camp — a well-meaning but futile effort at segregating infectious patients — with the perimeter fence thirty feet beyond. Their plan was to breach the wire directly behind the hospital building, which was sheltered from the view of the rest of the camp.

Joseph whispered to Lina to wait, then pushed the door to again, leaving an inch through which he peered for the next few minutes. As he glanced at his watch to check the time, he was alerted by the sound of footsteps crunching in the gravel around the side of the building. He stood holding his breath as two soldiers passed, laughing at something Joseph did not catch. As their footsteps receded, he opened the door, checked in both directions and stepped carefully down the wooden steps. Lina and the children followed and they crept along the side of the building until they turned the corner of the wall running parallel with the perimeter fence. Halfway down, they stopped.

Joseph walked rapidly towards the wire, hoping like hell their scrunching footsteps would not be heard. The further away from the shadowed safety of the back of the building they moved, the more wildly his heart pounded. They had about seven minutes.

He grasped two of the lower wires strung four inches apart all the way up the fence, put his foot on the bottom one and violently wrenched the top one up, making a gap of about eighteen inches. He suddenly panicked, realising that while the children would fit easily, Lina in her long full skirts would not be able to wriggle past the barbs. In desperation, Joseph yanked harder, feeling sweat pop out on his face and the wire bite into his hands. The gap increased by a further inch, but it would still not be enough. Behind him he could hear Lina ripping at her clothes.

'No!' he hissed. 'There isn't time!'

Not stopping to consider the wisdom of what he was about to do, he squatted, one foot still on the lower wire, put his head and shoulders through the hole, and straightened up as far as he could, forcing the gap open an extra half foot. Straining, he heard his uniform jacket rip as the barbs bit into the fabric. 'Go!' he urged over his shoulder.

Lina pushed both children through one after the other, their small bodies easily clearing the wire, followed by the pack, then crouched down, her skirts bunched up around her white thighs. She lowered her head, flattened her back and ducked through. On the other side she hefted the pack over her shoulder then turned back to Joseph, reaching for the top wire so he could release himself.

He was stuck fast, the barbs holding his jacket as viciously as the teeth of a starving dog. 'Take the jacket off!' she said. He couldn't; his webbing was buckled tightly over it, trussing him as securely as a lunatic's straitjacket. 'Go!' he said again. 'Go, Lina! Now!'

She looked at him for seconds that felt to Joseph like hours, then reached out and touched his lips with her fingers. 'Goodbye, Joseph Deane,' she whispered. Then she stood, grasped each child by the hand and ran into the darkness.

Joseph knew the ten minutes were almost up. He felt like a miserable little monkey he had seen on leave, squatting in a cage, a hunched and dejected captive. He closed his eyes and waited for the guards to spot him as he heard footsteps approach.

'You in the shit, mate?' asked an amused Australian voice. Joseph couldn't turn but knew it was Gabriel Lightfoot. He listened as the Aborigine removed his ragged shirt, then felt him slip into the gap in the fence next to him.

'When I push up, move forward and unhook yaself, then back out,' Gabriel directed.

Joseph did just that, releasing himself and landing on his arse inside the fence. Gabriel was still within the wires, the barbs digging into his naked back. As he heaved backwards to extract himself, Joseph winced at the sound of wire scraping on flesh.

'Fuck,' said Gabriel mildly as he snatched his shirt off the ground. 'Let's go, mate.'

They scrambled for the hospital building just as a shadowy figure turned the corner at the far end of the wall. Joseph and Gabriel didn't dare breathe. The guard stopped for a moment, had a cursory look around, farted in what he believed was complete anonymity, then walked off again, his heavy footsteps receding.

'Wondered what you were up to,' whispered Gabriel as they slunk off in the opposite direction. 'It were that nurse aid, eh?'

Joseph nodded.

'Ya silly prick,' Gabriel admonished. 'Hope it were worth it.'

'It was,' replied Joseph.

In his room he examined Gabriel's back by candlelight, sickened by the deep scratches torn by the barbed wire. 'Does it hurt?' he asked.

'She'll be right,' came the stoic reply.

Joseph did what he could to wipe the blood away.

'Thanks,' he said eventually. There was nothing else he could say.

'No worries, mate.'

Lina's absence was noticed at eight the next morning when Sister Abercrombie knocked on her door and received no answer. Going in, she saw the room was empty. She knocked on Joseph's door next, ignoring the fact he was in his underpants when she opened it without being invited.

'I suppose you don't know where Lina Van der Hoeven is?' she asked.

'No,' replied Joseph, reaching for his trousers. 'Why, is she missing?'

'It seems so.' Sister Abercrombie glanced at Joseph's uniform lying on the floor. 'Why is the back of your jacket ripped?'

'Caught it on a nail yesterday.'

Sister Abercrombie stared at Joseph for a moment longer, then left, closing the door behind her.

Joseph cursed himself for not having the sense to shove his torn jacket under the cot. He got dressed slowly, wondering when she'd be back and who she would have with her — guards or the camp commander.

But when Sister Abercrombie returned fifteen minutes later, she was alone. She tossed a khaki jacket onto the cot, picked up the torn one and said, 'You should be careful, Private Deane. You'll get into trouble one of these days.'

Joseph lifted the uniform and examined it curiously. 'It's a New Zealand one,' he said. 'Where did you get it?'

The sister tapped the side of her nose. 'Don't ask, son, just put it on. And I suggest you keep out of the way until you're ready to leave. I'll have to report Lina Van der Hoeven and her children are missing. It would be more than my job's worth not to.'

It was sensible advice. There was a furore when the commander was informed. Soldiers were ordered to search the camp, Joseph happily estimating Lina would be miles away by now. Careful not to ask about the missing prisoners, he filled in the morning entertaining the children in the hospital ward and chatting with Gabriel, who would be going home himself in a few days. Neither of them mentioned the escape.

At midday, a provisions wagon arrived at the camp and Joseph caught a lift when it returned to Pretoria. He made his way to the railway station and sat in a bar for several hours until it was time for his train to leave.

The long trip from Pretoria to Cape Town was pleasant enough, although Joseph discovered he had to pay for it himself unless he wanted to ride in the guard van. He opted for the comparative luxury of a carriage but woke during the night slumped over in his seat with a painful crick in his neck. Reflecting that he might have been better off sleeping on mail bags after all, he made a point of disembarking at every opportunity to stretch his legs.

He had twenty-four hours in Cape Town before his ship sailed. The Fourth and Fifth Contingents had also arrived after a rest period at Worcester in Cape Colony, but before joining them Joseph shopped for souvenirs and went sightseeing, riding in a little cart pulled by a barefoot African wearing a spectacular headdress incorporating a huge pair of bullock horns. After lunch he set out to find the New Zealanders, although he didn't have to look far; most of them had congregated in the hotels.

To his delight he met up with Sergeant Bob Thornton and they embarked on a tour of the town's bars. The next morning, somewhat worse for wear, the New Zealand contingents made their way to the docks where they spent hours waiting to embark.

The troopship SS *Tagus* sailed later the same day, expecting to arrive in New Zealand in under a month. The seas deteriorated as the ship turned east across the bottom of South Africa and sailed into the southern reaches of the Indian Ocean, but she was able to maintain an average of three hundred and twenty miles a day. This was little consolation to her passengers, who were anxious to be home.

Joseph had plenty of time to reflect on his experiences in South Africa. He came to the ambiguous conclusion, shared by many of his shipmates, that had he known in advance what it was going to be like he wouldn't have gone, but given the chance he would probably do it again. He thought about poor John Adams, and Jimmy Malone who would be unable to go back to shearing with only one arm, and wondered if it had been worth it.

The war looked like grinding on for some time yet. The British military commanders were both amazed and profoundly frustrated by the Boers' tenacity, but refused to go home. The war had been all but won as far as they were concerned, and it certainly looked that way on paper, as all of the major towns in the Transvaal and Orange Free State were under Imperial control, but still the Afrikaners would not surrender. Joseph remembered Lina and smiled.

Towards the end of June the ship called into port at Albany in southern Australia to take on more coal. General leave was granted, giving the troops a welcome respite on shore, although their commanders regretted the liberty by the end of the day and were forced to send military police to round everyone up. Along with almost everyone else, Joseph got into a fight with a crowd of Australian troops and received his first war wound — a broken nose. All shore leave was cancelled and the New Zealanders were confined on board the *Tagus* until she sailed two days later.

That, plus the deteriorating food and the close proximity of home, caused unrest amongst the troops and mutiny was seriously discussed, although nothing came of it. Several days later the ship anchored off Melbourne Heads to take on fresh fruit and vegetables, but only enough for the officers, which rekindled the grumbling and general resentment amongst the enlisted men. So close to home, however, no one considered the insult worth avenging, and they went back to rehashing and embroidering their daring exploits in South Africa, a time-honoured soldiers' tradition.

By the time the *Tagus* reached Port Chalmers, her passengers were more than ready to disembark. As she moved slowly towards the docks, the troops heard the faint sounds of a band striking up. They looked at each other and grinned broadly; this was more like the treatment they were expecting as returning heroes. The closer to the docks they came, the more they could see of the gathered crowd. Although not as big as the one which farewelled them, it was nevertheless a sight for sore, tired and homesick eyes. Every man crowded to the shore side, scrambling for a place near the rails.

Joseph squinted but couldn't see anyone he knew, which didn't surprise him as there were thousands of people on the dock. He assumed someone would be here to meet him, as he had written advising his father he expected to be on the next troopship. He stepped back and let someone else take his place, then went below to collect his kit. By the time he came back up, the ship had docked and the gangway had been lowered.

The first to disembark were the wounded, and the crowd hushed as a line of stretcher bearers appeared, two men to a litter, and began to file slowly down the gangway. After a decent interval during which the wounded were despatched to waiting ambulances, the crowd erupted into cheers as the first man stepped off the ship.

As his turn came, Joseph found himself being propelled down the gangway towards the crowd. He had still not glimpsed a familiar face, and was wondering how he could possibly locate anyone in the jostling mass of people, when someone yelled his name. He turned to the left and caught sight of his mother waving at him, her lovely, welcoming face dissected by a huge smile. '*Joseph!*' Tamar shrieked in a most unladylike fashion. 'Over here!'

He raised his hand in answer, the smile on his face matching her own. People stepped aside as he moved towards her, smiling indulgently at their enthusiastic reunion. 'You've *grown!*' exclaimed Tamar. 'You're not a boy any more!'

'*Mam,*' he grumbled as he straightened her hat, knocked askew during their embrace. 'Is *Papa* here?'

'No, he's been away, but he should be home by the time we get back.'

'And Andrew?'

'Same thing, I'm afraid. Riria's here though. She's been rather strange since John died.'

At that moment he saw Riria elbowing her way towards them. 'Hello, Joseph,' she said, kissing him fondly on his cheek. 'I am looking for John. Was he with you on the ship?'

Joseph didn't know what to say and looked at Tamar helplessly.

'Riria has spoken to a *tohunga* who has advised her John is still alive.' Behind Riria's back Tamar's face clearly expressed her discomfort and distress. 'She's hoping to meet him when he comes home.'

Oh Christ, thought Joseph. 'No, not as far as I'm aware, Auntie Riria. And I'm sure I would have known.'

'Oh, well,' replied Riria, not at all put out. 'There will be more troopships. If you will just give me fifteen minutes to talk to the captain, I will ask to see the manifest and if he is not listed, we can go.'

As she marched purposefully off in the direction of the gangway, Tamar said, 'I'm at my wits' end. What will she do when the last ship comes home and he's not on it?'

'Have you tried telling her straight out? That John has gone.'

'Well, of course I have, but she's adamant he hasn't. She puts great store in that damned medicine man, or whatever he is.'

'They're not all charlatans, Mam.'

'I know, but I wish this one had picked someone else to imbue with eternal hope. She will be devastated when she finally realises.' Tamar turned to her son. 'He *is* dead, isn't he?'

'Yes, he is,' Joseph replied, sadly noting the flicker of hope in his mother's eyes. 'There was a burial for him. Full military honours. And I've talked to someone who was there.'

Tamar sighed. Oh John, she thought, why the bloody hell did you have to go off and leave us all?

June 1902

Tamar and Andrew were in Napier when the news broke on 2 June. The war in South Africa was over and the Treaty of Vereeniging, signed on 31 May, had granted the Boers favourable terms.

'Thank Christ they've come to their senses,' said Andrew as they hurried to join the crowd outside the offices of the *Daily Telegraph*. On the front steps a paper boy in short pants warbled '*War over! Boers defeated!*'

They waited impatiently until the morning edition came off the presses, the ink still tacky on the pages. The treaty was front-page news. Andrew had a quick look at the lead story then rolled his paper up and stuck it under his arm to read properly later.

'This means they will all be home soon,' said Tamar, thinking of Riria.

'Yes, it does,' Andrew replied, knowing what was going through her mind. After almost fifteen years of marriage, he knew his lovely wife very well. 'All I can say is thank God it's over,' he added.

When the British Government had approached Seddon in 1901 about providing yet another contingent, the Premier had conceded to raise a further unit of one thousand men. The Eighth left New Zealand the following February, trailed closely by the Ninth and Tenth Contingents in March and April. Andrew thought it had all gone too far and had been firmly against the sending of the last three contingents, but now it was over the troops would come home.

New Zealand celebrated as if the war had been waged and won on her own shores. Most major centres declared a holiday as people delirious with patriotism poured into the streets waving flags, letting off fireworks and ringing every bell they could lay their hands on. There were endless parades and processions, culminating in longwinded speeches by dignitaries expressing the hope that a successful and fruitful reconciliation could be achieved with the brave Boers. Andrew thought this was appallingly hypocritical, given the rubbish slung at the Afrikaners in the newspapers over the past three years, but wisely kept his opinions to himself.

The press was saturated with stories about the huge contribution made by New Zealand troops to the Empire's victory and the extent to which they had so favourably impressed the British commanders. Better than the Canadians, wrote xenophobic editors, and certainly better than the Australians, who had behaved little better than rascals. Much was also made of the fact that, proportionately, New Zealand's contribution had been one of the most substantial of the Empire's colonies, and the tenor of most editorials implied New Zealanders had a right to be proud of their ability to produce such natural and fine soldiers; troops who were brave, resourceful, gallant and, to a man, excellent shots.

Within a month dozens of war memorials dedicated to the brave and noble young men who had fallen sprouted throughout New Zealand, some even before the last troopships arrived home. There were endless Troopers' Balls and functions, during which returned soldiers were fêted and celebrated, and plans were launched by Lord Ranfurly to build a home for war veterans in Onehunga as a national memorial.

Many of the celebrations had ended by the time the last three contingents returned to New Zealand in August, all having arrived in South Africa too late to play a significant part in the war. Four days after the treaty had been signed, Lieutenant Robert McKeich of the Ninth became the last of the Empire's soldiers to die when he was shot near Vereeniging by three Boers unaware the war had ended.

Riria met the Ninth when it came home, waiting in a crowd significantly smaller than those which had greeted the earlier contingents. The public response was even more apathetic when the Eighth arrived a week later. Riria, standing at the edge of the dock when the ship berthed, was as horrified as everyone else when the seriously ill were stretchered off. The SS *Britannic* had been struck by an epidemic of measles soon after leaving Durban, and twenty soldiers had died on the voyage. As litter after litter was carried off, the small crowd became utterly silent, quiet enough to hear the first man who could walk unaided stifle a sob as he shuffled down the gangway. As it became clear the returning troops, although unblooded, were physically and emotionally shattered, a curious mix of shame, disgust and sympathy flickered across faces in the crowd as they silently looked on.

Riria saw John Adams was not amongst them, and neither did he arrive home with the Tenth a week later.

EPILOGUE

Riria was finally forced to consider her beloved husband had indeed died in South Africa, although she refused to say the words. But her last remaining shred of hope dissolved when she received in the mail an image of John's grave, photographed and forwarded by John's British commander, Major Mellor, in the hope she might take comfort from it. It had the opposite effect and she collapsed.

Tamar was summoned by Simon, and she and Andrew packed up the children and went to Auckland immediately. John's friend Basil Stokes was contacted and asked to attend Riria, although she was beginning to recover physically by the time they arrived.

Simon confessed he was very worried about his mother. After the photograph had arrived she had taken to her bed, locking the bedroom door and refusing to eat for days. Simon was frightened she'd lost her mind and had climbed up the side of the house, broken a window and found Riria sitting silently on the floor, hugging a photograph of John in his army uniform to her chest. After he pleaded with her, she had conceded to come out of her room, but remained withdrawn.

'I think I know what might be distressing her,' Simon confided to Tamar. 'There is nothing for her to grieve over. Father didn't come home, and there was no *tangi*. There's nothing to … there's no grave.' He swallowed and looked away for a moment. 'There's no *body*, Auntie.' Tamar held his hand as he struggled for control.

'*Mama* needs something to help her bring things to a close. And so do we.'

'Would a memorial service help?'

Simon looked at her. 'I'm not sure, Auntie. Shall I ask *Mama*?'

'Do you think it would help *you*? And Rose and David?'

Tamar watched as he considered the idea. Poor Simon, she thought, only seventeen and already having to shoulder the responsibilities of a man. However, she was sure he was capable of it; he was very self-sufficient and mature for his age, handsome and strong like his mother, with his father's sense of humour and kind heart.

'It might,' he replied. '*Mama* is used to doing things the Maori way, but we have grown up with both cultures. Yes, I think it might help.'

Riria agreed to a memorial service, not for herself, but for the children and for John's many friends. The date was set for the end of the following week, more than a year since John's death. A church was booked, the minister consulted and Riria sent word to her family at Kainui.

On 5 September, as pink and white blossom began to appear on Auckland's fruit trees, John Adams' family and friends gathered at the Anglican church in Parnell to say goodbye.

The church was full twenty minutes before the scheduled starting time. The Murdochs sat in the front pew on one side of the church while a composed but sad-looking Riria sat with her children and her parents in the other. Behind them were squeezed several hundred people — John's friends, colleagues and many of his ex-patients, and what appeared to be half of Kainui village.

Just as the service was about to begin, the big church doors creaked opened. Tamar turned and was astounded to see a crowd of people standing outside. As they began to file solemnly in, she saw they were all Maori, dressed from head to toe in black and adorned with fresh greenery from native trees. Their mostly bare feet whispered on the wooden boards as they came, the smell of the forest accompanying them as they settled themselves on the floor before the altar, in the aisle and at the back of the church. Tamar's eyes filled with tears as she realised who they were — the local Maori John had insisted on treating free of charge.

The minister, convinced no one else could possibly fit into the church, began the service. Tamar, only half listening to his droning words, frowned up at the large cross on the wall above the altar; she still had several bones to pick with God and this would be another one. Why did John have to die when there were plenty of others the world would barely miss? People like the sort of person Peter Montgomery had been. She gave a small start; she hadn't thought of Peter in such a long time. Why would she, with five children whom she cherished, and a loving and attentive husband? Her lips curved in a gentle smile as it occurred to her that now, in the summer of her life, she had exactly what she'd always wanted.

She looked over at Riria. Her friend, clothed at last in the black of mourning, sat with her back straight and her head high. Her parents contemplated their daughter with loving concern but Tamar could see that under her veil Riria was dry-eyed. And neither were her children crying. They sat regally, with the grace and dignity Riria had instilled in them since they were tiny.

Tamar glanced at her own children. Keely was sniffling but her boys were still as statues, eyes big and blinking but clear. She could see they were struggling, and hoped she would not cry herself and set them off. At the end of the pew sat her precious first-born, Joseph, out of uniform now and staring resolutely ahead with only the white knuckles of his clenched fists suggesting the grief and anger he felt. She could hear several people weeping openly in the pews behind her, one of them poor Basil Stokes.

Finally the minister stopped talking and the congregation sang several hymns, the Maori voices soaring to the rafters and filling the church with clear and beautiful harmonies, then the service drew to a close.

As they stood to leave, an eerie, ululating cry rang out over the shuffling of hundreds of feet, a cry so poignantly heartfelt the hairs on Tamar's arms stood up. The Maori sitting on the floor rose as one and moved back towards the ancient woman voicing the lament. There was a moment of utter silence, then the group began a *haka*, slow at first then gaining energy and momentum. As the men moved backwards and forwards between the lines of women they hissed and slapped their chests and rolled their eyes. The women, their feet rhythmically striking the floor, swayed in unison as their voices rose and fell above the men's chant.

Tamar was transfixed. This was a tremendous tribute to John's memory — a war *haka* for a deeply respected man who had fallen bravely and honourably in battle. She looked over at Riria and saw she had discarded her hat and veil and was weeping uncontrollably and clutching her children. Tears coursing down her own face, Tamar felt her heart contract briefly, then release; none of their lives would be the same without John, but at least Riria could begin to live hers again.

As she and Andrew walked out of the church into the early spring sunshine, she saw her husband was weeping. She gave him a watery smile and he reached out a loving and supportive hand, as he always had, and he always would.

In a tree nearby, a fantail laughed joyously.

CHILDREN OF WAR TRILOGY

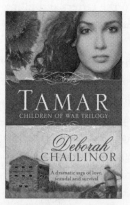

TAMAR

When Tamar Deane is orphaned at seventeen in a small Cornish village, she seizes the chance for a new life and emigrates to New Zealand. In March 1879, alone and frightened on the Plymouth quay, she is befriended by an extraordinary woman. Myrna McTaggart is travelling to Auckland with plans to establish the finest brothel in the southern hemisphere and her unconventional friendship proves invaluable when Tamar makes disastrous choices in the new colony. Tragedy and scandal befall her, but unexpected good fortune brings vast changes to Tamar's life. As the century draws to a close, uncertainty looms when a distant war lures her loved ones to South Africa. This dramatic story — the first in a sweeping three-volume family saga — has a vivacious and compelling heroine who will live with the reader long after the final page has been turned.

WHITE FEATHERS

In 1914, Tamar Murdoch's brothelkeeping days are behind her. Her life is one of ease and contentment at Kenmore, a prosperous estate in the Hawke's Bay, as storm clouds over Europe begin casting long shadows.

In this gripping second instalment of Deborah Challinor's sweeping family saga, Tamar's love for her children is sorely tested as one by one they are called, or driven, into the living hell of World War One.

During the Boer War, Joseph, her illegitimate eldest son, fought as a European, but this time he is determined to enlist in the Maori Battalion, despite his growing attraction for his childhood friend, Erin. As loyalties within the Murdoch clan are divided, and the war takes Tamar and Andrew's only daughter far from her sheltered upbringing, the people and experiences their children encounter will shape the destiny of the Murdoch clan for generations to come.

BLUE SMOKE

On 3 February 1931, Napier is devastated by a powerful earthquake — and Tamar Murdoch, beloved matriarch of Kenmore, is seriously injured. As she recovers, Tamar is preoccupied with the ongoing effects of the Great Depression. When her grandson threatens to leave for Spain to join the International Brigade, she feels a familiar dread — once again her family is threatened by war and heartbreak, as Hitler's armies march.

In this final volume of the Children of War trilogy, the story of the feisty Cornish seamstress who became a brothelkeeper and landowner is brought to a stirring and memorable conclusion.

On the Trail of
Mary, Queen of Scots

Roy Calley

AMBERLEY

First published 2017

Amberley Publishing
The Hill, Stroud
Gloucestershire, GL5 4EP

www.amberley-books.com

Copyright © Roy Calley, 2017

The right of Roy Calley to be identified as
the Author of this work has been asserted in
accordance with the Copyright, Designs and
Patents Act 1988.

ISBN 978 1 4456 5942 8 (hardback)
ISBN 978 1 4456 5943 5 (ebook)

British Library Cataloguing in Publication Data.
A catalogue record for this book is available
from the British Library.

Map illustration by Thomas Bohm, User
Design.

Typesetting and Origination by Amberley Publishing
Printed in the UK.

CONTENTS

Mary/Marie's Movements in Chronological Order   8

Introduction   9

1   Scotland, 1542–1548   16

    Linlithgow – Mary's birthplace   16

    St Michael's Parish Church – Mary's baptism   22

    Stirling Castle – Mary's infancy and her return as queen   25

    Inchmahome Priory – A brief sanctuary for the child queen   40

    Dumbarton Castle – Farewell to Scotland   43

2   To France, 1548–1560   51

    Roscoff – A first glimpse of her new home of France   51

    Carrieres, Saint-Germain – Marie meets King Henry
for the first time   57

    Chateau Royal de Blois – The influence of Catherine de Medici   65

    Chateau de Fontainebleau – A young queen's royal residence   68

    Blois – Mary of Guise's arrival   75

    Notre Dame – A royal wedding between Marie and Francois   80

    Hôtel des Tournelles – The death of King Henry   92

Reims Cathedral – The coronation of a new King of France 97

Amboise – The massacre of the Wars of Religion 99

Chambord – Marie hears the news of the death of her mother 103

Hôtel Groslot D'Orléans – The death of Francois and
Marie's grief 108

3 Queen of Scotland, 1561–1567 115

Leith – A return to Scotland 117

The Palace of Holyroodhouse – A queen's rule, the arrival of
John Knox and Lord Darnley, and the murder of David Riccio 124

Edinburgh Castle – A turbulent rule and the arrival of
the Earl of Bothwell 147

Jedburgh – The queen falls seriously ill 167

Hermitage Castle – Tending to Bothwell 172

Kirk O'Field – The murder of Darnley 177

Dunbar Castle – Bothwell abducts Mary and
he becomes her third husband 187

Carberry Hill – Mary surrenders to the Lords and
her imprisonment begins 194

4 Captivity, 1567–1587 200

Lochleven Castle – An island prison as the queen is
forced to abdicate 200

Dundrennan Abbey – A last look at Scotland as
she flees to England 208

Workington – A first glimpse of England as sanctuary 213

Carlisle Castle – The first hints of captivity 216

Bolton Castle – The beginning of imprisonment and
the introduction of 'The Casket Letters' 222

Tutbury Castle – Her most hated prison   230

Sheffield Castle and Sheffield Manor – A respite from the
rigours and discomfort of Tutbury   259

Wingfield Manor – Brief links to the imprisoned queen   263

Chatsworth House – Hawking and needlework   265

Buxton – Visits to the spa   267

Tixall Gatehouse – The Babington Plot   271

Chartley Manor – Her final stop before trial   272

Fotheringhay – Trial and execution   273

Peterborough Cathedral – First resting place   288

Westminster Abbey – Final resting place   294

Imagining Their Past in the Future   296

Acknowledgements   300

Bibliography   302

Mary/Marie's movements in chronological order

3 Inchmahome Priory
2 Stirling Castle
4 Dumbarton Castle
1 Linlithgow & St Michael's Parish Church
•24 Lochleven Castle
23 Carberry Hill
•22 Dunbar Castle
16 Leith • 17 Palace of Holyrood
18 Edinburgh Castle 21 Kirk o'Field
19 Jedburgh
20 Hermitage Castle •
25 Dundrennan Abbey •
•27 Carlisle Castle
26 Workington
•28 Bolton Castle
32 Chatsworth House • • 30 Sheffield Castle & Manor
33 Buxton • •31 Wingfield Manor
35 Chartley Manor •
34 Tixall • •29 Tutbury Castle
36 Fotheringhay • •37 Peterborough Cathedral
38 Westminster Abbey •

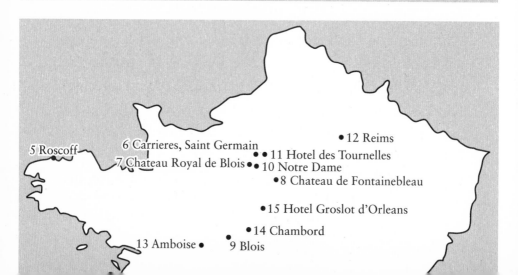

5 Roscoff
6 Carrieres, Saint Germain
•12 Reims
7 Chateau Royal de Blois • • • 11 Hotel des Tournelles
• 10 Notre Dame
•8 Chateau de Fontainebleau
•15 Hotel Groslot d'Orleans
•14 Chambord
13 Amboise • 9 Blois

INTRODUCTION

In My End Is My Beginning

These prophetic words, embroidered on her cloth of estate, and associated with her ever since, have effectively defined how Mary Stewart/Stuart has been remembered by those who know about her and those who have had a passing interest. On 8 February 1587, possibly one of the most controversial monarchs in history, and certainly one who divided opinion more than most, was executed. This was done on the orders of a fellow sovereign, her cousin and her 'sister' as Mary liked to describe Elizabeth I, after a trial that was as unjust as it was needless. Mary, Queen of Scots lived a life that was both extraordinary and tragic, and one that has been discussed, investigated and written about countless times in the centuries since her own time. During her life, she was the most divisive figure of her time as she sought to unite the two countries of England and Scotland with her belief that she was the true queen of the first, while ruling the second. Ironically, her death, after years of miserable captivity at the hands of the queen of England, set in motion the process that saw her son James eventually unite the kingdoms to form the union that is known today.

Mary was an emotional but intelligent woman whose decisions at crucial times were her undoing. There were her disastrous marriages, first to Lord Darnley and later to the Earl of Bothwell; she was clearly implicated in the death of the first. Later there was her later apparent involvement in the plot to assassinate Queen Elizabeth. Mary was loved and reviled in equal measure in her own time, something that has continued to the present day. Yet even her detractors should be able to see her legacy, a Scotland transformed from a warring nation at odds with itself to the country we see today, worthy of respect. More than four hundred years later, Mary's light still burns brightly. Books are still being written about her (like this one, of course), films and plays are still being produced and the buildings and castles that she graced in her lifetime are still being visited. Everyone who knows something of her life will have an opinion. She is cast as either the poor victim of unfortunate decisions and circumstances, who seemed incapable of showing cold judgement when it was needed, or she is perceived as a wanton harlot who used her stunning beauty and her feminine wiles to connive and cheat to get her way while she wore the crown. The author is firmly part of the former camp.

Mary has interested and fascinated me for many, many years, ever since the 1971 film starring Glenda Jackson and Vanessa Redgrave came to the cinema. I was entranced by the story and by beauty and sensuality that

Mary was supposed to have possessed – sadly, there are few contemporary paintings of her that prove this – and in the years that followed, I avidly collected as many books as I could on her, even spending a fortune on a few first editions. In my eyes, they were worth it. I spent time visiting and revisiting the castles in Scotland and northern France where she either visited or lived, and occasionally I had a vision of her presence. Once, while at Bolton Castle in England, I convinced myself that I'd had a conversation with her as I sat on the stone bench that looked towards the hills separating Yorkshire from Scotland. At times, as I walked through the very same halls and rooms that she had frequented, I felt a caress of her presence, a fleeting glimpse of her form as if it was only time that separated us. I remain convinced that somehow we connected. I believe that if we had been born in the same era, I would have been one of her most fanatical supporters. Maybe the four centuries that divide us are for the best.

This book is not necessarily just for those who have an interest in Mary's life, although there are many. Instead, it more for the person who loves history and likes to explore; it gives the reader a chance to visit the actual places that played such a big part in her life, even if she didn't always play as big a part in the history of those places. Whether in Scotland, northern France or England, the reader can pick and choose which location to visit and, hopefully, learn something interesting, maybe even fascinating, along the way. I certainly don't intend this to be another biography because there are so many of those and I couldn't possibly add anything new to Mary's story, but I do hope you gain some pleasure and insight into this fascinating subject by following in her footsteps.

I've divided the book into four parts to tell the story of her life, as well as making it easier to follow. I've also followed the example of Antonio Fraser, who wrote the standard-setting biography of Mary, in using a straightforward dating process. In the sixteenth century, the year used to start, almost incomprehensibly, on 25 March – and there were at least ten days difference between English and Continental dates, which adds to the confusion. For that reason, I've simplified things for twenty-first century readers and used the familiar 1 January as the year's start.

The Early Years: This section covers Mary's birth in Scotland, and her flight from the country during the years of Henry VIII's 'rough wooing', as the punitive expeditions into Scotland that were designed to reinforce Henry's aim of seeing Mary married to his son Prince Edward were called. Mary's infant years were a constant concern to those who cared about her; they were forced to move her from one stronghold to the next as the advances of the English increased. She had become Queen of Scotland within days of her birth, after the death of her father, so her role as a future royal bride became a reason for warfare then and, apart from relatively brief periods when she was married, it continued to be a threat to her own, and several countries', peace for the rest of her life. She left behind a grieving mother, Mary of Guise, who, as a widow, tried unsuccessfully to steer a divided Scotland towards unity, hindered by disloyalty from all around her and her own rapidly failing health.

Her Childhood in France: These are the years when Marie appeared to be at her happiest while she grew up in France, raised in luxury. She was loved and treasured by the king, embraced by her new adopted country, educated in the arts and culture of the Renaissance and taught the values of her Catholic religion. She was groomed for marriage to the Dauphin Francois, which later took place in the splendour of Notre Dame cathedral in Paris. As a result, she rightfully wore the crown of Queen of France, with her husband at her side. Only the unexpected deaths, in rapid succession, of her mother, the King of France and her husband Francois, brought her glorious time in France to an end. When she left, she was on a life journey that would not offer her such stability again.

Queen of Scotland: From the moment she landed on the eastern shores of the country, to the moment she fled to south of the border in the naïve belief that she could throw herself on the mercy of her cousin, the Queen of England, Mary's life was in almost constant crisis. From the regrettable decision to marry the entirely unsuitable Lord Darnley, to the almost incomprehensible later one to then wed the Earl of Bothwell, she was careering from one drama to the next. The savage murder of her secretary in front of her eyes set off a set of circumstances that few people would be capable of dealing with, never mind an emotional and misguided young woman who was surrounded by intrigue. When she looked to those she felt she could trust for advice and assistance, she received disloyalty and betrayal. Mary's years in Scotland were partly due to the actions of others, yet her inability to make the right decision at times of crisis was also responsible for her undoing. These are the years that have come to define her reputation.

Captivity: The last nineteen years of her life were often emotionally miserable and due to her ill health painful too. Her limited choice of companions and restricted movements were the complete opposite of the life she led during her two reigns. Her execution brought an almost fittingly dramatic end to a tumultuous and turbulent chapter in history. The sadness that accompanied these last years can only be guessed at – each new place where she was held captive was worse than the last and her health, never good at the best of times, became an increasing torment. The frail, sickly woman who had to be helped as she walked to her execution in Fotheringhay bore no resemblance to the vision of beauty who had so allured the men who met her that they fell under her erotic spell. Yet even at this moment, in the final moments of her life, Mary's regal presence stood proud. She accepted her execution with dignity, forgiving those who had mistreated her and praying for those who had stood by her, leaving a legacy that still exists today.

One of the astonishing aspects of Mary's life story is that there is not a single building or structure that was commissioned for her, or by her, yet many of these places now have her presence indelibly left on them. There are many houses, gardens, rooms and trails that are now renamed after the Queen of Scots yet, in many cases, this is just a flight of fancy aimed at attracting tourism as opposed to being based on historical fact. Although Mary didn't build anything, plant anything or name anything, every place described in this book has her presence lingering in them. Many of the places she did visit have benefited from her touch, whatever the circumstances of her being there might have been.

This book is not just Mary's story; it is a glimpse of the trail she left behind, like whispers in the wind. Her footsteps were sometimes light, sometimes heavy, but I hope we can retrace them as we follow her trail and visit various destinations, stand in the same spaces as she once did, only separated by the time that has passed.

I

SCOTLAND
1542–1548

Linlithgow

Mary Stewart was born on a bitterly cold winter's day on 8 December 1542 (although there is a suggestion that it was a day earlier, but Mary herself always referred to this date as her birthday) in the Royal Palace of Linlithgow, to father James V and mother Mary of Guise. I have deliberately referred to her as Mary Stewart as, at that time, that was how she was named. As the years passed, the spelling of both her names changed, depending on where she was, and the complexity of the sixteenth century – I will explain the constant changes as we arrive at those points in her story.

Her birth took place during one of the coldest winters on record; it had caused the sea to freeze over, with boats trapped for weeks off the coast of Newcastle. When Mary was born, King James already had at least seven living children, born to five different mothers, Elizabeth Shaw, Elizabeth Beaton, Elizabeth Stewart, Euphemia Carmichael and Margaret Erskine; the latter, in a strange coincidence, re-appears in Mary's story as the mother of her jailor on Loch Leven. Mary of Guise had given birth to two sons with James, but both had died in quick succession. Earlier, she'd had a son whom she'd been forced to leave behind in France when she married James and came to Scotland.

Mary Stewart's life started as it was to end, in tragedy. James was broken-hearted after the defeat of his forces by the English army at Solway Moss. This was apparently due to the incompetence of the Scottish generals, whose lack of military leadership resulted in thousands of brave Scots being massacred by the superior English forces. As he lay in his bed dying from what, at the time, was described as a melancholia, he received the news of Mary's birth with the words 'Adieu, farewell, it came with a lass and it will pass with a lass.' He was referring to the fact that the Stewart family had come to the throne through the marriage of Marjorie Bruce, the daughter of Robert the Bruce, and Walter Stewart, and that the birth of a girl had dashed his hopes of continuing the family line. It didn't help that Mary was also described as a '...very weak child and not likely to live, as it is thought'. James died six days later. Yet his daughter grew stronger, and became Scotland's queen – so her father's words were not to be fulfilled through Mary.

Linlithgow Palace was a fitting place for a queen to be born. Today it stands overlooking the loch and, despite it being roofless and parts of it in ruin, its grandeur is there for all to see. Mary's birthplace is now an empty space without a roof and nothing is left of the original room, but it is possible to imagine the surroundings as the rest of the castle is reasonably well-preserved. Inevitably, a building the size and stature of this one has had a remarkable history, and Mary Stewart's birth was just one part of it.

Linlithgow – meaning 'the loch in the damp hollow' has had a royal connection for centuries, with David I of Scotland being the first to build a fortress on the site in the twelfth century. He also founded the town that sprang up alongside it, but it wasn't until the fourteenth century that it became an important feature in Scotland's history. When Edward I of England was campaigning to annex the northern country, he fortified the existing manor house to accommodate a garrison of occupying soldiers, something he used to good effect. The building was later used as a base for the siege of Stirling Castle but, within eight years, Edward and the English had been defeated by Robert the Bruce.

Recorded with Sir William Wallace, who was executed in 1305, other leading names in the fight against the invaders were Sir James Douglas and Sir Thomas Randolph, but one man of humbler origins had also a part to play in Scotland's freedom at that time. William Bunnock was a farmer from Linlithgow whose hay had been requisitioned by the English garrison and he devised a clever plan to help Bruce capture the fortress.

A number of armed men hid in the hay, while others took up positions in the tower itself. As the hay cart passed through the gateway, the horse was cut loose, leaving the cart in the entrance and preventing the portcullis from being lowered. The guards were overpowered, the tower was captured and all the inhabitants were savagely massacred.

It was a brutal ending, but Bunnock was later rewarded by Bruce with a grant of land.

In 1310 the fortifications of Linlithgow were dismantled and it ceased to be a defensive stronghold. For the next hundred years or so, the building was occasionally used as a royal manor house. In 1424 any trace of the original building was erased though, when a fire swept through it and completely destroyed it. That gave James I the ideal opportunity to build a structure on the site that he could cherish and furnish in the style to which he had become accustomed to over the years – and so the current Linlithgow Palace came into being. The result was a hugely impressive quadrangular palace, with four ranges grouped around a central courtyard. It is certainly a tribute to James, who made the palace his lasting legacy.

James had spent eighteen of his twenty-nine years in English captivity after he was captured by pirates while sailing to France for his own safety. His imprisonment spanned the rules of Henry IV, Henry V and Henry VI, but as a royal, his was a privileged captivity, and so his love of architecture and the trappings of wealth were born. Once he had been released, he was crowned in 1424 at Scone Abbey. It was the same year that Linlithgow Palace was destroyed by fire so he immediately began constructing the building we see today. Approximately £4,500 was put towards the structure, with tiles imported from Flanders and the king's painter in charge of all of the decorations. The palace was built for James I and his wife, Lady Joan Beaufort, and after it was built, for years it became their favourite residence. It was clear that he had built it to be among the grandest and most impressive of the buildings in Scotland. To give some indication of how much thought and care had gone into the architecture, there is an unusual window on the eastern wall – what used to be the wall of the Grand Hall – where fourteen small apertures reflect the sunlight to illuminate what was a brightly painted ceiling. However, it was some time before the palace was afforded such royal favour again.

The next ruler to have an impact on the building, James VI, spent thirteen years on the Scotland throne, but it was a tempestuous time for him and the country. However, he managed to introduce a glamorous court life and the changes he made to Linlithgow can be seen today. The fountain, which quite recently has been restored and is now fully functioning, was commissioned and built with its naked musicians as part of a tribute to James and both of his French wives. At that time Linlithgow had a huge public profile with its vast hall the centre for banquets and entertainment. Gastronomically, it couldn't be bettered with such delicacies as swan, peacock, sturgeon and porpoise. The plays and sonnets that were part of the entertainment presented there were both political at times and certainly quite long – the original performance of *Ane Satyre of Thrie Estaits* by Sir David Lyndsay was of more than five hour's duration!

Both James IV and James V made changes and additions to the structure with new rooms and passages. It was the latter, of course, who brings us to the time of Mary. In the autumn of 1542, James V's life ebbed away. After mustering forces against Henry VIII at Solway Moss (where the Scots easily outnumbered the English), the resulting battle saw military ineptitude followed by low morale among his forces and so the battle was lost. James was laid low by what we now would describe as depression, yet that word would have been unknown in the sixteenth century. He visited his pregnant wife, Mary of Guise (who had already lost two children at birth) and then withdrew to Falkland Palace. There he retired to bed. When he was told of the birth of a daughter, he apparently turned his back and faced the wall and uttered the famous words 'It cam wi' a lass and it will gang wi' a lass', or, if you believe his chronicler Pitscottie, 'He turned upon his back, and looked up and beheld all his nobles and lords about him, and gave up a little smile of laughter, and thereafter held up his hands to God and yielded up his spirit.' Whichever version of the story is the true one, and whatever he did say, Mary's birth was not well received.

For Mary of Guise, the following months must have been traumatic, as she mourned the death of her husband and juggled the political ramifications of her daughter becoming queen when Mary was only six days old. It is not surprising that within eight months of Mary's birth, the child had been transferred to the comparative safety of Stirling Castle. James, Earl of Arran, who had assumed the regency, was affiliated with Henry VIII, who was more than a little interested in the wellbeing, or otherwise, of the infant queen. Linlithgow Palace was not a military fort, so the removal of the baby to Stirling Castle by her mother made perfect sense.

Linlithgow would hardly be a place for which Mary Stewart would have much affection during the years of her personal reign. Despite it being her birthplace, she seldom seemed to visit it. In fact, the palace was usually only used as a stopover on her many progresses throughout her kingdom. Mostly her attention was on the splendour of Holyrood – yet, as the years went by, Linlithgow returned to prominence during the reign of her son James. He summoned the Estates there in 1585, despite warnings that part of the building was unsafe. In fact, the western quarter of the palace collapsed in 1597, bringing down part of the northern wall with it, so a huge rebuilding process took place, which was not finished until 1620.

Sadly, Linlithgow was then left to rot away slowly as fewer and fewer royal visits took place and the palace almost became a forgotten relic. Only Charles I showed any interest in the place in the seventeenth century. Then a hundred years later, fires effectively brought an end to the grandeur as Bonnie Prince Charlie's Jacobite Rebellion saw numerous buildings suffer the same fate. January 1746 saw the end of Linlithgow Palace as an important structure as fire swept through it. Fortunately, restoration in the twentieth century, which continues today, has seen a re-emergence of the glories of what was once an important focal point in Scotland's history.

St Michael's Parish Church

Standing next to the palace is St Michael's parish church, a building that appears to have fared far better down the years than its more illustrious neighbour. It was here that Mary was baptised in what seemed to be a remarkably low-key affair. There is hardly any documentation available; her brief connection is almost a footnote to a far greater history.

The earliest mention of a church on the site can be traced back to the twelfth century, when David I gifted it to the Cathedral of St Andrews, and the building was dedicated in 1242. For some time after that it was also used as a weaponry and fodder store. The fire of 1424, which so damaged Linlithgow, also caused extensive harm to the roof so a full restoration was required. Funds were found for the rebuilding, not least from the locals who were fined each and every time they allowed their chimneys to blaze out of control. The duties were directed towards the upkeep and restoration of the chapel, so at least it appeared to be towards a good cause.

The nave and chancel were finished in the fifteenth century and by 1531, St Michael's became what we see today, with the completion of the apse. Two years later, Linlithgow was granted a royal charter, which was only possible after the full restoration of the chapel. As part of that charter, the citizens of the town have to undertake the duty of annually inspecting the boundaries, something they do with enthusiasm. The building where Mary was baptised is essentially the same one we see now, except for its obviously different adornments. In Mary's time, there were twenty niches above the buttresses, with statues depicting various saints. Now only St Michael remains, due to John Knox and his followers who, in 1559, systematically 'cleansed' many of the churches in their Protestant zeal. There were also twenty-four altars within the church in Mary's day, but they too have gone – for exactly the same reason. The church has been used for many things in addition to being a traditional place of worship, from a timber store to extra classrooms for Edinburgh University during the plagues of the seventeenth century, as well as a dormitory for Cromwell's soldiers. Down the years it has changed little. However, the stone crown we see on top of the tower is, in fact, a modern interpretation from the 1960s, when the original was replaced for safety reasons. The current design is effectively an impression of the original, as no drawings or paintings existed depicting the first structure.

As a final link to the past and Mary's time, let's look at the assassination of Mary's once-loved and respected half-brother, James Stewart, the Earl of Moray. He had become regent when she was forced to abdicate in 1567. Three years later, it was in Linlithgow that he lost his life at the hands of James Hamilton of Bothwellhaugh. The reason for the murder is unclear; a personal grudge cannot be discounted, despite political conspiracies of the time being the favourite theory. Moray was a man to whom history has not been kind. Despite his obvious political abilities and his naked ambition, he is remembered as someone following the winds and fancies of the day as he attempted to mastermind Mary's policies, and his later alignment with Elizabeth I and the English government. He had become a staunch Protestant and had struggled to accept his sister's faith, yet he had defended it when necessary. It has been said many times by noted historians down the years that he could and should have been the regent that Mary was not. He had the ability to guide

Scotland through its most turbulent times and may have seen the union with England created at a far earlier date. Also, twenty years later, when Mary was facing execution, Moray's intervention could have prevented that act and so history would have certainly been different from the one we know. Some say his death was at the hands of a vengeful wronged husband, who had fought for the queen and had his property confiscated as a result, leaving his wife 'stark naked' and 'all her goods taken from her'. Whether that is true or not, Moray's death robbed Scotland of a potentially great leader who has become a forgotten name in its past. How the two paths of sister and brother diverged.

Visitor Information

The palace is situated in the town of Linlithgow, West Lothian, some 15 miles west of Edinburgh. It is open for public tours, and at times local children can be seen acting as guides. This includes the parish church next door. Whereas many of the buildings in this book seem to be haunted by Mary's ghost, Linlithgow is unusual in that it is her mother, Mary of Guise, who is said to walk the empty spaces of the castle. There are some spectacular views from Queen Margaret's Bower, overlooking the loch and countryside, with the former being designated a Site of Special Scientific Interest. The postal code is EH49 7AL.

Stirling Castle

If Linlithgow was not a place that endeared itself to Mary, then Stirling Castle certainly was. This was the place that the infant queen was brought to for her safety at the age of just eight months; it was the place where she later soothed the fevered brow of her future husband Lord Darnley but also where she said goodbye to her new son at the age of just ten months, never to see him again. Mary spent most of her early childhood in the castle and her life at that point appeared to be as happy as that of any other child between the ages of one and five years old.

Stirling Castle is an astonishingly powerful looking building; it was understandably called the 'Gateway to the Highlands'. It occupies a position on what was once the only route from the Lowlands to the Highlands, guarding what was at that time the only bridge that crossed the River Forth. It also sits close to the meeting of three rivers, the Forth, the Teith and the Allan and, in fact, its original name 'Stryvelin' denotes that, but in later years the name Stirling became derived from 'ster', meaning a mountain, and 'lin' denoting a river. The castle sits at the top of Castle Hill, a crag that forms part of Stirling Sill – a geological formation – and it is surrounded on three sides by very steep cliffs so it is in an ideal defensive position. It is believed that the exposed area is around 350 million years old, and there are some suggestions that before historical records of the place began, the natural rock was occupied as early as the ninth century. Even earlier than that, the Romans chose not to develop the area and bypassed it completely, preferring to build a fort at nearby Doune. Some of the castle's earliest history includes it being given to Henry II of England in 1174 as part of the ransom for William the Lion.

There are also records of a chapel standing nearby even earlier, in 1110. It became a royal centre and soon Stirling had become a royal burgh and an administration centre for the governing of Scotland, so it became a bone of contention for the warring factions from both sides of the border. Indeed, over the next centuries, the easiest way for England to secure power over Scotland was to capture Stirling Castle, something that happened with regularity. After Henry II's acquisition of the fortress, he never appeared to take up residence there. Later, in 1189, Henry's successor, Richard I, gave it back into Scotland's control. It then continued to be a favourite of the royals and monarchy throughout the twelfth and thirteenth centuries, with a deer park added by Alexander III in 1262. Also in the thirteenth century, the Earls of Menteith and Buchan captured Alexander when he was just sixteen, and kept him there. He died in 1286, without leaving an heir. His death was unusual to say the least as it came about by falling off a cliff while riding his horse. His wife Yoletta was able to remain in Stirling Castle as she awaited the birth of a child, a possible heir, but after twelve months it seemed she'd either made a horrendous mistake or it was all part of a charade; she was hastily removed and escorted out of the country.

The castle remained under the guardianship of Edward I of England but after the Wars of Independence in the late thirteenth century, the Scots regained control of Stirling. It didn't last long though. Edward marched into Scotland with a huge army and, on the route from Linlithgow, heard that the castle had quickly been deserted as his terror tactics had wreaked havoc throughout the country. Indeed, on arriving, he found the keys to the gate nailed to the door! From then on, Edward claimed overlordship of Scotland and ensured the country was under the direct rule of the English.

One year later, the Scottish rebel William Wallace achieved a famous victory over the English at Stirling Bridge, and so recaptured the castle, but it soon changed hands again. This to-ing and fro-ing of ownership, including the bloody upheavals that accompanied it, continued. By 1299 it was in Scottish hands again following a siege by the lords, helped by the fact that the ninety English soldiers were effectively running out of sustenance and had to eat three grey mares 'for default of other food', but just four years later, it was England's again. This time the English army overcame William Wallace and his soldiers and, in an attempt to stop any more raids on what they believed was theirs, they hung and quartered the rebel and displayed his body from the ramparts. In 1314 it was Scotland's turn for revenge, this time under the now famous Robert the Bruce. His brother, Edward Bruce, had been laying siege to the castle for well over a year when Edward II brought a massive English army north to defend Stirling. The crushing defeat that followed at Bannockburn became part of Scottish folklore. The victorious Robert then had the castle and its adjoining towers levelled so as not to attract the unwanted attentions of the English again. However, that was of no use, as in 1535 Edward II had retaken it, restored its towers, ramparts and fortifications and installed a garrison of 200 soldiers to defend it. The conflict didn't end there. England was distracted by a war with France, which was to continue off and on for well over hundred years. This meant the defence of Stirling, and indeed control of Scotland, was little more than an annoyance and financially unsupportable and so, in 1542, the castle was given back to Scotland and specifically to Robert Stewart, who became its guardian. From then until the present day it has remained in Scottish hands.

Of course the castle, which had seen constant bloodshed, continued to be a place of dark deeds and bloody events, even if it did have a relatively peaceful hundred years or so following the Stewart guardianship. The 'Douglas Room', which is part of any history tour of the castle, came to have this name after an event in 1452 when the Scottish king, James II, summoned the Earl of Douglas to Stirling to answer charges of treason, including plotting against him. He promised him faithfully that he would be safe, but the moment Douglas arrived, the king plunged a dagger into his neck and then assaulted him with the help of a handful of loyal lords, before throwing the bloodied and battered corpse out of the window. The site of this murder became a fascinating story about the Stewarts in years to come and although they certainly made many attempts to effectively erase that part of their history, their failure is shown by the fact that the room has been remembered ever since as the 'Douglas Room'.

Despite this, Stirling Castle became a favourite of the Stewart family. Its rebuilding took place throughout the reign of James IV. The great hall, the Renaissance Palace and a new Royal Chapel were commissioned and completed. The chapel was especially important to James. Many years before, his father, James III, was murdered by a rebel group of which James IV was at the head. This so traumatised the young James that afterwards he visited the chapel daily and repented by attaching an iron girdle to his body, which was never removed. It also increased in weight every year. So it is thanks to James IV that we can still see what is standing today. During a twenty-five-year period between 1488 and 1513, he undertook the huge renovation project, which saw the King's Old Building, the great hall and the Forework all completed, plus the establishment of a college for priests, granted by the Pope in 1501. The Forework, of which virtually nothing of the original remains, was a large gatehouse that had conical towers on either side and effectively stretched to the whole width of the castle. It had French influence and can be compared quite readily to the similar structure at Linlithgow Palace, so although we can't see it today, we can imagine it. The castle we see today is much smaller than the one that grandly sat there in the sixteenth century but it is nevertheless impressive.

Stirling was very much the centre for royal visits and patronage, with artisans from all over Europe attaching themselves to the area as they used their talents to add to the walls' spectacular new engravings and statues. It became a place of revelry and excitement with parties and masques replacing the violence and bloodshed of earlier years. There is a story told of an Italian who wanted to prove to the world that he could fly, so he threw himself off the ramparts with a couple of handmade wings attached to his shoulders – predictably, it didn't end well. The castle had not seen such peace and happiness before and the 'Gateway to the Highlands' also became a place where ordinary townsfolk could come and sell their wares at a market immediately outside the huge stone walls. For a brief time, it was a happy place to be and to see.

When James IV died, his son James V was brought to Stirling (very much like his daughter years later) and he subsequently spent nearly his entire life there. One of the few occasions he did leave the area was in 1536, when he travelled to France to bring his new bride, Mary of Guise, back to Scotland. They appeared to live a happy life, despite the problems with his bride's pregnancies. Finally, the king's 'despair' over losing a battle and the knowledge the baby his wife had just given birth to was a girl coincided with his last days. Seven months later the infant Mary was brought to the castle by her mother as Henry VIII's 'rough wooing' had caused havoc and misery throughout the country, and so Stirling Castle again became the fortress that stood between Scotland and another possible English invasion.

Mary was baptised in Stirling Castle in a ceremony that appeared to be small and rather underwhelming. In fact, it was reported back to King Henry that it was a baptism of 'such solemnity as they use in this country, which is not very costly'. That gave the king another reason to attempt a kidnap of the baby queen and within two days he ordered a full onslaught on the castle. Stirling was now almost impregnable and, despite the betrayal of a number of Scottish lords, the castle and its two most important occupants – Mary of Guise and her child Mary, Queen of

Scots – remained safe. Henry's obsession with the capture of the new queen and the proposed English marriage that he so wanted in order to control Scotland once more, brought about many new and restrictive rules that affected Mary's upkeep. It was decreed that 'no noble in the realm might enter the castle with more than two servants in the company' and only her mother could be alone with her. Today the idea of arranging a marriage for an infant child is strange to most modern eyes, yet in the sixteenth century such a plan was an acceptable part of political machinations. Henry VIII was desperate for a marriage between Mary and his son Edward as a form of unification and to effect that, the Treaty of Greenwich was drawn up on 1 July 1543. This would respect Scotland as an independent country but it would be beholden to England. The treaty would also safeguard the young queen from the advances of France, Spain and Austria (which had all made claims to the infant's hand) but she would be forced to relocate to the English court, where her upbringing would be taken care of. This last stipulation was the main stumbling block for the Scots, who argued that she should not be allowed to leave her country until she was at least ten years old.

Two years later, when she was approaching her third birthday, her protection was put into the hands of the Lords Erskine and Livingstone at the then immense cost of £60 per month. They were not particularly successful though, as the battle of Pinkie Cleugh in 1547 saw the Scottish army completed routed. This happened after the death of Henry VIII, proving that the annexation of the northern country was as high on the agenda of the English monarchy as it had always been. With the claims on Mary now becoming almost irresistible, she was moved to the isolated island of Inchmahome on the Lake of Menteith. This will be dealt with in the next chapter. Mary said goodbye to Stirling Castle – effectively her childhood home – and didn't return for another fourteen years, when she re-entered it as a reigning queen.

Although we deal with Mary's return to Scotland in later chapters, it makes sense to deal with her link to the castle in this section, even if the story inevitably jumps out of chronological order. It wasn't until September 1561 that she returned to the castle, and by this time she was Queen of Scots. She'd left her familiar home of France and, as queen, had made a triumphant progress through her kingdom. Her popularity was as great as it ever had been, or was ever going to be. Surprisingly, her first return to the castle that had served her so well as a child nearly ended her life as an adult. During her two-day stay, a burning candle set the bed curtains alight while she was asleep and it was only chance that saved her, as she was discovered with the room smouldering.

Four years later, the queen tended to her cousin and husband-to-be, Henry, the Lord Darnley, through his sickness. It was this period of close proximity that led to her becoming besotted with this good-looking young man, and resulted in her second marriage. He was tall and, unusually for those days, clean shaven with an allure that impressed both women and men alike. It is fair to say she was completely infatuated by him. It turned out very quickly that she could not have made a worse choice

for a marriage partner than she had with this callow
and arrogant youth. Initially he appeared to be the most
perfect man to carry Mary away on a wave of passion.
He was also perfect in that he carried a bloodline that
combined the Tudor and Stewart dynasty, so that any
future claim to the English throne was made stronger by
the marriage, despite the fact that her illegitimate half-
brother, James Stewart, 1st Earl of Moray, was completely
against the union. Quite simply, the young queen, who
had endured a marriage with Francois in France that was
devoid of any type of meaningful passion or intimacy, was
totally overwhelmed by her desire for this youth and the
consummation appeared to have taken place extremely
quickly. She was probably still a virgin when she met and
married at the age of twenty-four – and already a widow
it has to be remembered – so the delights Darnley offered
in the matrimonial bed must have been a revelation for the
young woman. However, his charms were merely a cover
that hid a personality of selfishness, greed and downright
arrogance – as she found out the hard way.

One year later, Stirling Castle was the venue for the
christening of their child, James. Yet this could not have
been in more testing and trying circumstances. By then Mary
had undergone a complete reversal of her feelings towards
Darnley. She had begun to hate every part of him so they
had effectively become separated and were only connected
by the royal titles that Mary had bestowed on him,
which she was now desperate to erase. Her dislike of her
husband was brought to a head by the horrendous slaying
of her secretary Riccio, with Darnley not only complicit,

but actually physically at the head of the group that had stormed into her chambers to murder the unpopular Italian. Darnley's act of then pressing a knife to her swollen stomach had ended any hope of a reconciliation between the two of them, although Mary's pretence of contrition and forgiving him in the immediate aftermath of the stabbing was some of the most dramatic playacting in history. It was this that saved not only her life on that night, but also the life of her unborn child.

The christening was a sad but extravagant affair, taking place in December 1566. It was sad because Lord Darnley had decided to take no part in it and had stubbornly and rather childishly remained in his bedchamber while the partying continued. It was extravagant because the celebration was also intended to impress the foreign ambassadors who attended and, hopefully, Mary's cousin, Queen Elizabeth. But Elizabeth I chose not to grace the gathering and instead sent the Countess of Argyll as her proxy. In fact, the two queens never met, despite Mary's almost obsessive desire to meet the woman she described as her 'sister'. It was a Catholic service. The Earl of Bothwell, who was by now Mary's most trusted advisor and soon to be her third husband, refused to attend even though he had been entrusted with the arrangements. Bothwell was Protestant and he, and many of the lords, stood outside while the ceremony took place. It was a traditional christening, with the only change being that Mary dispensed with the rather distasteful act of the spittle being deposited into the baby's mouth. The ceremony was a huge success. The cloth of state for the baptism was of crimson velvet with gold edging, the baby's bedspread was at least 10 yards of silver cloth and there was a huge golden font (actually a present from the absent Queen of England). The event, according to the description of the time, 'combined elegance with value' – something that was essential for Scotland's rather cash-strapped monarchy. Later in the evening, there were parties and theatrical plays. A pyrotechnic display lit up the sky as the guests enjoyed a feast that seemed never-ending. Until that time, it was probably the most lavish party ever seen in the castle – certainly the most expensive! The next day there was hunting in the park for all the dignitaries and yet more plays and fireworks. It was huge, ostentatious and overwhelming, but the extensive celebration was completely ignored by the father, who didn't once set foot into the great hall to see how his newborn and all the important guests were faring.

Three months later, the baby was given into the hands of the Earl of Mar for safekeeping as the civil war caused by the death of his father, Lord Darnley, in rather suspicious circumstances, meant that nowhere was now safe for the infant. In April 1567, Mary rode to Stirling to see her new son and then left, never to set eyes on him again. It was the beginning of a long and ultimately distressing time for Mary, Queen of Scots.

Of course life and death in the castle continued, with further light imprints relating to Mary in its long history. The spectre of her husband Lord Darnley continued; four years after Mary's last visit in 1571, the Archbishop of St Andrews, who was one of the many accused of the murder of Darnley, was hanged there. Also later that year,

Darnley's father was shot in a disagreement in the town of Stirling. That was followed by the Regent Mar also dying in the castle.

The great building saw better times too and at the end of the sixteenth century there was another splendid baptism held in the huge hall, this one for Prince Henry, James VI's son and thus Mary's grandson. Among the many great displays was a 40-foot high model ship that took centre stage. The hall itself was at the time one of the grandest and most impressive in Europe and its fame was acclaimed by many but, as the years passed, both the hall and the castle lost their allure and soon became an almost forgotten landmark. Prince Henry died at the tender age of 19, so Charles I became the heir apparent and, with the union of Scotland and England now complete, the court removed itself to London, effectively abandoning Stirling Castle. In fact, the last person to actually live in the castle was James VI. However, Stirling was not yet completely left out of the history books. In 1651, incredibly, the castle was captured again, for the last time. The Covenanters, who were opposed to the Stuart kings regarding themselves as the spiritual heads of the Church of Scotland, seized it. It was again besieged by the English army but to no avail. Some ninety-four years later, Bonnie Prince Charlie made an effort to take control of the fortress; the battle of Falkirk was prolonged until the Duke of Cumberland arrived with his army and compelled Charlie to retreat. That in turn led to the battle and tragedy of Culloden. The castle has not had to stand firm against any invaders since.

Among the many wonderful and impressive adornments that can be seen even today, following years of restoration, there are some visible reminders of the days of Mary Stewart. On one of the ramparts the initials M.R. (standing for Mary Regina) can clearly be seen; this area is called Queen Mary's lookout as this was the place she liked to sit and look out upon the lands and forests below and to enjoy the fresh air. Also on the south side of the ramparts there are classical sculptures, which include both Mary and her father James V, both of them disguised as commoners. This is because they each had a passion for dressing down and taking to the streets of Stirling or Edinburgh to mingle with the people without being recognised. James adopted the title 'Laird of Ballangleich', a name that means 'windy pass' which adequately describes the pathway that James would use to the inner gate when leaving the castle for these excursions.

Once the Stewarts had departed, the castle's role as a regular royal residence declined and it then became a military centre. In the seventeenth century it was used as a prison for high-ranking officers and throughout the century only Charles I and II spent any time there. Charles I was due to stay there for a period of time and the castle had been prepared for such a visit for some eight years before his eventual arrival in 1633 – he was to spend just two nights there. His son Charles II stayed there around 1650 and became the last monarch to use the place as a royal home. Then the military used it more and more over the next 150 years. As it became a strategic place for defence, they even constructed a gunpowder magazine in the gardens.

From 1800 to 1964, Stirling Castle was owned by the War Office and it became a barracks and training ground for the Argyll and Sutherland Highlanders. The great hall fell into disrepair as it was used as an accommodation block. The Chapel Royal was used as a theatre for lectures and also as a large dining hall, the King's Old Building as an infirmary and the Royal Palace as an Officer's Mess.

Thankfully, since 1964, extensive renovation and restoration work has taken place. The Royal Lodgings were completed in 2011 at a cost of £12 million; the work took ten years to complete. Also, since 2002, the *Hunt of the Unicorn* tapestries have been faithfully recreated by the Tapestry Studio in West Dean. The weavers went to New York to view the fifteenth-century originals, now on display on The Cloisters in the Metropolitan Museum of Art. The weavers incorporated original techniques in an attempt to recreate the tapestries and their completed work now takes pride of place in the Queen's Presence Chamber in the Royal Palace. This project was completed recently and the hangings add to the atmosphere of the building, as they were almost certainly a part of the royal collection during James IV reign. The castle itself still plays host to the Argyll and Sutherland Highlanders, but they are no longer in residence.

Visitor Information
The castle is certainly a place you should visit on our Mary trail. Whether it is because it is the place where she was christened, or where she was seduced by the charms of her second husband-to-be Darnley, or where she said goodbye

to her son James, this is a place where Mary left many footprints. The castle is easily spotted in its lofty setting and easily reached, whether by car, train, bus, bicycle or on foot. It is open daily for tours, guided or not. There are magnificent views to be seen of Stirling and the surrounding countryside. There are also many events that take place there, some recreating moments in history, so it is worth checking in advance to find out if any Mary-related spectacles are due to be held before you plan your visit. The postal code is FK8 1EJ.

Inchmahome Priory

Although Mary only spent three weeks on this idyllic island at the tender age of four, it is such a pleasant and scenic place to visit, I feel it has to be included in any tour on the trail of Mary, Queen of Scots. Situated in the centre of the Lake of Menteith (the only natural 'lake' in Scotland thus named, probably after Dutch cartographers misunderstood the word 'laigh', which means low ground), the Priory of Inchmahome is a ruined building dating back to 1238. It stands some 15 miles from Stirling, and 5 miles east of Aberfoyle. The only way to get there is on a twelve-passenger motor boat, run by Historic Scotland. Once on the small island, the peace and tranquillity give a glimpse of the safe haven that Mary would have experienced after she and her mother fled from Henry VIII's 'rough wooing'.

The priory was founded in the thirteenth century by Walter Comyn, scion of one of the richest and most powerful families in Scotland at that time. However, there are suggestions there had been a church of some description on the island even before then. It is believed that Comyn founded the monastery as a place where his family could worship, and have a final resting place that befitted their standing in the community. The Chapter House, with a newly renovated roof, houses a number of grave slabs and effigies, which have been removed from the ruined church to protect them from the sometimes wild elements. By far the oldest is a double effigy of the first Stewart earl, Walter, who died in 1295, along with his countess Mary. His son, also named Walter, married Marjorie Bruce, the daughter of Robert. Their son then succeeded David II to the throne, as Robert II. Robert the Bruce had visited the priory in 1305, 1308 and 1310 and signed documents to that effect, and Robert II stayed there too. As the years passed, the influence of the priory declined and a local landowner who had become an appointee, handed it over to Lord Erskine, who was a guardian of the infant Mary, Queen of Scots. This is how the island and priory came to be used for her safekeeping in 1547, before she travelled to France a year later. By 1560, the priory housed eleven canons, but the Reformation meant that there were no new priests and in 1606 the property passed from the Erskine family to the Marquis of Montrose but, with the rising costs, in 1926, the 6th Duke of Montrose handed it over to the State. The priory is now a ruin, but a certain amount of imagination can recapture what it looked like in Mary's day. The most sacred part of the building, the choir, can be seen clearly. This contained the high altar and was lit by the huge, spectacular east window with five lancets. The arches of the choir contain the seating for the celebrant and his assistants, used during the religious services, and which can be seen today. Inside the choir are more grave slabs. One of them belongs to R. B. Cunningham Graham, the co-founder of the Scottish Labour Party in 1928. There are also numerous wall plaques dedicated to the Graham family. Alongside, the cloisters were the main domestic buildings of the priory where the community met; as well as including the chapter house, it also held the dormitories.

The Priory of Inchmahome has some references to Mary's stay there. These include such delights as Queen Mary's Garden, Queen Mary's Bower and Queen Mary's Tree but these must be regarded as merely attractive labels (or more harshly, tourist traps) as she arrived on the island between 11 and 18 September, and departed after the English invading army had re-crossed the Tweed on the 29th. It is possible she returned in her later years, but there is absolutely no evidence to support this. So the chances that the young child was responsible for planting a garden and a tree at a time of such tumult, and in such a short space of time, are slim to say the least. Nevertheless, Inchmahome is a truly glorious place to visit. Although it is one where Mary's footprint was among its faintest, it is a place that belongs in her history and story too. Her three-week stay certainly didn't define the place, but I would urge you to take the time to pay a visit.

Visitor Information

A boat ferries passengers, twelve at a time, to the priory from the Port of Menteith, on the B8034, off the main A81. There are set sailing times. The island is closed to the public during the winter months, between November and March. There are few places I have found that can match the tranquillity of the island, and I would highly recommend a visit. The postcode is FK8 3RA.

Dumbarton Castle

Of all the places that Mary stayed, lived or visited, Dumbarton Castle could arguably be said to have given her the greatest feeling of safety and wellbeing. She was transferred here from Inchmahome Priory, in February 1548, at the age of just five, to be guarded by French soldiers until the treaty of marriage between her and the equally young Dauphin of France was signed some five months later. Within another month, she would leave the country of her birth, not to return for another thirteen years.

Dumbarton Castle is imposing, as most castles are, but this one stands on its rock in the Firth of Clyde. For many years it was one of the most strategic places in the west of Scotland. Although its history is clouded in uncertainty, there are suggestions that the Romans occupied it. There is also the familiar connection with King Arthur, although there is little proof that this is based on fact. It is also suggested that this was the birthplace of St Patrick, who became the patron saint of Ireland, but again this could be mere legend. What is known is that Dumbarton was originally the capital of the area known as Strathclyde, a far more important and larger place than the one we know today. In the tenth century, it stretched from Loch Lomondside to Morecambe Bay, with its strategic rock – named 'Alclur' by the Britons and Welsh – being the centrepiece of the whole kingdom. Only in 1034 was Strathclyde made a part of a new, unified Scotland.

A new Dumbarton Castle was built in the thirteenth century; it was recorded in the charter of 1222 by Alexander, who also founded a new royal burgh. He installed a sheriff who kept the castle, in addition to his other duties as custodian of the burgh. One of the earliest names to be linked to Dumbarton was Sir John Menteith, a man who gained notoriety by betraying William Wallace for a £100 fee and the Earldom of Lennox from Edward I. Wallace was kept prisoner in the castle, before he was removed to London for trial and eventual execution. Many historians have pointed out that the trial was anything but fair and the execution was hasty, to say the least. These events led to the rising of Robert the Bruce – joined, by the way, in his campaign by Menteith, after a change of allegiance. Bruce afterwards played a huge part in Scottish history, notably the independence of Scotland following the Treaty of Northampton. As the years passed, Dumbarton gained a more important standing in Scotland, not least by being a gateway to trade with Scotland's friendly neighbours and protectors in France, thus bypassing the enemy England. It was in the fifteenth and sixteenth centuries that this took on a magnitude that transformed the history of the two nations.

To demonstrate how history has a habit of repeating itself, in 1436 the daughter of James I and Joan Beaufort was sent to France to marry the Dauphin of France. She was eleven at the time and he was fifteen, and their pledge had lasted for eight years before Princess Margaret was put on a ship, amid much splendour. Sadly, the story didn't end well. In addition to dreadful homesickness, Margaret was sickly; she suffered, and then died at the young age of twenty. A century later, Mary would also set off on a similar journey as her own Dauphin of France awaited.

In the sixteenth century, the hereditary title to Dumbarton Castle lay with Matthew, the Earl of Lennox, a man who in later years would become Mary's father-in-law. Lennox had been in the service of French royalty as the king's Scots guard, but at the age of twenty-seven had left their employ and arrived in Scotland. He also arrived with a credible claim to the throne of Scotland through his ancestor, Mary Stewart, the daughter of James II, but he was thwarted by the Earl of Arran, who seemed to have a stronger case and had already been named 'second person' by Parliament. The two were immediately at loggerheads, especially as Lennox was handed the keys to Dumbarton Castle for its safekeeping by Mary of Guise, who correctly believed he was a Francophile and sympathetic to her cause. Arran, meanwhile, was constantly urged by Henry VIII to eliminate his rival and acquire the stronghold that was Dumbarton. Lennox and Arran never found common ground. As was to be proved in future years, though, Lennox was not everything that he seemed. An intensely ambitious man, he saw that his prospects could be seriously improved by a convenient marriage – not unusual for the sixteenth century – and to that end he wooed Lady Margaret Douglas, a niece of Henry VIII's. There was reason for his union with Lady Douglas, and it had precious little to do with love. She had a distant claim to the throne; Mary I of England once suggested that Lady Douglas was better suited to the throne than anyone else. As if that wasn't enough, he also went on a bizarre mission to woo Mary of Guise also, now a widow, of course, but with poor results. She was twenty-five and the competition to wed her was described as a desperate kind of male beauty pageant at the time: 'they daily pursued the court and the queen mother with bravery, singing, dancing and playing on instruments, arrayed every day in sundry habilliments and prided who should be the most gallant in their clothing.' The other person referred to by the use of the word 'their' was the Earl of Bothwell who, in later years, would successfully capture Mary Stewart, in body, if not in heart. Eventually Lennox was forced to concede defeat, because Mary of Guise ignored him and so, in 1544, he married Lady Douglas. They had a son, Henry, Lord Darnley, who would later play an important part in Mary, Queen of Scots' life. So Lennox and Bothwell were both part of Mary's later story.

By 1547 Scotland was again under attack from the English, despite the death of Henry VIII. This time it was under the stewardship of the Duke of Somerset, who humiliated the Scots army at the battle of Pinkie Cleugh. The Scottish forces were larger than those of their foe, but in terms of morale and battle tactics, they suffered badly and the defeat became known to the Scots as 'Black Saturday'. English garrisons were established in many areas of Scotland, including Haddington, which was near the strategic centre, Edinburgh. It was with this as a backdrop that Mary of Guise removed her daughter firstly to Inchmahome and then to Dumbarton Castle for her safety.

Once at Dumbarton, young Mary was safe, as the castle was heartily defended by French soldiers, but the story of Mary, Queen of Scots very nearly didn't happen as the young child fell victim to a terrible virus that almost killed her. Historians have never established if it was measles or smallpox, but it was sufficiently virulent to spread rumours of her death throughout the kingdom. She recovered, though, and by August 1548, was waving goodbye to her mother, her friends and her country as she set sail for France and thence to Paris to meet and then marry the young Dauphin of France. The agreement for her transfer meant that Scotland was now under the sovereignty and protection of the King of France with a proclamation that read:

...the which day Monsieur d'Esse, Lieutenant General of the navy and army sent by the most Christian King of France for support of this Realm at this present time, show that the said most Christian King had set his whole heart and mind for the defence of the Realm, desired in his said Master's name for the more perfect union and indissoluble bond of perpetual amity and confederation the marriage of our Sovereign Lady to the effect that the said most Christian King's eldest son and Dauphin of France may be joined in marriage to her Grace, observing and keeping this Realm and the lieges thereof as have been in all Kings of Scotland in all time past, and shall maintain and defend this Realm and the lieges thereof the same as he does the Realm of France and the lieges thereof...

It was a wordy, and to our eyes an almost incomprehensible, statement and presumably its significance would have been completely lost on the child that Mary was then, but what would not have been lost on her was the knowledge that she was leaving behind everything she knew, including her mother. However, it is worth remembering that the way of life in the sixteenth century, especially for royalty, was nothing like it is today. Although she would clearly have been sad to wave goodbye to her biological mother, her closeness to Mary of Guise would have been fragile at best, because she would have been raised by a succession of nannies and relatives with precious little input from the queen mother. In fact, one of Henry VIII's stipulations included in the conditions for a possible marriage of the young queen to the heir to the English throne was that she was to be brought up by courtiers, with minimal contact with her mother. Mary was accompanied on the trip to Northern France by her governess and aunt, Lady Fleming (who was terribly seasick on the voyage and wouldn't have been much company for the child Mary anyway), as well as four companions, later known as the 'four Maries', Mary Seton, Mary Livingstone, Mary Beaton and Mary Fleming, all of who had been, and would continue to be, her closest confidantes. As an aside, the name Marie was quite common and it also implied the term 'maid', so although having four assistants with the same name must have provided some amusement to the young queen, it wasn't unusual. Mary was now under intense scrutiny as she sailed towards France and to give some idea about how she was monitored, a letter sent on the voyage from her governor, Sieur de Breze to her mother states '....I desire to assure you

Madame, that in spite of the very heavy winds during the last few days, which tossed the galley most severely, the Queen has never been sick, this makes me think she will suffer but little on the open sea...'

With Mary gone, the Earl of Arran continued to hold Dumbarton Castle in the hope that maybe one day the young queen would return to a union with his son 'the young Arran'. That hope was rekindled when Mary returned to Scotland thirteen years later, following the death of Francois. Despite Mary being in mourning for her first husband, Arran went on the offensive to lay claim to her for a possible marriage, either to him, or to his son, but his entirely unacceptable plans were thwarted by Mary's half-brother, Lord James Stewart, and Arran was put under strict supervision until his death in 1609.

By 1565, Mary had married Darnley, quite possibly the most unsuitable husband she could have chosen; yet as we have noted, initially she was completely infatuated with him. Despite this, she nevertheless had the presence of mind not to sign over the castle to her husband, although this may have had a lot to do with her innate mistrust of Darnley's father. Instead, she put the castle into the hands of another cousin, Lord Fleming.

Dumbarton Castle continued to play a part in her life as, step by step, it started to unravel in a most extraordinary way. It was to this castle that she attempted to flee after escaping from Lochleven. She wasn't successful, as Moray's troops cut off her path. The castle was captured by Captain Thomas Crawford of Jordanhill, which effectively ended any links between the Scottish

Queen and the place she had once regarded as her safe haven. The castle continued to exist but it had to withstand more attacks; in World War II, it was bombed four times by the Germans as they targeted a nearby aircraft factory. As before, Dumbarton Castle stood firm.

Visitor Information

Dumbarton Castle still stands today in all its majesty and glory. It sits on a volcanic rock in the Firth of Clyde and looks almost inaccessible from the sea. It lies nestled between two large hills, and offers some spectacular views. The gatehouse, which Mary would have used when boarding the ship, was swept away into the sea in 1735. However, the castle is essentially the same as it was in Mary's day. It is open to the public, but opening and closing times differ from season to season. It can be accessed easily from Dumbarton, and is found on the predictably named Castle Road. The postcode is G82 1JJ.

2

TO FRANCE
1548–1560

Mary's story now moves into France and for that reason
we shall now use Marie as her first name, plus changing her
surname from Stewart to Stuart. She was certainly born as
a Stewart then later became a Stuart through marriage to
her cousin Lord Darnley, but once she arrived in France,
her surname was always referred to as Stuart. Her Christian
name became Marie, in the French way, whenever she signed
her name – although as Antonia Fraser rightly points out,
little importance should be attached to the actual name that
was used, as people of the sixteenth century would regularly
changed the spelling or pronunciation of their names with
indifference.

Roscoff

For many years, historians have argued about the landing
place of young Marie on 15 August 1548. Although it
is now accepted that she landed safely in Roscoff, there
have been schools of thought that suggested either Brest

or St-Pol de Léon as the landing place; but the first was eventually discounted and the second seemed unfeasible as at that time the town was at least a mile inland from the water. The most accurate description of the landing of the ships and their company came from Monsieur de Breze, the man who had been sent by Henry II to ensure a safe passage for the queen:

> When the galleys had arrived in the port of Roscoff, I did not fail, three or four days after the landing of the little Queen of Scots, to send them to Rouen, to await the king's instructions.

That letter was sent to the Duc d'Aumale and clearly mentions Roscoff. The reason there has been so much confusion since is because on the same day, 18 August, he also wrote a letter to Marie's mother stating that the landing place was St-Pol de Léon, but as that was impossible in the sixteenth century, that can be regarded as an innocent mistake (although if he knew the trouble that biographers have had since, he may have been a little more attentive to detail!). Saint Pol is, in fact, some miles inland, and as for Brest? There has never been any real evidence to suggest that it was the place that she first saw as she drew nearer to the French coast, and so we now go along with the accepted idea that Roscoff was indeed the first landing place, although the captain of the fleet must have been an extraordinarily talented seaman to negotiate what was then a hazardous approach through strong currents and hidden marshes.

Roscoff today is, of course, a completely different place and virtually unrecognisable from the small fishing village that Marie first saw in 1548. Today it boasts a ferry port for Brittany Ferries, specifically founded for journeys from Plymouth to the French coast as the government made the decision in 1968 to build a deep water harbour to attract tourism, and the reluctance of existing ferry companies to change their routes to a less populated part of the northern coastline led to Brittany Ferries being founded. The small but bustling port is essentially a waypoint for tourists and few take the time to explore what is a quite stunning part of northern France. For Marie-watchers, it is sadly a disappointment. Just near the entrance of the port there are two buildings calling themselves 'Marie Stuart houses' where the legend is that the infant queen and her company stayed here for a few days. However, that story is most likely opportunistic tourist-bait as opposed to real history as both houses were built at least ten, and possibly twenty, years after she arrived and, in fact, at that time there only existed the St Ninian's Chapel at the head of the landing stage. That building too has an unusual legend attached to it. The story goes that the outline of Marie's foot was traced on a rock as she set foot on land, and it was there that the chapel was extended to what it became in later years. Like all legends and stories, there is a mixture of truth and fantasy involved. The company comprising the queen and the courtiers almost certainly departed immediately for St-Pol de Léon, thus beginning the initial confusion.

Although Roscoff is not an essential place on the Marie trail, if you should decide to visit it, here are a couple of quirky facts about the place. The Kouign Amann cake served in the town is an artery-hardening, heart-stopping mixture of sugar and butter and shouldn't be taken lightly, or at all if one is health conscious, and the 'Onion Johnnies' originated from Roscoff. They were the Breton farmers who, in the early part of the twentieth century, dressed in their traditional costume of a black beret and a black-and-white striped jumper, rode their bicycles through the English countryside with pink onions for sale hanging around their necks, and so creating the caricature of French countrymen. Even the French don't recognise this image – unless they come from Roscoff!

On 20 August, the queen visited Morlaix, some miles inland from her landing place. This was confirmed by a story from Albert le Grand who was born in the town in the late sixteenth century and had been told of her coming by his parents and peers. He was later to write in his book *Catalogue of Bishops* under the heading 'Jean Juvenal des Unions' the following:

There arrived in the same town by sea the most noble and puissant princess, Marie Stuart, Queen of Scotland, who was on her way to Paris for her marriage with the Dauphin, Francois, afterwards the second king of that name. the Lord of Rohan, accompanied by the nobility of the country, went to receive her, and she lodged in the Dominican Convent. When her Majesty, in returning from the church of Notre Dame, where the Te Deum had been sung, had passed the town gate which they called 'the Prison', the drawbridge, which was overladen by the weight of the horseman, broke and fell into the river, although without any loss of life.

The Scottish gentlemen in the queen's suite who had remained in the town feared that some mischief was intended, and began to shout 'Treason, treason!' but the Lord of Rohan, who was by the side of the queen's litter, shouted to them at the top of his voice, 'No Breton was ever a traitor!'

During the two days on which the queen remained at Morlaix, in order to refresh herself after the fatigue of the voyage, he caused all the gates of the town to be taken off their hinges, and the chains of the bridges to be broken.

From Morlaix, the queen travelled to Saint-Germain, something which was confirmed by the reliable de Breze, who advised of the journey in a letter on 18 August, also confirming that the Duke and Duchess of Guise were coming to meet her. The Duchess (Marie's grandmother) was at pains to let her daughter in Scotland know of her love and care for the young queen:

Madame, I felt happier than I can say when I heard that our little Queen had arrived in as good a health as we could wish for her. I grieve for the anxiety which I think you must have had when she set out. You have had so little happiness in this world, and are so much accustomed to have trouble and care, that I think you can hardly know what pleasure means, except that through her absence and loss you hope for some rest for this little creature, with honour and more good fortune than ever, if God will. I hope to see you sometimes again before I die. I will start this week, God willing, to meet her as quickly as I can, and bring her to Saint-Germain, according to the King's instructions.

As it was, the Duchess outlived her daughter and granddaughter by many years.

Sadly, not everyone was as cared for and healthy as Marie, as both Lords Erskine and Livingston were seriously ill on the journey, and one of the courtiers, 'le petit Ceton' (the young Seton), died on the way of a stomach flux. The young queen was already attracting attention and in another letter, sent later on 1 October, the Duchess, Antoinette de Bourbon, wrote to her son,

> She is very pretty indeed, and as intelligent a child as you could see. She is brune, with a clear complexion, and I think that when she develops she will be a beautiful girl, for her complexion is fine and clear, and her skin white. The lower part of the face is very well formed, the eyes are small and rather deep set, the face is rather long. She is graceful and self-assured. To sum up, we may be well pleased with her.

Unfortunately, she had few good things about the rest of the Queen's train, saying that with the exception of Lady Fleming they were '*et sy pey propre quy lest possible*' – basically, they were not handsome.

There is confusion as to the exact date that Marie and her train arrived at Saint-Germain, but 16 October is accepted as when they were expected to arrive. King Henry, who was very keen to meet his new 'child' had made arrangements for them to stay in the house of Carrières near Saint-Germain for her reception. The chateau was to be cleaned and the surrounding village to be significantly smartened up, and an instruction was sent out that no workman or stranger would be allowed to enter Saint-Germain, and especially the palace, who had come from any place that carried an infectious disease. The king also ordered that as soon as Marie arrived at Carrières, all foreign nationals who travelled with her were to be sent home as he wanted her to be served by the same French officials who served his own children. He wrote on 18 October

> ...since all who have come here after seeing her praise her as a wonder. This doubles the desire I have to see her, as I hope to do ere long.

Visitor Information

Roscoff is certainly off the beaten track of our trail so, if you do decide to visit, don't expect too much in the way of Marie connections. However, here are things to do about the town. The port area has charming restaurants and cafés, and close by there are some magnificent beaches. The Onion Johnnies, as mentioned, are celebrated each August in the two-day Onion Festival, which is actually far more enjoyable and interesting than it sounds. There are also some excellent and reasonably priced hotels, especially near the port. The town of Morlaix is nearby, and of course this is also part of Marie's journey when she first landed in France. The French postal code is 29239.

Carrières, Saint-Germain

The king had asked for miniature paintings to be made ahead of his first meeting with Marie so that he could recognise her, and it is fair to say that he wasn't disappointed at all when the meeting took place. He didn't see her until the second week of November because he had an insurrection to deal with as the people of the south had risen up against the collectors of the salt tax. It was quelled in a ruthless and efficient style by Colonel Montmorency, who, with his pride in torture, watched as peasants were either burned at the stake or broken on the wheel. When the king finally arrived, after having watched the wedding of Jeanne d'Albert, the daughter of Henry's aunt, he described Marie as: 'The most perfect child I have ever seen.'

Just as importantly, Marie and the Dauphin, Francois, also seemed to like each other, although one has to remember that she was five years of age and he was a year younger. She arrived speaking the 'barbaric' language of Scots and he, of course, spoke aristocratic French. She was a tall girl for her age, perfectly healthy, and beautiful by sixteenth-century standards, whereas he was frail, small, sickly and spoke with a stammer. At that tender age there were of course no romantic feelings between the two children, but it was clear that Marie looked upon Francois as a playmate whom she could care for, whereas he looked up to her with a sense of awe and wonder. The French-Scottish accord was safe as long as they both liked each other.

The king was entranced with Marie and instructed that she should take precedence over his biological daughters as she was a queen and was betrothed to his son, but he was ruthless when it came to her companions, sending the four Maries away to a convent to learn French. The mother of one of the Maries, Lady Fleming, was kept at court and for reasons that quickly became very obvious. She was a fluent French speaker but far more importantly, was ravishingly beautiful and Henry immediately fell for her. They embarked on an affair during which she became pregnant and, after rather brazenly broadcasting the news to many at court, she was banished back to Scotland – and so was taken away from her daughter.

To show how much the king was entranced with Marie, Monsieur de Breze wrote this letter to her mother in Scotland:

He holds her today for no less than his own daughter, and I do not doubt that if she and the Dauphin were of marriageable age or approaching it, the King would soon put the business in hand. Meanwhile the King wishes them to be brought up together and that their people should make one household. The reason of this is that they may early grow accustomed to each other's society. I assure you Madame, that the King thinks her the prettiest and most graceful princess he has ever seen. The same opinion is held by the Queen and all the Court.

There is also another rather interesting story about the first meeting that Marie had with the French court, and that concerns Francois's mother, Catherine de Medici. Catherine had arrived unannounced in the nursery after Marie and Francois had met, and she stood and watched without introducing herself causing Marie to ask if she knew that she was in the presence of the Queen of Scotland. Catherine took this badly and immediately responded by asking if she knew that she was stood in the presence of the Queen of France. From that moment onwards, the two disliked each other intensely. It must be said that Catherine was a woman who had a lot to bear. Her husband, a notorious womaniser, had a long-standing and passionate relationship with Diane de Poitiers, so much so that she attended royal engagements, effectively the woman by his side, something which Catherine had to accept for her family's sake and the future claim to the throne. She had been barren for ten years before finally giving birth, and the king's dislike for her was so immense that it was his mistress Diane who had almost to force him to the marital bed to procreate an heir. Catherine, who played such a large part in the history of France once her husband had died, went on to have twelve children, of whom ten survived. All of them, including Francois, were frail and suffered from many illnesses and ailments. Her dislike of Marie was to play a large part in the young queen's future in years to come. The king though, was thoroughly smitten, as shown by these words to Mary Guise in a letter written in December 1547:

I should like you to know Madame, my good sister, that I have invited to the wedding of my cousin the Duke of Aumale, your brother, all the Ambassadors of the various princes who are with me. He of England was not absent, and in his presence I took the opportunity of making my son the Dauphin dance with my daughter the Queen of Scotland [note how the king now refers to Marie as *his* daughter], and as he was talking with the Emperor's Ambassador, my cousin the Cardinal of Guise approached him, to whom I said that it was pretty to see them. My cousin replied that it would be a charming marriage. The English Ambassador merely answered that he found much pleasure in watching them. Yet I am sure he found hardly any, and liked as little the caresses which he saw me give them. Such Madame, my good sister, are the tidings of my nursery, which I wished to tell you, so that you may feel, over there, something of the pleasure which I enjoy constantly, and which increases from day to day, when I see my daughter and yours going on always better and better.

Henry was not a great king as he seemed to lack the intellect to govern successfully, although he was without doubt very brave. He was passionately in love with Diane, someone he had met when he was still a child when he had grown to love her, and he was a gentle giant around his children, notably Marie, but he was also capable of terrible cruelty. When a poor Huguenot tailor ventured to reprove Diane de Poitiers, Henry swore that, with his own eyes, he would see him burned. From a window in the Rue Saint-Antoine, he watched the dreadful event. The man though performed the final act in this horrendous spectacle as he directed his dying gaze so fixedly on the king's face that Henry shrank back, pale and trembling. Never again, he declared, would he witness so horrible a scene – yet the ashes of persecution were never cold during his reign.

It is interesting to see how the expenditure rose so dramatically in the royal household once Marie and her entourage had joined the French court. The treasurers' accounts for 1551, while in Saint-Germain, prove that Marie was richly provided with clothes. Rene Tardif, silversmith to the king, supplied lengths of violet, crimson and yellow velvet, fine Holland linen, white satin from Venice, and pieces of violet, black, red and white taffeta, which were to be made up into garments for the Queen of Scotland. The catalogue includes frocks of golden damask and cloth of silver, linings of white silk and satin, and muffs of velvet trimmed with sables. Sixteen dresses were made for her in 1551 alone. Mathurin Lussault, a goldsmith, furnished gloves, pins, combs and brushes. Another goldsmith provided twelve dozen crescent-shaped buttons, enamelled in black and white, which were to trim a pair of sleeves and a coif of violet velvet. Marie possessed a golden girdle, enamelled in white and red, and her jewels were so numerous that three brass chests could scarcely hold them.

The expenditure for food in the chateau is quite extraordinary and makes you wonder how on earth they could afford to keep the royal household. The provisions for just one day include two calves, sixteen sheep, five pigs and seven geese, besides pieces of choice beef, chickens, pigeons, hares and one pheasant. Thirty-six pounds of cutlets are on the butchers' bill for that one day, as well as calves' feet, partridges and larks.

Seventy-two dozen loaves were supplied by the baker, and five different merchants provided wine. The fruiterer sold, besides his own special goods, white and yellow wax for household and church use. It's a quite exhaustive list and gives the impression that all the royal train did all day was to eat! In fact, one of the reasons for Catherine de Medici's many ailments in later life was put down to excessive eating.

We also learn from the accounts of the same year that the royal children had many animals as pets too. Among them were four bulldogs 'well muzzled', and twenty-two little drawing-room dogs. They had horses and ponies, tiercelets (male falcons) and tame birds in a cage. The greatest nobles in France sent them horses and dogs. The Dauphin's favourite horses were named 'Fontaine', 'Enghien', and 'Chastillon', the Queen's were 'Bravane', and 'Madame la Reale'. Wild animals and serpents from Africa were shown to all the children. Wolves were brought for them to see as well as boars caught in the snare. The Count of Saint-Aignan gave the Dauphin a hind, which he became extremely fond of. The Sieur des Carpentils and the Marshal Saint-André each sent him a bear.

Marie's health was also well looked after at this early stage. A letter from Giovanni Ferreri to the Bishop of Orkney gives some clues as to how her physician was appointed:

Inquiries are being made here about a medical adviser who may pay attention to her health according the custom of the Courts. There are many French who desire the office, but in my opinion it would not be the prudest (sic), nor the very fitting for her Majesty. The greater part of them either do not appreciate the importance of their art, or are not the persons to comprehend a Scottish temperament. They will all rather do harm than good to the young Queen. Only one is of Scottish race, William Bog, Doctor of Medicine. He is so learned that he will bear any comparison with any Frenchman and is by far the best in diagnosing Scottish temperaments. All the Scots at Court ardently wish him to get the post, but the modest man hesitates to accept such a responsibility until he has won the Queen Mother's consent. As he cannot find a man of authority and note to obtain that consent for him, he has dealt with me to request you not to fail him, or rather not to fail the Queen in a matter like this. I know that you are so acceptable to the Queen Mother that she will not refuse this favour, be it what it may, if only she knows that it is sanctioned by your advice.

As for the chateau at Saint-Germain-en-Laye, there is little remaining to remind us that Marie spent a large part of her childhood there, with Henry's other children, and for a time, the four Maries too. The chateau was a glorious looking structure, built in 1122 by Louis IV and originally called Le Grand Chatelet. It was expanded by Louis IX in the thirteenth century but was burnt to the ground by the Black Prince in 1346, before being completely rebuilt by Charles V on the original foundations in the late fourteenth century and and became named Chateaux Vieux. In fact, the parts of the castle that we can identify with Marie had only just been built at the time of her arrival.

Francis I had extended the original building in 1539 and, during Marie's childhood there, King Henry, who was so unimpressed with the 'coldness' of the building, chose to build a second chateau – Chateau Neuf – at the crest of a slope nearby. Again, Marie's time there can hardly be traced. The tenure of the building was relatively brief, as it was eventually abandoned after Henry died and was demolished in 1660.

Chateaux Vieux continued to have a long and rich history, most notably concerning Louis XIV who was born there in 1638. It became a place of royal residence before it was turned over to James II of England after his exile in 1688, following Louis' earlier move to Versailles for good in 1682. In more recent times, the castle was the scene of the Treaty of Saint-Germain-en-Laye when hostilities ended between the Allies and Austria on 10 September 1919, and in World War II the German Army used it as their headquarters during the occupation of France. Today it is home to the Musée d'Archeologie Nationale.

Visitor Information
The chateau can be found in the department of Yvelines, about 19 kilometres west of Paris. It is a truly awe-inspiring building and the museum housed there is certainly a 'must' when visiting, whether you have an interest in archaeology or not. Check for visiting days as, like many museums in France, it is often closed on Tuesdays. The postcode is 78100.

Chateau Royal de Blois
The Chateau of Blois is situated in the heart of the city of Blois and today visitors will see a wonderful example of French and Italian architecture, with spectacular views over the nearby River Loire. Sadly, Marie-watchers will find it a disappointment as very little remains of her time there, either as a child or later as a young woman married to Francois. Most of the castle was badly damaged during the French Revolution and, indeed, had been virtually

abandoned for more than 150 years, so what you see now is the result of a massive renovation from 1841 under the direction of Felix Duban. Unfortunately, hardly any original furniture remains, due to long-lasting damage, so what you see are reproductions, but a sense of the grandeur has been achieved. It was also at this time that Chateau Blois was turned into a museum. Now it has become a tourist attraction under the stewardship of the city council.

Although Marie did spend many years there as part of her French upbringing, and later with her first husband, attempting to find anything that connects to her is extremely difficult – except for a portrait of her as a young woman. There is, however, the wonderful 'chamber of secrets' belonging to Catherine de Medici, which is worth visiting. This was not a series of dark poison cabinets, as speculated, but was more likely to have been a place to show precious artefacts to guests. Catherine had gained a reputation for her interest in astronomy and astrology. She had also regularly turned to potions to cure whatever ailments she had, and some of these were regarded as lethal. She used her potions when she was attempting to become pregnant.

The Queen's Chamber on the first floor is reputed to be the place where Catherine died in 1589 and you can see the walls that are decorated with her and Henry's monograms, although these were added at a later date as Henry's passion for his mistress was far more pronounced than any affection for his wife.

Blois Chateau has a long and rich history. One of its greatest moments was in 1429, when Joan of Arc was blessed there by the Archbishop of Reims, before she travelled to Orléans with her army with the aim to drive out the invading English. The chateau is enormous with 564 rooms and seventy-five staircases, including the renowned spiral staircase in the Francois I wing, where, if you look closely, you can see the initials of Catherine de Medici and Henry II on the ceilings of the adjoining rooms, although they can also be seen as monograms of Henry and Diane, something far more likely in intention owing to the love he had for his mistress.

The castle was purchased in 1391 by Louis Duc D'Orléans, the brother of Charles VI, and, after his death, his widow Valentina Visconti saw out her later years there. Her son, Charles, inherited it before being captured by the English and held hostage for twenty-five years. When he returned, he completely renovated it to make it a more comfortable dwelling. His son, Louis XII, used it as a royal residence. It was during the sixteenth century that the entrance was rebuilt and an Italian garden was designed (destroyed in 1890 when the Avenue Victor Hugo was extended across the grounds) and it is here that a statue of King Louis stands tall at the entrance to the castle. Queen Claude and Francis I refurbished the chateau in 1515, as they intended to leave their residence in Amboise, but nine years later, Claude died and Francis lost the will to spend any more time there. He did, however, leave what was, at the time, the country's biggest and most exhaustive library, only for it to be moved to Fontainebleau soon afterwards, where it remains to this day.

Although Marie enjoyed the benefits of the castle, her footprint seems to be significantly lighter here than at many other places she frequented, as her time is rarely acknowledged in the long history of the place. Don't let that put you off, though, as this would be a visit in the heart of some of the most exquisite countryside and a chance to enjoy the beauty in the area. Walking through the gardens, you can get the sense of what it must have been like for Marie and her train in those heady and exciting times for the young queen.

In later years, a darkness spread over the castle after the assassination of Henry, the Duke of Guise, during a convention in December 1588. He was killed by Henry III's bodyguard and the following day, the Duke's brother, Louis II, the Cardinal of Guise, was also killed. They were bitter enemies.

The castle then became the place of exile for Marie de Medici after she was expelled by her son from the royal court and, from the seventeenth century onward, the chateau was handed down from one royal family member to another until the council of the City of Blois took control and it is now run as very impressive tourist attraction.

Visitor Information

The chateau can be found in the centre of the city of Blois, which is located in the Loir-et-Cher department of the Loire Valley. It is open to the public, although it is worth checking ahead for opening dates and times. The royal apartments now house an art museum – a word of warning though, the guides are in French, so if you don't understand the language, then it may be easier for you to make your own relaxed way around the building. The postcode is 41000.

Chateau De Fontainebleau

Fontainebleau is another of those magnificent chateaux that Marie spent time in, yet it is not remotely touched by her fleeting presence. Situated south-east of Paris, some 34 miles distant, it is another wonderful example of French architecture. The building was upgraded during the Renaissance and is now seen as so important that the royal residence is now a UNESCO World Heritage Site. The earliest records of this castle date back to 1137, when it had become a favourite residence of the kings of France because the area was renowned for hunting. It took its name from the nearby spring, the Fountain de Bliaud, which is now located in the English garden that was built in the seventeenth century. Down the years, the chateau was used by Louis VII, for whom Thomas Becket consecrated the chapel in 1169; Philip Augustus; Louis IX, who built a hospital and convent; and by Philippe le Bel, who was born there. Our interest, though, lies in the chateau as it was during the time Marie visited it.

For many centuries the castle had effectively been untouched but in the reign of Francis I (1494–1547) it was rebuilt in a Renaissance style, recently imported from Italy. It is interesting that many of the cultural aspects that we so identify with France, such as architecture, cuisine, the arts, etc., were originally imported from Italy, and Catherine de Medici, in particular, who was born in Florence, was responsible for changing the country. A new oval courtyard was built on the site of the original castle, which included the impressive stairway – the Portique de Serlio – which gave access to the royal apartments in the northern wing. One of the main changes to the chateau was the construction of the Gallery Francis I in 1528, which linked the apartments to the Chapel of Trinitaires. Italian architect Sebastiano Serlio and painter Giovanni Battista di Jacopo rebuilt and decorated the new gallery, effectively introducing the Renaissance to France.

There was also another addition during the time of Marie's presence, that being the completion of a new square of buildings, built around the courtyard – the north wing of the Ministers, the east wing of Ferrare and the south wing of the Galerie d'Ulysse. A new park also was constructed surrounding the chateau, in the Italian Renaissance style, with pavilions and monuments in tribute to Ulysses. It was during this time that Marie would regularly visit the castle with her companions and must have delighted in the constant adjustments and improvements.

After the death of Henry II, his widow Catherine de Medici stayed on in the chateau and continued the planned reconstruction, which included a new wing called Belle -Cheminée. It had (unsurprisingly) elaborate chimneys and two opposing stairways. A moat was also built, as the likelihood of attack was increasing. Of course, by this time, Marie had returned to Scotland to rule the country of her birth, never to return to France.

The chateau went through so many changes in the following centuries that it now bears hardly any resemblance to the place of wonder that Marie had resided in. During the seventeenth century, Henry IV seemed to have been obsessed with rebuilding, or adding to, or improving on, virtually every aspect of the castle. Two more pavilions were constructed around the oval court, a new gateway was constructed on the east side, called Porte du Baptistère, which was distinguished by a huge dome. All the façades in the courtyard were remodelled and a new courtyard was also built called, inevitably, Quartier Henry IV. He didn't stop there as two new galleries, Galerie de Diane de Poitiers and Galerie des Cerfs (stags), were built, enclosing the old garden of Diane, which, when originally built, had a huge monument to Diane as its centrepiece.

Just to add to all this splendour, the largest indoor tennis court in the world was constructed, although this, it has to be remembered, was a court for 'real' tennis, a game very popular in Europe at the time, but which has no connection to the sport of lawn tennis as we know it today. Finally, Henry commissioned a new park, with a wondrous array of plants and trees that also enclosed a canal some 1220 metres in length.

Within seventy years of Marie's time there, Fontainebleau had been almost completely transformed. Henry's son, Louis XIII clearly inherited his father's passion for the place and the ingrained desire to leave a legacy of his time there too. The Chapel of Trinity was completed and a horseshoe stairway was added on the courtyard, known as the Cour de Cheval Blanc. He also completely redecorated the residence leaving little or no trace of its past. His son, Louis XIV, loved the place and spent most of his reign there. He wasn't quite as sweeping regarding changes to the chateau, but he did build an apartment for his 'companion' Madame de Maintenon, as well as demolishing other apartments to accommodate the royal princes. He also made some major changes to the park that Henry IV had created, replacing the

Hanging Garden with a large pavilion on an island in the centre of a new man-made pond.

Like all castles or chateaux, there is a tale of darkness and for Fontainebleau that came on 10 November 1657 when the former Queen of Sweden, Christina, was a guest, after only recently abdicating. She was suspicious of most people around her. That included her lover, the Marchese Gian Rinaldo Monaldeschi, whom she had stabbed to death by her servants in one of the great halls after accusing him of treachery and colluding with her many enemies. There is also the story of the Russian Czar, Peter the Great, visiting in 1717, when great hunting expeditions were arranged as sport for him – but it seems he didn't enjoy a single moment of his two days there and he left complaining about French tastes, not least their abundance of wine, which he hated.

Still the building continued. Under the control of Louis XV, a huge new courtyard – Cour de la Conciergerie – was constructed on the east of the Gallerie des Cerfs. He also demolished the Galerie d'Ulysse and replaced it with a brand-new stone building extending into the parkland. A new wing was built and a larger pavilion replaced the original Pavilion des Pouêles, which had stood for barely a hundred years. A grand theatre was also constructed on the first floor in the Belle-Cheminée (although that was destroyed by a fire in 1856, to be replaced by a new one a year later by Napoleon III). His son, Louis XVI barely diminished the speed of the rebuilding as he added to the chateau with more apartments for his courtiers, plus refurbishing numerous rooms, not least the apartment of Queen Marie-Antoinette in Turkish style, plus a new boudoir in the style of Arabesque architecture. Rather surprisingly, the palace suffered virtually no damage during the French Revolution, and hardly any major changes took place – they happened in peaceful times. The furniture was sold and the castle was occupied by the Department of Seine-et-Marne until 1803, when Napoleon I used it as a military school. A year later, the historic meeting between Napoleon and Pope Pius VII took place at Fontainebleau, where Napoleon was crowned Emperor. He had extensively refurbished the building for the meeting and in later years the only change made to the exterior was one of the wings – Aile de Ferrare – being demolished so that the front of the palace could be made visible through an elaborate iron fence. He also transformed the parkland into an English garden, designed by Maximilien-Joseph Hurtault.

In 1812, Pope Pius, whose previous visit to Fontainebleau had been to crown the Emperor, found himself incarcerated there for two years, although the comfort of the place would have somewhat eased his imprisonment. In turn, Napoleon abdicated there on 4 April 1814 and left just under a year later for his final prison and resting place of St Helena. In his memoirs, written while on the island, he described Fontainebleau as '…the most comfortable and happily situated palace in Europe'.

In 1861 a museum was opened by Empress Eugenie, which contained gifts from the King of Siam and also artworks seized during the pillage of the Summer Palace in Beijing. The Emperor, meanwhile, built his offices and these were effectively the last two rooms built by residents, as the castle has remained essentially the same ever since. In 1870 the

Empire fell during the Franco-German war and the Chateau was closed. In fact, Eugenie became the last royal resident to spend any time in the castle when she revisited it in 1920, but since 1870, it has become a tourist attraction and also a premier site for museums and art collections.

The façades of the building were given historical protection in 1913, and a full World Heritage Site status by UNESCO in 1981. The Ecoles d'Art Américaines opened in 1923, and still exist today. Four years later it also became the French National Museum, an honour it still retains.

It was occupied by German military forces twice in World War II, in 1940 and 1941; it became the headquarters of Allied Forces, Central Europe, from the end of the war until 1966.

Fontainebleau is a truly wondrous place to visit and it could take you a long time to see all of it and appreciate its beauty and history. Marie's vision of it would have been so different to the one we have now as barely anything she saw still stands, so we have to be clever in using our imagination. Then, as now, it was a magnificent building that dominated the country, never mind the surrounding countryside, and was an important place in the history of France. It's fitting that Marie stayed there but traces of her are all but gone, unlike many other important places of her time.

Visitor Information

The chateau is situated some 55 kilometres south east of Paris and is described as one of the largest royal chateau in France. It's an astonishing building that, even though it has little of Marie in it, is still an amazing place to visit.

The Gallery Francis I, completely decorated a decade or so before Marie's stay, is spectacular in its grandeur and opulence. The horseshoe stairway at the entrance is the focus of numerous photographs, and the boudoir of Marie-Antoinette is a room not to be missed. The list of attractions include St Saturnin's Chapel, the Stairway of the King, the Queen's Bedroom, the Throne Room of Napoleon and the museum, the Chinese Museum, plus the theatre where numerous plays and concerts took place. The English gardens are also a must-see when visiting the chateau. Although not strictly a 'Marie' building, she did spend many happy days here, even if it now bears no resemblance to the one she frequented. The French postal code is 77300.

Blois – Mary of Guise's Arrival

In 1550, the eight-year-old Queen Marie was beside herself with joy and happiness at the news that her mother, Mary of Guise, was travelling to France to see her, as well as dealing with numerous political matters. She was to stay for most of the winter at Blois, but entered the country of her birth at Rouen in Normandy on 25 September. On the king's orders, she was received with the highest honour by all the estates of the town. The young Marie was brought to Normandy by the king and she, with her mother, witnessed the spectacle of the official arrival of the King of France on 1 October. It was described in contemporary reports like this:

First in the state procession came the religious orders, then the secular clergy with their gold and silver crosses, next the tradesmen of the city in costly apparel. The powerful corporation of the salt merchants rode in costumes of grey taffeta with black velvet caps adorned with white feathers. The drapers wore white satin doublets, and gold buckles shone in their caps. The fishmongers had doublets of red satin. Twenty-four councillors passed by in their black satin robes. A high official of the Parliament was resplendent in scarlet, with ermine cap surrounded by great pearls. The horses were apparelled hardly less sumptuously than their masters. After the riders came gay companies of footmen, some dressed in white and green, others in white and red. Surprising indeed to the child Queen must have been the sight of the triumphal cars, bearing goddesses and nymphs. In one car sat a mimic king, robed in white velvet, and behind him stood a beautiful woman, holding a crown over his head.

The most astonishing show was the procession of six elephants. The first carried on its back a tray of lighted lamps; the second, a church; the third, a villa; the fourth, a castle; the fifth, a town; and the sixth, a ship. Here was a company of soldiers in Turkish costume, there a group of men, each of whom carried a live sheep. The Constable Montmorency bore the naked sword before Henry II, who rode alone on a chestnut horse, followed by the anchors of the guard. His costume was of white velvet and cloth of silver, with a white plume in his hat. Entertainments of 'strange device' were provided for him on his journey – in the suburb of Saint Sever he had received addresses from public bodies, and as he approached the main bridge, there crept out from behind a huge artificial rock Hercules and the seven-headed hydra. Within the cave, Orpheus sat on a throne, while fairy-like girls around him played soft music. The procession halted while Hercules fought with the serpent and crushed it into the dust. The first river marvel was a huge whale. Salvoes of artillery welcomed the king as he crossed the bridge. The people of Rouen had squandered money on this reception. Fifty Brazilian natives had been landed at the port, and they joined in combat between two ships, one of which was given over at the end to the 'savages', who pillaged and burned it, while the crew took refuge on an island. The most impressive sight of all was shown to the king near the bridge of Robec. There was displayed a green enclosure, described by Masselin as 'an Elysian field of earthly paradise'. Within the enclosure lay two figures representing Francis I and Henry II, with a goddess watching their slumbers. Latin inscriptions were placed on either side: *'Sedes ubi fata quietas ostendunt'* and *'Ut requiescant a laboribus suis'*. The king heard Mass in the Cathedral and dined at the Abbey of Saint-Ouen. On the following day Catherine de Medici made her entry, accompanied by the ladies of the court: Madame Margaret, the king's sister; and the Duchess of Valeninois. Catherine was dressed in cloth of silver, and her ducal cap was covered in gems: 'The eye sank before the vision of her magnificence.' Diane de Poitiers was in black velvet, trimmed with ermine, and each lady in the queen's procession wore a white feather. It was an astonishing parade and makes most spectacles in modern times seem dowdy in comparison. The Dowager Queen then moved to Blois, where the festivities continued. In the first week of

February 1551 there were processions, tournaments and masked dances, to which all the ambassadors were invited. A banquet was given by the Cardinal of Lorraine at which the king was actually the steward and the Constable, clerk of the kitchen. Sir John Mason wrote, 'A man would have thought that all the jewels in Christendom had been assembled together, so gorgeously were the dames beset with great numbers of them, both their heads and their bodies.'

It was later in February that King Henry appeared to be set on war with England and so it was suggested that Queen Marie 'be sent away with all good speed and with 300 or 400 men of arms and 10,000 foot'. Thankfully this didn't come to pass, but Mary of Guise must have felt some melancholy as she watched the festivities in her birth country, and compared them to the harshness of the Scotland she ruled and the Scotland that would soon be her daughter's.

At this time Marie's schooling was under way, including tutelage by her mother. As it was described at the time, one of her greatest assets was her singing: 'She sang very well,' wrote Brantome,

> ...attuning her voice to the lute, which she played very prettily with that fair white hand of hers, and those well-shaped fingers, which were lovely as the fingers of Aurora. In the excellence of her singing, she profited greatly by a certain natural – and not acquired – modulation of her voice. She played well on the cittern, the harp and the harpsichord, as they called it. She danced excellently to music on account of

her wonderful agility of body, yet gracefully and becomingly, for by quiet and gentle motion of her limbs she could express any harmony of the strings.

The praise didn't stop at her singing. It was also observed that,

She devoted great attention to acquiring some of the best languages of Europe, and such was the sweetness of her French that she was considered eloquent in it, in the judgement of the most learned. Nor did she neglect Spanish or Italian, which she enjoyed more for use than for show or lively talk. She understood Latin better than she could speak it.

She was also taught needlework at this time and was tutored with such skill and care that the exercise of the womanly art became to her no mere task but a pleasure and recreation for the rest of her life. In fact, the long and gloomy days incarcerated in English prisons were made slightly more bearable by her attention to the skill and the pastime she so loved.

As the young Marie was growing up, it seemed that there was nothing that she wasn't either good at, or capable of, if you were to read the letters written concerning her talents. She was supposedly a fearless and graceful horsewoman, and she bore herself gallantly when an accident occurred, as you might expect. On an autumn afternoon in 1559 when hunting near Blois, she was caught by the bough of a tree, and flung off her horse with such force that she was unable to cry for help. Several ladies and gentlemen of her suite had, in the excitement of the rush, passed on before she was noticed,

> ...and some of their horses rode so near that her hood was trodden off. As soon as she was raised from the ground, she spoke and said she felt no hurt, and herself began to set her hair and dress up her head, and so returned to the Court, where she kept her chamber until the king removed. She feels no incommodity by her fall, and yet has determined to change that kind of exercise.

There is no doubt that the child was adored, albeit somewhat falsely by her courtiers at times, but it showed that she was being educated in the strictest fashion to become the gallant queen that both Scotland, France and, hopefully, England needed.

Notre Dame

The marriage of Marie and Francois in April of 1558 was inevitably a particularly grand affair. She was fourteen and Francois a year younger and they captivated the hearts and minds of the French people, who lined the wedding route in their thousands. The wedding had, of course, been preordained but the two youngsters had genuinely grown to love each other in the childish type of affection that grows between playmates. They had spent all their time together, and it was a huge relief to all that they had grown so fond of each other. After all, if there had been a strained relationship between them, then any Franco-Scottish accord in the future could be put in jeopardy. They had been gently and gradually pushed together by the courtiers and there was never a question of the marriage not taking place. It may not have been romantic love, but it was a genuine and deep friendship. The day of the wedding would be one that would live in the memory of so many. The ceremony has been described many times but this is the best version, published in *The Girlhood of Mary, Queen of Scots* by Jane T. Stoddard (1908):

It was eleven o'clock when a fanfare of trumpets announced that the bridal train had left the Episcopal palace. The pressure of the people in the Cathedral square and the surrounding streets was overwhelming. The humblest Parisian wished to a have a glimpse of the lovely bride, as she passed along the arcaded gallery with its bower-work of green. First came the Swiss halberdiers carrying their pikes, and followed by the band of their regiment. Francis, Duke of Guise, who performed the duties of Grand Master in the absence of Montmorency, saluted Bishop du Bellay, who was accompanied by his cross-bearer, and by the choirboys carrying lighted tapers in silver candlesticks. The great soldier then turned to the people, and observing that the lords and gentlemen on the dais were crowding so as to obstruct the view, he bade them stand aside. Musicians playing on many instruments advanced along the gallery and these were followed by a hundred gentlemen of the royal household, and by the princes in splendid array. In the procession walked eighteen bishops and abbots, six cardinals – Bourbon, Lorraine, Guise, Sens, Meudon and Lenoncourt – besides Cardinal Trivulzio, the Pope's Legate.

After these came the bridegroom and bride. The Dauphin was conducted by the King of Navarre, and accompanied by his brothers, Charles and Henry. Queen Marie walked between Henry II and the Duke of Lorraine. The Hôtel de Ville chronicler says that her robe was covered with jewels and decorated with white embroidery. She must have seemed like 'a lady walled about with diamonds'. Two young girls bore her long and sweeping train. The great carbuncle in her tiara was valued at 500,000 crowns.

Immediately after the bride walked Catherine de Medici with the Prince of Conde, the Queen of Navarre, Madame Margaret, sister of the king, and other ladies. On reaching the main door of Notre Dame, Henry II drew from his finger a ring which he handed to the Cardinal de Bourbon, Archbishop of Rouen. It was this prelate, brother of the King of Navarre and the Prince of Conde, and nephew of the Duchess of Guise, who performed the nuptial rite in the presence of all the people. The Bishop of Paris delivered an address.

The Duke of Guise, who loved to court the favour of the Parisians, again exerted himself to keep back the crowd of gentlemen, so that the masses might enjoy an uninterrupted view. As the king entered the church, money in great quantities was thrown by the great heralds, with a cry of 'largesse' three times. A frantic struggle ensued, and in the effort to capture a coin or two, lives were nearly sacrificed. From the panting and exhausted multitude voices were at length heard calling to the heralds to throw nothing more.

Mass was celebrated by the Bishop of Paris, and immediately afterwards the royal party returned to the episcopal palace for the wedding banquet. During the meal, the king asked two gentlemen, Messieurs de Saint-Sever and Saint-Crespin to hold the crown above the head of the bride. The civic party did not accompany the Court to the palace as their invitation was for supper. They dined in a small house on the Place de Parvis, and the town chronicler observed that the house was very inconvenient and it would be inadvisable to return there on a similar occasion. The royalties had a dance after dinner, the king choosing Queen Marie as his partner, and the Dauphin his mother. Fourteen of the greatest personages in the kingdom led this impromptu ball, which ended soon after four o'clock, when the bridal party proceeded to the Palais de Justice for the evening revelries. Catherine de Medici and Marie Stuart were in the same open litter, with the Cardinals Charles of Lorraine and Charles of Bourbon on either side, and the Dauphin riding behind followed by the other lords.

At five o'clock the city fathers set out for the Palais de Justice, where they were welcomed with stately ceremony. At one end of the magnificent hall were ranged statues of all the French kings and in the centre a white marble table where the family sat down. Twelve masters of the household assisted the Duke of Guise, who was sumptuously dressed in frosted cloth of gold, adorned with jewels. Each dish was presented to the sound of music. More dancing followed the supper, and then began the entertainment which the contemporary chronicler describes as 'masques, mommeries, ballades et autres passetems'.

Out of the Golden Chamber came seven planets, for this great marriage was to be represented to the people as a pageant gazed upon by unearthly spectators. Mercury passed by, arrayed in white satin with golden girdle, spreading wings and the caduceus in his hand. Mars was clad in costly armour. Venus in floating draperies. After the planets came the childish fancy of the twelve hobbyhorses, caparisoned in gold and silver, each mounted by a young prince in golden costume. Lackeys carefully led the wicker horses, on which were seated the Prince Charles and Henry, and the children of the Dukes of Guise and Aumale. A train of coaches followed, carrying pilgrims. Lastly there entered the pageant of ships, decked with cloths of gold and crimson velvet and carrying silver sails. Slowly they advanced, dipping gently to an artificial breeze and gliding as if on the surface of deep waters. On each deck there were two seats of state, one occupied by a prince, the other waiting for his chosen one. Through the wide hall moved the ships, as if on woven wings, until they passed near the marble table, at which the ladies were sitting. The king, a bold mariner, drew the bride to her place beside him; the Dauphin took his mother, the Duke of Lorraine the Princess Claude, Antoine Navarre his own wife, and the Prince of Conde the Duchess of Guise.

Giovanni Michiel, writing to the Doge and Senate on 25 April, described the marriage festivities:

These nuptials were really considered the most regal and triumphant of any that have been witnessed in this kingdom or many years, whether from the concourse of the chief personages of the realm both temporal and spiritual thus assembled, there being present and assisting at all the solemnities the Cardinal Legate and all the other ambassadors, or from the pomp and richness of the jewels and apparel, both of the lords and the ladies; or from the grandeur of the banquet and the stately service of the table, or from the costly devices of the masquerades and similar revels.

The two youngsters must have made an unusual looking couple. Francois, the sickly Dauphin with a constantly runny nose, a boy who seemingly hadn't reached puberty and who suffered from an overall weakness of physique, alongside the very tall (for sixteenth-century standards) and beautiful Marie. They were to be known as the Queen-Dauphiness and the King-Dauphin, which gave Francois the additional title of King of Scotland by his marriage.

There is a story that in the aftermath of the festivities to celebrate the wedding, Marie nearly collapsed while wearing the extremely heavy crown on her head. It was removed and a lighter version replaced it. This became the source of stories that suggested Marie was not strong enough to govern, apparently shown by her inability to withstand the pressure of a crown. That crown, of course, denoted Scotland too, a place far, far away but on the wedding day, the cannon of Edinburgh Castle, Mons Meg, was fired with the shot almost reaching as far as Wardie Moo and the noise heard for miles around.

It may also be worth mentioning that Marie also had a seemingly rightful claim to be the heir to the crown of England too. On 17 November 1558, a few months after Marie's marriage, the Queen of England, Mary Tudor, died childless, leaving the throne to her half-sister Elizabeth.

Elizabeth I was unmarried and without children. This meant that until such time that Elizabeth was wed, and bore a child, then Marie was the next heiress by virtue of her descent from Henry VII, her great-grandfather. Even that wasn't so simple, though.

Elizabeth's father, Henry VIII, had divorced his first wife, Mary Tudor's mother Catharine of Aragon, and that divorce had never been recognised by the Catholic Church (resulting in Henry cutting all ties to the Church of Rome, and the creation of the Church of England followed). So, in the eyes of Rome and of Catholics, his daughter Elizabeth was a 'bastard' and no illegitimate man or woman was allowed to inherit the throne. This meant that, by rights, Marie should have followed Mary Tudor as Queen of England. An Act was passed in 1536 to that effect, but it was overturned in 1544. This belief that she was the rightful queen of England stayed with Marie for the rest of her life.

Notre Dame Cathedral is one of the most famous and recognisable structures in the world, but as with many other places linked to Marie, her footprint was light and brief in the context of the building's rich and varied history. It is widely considered to be one of the finest examples of French Gothic architecture and its position in the fourth arrondissement of Paris affords a spectacular view of the city from the top of its steeple that commands the area all around.

The building of the cathedral started in 1163, three years after the Bishop Maurice de Sully had the previous church there demolished on the grounds that the building wasn't suitable for its standing as the 'Parisian church of the Kings of

Europe'. This was later to be proved incorrect as researchers and archaeologists in the twentieth century unearthed foundations that suggested the original church was as big as the current cathedral so, in fact, it is folly that the Bishop decided to rebuild it under his stewardship. The Bishop de Sully died in 1196, by which time only the apse and the choir had been completed. It was bitter-sweet as he had devoted most of his time and indeed his wealth to the project. His successor, Eudes de Sully – who was, by the way, no relation – saw the completion of the transepts and the nave, and also the near-completion of the western façade before his own death in 1208. From then on there were many different architects who oversaw the continuation of the building, as can be seen by the different styles around the cathedral. The heights of the 'matching' towers are unequal, as separate architects and designers were involved in those constructions. The western towers and the north rose window were completed by 1250 and, at the same time, the transepts were re-modelled by Jean de Chelles and Pierre de Montreuil in what was then the latest Rayonnant style. It was the biggest change to that date.

By 1345, when the building was completed, Notre Dame effectively looked as it does today, towering over the city of Paris with its unique flying buttresses, something which came about more by circumstance than design, as the thin outer walls were beginning to show signs of stress under the weight of extra building.

The cathedral has, of course, been damaged during the intervening years, in 1548 when the Huguenots considered the cathedral and its contents idolatrous, and during the French Revolution in 1793 it was renamed the 'Cult of

Reason' and then the 'Cult of the Supreme Being'. During these times many of the treasures were destroyed or stolen and the original thirteenth-century spire was torn down. In an almost surreal moment, the statues of the biblical kings of Judah (located on the façade) were beheaded as they were mistaken for the previous kings of France! The dismembered heads were found in 1977 when workers were excavating the site. Also during these turbulent times, the Virgin Mary was replaced by Lady Liberty and the cathedral was used a storage warehouse for food. World War II saw more damage as many of the stained glass windows were hit by stray bullets and were replaced after the conflict. Thankfully, though, that was the extent of the damage and the building came through the invasion relatively unscathed. By 1991, the French government decided a major renovation project was required, something that was only initially planned to last a decade, but still continues to this day. The cleaning of the delicate structures has caused the major delay in its completion.

Notre Dame has witnessed many historic events, with Marie's marriage to Francois just one footnote in a lengthy existence. Some are listed below, but they merely scratch the surface of this quite wonderful building.

1239 – The Crown of Thorns is placed in the Cathedral by St Louis.

1431 – Henry VI of England is crowned King of France.

1537 – James V of Scotland is married to Madeleine of France, one year before Marie and Francois

1804 – The coronation ceremony of Napoleon I and Josephine, with Pope Pius VII officiating.

1909 – Joan of Arc is beatified.

1920 – Joan of Arc is canonised.

1944 – The liberation of France is celebrated with the Te Deum Mass.

1970 – Requiem Mass of Charles de Gaulle takes place.

1980 – Pope John Paul II celebrates Mass

1996 – The Requiem Mass of Francois Mitterand is held.

As an aside, under a law passed in 1905, the cathedral is one of seventy in France that is owned by the French State. The Catholic Church is the beneficiary and has the exclusive right to use it for religious purposes in perpetuity. The final word must go to John of Jundun, who described Notre Dame back in 1323, when it was still not fully completed:

The most glorious church of the most glorious Virgin Mary, mother of God, deservedly shines out like the sun among stars, and although some speakers, by their own free judgement (because they are only able to see a few things easily) may say that some other is more beautiful, I believe however, respectfully, that if they attend more diligently to the whole and the parts, they will quickly retract this opinion. Where indeed, I ask, would they find two towers of such magnificence and perfection, so high, so large, so strong, clothed round about with such a multiple variety of ornaments? Where I ask would they find such a multipartite arrangement of so many lateral vaults above and below? Where I ask would they find such light-filled amenities as the many surrounding chapels? Furthermore let them tell me in what church I may see such a large cross, of which one arm separates the choir from the nave? Finally, I would willingly learn where there are two such circles situated opposite each other in a straight line, which on account of their appearance are given the name of the fourth vowel (O); among which smaller orbs and circlets, with wondrous artifice, so that some arranged circularly, others angularly, surround windows ruddy with precious colours and beautiful with the most subtle figures of the pictures. In fact, I believe that this church offers the carefully discerning such cause for admiration that its inspection can scarcely sate the soul.

Visitor Information

The cathedral is easily located as it sits alongside the River Seine. The flying buttresses on the exterior are remarkable in their design, even if they did come about almost by accident. Once inside, there are so many things to see, which, unfortunately, don't necessarily include Marie. Today Notre Dame is still a working church so visitors are requested to respect it as such.

Inside the cathedral, the north rose window is a spectacular vision of Gothic Rayonnant style and a statue of Joan of Arc stands tall in the interior. The bells, of which the largest is called Emmanuel, are located in the south tower, and toll to mark the time of the day. The Archaeological Crypt was created in 1965 to protect various discoveries; you can see the under-floor heating built by the Romans. These are just a few of the many and great artefacts that can be seen. Notre Dame is a wonderful place, but inevitably very, very busy. The postcode is 75004.

Signing away her country

What took place following the wedding was of such grave importance that it haunted Marie's life thereafter and set her on a path that she couldn't be diverted from. On 4 April, at Fontainebleau, three documents were given to the fifteen-year-old girl by her courtiers, which, in naivety and out of a fierce loyalty to her new family, including King Henry, she signed without hesitation.

The first promised that the kingdom of Scotland would be given to the King of France as well as all her rights to the kingdom of England should she die childless. This was explained in the document as such:

> The King of France has always shown singular and perfect affection in protecting and defending Scotland against the English, ancient and inveterate enemies of the Queen and her predecessors, and that Henry II had shown great kindness to the Queen during her minority, having maintained and still maintaining her establishment at his own cost.

The second, following the advice of her uncles, the Cardinal of Lorraine and the Duke of Guise, she signed to proclaim that if she did not have an heir she transferred to the King of France, the kingdom of Scotland until or unless a million in gold had been paid to him. This was explained with the words

> ...but for the expenses incurred and still to be incurred, the kingdom of Scotland would have been in evident danger of total ruin, so that its preservation is entirely due to the Kings of France....

Marie was in no position to argue against the claim, even though it seems fragile, to say the least.

The third document, which was signed by Marie and Francois, refers to the Scots Commissioners suggesting that should she die without an heir, then the transfer of the kingdom should be to 'certain lords of the country, thus taking away from her, the true Queen, all right and liberty to dispose of it in any way, to her great regret and prejudice.'

These three documents, signed by a young and impressionable girl, who would no more have thought of standing up to her uncles than flying to the moon, were to create a cloud of despair that inevitably affected her reign in Scotland. They effectively gave Scotland to the house of Valois should she die without an heir, only to be redeemed at an absolutely ruinous cost. As was accurately surmised afterwards: 'The young Queen, only in her sixteenth year, probably signed these deeds without fully realising their import.'

Hôtel des Tournelles

The health of the young queen was always suspect, as indeed was that of the feeble dauphin, and in 1559 there were serious concerns for her welfare with Sir John Mason writing that 'The Queen of Scots is very sick, and we fear she will not long continue. God take her to Him so soon as may please Him.' Six days later, on 24 May, Throckmorton, who represented the English government in Paris, visited Marie in her chambers and afterwards reported similarly:

Assuredly, the Scottish Queen in mine opinion looketh very ill on it, very pale and green, and withal short-breathed, and it is whispered here among them that she cannot long live.

By June of that year, he was reporting that she had been 'evil at ease' in church and had kept from fainting by wine brought from the altar. Add to that the inherited weakness of constitution that Francois suffered from and the hopes of a fruitful reign for the two of them were slim at best.

Sadly, their health wasn't helped by the untimely death of Henry II caused by a jousting accident at the Hôtel des Tournelles on 1 July. The joust was part of the festivities to celebrate the double marriage of the king's sister Marguerite de France to the Duke of Savoy and Elisabeth de France to Philip II of Spain, plus the signing of the Treaty of Cateau-Cambrésis, which brought to an end France's and Spain's series of ruinous wars over Italy. It was also the climax to a three-day tournament held on the widest street in Paris, known as La Grande Rue Saint-Antoine.

This was part of a huge complex of numerous buildings that the court had lodged at, despite it being a very unpopular place with the royal couple. For days beforehand, pavement slabs were raised and replaced by jousting lists with spectator stands being erected for the hundreds, if not thousands, who wished to attend. King Henry was a keen participant in jousting (indeed his bravery in the battlefield was also legendary despite the constant warnings from his entourage) so it was natural he would take part in the festivities that had brought so many spectators and visitors to this area of Paris during a balmy, sunlit week in June and July. The jousting started on the Wednesday, six days after the successful marriage of Elisabeth and Philip, and on the third day (Friday) Henry was ready to compete. The previous evening, Catherine de Medici had a dream (or a vision as she later described it) in which she saw her husband wounded in the eye in the tournament. The next morning, she had begged him not to enter the competition but instead to satisfy himself by watching from the comfort of his chair. Add to this a prophesy from an Italian astrologer, Luca Gaurico, that the king must take care in his fortieth year to avoid 'all single combat in an enclosed space', and the omens were clear to all but Henry. Even the prediction from Nostradamus: 'The young boy will overcome the old, in a field of combat in a single fight. He will pierce his eye in a golden cage, two wounds in one, he then dies a cruel death' (published in 1555) seemed to suggest a tragic ending. Of course the king took no notice and, wearing the familiar black-and-white colours of his mistress Diane de Poitiers, he proceeded to joust vigorously. In the third clash with his opponent, Gabriel de Lorges, the lance violently struck the king's breastplate, which shattered the lance and a splinter entered Henry's right eye. Throckmorton later reported the incident:

> de Lorges gave such a counterbluff, as he drove a splinter right over his eye on his right side, the force of which stroke was so vehement and the paine he had withall so great, as he was too much astonished and had great ado to kepe himself on horseback.

The king was taken back to the palace, where he was initially diagnosed favourably – but even with the best efforts of Charles V's celebrated doctor, Andreas Vesulius, Henry II died of his injuries on 10 July, only once recovering consciousness. The great hall of the palace was transformed into a death chamber and Paris into a city that mourned heavily for its popular king. Marie and Francois were both inconsolable. Catherine, in a genuine state of mourning, immediately banished Diane after years of effectively living in her shadow, recovered all of her jewels and began ruling France through her weak son.

Unfortunately for us there is nothing left of the Hôtel des Tournelles, as it has now been completely demolished and only the most vivid imagination can transport you back to the grand rectangle that made up the buildings of the Tournelles, named after the numerous small towers attached to it. It was built in the early fourteenth century but at that time was just a house, inevitably called Maison des Tournelles. Over the next 200 years, successive royals either stayed there (albeit briefly in many cases) or added a more luxurious apartment to make it worthy of a royal residence. The rectangle was made up of the Rue St Antoine, Rue des Tournelles, Rue de Turenne and Rue de St Gilles, which surrounded the park of the royal estate, while the main palace was said to be capable of holding 6,000 people.

After Henry's death, Catherine de Medici saw the palace as more or less cursed and after gaining complete power, she ordered that the structure should be demolished and the brickwork sold off. This was done over a period of thirty years, and much of the original building became part of new structures she built in Paris, notably the chateaux of Madrid and the Tuileries. Catherine moved to the Louvre Palace. The Hôtel des Tournelles was never a popular place and its shadowed majesty diminished as what remained of it became an arsenal and later a horse market where hundreds of horses were sold every weekend. By 1603 Henry IV, unsure of what to do with the remaining buildings on the site, attempted to create a factory for the production of silk, gold and silver, with the help of Italian artisans, but it failed spectacularly. Eventually the Place Royale was to spring from the ashes of the much-derided hotel, which in turn became the Place des Vosges.

A visit to the site is certainly not a must for any Marie-watcher, but if you happen to find yourself in that part of the bustling modern city of Paris on the rue de St Antoine, it will take a huge amount of mental discipline to block out the sights and sounds of the 21st century to imagine the young Marie and her husband watching his beloved father die in terrible agony.

Visitor Information

There is nothing in the way of information, simply because this place no longer exists! If you do want to visit the bustling street of Paris, then the French postal code is 75004. Unfortunately, you may not find it quiet enough to be able to imagine yourself back in Marie's time, but good luck nonetheless. No matter, the rue de St Antoine was considered the most beautiful Parisian thoroughfare in the seventeenth century and the Place des Vosges is in effect the prototypical residential square of the whole of Europe.

Reims Cathedral

After Henry's death, Francois travelled to the traditional coronation city of Reims to be crowned King of France, a journey that took four days. He arrived in wet and stormy conditions on 15 September and was met by the Cardinal-Archbishop, who was accompanied by many of the clergy. By all accounts it was a sombre affair, although the citizens had certainly made efforts to recognise the importance of proceedings despite the grief over Henry's recent death. Francois rode on a white horse along gaily decorated streets. There was an artificial fountain at the cathedral square, pouring out red wine, with all manner of fruit displayed in a huge basket. His canopy was made of red velvet. Twelve trumpeters proceeded him, clad in violet velvet. Marie, who was not due to be crowned as she was already a queen in her own right, arrived the day afterwards.

The coronation itself was conducted slowly and intently with all the ladies, save Marie, wearing the colours of mourning. It had been decreed beforehand that no one should wear any goldsmith's work or embroidery, but only silk or velvet, and on the next day the mourning should resume. There was also no sermon after the event, but this was probably due to Francois's ill health. In fact, after the ceremony, which finished before 12 noon, the royal party retired to the Archbishop's palace next to the cathedral, where a grand but efficiently quick meal was served and then the new king was left to rest in his quarters.

As with the death of Henry II, Francois's coronation involved Marie playing a peripheral part in the occasion – watching from a distance – so the reason for visiting the cathedral of Reims is more for the sheer splendour of the building than to go in search of Marie's presence. The cathedral is a major tourist destination and receives up to a million visitors annually, benefiting from becoming a UNESCO World Heritage Site in 1991. It was built in 1211 after the previous church was destroyed by fire. In the following centuries, it has been modernised, repaired and extended like any other building with such a long history.

The grand, ornate building that Francois stepped into in the sixteenth century would look similar today, except for changes to the interior design. By 1875 the façade and balustrades were in such poor condition that the French National assembly agreed a sum of more than 620,000 French francs for repairs (approximately £80,000), which was a huge amount for that time. By World War I, the cathedral had been requisitioned as a hospital but that didn't stop large parts of the building being damaged by German shellfire. Once the war was over, renovation started in 1919 – financed in some parts by the Rockefeller family – and it continues to the present day. In 2011, the cathedral celebrated its 800th birthday, and celebrations took place between May and October with street parties, fireworks, performances and the inauguration of six new stained glass windows on either side of the apse.

This is not strictly a Marie building; it is a place that she visited during her duties as Francois' wife, but although the chapter on this is sparse, I would still encourage everyone to visit this wonderful cathedral. Reims itself is a great city, which has changed beyond recognition since those days, but the cathedral has remained constant. Again, another dose of imagination will help the Marie-watcher to picture her as she and her new king walked serenely by on the day of his coronation.

Visitor Information

The Cathedral Notre Dame de Reims can be found on the Rue Guillaume de Machault in the city. It is a beautiful building and it dominates the area around it. Again, as mentioned regarding Notre Dame, this cathedral is above all a place of worship so respect should be shown when visiting. The city of Reims was the traditional coronation place for all royals, so there are many reminders, including such attractions as the Palace of Tau and Saint-Remi Basilica. In one of the main squares of the city, you can see the statue of Louis XV, plus one of Joan of Arc on horseback. Reims is also one of France's main centres of champagne production and there are many guided tours, which are enjoyable. The postcode is 51100.

Amboise

In keeping with the last few places of interest, Amboise was another that had a strong link to Marie and even if she was an outsider, it was important nonetheless. The Chateau D'Amboise was one of the many grand palaces where the young queen was raised by King Henry and his wife Catherine de Medici, with their own children, but it has long been preserved in history as the place of one of the worst massacres in France's history.

The French Wars of Religion were taking place in 1560 with the House of Guise – which then virtually ruled France in the name of Francois – uncovering a plot against them by the Huguenot house of Bourbon. Their reaction was swift and brutal, with more than 1,500 Protestants rounded up and murdered in truly barbaric fashion. As it was described by a contemporary writer: 'Blood flowed in great waves through the town of Amboise, the Loire bed was covered with the corpses of those who had been flung into its waters. The streets were choked with dead bodies, and the public squares were not large enough to contain the gallows and scaffolds. More than fifteen hundred persons perished during the executions.'

The punishments were horrific and to a twenty-first century reader, almost incomprehensible in their cruelty and savagery. Many were hanged while others were locked in barns and burnt to death. In some instances, Protestants were tied in a sack and thrown into the river to drown, some were tied to the wheel and their limbs broken until they died in agony. The executions in the form of hangings took place 'after the dinner-hour', which would be early afternoon, after twelve, and they were played out as a form of entertainment. Régnier de la Planche wrote:

> The Guises did this on purpose to give some amusement to the ladies who were getting tired of being shut up so long in one place. The truth is the lords and ladies were placed at the windows of the castle, as if some mask or mummery were to be witnessed.

He adds: 'The king and his brothers appeared at these spectacles and the Cardinal pointed out the sufferers to them with signs of joy. The lordly spectators showed no signs of sympathy or pity.'

Agrippa d'Aubigné who, like de la Planche, was a first-hand witness of the scene, wrote, '…the sight of the executions amazed the king, his brothers and all the ladies of the court, who watched from the terraces and windows of the castle.'

There has never been any suggestion that Marie was complicit in any of these brutal acts; she was, after all, only 18 years of age, but it is inconceivable to think that she didn't witness the murders or see the battered bodies hanging from the iron hooks that were attached to the town walls. In a more recent history of a century ago, Principal Lindsay describes her as '…leading her boy husband and her ladies for a walk around the Castle of Amboise to see the bodies of the dozens of Protestants hung from lintels and turrets and to contemplate the fair clusters of grapes which the grey stones had produced'. Whatever the truth, this event, so shocking and so defining, must have had some effect on the mentality of a young girl and her future aspirations as queen of France, and soon to be of Scotland.

A peace treaty was signed in 1563, by which time the royal family had departed Amboise (some reports suggest it was due to the stench of the rotting corpses) and the chateau very quickly fell into decline. In the 'edict of pacification' Protestant services were allowed, yet had to take place outside the borders of towns, but it was a short-lived truce.

Amboise became a derelict building within forty years as the royal court never returned, which is hardly surprising bearing in mind the horrors that took place. By the seventeenth century it had been transformed into a prison under the Crown. The French Revolution virtually destroyed the original building that Marie had spent many days in. Although it was given 'Monument Historique' status in 1840 by the French ministry, it barely survived the ravages of World War II.

Today's visitor can only see approximately a fifth of the original building. Marie can be traced by recognising the gardens where she and Francois walked daily, before the horrors that came to define the building, but Chateau d'Amboise has become just as famous for another event. Leonardo da Vinci, who visited and worked in the castle, was buried in the church of Saint-Florentin, attached to Amboise. At the time of Napoleon, the church was in such a dreadful state that it was demolished and the stones used to repair the crumbling chateau. It was then that a skeleton was found, with fragments of stone with letters of da Vinci's name engraved on them, and under the assumption it was him, the collection of bones was carefully removed and can now be viewed in the chapel of Saint-Hubert.

The chateau, which was built above the River Loire, is worth a visit for its magnificence and its surroundings. It dominates the skyline of the town of Amboise and a modern-day visitor can still glimpse the stately progress of the royal court during Marie's formative years. Despite the horrors attached to it, this was one of the many places that she yearned for in later years as an example of regal and comfortable living, something which she was rarely to experience again.

Visitor Information
The chateau is located in the centre of the city and is one of the smaller ones that can be visited. Tours are available every day, apart from Christmas Day and New Year's Day. Most tourists comment on the splendour of the gardens, rather than the interior of the building. Again, it is not a 'must' for Marie-watchers and probably has more interest arising from the terrible atrocities that took place there as well as being the burial place of Leonardo de Vinci. The postcode is 37400.

Chambord

If 1559 had been a tragic year for Marie, the following year was to get a lot worse as both her mother and her husband died within a few months of each other. On 10 June Mary of Guise died in Edinburgh, at the age of 45, from the blood-related illness, dropsy. She had been in ill health for some time and the stress of attempting to keep the country of Scotland together despite being formally deposed as regent a year earlier – something which she and her courtiers ignored completely – and the Lords of the Congregation entering the city of Edinburgh triumphantly pulling down friaries and abbeys that did not observe the Reformation, sadly became too much for her. The regent was isolated, and misfortune followed her every step of the way. Her youngest brother, René, Marquis d'Elbeuf, set sail from France to rescue her but was driven back by storms and, as the Protestant uprising closed in, she retired to her chambers and peacefully passed away. She was regarded later in history as a great leader of the warring Scottish nation as this passage from the book *A History of Scotland*, published in the nineteenth century by Professor Hume Brown confirms:

> Alike by her own character and gifts, and by the momentous policy of which she was the agent, Mary of Lorraine is one of the most remarkable figures in Scottish history. It was her misfortune – a misfortune due to her birth and connections – that she found herself from the first in direct antagonism to the natural development of the country of her adoption, and that the circumstances of which she ruled were such as to bring into prominence the least worthy traits of the proud race of which she sprang. Yet in personal appearance as in courage and magnificence, she was the true sister of Francis of Guise and the Cardinal of Lorraine, the Pope and King of France.

Marie wasn't informed of her mother's death until 28 June, despite the royal entourage being aware of it ten days earlier. Giovanni Michiel wrote on 30 June:

> The death of the Queen Regent of Scotland, her mother, was concealed from the most Christian Queen until the day before yesterday, when it was at length told her by the Cardinal of Lorraine, for which her Majesty showed, and still shows such signs of grief, that during the greater part of yesterday she passed from one agony to another.

Marie truly was grief-stricken and lay in her chambers in Chambord for many days apparently unable to move, so that physicians were seriously concerned for her welfare.

For a young girl who had been separated from her beloved mother for so long, to hear of her death weeks after the event must have been painful to bear. Although the funeral sermon for Mary of Guise took place at Notre Dame in Paris on 12 August, the remains of her body were not sent to France until the following year, by which time Marie had returned to Scotland as ruler.

At the time of Marie, Chambord was a huge chateau at the centre of a large and well-stocked park. It was regarded as one of the most beautiful buildings north of the Alps. Alfred de Vigny wrote:

Far from any road, you suddenly come upon a royal or rather a magical chateau... from some country of the sun to conceal it in mistier lands. The palace is hidden away like buried treasure but its blue domes and elegant minarets rounded where they stand might suggest you were in the realms of Baghdad or Kashmir.

It had over 400 rooms with enormous towers and staircases, yet it was a cold place, miles from any nearby town. This meant furniture and provisions had to be physically taken to the castle by servants and courtiers on an almost daily basis. It was impractical at best and during Marie's time there, it was still undergoing final construction. Building first began in 1519; Chambord was originally built as a hunting lodge for Francis I, who kept residences at both Blois and Amboise.

There is some uncertainty as to who originally designed the structure, but Leonardo da Vinci is strongly linked to it without any firm evidence to prove he was involved. It took twenty-eight years for the chateau to be completed, by which time it had changed its appearance many times. Its Renaissance style saw the huge building composed of a central keep with four enormous towers at each corner. There are also two more large towers at the front wall. The interior consisted of 440 rooms and eighty-four staircases, the most impressive being the central double spiral open staircases that reaches the third floor, again attributed to da Vinci.

One of the unusual visible features of the chateau is the roof, which can be compared to a city skyline with its many different turrets and towers. The story is that Francis I wanted the roofscape to resemble the city of Constantinople.

The building has 800 sculpted columns and a fabulously decorated ceiling, with the whole construction surrounded by a 13,000-acre park and woodland incorporating a game reserve, enclosed by a huge wall that stretches for 20 miles. The king originally wanted to divert the River Loire to surround the chateau, but that grandiose scheme fortunately never came to fruition. Despite building the chateau, Francis I hardly spent any time there and it was a sad coincidence that he died of a heart attack in the year that the great building was finally completed. Despite the impressive nature of the construction, it was never a popular place with successive royals, including of course Henry II, but Marie does seem to have spent many carefree days there.

Following the death of Francis I, the chateau was barely used for the next eighty years or so and was virtually abandoned by the end of the sixteenth century, but in 1639 it was given by Louis XIII to his brother Gaston d'Orléans, and he carried out renovations. Later, a huge stable was added by Louis XIV so that it could again be used as a hunting lodge, but even then it was virtually unused for another century excepting a brief few years when the former King of Poland (Stanislas I) lived there.

The major change came during the French Revolution when in 1792 the government ordered that all the furnishings be sold off and the wooden wall panels and flooring were also removed and sold. The chateau was now a bare shell and despite it changing hands many times (Napoleon Bonaparte gave it to Louis-Alexandre Berthier, whose widow in turn handed it over to Henri Charles Dieudonné d'Artois, who then gave it to his grandfather Charles X) it was a sad and forlorn place, even becoming a field hospital in the Franco-Prussian War in the nineteenth century.

The twentieth century wasn't any kinder to the magnificent building, with all types of restoration ceasing at the onset of World War I. In fact, it was confiscated as enemy property in 1915 and only after a lengthy court case, lasting some seventeen years, did it return to French hands in the shape of the family of the Duke of Parma. After World War II, the French government made the decision to fully restore the building and, in 1981, it officially became a UNESCO World Heritage Site, saving it from any further neglect.

Today the chateau is in good condition and is a huge draw for tourists from all over the world, enticed by its chocolate-box appearance. Its history was varied and it was not necessarily as an important a place in French history as one might imagine. The surrounding areas were damaged quite badly in June 2016 after heavy flooding, meaning yet more money would be needed for repairs. It is nonetheless worth a visit.

Visitor Information

The chateau is one of the largest in the Loire Valley, and its structure makes it instantly recognisable around the world. It is open to the public, but gets very busy, so it is worth booking in advance. The gardens are huge and it could take a whole day just to explore them on their own. Inside there may not be much that is historically of interest, but the architecture is incredible. Although there is little in the way of Marie Stuart connections, it was a place she did stay at. The French postal code is 41250.

Hôtel Groslot D'Orléans

Francois's health was always fragile. Astrologers had predicted that the sickly child wouldn't live beyond his eighteenth year, and they had good reason to feel confident that they wouldn't be proved wrong as numerous illnesses blighted him from his infant years. The marriage of Marie and Francois was almost certainly not consummated, not just due to his weakness of body, but also due to the fact that neither of them was sufficiently mature enough, either physically or mentally. There was also a suggestion that Francois wasn't 'fully formed' and that one of his testicles hadn't dropped, but that didn't stop Marie once convincing herself that she had become pregnant and she went into the routine of retiring to bed in preparation, before realising that it was a false alarm. Theirs was a political dynastic marriage between two childhood friends who genuinely cared for each other, but at no time did there appear to be a physical union between the two. Sadly, what union there was ended in the traumatic year of 1560 with Francois's death at the age of just seventeen.

With the bitter, violent and bloody battle between the House of Guise and the Huguenots still raging, with persecutions continuing, and with Francois and Marie refusing to ratify the Treaty of Edinburgh following Mary of Guise's death, it was a tense royal procession that made its way to Orléans in October. The streets, belying the unsure nature of the times, were decorated in a gay manner with flags and banners made up of the king's and queen's colours. Francois made his entry into the city on 18 October, greeted and escorted by 400 archers of the guard, 200 gentlemen of the household and musketeers of the new guard. A triumphal arch had been erected at the city's entrance with the words 'Vive Le Roy' hung above the arch. A few hours later, Marie, riding a white horse and accompanied by the princesses and duchesses of the court, also entered the city. Her arrival was predictably written about in glowing terms. Orléans historian Francois Le Maire later wrote:

If the silvery moon had appeared shining in the midst of her stars, her lustre would have been dimmed beside such rare perfections and such dazzling loveliness.

The royal couple were accommodated at the Hôtel Groslot in the centre of the city, a sumptuous, huge mansion that dominated its surroundings. In time they were joined by numerous guests, including Renée of Ferrara, the mother of the Duchess of Guise.

Unfortunately, Francois's health started to give cause for concern and by the third week of November, there was enough alarm surrounding the king for physicians to order him not to go hunting in Chambord, but remain in his chambers. The cause of the initial illness seemed to be a chill that soon turned into a fever and shivering fit. Francois had long been plagued by a catarrhal flux that manifested itself with discharge from his right ear, which in turn caused severe pain in his jaw and teeth. A swelling occurred behind the ear with a bump the size of a nut and his doctors advised that the change of weather in Orléans had brought the illness about and he should rest until the climate improved. To our modern-day understanding this seems woefully inadequate, but in the sixteenth century there was a genuine belief that maladies would cure themselves no matter how severe. At the time, there were many people who feared that the king suffered from leprosy, mainly due to the hue of his skin, purple with patchy red marks. In addition, his rotten breath gave away the fact that his body was failing him.

By the end of the month it was feared among his courtiers that Francois would not survive. Marie kept vigil at his bedside constantly administering soothing flannels to his fevered face but was helpless as her dear childhood sweetheart drifted in and out of consciousness. The foul-smelling pus that oozed from his infected ear irritated his skin and his fever rose unabated. On 28 November Throckmorton reported:

> The constitution of his body is such as the physicians do say that he cannot be long-lived, and thereunto he hath by his too timely and inordinate exercise now in his youth added an evil accident. Some say that if he recover this sickness he cannot live two years. Therefore there is talk of the French Queen's second marriage. Some say the Prince of Spain, some the Duke of Austria, others the Earl of Arran.

Marie wasn't thinking of such things and her fears were realised when, at around ten o'clock on the evening of 5 December, Francois passed away. His death was expected and it had been suggested that the king had promised to all those who would listen that if life was given to him, he would continue the persecution of the heretics as had been done since the summer. Calvin wrote to Sturm in a characteristic way:

> Did you ever read or hear anything more timely than the death of the little king? There was no remedy for the worst evils when God suddenly revealed Himself from heaven, and He who had pierced his father's eye struck the ear of the son.

Marie had lost her adopted father, her mother and now her husband in the space of just eighteen months, almost too much for anyone to bear, never mind for someone of such a tender age. The next day, stricken with grief, she was shocked to hear that Francois's mother, Catherine de Medici, had immediately demanded the return of the crown jewels and had left Marie to mourn wearing the traditional white, in a black velvet room. It was clear that Marie was now no longer required at French court as she was no longer queen – that honour was now held by Catherine, who intended to rule France.

Marie was also the subject of marriage advances on behalf of Don Carlos of Spain in an attempt to unite the two countries, immediately after her husband's death. Fortunately for her, Don Carlos, a small and frail epileptic who had been brain damaged after a fall down the stairs and who had an obsession with cruelty to animals and people, wasn't encouraged by his family or by Catherine. The new French queen very quickly wanted to get rid of Marie, but any marital union with the Spanish prince would be with one of her own daughters.

In the immediate aftermath of her husband's death, it seems unlikely that Marie was thinking of her long-term future, but she had signed a contract to say she had a right to choose to stay in France in one of the many properties that belonged to her through marriage, or she could return to Scotland. That would be a decision for after the funeral.

The Hôtel Groslot was constructed in 1549 by the architect Jacques Androuet du Cerceau and has been designated as a Historical Monument (Monument Historique) since 1862. It is situated in the centre of Orléans, near the cathedral of Sainte-Croix. It takes its name from Jacques Groslot, who commissioned the building. The construction took many years to complete and only with the help of his two sons, Jerome and Henri, was it finished by 1560. For all of that time the Groslot family lived in the heart of the hotel and of course it was in this completed state that the building housed the ailing Francois and Marie. It should also be pointed out that Jacques Groslot was totally against the king and queen staying there, as he was a Reformed Protestant and had no taste for Catholicism – despite the orders of the Royal Court.

The hotel is a brash, extravagant building that catches the eye today just as it must have done in the sixteenth century. Of red brick, it has a central battlement with two Renaissance-style staircases and a statue of Joan of Arc in the main square. The building basically consists of four large rooms: *le salon d'honneur, l'ancienne salle du conseil municipal, l'ancien bureau du maire* and *la salle des marriages*. All rooms are decorated in a gothic troubadour style, but this was done between the years of 1850 and 1854, so there are no reminders of Marie and Francois, despite the history attached to their tragic visit. Instead there are numerous artefacts relating to Joan of Arc throughout the building.

There is, however, a painting depicting the death of Francois by French painter Pierre Dupuis. This is usually seen in the main room but has been known to be moved elsewhere so if you are visiting, it would be advisable to ask about it if you don't see it immediately. The gardens, which can be accessed from the Rue d'Escures, have a wall that is also classed as a Historical Monument (since 1846) as it was once part of the Saint-Jacques Chapel.

Visitor Information

This building is now a very popular place for weddings and banquets. Next to the cathedral, the hotel has free entrance and allows tourists to look around the rooms and gardens. Many of the rooms are decorated in traditional Renaissance style and the owners appear to be happy to answer any questions concerning its history. This was where Marie's beloved Francois died, so there may be a heavy pall hanging in the air if you're a Marie-watcher and you can imagine the pain and heartbreak that was felt when that happened. The French postal code is 45000.

3

QUEEN OF SCOTLAND
1561–1567

After Francois's death, Mary (we will now revert to the non-French version of her name as she was about to leave the country) collapsed with such grief that the English ambassador wrote to Queen Elizabeth in January 1561 that after the French king's death, Mary had been left 'as heavy and dolorous a wife as of right she had good cause to be, who, by long watching with him during his sickness, and painful diligence about him, had worn herself out and made herself ill'. Mary then observed the accepted forty days of mourning, dressed in white (which was traditional in France), only seeing esteemed guests who had the rank and authority to visit a queen in mourning. Of course, her future was a matter of some speculation. As well as being regarded as suitable marriage material for almost every high-born single male throughout Europe, there were also political machinations at work, which she had to accept. In fact, it was during this time that she was visited in an official capacity by her future husband, Henry Stuart, Lord

Darnley. He was only fifteen years of age at that stage and had been sent by his ambitious mother Margaret, Countess of Lennox, as a possible marriage suitor in an attempt to strengthen her family's ties to the English crown. There are no records as to how he was received by Mary, but it is unlikely that their future romance blossomed under such trying circumstances.

After attending the memorial service for Francois at Orléans on 18 January (his heart was later removed and enclosed in a leaden vase to be taken to the cathedral at Saint-Denis as tradition dictated), Mary then seemed to make up her mind to return to Scotland. It was a brave decision because her birth country would have been virtually unknown to her as her memories had faded away, and the now-Protestant Scotland had no real knowledge of Mary Stuart, so there was no certainty that she would be taken to people's hearts. She had decided, at the age of eighteen, to return to the country of her birth and to rule it as her mother had done. It was an unexpected decision and one that moved her life completely towards intrigue, drama and tragedy. Instead, she could have had a cosseted and luxurious existence in the French court, to which she still had a claim – despite the aggression now emanating from Catherine de Medici.

After a three-month tour of her French relations, taking in Reims, Nancy, and Blois, she said farewell to her adopted country for the first and last time. On a misty August day, she set sail from Calais in an emotional state. This hadn't been helped by the scene of a fishing boat capsizing in the harbour before her eyes; she saw all on board drown.

Nevertheless her 600-mile journey had begun. There had been no guarantee of a safe passage from the English queen, who was frustrated that Mary had still not signed the Treaty of Edinburgh – the treaty would have effectively seen Scotland as Protestant and French soldiers retreating back to France. There was no passport either, but the two galleys set sail. The English Ambassador wrote these words to his queen: 'The bravado of the gesture must be applauded. Even if his watchful eyes had been able to spy into the great white galley and discern the tragic weeping figure on its poop, he might scarcely have recognised this tormented being for his modest self-controlled young queen.' Mary, Queen of Scots was standing at the stern, looking at the receding land, crying out '*Adieu France, adieu France. Adieu donc, ma chere France... Je pense ne vous revoir jamais plus.*'

Leith

Thirteen years after leaving the country of her birth, Mary returned on a foggy August morning. The journey had been uneventful and had taken only five days, far quicker than planned, and the expected interference from the English had not taken place either. Queen Elizabeth had eventually granted them safe passage, but Mary had already left France by the time the letter had arrived. The galleys, one in brilliant white and the other red with the blue arms of France flying from the stern, were shadowed by numerous English ships but, apart from a salute, there was little in the way of contact. Mary arrived early in the morning, too early, in fact, for an official welcome. On 19 August 1561, at around 9 a.m., she stepped back onto

Scottish soil, to be met by virtually no one. The day was unpleasant and grey and we can only imagine what was going through the young woman's mind as she surveyed her new kingdom and compared it unfavourably with the glorious French court that she had left behind. This was a barren and apparently savage country, completely at odds with everything that France stood for. As there was little in the way of welcome and Holyrood Palace was not yet ready, she dined at the house of provost Andrew Lamb before being taken to Edinburgh, a few miles further on. Her horses had been impounded and the sorry-looking nags that were eventually provided were not exactly what the queen was expecting, but as she made her progress, she must have been heartened to see that many peasants had left their homes to gawp at their new ruler. It was probably owing to curiosity more than adoration but, as she was able to speak to them in her native Scots (something she never forgot despite being brought up in the French language), she became more and more comfortable with the people and her surroundings. They, in turn, must have felt comforted in the knowledge that they had a ruling monarch again, after a haitus following the death of her mother. It was ironic that Leith was the port that, just one year previously, had seen Mary of Guise defeated by the Protestant Scots and English forces and then lose the struggle against the Reformation.

While following Mary's trail, Leith is certainly worth a visit. It is a bustling port that lies on the coast at the Firth of Forth. Although it is a few miles north of Edinburgh, it lies within the council area of the City of Edinburgh.

There were religious foundations there from the twelfth century, as it was mentioned in the royal charter that authorised the construction of Holyrood Abbey. About two centuries later, the port became an important trading post for Scotland following the destruction of Berwick. Trade with Norway and the Low Countries and, of course France, were commonplace, but as Leith was not a royal burgh at that time, no profits could be taken, and instead the city of Edinburgh took advantage. It wasn't until 1920 that Leith was merged with the royal burgh of the capital city (even though the local populace voted four-to-one against the move).

At the start of the sixteenth century, James IV was building up his Scottish navy, but Leith's waters were too shallow, so nearby Newhaven was where a shipbuilding yard was situated. However, nearly all the workers there, and the sailors for the ships too, were from Leith. They were renowned for their battle-hardened temperament, viciousness and, in some cases, their piracy too.

Leith was also the place where two previous queens (part of the ancestry of Mary Stuart) had taken their first steps on Scottish soil. In the fifteenth century, Mary of Guelders arrived from the Low Countries to marry James II and then, twenty years later, in 1468, her daughter-in-law, Princess Margaret of Denmark, arrived to marry James III. Margaret brought with her the dowry of the Orkney and Shetland Isles, which are still part of Scotland today. Both these queens had set foot on Scottish soil at a place called King's Wark, but that, like the rest of Leith (and indeed most of the surrounding areas of Edinburgh) was badly damaged by the destruction of Henry VIII's 'rough wooing' for the hand in marriage of the infant Mary, Queen of Scots. The English soldiers who had docked in 1544 had been given the instruction to 'sack Leith, and burn and subvert it, and all the rest, putting man, woman and child to fire and sword without exception, when any resistance shall be made against you'. This they did with ruthlessness, leaving the town in ruins. Three years later – after the death of Henry VIII – they returned and the famous battle of Pinkie Cleugh took place, when 36,000 armed Scots were massacred by the English forces. Once again, the rebuilt Leith was the focus of English rage and was sacked and burnt to the ground. In 1560 Mary of Guise had moved the Scottish court to Leith. It was established on a site that is now Parliament Street, with her palace on Rotten Row now renamed Water Street. Her sculptured coat of arms can be seen in the South Leith Parish Church, and artefacts from the palace are on display in the National Museum of Scotland. With the town under attack again, Mary of Guise commissioned the building of a great wall to surround it, in an attempt to resist the English. This worked insomuch as no gunfire could reach the people of Leith and the large stone-built forts also resisted an invasion, but the English then came up with the rather ingenious idea of building two earth mounds – known as 'Giant's Brae' and 'Lady Fyfe's Brae' – built at the south of Leith and adjacent to the present Pilrig House respectively. This was done so that they could effectively fire down from above. However, they weren't as successful as they desired because the position of the mounds was too far away to cause any major damage. These two mounds, which are still visible, are now listed as scheduled monuments. As the attack was unsuccessful, it was followed by a further attempt on 7 May when English forces tried to breach the walls of Leith with ladders that were too short, causing the deaths of around 1,000 English soldiers, something which was enthusiastically celebrated by the Scots. Eventually the hostilities ceased and on 6 July the governments of France and England signed the now-famous Treaty of Leith (also known as the Treaty of Edinburgh) which demanded a withdrawal of French and English troops from Scotland. Sadly, by then, Mary of Guise had died from dropsy, broken in spirit and body.

Leith continued to play a big part in the violent history of Scotland and after Mary Stuart fled the country in 1567, the ensuing civil war saw troops loyal to her son, James VI, fighting his mother's supporters in Edinburgh Castle. This became known as the 'Wars between Leith and Edinburgh', fought between 1571 and 1573. Eventually James won. Over a century later, Leith was the centre of another battleground when the Army of the Covenant built an earthen rampart around the town and the northern approach to the capital city, to defend it against Oliver Cromwell's forces. This rampart became what is now one of the longest streets in Edinburgh – Leith Walk. Following that, a fort called Leith Citadel was erected in 1656 with the aim of regulating the port traffic, but that was destroyed and only the main entrance survives, which can be seen in Dock Street. A curious episode in Leith's long and fascinating history took place during America's War of Independence. Scotsman John Paul Jones (then living in

America and credited with founding the US Navy with John Barry) sailed to Leith in an attempt to capture the town and hold it to ransom, and also to disrupt any British commerce from the port. His plan failed spectacularly when his ships were stranded on the Firth of Forth in September of 1779, with severe gales lashing his squadron of seven ships. However, this event concerned the citizens of Leith enough that they erected a quickly built armoury, called Leith Fort. In later years it was used for National Service training, and was active until 1955 when it was demolished for council flats. The gatehouses and part of the outer wall are still visible on the site. The council flats were also demolished in recent years.

The port of Leith officially became the docks of Edinburgh and in 1806 the first new wet dock was opened with many local and national dignitaries taking part in a lavish procession. Eleven years later the second wet dock was opened and for many years Leith was again an important trading post and effectively the gateway to Scotland from the sea. Unfortunately, the area rapidly declined and by the 1950s it was a shadow of its former self, with trade disappearing and a reputation for seediness and criminality replacing it. There has, however, been a time of renovation and regeneration and, like many old towns, Leith has found a new lease of life with cruise liners crossing the same waters to dock on the shore and a feeling of vibrancy with new pubs, cafés and restaurants dotted around the shoreline.

There have been many industries associated with Leith such as whisky and wine production, glass-making, soap and lead factories, but two are worth noting for their 'quirkiness'. The first is the production of lime juice, starting in 1868. This was made by Lachlan Rose on Commercial Street and was initially meant to supply Vitamin C to help fight the sailors' worst fear, scurvy. This is where the phrase 'Limeys' comes from when Americans, in particular, refer to the British thus as a term of affection, or perhaps otherwise. The second is that Leith was well-known for the now unacceptable (to most nations) industry of whaling. The Christian Salvesen company was heavily involved in whaling in the Arctic and the Antarctic, with stations based in South Georgia and the Falkland Islands (where the base is called Leith Harbour). It was a successful venture for many years, especially in the Icelandic waters, but faded away as whaling became less profitable and then unacceptable in recent years. The company actually left Leith and Edinburgh in the 1990s.

Visitor Information
A visit to Leith can be thoroughly enjoyable, especially as the Ocean Terminal is the permanent mooring of the Royal Yacht *Britannia*. This is now a five-star visitor attraction. As well as trying to follow Mary's trail, and visiting the many historical sites still dotted around the town, you could even follow the trail of the characters in the film *Trainspotting* and its sequel. The two movies tell the story of a group of Leith heroin addicts (quite brilliantly); the films became international hits. Leith is also the home of Hibernian Football Club, whose fans are known as 'The Hibees', pronounced Hybees, and, remarkably, the official rules of golf were first devised in Leith in 1744, later to

be implemented by the Royal and Ancient Golf Club of St Andrews. The postcode for the Leith district is EH6 and the town can be found to the north of Edinburgh.

The Palace Of Holyroodhouse

After Mary made her way along the short distance to Edinburgh, she had an official royal entry to the city a few days later. Townsmen dressed up in elaborate costumes of yellow and black, a stage was set up at the Tollbooth with four virgins representing virtue. Wine flowed from the fountains at the cross. The celebration had a strongly Protestant tone, though, with a child descending from a model of a wooden gateway, as if floating from a cloud, to demand that Mary accept the Bible and Psalter, and with another child then asking the queen to abandon Mass. The new Protestant religion had covered the country almost completely and Mary's Catholicism was something that was no longer acceptable. She would have been looking at a Scotland almost completely unknown to modern eyes. I'm indebted to Antonia Fraser's wonderful biography for the topography of the country in the sixteenth century.

Scotland was a country almost devoid of trees, with the huge forests of centuries before all but disappeared, apart from in the Highlands. There were large forests near the lochs of Ness and Maree, but elsewhere what had once been forest was now copse. Legislation at the time demanded the planting of trees to make the land more fertile. It was also extremely cold, far colder than we would experience today. This was mainly due to a 'Little Ice Age' that took place between 1550 and 1700, making the prospects of happiness for Mary even more bleak, the summers were known for their wetness and being mild, rather than warm. It looked different too. In the sixteenth century, lochs criss-crossed the countryside, making it extremely difficult to traverse and any journey, no matter how short, was treacherous in the extreme. A lot of these lochs have now disappeared with the progress of industrialisation down the years.

The Scotland that Mary returned to couldn't compare to the France she had left – in climate, scenery, culture or splendour. It was also a lot smaller in terms of population. Whereas France had around fifteen million citizens, Scotland played host to only around 600,000, and many of them were separated from each other, serving lairds or kinsmen. The battles in the country, of which there were many, nearly all resulted from powerful families fighting over land or property, and any suggestion of their being 'Scots' to the peasants working the land would have meant very little – they pledged allegiance to their nobles, and not to the country.

Mary must surely have wondered what she had let herself in for, once she had installed herself in the royal apartments in the north-west corner of Holyrood Palace – even more so when her first night's rest was disturbed by around 600 amateur musicians gathered outside her window to serenade her. Unfortunately, their playing of the fiddle and rebec (not bagpipes as has been regularly reported) was so poor that it was painful to listen to. At least she had the good grace to appreciate the gesture and suggest they return the next evening too.

The apartments she inhabited were splendid for those days. She had a private chapel and the ante-room was decorated in spectacular fashion, despite her rooms being strictly guarded, with iron railings on all the windows. Her apartments occupied the second floor and consisted of two main rooms and two much smaller ones. They were entered from the stair tower in the north-east corner. In the outer chamber, Mary received ambassadors, and held state and formal banquets. The inner chamber held her bed, which was a four-poster with curtains that were closed at night. This inner chamber was also the room that she used as her private living area, and it was here where she would have been alone with with Darnley at the beginning of their relationship. There were also two small rooms that led off from the inner chamber, one where she dined with friends – later to be the scene of the murder of her secretary – and the other had a water closet. All the rooms were decorated by Mary, as tapestries and hangings from previous regents had been badly damaged, and Mary brought numerous upholsterers and embroiderers with her from France to redecorate the apartments. Immediately beneath her rooms were the apartments for the king, which Darnley used and later, to a lesser extent, Bothwell too. It wasn't what she'd been used to in France, but it wasn't uncomfortable.

Holyrood Palace is a place that is more identified with Mary, Queen of Scots than anywhere else, so, for that reason, this chapter on it is longer than others. We will look at the palace's history presently, but as so many events in Mary's life took place at Holyrood, it will make for easier reading if we break them down into segments, as chronologically as possible, while also dealing with some of people who had the most influence on her life, starting with John Knox.

John Knox – Protestant evangelist

John Knox was Mary's nemesis – the person who followed her every move and more often than not, heaped scorn and ridicule on her. Born in Gifford in 1514, he had trained for the priesthood at St Andrew's University, after being influenced by the Protestant preacher George Wishart. Knox had witnessed Wishart being burned at the stake by Cardinal Beaton. In his desire for revenge, Knox joined a party that besieged Edinburgh Castle and captured Beaton, who was then himself murdered. In 1547 the castle was taken by French and English soldiers, and Knox was captured and made to work as a galley slave on a French ship. Eventually, he was released and returned to England. There he became a ferocious preacher, but had to flee back to Scotland once the Catholic Mary Tudor succeeded to the throne. After a brief spell in Geneva, where he fell under the spell of Calvin, Knox's brand of Protestantism became even more fiery and he sailed back to Scotland to take on his mission with zeal. He was now the victor of the Scottish Reformation, a firebrand preacher who from the pulpit promised hell and damnation to anyone who didn't follow the true religion. In 1558 he had written the book, *First Blast of the Trumpet against the Monstrous Regiment of Women,* aimed at Mary Tudor, but of course it also applied to Elizabeth I, Mary of Guise and Mary Stuart. In it he had declared that to make any woman, seeing that women were in his view 'weak, frail, impatient, feeble and foolish creatures', into a leader was a 'subversion of the good order, of all equality and justice'. This was the man that Mary called for his first interview to Holyrood on 4 September.

Knox had railed against the arrival of the Catholic queen, speaking publicly against her presence and her religion. In the presence of Mary's half-brother Lord James (who had effectively ruled Scotland with Knox in the time between Mary of Guise's death and the arrival of Mary Stuart), the two faced each other in Mary's ante-room. It was a predictably heated meeting at which neither of them would back down. At one point, in sheer frustration, Mary burst into tears. As a queen, she was unused to being spoken to in the harsh tones used by Knox. Although he acknowledged that she couldn't do anything about her sex, and that the country would not necessarily be brought to disaster due to her gender, he believed that: 'Conscience requireth knowledge, and I fear right knowledge you have none.'

Knox was actually secretly impressed with both Mary's beauty – she was 'pleasing' – and her intelligence, despite his damning statement. He was later to tell friends: 'If there not be in her a proud mind, a crafty wit and an indurate heart against God and his truth, my judgement faileth me' and that he had 'spied such craft as he had not found in such an age.' It would be easy to believe that Knox, the firebrand and preacher, hated women but, in fact, that wasn't the case. He had numerous mistresses and later in life fathered a child by a much younger woman. He just hated Catholicism and queens! He also lived in one of the sumptuous houses on the Royal Mile (as it is now known) with a bay window jutting into the street so that he could observe all. He was given an annual salary of 400 Scots pounds and lived a charmed and protected life. This was one of several meetings Knox and Mary had, but none brought about any kind of accord between them. He continued to harangue Mary and her religion for all the time she was queen, and he lived long enough to see her downfall and imprisonment. At another meeting, Mary ranted and raved at his disrespect towards her when she was thinking about her future betrothal and a possible marriage to Don Carlos of Spain. Knox had thundered from the pulpit in Edinburgh with his usual viciousness. Then he had to listen as Mary lectured him,

...had she not borne with him more patiently than any other ruler, in all rigorous manner of speaking both against myself and my uncles. Yea, I have sought your favours by all possible means. I offered unto you presence and audience whensoever it pleased you to admonish me, and yet I cannot be quit of you.

Knox died in 1572 just a few days after delivering his last sermon, almost inaudible due to his faltering and weak voice. His body was frail but his spirit was as strong as ever. He was buried in St Giles churchyard, but there is now no trace of it as it has been covered by numerous buildings down the years – an obscure end to a fierce man.

Lord Darnley – Mary's Second Husband
Of all the people that Mary came into contact with throughout her life, Henry Darnley was the one who had

the biggest impact and who changed her life in ways that could not have been previously predicted. In our own lives, most of us develop romantic feelings for a person who is ill-suited to us but thankfully few of us are affected in such a way that it becomes life-threatening. There cannot have been many decisions taken that were more catastrophically wrong than Mary's. She fell in love with him (admittedly this isn't a decision but she could have fought against the attraction), then she decided to marry the arrogant and vain young man.

Mary's marriage plans were foremost in her mind and indeed her courtiers' in 1565. For at least two years she had been linked with many prospective spouses at a time when marriage for a queen was a political necessity as opposed being based on desire or love. Many suitors had staked their claims. Her leaning was initially towards the son of the King of Spain, Don Carlos, no matter how unsuitable he was as a potential husband. He was an epileptic who weighed around five stone and was physically stunted. He had a seriously cruel streak after brain damage following a fall down the stairs, and was soon to be declared insane. Yet he was a potentially perfect match as the marriage would bring the might of Spain to align with the lesser power of Scotland. Eventually Phillip II of Spain changed his mind, though, after hesitating and blocking negotiations for months, so other suitors were sought. There was a suggestion that Robert Dudley – the favourite of Queen Elizabeth – would be the obvious match, something that, rather oddly, seemed to have been supported by Elizabeth herself, but this suggestion came to nothing.

Eventually, with the cunning ambition of his mother Margaret, the eighteen-year-old Darnley presented himself at the Scottish court. He made an attractive option. Despite his rather feminine looks, 'beardless and baby-faced' is the way Melville described him, he was tall (around 6 feet 2 inches, which made him perfect for the unusually tall Mary – 'yon long lad' as described by Elizabeth I) and pleasing to the eye. He was schooled in the arts, played the flute admirably and danced well. He had been educated in exemplary fashion and was quite clearly the apple of his mother's eye – and therein lay the problem, he was a spoilt young man. Darnley originally arrived at Holyrood, but Mary was hunting in Fife, so he immediately headed to the house of the Laird of the Wemyss where, on 17 February, he met the queen for the second time. From contemporary reports, it seems that Mary wasn't particularly physically attracted to him. Then in April he fell ill with measles and was confined to his bed at Stirling Castle for weeks. Her ministrations to him on a daily basis in the small confines of the bedroom (although there is no suggestion of any intimate relationship at this time) turned her natural caring into a complete infatuation that totally overwhelmed her and threatened the very fabric of court life. From soothing his brow and changing his bed linen, serving him hot and cold meals and nursing him – proving that Mary was a genuinely caring person and became radiant when she could help anyone who was suffering – she fell hopelessly in love with Darnley, and couldn't seem to function without his presence. It was a new feeling for her as there could have been nothing remotely similar in her union with

Francois, so this was an exciting and devil-may-care time. Sadly, she had fallen in love with just about the most unsuitable man on earth and it would only be a matter of time before she realised it. In the meantime, his boorish behaviour towards all around him – this included constant physical attacks against courtiers and advisors who were in no position to retaliate – were ignored and overlooked by a doting Mary. His behaviour, born of enjoying a position of wealth and high standing and nurtured by an overindulgent mother, was so bad that Randolph had written of him and his unpopularity with friends: 'I know not, but it is greatly to be feared that he can have no long life among these people'. The other problem was that he had virtually no interest in matters of the mind, despite his intelligence, and preferred to pursue whatever gave him pleasure. No matter, Mary loved him and against the wishes of all (including her four Maries, who were still in attendance and equally disliked Darnley), she married him at Holyrood Chapel at 5am on 29 July.

The festivities were grand, although not apparently as lavish as the ones in Paris after her marriage to Francois. Mary wore all black to signify that she was still in mourning for her deceased first husband – although the usual mourning colour for royalty in France was white – and then allowed everyone around her to take one pin out of her garments to show she was gradually leaving that state for a happier future. After the wedding, Darnley left her in the chapel to hear Mass because, although he professed to be of the Catholic religion, he had followed the Protestant faith in England. He then awaited her in the bed chamber. He was now King of Scotland, a title he neither deserved nor lived up to in future years.

There is an interesting issue regarding the wedding that has been virtually lost in the maelstrom of intrigue and deceit that followed Mary's union with Darnley. As he was her cousin, she needed a dispensation from the pope in Rome for the wedding to be sanctioned, and she naturally assumed permission would be granted. Yet records later showed that, in fact, the pope hadn't agreed until between the dates of 1 and 25 September, almost two months after the wedding. This means the marriage was technically invalid. If only the more practical part of Mary's mind could have grasped this fact, or if she'd had more astute advice, then a lot of the future suffering would have been avoided and the story of Mary, Queen of Scots may have been a happier one.

Mary's love for Darnley lasted for as long as it took for her infatuation to die. Whether it was a sudden realisation that the person she'd married was not the person she wanted, or whether it was due to Darnley's almost unforgiveable behaviour, by the time the summer ended, her feelings towards him had completely changed. However, by then she was pregnant. Darnley had become almost unbearable at court. He sulked constantly after Mary had refused to give him the crown matrimonial, something with which Francois had been honoured. The title would have meant that he had equal powers with his queen, but it could only be given by an Act of Parliament, something which Mary and her lords became more and more reluctant to enact. Darnley did little to help his cause, as Knox was to observe: 'As for the King, he passed his time in hunting and hawking and such other pleasures as were agreeable to his appetites, having in his company gentlemen willing to satisfy his will and affections.' It wasn't just the regular hunting expeditions (he was never at court to help make decisions and so, eventually, a stamp was made with his signature on it so that any law could be passed without requiring his presence), but it was his drinking too. He was regularly inebriated and spent many evenings touring the streets of Edinburgh looking for pleasure, accompanied by his like-minded courtiers. Obviously, by this time Mary had tired of him and would certainly have been unwilling to share her bed with him, as she probably no longer saw him as her king. It's interesting that a number of special coins had been commissioned following the marriage, but the only one that saw Darnley's name first (i.e. on the left before Mary) was quickly withdrawn from circulation, a further confirmation that she had no intention of giving him the crown matrimonial. For Mary, the marriage was now a sham and something she bitterly regretted, yet Darnley continued to behave in a manner that was never likely to win her back. His arrogance and his disdainful attitude had made many enemies, even for such a young man. However, it was to be these very same enemies who would use him in their attempt to remove the queen.

Despite Mary's popularity with her people, mainly due to the fact that she hadn't attempted to impose the old religion on the populace, but also because she was beautiful and engaging, she was unfortunately becoming increasingly unpopular with the lords at court. The Chaseabout Raid was a significant event in Mary's history and one that contributed to her life spiralling towards a tragic conclusion. Her half-brother, the Earl of Moray, who had always been supportive of her, had been dismayed by her proposed marriage to Darnley and fought against it. Later, he believed that the cause of Protestantism was being harmed and so he attempted to enlist the help of the English queen, Elizabeth I, to support an uprising against his half-sister. This never came about and when Mary learned of his treachery, she immediately impounded his properties and those of his accomplices, notably Rothes and Kirkcaldy. In turn, Moray gathered a fighting force, but it couldn't match Mary's army so, after some fruitless chasing around the immediate area of Edinburgh (hence the name Chaseabout), Moray fled to England to regroup his forces and plan another attempt, but instead of using military force, it didn't take long for him to realise the best way of getting to Mary would be by attacking her weak link, and that would be her husband. Moray looked to Darnley as the man who could take the crown matrimonial and usurp the queen's power, even though he had absolutely no qualities as a king. In fact, Darnley had continually embarrassed not only Mary but all the lords, such as when he appeared at a meeting of merchants when he was drunk and openly insulted her. At one stage he made a comment that it was possible to 'work a mare when it is in foal', in response to which Mary stormed out of the room in floods of tears. For Moray though, a weak King Darnley who could be made to bend to whatever demand was put on him, was preferable to a strong Queen Mary, who was obstinate and knew how to rule. Moray had, after all, acted as regent after Mary of Guise's death and before Mary, Queen of Scots returned to Scotland.

At this point Mary's story has become entwined with that of her Italian secretary, David Riccio (this is the actual spelling of his name, not 'Rizzio', as it has repeatedly been mistaken to be). However, her relationship with Riccio was not as literally entwined as Darnley was led to believe by Moray and his cohorts who, knowing how weak Darnley was, put into his mind the idea that the reason Mary was no longer sharing his bed was simply because she was sharing hers with the Italian. This seems unlikely to say the least. Riccio, employed from 1561 as the king and queen's secretary, seemed to share the same arrogant characteristics as his male master, but there the comparison ends. Unlike the good-looking young Darnley, Riccio was thirty-five and not in the least bit attractive to the fairer sex, despite his love of expensive clothes. He was hunchbacked and short and was described as 'ugly' and 'ill-favoured' by many, but he had a talent for languages and was an accomplished singer and musician, something which immediately appealed to the queen with her love of the arts. The problem was that as well as being Mary's secretary he appeared to be her only confidant. He would spend hours locked away in her company, in private, which inevitably led to rumours, gossip and scandal. It was this suspicion of intrigue that was fed to Darnley by Moray and his supporters, who now included Morton, George and Ruthven Douglas, Maitland, Rothes and Boyd. A bond was drawn up, which most signed; the fifth item made their aims clear: 'So shall they not spare life or limb in setting forward all that may bond to the advancement of Darnley's honour.'

On Saturday, 9 March 1566, late in the evening, Mary was hosting a small supper party in one of her chambers in the north-west tower of Holyrood Palace. It is an extremely small room. Visitors today regularly question how the events about to be described could have actually taken place in so small an area. Riccio was there, wearing a gown of furred damask, a satin doublet and red velvet hose. He was entertaining the ladies as they took their meal, when Darnley unexpectedly appeared in the doorway, followed by the very frail and sick Lord Ruthven. They both demanded that Riccio go with them. The Italian, clearly aware of the peril he was in, shrunk back and attempted to hide against the window bay. Soon they were joined by others as Ruthven and Darnley accused Riccio of offences against the queen's nature and person. In the melee that followed, the meal table was overturned, a dagger was lunged at Mary, and in the confusion there was a suggestion that a shot rang out, also just missing Mary. Riccio was seized, despite clinging miserably onto his mistress's skirts. As he was dragged out, he cried; '*Justizia, justizia. Sauvez ma vie, Madame, sauvez ma vie.*' His body was found downstairs, lying over a chest, after between fifty-three and sixty dagger wounds had been inflicted. It was a horrifying, vicious attack, and shocking too because of who it involved. After all, Mary was the Queen of Scotland, and pregnant, yet she was fending off armed men in the sanctuary of her own chambers. Showing an incredible presence of mind, Mary produced an acting performance, decided upon within a split second, to save the life of her unborn child (she genuinely felt it had been in mortal danger during the attack) by appealing to Darnley and pretending to be reconciled with him. This seems incredible, but she had just survived an attack that was not only aimed at Riccio but her too, and after furiously challenging her weak husband, she correctly reasoned that he was merely a pawn in a bigger game. Continuing to show presence of mind, she devised an escape the next day, after appearing at the window of the palace to allay the fears of the townspeople who had come rushing to their queen's aid, then evading the guards who had been sent to ensure her incarceration. She and Darnley fled on horseback to Seton and then on to Dunbar. Darnley was in the lead, now fearful for his own life as the reality of what had taken place finally dawned on him. It seems incredible that this young man, or overgrown boy, should show so little understanding of the world around him. Typically, he showed little grace and screamed that they could make another baby if this one should die as a result of the frantic ride over rough countryside. This was Darnley's last connection with Holyrood Palace, although his story with Mary continued. He will return to our trail of Mary, Queen of Scots later, but only for a brief period.

Holyrood Palace (or the Palace of Holyroodhouse, as it is correctly known) was a relatively new building when Mary first arrived, but its appearance has changed dramatically since the sixteenth century. It's fair to say that of all the buildings that are associated with Mary Stuart, this is the one with the strongest links to her life. Visitors here are nearly always impressed by the rooms and artefacts that still link us to Mary's time. As mentioned previously, during her reign as queen, there wasn't a single building commissioned by her or for her, except for Queen Mary's Bath House in Holyrood, which, despite its name, was most likely used as a summer pavilion or dovecote.

Holyrood Palace was built alongside the Holyrood Abbey, which itself dates back to 1128. The story of the founding of the abbey is predictably shrouded in mystery and legend. It was said that the Holy Rood appeared after King David had gone hunting in the grounds of Edinburgh Castle, despite the protestations of his courtiers who had seen a bad omen and would also have preferred him to spend the day in prayer. The king ignored their pleas. While leading the chase, he was thrown off his horse and found himself alone, apart from the attentions of an extremely angry stag. This animal was about to end the king's life when a mysterious mist shrouded it and, in stretching out his hand to protect himself, the king grasped a cross between the stag's antlers. Then the animal disappeared. Later that evening, King David had a dream that it had been divine intervention that had saved him, with a plea for an Augustine monastery to be built on the spot, which he ordered. Another explanation, and one that is now widely accepted, is that the name Holyrood comes from a relic of the True Cross known as the Holy Rood or Black Rood, which had belonged to Queen Margaret, David's mother. It took more than fifty years to build the abbey, which now, sadly, lies in ruins alongside the splendour of the palace following the 'rough wooing' of the English; it was never truly repaired. When finished, the abbey had huge towers that dwarfed the church. The complex also included guest houses and an infirmary, a brewery, stables, dormitories, a refectory and extensive vegetable and herb gardens. The abbey was one of the richest and most powerful buildings in Scotland, and it generated a huge income. As the years progressed, it played host to many significant moments in history. In 1177 a papal legate was received and, twelve years later, the nobles met there to discuss a possible ransom for the captive king, William the Lion. David II was the first royal to be buried there, in 1370 – and James II was born, crowned, married and died at the abbey. His son married Margaret of Denmark in the abbey in 1469. The abbey granted rights of sanctuary, which continued right up to the start of the twentieth century. The boundary for sanctuary lay at the foot of the Royal Mile, at the site of the Girth Cross, and it extended over the total area of Holyrood Park. Most people looking for sanctuary were debtors and one can imagine their sense of relief once they crossed the border as their creditors cursed and shouted, knowing they couldn't lay a finger on them in that restricted area. The most famous person to seek shelter was the Conte d'Artois, younger brother of Louis XVI, who stayed there after the French Revolution, remaining there from 1796 to 1803. It would be interesting to see how such a concept would work today.

It's also worth noting that the abbey wasn't used by Mary for her own private Mass; instead she used the building that became known as the chapel royal in the palace. The

Abbey of Holyrood became the chapel royal in the reign of Charles II.

Holyrood Palace was built by James IV between 1500 and 1505, but was virtually complete in 1503. He wanted it ready for his new bride, Margaret Tudor, and they were married in August of that year. It was originally built around a quadrangle and contained a chapel (as previously mentioned), the royal apartments and a huge great hall. However, it was also originally rather drab and gloomy inside due to its thick, heavy walls and deep-set windows. Over the next few years the king constantly added to the palace, with extra rooms and kitchens being built. His lodgings were in the west range and soon a gatehouse was constructed, which can still be seen in the adjacent abbey today. A lion house was also built to house his many exotic animals from around the world, an example which Mary and her courtiers followed. The northwest tower was erected in 1536. This stood out and made the entrance to the building look grand but at that time there were no plans to mirror it with a southwest tower. The architecture owed much to the French style – which in turn had been developed from an Italian influence many years before – so its design must have made the palace pleasing to Mary's eyes, bearing in mind the luxury she had been used to in France. Its quality was also due to the fact that many of the stonemasons and other builders had been imported from France. Holyrood Palace was built outside of the city walls of Edinburgh; this was probably unavoidable due to the grand size of the building, and it meant it was surrounded by countryside that included the magnificent natural feature of Arthur's Seat and quite breathtaking scenery. Of course the 'rough wooing' regularly referred to in this book caused an enormous amount of damage to the palace. In 1544, Holyrood was sacked and burned, and despite repairs being made, the Scottish Reformers caused extensive damage again, and virtually destroyed the abbey. The interior was removed and any 'offensive' items destroyed.

When Mary first arrived, she was housed in the north-west section of the palace, in apartments that were, for the country at that time, grand and stately. She also had her own private gardens where roebuck and stags were brought for her hunting pleasure. These animals were rounded up from forests as far north as Falkland and deliberately left to roam in the royal park, while some boar had been especially imported from France at the considerable cost of 189 Scots pounds for every beast. No wonder the royal household was constantly financially embarrassed! Hunting and hawking were such vigorous pastimes for Mary that there were times when anti-poaching laws were made for the rest of the kingdom so that her pleasure wasn't interrupted. The problem was described at the time: 'The deer were so destroyed that our Sovereigns can get no pasting of hunting.' If hunting wasn't available, Mary could enjoy her own archery range, a sport at which she was exceptionally good.

Of course the most dramatic moment in not just Mary's life, but Holyrood's, has to be the murder of Riccio. Queen Mary's apartment can still be seen in almost the same state as it was at the time of the tragic and violent event, which is markedly different from virtually every other building in Scotland and England that links to her, as they are all for the most part in ruins. A word of caution, though; don't assume the staircase that connects the lower room used by Darnley with Mary's is the one that played a part in that terrible night, as that one is hidden behind the panelling installed by Charles II. The room, however, can be seen by visitors and gives the strongest possible connection to Mary and has been described, rather romantically, as the most famous room in the world. For the author, it is one of the places on the Mary trail that really connects us to a woman who lived more than 450 years ago. Inevitably, it can be quite busy at times – but if you do get the brief opportunity for a moment alone in her chambers, then it is just possible to hear a whisper of her presence.

You can also see the prayer niche at the far end of the Outer Chamber, which, in her time, looked directly at the entrance to the abbey. As a further bonus for Mary-watchers, the ceiling was uncovered in a recent renovation and the original panelling can now be viewed. It's worth lingering in the hall attached to Mary's room as many souvenirs from her time can be viewed in glass cases; of course they are guarded – but these are the moments that can be so rewarding.

As with all of the buildings that have Mary's footprint in them, Holyrood Palace and the abbey continued their history well after Mary had departed, even though nothing has taken place at the palace to quite match the six years of her reign. In 1590, the abbey was where her son James VI's wife, Princess Anne of Denmark, was crowned Queen of Scotland. Thirteen years later, James became the King of England and moved the royal court to London. In 1633, Charles I was crowned King of Scotland in the palace after extensive renovation work had taken place, as the palace was now all but abandoned and only used for ceremonial occasions. It fell into further disrepair in 1650 while it was being occupied by Oliver Cromwell's soldiers, when a fire destroyed the eastern part of the building, while the rest of the palace was being used as an army barracks. The splendour of Mary's day had virtually disappeared. In 1670, the Privy Council in Scotland put money aside for the repair of the building, which by then had become an embarrassment compared to the opulence of Edinburgh Castle at the top of the Royal Mile. It was decided to build a southwest tower to match the existing tower that had been built more than 100 years earlier. This is the image we see today when we enter Holyrood, with its two towers standing guard over the entrance, something Mary did not witness in her day. The interior of the palace was also extensively refurbished by Sir William Bruce, the king's surveyor, and new royal apartments were created (although Mary and Darnley's rooms were left intact), but his position was terminated in abrupt fashion and Lord Hatton saw out the remainder of the work.

By 1679, Holyrood Palace effectively became what we see today, with the help of Dutch carpenters and painters, notably Alexander Eizat and Jacob de Wet II. A Jesuit college, which had been set up by the Catholic king, James VII, was destroyed by an anti-Catholic mob after the start of the Glorious Revolution in 1688 and, three years later, the abbey was replaced as the local parish church by the Kirk of the Canongate. This is where Elizabeth II attends services when she resides at Holyrood Palace.

By the eighteenth century the palace had lost its importance, as the government was run from London after the union of England and Scotland. Many parts of the building were abandoned, not least the king's apartments, which gradually fell into disrepair. The roof of the abbey collapsed in 1768, never to be repaired, so it remains the same today.

Fortunately, in 1822, George IV ordered repairs after becoming the first reigning monarch since Charles I to visit, although he stayed at Dalkeith Palace as Holyrood wasn't fit for habitation. Mary's rooms were preserved as they were (something for which we should now be very thankful), but the buildings at the north and south end of the quadrangle were demolished to be gradually replaced.

By 1871, Queen Victoria was able to use living quarters on the second floor after extensive renovations, with the former royal apartments and great hall now open to the public as tourist destinations.

The real transformation into what we see today at Holyrood Palace as a tourist attraction took place at the beginning of the last century. George V was due to visit in 1911 and he commissioned the installation of electric lighting, central heating and a sewerage system, with renovations to the kitchens taking place a decade later. It was then that the palace became the official royal residence in Scotland, something which it still is today.

Elizabeth II now spends one week per year at Holyrood, where investitures, audiences and garden parties are held. The Ceremony of the Keys is an important part of her stay, when she is presented with the keys to Edinburgh by the Lord Provost at a traditional gathering. Since it became the official residence for the monarch in Scotland, Holyrood has also welcomed many visiting dignitaries, including Nelson Mandela, Vladimir Putin and Pope Benedict XVI. The renovations and repairs, which are necessary for any historic building, continue apace at the Palace of Holyroodhouse. A multi-million-pound project is underway to update and modernise the grounds and forecourt surrounding the palace, which also includes Holyrood Abbey, and the hope is that by the end of 2018 these works will be complete.

Visitor Information
For a Mary-watcher, a visit to Holyrood Palace is absolutely essential as this building, more than any other castle, palace, chateau, or abbey, contains such important links to her past. Her footprint is heavy here (and let's not forget that she married her third husband, Bothwell, here in the great hall), despite the relatively short period of time she inhabited the buildings. Just a walk around the area, with some of the views that are almost unchanged in the last 500 years, gives you a sense of the drama and intrigue that attached themselves to her life. I can't recommend Holyrood enough. The palace can be found on Canongate; the postcode is EH8 8DX.

Edinburgh Castle

Standing at the top of the Royal Mile and dominating the city of Edinburgh is the castle, arguably the most famous landmark in Scotland. Although there have been many changes to the fortress since the sixteenth century, what Mary saw as she made her ceremonial way into Edinburgh following her return from France would be effectively be the same view we have today. It is an overwhelmingly grand castle that dominates the skyline and attracts more tourists every year than any other destination in Scotland. It was here that Mary, Queen of Scots gave birth to her son James, in 1566. Following the traumatic events surrounding Riccio's death, Mary certainly had no desire to return to Holyrood Palace for the birth of her child. So her courtiers, who still greatly feared for her safety, suggested the far more impenetrable Edinburgh Castle as the obvious solution. Mary lodged there from April, surrounded by high levels of security. The chambers had been decorated with Turkish carpets, and elaborate oak tables had been installed. Mary also had many tapestries made,

...eleven of gilded leather, eight of the Judgement of Paris, five of the Triumph of Virtue, eight of green velvet, ten of cloth of gold and brocaded taffeta, thirty more of massive cloth of gold, one bearing the story of the Comte de Foix, eight bearing the ducal arms of Longueville, five having the history of King Rehoboam, one the tale of Tobit, and four the Hunts of the Unicorn.

It was a remarkable collection and it was certainly impressive how quickly they had been produced.

At this time also, Mary made her will; it was not unusual to do this as, in those days, childbirth was extremely dangerous, but with the threat on her life still as strong in her memory, it was clearly very important to her to have her wishes recorded. Among the many hundreds of people who would benefit from the will, she left Darnley 26 bequests, but this was probably due to the fact that as queen, it was an act of duty. It had been suggested by George Buchanan (a staunch supporter initially but later to become her nemesis after her abdication) that she completely ignored Darnley in her will, but as that was actually an illegal act, it was highly unlikely she would follow his advice. Among other things, she left Darnley a diamond ring, accompanied by a letter that said, 'It was with this that I was married. I leave it to the King who gave it to me.' Hardly words of romance or even affection, though.

Mary took to her lying-in chamber in a predictably ceremonial fashion on 3 June, following royal tradition. It had been extensively decorated by her midwife Margaret Asteane with the huge bed hung with taffeta of blue, and velvet of the same colour, the baby's cradle decorated in the same way. The room was in the northeast part of the castle overlooking the town, but the actual birthplace was an extremely small room that lay off the main chamber (now known as Queen Mary's Room). On 19 June, in the mid-morning, after a long, painful labour, during which a piece of quasi-witchcraft was even used to ease the pain when Lady Reres, who was to become the wet nurse, lay down on the bed and attempted to embrace the pain herself, James was born. The celebrations around the city to mark the safe arrival of the new heir were grand, with bonfires being lit and the artillery of the castle being discharged. St Giles Church, a Protestant place of worship, was full as the lords and nobles packed in to thank God for the birth of a new male heir. It was an event that was welcomed with much pleasure throughout the realm, but, of course, it wasn't received in quite the same way by Queen Elizabeth of England. She'd received the news after Sir James Melville rode for five days to reach London and she immediately responded with the now famous line 'Alack, the Queen of Scots is lighter of a bonny son, and I am but of barren stock.' Bearing in mind that Elizabeth I had refused point blank to even discuss the possibility of marriage, her remark about her cousin was made from jealousy rather than joy.

When you visit the bedchamber where James was born, you can see easily visible on the ceiling the initials of mother and son, MR and JR, and the date of birth. Darnley was now further down the line of succession for both the English and Scottish crowns, something that inevitably fuelled his mood swings, and Mary's proclamation after the birth gives an insight into her state of mind and the suspicion under which was Darnley still held. In front of her courtiers and her husband, she held her newborn high and said in a loud voice,

My Lord, God has given you and me a son, begotten by none but you ... here I shall protest to God that I shall answer to him at the great day of Judgement, that this is your son and no other man's son. I am desirous that all here, with ladies and others bear witness ... for he is so much your own son, that I fear it will be the worse for him thereafter.

The final sentence clearly aimed a barb at Darnley, who could now be under no illusion as to how much Mary despised him.

There is an interesting story that arose in the nineteenth century that, in fact, Mary's child had died at birth and she had very quickly replaced it so that she could fool Darnley and stop him from seizing the throne. This theory followed the discovery of a child's skeleton in the walls of the castle by workmen who were involved in its renovation. The body was wrapped in a woollen cloth. With the added 'incriminating' evidence of a painting discovered at the end of the same century of a wedded James VI looking remarkably like the 2nd Earl of Mar, no wonder the conspiracy theory arose.

It was down to Antonia Fraser to completely debunk this theory in her biography of Mary, pointing out, quite rightly, that it would have taken a ridiculous amount of subterfuge and cover-up to arrange something that quickly (not least the Archbishop Hamilton having to agree to it, despite having legitimate family claims himself). In addition, the painting was typical of an era when many lords and nobles looked similar due to the dynastic family connections throughout Scotland. No evidence of any kind ever backed up the story and, as Antonia Fraser says, the child's remains were probably the result of an unfortunate tryst by a lady-in-waiting.

The birth of James had been successful but it had increased Mary's health problems. She had never been the healthiest of people and throughout her life had been prone to fainting fits at times of stress, of which there were many, and a regular propensity to fall into a paralysed state from which it seemed she would be unlikely to recover. We will deal with an extreme example of this shortly at Jedburgh after an extraordinary 50-mile journey by horse to Hermitage Castle and back. After the birth, though, and after sending little James to Stirling Castle and his foster parents – a regular routine in the sixteenth century for royalty and something which in no way suggested a lack of maternal love from Mary for her son – she took to Newhaven and Alloa to savour the sea air in the hope of improving her well-being. It seemed to work, but sadly the sea air couldn't resolve her now total disgust with her arrogant and wayward husband. Despite the appalling circumstances surrounding the death of Riccio and his involvement in it, Darnley's behaviour was as bad and as distasteful as ever. He was despised by the nobles – not least the ones who were complicit in the secretary's death and who now felt betrayed by him after his flight from Holyrood with Mary – and ways were beginning to be found of ridding the queen of him. This was originally in the form of divorce but it soon became clear that more sinister actions were being planned. At a meeting between the queen and king in front of the lords, Mary asked Darnley specifically what she had done to offend him but he, in typical fashion, had a tantrum and announced he was leaving for 'abroad', much to the exasperation of her courtiers. This led to the meeting of Huntly, Argyll, Moray,

Maitland and Bothwell who, between them, suggested to Mary that other means could be used to rid her of him (as divorce was highly unlikely from Darnley's point of view bearing in mind everything he and his family would lose) and if she pardoned Riccio's slayers, then Moray would 'look through his fingers' and that they would 'guide the matter among us, and your Grace shall see nothing but good, and approved by Parliament'. It's at this point that Mary's degree of involvement has always been questioned. Many believe that she knew exactly what would happen, and so her reputation was decided. On the other hand, a bond was apparently written, which stated that Darnley could be charged with treason and then executed, but this bond no longer exists despite suggestions that it was seen by all and was apparently in Mary's possession when she was imprisoned. This is the moment when the story of Mary, Queen of Scots becomes the fascinating tale of intrigue that has had history lovers spellbound.

James Hepburn, 4th Earl of Bothwell

It is at this point that we should now introduce the man who was the person who sent Mary to such a tragic and disastrous end. James Hepburn was a controversial and powerful nobleman who was an ally of Mary's mother in her battle against the Scottish Reformers. He was the son of Patrick Bothwell and Agnes Sinclair. His appearance was the type to get him noticed; he was 5 feet 6 inches tall with a broken nose and sensual lips under his carefully manicured moustache. He had a build that was completely different from the almost-effeminate Darnley and his bravery in the field of war was legendary, even at this time of his life. He was a ladies' man, well educated and he spoke both Scots and French and was certainly one of the most travelled men from his native country. His power stretched across the southeast of Scotland, with his base of Hermitage Castle standing tall and alone on the windswept fells. He'd successfully helped Mary of Guise in 1559 when he had stolen 6,000 English crowns meant for the Protestant Lords of the Congregation at Haddington. With the help of a handful of his most loyal men, he had ambushed the Laird of Ormiston, causing him serious injuries. In retaliation, the Protestant leader, The Duke of Châtelherault, sent his son, the Earl of Arran, to seize Bothwell's home of Chrichton Castle in an attempt to force him to abandon the Scottish Regent. Bothwell stood firm and it was his loyalty to her mother that so appealed to the young Marie when they first met at court in Paris, she as the French Queen still married to Francois.

The first meeting has been described by many as a future love-match for the couple, but there is no contemporary evidence to back this up. Marie was in her teenage years and married to her sickly husband, while Bothwell was much older and had already entered his first marriage to the Norwegian noblewoman Anna Throndsen. In fact, the reason for his visit to Marie's court was to secure funds for the forthcoming wedding. It is fair to say, though, that the swaggering Bothwell, who didn't stand on ceremony with his crudeness, even in front of a queen, left a lasting impression on the young Queen of Scots. He was later to write, 'The Queen recompensed me more liberally and honourably than I had deserved,' as he received a retainer and the position in the French King's chamber. There was no suggestion though that Bothwell had any physical attraction to Marie, or she to him, despite the varying accounts that were written many years later as a way of blackening her name even more.

His relationship with Anna, whom he'd met on his travels in Denmark, was tumultuous and unpredictable. On his return he'd asked her to sell all of her possessions, which she did, then he approached her rich family for more funds, but his abandonment of her was to prove his eventual downfall. Anna was desperately in love with him and wrote him long, flowery letters of desire when they were apart, without realising how these very same letters would be used against him and Mary Stuart in years to come. He'd had a relationship with Jean Beaton, a woman who had five husbands and numerous lovers (she was in her fifties and he was twenty-four when they became 'hand-fasted' together – a ritual one step removed from marriage) but he eventually married Jean Gordon, the very rich sister of Huntly. The wedding contract showed that it was the bride who was making the marriage settlement and not the traditional other way round, which says everything there needs to be known about the relationship and what it meant for both parties. James Bothwell easily separated the act of union from any other feelings, as at the same time he was involved with a mistress, Bessie Crawford, with whom he had many secret meetings. Frustratingly for him, these secrets were not kept hidden for long as his wife discovered his infidelity and divorced him. Eight days later he was married to Mary, Queen of Scots. Of that, there is more to come.

Bothwell had already seen the inside of Edinburgh Castle long before his burgeoning working relationship with Mary and the Scottish court began, as he was imprisoned there without trial in 1562. This came about after the Earl of Arran, who was later described as being insane, implicated Bothwell in a plot to kidnap the queen in order to force a marriage with the earl. This, in hindsight, seems to have been completely absurd, as Bothwell had shown nothing but complete loyalty to Mary and her mother down the years, but he was sent to prison nonetheless, probably due to the fact that he had become an irritant to certain members of the royal household. After four months he escaped, with the help of his servant, by pulling the bars from his cell window and climbing down the rock, hazardous to say the least. The fact that his servant helped at all is testimony to the loyalty shown, as it was common knowledge that Bothwell regularly mistreated his servants. Two years later, Bothwell managed to escape again, this time from the Tower of London after attempting to flee to France.

Mary had originally sent for Bothwell at the time of the Chaseabout Raid and soon he became one of her closest advisors as a trusted noblemen. He had been against the marriage of his queen to Darnley and had little time for him, or their secretary Riccio. Of course his later involvement in the death of Darnley was to define Bothwell's life. We shall hear much more of Bothwell later.

Edinburgh Castle is certainly not defined by Mary Stuart as its long and rich history has so many tales to tell and a tour of the impressive structure perfectly shows its remarkable story. The castle looks effectively the same as it did back in the twelfth century, yet few of the buildings predate the sixteenth century. There has been human occupation of the site since the Iron Age in the second century, according to archaeologists, but the oldest remaining building, and indeed the oldest building in Edinburgh, is St Margaret's Chapel, which dates from the eleventh century. It was built by the pious queen of Malcolm Canmore, the first king of a united Scotland.

The city they inhabited was originally the capital of a Celtic tribe called the Gododdin known as 'Dinas Eidyn,' which in a rather convoluted way became 'Dun Eadainn' (Dunedin in modern language) and that was reversed to have Edin ahead of burgh. Queen Margaret's death is a tragic story. She died upon hearing about the slaying of her husband and son on the battlefield. Her body was prepared for burial at Dunfermline Abbey, but that was blockaded by Malcolm's brother, as he was now laying claim to the throne. That meant that her remaining sons had to carry the coffin down the craggy rock face from the chapel, fortunately camouflaged by a thick fog, one of the earliest legends to be associated with Edinburgh. The castle itself stands on the site of an extinct volcano and is 430 feet above sea level with cliffs to the south, west and north that rise to stand 260 feet above the surroundings. It's quite clear why a fortress should be built in such a spot and no matter how many times you see it, the building can always take your breath away. Edinburgh Castle was at the centre of the battles during the Wars of Independence and was the subject of numerous sieges. In 1296, Edward I invaded Scotland and the castle fell under the control of the English. After his death in 1307, the Scottish forces looked to take control again, despite a huge garrison of soldiers stationed there. By 1313 the fortress was again under siege by the Scots, led by Robert the Bruce and it was at this time a famous event took place. Randolph, the Earl of Moray, had found breaching the castle almost impossible, but one of his soldiers then came up with a rather unusual plan. Twenty years earlier he had got into the routine of climbing up and down the rock face using a rope ladder to visit a girl in West Bow, the gates being closed at dusk every day. Now, he suggested that a small group of soldiers do the same, despite it being a bitterly cold winter's day in March with the rock dangerously covered in ice and snow. It was agreed, and they bound the rope ladders together and clambered up the treacherous rock, enabling them to breach the defence and surprise the garrison. They took the castle. Later Robert the Bruce stripped it of its defences to deter any future re-occupation by the English. For a quarter of a century the castle lay threadbare and desolate, giving no protection to Edward II or Edward III as they both attempted to take possession of the city, with soldiers pursued through the warren of streets in the city and slaughtered. In 1328, Edward III in Northhampton and Robert I in Edinburgh Castle agreed a treaty that made Scotland independent, but the treaty didn't hold. By 1337 the castle was back in English hands again after another invasion by Edward III. In 1341, though, the final to-ing and fro-ing came to an end in a remarkable fashion.

Sir William Douglas devised a plan that was simple but effective. A priest disguised as a captain of a trading vessel approached the governor of the castle and offered him the first choice of his goods, which included French wines and food, at which the guardian, who was always seduced by such luxuries, agreed to buy the whole shipment and arranged for it to be delivered the next morning. When the first cart pulled up under the portcullis, it was overturned, preventing the gate from being closed, and the seamen accompanying the shipment showed themselves to be soldiers and rushed into the castle, retaking it successfully by completely overwhelming the occupying garrison. This was to be the last occasion Edinburgh Castle was in the hands of the English until the Act of Union in 1707.

The Wars of Independence ended in 1357 with the Treaty of Berwick and the castle then went through a significant spell of renovation and rebuilding. Robert the Bruce's son, David II, was responsible for the work and at that time 'David's Tower' was built on the north side of the castle, but David himself died before it was completed. The tower stood around 60 feet high and looked down on the surroundings with a large pit encircling it, making it virtually impossible to scale and so adding to the impregnability of the castle. The tower is now the site of the Half Moon Battery, which was built in 1573, although the lower two storeys of the tower are still standing and can be viewed.

By the mid-fifteenth century, Edinburgh had been reinstated as the capital of Scotland and has retained that honour until the present day. This was in no small part down to James II. He was crowned at the age of seven, but his early life was beset by constant attempts by the lords to control and exploit him. Fortunately, his mother was a resourceful, intelligent woman and, after smuggling him out of the castle in a small chest (after the Lord Chancellor Crichton had refused permission for anyone to see him, making the king and his mother virtual prisoners) she took him to Stirling Castle. A civil war nearly ensued between Crichton and Regent Livingston of Stirling over the boy, but this was averted by the Bishop of St Giles, who presented a compromise.

One of the most horrendous acts to take place in Edinburgh Castle happened in November 1440. This shows it wasn't only Mary who had to witness violence and horror during her brief reign. On this occasion, the sons of the Earl of Douglas, the lieutenant of Scotland, were summoned into the king's presence. The earl had recently died and had left great wealth to his children. It matched that of the king, and so when the 10-year-old monarch invited William and David to the castle, it was with a sense of foreboding that they accepted. William, the elder of the two at eighteen, was an arrogant young man who regularly rode out with around 1,500 warriors and it had become common knowledge that the monarchy regarded him as an enemy to the crown. Despite this, the king welcomed them both warmly, although William's soldiers were not admitted to the castle due to their sheer numbers. A feast was held and midway through it, to the shock of the child king and his guests, a blackened bull's head was produced, called 'the black dinner'. Under ancient Scottish custom, this meant there was to be a death among the main guests, something which William and David fought valiantly against, but despite their efforts, they were beheaded in front of the child king, who couldn't hide his horror. A popular rhyme was written and sung, which commemorated this act of treachery:

> Edinburgh Castle, tower and tower,
> God grant thou sink for sin,
> and that even for the black dinner,
> Earl Douglas gat therein.

The banqueting hall where this took place is still used today for state visits and functions.

During the fifteenth century James II continued to live in the castle. He married Mary of Guelders; and it was he who commissioned the Nor Loch, which was a defensive artificial lake in the heart of the city. It was eventually drained 300 years later, when the new town was built, and it is now the site of Princess Street Gardens and the entrance to Waverley train station. Also as part of the defensive improvements to the castle, armaments were purchased, including the Mons Meg cannon (previously mentioned). This was the largest and most powerful cannon ever seen at the time and can still be found today in Edinburgh Castle after its return from England. James II's desire to arm the castle as much as possible would indirectly cause his early death – as one of his own cannons exploded near him during the siege of Roxburgh Castle.

As we have seen, James IV constructed Holyrood Palace in the sixteenth century, but he was still residing at Edinburgh

Linlithgow Palace, 1500s. Mary was born here. (Author's collection)

Linlithgow Palace is a magnificent edifice overlooking the loch. However, it didn't appear to be a favourite place of Mary's in her later life. (Author's collection)

Linlithgow Palace is now an empty shell. The place where Mary was born is on the first floor. (Author's collection)

Stirling Castle's entrance. Mary was brought here as a baby and she spent several happy years in the castle before she had to be moved again for her safety. When she returned to Scotland, Stirling Castle was also the place where she soothed the fevered brow of her future husband, Lord Darnley. (Author's collection)

Dumbarton Castle. It was from here that Mary would have said farewell to her mother, Mary of Guise, before being sent to France at just six years old. The gateway she left from no longer exists, but the building is effectively the same some 450 years later. (Author's collection)

Above left: Mary grew up in France, raised in luxury while she was groomed for marriage to the Dauphin Francois. This portrait of him is from 1560. (Author's collection)

Above right: Marie aged nine. (Author's collection)

Blois Chateau has a long, rich history and still exists, although not as it was in Marie's day because it was attacked during the French Revolution. What you can see now is the result of renovation from 1841, under the direction of architect Felix Duban. (Author's collection)

The chateau is enormous with 564 rooms and seventy-five staircases. (Author's collection)

Chateau De Fontainebleau, situated 34 miles south-east of Paris, is a wonderful example of French architecture and is now a UNESCO World Heritage Site. For many centuries the castle was untouched but in the reign of Francis I (1494–1547) it was rebuilt in a Renaissance style, recently imported from Italy. Many of the cultural characteristics we so identify with France, such as aspects of architecture, cuisine and the arts, were imported from Italy; Catherine de Medici, born in Florence, was a strong influence. Marie was sought out at Fontainebleau by the English Ambassador Nicholas Throckmorton seeking the ratification of the Treaty of Edinburgh. (Author's collection)

Above: **Notre Dame Cathedral.** The marriage of Marie and Francois took place here in April of 1558. She was fourteen and Francois was a year younger. The royal couple captivated the hearts and minds of the French people, who lined the wedding route in their thousands. (Courtesy of Stevan Nicholas under Creative Commons)

Right: **Reims Cathedral.** After the death of Henry II, Francois travelled to Reims to be crowned King of France. Marie, already a queen in her own right, had only a peripheral role in the occasion. The cathedral was built in 1211 and modified over the centuries, but the grand building Francois stepped into in the sixteenth century looks similar today, except for changes to the interior. In 2011, the cathedral celebrated its 800th birthday, with the inauguration of six new stained glass windows on either side of the apse. (Author's collection)

The Royal Yacht, Leith. These days, the Royal Yacht is a big tourist attraction in Leith, and well worth visiting. Leith is also where Mary first stepped back on to Scottish soil on 19 August 1561, when she returned to rule the land of her birth. (Author's collection)

John Knox preaching before the Lords of the Congregation, 1559, by David Wilkie RA. (Courtesy Rijksmuseum)

Edinburgh, John Knox's House. The home of the Protestant preacher, who was one of Mary, Queen of Scots' strongest critics, is situated halfway up the Royal Mile. His room overhangs the rest of the building so that he could watch the citizens walk by. (Author's collection)

Right: **Mary's bathhouse.** This building, the only one commissioned during Mary, Queen of Scots' reign, is situated on the edge of the grounds of Holyrood Palace, but it was unlikely to have contained bathing facilities, it was more likely to have been a summer pavilion or dovecot. (Author's collection)

Below: **Holyrood Palace.** (Courtesy of Christoph Stässler, Creative Commons)

David Riccio, *above left*, was the king and queen's secretary, and although he was not as good-looking as **Lord Darnley**, *above right*, Mary's enemies convinced her second husband that the 35-year-old hunchback was behaving improperly with the vivacious **Queen of Scots**, *left*. Riccio was dragged from the Queen's private chambers and stabbed to death. (All author's collection)

Mary's bedroom in the **Palace of Holyrood House**. (Author's collection)

Edinburgh Castle. (Courtesy of Philip McErlean, Creative Commons)

Interior of Hermitage Castle. The first floor is where Bothwell lay seriously injured and it was here Mary spent two hours with him after her horseback journey from Jedburgh. (Author's collection)

Jedburgh. It was in this town that Mary, Queen of Scots conducted a royal justice eyre, then went to see James Hepburn, the 4th Earl of Bothwell, an exhausting 56-mile round trip – after which she became seriously ill. This may be the house where she stayed, but there are suggestions it was built during the time of her son, James. (Author's collection)

Exterior of Hermitage Castle. This windswept, barren castle looks little different from Bothwell's day. It is claimed there is no-one brave enough today to spend a night inside the ruined building.

Dunbar Castle. There is so little left of the castle now that it's difficult to imagine the events between Mary and Bothwell taking place here. Attached to the modern harbour, this picturesque ruin is out-of-bounds to the public. (Author's collection)

Lochleven Castle on the island in the middle of the loch. Note the water levels, compared to the picture on the next page. (Author's collection)

Left: **Mary's chambers, Lochleven.** Although now closed to the public, the balcony is part of the two storeys that contained Mary's apartments during her imprisonment. It was in these rooms that Mary miscarried twins from her relationship with Bothwell. (Author's collection)

Below: **Lochleven Castle.** This was to be Mary's first prison where she was forced to sign her abdication papers. (Author's collection)

Above left: **Dundrennan Abbey.** This was the spot where Mary spent her last hours on Scottish soil before fleeing to England. There is confusion as to whether she stayed here in the abbey, or at a nearby farmhouse, but she certainly saw the place as she walked to the shore to sail into her eventual captivity. (Author's collection)

Above right: Mary, as she looked when she was at Carlisle Castle. (Author's collection)

Carlisle Castle. The Warden's Tower, where Mary was lodged, was demolished many years ago, but she and her 'Maries' took regular walks along the ramparts of the castle – now renamed The Lady's Walk. (Author's collection)

Left: **Bolton Castle.** A personal favourite of the author's, this castle is as outstanding today as it must have been in the sixteenth century. At this stage in her story, Mary was becoming aware that she was a prisoner and not a visitor. (Author's collection)

Below: **Tutbury Castle.** The much despised Tutbury Castle. Now in ruins, this was the place Mary hated more than any other. (Author's collection)

Gateway, Tutbury Castle. Each time Mary entered through this gate, her heart must have sunk even lower, as it was a loathsome place to be held captive. (Author's collection)

MARIE Stuart Reyne d'Escosse souffre le Martyre pour la Foy: et par la constance de sa mort, renouuelle en ces derniers temps, les exemples de l'ancienne Eglise.

Above left: **Mary**, imprisoned in Sheffield. (Author's collection)

Above right: **Mary**, by Abraham Bosse. (Courtesy Metropolitan Museum)

Fotheringhay Castle. All that is left of the place where Mary spent her last seconds on earth is this mound where the castle stood – an atmospheric and unbelievably sad place. (Author's collection)

Castle and presiding over many galas and banquets, plus numerous jousting contests. These took place in the south-western corner, and one particular contest took place in 1503 when only the king's intervention stopped one of the knights being killed on the spot. A soldier from the Low Countries had challenged Scotland's best knight, Sir Patrick Hamilton, to a fight to the death, but he was well beaten and only the compassion of James enabled him to walk free and relatively unscathed. The king was killed in the battle of Flodden Field in 1513, and with the English laying siege to the city again, the Scots hastily constructed a border wall to augment the defences of Edinburgh and its castle.

James V was only five when he came to the throne, but he was responsible, in his later years, for the extensive addition of defences that became necessary. Henry VIII's 'rough wooing' was underway once James had died, just after the birth of his daughter Mary. His wife, Mary of Guise, built herself a separate residence on Castle Hill, as she attempted to stand firm against both the English Army and the Scottish Reformers. The end of her days was tragic, as we have seen, with her daughter removed to France for her own safety. Mary of Guise was suffering from dropsy and could only hobble with the aid of a walking stick. She had thrown herself on the mercy of the opposition leaders in the castle. Her forces were being overwhelmed by the combined armies of England and Scotland and, after her brief stay in Leith, she returned to Edinburgh and took to her bed, too ill to stand. It was there that she summoned the nobles in an attempt to create a peace, but sadly they didn't heed her call. John Knox had warned many of them not to attend in case the 'Guisian practice should prevail' and he also declared that Mary could 'enchant' them should they see her face-to-face. She died on 11 June 1560, in the bedchamber that would be where Mary Stuart would give birth to her son. Mary of Guise died twenty-two years after the date of her arrival in Scotland. There is an epitaph set on the wall of the royal apartments that says:

Mary of Lorraine, Queen of James V,
Mother of Mary, Queen of Scots, and Regent of Scotland from 1554–1560,
died here 11 June 1560. A lady of honourable condition – of singular judgement – full of humanity – a great lover of justice – helpful to the poor.

As I have referred to before, Mary of Guise was a truly inspiring leader of her adopted country and history hasn't necessarily been kind to her; she is chiefly remembered only as the mother of Mary Stuart, but her achievements were arguably greater than the subject of this book, and the wisdom she showed in the face of constant adversity was a trait that didn't seem to have been handed down to Mary, Queen of Scots. If her daughter had inherited her mother's sense of leadership, then the story of Scotland in the sixteenth century may have been a radically different one – but then that story would probably not have been remotely as interesting.

Following Queen Mary's imprisonment, many of her nobles remained faithful to her; but a civil war was taking place. The sides were divided into the 'Queen's Men', headed by Sir William Kirkcaldy of Grange, who had been on the side of Moray when Mary was incarcerated but soon changed sides after the regent's death, and the 'King's Men', headed by the new regent, the Earl of Lennox. Mary's strongholds fell one by one until only Edinburgh Castle remained, and that lay under siege for more than two years as the King's Men battered at the fortified walls without success. At one stage Lennox attempted to starve the garrison out of the fortress, but he didn't know about the underground tunnel that ran from the castle to the Royal Mile, enabling stocks to be smuggled in. Eventually, though, the bombardment caused the defences to weaken, helped by around 1,500 of Queen Elizabeth's men armed with huge cannons. These were all fired at once and continued for a week, finally breaking through when David's Tower collapsed. This led to the destruction of the battlements and other towers and, after negotiations and a promise of safe conduct, Kirkcaldy surrendered. He was hanged publicly at Mercat Cross three months later.

James VI never lived at Edinburgh Castle as it had effectively become a ruin, but the Regent Morton went about rebuilding it, including the Half Moon Battery, later to be described as an ineffective battlement that appeared sturdier than it actually was, and Portcullis Gate. Successful rebuilds took place during James VI's reign, but he took up residence in London and used Holyrood Palace when he was in Scotland. His successor, Charles I, became the last monarch actually to reside in the castle, but that was for one night only, on the eve of his Scottish coronation. Sadly, more parts of the building were destroyed by Oliver Cromwell in 1650 when Charles II was crowned King of Scotland. Cromwell invaded again and, after a ruinous three-month siege, the castle was taken with extensive damage inflicted but, once the exiled Charles was restored to the English crown, he agreed to maintain a garrison there based on Cromwell's New Model Army. That garrison was kept at the castle until 1923.

The number of sieges that the castle had to endure seems almost endless, with 7,000 soldiers blockading it in 1689 as part of a religious dispute, the Jacobite uprising in 1715 where around 100 Highlanders attempted to scale the walls with rope ladders, and a further uprising in 1745 when yet more damage was done with Jacobites attempting to invade the castle against the Deputy Governor George Preston. After buildings were destroyed and soldiers killed, the Jacobites returned to England. Thankfully, that was the last military action the castle was to see. Throughout the ages it has survived constant attacks and sieges and somehow, with many alterations, has survived.

From the eighteenth century, Edinburgh Castle's main purpose was as a prison. Of course Lord Bothwell was the most famous early prisoner, as we have seen, but captured soldiers from the Seven Years War, the American War of Independence, and the Napoleonic Wars were all sent to the vaults of the castle. By the early 1800s though, the vaults were no longer suitable to be used as a jail, underlined by the fact that forty-nine prisoners had escaped in 1811. Edinburgh Castle became what we know it as today, an historic monument. In 1818 the Crown of Scotland was rediscovered and put on display for the general public, numerous buildings were renovated or completely rebuilt over the years, such as the Argyle tower, the great hall, a new gatehouse was built and the hospital restored. Despite a brief period during World War I when it was again used as a prison, the castle continued to be a popular attraction for both public and royalty alike. George IV visited in 1822, the first monarch since Charles II had done so 171 years previously. Again, it was used briefly as a prison in World War II, but by then it had transferred from the War Office to the Office of Works. At the end of the twentieth century, it was in the care of Historic Scotland and became a Scheduled Ancient Monument in 1993. The buildings are protected by twenty-four listings, some at the highest A level, while the city of Edinburgh is now recognised as a World Heritage Site by UNESCO. The National War Museum is housed south of the courtyard leading from the Governor's House. It covers the history of war-torn Scotland. The Royal Palace, built in the mid-sixteenth century for the Stuart family, and, of course, Mary's Room in particular, is of interest to us. It is on the ground floor and is more remembered for the birth of Mary's son James, than for the death of Mary's mother. The great hall is the area that attracts the most attention and visitors. Built in the early 1550s, it measures 95 x 40 feet and took it took many years to complete its luxury. It has also had moments when it fell from grace; it was turned into a barrack for Oliver Cromwell's troops in 1650, and then redesigned in 1737 to house soldiers in three separate storeys. By 1897 it had become a military hospital, but by the twentieth century it was restored to what we see today.

Edinburgh Castle is a place that everyone should visit if they are touring Scotland's capital city but, of course, our reason is we are on the trail of Mary Stuart. Her footprint was heavy here as we have established, although as previously stated, the building is not as much defined by her brief presence as Holyrood Palace is. It is fascinating to look at Mary's Room and imagine the import of the events that transpired there, but of course the castle holds so much more than I'm able to convey in these pages, simply because it can sustain a book in itself (and has done so several times).

Like so many historical monuments, its history is vast and to delve into every facet would be difficult for author and reader alike. Sometimes it is just easier to experience a place for yourself. If you do visit (and I urge you to) you may be in a position to hear the one o'clock gun. This is a time signal fired every day at that time – apart from Sundays, Good Friday and Christmas Day. It was originally fired for the ships in Leith harbour from 1861 as a way of aiding them with departures during the tides, but the tradition has survived and continues to this day. Also, if you happen to find yourself there at the turn of the New Year (Hogmanay), then the annual fireworks display is the focal part of the city's celebrations. They mark the end of the Edinburgh Festival in the summer. The castle dominates the skyline and, with Holyrood Palace, is likely to dominate the thoughts of anyone who makes the journey to follow the trail of Mary, Queen of Scots. It's essential to visit both if we are to truly understand the life of our heroine.

Visitor Information

Visitor Information

Like Holyrood Palace, Edinburgh Castle is extremely easy to find because it dominates the city's skyline. It can be found on Castle Hill, postcode EH1 2NG.

Jedburgh

We've already heard how Mary suffered from a variety of illnesses throughout her life, but none quite matched the terrible torpor she fell into while at the small border town of Jedburgh. In October 1566, the queen had arrived at the town to hold a justice eyre, a regular administrative duty for monarchs. It's interesting to see at this point how differently she and her half-brother Moray had dispensed justice at moments like this. Mary was constantly criticised for her leniency towards her subjects, but when Moray was the arbiter of felonies, he ruled with an iron fist. In the market place, he issued a proclamation prohibiting succour to known thieves on the point of death. He proceeded to have eighteen prisoners drowned in a large pool to prove his point. For the justice eyre, Mary resided in a fortified house on the main street and while in session, she learned that Bothwell had been seriously injured in a skirmish and was close to death. He was at his ancestral home of Hermitage Castle (although it had only been in the family for around seventy years) and wasn't likely to survive his wounds, so she made the decision to ride the 26 miles to visit him and return on the same day, a gruelling journey of some 52 miles on horseback. It's here that many historians have disagreed over her reasons. Some argue that by now Mary – who was still married to Darnley – and Bothwell were lovers, because riding so many miles in one day surely proves the love she had for him because it was dangerous and so close to the English border that she was putting herself and her men at risk. What is easily forgotten among the accusations is that she didn't actually leave Jedburgh for six days, until she'd completed her royal duties. It can also be argued that she had to visit Bothwell as, by that time, he had become her lieutenant and chief advisor, so it was natural that she was concerned for his welfare and continued to need his advice on the border skirmishes. The conflicting points of view are demonstrated in the following two statements. The first is from her secretary Nau (who had succeeded Riccio):

> The Earl of Bothwell was so dangerously wounded that everyone thought he would die. Such being the case, her Majesty was both solicited and advised to pay him a visit at his house, called the Hermitage, in order that she might learn from him the state of affairs in these districts, of which the said Lord was hereditary governor.

An alternative view came from George Buchanan (who had at one stage been a staunch supporter of Mary's but changed to be against her in later years):

> While Bothwell was conducting himself there in a manner worthy neither of the place to which he had been raised nor of his family and what might have been expected of him, he was wounded by a dying robber. He was carried to his castle of Hermitage in a condition such as to make his

recovery uncertain. When this news is carried to the queen at Borthwick, although it was a severe winter, she flies like a madwoman with enormous journeys first to Melrose and then to Jedburgh. Although reliable reports about his life had reached that place, her eager mind was unable to retain self-control and to prevent her from displaying her shameless lust. At an unfavourable season, in spite of the dangers of the roads and the robbers, she threw herself into this expedition with such an escort as no one slightly more honourable would have dared to entrust with life and fortune.

She set off with her half-brother Moray and a band of soldiers and made the journey there and back within one day. This was partly due to the fact that Hermitage Castle was not ready to welcome a royal party but also because it was so close to the English border that it was in a vulnerable position. In the author's opinion, if Mary had been in love with Bothwell, she would have closed her eyes to such dangers, set off immediately instead of waiting six days, then stayed there to minister to him in the way she had for Darnley years before.

What is indisputable is that when she returned she became violently ill. It's clear that exhaustion after the ride played a big part in her condition. It was so pronounced that many were convinced she was close to death. There could be many reasons for her failing health, but the stress over her relationship with her husband must have played a large part. Maitland had written a letter to Archbishop Beaton stating that, '(Darnley) misuses himself so far towards her that it is an heartbreak for her to think that he should be her husband.' It seems this stress and her frail constitution brought about the most serious collapse of her life. She vomited up to sixty times, falling into unconsciousness and became almost paralysed on the bed, unable to speak or move. Her arms and feet were stiff with cold and her face had become distorted. The case was so severe that she was prayed for in the churches of Edinburgh. At one stage she was actually pronounced dead and her servants began to air the room by opening the windows, while her less-than-loyal brother Moray had started to help himself to her belongings, something he later denied. She was saved, seemingly at the last minute, by her physician Arnault. He had seen signs of life and bandaged her arms and legs very tightly (a treatment that is incomprehensible to modern-day readers), followed by forcing wine down her throat. The queen choked, then vomited up a large amount of blood, and slowly began to recover. For a thirty-minute period, the Queen of Scotland was believed to have died. This episode obviously concerned the queen as she then made arrangements for the crown to be passed to her son in the event of her death; it was not to be taken by her husband. Her writings make this very clear:

> My Lords, you know the goodness that I have used towards some whom I have advanced to a great degree of honour and pre-eminence above others, who notwithstanding, has used ingratitude towards me, which has engendered the displeasure that presently most grieves me, and is also the cause of my sickness. I pray Lord mend them.

Darnley, who was unaware of her proclamation, did not ride to see his stricken wife for eleven days but, in his defence, it was reported that he actually did not learn of her illness until 27 October because he was hunting and hawking, and that he set off the next day. Unfortunately, his defence is not strengthened by the fact that he did not stay long, as he returned to Edinburgh almost immediately.

Visitor Information
While on the trail of Mary, Queen of Scots, today Jedburgh is a pleasant place to visit. It is a pretty market town and is easily accessible off the A68. The house the queen stayed in is clearly signposted and worth a visit, as it is now a very enjoyable museum. It is interesting to stand on the upper floor and imagine the concern her courtiers had as they ministered to their stricken queen and, looking out of the windows, you can imagine the scene with the ruined abbey overlooking the town. Visiting that building too is a must, although there are no direct Mary links to it, apart from the constant border wars of her time and the ransacking of it by the invading English army. The abbey was founded in 1147 but suffered severe damage in the aforementioned wars, so now it stands roofless but still retaining the grandeur of its Norman architecture. Other visitor attractions are the Jedburgh Castle Jail, and Carnegie Library. Mary, Queen of Scots House is located on Queen Street. There are numerous artefacts from Mary's time on display and there is a theme as you enter each room. A Rogue's Gallery shows you the people who played a part in her life, and the Last Letter Room is a poignant tribute to her final thoughts. Jedburgh

council bought the house in 1927 and they have run it as a tourist attraction ever since. One slight concern is that there are suggestions that this is not the original house that Mary stayed in, as some historians say it was built at the time of her son, James. It is, however, on the same spot as the house associated with her. It is open only between the months of March and November, and be sure to check for opening times too. A benefit is that there is free entry to the exhibition – a wonderful way to spend a couple of hours. The postcode is TD8 6EN.

Hermitage Castle

Hermitage Castle is an isolated and forbidding building standing in a windswept, barren landscape, which offers no comfort today and certainly offered little in the sixteenth century. Built 300 years previously, it stands in Roxburghshire, close to Hermitage Water, from which it takes its name. It has a history of unrelenting violence and was once described as the 'guardhouse of the bloodiest valley in Scotland', something that appealed to the Highland warrior, Bothwell. At one stage, the castle could house 1,000 soldiers, yet at times it had been overrun by warring factions and families looking to strengthen their cause with the capture of the garrison. The building does give the impression of being completely built as one fortress, mainly because the architecture is similar, but it has been added to and extended over the centuries. It was first built in 1240 by the Norman family of Nicholas de Soulis, then passed down to the Douglas family, who held it for two centuries. Lord Soulis was reputedly a man who took terrible vengeance on his enemies, with the legend that he melted his victims in boiling lead, as the popular verse of the time describes,

> They wrapped him up in a sheet of lead,
> a sheet of lead for a funeral pall,
> they plunged him into the cauldron red,
> and melted him – lead, bones and all.

Later, in the fourteenth century, Sir William Douglas imprisoned Englishman Sir Ralph de Neville there. When the Douglas clan were outraged at losing the Lieutenant of the Border title, Douglas seized his rival Sir Alexander Ramsay and threw him into the dungeon, where he starved to death. The Hepburns of Bothwell became the keepers of Hermitage Castle in 1492 after James IV ordered the Earl of Angus to relinquish the fortress due to his suspicious relationship with Henry VII of England. At the time of Mary's now famous ride from Jedburgh, the castle was in the hands of the 4th Earl of Bothwell. After his eventual incarceration in Denmark, Hermitage became the residence of his nephew, Francis Stewart, a grandson of James VI, but he fared little better as he was imprisoned, not once but twice, in a three-year period for intrigue against the Crown, despite receiving a royal pardon following the original crime. By the seventeenth century Hermitage Castle was effectively abandoned following the Union of the Crowns and for the next century it fell into serious disrepair. Then in 1820, the Duke of Baccleuch attempted to restore its faded glory, yet little was done that was permanent. At that point it was in the possession of the Scott clan, but by 1930, without any reason for continuing their possession of a ruin that brought in no income, it was handed over to Historic Scotland, who now take care of the running of the building as a tourist destination. If you want to visit, and again it is a place that I would urge you to see, you will have to be careful with your arrangements as it is only open from April until September, the winter season making it difficult to approach.

Hermitage Castle is an astonishing place in that it is one of the bleakest and most miserable places as we follow Mary's trail, but it has splendour and fascination attached to it. It's difficult for modern day watchers to imagine how on earth anyone could have lived there, especially during the harsh winters when attempting to keep the cold at bay would have been an almost impossible task. Despite it having just a fleeting connection to Mary, it set the stage for a moment in her life that has often been discussed down the years. There is supposed to be a Mary ghost walking around the ruined building but, as much as that would be fascinating and rewarding to experience, I can't but help think there must be far more important structures that Mary would want to continue to visit.

Visitor Information

The castle is only opened during the summer months, and it is easy to understand why. Access is down an old drover road, which is very narrow, off the B6399 and A7, south of Hawick. Once there, though, it is a truly awe-inspiring spectacle in the bleakness of its surrounding. Plaques are displayed around the inside, explaining its history and, on a summer's day, it is a lovely picnic setting. The postcode is TD9 0LU.

Honourable mentions

Before we move on to the most important moment in the life of Mary, Queen of Scots, I have to mention some of the places that I haven't fully covered in the trail. This is mainly because, as regent, she visited so many places during her progresses, some just fleetingly and some purely for pleasure. **St Andrews** certainly falls into that category, a place she visited on numerous occasions to enjoy the sea air as an aid to improving her health. It was at St Andrews that one of her suitors, the French poet Pierre de Chatelard, managed to hide under her bed in an attempt to seduce her. He can be forgiven, to a certain extent, as he'd done the same thing at an earlier date at Holyrood and then Mary hadn't been offended. In fact, she had taken to kissing his neck and embracing him publicly, something that was frowned upon by her courtiers. Unfortunately for the lovesick Frenchman, on this occasion Mary was terrified and she demanded that her half-brother Moray immediately put him to death. De Chatelard was hanged, with Mary watching from the battlements as he sang an ode to her called *Hymn to Death*. There was a suggestion that his behaviour was engineered by Mary's enemies in France but, whatever the reason, on this occasion she didn't show any leniency at all. St Andrews is now a picturesque ruin that has suffered the ravages of time and the approaching sea, but it can be visited.

Wemyss Castle in Fife was the place where Mary first met Darnley. This wonderful pink sandstone building stands above the Firth of Forth and was a place she visited as part of her royal progress. **Inverness Castle**, much further north, was the place where she was refused entry by the son of Huntly, Alexander Gordon, who was under orders from his father, but for his actions he was captured and hanged with his head put on a spike for all to see. The castle that stands there now is unfortunately not the one where this dramatic act took place as it was completely rebuilt in the nineteenth century. The same can be said for **Glamis Castle,** where Mary stayed on the first of her visits, but that was completely rebuilt in the seventeenth century and little remains of the original. It is now more famous for being the seat of Macbeth and the birthplace of Princess Margaret. Let's not forget **Falkland Palace** where Mary's father learned of the impending birth of his daughter and turned his face to the wall to utter those famous words. As well as that fragile link to Mary, there is the tennis court that was uncovered in the early part of the last century, where Mary used to play the game real tennis. It was also there where she was scandalising the court by wearing men's breeches while playing. **Seton Palace** was a much-loved escape for her as she regularly visited, and it was the place where Bothwell followed her and suggested marriage after the death of Darnley. This is another venue that cannot be visited, as it was completely demolished in 1789, but standing in its place now is the grand Seton Castle, of which much of the stonework came from the palace. Finally, there is **Edzell Castle,** which has at its centre a wonderful garden that owes much to Mary's son James, but was still elegant enough in her time for an extended stay.

All these places were touched by Mary, albeit briefly in some instances, and with John Knox's house on the Royal

Mile or the house in St Andrews, which now belongs to the university and is used as a library, they can all be visited or seen if time allows.

Kirk O'Field

One place that really defines Mary's life, and certainly her demise, is a place that we cannot visit as it no longer exists. Kirk o'Field is where Darnley was murdered and where Mary effectively put herself at the centre of one of the most shocking episodes in Scottish history.

Just two months after Mary's serious illness at Jedburgh, Darnley became extremely ill with what was originally described as smallpox, but later historians have attributed to syphilis. Mary, still looking for ways to be rid of her appalling husband, actually sent a doctor to see him in Glasgow, while at the same time pardoning the nobles such as Morton for their involvement in Riccio's death, only further strengthening the belief that she was involved in the events that were to follow. Almost lost in the controversy of Kirk o'Field is that at the start of 1567, Darnley was seen to be plotting against his wife with letters to the pope and the King of France in an attempt to overthrow Mary and claim the throne for himself. It was with this background of intrigue that on 20 January the queen set off to Glasgow to bring her wayward husband back to Edinburgh. As with nearly all of Mary Stuart's life, there has been speculation surrounding her actions and motives. She returned to Edinburgh with her sick husband following in a litter, and that in itself is cause to question why. She no longer loved him, she blamed him for Riccio's murder and she was aware of him plotting against her. She wanted rid of him, preferably by legal means, but there had been discussions, as we've seen, about other more sinister methods. So was she bringing him back to put him in a position for him to be disposed of, or was it make sure she was keeping her enemy – as Darnley surely was by now – as close as possible? There could even be the suggestion that due to her natural caring nature, she felt sorry for this now pathetic creature. No definitive reason has ever been provided. What we do know, though, is that Mary lodged Darnley in a provost's house in a quadrangle of buildings called Kirk o'Field, about ¾-of-a-mile from Edinburgh Castle. Again, this gives the Mary accusers ammunition, though it has to be remembered that she had originally intended for Darnley to go to Craigmillar, but he refused as he didn't feel safe there. The house, certainly not the largest of the buildings that surrounded the courtyard, was skirted by the city walls and had pleasant gardens attached to it. Darnley was installed in the upper bedroom, where he took to his bed, hideously marked on his face so that he had to wear a taffeta at all times. His illness also meant that he had the most horrendous bad breath, which was putrid enough for courtiers to visibly wince when they entered his chamber.

The timeline of the next week is fascinating as we see how the events unfolded in what became the last few days of Darnley's life and the last few weeks of Mary's reign as Queen of Scotland. On Saturday, 1 February, Darnley was installed in his chamber, with all his furnishings arriving shortly afterwards. He was attended to by his doctors and a full recovery was expected. By Wednesday, relations between Mary and Darnley were good enough for her to sleep in her own chamber downstairs, immediately beneath her husband's, and by Friday they were talking together about the plots that she had heard about. He denied them and the accord was strong enough for her to sleep downstairs again – but two days later Darnley breathed his last. It was the last Sunday before the start of Lent and, with that, came the celebrations. In addition, Mary had two formal functions to attend. In the morning her valet, Bastian Pages, was to marry Christiana Hogg, and then in the late afternoon she was the guest at a dinner in Canongate, held by the Bishop of the Isles. Both needed her presence, but she had planned to sleep at Kirk o'Field that evening after promising her husband that the next day he could return to Edinburgh. With many courtiers in her retinue, including Huntly, she stayed in Darnley's room for a few hours while the nobles played dice, or listened to music, and drank wine. It was a calm and enjoyable atmosphere, but at ten o'clock she left abruptly after being reminded that she had to attend the wedding masque. Darnley was upset, but she gave him a ring to pledge her goodwill and said goodbye, walking down the stairs where her horses were waiting. It was then that she saw Bothwell's former servant, the much-abused Paris, and was shocked at his countenance. 'Jesu, Paris. How begrimed you are!'

During the day a huge amount of gunpowder had been deposited in the cellar with the aim of blowing up the house. As Antonia Fraser points out, the gunpowder of the sixteenth century was weaker than today, so an enormous amount would have been needed to cause the kind of explosion that followed, leaving the unanswered questions – who had planted it there, and how did they do it in broad daylight? This is the point at which Bothwell is suspected of being guilty of the murder, but there were so many unsolved puzzles surrounding his whereabouts and motives that it has never truly been proved. This is not the place to investigate much further as the events are so complicated and contradictory that it is now impossible to be confident of fthe acts surrouding that night. All that is known is that Mary rode back to Holyrood after spending a few pleasant hours in a house that had enough gunpowder in it, ready to be lit, to destroy the house and all those in it.

At 2am the city was awakened by the huge explosion, the sound of it being likened to that of thunder. The house was completely destroyed, yet Darnley hadn't been killed by the blast. His body, and that of his servant Nelson, were found in the garden, the king wearing his nightshirt and next to him lay a cloak, chair, dagger and some rope. He had been strangled to death. It was clear that he'd been awakened by the noise and had escaped by means of the articles left with his body, but someone was waiting – and he died of strangulation.

History hasn't been kind to Darnley. He had a man's estate but his behaviour was that of a spoilt brat, to use modern terminology. His end was abhorrent and violent. People who lived nearby apparently heard his pleas as he died at the hands of the Douglas men who by now hated him: 'Pity me, kinsmen, for the sake of Jesus Christ, who pitied all the world.' What can easily be forgotten is that with all his shortcomings, he had been brought up in an environment of luxury and wealth, with nothing denied him by his doting parents: nature or nurture? He died at the age of just twenty years.

It seems unusual to include a chapter on a place that we can no longer see as part of the Mary trail, but this was *the* defining moment of her life. Kirk o'Field lies beneath the university of Edinburgh and absolutely no trace of it remains, and recent archaeological digs have failed to establish the exact place where the house stood. At least a walk past the university means you're sharing the same space as Mary did all those years ago.

So who did kill Darnley and why? Well the obvious answer as far as contemporary judges and historians are concerned was Bothwell. He was in a position to dispose of the king and it certainly furthered his cause as he was in serious financial difficulty and the prospect of disposing of the hated Darnley and replacing him as Mary's husband and future king was something he wouldn't shy away from. He had accomplices though, especially Morton and Maitland and the possible involvement of Mary's half-brother Moray. All had reasons to want to be rid of Darnley; yet in the immediate aftermath, there were strong suggestions that the plot had been aimed at the queen and she was in imminent danger herself. Whatever the truth, the fact is that following the explosion and the subsequent discovery of the dead Darnley, Mary completely lost control and suffered what would now be described as a mental breakdown as she failed miserably to deal with the storm that was engulfing her.

On the day of the explosion, Monday, 10 February, she wrote a letter to her ambassador Beaton in Paris and also to Elizabeth I in London, where she expressed horror and revulsion, although there seemed to be little in the way of grief shown for her deceased husband:

> The matter is so horrible and strange as we believe the like was never heard of in any country … with such a vehemency, that of the whole lodging, walls and other, there is nothing remaining, no, not a stone above another, but all carried away, or dung in dross to the very groundstone. It must have been done with the force of powder, and appears to be a mine … the diligence our Council has begun already to use … the same being discovered … we hope to punish the same with rigour as shall serve for example of this cruelty to all ages to come … Always who ever have taken this wicked enterprise in hand, we assure our self it was dressed always for us as for the king; for we lay the most part of all the last week in that same lodging, and was there accomplished with the most part of the lords that are in this town that same night at midnight, and of very chance tarried not all night, by reason of some mask in the abbey, but we believe it was not chance but God that put it in our head.

It's worth pointing that this is a translation from the original sixteenth-century French. Mary spoke Scots-Gaelic at the beginning of her life and relearned it when she returned, but she was brought up in France, so French became her first language. She didn't actually speak English until she was imprisoned in England in her later years.

Bothwell, who surely was the instigator of the plot and had allegedly forced his servant Paris to steal the keys of the lodgings so that the gunpowder could be packed in the cellar, had returned to bed after hearing the explosion. This was for use as an alibi, but on being 'awoken' by his servant, he had risen quickly shouting 'Fie, treason!' and immediately raced to the scene – that he'd just left – with an army of soldiers to do his city sheriff's duty. Darnley's body, which had 'no mark of fire' was removed and carried into the lodgings next door, where it was examined by a surgeon, the Privy Council, and rather bizarrely, by the general public, which was their right in those days. They themselves had reacted in horror at the murder of their king and it needed strong actions by Bothwell and his men to calm down a possible insurrection; most at that time believing the queen was also in danger.

The court immediately went into forty days of mourning and Mary, as well as decorating the rooms in black (so forsaking the French tradition of white for mourning) seemed to fall into a melancholic state of shock, although she was able to attend the wedding of her bedchamber maid the next day. She went to her favourite spot of Seton Palace for recuperation, but on her return to Edinburgh she received long and damning letters from her former mother-in-law Catherine de Medici, who was now the Queen of France, and Queen Elizabeth of England, both demanding that she bring the culprits to justice, and confirm that she had played no part in the proceedings. Rumours were now rife among the people of Edinburgh as stories seeped through of the involvement of many of the people closest to Mary, with servants especially playing on the idea of her being close to the perpetrators. It didn't take long for the citizens to start to accuse and turn against the queen, conveniently ignoring the base behaviour of their king in the past. This was encouraged by Darnley's father, who shouted for justice, accusing the queen of wanting his son dead. It was an outpouring of emotion that wasn't placated by Mary's apparent detachment and this fed the antipathy growing against her.

It was at this time that placards were hung on trees in the city which expressed the strength of public feeling and the fact that Mary, their beautiful and once beloved queen, was now the focus of their disgust and anger. Placards had been an invention of the French and had only recently become popular in Scotland as a way of expressing any opinion, and they were certainly used to good effect after Darnley's murder. The most famous was of course the one that depicted Mary as a mermaid, naked from the waist upwards, with Bothwell as a hare, with a crown on Mary's head and the crest of the Hepburns surrounding Bothwell. At the time, a mermaid was a symbol of a prostitute. Now was the time for the queen to act decisively, but as history has recorded, she did anything but.

It was probably her state of mind that showed itself at this point, added to the ongoing ill health that she'd suffered the past few years, but Mary failed to bring anyone to justice, despite the Privy Council putting up a 2,000 Scots pounds reward for information.

Moray had disappeared again – as he was want to do at times of crisis when he was involved – while most of the others who had been implicated had just gone to ground, except of course one man, Bothwell. He effectively took charge in the queen's mental 'absence', removing Lord Mar from the title of governor of Edinburgh Castle and replacing him with his close ally, Sir James Cockburn. He ordered the makers of the numerous placards to be arrested and replaced them with those of his own challenging any man to meet him in hand-to-hand combat if they continued to accuse him, and he also divorced his wife Jean Gordon, giving her grounds following his adultery with Bessie Crawford, leaving the way clear for his plan to gain the kingdom. While Mary fell into a stupor, Bothwell showed his strength and cunning. It's also fair to record that down the years, Mary had relied on strong men in times of crisis, and Bothwell had always been a staunch ally and supporter of Mary's, and her mother before her, so she must have felt protected by him, despite his obvious plotting for his own gain.

After forty days of mourning, Darnley's death was remembered in a Requiem Mass, but shortly afterwards, and after constant demands by Lennox, Mary went through the process of charging Bothwell in a private hearing in front of Parliament. This appeared to be more a case of being seen to do something as opposed to any real investigation, as by this time Mary had lost any sense of leadership and was now a lost soul in the corridors of Edinburgh Castle.

Killigrew, Elizabeth's envoy, said that when he met her, 'She was in a dark chamber, so as I could not see her face, but by her very words, she seemed very doleful, and did accept my sovereign's letters and messages in a very thankful manner.'

The 'trial' of Bothwell was a sham. In typical robust and arrogant style, he rode with 4,000 of his men down the Canongate, with Morton and Maitland alongside, daring anyone to accuse him. The proceedings went on for seven hours until Bothwell was inevitably acquitted, much to his obvious pleasure. The next week he rode again, this time with a compliant Mary, to the Parliament, and listened impassively as the lands that belonged to Darnley – including Dunbar Castle of which we will hear more of soon – were handed to him and Huntly. Bothwell's rise to power was almost complete, but he needed his innocence confirmed and official backing for his plans to succeed the king to work, so on the 19 April he invited twenty-eight nobles to a grand feast at Ainslie's Tavern in the city, plied them with more than enough drink, and by his sheer force of personality, got each and every one to sign a bond (called inevitably the Ainslie Bond) stating that the queen 'was so destitute of a husband, in which solitary state, the commonwealth may not permit her to remain ... if the affectionate and hearty services of the said Earl, and his other good qualities might move the queen to select him as a new husband ...(she) would prefer one of her native-born subjects unto all foreign subjects.' It was agreed, and now all he needed to do was marry the queen.

Visitor Information

There is nothing to visit, unfortunately, as Kirk o'Field has now completely disappeared. The closest you can get is the Old College at the University of Edinburgh, as it is believed that is built over the original site. That can be found at South Bridge, postcode EH8 9YL.

Dunbar Castle

Dunbar Castle is now a complete ruin, but what remains holds the dark secrets that were shared between Mary Stuart and the Earl of Bothwell in the weeks following the murder of the king of Scotland, and those secrets are most unlikely to be revealed. The castle is not open to the public, but what its standing was we can imagine by what is still there, as it fights the onslaught of time and the incessant battering by the sea.

There had been a castle on that spot well before the now ruined walls of the building that are slowly giving into the ravages of time. Edward I fought for it in 1296, but in the fourteenth century it stood resolutely against the English forces, led by the Earl of Salisbury, as two enormous galleys and hundreds of smaller ships blockaded the fortress. It was ably stewarded by the redoubtable Countess of Dunbar, or 'Black Agnes' as she became known, a woman of great bravery who marshalled her forces as well as any general. An interesting story, which may or may not be true, was how she and her handmaidens dusted down the battlements each night with handkerchiefs after the guns had stopped firing to make the castle look clean and tidy for the aggressors the next day.

A century later, Queen Joan, the widow of James I, was also at the heart of the defence of the castle against another English siege. In 1488, Parliament, tired of the constant advances against the building by the English, ordered the destruction of the castle; 'cassyne doune and alutterly distroy it in sic wise that only fundment tharof be occasion of biging nor reparacione of the said castell in tyme to cum'.

Eight years later it was rebuilt by the king himself, who finished the project in 1501. By the time Mary, Queen of Scots arrived, at the time that she was fleeing for her life following the murder of Riccio, with Darnley well ahead, in a state of terror, it had been rebuilt once more following sixty years of abandonment. The French had extensively changed its internal features and increased its size so that at least another 1,500 extra soldiers could be garrisoned, but once the Treaty of Leith was signed (ending the Franco-Scottish alliance), these embellishments were summarily destroyed.

Mary had gone to Seton again for solitude and a way of recovering her senses, but Bothwell followed with Maitland, and immediately pressured her with suggestions of a marriage. Clearly the queen had no idea what to do and this unexpected development must have confused her even more. As Nau wrote,

> This poor young princess, inexperienced in such devices, was circumvented on all sides by persuasions, requests and importunities, both by general memorials signed by their hands, and presented to her in full council, and by private letters.

Her closest advisors were also proposing the marriage, mainly because Bothwell was strong and in times of crisis could be relied on in his loyalty. She then travelled to Stirling to be with her son, spending two days with James, not knowing at the time that it would be the last time she would ever see him. Then she made the journey back to Edinburgh in a melancholic mood. Her health was poor again, so much so that on the journey she was seized with a pain and had to rest in a small cottage while her nobles fussed and fretted. She recovered but, when she resumed her journey, she was stopped at the Bridges of Almond (around 6 miles from the city) by Bothwell and around 800 of his men. He warned her of danger if she returned to Edinburgh and said he would escort her to Dunbar Castle where she could be protected. Although many of her retinue complained and argued, Mary was compliant and agreed to the change of plan, apparently meekly following Bothwell. Some speculate that Mary knew of the plan in advance, and certainly many of her nobles appeared to be wise to the events days before, with Lennox and Kirkcaldy both aware. Her actions do give us cause to believe that she had been told well in advance that she would be 'abducted'. It could also be that she was in such a state of despair and on the verge of her mental breakdown that, in fact, she was prepared to follow anywhere the one man who had been her loyal companion in these difficult times. She wrote to the Bishop of Dunblane later: 'Bothwell awaited us by the way, accompanied with a great force, and led us with all diligence to Dunbar.'

What took place once they arrived at Dunbar is again the subject of controversy and discussion among historians who have studied Mary's life. Many believe Mary was in love with Bothwell and had already been intimate with him, although there doesn't appear to be any contemporary evidence that this was the case. A whole industry has evolved down the years with books written about the so-called love story of Mary, Queen of Scots and the Earl of Bothwell, but I believe this to be fantasy and nothing more. A far greater number believe that on the first evening, Bothwell raped the queen and so now controlled her, meaning she had to marry him as they had 'consummated' their relationship. Melville, who was part of Mary's retinue in the castle, wrote: 'The Queen could not but marry him, seeing he had ravished her and laid with her against her will.' Later Mary was to say, 'Albeit we found his doings rude, yet were his words and answers gentle.' It was clear that they had had some kind of intimate encounter that evening, but it also seems likely that this was against her will – rape was not something that Bothwell would shy away from.

Despite the infatuation that Mary had with Darnley at the beginning of their relationship, there has been no suggestion that she was the wanton whore that some people had painted her to be. Her marriage to Francois was a childhood friendship and unlikely to have been consummated, and the distaste she had for her second husband was obvious after only a few weeks following their first intimate moment. Lustful passion simply does not seem to be part of Mary's makeup, or at least not to such an extent that she would hazard her own reputation, still less her immortal soul. Her confessor, Mameret, had sworn that he had not come across a more virtuous and upright woman than Mary, so the union of the queen and Bothwell was almost certainly due to the desire to see Scotland ruled strongly, and with Mary in a state of complete abandonment mentally, he was the strong leader the crown needed. She would also have seen the Ainslie Bond, supplied by Bothwell, meaning that any suspicion cast on her new husband over the death of Darnley, had been officially rebutted by the nobles' signatures. With this on her mind, she returned to Edinburgh with Bothwell and married him on 15 May, three months after the death of her second husband. As mentioned earlier, Bothwell had successfully divorced his wife Jean just twelve days earlier, his adultery with Bessie Crawford cited as grounds.

The wedding took place in the great hall of Holyrood Palace and unlike her previous two weddings, this one was conducted in a solemn fashion. It was a Protestant ceremony, although Mary heard Mass earlier in the day, and afterwards there were no celebrations or masques or dancing, just a simple wedding dinner attended by a handful of nobles. There were few gifts exchanged between the two, totally against the tradition of the time when royal marriages involved huge presentations of extravagant presents and gestures, and it was reported that soon after, Mary was seen to be in floods of tears when explaining her actions to John Leslie, the Bishop of Rome. This was clearly not a marriage of love and passion, but more an act of convenience and circumstance. To the Bishop of Dunblane, she wrote:

As envy follows virtues, and this country is of itself somewhat subject to factions, others begin to mislike his proceeding, and so far by reports and misconstructing his doings, went about to put him out of our good grace ... He obtained an writing subscribed with all their hands, wherein they not only granted their consent to our marriage with him, but also obliged them to set him forward with their lives and goods ... This realm being divided in factions as it is, cannot be contained in order, unless our authority be assisted and forthset by the fortification of a man who must take upon his person in the execution of justice ... the travail thereof we may no longer sustain in our own person, being already wearied, and almost broken with the frequent uproars and rebellions raised against us since we came in Scotland.

These words more than any must surely explain why Mary so easily gave into the demands from Bothwell that she marry him.

Unfortunately, Bothwell then showed his true self by completely controlling her and treating the queen in such a fashion that she was effectively his prisoner. Harsh words were constantly spoken by him and a jealousy seems to have taken hold as he stopped her from any happy pursuit or diversion and refused to allow her to meet any male member of her entourage unless he was present.

At this time, he was also in complete charge of State affairs and hardly involved the queen in any decisions, something which only added to her continuing loss of strength, both physically and mentally. Her health declined rapidly and she started to experience epileptic attacks. After overcoming the trials and stresses of the deaths of Francois and her mother, the murder of Riccio and the assassination of Darnley, she seemed to be in a hopeless position and all her well-known resolve and strength had virtually disappeared. At the same time, the people of the country hardly took to the wedding of their once-adored queen to the man they believed to be the instigator of the murder of the king. Also, Maitland, who was always a supporter of Mary, left the court owing to his huge dislike of Bothwell, looking for ways to defeat him, and with that came yet another prospect of civil war.

To return to Dunbar Castle, as a final act following the debacle of Carberry Hill (of which we will read more of soon), Parliament for the second time ordered the destruction of the building and by 1568 it was no longer in existence.

If you search closely, the northwest part of what is left houses the apartment where Mary resided on the occasions she came here under tremendous stress. It is about 12 feet square and virtually impossible to access but it is there nonetheless.

Dunbar is important on the trail of Mary as it was the place she stayed at when she was involved in the fruitless Chaseabout Raid, the place she stayed after the horrendous death of her secretary, and of course the place she was effectively held against her will, as Bothwell implemented his plans and made it impossible for her to release herself from his clutches.

Visitor Information
Obviously there isn't a postcode as the castle is now a complete ruin and no longer open to the public, but it can be viewed from a distance, even if little remains.

Carberry Hill

Mary's last day of freedom and as a reigning monarch was at Carberry Hill, a place just 2 miles from Musselburgh, on the edge of the village of Carberry, and a more unremarkable spot for the demise of a queen cannot be found.

On 6 June, Bothwell took Mary to Borthwick Castle, a fifteenth-century fortress 12 miles south of Edinburgh. The mood of Scotland had changed dramatically towards their queen and for the first time since returning to the country, Mary no longer felt safe. Her marriage to Bothwell, the man who was responsible for the murder of Darnley in the people's minds, was the act that had turned her subjects against her. There was little sympathy from them, as they demanded justice for the murdered king. Mary and Bothwell were pursued and the castle was surrounded, with all four walls besieged by those who hated Bothwell and those who were now against Mary after the events of the previous few months. Her third husband, always the warrior and great military tactician, realised the castle wasn't strong enough to withstand these forces and made his escape, leaving Mary to defend it herself.

She sent messengers to Huntly asking him for help, but the besiegers, led by Morton, captured them and had them executed. She then showed some presence of mind by disguising herself as a pageboy and escaping under the cover of darkness. Mary fled to Black Castle at Cakemuir and met up with Bothwell again, then the two of them returned to Dunbar. At this point she was assured by Sir James Balfour that she would be able to return to Edinburgh in safety as his guns would protect the royal entourage. Balfour was the laird of the castle, but his deceit became all too evident after Mary and Bothwell left the strong fortress of Dunbar. By the time she arrived at Seton Castle, she was supported by around 600 men following her, including her staunch supporter Lord Seton himself, but many of the men who had professed their allegiance to the queen, including the likes of Lord John Hamilton and Fleming, were nowhere to be seen.

After a night at Seton (the last time Mary would see the place), the royal soldiers made their way to Carberry Hill and took up position on the high ground. There they faced the Confederate Lords with Morton, Home, Atholl, Mar, Glencairn, Lindsay and Ruthven and their armies outnumbering the royal soldiers. It was 15 June 1567, and a blazing hot day, and with Mary's forces seemingly ill-equipped to cope with the heat due to a lack of water and food, the stand-off dragged on for far too long. Bothwell, in his usual belligerent style, had offered hand-to-hand combat to anyone who cared to take up the challenge in an attempt to end the confrontation, but no one rose to the bait, knowing that they had superiority in numbers. Mary was asked to abandon Bothwell and return to Edinburgh as queen, but she resolutely refused, pointing out that the lords who were facing her were the same ones who had signed the Ainslie Bond agreeing to the marriage. At this time, she could not trust anyone, and had put her life totally into Bothwell's hands. It was also believed that she was now pregnant with his child (she miscarried, at Lochleven, in July), and so with a second possible heir to the throne, there would be little chance that she would give up her husband.

Her loyalty did her little good. Her own army, combined with her husband's, gradually deserted as the sun blazed down. They were ill-equipped for such a stand-off and the reinforcements that had been promised just didn't materialise. Bothwell decided they should retreat to the safety of Dunbar, but when the lords then suggested that they would allow a safe passage for him providing she followed them into the city where her crown would be restored (under their guidance), she quickly agreed. Bothwell, after initially arguing against the agreement and then handing over the bond that had been signed at Craigmillar stating the guilt of Morton and Maitland in the murder of Darnley, embraced her and rode off. After just five weeks in power, he disappeared and Mary never saw him again.

Mary had been duped. She was immediately seized by the soldiers, who leered and made crude jokes about her, their anointed queen, as she was still wearing the men's clothes that she had stolen when she escaped from Borthwick. Her garments were hardly those of a queen, with a red petticoat only just covering her knees, much to the ribald pleasure of the lords and soldiers who now handled her roughly. She cried out, 'How is this my Lord Morton? I am told that all this is done in order to get justice against the king's murderers. I am told also that you are one of the chief of them.' In reply the soldiers chanted, 'Burn the whore, burn her, she is not worthy to live.' Mary was now in fear of her life and if she ever had any thoughts that she would be saved by any of the nobles who had made the promise of safe conduct, or by her subjects who once loved her, as she returned to Edinburgh they disappeared as quickly as Bothwell. The citizens took to the streets and shouted 'Kill her, drown her.' She had to endure the taunts and physical attacks as she was led through the streets of the city as they only saw an adulteress and murderer instead of the beautiful young queen of just a few months previously. In desperation, she cried out to the people proclaiming her innocence of Darnley's murder, but her shouts were drowned out by the screams of the people. This was the lowest point in Mary's reign as Queen of Scotland.

If you visit Carberry Hill, and it is a very important stop on our Mary trail. There is a plaque that was erected in 2004 by the Mary Stuart Society which reads: 'M.R 1567. At this spot Mary, Queen of Scots after the escape of Bothwell mounted her horse and surrendered herself to the Confederate Lords 15 June 1567.' A little further on, there is another information panel that tells the story of that fateful day. Carberry Hill itself can be seen behind the stone wall that holds the monument and the scene is quite easy to imagine. This description of the non-battle is from the diary of Burrel:

> The 15 day being sonneday, the armies came within view. The one stood upone Carberry Hills, with 4 regiments of shouldiours, and six field-pieces of brasse, the other armey stoode over against it; messengers going betwixt them all day till neir night: dureing which parley the Duke fled secretly to Dunbar, and the Queine came and rounded herself prisoner to the Lords, quho convoyed her to Edinburgh to the Provost's Lodgeing for yat night.

As the diary states, instead of being taken to either Edinburgh Castle or Holyrood Palace, she was lodged in the house of the provost, locked in a small room with guards constantly in her presence. She was given no nourishment and still wore her clothes 'all spoiled with clay and dirt'. In desperation she stood at the window pleading her cause, but this was received with more abuse and shouts from the angry people. She saw her once-loyal secretary Lethington walk past and called out to him, but he pretended not to hear. At one stage her sheer despair was so evident that she stood screaming from the window, her hair hanging down, and her bosom exposed as she had rended her clothes apart in anguish. It was just four weeks since she had married Bothwell. Her previous life had been destroyed.

So what became of Bothwell? He fled and was pursued by his enemy Kirkcaldy of Grange but, after a chase through the Orkneys, he managed to escape to the coast of Norway, presumably to raise a force strong enough to return to Scotland and take back the crown. This was probably not due to any feelings of love or compassion for Mary, although he had always been strictly loyal to her cause, but more for his own ambitions.

Unfortunately for him though, he ran into relations of his former mistress Anna Throndsen, and many of his creditors still chasing him. After initially escaping, he was incarcerated in Copenhagen Castle. The King of Norway at first looked upon him as a possible hostage for future negotiations with Scotland, but soon forgot about that and, indeed, about him. When it became clear that Mary would not regain the throne, he became insignificant as a bargaining tool; there is some poetic irony in this, considering his earlier exploitation of Mary.

Bothwell, so long the mighty warrior who boasted that no prison could ever hold him, was chained to a large post in a dark dungeon without the means to stand properly. His food was passed down on the end of a rope and he was never to see the light of day again. After about ten years of captivity, he died completely insane.

Visitor Information

As the Mary Stuart Society accurately says on its website, Carberry Hill is not the easiest place to find. Carberry is located in East Lothian off the A6124 and its postcode is EH21, but the scene of the famous stand-off between Mary and her opponents needs some searching for. You can find it via a pleasant walk through the woodlands, about 2 miles outside of Musselburgh, in the village of Carberry. If you go past Carberry Tower, then you will see an opening in the wall and that takes you to the woodlands. Continue the walk until you see the plaque erected by the Society. There is no parking in the area, so it requires effort to get there, but once you do, then you are sharing a real moment in time with our heroine.

4

CAPTIVITY
1567–1587

Lochleven Castle

After only one night in the provost's lodgings, Mary was briefly taken back to Holyrood Palace, where she was re-united with two of her 'Maries'. She was given a meal, her first for nearly two days, but midway through it, she was told she had to leave immediately as her horses were waiting outside. She believed she was to be taken to Stirling Castle to be with her son but, sadly for Mary, that wasn't so. The departure was so quick that she wasn't allowed to take any of her clothes and she could only be accompanied by two of her personal chambermaids. They travelled at speed some 50 miles north of Edinburgh, where they arrived at the huge expanse of water known as Loch Leven, with Lochleven Castle occupying one of the islands.

Lochleven Castle today is a ruin, but happily can be visited by the public, as it is another location cared for by Historic Scotland. The scene that greeted Mary back in the sixteenth century doesn't differ a great deal from what we can see today, except that the loch's waters have receded somewhat, so that they no longer wash against the stone walls as they did in Mary's time. It is a forbidding castle, as they all are for obvious reasons, and one can only imagine the sheer desperation she must have felt as she was rowed across the loch to her prison. She knew the castle, as she had been there many times before, in better circumstances than she was in now; she had had one of her famous meetings with John Knox in the castle where for two hours he had lectured her following her complaints of Catholic monuments being defiled in Edinburgh and surrounding areas. She had also visited it briefly during the Chaseabout Raid, and Darnley had been a regular visitor, as the surrounding woods were ideal for his passion of hunting and the loch supplied a remarkable amount of trout.

The origins of the castle are confusing. In David and Judy Steel's excellent book *Mary Stuart's Scotland*, published in 1987, they point out that the castle was the baronial residence of the feudal superior of the second smallest of the old Scottish counties, Kinross – this means the Douglas family were in possession for 350 years from the late fourteenth century, but the castle's history dates from further back. The priory on the neighbouring island was built in 511. Tradition suggests the castle was built at the same time, although nothing from that time remains. Lochleven played a big part in the Wars of Independence, when the great Scottish patriot William Wallace, seeing it was garrisoned by the invading force of the English, swam across the loch with his sword tied around his neck, stole a boat and then helped the Scottish army to liberate the fortress from the unwary soldiers.

A quarter of a century later, the castle was besieged again, despite Scotland now officially being declared independent and, for more than nine months, boats battered at the walls with stone shots, and a temporary fort was erected on the mainland to intensify the blockade. A dam had also been constructed in an attempt to flood the castle, but this proved to be ineffective. The siege only ended when the besiegers left to attend a religious festival in Dunfermline, in honour of Saint Margaret of Scotland, and the temporary fort was then destroyed by the defenders. By the late fourteenth century, Lochleven Castle was being used as a prison, with the future King Robert II and his son among the first inmates. When Robert III succeeded to the throne, he actually presented the building to his second wife Euphemia Ross, proving their stay there wasn't quite the desperate time it could have been.

It later became a marriage gift to his niece's bridegroom, Sir Henry Douglas, but despite being owned by the Douglas family, it could still be commandeered by the Crown. It was to this castle, now run by the stern Lady Margaret, mother to Moray by Mary's own father James V, that the queen was transported, arriving during the night after a tiring and dangerous journey. She was not shown to one of the royal apartments that had been available to her on past visits – there is evidence to suggest that they had been prepared many years earlier with vast furnishings of tapestry, green velvet hangings and draperies of gold and silver – but was shown to the stark laird's room. Secretary Nau wrote:

At the edge of the lake she was met by the Laird and his brothers, who conducted her into a room on the ground floor, furnished with only the Laird's furniture. The Queen's bed was not there, nor was there any article proper for one of her rank. In this prison, and in the midst of such desolation, Her Majesty remained for fifteen days and more without eating or drinking or conversing with the inmates of the house, so that many thought she had died.

Mary again had fallen into one of her many bouts of illness and withdrawal; but this one in particular could be explained. She had miscarried twins in July in what appeared to be a life-threatening moment for her, so that now all connection to Bothwell was lost.

Earlier the lords had issued a warrant for the queen's imprisonment (the same ones who only eight weeks earlier had signed the Ainslie Bond) and all her jewellery and furniture were confiscated. Some of the jewels were taken by her half-brother Moray, who then sold them to Queen Elizabeth, only saving a handful for a present for his wife.

At the same time, the lords were pursuing anyone remotely connected with the death of Darnley, with William Blackadder captured then hung, drawn and quartered and his limbs posted on the gates of the entrance to Edinburgh. Others followed, with John Hepburn and John Hay executed, Bothwell's loyal servant Paris was hanged after making a confession under torture, and George Dalgleish, Bothwell's servant and tailor, was caught and executed.

Of course the main instigator was now far away from Scotland but facing his own horrendous demise. Two days after Mary's miscarriage, she was forced to sign her own abdication papers. In a state of mental stress and physically unable to move due to the loss of blood, she was threatened with having her throat cut by Lord Lindsay, with the support of Lord Ruthven, if she did not sign. Despite this, she demanded that there should be a parliamentary enquiry, but as it was clear that her life was in serious danger (she had also suffered a disease of the liver, which she feared was poisoning), she signed the papers that ended her reign as Queen of Scotland and forfeited any rights to the Crown of England too. In her own mind she may have believed that she would escape and then be able to retract the documents as her signature had clearly been forced from her under duress. One can only imagine the depths of despair this poor twenty-four-year-old woman was falling into.

Five days later, her thirteen-month old son James was crowned King of Scotland, with James Stewart, the Earl of Moray, proclaimed as regent. To show the level of disregard in which she was now held, cannons were fired from the battlements of the castle and bonfires lit to celebrate the crowning of a new king. Mary saw the festivities, and returned to her room weeping and desperate. If that wasn't enough, shortly afterwards Moray visited her and, instead of showing the natural brotherly love she hoped for, he lambasted her for past actions and at one stage suggested she might even be executed for her role in the death of Darnley. After two days of loudly haranguing her, he left – leaving her utterly desolate and alone.

Despite the depths of despair she had been forced into, Mary still seemed to have the ability to captivate and charm with her beauty and demeanour. She had asked for and finally received after a wait of many months some of her clothes from the royal apartments in Edinburgh, including petticoats and satin sleeves, plus powder and soap, and leather shoes. Her keepers had moved her to a more comfortable room in the main tower, although that came with higher security. She now indulged in pastimes to keep her mind occupied such as needlework, card-playing and dancing.

This all helped her state of mind and it was at this point that she became aware of the attentions of the young George Douglas. He was clearly falling in love with her and so was willing to help her in any scheme that would eventually set her free. To that end, he started by smuggling out letters to Catherine de Medici and the Queen of England on her behalf, both of whom failed to reply to her entreaties that she had been unjustly arrested and was now in fear for her life. In fact neither queen had further interest in Mary – and the request to Queen Catherine to send French soldiers to free her from her island prison was met with ridicule.

George looked for ways of freeing Mary as he had fallen deeply in love. There was no suggestion that she reciprocated those feelings but she was very fond of him and he stayed in her court for the rest of her life. After initially being banished from the island by his father and brother, he forewarned staunch supporter Lord Seton that Mary was soon to escape. Sadly, the first attempt failed when she took the place of a laundress in a pre-planned switch. With her face shrouded by a scarf, she sat with the others who were returning to the mainland after collecting the laundry. It looked as if it would be a pretty straightforward journey across the loch, but the boatman very quickly realised who she was after seeing her delicate hands and the long fingers she was well-known for, and he returned her without alerting her keepers. That was to his credit, but it meant that Mary was still imprisoned.

The second attempt shortly afterwards was a success. With the help of Willie Douglas (a young lad who had also fallen under Mary's spell), she escaped by simply walking through the main gates dressed as a countrywoman. George had arranged for all the boats to be scuttled, bar one, and alerted the nobles to be ready with horses on the shore, while Willie, who was an incredibly intelligent boy of fourteen, had managed to get the Douglases very drunk at a late-night feast and simply stole the keys to the guard-gate by covering them with a napkin when serving the laird. George, who had been given a pearl earring by Mary and told that he was to return it to her when the plans for the escape were at hand, duly did this by giving it to a handmaiden, saying he had found it at the bottom of a boat and it had clearly been stolen. She then returned it to Mary under the less-than-watchful eye of Lady Margaret, who didn't suspect a thing. The scene was set and while the feast and party continued (although her jailor, the laird, had shown a certain amount of interest at George's tampering with the boats, which he couldn't understand but didn't bother to investigate), Mary and Willie simply got into the boat and rowed across the loch to the waiting George Douglas, Lord Seton and John Beaton. As an aside, Willie was also devoted to Mary and spent the next twenty years with her until she died.

For now, she was free and as the entourage rode through the land, peasants came out of their homes and cheered her as she passed, so different to the reception she had received in Edinburgh nine months previously. Meanwhile, the laird, seeing that his prisoner had escaped with the simplest of ruses, tried to take his own life with a dagger.

Lochleven Castle wasn't to see such high drama again, unless you count the Earl of Northumberland being captured in 1570 after the failure of the Catholic Uprising. He was imprisoned for eighteen years before being sent to England for execution. By the seventeenth century, Lochleven was no longer a dwelling, but owned by Sir William Bruce who, as well as building Kinross House on the lake shore (later demolished), used the castle as the centrepiece for his gardens. For the next two centuries it was left to fall into ruin and was inaccessible, but in the early twentieth century it was given to the State. Historic Scotland run and maintain the building and the loch.

Lochleven Castle was one of the places at which Mary stayed for the most consecutive days, albeit as a prisoner, and so for that reason alone it is certainly worthy of inclusion on our Mary trail. It can be accessed by a twelve-person passenger ferry. The building offers glorious solitude, peace and tranquillity, completely at odds with its history. Parts of the ruins are now a Scheduled Ancient

Monument and the castle itself has the highest category listing, meaning it should now be preserved for generations. It is only open to the public at certain times of the year, so it is worth checking in advance. Of course, like many places that are now associated with Mary Stuart, there is a ghost that has been seen walking the walls, reputedly Mary. Much as I would love to believe it, I still maintain that there are far more worthy buildings for her spirit to occupy than the castle that saw her first imprisonment. I will return to this subject later.

Visitor Information
As mentioned, the castle is reached by way of a small ferry, which takes about 10 minutes. It can be a popular spot with tourists and is ideal as a picnic site on a summer's day. The castle is closed for the winter and the website strongly suggests that you book a visit in advance due to its popularity. It can be found on Pier Road, Kinross, postcode KY13 8UF.

Dundrennan Abbey
So Mary was free. After nine-and-a-half-months, she had her liberty gain, but if she thought that would be the last time she would be incarcerated, she couldn't have been more wrong; her imprisonment at Lochleven was just a taste of what was to come. Her first instinct was to flee to the relative safety of the fortress that is Dumbarton Castle, which was still firmly a pro-queen stronghold, and following several proclamations with earls, bishops and lairds all offering their support, she made her way in that

direction. Unfortunately, her half-brother Moray stood against her. He had refused any negotiation with Mary and was determined to see her captured once more, and to that end, his forces (much smaller than Mary's) assembled to do battle at a small village called Langside.

In what has become a regular occurrence in Scottish military encounters, the smaller army completely out-manoeuvred and out-battled the larger, and Mary's forces were decimated with more than 100 killed and a further 300 taken prisoner. The reason for this complete catastrophe was the incompetent leadership of the Earl of Argyll, who failed miserably to press forward an advantage when he had one. He also mysteriously had a fainting fit at the exact time he was needed to show command – something he'd been given because he had supplied the most men – but as he was Moray's brother-in-law, the reasons probably don't need to be explained.

For Mary, it was an absolutely crushing blow; despite at one stage personally riding into the battle and exhorting her soldiers to fight, she had found them confused and fighting among themselves. She fled the scene, and as Dumbarton was now cut off by Lennox's men and the pursuing Moray, she changed direction and headed south, where she still had large royal and Catholic support. The journey was difficult, as was shown by her own account to her relations in France in which she wrote:

I have endured injuries, calumnies, imprisonment, famine, cold, heat, flight not knowing wither, 92 miles across the country without stopping or alighting, and then I have had to

sleep upon the ground and drink sour milk, and eat oatmeal
without bread, and have been three nights like the owls.

The party had made its way through the Glenkens and the
west shore of the River Ken, before resting at the peak of
the valley of the Tariff, now called Queen's Hill. Later, Mary
stopped at a peasant's cottage to share the sour milk and
oatmeal as mentioned in her letter. Legend has it that the old
woman who served her was so overcome by her presence
that she was almost speechless. In return for her hospitality,
Mary granted her the freehold of the cottage for the rest of
her life, which would have been a welcome gesture for the
old woman, who presumably had been paying rent to the
landowner.

Eventually Mary arrived at the Maxwell Castle of
Terregles, and then travelled down to the Abbey at
Dundrennan, and it was here that she made the most
disastrous decision of her life, even surpassing that of
marrying Darnley and then allowing herself to be controlled
by Bothwell. Time and again in her life, Mary had shown
that she was a slave to her emotions and when cool,
practical decisions were needed, she was found wanting.
It was this same headstrong feeling that made her decide,
against all of the advice of her nobles, to flee to England
and put herself at the mercy of her 'sister' and 'cousin'
Queen Elizabeth. Despite there being absolutely no
encouragement from the Queen of England – rather if
anything there was consternation in London about the
events of the previous few months in Scotland and her
escape – Mary was sure that a fellow sovereign would take

pity on her and aid her, especially one she seemed to have such an affection for. It had been said many times by those who were attempting to arrange marriages for both queens that it would have been so much easier if one of them had been a man, as they would make a perfect husband and wife, and Mary herself seemed to have an extremely strong connection to Elizabeth; but history has shown that the affection was not reciprocated.

With the benefit of hindsight (and Mary probably wouldn't have acknowledged the truth anyway if she had been given it), it would have made a lot more sense if she had stayed in Scotland and stood her ground until more support came or, more likely, if she had returned to France. There she was still highly regarded and, as a Guise, had the backing of family and the income of a royal dowager. She could have either remained there and still lived a happy life, or she could have raised an army sufficiently large to invade Scotland and re-take her crown – but instead she made the now seemingly incomprehensible decision to cross into England.

It was at Dundrennan Abbey that she spent her last night in Scotland, never to return. Her nobles despaired and one wrote to the deputy-governor of Carlisle Castle asking for permission for Mary to take refuge there, but she didn't bother to wait for the reply, such was her eagerness to act on the decision that she alone had taken. There is some confusion about whether or not Mary actually stayed in the abbey, as it has been suggested that she lodged in a private house, but it is certain that she saw this beautiful twelfth-century building as she made her way to the shore, even if its radiance could well have been lost on her at that time. She was also looking increasingly un-regal in the torn clothes she was wearing, and with her head now shaved to avoid recognition, so her last night in her country wasn't the stately occasion that she was used to and certainly did not match her return to Scotland all those years before as queen.

Dundrennan Abbey is a beautiful sight, even if it is now more or less a total ruin. Established in 1142 by Fergus of Galloway, David I of Scotland and the monks of Rievaulx Abbey, there is little now remaining, but what can be seen gives an impression of the splendour that this historically peaceful abbey once had. Its Cistercian background gives it the simplest of form and down the centuries the grey sandstone has weathered well. The history of the abbey is unremarkable and Mary's stopover is probably the most unusual moment. In 1606 it was disestablished, after being passed to the Crown following the Scottish Reformation.

As with all the buildings associated with Mary, it is worth a visit simply because it was from this spot that she had her last moments on Scottish soil and it was also one of her last days of freedom, even if she was blissfully unaware of it at that point. It's also worth imagining what was going on in her mind as she walked down to the shore after making the momentous decision to go to England. Did she doubt whether she was doing the right thing? Was she convinced Elizabeth would help, bearing in mind Mary still harboured hopes of gaining the English Crown too?

This is a very important spot on Mary's trail, but make prior enquiries before visiting as, although it is controlled by Historic Scotland and is a tourist destination, sometimes adverse weather conditions can cause an unplanned closure.

Visitor Information

The abbey is very popular with tourists, but is closed in winter so pre-planning is essential. The guides are very helpful and knowledgeable, with Glyn from Historic Scotland a passionate orator on the building's history. The postcode is DG6 4QH.

Workington

On Sunday 16 May 1568, Mary Stuart boarded a small fishing boat with a small band of followers, Lord Herries, Lord Maxwell, Lord Fleming, Lord Claude Hamilton and a few attendants, and set sail for England. As with most things connected to Mary, there is a myth that has developed that the place she departed from, Port Mary, and the place she set foot on in England, Maryport, were both named after her, but this is not the case as the place in England was named, well into the seventeenth century, after the mayor's wife, but it is an understandable mistake.

The four-hour journey was difficult and it has been suggested that midway through it, Mary had a change of heart and asked to be taken to France instead, but the winds and tide were totally against her so she continued her journey to England. Once she arrived in the small town of Workington, legend again has it that she lost her footing stepping onto land as it was slippery underfoot and, if that wasn't taken note of at the time, in later years it has been suggested that it was a bad omen for the queen who had chosen to go into exile. Hindsight can play a big part in history's telling.

Mary went to Workington Hall, a grand building just on the outskirts of the town, and there she rested but also wrote and sent another beseeching letter to Elizabeth asking for aid and sanctuary:

> Alas! Do not as the serpent that stoppeth his hearing, for I am no enchanter but your sister and natural cousin. If Caesar had not disclaimed to hear or heede the complaint of an advertiser he had not so died ... I am not of the nature of the basilisk and less of the chameleon, to turn you to my likeness.

The residents of Workington, unused to anything remarkable taking place in their town, had already become aware that they had what we would now call a 'celebrity' in their midst, as this tall and shaven-headed young woman was attracting attention and it soon became common knowledge that she was indeed the famous Scottish queen. A force of around 400 men arrived shortly afterwards with Richard Lowther, the deputy-governor of Carlisle at its head, with express instructions to escort the young queen to Carlisle Castle, something she immediately objected to. She pointed out that she had requested the assistance of Queen Elizabeth against her disloyal subjects, and to that effect had sent John Beaton to London to have a face-to-face counsel with the English queen, but Lowther was unmoved. The following day, Mary was taken to nearby Cockermouth, and then on 18 May she was lodged in Carlisle Castle. At that time, to her, it was just a stopping-off point before she could meet Elizabeth and plead her cause, but unbeknown to Mary, this was the start of the imprisonment that she was to endure for the rest of her life.

Workington is not the type of place to be found on the usual tourist destination list. Located at the mouth of the River Derwent, it has a small population. It became an unemployment black spot once the traditional production of coal and steel came to an end. Like many northern towns though, it has a unique history (although very little of it has any connection to Mary apart from her very brief stay) and has regenerated over the past fifteen years. The surrounding areas are beautiful, with the Lake District nearby, and it is this that inevitably draws the most visitors.

Workington is included in our trail of Mary, Queen of Scots simply because of the importance of the moments she spent here. It was here that she first set foot on English soil. It's here that she unwittingly became a prisoner of Elizabeth, despite her naive hopes and beliefs, and after 17 May 1568, she was never to be free again. This part of our trail is essentially a stopover to see the plaque commemorating her arrival. It was unveiled in 2005 on the quayside, even though there has always been a dispute as to the exact location of that fateful step ashore (many historians argue that it was between Siddick and Workington and not in the town itself), and there is also a new heritage trail that marks her walk from the harbour to Workington Hall, although, again, this is the subject of more conjecture. It's good to see, though, that the town has recognised the immense impact that that day had on history.

Visitor Information
Should you wish to see Workington Hall, it can be found on Ladies Walk, postcode CA14 4YB.

Carlisle Castle

Carlisle Castle is situated in the town and is near the ruins of Hadrian's Wall. With it being nearly 1,000 years old and close to the Scottish border, it has had its fair share of skirmishes. In fact, it has endured more sieges than any other place in the British Isles, according to the English Heritage website. It was built when Cumberland (now called Cumbria) was still part of Scotland in the eleventh century, and was originally constructed on the site of a Roman fort. In the twelfth century, the King of England, Henry I, ordered it to be reconstructed as a stone building and extended the city walls so as to block the flow of invading Scots who coveted the site as a base for their attacks. They managed to take the castle no fewer than seven times between 1173 and 1461. Probably the most famous, and the most dramatic, siege was by Robert the Bruce after he overcame the English in the Battle of Bannockburn, but his attempt failed and his forces retreated to Scotland. The bloodiest, though, would have been during the War of the Roses, when the Houses of Lancaster and York battled for supremacy, with the Lancastrians seizing the castle with the help of Scottish soldiers. Of course, the fortress changed hands many times down the years; by the middle of the thirteenth century, it became the base of the Western March, which was a buffer zone protecting the western part of the border between England and Scotland.

This continued until Henry VIII reconverted the castle into a military barracks, and it was in this that Mary found herself a prisoner during 1568.

When she arrived at the castle, she was without adequate clothing and certainly without funding to present herself in the regal style to which she had become accustomed, and so her new keeper, Lowther, helped her by sending for clothing from nearby merchants and also paid for the expense of the trip from Workington to Carlisle. She was beholden to Lowther, even if at that time she had no idea she was taking one more step closer to incarceration for the rest of her life. Naively, she still believed that Queen Elizabeth would come to her aid, or failing that, her French relations would send an armed force to rescue her and return her to the throne of Scotland.

At this stage in her life, she was grasping at any straw. Elizabeth herself at that time probably had no idea how to treat the exiled queen and possibly wished the problem would just go away. After all, Elizabeth was a Protestant queen and Mary a Catholic, and at a time when that statement meant everything, it would have been inconceivable for the English queen to help restore Mary to her throne, especially considering the hopes that the Scottish and French queen had always had of inheriting the English crown too.

So Elizabeth sent her counsellor, Sir Francis Knollys, to Carlisle to negotiate with Mary, hoping that she would agree to a trial over the murder of her second husband, before any hope of being presented to Elizabeth could be considered.

The Scottish queen seemed to have made a favourable impression on Sir Francis in their many meetings and it is fair to say that he became quite fond of her, as many who met her eventually did. He later wrote of her:

>...she was a notable woman because she had no care for ceremonies beyond the acknowledgement of her royal estate; then she spoke freely to everyone, whatever their rank and showeth a disposition to speak much and to be bold and to be pleasant and to be very familiar.

Unfortunately for Mary, this did nothing to sway Elizabeth, who decided that she could not be presented at an English court until she had been completely cleared of the accusation of being involved in Darnley's murder, and the only way that could happen would be for her to endure a trial. Mary took the news badly and fell ill once more, after a waterfall of tears.

The apartments that Mary Stuart occupied at Carlisle were less than stately; in addition, she was now more alone than before because many of her ladies-in-waiting had not been permitted to stay, with only the loyal George Douglas constantly by her side. Most of her entourage had to sleep away from the castle and many were not permitted to visit her during the evening hours for fear of a possible escape. The chambers where she lodged were secured at night and any attempt at leaving during the day was impossible as iron gratings covered the windows. If she hadn't realised it before, then by now surely she must have understood that she was a prisoner of the English crown. Elizabeth paid for her upkeep, the not inconsiderable sum of around £56 per week in food and wine for Mary's small entourage. Mary's clothing was replenished by stocks from Lochleven, after a request to Elizabeth had been met with a frugal response, and one of the 'Maries' returned to her service, in the form of Mary Seton, meaning a familiar childhood friend could help her while away the long hours of boredom. Mary never gave up on the belief that her 'sister' would eventually come around to her way of thinking and would rescue her from the situation she found herself in.

She wrote many letters to Elizabeth, plus some rather romantic poetry. One letter was written in both French and Latin – she still couldn't speak English well enough to write fluently in it at this point – and her words are worth showing here as they give an insight into her desperation. This is the English translation:

A longing haunts my spirit, day and night, Bitter and sweet, torments my aching heart, Twixt doubt and fear, it holds its wayward part, And while it lingers, rest and peace takes flight ... Ah! I have seen a ship freed from control, On the high seas, outside a friendly port, And what was peaceful change to woe and pain, Even so am I, a lonely trembling soul, Fearing not you, but to be made the sport, Oh fate, that burst the closest, strongest chain.

The letters continued to be beseeching, but one sent in late May was almost threatening in its tone, suggesting that if she didn't receive help from London, she would then seek it from France. Her letter never arrived in Paris though, as its bearer, Lord Fleming, was not allowed to proceed across the Channel after it had been read by Elizabeth.

At the same time, her half-brother (and now her arch-enemy) Moray produced a number of letters supposedly written by Mary at the time of Darnley's death, which clearly implicated her in that event. These letters had lain untouched and unseen with Morton for some time and seemingly had little importance, but once Mary had fled to England, they were used against her. The validity of these letters was doubtful from the very beginning, as they had been written in French then translated into English; plus there was scepticism about whether they had been written by Mary at all, as they appeared to be completely inaccurate in their descriptions of the events surrounding Darnley's murder.

It would be fascinating to be able to study these documents today, but sadly none of them survived. With the uncertainty about what to do with the exiled queen, especially as she completely refused to be put on trial by a fellow sovereign and someone she regarded still as her 'sister' and 'cousin', Mary was removed after just a few months to a castle further into England, Bolton Castle in Yorkshire. This was a far more secure place in which to keep such an important prisoner as it was not as close to the Scottish border as Carlisle.

The place where she was lodged at Carlisle, the Warden's Tower, built in 1308 in the south-east corner, was demolished in 1835, frustratingly for us, of course, but like many of the places associated with her, Carlisle Castle carried on its history without so much as a by your leave.

It was central to the English Civil War in 1644, when it was besieged for months, and then it played a central part during the second Jacobite Rising, well after the Act of Union between England and Scotland. That, though, would be the last battle seen at the castle and, as it was of no use with no border skirmishes taking place, it was neglected. French Prisoners of War were held there in the eighteenth century, but by the nineteenth century huge parts of the castle had been demolished due to it having fallen into ruin and materials were taken for other buildings. The Army occupied it for many years. In 1820, the government feared a revolution so it was refurbished and heavily fortified once more. That military presence has continued to the present-day with the Border Regiment.

The King's Own Border Regiment Museum is within the building and certainly worth a visit, plus the castle, which is now run by English Heritage, has an excellent tour relating to Mary's time there, even if the actual tower where she first experienced English imprisonment has now disappeared. It's also interesting to note that with Mary's brief stay at Carlisle Castle, she became the last royal to actually live there, despite many visits by monarchs since.

Again we have come across a place where Mary's presence has faded due the brief amount of time she was there, but Carlisle Castle is an important stop on our Mary trail because her life changed beyond anything she could have feared when she fled to England. The slow realisation that she was now a prisoner and not a 'guest' of Elizabeth, would have taken place while she was here, so you can imagine her sense of desperation while visiting it.

Visitor Information

The castle is an extremely popular tourist destination and visitors can certainly find enough to do with Mary to make it worthwhile to visit it. The building can be found on Castle Way, the postcode is CA3 8UR.

Bolton Castle

When Mary first learned of her proposed removal from Carlisle to the comparative seclusion of Bolton Castle, she wept with rage. Her keeper, Sir Francis Knollys, tried to placate her by saying it was his queen's wishes (Elizabeth) that she be moved so that she could be closer to her, to which Mary responded in melancholy fashion that she was in her hands and that she might dispose of her at her own will. Eventually, after much disagreement, the journey took place, taking two days with overnight stays at Lowther Castle and Wharton, before arriving at the high-walled fortress that is Bolton Castle. Again, when she arrived, she found that the rooms had not been made ready for her and furnishings had to be sent for from Sir George Bowe's house some distance away.

Bolton Castle was at that time completely cut off from the outside world, compared to Carlisle. The former was a thriving, busy border town where messengers and diplomats could easily travel, and news of the political manoeuvrings surrounding Mary could be transmitted to her, whereas Bolton Castle was in North Riding, Yorkshire, some 50 miles away, with no town to speak of. Today it is surrounded by a pleasant and busy community, but no such place existed then. For the exiled queen, it became one of the loneliest of places, despite her retinue of former courtiers still accompanying her – although they were gradually decreasing in number. She still believed, in an almost childlike fashion, in Elizabeth's good nature and still genuinely expected to be released and restored to the Scottish crown, even as the walls of captivity started to close in on her.

It was while she was at Bolton Castle that two 'trials' implemented by Queen Elizabeth, took place, neither of which Mary was allowed to attend. It was also where the famous Casket Letters first came to prominence, which effectively sealed Mary's fate, yet they have since been proven to be forgeries. We'll hear more of them shortly.

The first trial took place in York, some 40 miles away. It is worth noting that at the time England had no legal right to try a Scottish Queen, even though Elizabeth had promised that Mary would be restored to the Scottish throne if she were proved innocent, or indeed guilty, something she backtracked on shortly afterwards without Mary's knowledge. The *Book of Articles*, written by Calvinist historian George Buchanan, was published containing Mary's letters that were to be used in evidence against her. The trial was to be in the form of an examination where Mary and her accuser, her half-brother Moray, were to be allowed commissioners to represent their cases. Mary had John Leslie and three lords, Livingston, Boyd and Herries, while Moray attended personally with Maitland, something which Mary was forbidden to do. It started in October and ended shortly afterwards following an impasse where little could be proved, not least because the letters that had been offered as evidence were not seen by most of the parties present, and appeared to change in number from the originals. Elizabeth, rather wary of the atmosphere in the close confines of York, ordered the trial to be abandoned and reset in Westminster, but again forbade Mary to attend. Once more the Casket Letters were to be the main evidence.

The Casket Letters

The Casket Letters were pieces of evidence that brought about the downfall of Mary, Queen of Scots, yet at the time of her trial, the numerous letters – which seemed to increase in number as each new day dawned – did not appear to be as important as later centuries have suggested. In fact, as the years have passed, the importance of the Casket Letters has appeared to increase and they have been scrutinised and investigated, with books and studies written and mostly with the same conclusion. They were found, allegedly, under the bed of Bothwell's tailor George Dalgleish. He had played a part in the murder of Darnley in that he helped his master to acquire the keys to the property where the explosion took place and also helped him with a change of clothing following the gunpowder blast. It was under a series of tortures that Dalgleish finally produced a silver casket (now to be seen in the Lennoxlove Museum in Scotland) that appeared to contain love letters from Mary, although at that point there was no suggestion that they were to Bothwell, but more likely older romantic letters sent to Darnley when they were both in the first throes of passion. These letters weren't of any interest when Bothwell was forcing the nobles to sign his Ainslie Bond, and they then disappeared from view for months – until the trial at York and then Westminster. There were twenty-two documents, of which eight were letters, two were marriage contracts and twelve sonnets, which effectively made up one long poem. It has since been proved after rigorous inspection that only two were actually in Mary Stuart's own handwriting. It's clear they had been severely tampered with, while the rest were a mixture of old letters with dates conveniently added, or love letters to Bothwell that looked like had been sent by an ex-mistress (possibly Anna Throndsen?). Antonia Fraser considered that

> Every modern argument concerning the Casket Letters, and indeed every argument on the subject since the conference at Westminster in 1568, has of necessity had to leave out of account this most important consideration in any discussion of letters said to be forged – the question of handwriting – for the Casket Letters now disappeared from sight as mysteriously as they had appeared.

It's fair to say that such evidence wouldn't stand up in proceedings today. The reason for their admission was to prove that Mary was indeed culpable in her husband's death, they were the crucial part of the trial that convened in Westminster on 25 October, again without Mary's presence.

Moray, meanwhile, had been in Queen Elizabeth's presence on many occasions, so Mary then commanded her commissioners not to take part if she could not attend. The 'trial' went on until mid-January and during that time the Casket Letters were made available and scrutinised, with Moray and Maitland swearing to their authenticity. Mary's commissioners were just bit-part actors in the prolonged drama and at one stage Elizabeth asked Mary to answer the charges brought against her from Bolton Castle, but the Scottish queen refused, stating quite reasonably that she hadn't seen the evidence against her and so it was impossible for her to refute it. On 11 January, the conference was officially ended by Elizabeth with neither innocence nor guilt proved and the English queen pronouncing,

> There had been nothing sufficiently produced nor shown by them against the Queen their sovereign, whereby the Queen of England should conceive or take any evil opinion of the Queen, her good sister, for anything yet seen.

It meant that the letters hadn't conclusively proved that Mary was guilty, and in return the Scottish queen hadn't proved that her nobles had acted against her. Mary was to remain a prisoner in Bolton Castle.

Mary used her time there to good effect, learning how to speak and write English from Knollys. Her first letter was to him, after he had been absent for a few days, and it was clear that a relationship was forming between them, although from Mary's point of view, it probably wasn't romantic but more of an attempt to gain further favours from the man who was imprisoning her. The final words of that letter were; 'Excuss my ivel vreitin thes furst tym', which showed that she was learning fast.

She also seemed to toy with the possibility of accepting the Protestant religion into her life, something strongly encouraged by Knollys, but after disquiet from the Catholics in England, she went out of her way to convince them that she had absolutely no intention of changing her faith. It could have been another attempt to influence her keeper so that she could get closer to Elizabeth and the possibility of release.

At this time Mary seemed to be content staying at the rather uncomfortable castle so as not to incur the wrath of Elizabeth, so security around her was a lot slacker than previously, but she did write later after a period of inactivity that: 'If I shall be holden here perforce, you may be sure then being as a desperate person, I will use any attempts that may serve my purpose either by myself or my friends.' Yet there were reports of an escape attempt she apparently made in August when she was said to have been let down from a window, with horses awaiting beneath it ready to whisk her away, but the plan was foiled when one of her servants made too much noise and alerted the guards. This was never actually confirmed and it seems unlikely that Mary would have agreed to such a plan at this early stage, as she was still very much beholden to Elizabeth. After six months though, with no conclusion at Westminster, Mary was removed from Yorkshire to the complete security of Tutbury Castle in Staffordshire, a place that now became her home.

Bolton Castle is today a lovely place to visit, surrounded by the village of Castle Bolton, and a day out in the sunshine can be invigorating. With that in mind, it is sometimes difficult to remember that this was a prison for Mary, and the surrounding countryside would probably only have served to emphasise her seclusion.

The castle was built in the fourteenth century, begun in 1378 and finished eleven years later. It has some of the highest walls seen in any castle in the United Kingdom. It's now a Grade 1 listed building, for obvious reasons, but its history is not necessarily one of skirmishes and battles, but more of sanctuary. It was damaged during the English Civil War, but that was minimal and no major renovation projects were required afterwards. It's still in private ownership, which is unusual for a castle of such age and prominence.

The Abbot of Jervaulx used it as a sanctuary in 1536, during the Pilgrimage of Grace rebellion against Henry VIII's religious reforms, but he was eventually captured and executed. As part of the king's retribution, he ordered the castle to be burned to the ground, but this was impossible due to the sturdiness of the stone walls. There was some damage done to the interior, but renovations quickly followed, paid for by the owner, Sir John Scrope. The Scrope family have owned the castle ever since and it is now a popular tourist destination, making much of Mary's stay there.

There is a room, called Mary's Room, still intact, which looks gloomy even today, so one can only imagine the sense of it in Mary's day, but a word to the wise. This room is not the one that Mary lived in as she was housed in a now-demolished tower, but it is fair to say she did spend time alone there.

At the northern part of the castle are some magnificent gardens with spectacular views over the Yorkshire countryside, similar to the ones that Mary must have seen centuries ago, and the places where she was allowed to go hunting on her few days of relative freedom.

It's at this point that I have a confession to make (which I alluded to earlier), and one that I wondered if I should include. It was at Bolton Castle, many years ago, that I genuinely felt the presence of Mary when I was sat on one of the stone benches looking out on the countryside. To many, this will sound ridiculous, but to me it felt very real. I am convinced we had a 'conversation' about the length of time it would take me to travel to Scotland from that spot compared to how long it would take her. To this day I am convinced this mundane exchange took place. In a way, this is what this book is all about. If you have a passion for history (not just Mary Stuart), then these glimpses of the past are what make it all so exciting. We share the same space as that person did, so is there a connection? I believe there is, and I'm sure others feel the same, but I will understand if you're one of those who want to quickly move on to the next chapter! Sadly, Mary didn't want to move on quickly, and her journey to Tutbury was anything but rapid.

Finally, before we go on, Bolton Castle was the location for the film *Elizabeth* starring Cate Blanchett in the late 1990s. This was an excellent film, but certainly used artistic licence. If you want to know the real story of Queen Bess and Mary, then enjoy the film as an entertainment, but look elsewhere for history. Mary doesn't even get a mention!

Visitor Information

The castle is certainly one of the busiest on our trail in terms of the number of daily events it provides, and as a venue for weddings and banquets. Most of it is now in ruins, but the part that has been renovated can be toured with excellent explanations of the history, including of course reference to Mary. It's open daily and there is car parking, with the admission fee giving you access to the gardens. I don't expect you to sit on a bench and have a chat with our heroine, but maybe you'll get a real feeling for the place and Mary when you visit. It can be found at Castle Bolton, Leyburn, DL8 4ET.

Tutbury Castle

Once Mary was removed from Bolton Castle with instructions to relocate to Tutbury Castle, she could have had absolutely no doubt that she was a prisoner. Any hopes she had clung to about the goodwill of Queen Elizabeth were completely gone. The sense of betrayal must have been immense and one can only imagine her feelings as she looked back over the previous year, after she had made the decision to throw herself at her 'sister's' mercy by fleeing from Scotland to England.

The number of courtiers she had accompanying her was decreasing; although there were still well over fifty, this was not the size of the royal household she had enjoyed in the past. She no longer heard from her supporters; she now had very little contact with the outside world and her enemies were numerous – Moray was still regent of Scotland and he had Elizabeth's ear. Her keeper Knollys, with whom she'd had a pleasant relationship, lost his wife to a sudden illness so he was preoccupied with his own problems and did nothing to question the instructions to move Mary elsewhere.

As if that wasn't enough, the journey to Tutbury was difficult. The weather was bitterly cold. The north of England had been covered with heavy snow for most of the winter and it had turned to thick ice, which made travel on horseback treacherous. Most of the retinue suffered from some kind of sickness, with Lady Livingstone so poorly that she had to be left behind. Then Mary fell ill too. She was in such a state, mentally and physically, that she collapsed and the journey had to be halted between Rotherham and Chesterfield until she recovered.

Then there was a detour when news arrived that Tutbury Castle had not been prepared for her arrival so instead of going there, they were to head for the Earl of Shrewbury's home in Sheffield. He would be her new jailor, and he owned many huge properties spread across the north of England. While on their way to Sheffield, they were again stopped and informed that all the furniture and hangings had been sent to Tutbury after all, so they should change direction again. It was by all accounts a miserable and frustrating journey.

When she arrived at the castle on 3 February 1569, Tutbury turned out to be even further from the standards she had previously enjoyed; the medieval castle was not designed to house a queen but she would spend the majority of the next eighteen years of her life there, whether she liked it or not.

Mary expressed the view many times in the following years that Tutbury was the place she hated the most and the end of her life began the moment she entered the castle. The fortress occupied a hill, overlooking both Staffordshire and Derbyshire, but it was in a state of virtual ruin, and offered little if any comfort, despite the spectacular views from towers. It was damp and extremely smelly, mainly due to the poor sewerage system and a pungent marsh that ran alongside the walls. It was also very draughty; the windows were ill-fitting, due to the rotting wood of the window frames. During the winter, when Mary first arrived, it was breathtakingly cold with winds howling around the castle and into every chamber, so trying to stay warm was the main endeavour of every day. Although the castle had received extensive renovations a decade earlier, it was reported the repairs were 'indifferent'.

Another problem that was to face both Mary and her new jailor the Earl of Shrewsbury, was the lack of money to spend on the upkeep of the prisoner and her household. There were constant requests to Elizabeth for funds, which sometimes were accede to – but usually not. Although the earl was extremely rich, he was not keen to spend money on the upkeep of the exiled queen.

Mary also realised she had gained another foe in the shape of Shrewsbury's wife, Bess of Hardwicke. An formidable woman, who had had at least eight children and three other marriages, she was in charge of the household and dictated the finances. She was twice as old as Mary and quite different in personality. Surprisingly, however, the two women did reach some type of understanding and the early days of Mary's imprisonment were not as bad as they could have been, despite the unhealthy and uncomfortable conditions. Mary was allowed to put up her cloth of state and she continued her favourite indoor pastime of embroidery, something she found more and more pleasurable in her later years. It was an interest that the much older Bess shared too, so they were able to spend time together in a type of companionship.

Inevitably, the harsh conditions aggravated Mary's poor health. Within a couple of months she had again fallen seriously ill, necessitating her removal to the more agreeable Chatsworth and Wingfield (we'll come to both these places later) but those respites were never a full-time solution and Mary was never to experience full health again.

Her charm remained though, as a visitor Nicholas White wrote after stopping over at Tutbury to see how the queen was faring:

> She hath withal an alluring grace, a pretty Scotch accent, and a searching wit, clouded with mildness. Fame might move some to try to relieve her, and glory joined with gain might stir others to adventure much for her sake.

It was this charm that made her an attractive proposition for a future marriage, coupled with the fact there was still a possibility of a return to the Scottish throne. Thus, enter Thomas Howard, the Duke of Norfolk. Supported by many, including Moray for reasons too obscure to really appreciate, Norfolk made advances to Mary in the hope of securing her hand in marriage. The couple never actually met; they played out their romance in a series of letters and extravagant gifts to each other. Mary assumed this would be a way of pleasing Queen Elizabeth, in the hope that she would eventually be released from captivity because the marriage to Norfolk would strengthen her ties to England. At this time, there was no suggestion that Mary was looking to escape from Tutbury Castle by conventional means so a more legal and official departure seemed like a workable plan. Meanwhile, she still hoped that either King Philip of Spain or Charles IX of France would come to her aid; neither did. Norfolk was thirty-three, so older than Mary – although that was not usually a problem in the sixteenth century. He was the owner of vast estates and had a good lineage, and it was to this man that Mary started to write affectionate letters:

> My Norfolk, you bid me command you, that would be beside my duty many ways, but pray you I will, that you counsel me not to take patiently my great griefs … I trust none that shall say I ever mind to leave you, nor to anything that may displease you, for I have determined never to offend you, but remain yours. I think all well bestowed for your friendly dealings with me, all undeserved.

To our modern eyes, these words are a confirmation of love, but 500 years ago, they were predictable acts in an elaborate courtship ritual. Mary continued this correspondence and made a pillow for Norfolk with the Latin words *VIRESCIT IN VULNERE VULTUS* (meaning 'courage grows in adversity') embroidered across it. In return, she received an expensive diamond that she wore around her neck. All of this was done in the belief that Elizabeth desired a marriage for her imprisoned 'sister', and as late as 1570, Mary wrote again; 'Our fault were not shameful, you have promised to be mine, and I yours; I believe the Queen of England and country should like it.'

Of course there was still the curious problem of the marriage to Bothwell. How could Mary marry Norfolk when she was still officially married to the man who was now in a dungeon in Denmark?

Well, it was simple. Firstly, Mary had sent an envoy there to ask for her husband to sign a divorce paper but due to his growing insanity that never happened. This seems to show how little affection she had for the man who many historians had painted as her true love.

Then there were two other reasons why this marriage was not now an obstacle. At the time of the wedding, Bothwell was still officially married to Jean Gordon, so that meant that the vows were invalid. Secondly, Mary had married under duress following Bothwell's abduction and possible rape of her. So it seemed she had several reasons to believe she would be able to take another husband.

However, that left Elizabeth out of the picture. Far from being supportive of this union, as Mary had been led to believe, the Queen of England flew into a rage when she learned of it. In revenge, she had Mary returned to Tutbury (she'd been away from the castle because of her health and had been staying in Chatsworth), replaced her jailor with a man whom Mary detested called Huntingdon, severely cut down her entourage, and completely banned her from sending any messages to the outside world – or receiving any. The walls came closing in on the helpless Mary Stuart. There would be no help at all from Elizabeth, that much was now very clear.

The anger the English Queen felt towards her Scottish relation did not only come about entirely due to the 'secret' marriage proposal, but because there had been a Catholic uprising in the north of the country, which, inevitably, had Mary as its focus, even though she had little knowledge of it.

Very quickly after being returned to Tutbury, she was next sent to Coventry to ensure she was far away from the tumult instigated by the Earls of Northumberland and Westmorland. Mary was initially lodged in an inn because Coventry Castle was uninhabitable but Elizabeth had no intention of leaving Mary where she could enjoy herself, so she ended up at Caesar's Tower within the city. (This place no longer exists in the form it had in Mary's day). Queen Elizabeth now completely distrusted Mary and had begun to believe Mary was plotting against her, hardly surprising following the northern uprising, which eventually failed.

It was at this point that Mary's half-brother Moray was killed on the main street of Linlithgow. Mary received this news with little grief, and actually paid the assassin a pension. As mentioned earlier in the book, Moray could have been a great leader – he had certainly calmed the violence that followed Mary's abdication – but circumstances dictated that he was never to get the opportunity. His dislike of his sister's religion, and his belief that it was his destiny to be regent of Scotland, will always sour his actions in the eyes of Mary's supporters. What he might have achieved in future is lost to history. There were varying reports about who had committed the deed, but it was later established that a Hamilton had fired the shot that ended his life.

During this period, Mary was being regularly switched from Tutbury Castle to other locations for political reasons, as well as to give her some respite from the ailments that were making her every day difficult. So we should now take a closer look at this castle that was to be her home longer than any other residence in her life. As described, it is a splendid-looking ruin. There has been a suggestion following recent excavations that a building existed on the spot during the Stone Age. There has been a castle on the top of the obviously defensible hill for many years. From about 1068, there are records of the building erected by Hugh d'Avranches and, in the same year, the castle of Tutbury is listed in the Domesday Book. Nearly a century later, Tutbury was besieged by Empress Mathilda's son Henry of Anjou (later to become Henry II) and again in 1170, when it was overpowered and Henry ordered it to be destroyed. By the beginning of the thirteenth century, the chapel was built on the grounds, part of which we can still see today, and the castle itself was in the process of being rebuilt too but some fifty years later, Edward I attacked, causing considerable destruction.

This latest attack was against Robert de Ferrers, who was in conflict with the king. The castle was confiscated and given to Edward's brother, Edmund Crouchback. It was he who fully restored the fortress and made it part of the Lancaster estate, after being given the title of Earl of Lancaster. The renovations were vast and impressive, making the castle the splendid building it is today. A new garden was planted, and a vineyard and meadow were added. Inside, a huge new grand hall was designed. There was a gateway that towered over the main entrance, which can be seen today. Shortly after these improvements, Edmund's son Thomas was in conflict with the king and was heavily defeated after a battle on the River Trent. He retreated to Tutbury but, relying on Scottish soldiers who never appeared, he was captured, and executed. The castle was again demolished. An interesting aside to this brief description of the attack is that Thomas had with him a hoard of English, Scottish, Irish and European coins that were meant to pay his soldiers, but somehow they were lost in the River Dove during the battle, then discovered in 1831. buried in the banks. These coins, now known as the Tutbury Hoard, can be found in the British Museum.

In the fourteenth century, Tutbury was again rebuilt, this time by John of Gaunt, the Duke of Lancaster, who used it as a permanent residence. With the help of his second wife, Constance, the gardens were completely reconfigured and re-laid. By this time, due to John's title, the castle had become crown property and Henry III gave his permission for the improvements. Sadly, the decay to the building that had started much earlier was now taking effect, and constant improvements were needed to keep it in shape, costing far more money than was expected. In 1480 it had been reported that many of the adjoining buildings were shaky and dangerous, with some almost impossible to enter due to the hazard of falling bricks and masonry. In 1516, the kitchen roof fell in. Seven years later, a survey was made that suggested that most of the buildings were defective and needed extensive repair. It was to this castle that Mary was transported from Yorkshire, confirming her belief that it was not a building fit to hold a queen.

There were many plots aimed at freeing Mary to restore her to the Scottish throne, and to assume the English throne too. One was the Ridolfi plot in which Roberto Ridolfi, an Italian banker based in London, planned to have England invaded from the Netherlands with the help of Philip II of Spain, causing a Catholic uprising. Elizabeth would be removed and Mary put on the English throne, with Norfolk by her side. Norfolk, although he had been imprisoned in the Tower following his amorous pursuit of the Scottish queen, was now free.

The plot was ridiculous though, and never looked likely to succeed. The main problem was that Philip demanded that the English Catholics rise up first, before any invasion plans could be implemented, and, should they fail, the Queen of England's retribution was a grim certainty. The plot was a non-starter, and there has always been a question about whether Mary truly involved herself in it or not. There were claims that she wrote to Ridolfi giving instructions to him should the plot materialise, but the incriminating letters disappeared long ago, so we have to rely on conjecture. In these letters she was supposed to have bemoaned her position in the prison that was Tutbury, and to have said that she felt abandoned by her relations in France, and was quite willing for Norfolk to take care of all the details of the plot. She also apparently asked for her son James to be sent to Spain to be brought up in court there and hopefully to marry a Spanish queen.

At this time, Mary's attempts to communicate with her young son were being thwarted by Elizabeth, as none of Mary's affectionate letters were sent to him. As a result, James grew up seeing his mother as a cold-hearted adulteress who had abandoned him after murdering his father. By the time he was thirteen, in 1581, he had little knowledge of his mother and was busy learning how to be the king of Scotland, unperturbed by her imprisonment.

At about that time, Mary came up with a plan to restore herself to the throne, by suggesting that she and her son ruled jointly. This would have to be agreed by Elizabeth, so it was a plan that, in hindsight, seems too simplistic to be taken seriously. After all, James had now been brought up as a Protestant, so joint rule could never have worked, but Mary (obviously unaware of her son's coldness towards her) genuinely thought it would be a viable solution to her imprisonment, even agreeing to take up a position against France should her family there not agree to the plan. She was desperate to retrieve her freedom, no matter what it took, but four years after proposing the idea, she received the devastating news that James had rejected it, writing to Elizabeth; 'Association desired by his mother should neither be granted nor spoken of hereafter.' It was many, many years – well after Mary's death – before James finally learnt the truth about her and he went to some lengths to restore her reputation.

As well as writing letters to Ridolfi, Mary was also accused in the trials to come of sending financial support for the plot. Her envoy Leslie, Bishop of Ross, was involved and it was he who was to be the recipient of the plans sent by Ridolfi from Tuscany. However, the messenger Charles Bailly was arrested at Dover. This alerted the English queen and she immediately acted, arresting Norfolk once more and imprisoning him in the Tower. He was then sent to trial, accused of high treason, found guilty, and executed.

Mary wept when she heard the news, although her tears were probably more to do with the knowledge that yet another route to freedom had been blocked. Leslie completely betrayed her under fear of torture, proclaiming that Mary had murdered her second husband, and also had poisoned Francois too. Ridolfi was abroad when the plot was uncovered, so escaped punishment. Mary was castigated for her actions, whether deservedly or not, and even France's King Charles (Mary's brother-in-law) despaired of her, writing: 'Alas, the poor fool will never cease until she loses her head.' It should be added that it was Mary's old foe, Catherine de Medici, who had forewarned Queen Elizabeth of the plot that was being financed by Spain and Rome.

The English Parliament railed against Mary and she was described as the 'monstrous dragon' in a speech by one member and the queen penned what has now become a famous poetical diatribe against her 'sister':

No foreign banished wight shall anchor in this port;
Our realm it brooks no stranger's force, let them elsewhere
resort;
Our rusty sword, with rest, shall first his edge employ;
To poll their tops that seek such change, and gape for joy.

Despite these words, Elizabeth resisted the demands for Mary's immediate execution. In 1572, she passed a Bill saying that Mary now had been deprived of the right to succeed to the English throne, and if there were any more plots, then she would be put on trial by English peers as opposed to Scottish.

Mary's cause wasn't helped by the massacre that had taken place in France; the Guise family acted against the Protestant Huguenots, in August, on St Bartholomew's Day. As a result, any Catholic in the middle of Protestant England – especially an exiled queen – was looked upon with complete distaste and mistrust. Despite the obviously one-sided relationship between Mary and Elizabeth, it was to the English queen's credit that she did not acquiesce to the almost hysterical demands for the head of Mary – not at first, anyway.

The slow demise of Mary's strongholds continued, and one of the biggest blows was the loss of Edinburgh Castle in 1573. This had been held for her by her staunch supporters, Kirkcaldy and Maitland, but it suffered under a heavy siege from the English and their effective cannons, and eventually fell. Kirkcaldy was executed and Maitland committed suicide, the latter survived by his wife Mary Fleming, one of the 'four Maries'. Kirkcaldy's loss made Mary despair, even if she didn't show any grief for Maitland due to his, at times, rather fragile loyalty. The fact was, though, that her power in Scotland had, by now, been completely stripped away and there seemed to be no hope of any revival.

Having said that, the excommunication of Elizabeth in 1575 by Pope Pius V meant Mary's name was put forward once again as a possible successor to the English throne, supported by Pope Gregory XIII, the man who succeeded Pius. Still, Mary was very much relying on hope, as opposed to anything tangible.

Tutbury, as we have seen, was about the least attractive place in the world to Mary. She was fortunate that she was able to move around, especially when the castle needed cleaning, as most large buildings of the time were evacuated and the whole of the structure was cleaned while it was empty, allowing the sewerage works to be emptied too. That meant far more pleasant stays at Sheffield, Chatsworth and even Buxton (of which we will hear more) but gradually her entourage was decreasing in numbers, making her surroundings less regal than she had been used to since birth. She had around thirty servants, from her own attendants to chair-bearer. The cost of keeping them was becoming ruinous for Shrewsbury, despite constant pleas to Elizabeth for extra funds, which for the most part were ignored. He took on a fee farm in an attempt to raise finance. His weekly allowance had been cut from £56 to £30, meaning that many of Mary's retinue were released and so she was surrounded by fewer and fewer of her friends and supporters.

Shrewsbury was a kind jailor and had clearly a soft spot for his prisoner. He was constantly having to justify his actions to Elizabeth, who rightly thought that he was too permissive in his treatment of the Scottish queen, and this caused him to write to her once: 'I know her to be a stranger, a Papist and my enemy. What hopes can I have of good of her?' Despite this shrug of the shoulders, he continued to let her have as much freedom as was possible within the confines of the castle.

She was even allowed out to go hunting, still one of her favourite pastimes, and she took up archery again, at which she had always been proficient. She had many pets to keep her company, some of which were presents from supporters in Scotland and France, and the evenings were taken up with lute-playing once more. She had a billiard table installed and still spent a lot of her time on embroidery, either renewing or designing new dresses for herself. She still had the one remaining Marie with her. Mary Seton, the only one of the four not to marry, was a loyal and dear friend who had stayed throughout the troubles of her mistress. She had seemingly abjured any chance of romance and had taken a vow of chastity and, at the time of Tutbury Castle, she was still Mary's closest confidante. In 1583, though, with Seton now unable to cover the cost of her daily duties, Mary allowed her to retire to a convent in Rheims where she lived for many years, until her death in 1615.

As well as imprisonment, Mary's main problem was her appalling health, which had gradually got worse over the years. She had nearly died in Jedburgh in 1566, as we have seen, and unfortunately the maladies that afflicted her then regularly continued. There was a suggestion in later years by surgeons that she had a kidney disease and the blood-related 'dropsy' and this might explain the excruciating pain she had in her left side. She vomited constantly, which in itself must have put tremendous stress on her constitution. The constant setbacks in her attempts to free herself brought on even more distress.

When Norfolk died, she took to her bed and couldn't eat or drink anything due to vomiting. Her right arm swelled to such an extent that she could no longer write, and after once falling from her horse near Buxton, she badly injured her spine so she stooped when she walked from that day onwards. There was also a serious bout of influenza, which so afflicted her that the surgeons were convinced yet again that she was dying As she was now in her thirties, she was regarded as a middle-aged woman. Despite Shrewsbury's kindly treatment of her, he was at times sceptical of her illnesses, writing to Elizabeth: 'I perceived her principal object was and is to have some liberty out of the gates,' but after another terrible bout of vomiting, he agreed that her sufferings were genuine.

The illnesses that hit Mary so hard have been analysed down the centuries, and it is now accepted that she had the hereditary disease porphyria, something that afflicted her father and grandfather. It appeared to be worse at times of extreme stress, and the imprisonment in a totally unsuitable castle such as Tutbury would be stress enough to bring on any of these symptoms. The unusual aspect of this illness is that the sufferer can recover very quickly, so that was the basis for Shrewsbury's scepticism, at times, about Mary's suffering. Antonia Fraser points out that Mary's father died in a similar way after hearing of the birth of his daughter following the calamitous battlefield defeat, and so Mary was just unfortunate to inherit this sickness, to add to the other woes life had thrown at her.

If her health wasn't enough of a problem, Bess became another. The wife of Shrewsbury, overbearing and abrasive, had now completely turned against her prisoner. This was probably due to the huge expense Mary and her retinue were costing her and her husband, and Bess was certainly the kind of figure who would be aware of the financial implications of the situation. Her marriage was also in trouble, following the death of Shrewsbury's son Gilbert Talbot, so Bess took the opportunity to publicly accuse Mary of having an affair with her husband. This, in a way, was something that some people could quite easily have believed, as Shrewsbury had been a kind jailor to his prisoner, but there are no contemporary reports or any evidence whatsoever to prove that such a relationship ever existed. There were even rumours of Mary having two children with Shrewsbury, and a book was written on the subject, but again, there is no proof. The queen was outraged and railed against Mary, who was never allowed to leave her prison to plead her innocence, despite Bess hawking accusation upon accusation in the streets of London. Mary wrote a long letter to Elizabeth (which the queen of England never saw) detailing Bess's many wrongdoings and proclaiming her own innocence, while Shrewsbury appeared to diminish in size and stature under the force of his wife's personality. Although Mary was again frustrated that she had few options to explain herself, the scandal eventually burnt itself out.

At this point it's also worth noting how physically changed Mary had become. Through illness and the stress of her life, the young and beautiful princess had become a middle-aged woman who had put on weight and lost her best features. She still retained the sparkling charm that so entranced men around her, but her physical allure was now fading fast. Shrewsbury's interest (if there was one at all) would probably have come about due to the complete contrast of Mary with Bess, who was very masculine in her personality and appearance. It is possible there was a friendship, to which Bess objected, but it is difficult to believe that Mary had a passionate relationship with Shrewsbury.

Mary spend a long time in Tutbury, so it was became the focus of eighteen years of plots and intrigues, desperate attempts by her supporters to get her released. We've already heard of the ill-thought-out Ridolfi plot. That was followed by the Throckmorton plot, another which was supposed to see the invasion of England by Catholic Spain. This was something always feared by Elizabeth, as Spain was at that time the greatest power in Europe. Francis Throckmorton was the central figure in carrying messages to and from Mary, in secret, to relatives in France, in which the plot was outlined and she appeared to agree to it. The intrigue didn't get very far as Elizabeth's Secretary of State, Sir Francis Walsingham, a true master of espionage and spy networks, had Throckmorton arrested in November 1583, after discovering the messages. Throckmorton confessed under torture and then was executed, after implicating the Scottish queen in virtually every facet of the plot, despite her isolation from the outside world. This gave the English government all the ammunition it needed to portray Mary as a dangerous figurehead of a Catholic uprising, even if she was now a helpless figure wasting away in a cold and dark castle, miles from anywhere.

Another hare-brained plot was uncovered in 1585, when a Doctor Parry made his intention known of assassinating Elizabeth, with the help of Mary's agent in Paris, Thomas Morgan. This absolutely horrified Mary and she immediately wrote a letter to the English queen completely distancing herself from such a plan, but the damage had again been done. The exiled Queen of Scots was seen as evil by much of the population of England, they thought she would be willing to do anything to remove Elizabeth and put herself on the throne.

Parliament created a bond that instructed any plotters against the crown to be put to death once they were caught, and that included Mary, whether she had any knowledge of, or agreement with, the plans. This effectively guaranteed her future execution as plots were constantly being thought up by her supporters, so it was only a matter of time before one of them would be uncovered. The Babington Plot would be the infamous intrigue that finally sealed her fate.

After the Parry plot, Mary was returned to the loathsome Tutbury Castle (she'd been transferred earlier to one of the less odious buildings) and was now under the stern hold of a new keeper in Sir Amyas Paulet, the total opposite to Shrewsbury and a man who added to her discomfort with relish. It's fair to say that Mary's last few years on earth were the most miserable of her existence, and that misery was compounded by Paulet. He despised Mary and everything she stood for, not least her Catholic religion. With that ingrained hatred, his actions were as harsh towards her as possible. All the benefits that she enjoyed under Shrewsbury were immediately withdrawn, and that included removing the royal cloth of state. Mary wept and complained bitterly until she finally gained the return of the cloth, but she was forbidden from having it displayed above the chair she used. She was not allowed to leave the chambers she lodged in; this meant she was unable to enjoy the fresh air and the woman who had a passionate love of the outdoors had to spend each and every day with the smell of sewage. Any correspondence with anyone from the outside world was now strictly forbidden, making Mary an isolated prisoner with no means of knowing what was happening outside her chambers. One of the pleasures she'd had in recent years were visits to the waters at Buxton, but these too were now stopped. Any financial aid that the exiled queen had given to the poor people of Tutbury, something she had done with regularity when riding out, immediately ceased, as Paulet felt it was her way of gaining favour, nor was she allowed to pay any of the servants in the castle, in case this was bribery.

With Mary now in a complete state of desolation, she was finally moved from the draughty and stinking Tutbury to Chartley Hall (of which we will hear more in the next section) but not due to any charitable act on the part of

Paulet or his employer Queen Elizabeth. It came about because of the furious protests from the French court about her treatment at Tutbury. In that, they at least showed enough compassion to make her life slightly less difficult, even if there was little else in the way of help.

It's now time to take a look at Tutbury over the centuries. Following Mary's departure, it is interesting to see that there was still a family link, although under totally different circumstances. Despite the deprivation his mother suffered there, James seems to have had no problem spending time at the castle in pursuit of pleasure, as it was extensively used as a hunting lodge.

As the years passed, its defences were strengthened, especially during the English Civil War, when Tutbury was one of the last fortresses to hold out against the Parliamentary forces in 1645 for Charles I. It was finally seized by Sir William Bereton in 1646, and the castle's 'protector' Oliver Cromwell, paid for it to be demolished – the result we see today.

Little has changed since the seventeenth century, except for a few minor alterations. The mock ruin at the top of the hill was constructed in the late eighteenth century, and farm buildings were built around thirty years later. These are still in use today, but now as tearooms and kitchen. The castle became a tourist destination by the mid-1880s with the farms being closed down in 1952, and just a few years later, excavations discovered the entire foundations of the chapel. At the beginning of this century, the staircase of the great hall was re-opened to the public and now the castle plays host to many events, quite a few involving the life of Mary.

In fact, of all the places listed in this book linking us to the Trail of Mary, Queen of Scots, this is one of those that cannot be left out. She spent more time at Tutbury Castle than any other building, chateau, castle, inn or palace over the years. It is an essential stop and one that is worth exploring for as much time as you can allow. Today it stands in the natural beauty of the surrounding countryside, yet in Mary's day it was the darkest and most unpleasant of places and the one she hated the most. Tutbury Castle was the place where she began to fade away and die.

On Christmas Eve the journey was made to Chartley Hall, although Mary then fell into another of her illnesses and stayed bedridden for nearly eight weeks. It was under this stress that she entered into the final intrigue that would lead to her execution. The illness was again of sufficient concern that many of her servants fully expected her to die, and even Paulet was seen to show a glimpse of compassion but, as before, she was able to recover. Physically she regained her strength and it was with this new energy that she entered into the final acts of her life.

The Babington plot may not have been something she would have considered in her earlier and less isolated years, but there was the problem – Mary was now completely cut off from the outside world and had absolutely no knowledge of any political machinations between England and Scotland or indeed Protestant and Catholic. In her own mind, she still believed someone would come charging to her rescue, remove Elizabeth and the Scottish Regent, and install her on the throne of both countries. Her inner belief that she was still a queen inevitably meant that any possible actions taken by another to help her cause would be met with enthusiastic agreement.

At this stage, a man called Gilbert Gifford entered her life and put into place the events that led to her ultimate downfall. Gifford was a staunch Catholic and had trained in Rome as a priest, but for reasons not fully explained, he was expelled. He then spent time in Europe and seemed to have a particular fascination with spying. He engaged his cousin George to help him in a plot that would finally free the Catholic queen, then presented himself to the French embassy and promised to smuggle a batch of letters to Mary. The embassy was relieved to be rid of the letters, which could only cause them problems if found, and Mary was delighted that she had finally received correspondence from the outside world. The letters were smuggled by a local brewer who hid them in a waterproof container in the weekly barrels of beer delivered to Tutbury. Mary thought that she had at last found a friend and a means of communication that had been denied her for so long. Unfortunately, she was unaware that Gifford was working for Walsingham as one of his many spies.

After a period of time, a routine was set in place. Mary would write a letter in code, with the help of her secretary Nau, and place it in the hands of the brewer, who would hide the incriminating notes in a tube in the barrel. He would hand the letters to Gifford, who would then in turn hand them to Paulet. The letters would be deciphered (which seemed comparatively easy as the code was not of the highest level, even by the standards of the time) and then the letter would be read by Walsingham before eventually arriving at the intended destination in France. It was a profitable situation for all involved, for entirely different reasons. Mary was railing against her imprisonment and listening to any suggestions that the English queen might be assassinated, Gifford was of some use to someone and being paid, Paulet was happy that all of his convictions about his prisoner were being shown to be correct, and the brewer was being paid twice over (once by Mary and once by Paulet), so he happily continued. Walsingham was watching from afar. The letters, mostly to relations in France, were not necessarily incriminating, but there were constant pleas for help and descriptions of how she was imprisoned. All that was needed was for a plot to be outlined for Walsingham to rid England of this troublesome queen.

The Babington plot was named after Anthony Babington, a young English gentleman, who was a Catholic too. In 1586, he led a party of Catholic supporters who believed that Mary was the true queen and Elizabeth had to be deposed. He'd managed to recruit many to his band of rebels. He'd actually worked at Tutbury as a pageboy under Shrewsbury when he was younger, and so had seen the exiled queen regularly, and it is supposed had fallen for her charms like most men. He was also very rich, so could finance a scheme to realise his dream of freeing Mary with no problems at all.

He was popular among his cronies. 'When in London he drew to himself by the force of his exceptional charm and personality many young Catholic gentlemen of his own standing, gallant, adventurous and daring in defence of the Catholic faith in its day of stress, and ready for any arduous enterprise whatsoever that might advance the common Catholic cause,' was how he was described by Father Williams Weston. It was this daring that so appealed to Mary and gave Babington the belief that he could raise a foreign army to rescue her and overthrow Elizabeth. Mary was informed of his interest and soon entered into communication with him.

She wrote to Babington for the first time on 25 June saying,

> I have understood that upon the ceasing of our intelligence, there were addressed unto you from France and Scotland some packets for me. I pray you, if any have come to your hands, and be yet in place to deliver unto the bearer thereof who will make them safely conveyed to me.

Mary trusted Babington very quickly and so the scheme, unbeknown to her, was underway, as all correspondence was read by Walsingham. Unfortunately, Babington wasn't as discreet as he should have been and he replied in a lengthy letter that outlined the invasion of the foreign army, to be joined by many English Catholic sympathisers, the forcible release of Mary – 'for the effectuating of all which it may please your Excellency' – the removal of Elizabeth forcibly and eventually her being put to death.

Mary received this letter in July, but it had already been read by Walsingham, so any possible plot was doomed to failure even at that early point. Mary's next action was to breach the Act of Association, which forbade her, on pain of death, from conspiring against the realm. She replied agreeing to the schemes, including the assassination of Queen Elizabeth, and suggested various options for her escape:

> ...one day appointed for my walking abroad on horseback, in the moors between this and Stafford, where ordinarily you know that very few people do pass, fifty or three score men horsed and armed come to take me away there, as they may easily do, my keeper having ordinarily with him but eighteen or twenty horsemen, with their (heavy pistols). The second mean is, to come at midnight, or soon after, to set fire to the barns and stables, which, you know, are near to the house, and while my guardian's servants run forth to quench the fire, your company having every one a mark whereby they might know one another under night, might surprise the house, where, I hope, with the few servants I have about me, I were able to give you correspondence. And the third – some that bring carts thither ordinarily come early in the morning, their carts might be so prepared, and with such cart leaders, that being just in the midst of the gate, the cart might fall down or overwhelm, and you might come suddenly with some followers, and make yourselves masters of the house, and carry me away.

Legend has it that when the letter was sent to Walsingham, his codebreaker, Thomas Phelippes, drew a gallows sign on it and that indeed was what the reply would mean for Mary. Just to be sure of her complicity, Walsingham added a post script asking for the names of the conspirators.

They were revealed in the reply, so the plot was now completely revealed. Mary also heard at this time that a union had been agreed between England and Scotland, with a treaty signed by both Queen Elizabeth and Mary's son King James.

This meant she now played no role at all in the governance of either nation. If there was ever a more compelling reason to agree to outside help to release her from the life she was leading, then surely this was it. Her son had never looked upon her in an affectionate way and had no intention of aiding her release, and her relations in France seemed unwilling too. So Babington had shown her the only glimmer of hope and she had completely fallen in with his scheme, and that included the killing of her 'sister' and fellow sovereign Elizabeth. Walsingham, knowing she was in his snare, now acted.

Gifford fled to France as soon as he became aware that the plot was to be made public, as he felt his aid had helped to bring Mary down. In France, he eventually became a priest before being arrested in a brothel; he died in prison in Rheims.

The main instigator, Babington, becoming aware that his plan was not as watertight as he had originally thought, heard of the impending arrests and fled to St John's Wood, believing he would be safe. He wasn't, as on 14 August he was arrested and taken to the Tower, where under the threat of torture, he confessed all. He had destroyed Mary's letters to him before arrest, but under torture he recounted every line of them to Walsingham.

One month later he was tried for the attempted assassination of the English Queen – Mary's name actually wasn't mentioned in the trial as there was a fear that her supporters would rise up if they knew of the intrigues – and he was executed in the most savage and barbaric way. Alongside his fellow conspirators, he was hanged, quartered and disembowelled while still alive in front of a baying public, with his body left on display to deter anyone else who may have considered an act of treason.

Mary was unaware of any of these events when she was asked on 11 August by her previously arrogant and strict jailor Paulet, if she would be interested in going for a ride in the woods and a spot of hunting. The sense of release must have felt extraordinary to her after years of imprisonment.

Even if she might have felt slightly wary, she embarked on the journey with her two secretaries and her physician. They were heading in the direction of Tixall, with the party enjoying the fine fresh air, when a group of horsemen approached.

For the queen, there must have been that fleeting moment of hope in her heart and a knot in her stomach as she saw the men – maybe they were here to implement Babington's plot and rescue her? Again though, all Mary's hopes were to be crushed as she saw the leader of the group was none other than Sir Thomas George, the emissary to Queen Elizabeth. He dismounted and approached Mary with these now-famous words:

Madam, the Queen my mistress, finds it very strange that you, contrary to the pact and engagement made between you, should have conspired against her and her State, a thing which she could not have believed had she not seen proofs of it with her own eyes and known it for certain.

The end was nigh for Mary. Her companions were removed – she never saw them again – and she was forcibly taken to Tixall, an Elizabethan house nearby (described later), at one stage sitting on the ground and weeping and wailing loudly. At the same time her apartment at Chartley was raided by Paulet's men and all her possessions were removed, including eventually, every penny of the money she owned.

Two weeks later she was returned to Chartley Hall, while her two secretaries were cross-examined by Walsingham and in fear for their lives, completely implicated their queen in all of the intrigues. Nau, the closest of the two to Mary, was given money and actually stayed in the same house as Walsingham during the interrogations, before being returned to France. He was forever afterwards portrayed as a betrayer of his mistress.

On 21 September 1586, Mary, Queen of Scots made her final journey, from Chartley Hall to Fotheringhay, where she awaited trial and the inevitability of her death. By this time, she had all but given up any hope and at the age of forty-four was ready to say goodbye to a life that had been immensely cruel to her. Fotheringhay was to be the last place she would ever see.

Tutbury Castle is a working tourist attraction and seems to employ an all-things-to-all-people approach, which means there are constantly different displays on various subjects. There is a car park, which is inexpensive. Once inside, the casual observer may be disappointed at how little of the castle remains, but it's an excellent place to visit. Plays on the life Mary Stuart are sometimes presented. The castle can be found on Castle Street, Burton-upon-Trent, DE13 9JF.

Sheffield Castle and Sheffield Manor

Mary was moved to Sheffield Castle on 28 November, and it was a misty and cold day as she left the comfort of Chatsworth for the little town of Sheffield, which was dominated at the time by the large and impressive castle. The journey would have taken her along Baslow Edge and then Carbar and Froggatt edges. She would then traverse the estate of Longshaw before descending into the beautiful River Sheaf valley. Whether she was able to enjoy the splendour of the English countryside, however, is open to doubt.

Sheffield Castle was the place where Mary had the longest unbroken stay, albeit only two years. There is now nothing left of this magnificent fortress. For periods between November 1570 and late in 1584, Mary was housed in the castle but also in the nearby Sheffield Lodge, which, fortunately is a place we can still see today.

While at these two places, her retinue's upkeep remained prohibitively expensive and Shrewsbury would constantly ask for more money from Queen Elizabeth, mentioning the fact that the size of the joint household was only second to the English queen's. The menu is extraordinary: Mary would have two main meals a day, dinner and supper, which both comprised at least sixteen dishes, served to her servants too.

Reading the list today is an education – it lists the 11am meal as consisting of soup, veal, beef, mutton, pork, capon, goose, duck and rabbit, followed by another course of pheasant, partridge, lamb, pigeon, apple tarts and pears; with a similar arrangement of courses for the second meal at around 5pm.

If it was a Friday, which meant a 'fish day', the menu would comprise plaice, haddock, cod, turbot, skate, eel and pike, followed by another dish of trout, tench and herring. It is hardly surprising that Mary put on weight and suffered constant digestion problems as part of her regular illnesses, none of it helped by the comparative lack of exercise she was now allowed.

Sheffield Castle was built in the late twelfth century by William de Lovetot at the confluence of the Rivers Don and Sheaf, which provided a natural moat. About a mile away, on a hill, stood Sheffield Manor, a hunting lodge and the residence of the Shrewsburys in later years. The site of the castle is where the earliest settlement of Sheffield was founded in the later part of the first millennium, and it is referred to in the Domesday Book.

The original wooden castle was first mentioned in 1188 but it didn't survive long as it was burnt to the ground during the Second Barons War of 1266, the anti-monarchy army led by John de Eyvill causing the damage. The castle that Mary inhabited was built in 1270 by Thomas de Furnival, made of stone, and it extended from the River Sheaf to the River Don, a total area of around 4.2 acres. It completely dominated the hamlet that was Sheffield. Sadly for us, the castle was completely demolished after the Civil War in 1648, and only a few fragments of the wall remain underneath what is now Castle Market in the centre of the city. Despite the almost complete destruction – ordered by the Houses of Parliament – the Earl of Arundel bought the remnants in an attempt to rebuild it, but to no avail.

To make matters worse, there aren't any known surviving drawings or plans of the castle, so any attempt at establishing where Mary stayed is a matter of imagination and conjecture. In 1927, an excavation discovered the base of a gateway tower and part of the gateway itself and they were then listed as Grade II structures, but they are buried beneath the Castle Market.

The good news, though, is that these are open for viewing, so at least there is the faintest glimpse of what awaited Mary as she passed through the entrance to her new home on that misty day. You do have to pre-book, however, and there is an opportunity to see some of the other remains near the River Don, such as the surrounding wall. This also gives an impression as to how large the castle was.

There is better news regarding Sheffield Manor, where Mary stayed regularly while the castle was being cleaned. Situated on Manor Lane, it can be seen in most of its glory.

Also on view is the preserved Turret House that hosts a small museum.

Manor House is sited on the highest point in the centre of what used to be the deer park of the Lord of the Manor of Sheffield. It was originally a mediaeval hunting lodge, which was enlarged in the sixteenth century for Shrewsbury's summer retreat. As part of its history, Cardinal Wolsey was temporarily lodged there on his way to trial before Henry VIII on a charge of treason. He was seriously ill at the time, and despite being housed in grand apartments where his health improved, he died two weeks later at Leicester Abbey.

Wolsey Tower and Long Gallery still stand but in a ruined state; they were part of a quadrangle of buildings that surrounded a courtyard, covering about 4 acres. Manor House had its entrance between the tall towers, with a staircase that ran up to the grand hall. Also not too far away stands a smaller lodge of three levels, called Turret House.

This was reputedly built during Mary's stay in 1574. It has survived well, including original plasterwork and artefacts found in recent excavations, some of which were items from Mary's time.

It has been assumed that Turret House was built as a possible prison for Mary, but this has never been established, yet it is pretty certain that she used the building in its original capacity as a hunting lodge on the few occasions she was allowed to indulge in her favourite pastime. At the top of the building are the Queen Mary's Rooms, which are almost certainly the ones she used when she was there. Over the fireplace there is a heraldic motif, showing the arms of the Earl of Shrewsbury. The ceiling has plaster motifs, with the thistle of Scotland clearly visible.

The Turret House was restored in 1873 by the 15th Duke of Norfolk, as its walls were crumbling and the building becoming uninhabitable, and his work was instrumental in keeping the manor for future generations. It is now owned and run by Sheffield City Council, and recently they received a Heritage Lottery Fund donation of £1.2 million for the restoration of the Manor. As an aside, one of the few portraits of Mary that was commissioned in her later years was painted at Sheffield Manor. The now familiar image, of her standing wearing a black velvet dress and a white-peaked headdress lined with black lace, is the only surviving image we have of Mary the captive. Both the Manor and the Turret House are said to be haunted by Mary's ghost.

Visitor Information
Sheffield Manor is now a very popular place for weddings as well as a tourist attraction. It can be found at 389 Manor Lane, Sheffield, postcode S2 1UL. Like most places, it is advisable to check in advance for opening times.

Wingfield Manor
We can now take a look at some of the other places that played a part in Mary's captivity during those eighteen long years in England. Some played a big part in her life, and others were just a passing distraction. Wingfield Manor was a place that she, and her jailor Shrewsbury, liked, due to its position and relative comfort. Situated on a hilltop

overlooking the meadows that ran down to the River Amber, it was built by Oliver Cromwell and extended in 1455 by the 2nd Earl of Shrewsbury, and it is said that its design was actually the inspiration for Hampton Court Palace. It was a grand building, having an inner and outer court, with many outbuildings surrounding the centre. Mary was housed in apartments in the north west part of the mansion, which gave splendid views over the Ashover Valley and it was here that she was at her least unhappy as a prisoner.

Wingfield Manor is now a stately ruin and it is a sad sight bearing in mind how glorious the mansion used to be. It was another building that took the brunt of the English Civil War, being partially demolished after firstly being in the hands of the Royalists, and then the Parliamentarians. By 1648 it was in a state of ruin, but renovated shortly afterwards by Immanuel Halton. Sadly, it fell into neglect again by the 1770s when it was all but abandoned.

What can be seen today are the tower, the great hall (one of the largest in the country at the time) and beneath it a perfectly preserved crypt with a vaulted roof. This was used by servants as their quarters, as kitchens, with a wine vault. There are the remains of two ovens, used for baking bread, with two large fireplaces. You can also see damage done by cannonball fire on the walls of the towers; it has been established by historians that some of this was caused during the 1644 Civil War.

Mary was imprisoned here in 1569, 1584 and 1585 and the magnificence of the place is evident even in today's ruined state. The Manor is run by English Heritage and tours can be provided, but it is also home to a working farm so you are asked to respect the owner's privacy. Again, it is a place that has been defined by Mary's presence and certainly worth a visit.

Visitor Information

This is one of the more difficult places to visit as it appears to open irregularly. You have to book in advance on the English Heritage website for a guided tour. There is a sense of decay surrounding the site, which is disappointing; you can't help but feel it would need a huge amount of time and investment to bring it back to its former glory. It can be found in Alfredon, postcode DE55 7NY.

Chatsworth House

One of the most famous and most-loved stately homes in the country, Chatsworth House plays host to thousands of tourists each year but, sadly for us, it is not the Chatsworth House that Mary occupied during her captivity. The Elizabethan House was on the same site as the current one in beautiful countryside running along the River Derwent in Derbyshire. Bess of Hardwicke was responsible for completing the building of the house, which occupied exactly the rectangular part of the existing buildings. In the sixteenth century, the village of Edensor stood on the slope that overlooked the house and stretched beyond the brow of the hill to the present site of the village. The house was built with its frontage turned eastwards, and so effectively away from the village and its buildings to guard its occupants' privacy. Separating the house and the River Derwent was a large wall, which helped divert the water away from the building when the river overflowed. There is little remaining now from the time of Mary's captivity, as it was virtually rebuilt bit-by-bit in the seventeenth century. So Bess's house only stood for around 150 years. For Mary-watchers, the apartment where she lodged is now called the Queen of Scots Room, but of course this only depicts the space she inhabited as opposed to the actual room. It can be found on the top floor, and at least affords the same spectacular view that Mary enjoyed centuries ago.

The most obvious connection to Mary is the Queen Mary Bower. This was built in the 1570s when she was captive and tradition has suggested that it was constructed for the sole purpose of exercise for the exiled queen. According to Chatsworth's own website though, this is likely to be false and the bower was actually built as a garden feature. Again, there seems to be little of the original bower from the sixteenth century, as it was completely restored around 200 years later, but it is supposedly where Mary used to sit and embroider, sometimes with Bess. Originally there were three buildings in the water gardens to the northwest of Chatsworth. The gardens had seven large rectangular ponds with grassed walks and orchards planted alongside. The water gardens weren't just for ornamental use though, as they also provided fresh fish for the household.

Chatsworth House, and the Bower, must have been a pleasant place for Mary to have been during her long years of captivity if, of course, pleasant can be used to describe imprisonment. It was here that she had most freedom under Shrewsbury and regularly enjoyed hunting and hawking, plus doing her now famous needlework. A few of those valuable pieces can be seen at nearby Hardwicke Hall, alongside Bess's own efforts. It is certainly worth a quick detour. The current Chatsworth House is a magnificent stately home with its own history, but a visit for a Mary-watcher can still be satisfactory because the surrounding countryside is very similar to Mary's time there. On a lovely summer's day, there aren't too many better places to visit.

Visitor Information

A wonderful place to visit but, as part of our Mary trail, not vital because it is a completely different house. It can be found in Bakewell, postcode DE45 1PP.

Buxton

Buxton is included because this was one of the few places where Mary could actually enjoy herself in her last years. Suffering from rheumatism, she had pleaded with Elizabeth to be allowed to travel to the Roman town, to 'take the waters' in an effort to either cure or at the least alleviate some of her suffering.

Buxton is known for its water that is today freely available near the Old Hall Hotel, opposite the Georgian Crescent, and locals swear by its purity and restorative powers. In Tudor times, there used to be a well called St Anne's, which was the centre of regular religious pilgrimages, but under Cromwell and the Puritan revolution, the tradition was stopped and the baths closed down.

By the time of Mary's first visit, the baths were reopened and had become more and more popular. In 1572, a certain Doctor Jones wrote a paper called *The Ancient Baths of Buckstones*, in which he explained the healing powers of the water, and it was said that Bess Hardwicke had already looked into the profit that could be made by charging visitors to the baths, depending on their class. Visitors to the spa drank the water (as much as seven pints per day) and bathed in it too, then afterwards would engage in gentle games to help broaden the mind and improve the body, such as archery or the French game of boules. There would be opportunities to sit around the hot springs in the bathhouse, and also to air their clothes alongside the chimneys that blew out cool and refreshing vapours. At a time when personal hygiene was of little importance to most people, these sojourns to a spa were also a way of cleansing the body as well as attempting to erase the dirt and odours that gradually built up in clothes that were rarely cleaned.

Mary first visited in August 1573 and spent five weeks there. Over the next eleven years, she visited a total of five times and thoroughly enjoyed the recuperative quality of the waters, plus the opportunity of mixing with the people too. She met the Earl of Leicester during one of her visits, as he was attending to try to cure his gout, but it was suggested that he had been sent by Queen Elizabeth to spy on her Scottish cousin.

At one stage too, it looked as if Mary would finally get her wish and meet Elizabeth herself in August 1575, as the queen was at nearby Chartley House, but it was the closest she came to Buxton and the meeting never took place. It was always thought that Elizabeth feared she would lose any argument or disagreement between the two owing to Mary's legendary charm, so this could have been a reason not to meet. The closest occasion was the planned meeting shortly after Mary's arrival in England, at York, but Elizabeth had a last-minute change of mind because of the violent uprising in France.

Shrewsbury, who was her jailor at the time of the Buxton visits, was under constant criticism from Elizabeth for his lenient attitude towards his prisoner. Once, when Mary was enjoying the benefits of the baths, she spoke to a cripple and this was reported back to the queen, who then forbade Mary to speak to anyone again while she was in Buxton. She even refused one of Mary's requests to visit the area, but Bess took her anyway, using the occasion to continue her financial business in the town.

Once Paulet took over Mary's captivity, her visits to Buxton were at an end. During her final visit, in 1584, she obviously knew that she would never return, as she inscribed on a windowpane with her diamond ring these words:

Buxton, whose warm waters have made thy name famous, perchance I shall visit thee no more – Farwell.

This is the English translation from the original and the inscription can still be seen in the window of room 26 in the current hotel.

Mary's lodgings in Buxton were at the Old Hall, built by Shrewsbury and made into a private lodge for her, but this is not the Old Hall Hotel that we see today. That building does stand exactly on the same spot as the original. The oldest part of the current structure is the part of the tower that belonged to the house that Bess and Shrewsbury owned, but it was rebuilt in 1670. By that time, Buxton had become a popular destination and slowly it grew into the town that we see today, with the now-famous Georgian Crescent built between 1780 and 1786. On the front wall of the Old House Hotel is a plaque commemorating Mary's stays, and Buxton is certainly a pleasant place to visit, even without Mary's connection to the place.

One final word on the town. Nearby is a wonderful cave under a hill, called 'Poole's Cavern', and it certainly is worth the official tour, providing you don't suffer from claustrophobia. When I went, the guide referred to Mary visiting the cavern and saying words to the effect that she had never seen anything so beautiful in all her life, and indeed there is a stone pillar that depicts how far she walked into the caves. However, to me, this seems highly unlikely; Mary was suffering from serious rheumatism, so for her to venture into what would have been then a rather dank, wet and gloomy atmosphere seems improbable. I'd like to be proved wrong, but there doesn't appear to be anything to back up the claims of her visit.

Visitor Information
The Old House Hotel is situated just around the corner from the famous Georgian Crescent and near the theatre. The postcode is SK17 6BD.

Tixall Gatehouse

Tixall is worth mentioning as this was the first place Mary was taken to after her arrest following the Babington Plot. Tixall is situated near the town of Stafford. Of course, she saw little of the place as she stayed in her chambers for the entire two weeks she was there. For us, there is little left to see; it was a large Elizabethan house that had been built only around thirty years earlier, with the gatehouse, which is the only part remaining, constructed in 1580. The turreted gatehouse has Doric columns on the ground floor and Ionic and Corinthian columns on either side of the two upper storey windows. The two halls were demolished in 1927, but the gatehouse was eventually bought by Landmark Trust, given a Grade I listed status, and is now actually available to rent.

The legend has it that as Mary left Tixall to be taken to Chartley, she encountered poor beggars at the gatehouse and was to believed to have said,

> I have nothing for you, I am a beggar as well as you, all is taken from me … I am not witting or privy to anything intended against the queen.

It was only a brief appearance, but Tixall does play a part in Mary's last days.

Visitor Information

Tixall Hall's postcode is ST18 0XT and is worth visiting, even if what remains of the hall is now just the original gatehouse. It is a working hotel, which seems to be extremely popular for wedding celebrations.

Chartley Manor

This building played a large role in Mary's captivity in later years, as it was a welcome change from the appalling conditions of Tutbury Castle. It was the last place she stayed before her trial.

The manor was an Elizabethan house set in a park of nearly 1,000 acres between Stafford and Uttoxeter, which belonged to the 2nd Earl of Essex. The original castle stood on a hill with a large moat surrounding it, which made it more secure, and was built in the thirteenth century by Ranulph, the Earl of Chester. By the fifteenth century the castle was largely abandoned, and the manor was constructed nearby, and this was where Mary was kept prisoner for nearly a year.

It was chosen by Paulet as a prison mainly because of its security and the more mundane fact that the laundresses had enough water in the moat for their work. The owner, the Earl of Essex, protested against the Scottish queen being lodged in his house – he feared it would be damaged, that the trees in the woodlands would have to be felled to warm the house, and he was totally against a person such as Mary being kept as a prisoner in his house. He was summarily overruled by Paulet.

When she was returned from Tixall after her arrest and saw that all of her belongings had been riffled through and items taken, she cried out in anger; 'Some of you will be sorry for it' and then she declared that there were two things that couldn't be taken from her, her royal blood and her religion; 'which both I shall keep until my death'.

The manor house has now disappeared, destroyed by a fire in 1781, but what remains of the ruins of the mediaeval castle are certainly worth a visit. The keep, a curtain wall flanked by two impressive half-round towers and a twin-towered gatehouse, can clearly be seen on the hilltop of Chartley Park.

The site has been protected since 1925 and the castle ruins are now a Grade II listed building and a Scheduled Monument. The property is in private hands, so any visit has to be planned with care.

Although there is little left of what Mary saw centuries ago, it is an important stop as this was where Paulet exercised his complete control over his prisoner – and where the Babington Plot was first discovered. It provided a welcome relief from Tutbury, but was also completely cut-off from the outside world owing to its location, and it was here that Mary became less and less aware of the political machinations that were taking place in her world.

Visitor Information
The postcode for Chartley Manor is T18 0LN and the ruined building is a place definitely worth visiting but it is in private hands so make advance arrangements.

Fotheringhay
The trial of Mary, Queen of Scots at Fotheringhay has been described down the years as one of the greatest injustices in history, yet the age in which it took place had seen far worse. The participants in her prosecution would have

believed that Mary received a fairer hearing in England than she would have done if the trial had been in Scotland. Whatever the rights and wrongs at the time, the facts were that Mary, who had learned the English language late in life and had little knowledge of England or its customs, was totally alone as she sat facing her accusers; she was a weak, frail woman in mind and spirit. She wasn't given her own counsellors or allowed to view any of the incriminating documents.

For one-and-a-half days, she was verbally harangued by the prosecution, without any guidance from a legal expert, in a trial that she always believed was unlawful as she was still a queen of her own country (she had rejected her abdication as it had been signed under duress) and there were no grounds for her to be tried by the sovereign of another country.

When she left Chartley Manor on 21 September 1586, she was under the impression that she was to be removed to London as it seemed the obvious place to conduct a trial. It soon became clear though that she was not to be transported to the capital, or closer to Elizabeth. She was under escort with armed men travelling alongside, while her servants were locked indoors so they couldn't bid her farewell. The windows were blocked so that they couldn't see her and she couldn't see them. She was almost completely alone with no attendants or supporters making the long journey with her.

On the first evening, the entourage stayed at Hill Hall near Abbot's Bromley, where an inscription was scratched on a windowpane (this can be seen in the William Salt

Library in Stafford) saying: '*Maria regina Scotia quondam transibat istam villam, 21ˢᵗ Septembris, 1586 usque Burton Fotheringhay.*' According to Antonia Fraser, though, this was almost certainly not Mary's own work.

The following two evenings were spent at the Earl of Huntingdon's Lord's Place in Leicester, and then on 25 September, she finally arrived at Fotheringhay Castle. It dominated the area, standing tall with a large moat surrounding it. There was a polygon stone keep and a huge gateway that faced northwards, with an interior courtyard that was surrounded by a great hall and a chapel. There was a river to one side, crossed by a bridge, and a double moat system that secured the castle on the other three sides. The castle was probably built around 1100 by the Earl of Northampton, and thirteen years later it came into the possession of Prince David of Scotland. Then it was handed down to his descendants over the years. It was only in the thirteenth century that it was taken by King John of England, which led to it becoming a Yorkist castle. Richard III was born in the fortress, but by the sixteenth century it was a prison, and was described as a wretched place to be. Its reputation for discomfort had increased as the years had passed. It would be clear to Mary at this stage that this was probably going to be the final place she would see.

Mary was lodged in a very small apartment and she heard the counsellors from London arrive during the weeks that followed, taking up the other empty rooms. The ever-unsympathetic Paulet constantly prodded her to admit her guilt, but in one telling response she spoke these words, which summed up her defiance:

As a sinner, I am truly conscious of having often offended my Creator, and I beg Him to forgive me, but as Queen and Sovereign, I am aware of no fault or offence for which I have to render account to anyone here ... as therefore I could not offend, I do not wish for pardon; I do not seek, nor would I accept it from anyone living.

Those brave words notwithstanding, she heard shortly afterwards that she would be brought to trial under the Act of Association, an Act deliberately invented to deal with the Scottish queen. This meant that if she was found guilty of treason – although she was Scottish and not English – then she would relinquish any claims to the English throne and could be put to death if Queen Elizabeth ordered it.

There was no chance of Mary being acquitted. She was not to be allowed any witnesses in her defence or any counsellors. A request for a secretary to help her prepare was refused by Elizabeth too.

The evidence was to be withheld from her and she had no right to stand as an accused to state her defence. She was a lonely, frail and ill woman who had aged even more that would be expected over the almost twenty years of her imprisonment, so much so that her rheumatism made it almost impossible for her to stand, never mind walk, and she had to be carried into the courtroom.

By October, most of the prosecution commissioners had arrived and, again, Paulet threatened her if she refused to co-operate.

Again she replied in a stately and dignified fashion:

I am myself a Queen, the daughter of a king, a stranger, and the true kinswoman of the Queen of England. I came to England on my cousin's promise of assistance against my enemies and rebel subjects and was at once imprisoned. As an absolute Queen, I cannot submit to orders, nor can I submit to the laws of England, nor do I know or understand them as I have often asserted. I am alone, without counsel, or anyone to speak on my behalf. My papers and my notes have been taken from me, so that I am destitute of all aid, taken at a disadvantage. I came into this kingdom under promise of assistance, and aid, against my enemies and not as a subject, as I could prove to you had I my papers; instead of which I have been detained and imprisoned ... I do not deny that I have earnestly wished for liberty, and done my utmost to procure it for myself. In this I acted from a very natural wish ... can I be responsible for the criminal projects of a few desperate men, which they planned without my knowledge or participation?

She did, however, agree to make a personal appearance at the trial so that she could defend herself against the charge of an assassination attempt on Elizabeth.

The trial, which started on 15 October, was an obvious sham to modern minds. It took place in the great hall and Mary sat alone facing the Lord Chancellors, a Lord Treasurer, many earls (including the reluctant Shrewsbury), barons of the exchequer, knights, crown representatives and judges. In total there were twenty-four nobles and more than forty commissioners sitting before her, each and every one looking to find the exiled queen guilty. There was also a spectators' gallery full of Protestant supporters, who made their feelings known. The room, which was on the second floor of the chambers, was 69 feet long and 21 feet wide, with the larger area at the top of the hall used as a courtroom. At the upper head of the elevated stage, stood a chair beneath a cloth of state and emblazoned with the royal arms of England. This was to signify Queen Elizabeth in her absence.

Mary sat in the hall, with as much dignity as she could muster, wearing her dress of black velvet and white head-dress, only accompanied by her maid, who had helped carry her into the room. In a statement to the lords she said:

> I cannot walk without assistance nor use my arms, and I spend most of my time confined to bed by sickness ... My advancing age and bodily weakness both prevent me from wishing to resume the reins of government. I have perhaps only two or three days to live in this world, and I do not aspire to any public position, especially when I consider the pain and desperance which meet those who wish to do right.

The trial began at 9am and for the whole day, she was accused of plotting her escape, plotting to overthrow the queen of England and to murder her too. The Babington Plot was revealed in its entirety and of course the Casket Letters were produced. There were sworn statements from her two secretaries, Nau and Curle, confirming involvement, although these had been produced under torture, and even her assertion that she was the rightful heir to the English throne was used as another accusation. To make matters worse, all the prosecution evidence was shown to the lords but not to Mary, and each statement was read to them, and not in the direction of the accused. This meant that Mary constantly had to interrupt the proceedings to have her say. Many of the documents were presented in an ad-hoc way so that there was no chronological timeline, meaning that she had to strain to understand what was being said in a language she had barely mastered. She also struggled to remember the exact events as they took place, a ploy that the judges had hoped would catch her out as they jumped from one moment to the next.

She denied that she wanted to harm Elizabeth as she still hoped to fall on her mercy, and then stated that she had little time left in her life and she had no desire to be a queen of England, or indeed Scotland anymore, due to her ailments. By the end of the day, she was exhausted and not helped by the judges constantly attacking her, shouting that she was guilty of all charges. The account of physician Bourgoing shows he despaired of the treatment that this poor woman was receiving, and that the trial had become farcical due to the one-sided nature of it. It would be inconceivable that such a trial would be allowed today, but the nature of sixteenth-century justice was such that this was regarded as the norm.

The next day it continued and this time the accusation of enlisting the help of the Spanish to invade England was used. Again Mary defended herself, saying she had no knowledge of such plans as she was incarcerated and unable to dictate the affairs of a foreign nation. She was accused again of wanting to escape, to which Mary correctly stated that as a prisoner, and unlawfully held, she had the right to want to grab her freedom.

By mid-afternoon though, the trial was at an end, and the commissioners (who had arrived that morning dressed in their riding clothes showing that they had already made their decision) left to the words from Mary: 'My lords and gentlemen, I place my cause in the hands of God ... may God keep me from having to do with you all again.' She also asked that she be permitted to face Elizabeth and her accusers in front of Parliament, but this was met with indifference. Somehow, despite the ordeal that she had experienced, she had kept her dignity and been calm. She hadn't screamed in defiance and had, when she was allowed, replied to her accusers with a gentle and persuasive voice, unlike the judges who had shouted their demands in an attempt to unnerve her. That calmness saw her through the next few days as the commissioners met in London to discuss her fate.

They presented their conclusions to Parliament, in the Houses of Lords and Commons, then addressed Queen Elizabeth urging her to agree to the execution of Mary for her own future safety and the safety of the realm. Elizabeth, to her credit, refused to agree to their request and looked for another way in which justice could be done but, on 19 November, Mary was informed by Lord Buckhurst that she had been sentenced to death. It didn't come as a surprise as by this time she had accepted her fate and still showed the calmness that she had demonstrated in the trial, refusing the opportunity of repenting to a Protestant clergyman, maintaining her Catholicism right to the end. Her words to her maid were simple,

> Well, Jane Kennedy, did I not tell you this would happen? I knew they would never allow me to live. I was too great an obstacle to their religion.

For the next few weeks, while Elizabeth was closing her eyes to the problem and refusing to grant the execution order, Mary went about tidying up her life, writing letters to the pope and her relations in France. She wrote to her trusted advisors and also to her unloved mother-in-law from her days in France, Catherine de Medici. There was little else she could do but wait.

On 4 December, an official execution order was made public – but without a date. Bonfires were lit in celebration in London as the queen of England was now saved from 'this most wicked and filthy woman' as Sir Ralph Sadler described her. Mary received this news with tranquillity. She was tired and physically unwell. Her body was slowly giving up on her and the strain of her life had made her wish for a quick ending to the terrible dramas that were heaped upon her.

Mary saw what most historians now believe was a comet flying through the sky. She had a feeling that it was a bad omen. Three days later, on 1 February 1587, Elizabeth signed the death warrant. Comets were normally associated with the demise of well-known and famous personalities. Elizabeth casually signed the warrant while discussing the weather with her secretary, William Davison. Elizabeth signed several documents at the same time, apparently absent-mindedly, although she knew exactly what she was doing when putting pen to paper over the execution. For his trouble, Davison was later imprisoned and given a £10,000 fine, a sum which would have been almost impossible to pay in the sixteenth century. After the execution Elizabeth claimed he had disobeyed her instructions not to seal the warrant.

Mary was told by Shrewsbury on 7 February, while taking dinner, that she was to be executed the next morning at 8am. Plans had already been put in place. Extra garrisons of soldiers had arrived at Fotheringhay to ensure no last-minute escape, the scaffold had been built and the executioners were housed in the local village, ready to be called when required.

The Scottish Queen took the news calmly, unlike her servants who wept and wailed in despair. She told Shrewsbury,

> I thank you for such welcome news. You will do me great good in withdrawing me from this world out of which I am very glad to go.

With that, she went about organising the last moments of her life, including bequeathing the contents of her wardrobe to her trusted and loved servants and relations. Even her disloyal closest secretaries, Nau and Curle, received gifts, with the former being given his pension, something he had lost with his earlier confession against his employer. She also spent some time writing letters, the most intimate being one sent to her brother-in-law King Henry of France. In it she described all of the horrors of her life since returning to Scotland and her imprisonment in England, and by the time she'd finished it, it was two o' clock in the morning.

Today, after dinner, I was advised of my sentence. I am to be executed like a criminal at eight o' clock in the morning. I haven't had enough time to give you a full account of all that has happened, but if you will listen to my physician and my other sorrowful servants, you will know the truth, and how, thanks be to God, I scorn death and faithfully protest that I face it innocent of any crime. The Catholic faith and the defence of my God-given right to the English throne are the two reasons for which I am condemned, and yet they will not allow me to say that it is for the Catholic faith that I die. I beg you as Most Christian Majesty, my brother-in-law and old friend, who have always protested your love for me, to give proof now of your kindness on all these points; both by paying charitably my unfortunate servants their arrears of wages, and also by having prayers offered to God for a Queen who has herself been called Most Christian, and who dies a Catholic, stripped of all her possessions. Concerning my son, I commend him to you inasmuch as he deserves it, as I cannot answer for him. I venture to send you two precious stones, amulets against illness, trusting that you will enjoy good health and a long and happy life.

The great hall, immediately below the room where the trial had taken place, was now converted into an execution chamber, and it was to this room that Mary made her last journey. A large wooden stage, hung with black, had been erected, with the great axe standing beside the robed cushion that Mary was to use as she awaited the final act.

Flanked by her servants, who at first were refused entry but then admitted after Mary promised they would not disturb the proceedings, she entered wearing all black with a huge white veil plus the white headdress that had been seen at the trial. It was only when she was disrobed for the execution that the spectators – of whom there were at least 300 – saw that underneath she was wearing a crimson petticoat, silver stockings with green garters and black leather shoes. She stood in a regal fashion, holding her crucifix and rosary beads, and even smiled at the commissioners around her, and also giving the traditional forgiveness to the executioners for what they were about to do. She then started praying in the Catholic way, despite the Protestant Dean of Peterborough exhorting her to pray with him. She honoured her promise of never leaving her faith, right until the end. When her servants cried, Mary's final words to them were; *'Ne crie point pour moi. J'ai promis pour vous...'* asking them to observe the promise she had made at the entrance to the great hall that they wouldn't disrupt the proceedings. The whole occasion was conducted in virtual silence, apart from the cries and tears of her servants and Shrewsbury, who was genuinely upset at the acts that were to follow.

The actual execution was as dramatic as her life. After being blindfolded by her loyal maid Jane Kennedy, she cried to the Lord in Latin; 'Into your hands O Lord, I commend my spirit' and placed her neck on to the block.

The first blow, unleashed by a nervous axe man, missed her neck and buried into her head. She was heard to cry out 'Sweet Jesus', but the second blow virtually severed it, although the axe was then used in a sawing fashion to finally disconnect the head from the body.

Cries of 'God Save the Queen' were then shouted half-heartedly from the commissioners and spectators, referring to the regent of England, and when the executioner lifted up Mary's head to prove that she was dead (her lips continued to move for at least a quarter of an hour afterwards), the red wig she was wearing detached itself and the head fell to the ground. Her hair was grey and closely cut, showing the ravages of time on a woman who had lived through a personal hell for nearly two decades.

At the same time, her small Skye terrier, which had hidden under her petticoats, crept out and whined next to the dead body of its mistress. It later died without ever eating again.

The servants cried, but were quickly removed and locked away so they could not take any item of clothing. All her possessions were hastily gathered up. This was so that nothing could be used in future years to turn her into a martyr by her supporters. Her blood was washed away and her discarded clothing was burnt, and within an hour, all traces of the exiled queen were gone, including the block where she had been beheaded – burnt with the rest of the items. Mary, Queen of Scots was dead.

At one o' clock, four hours after the execution, Lord Talbot galloped to London to convey the news to Elizabeth, arriving at 9am the next morning. The queen received the news with indignation and anger, saying that she hadn't expected the order to be carried out, but in the streets of London bonfires were lit in celebration and banquets were held as a great danger to their queen no longer existed.

Meanwhile, Mary's body was inexpertly embalmed and then wrapped in a lead coffin, the heart removed, and kept in the confines of Fotheringhay Castle. The organs were buried deep beneath the building and eventually lost forever as no documents were made of the exact location. Her servants were imprisoned and not allowed to return to France, as had been promised before Mary's death, and most of her letters were not delivered. Whatever small concessions she had been allowed at the end of her life, were completely forgotten in her death. By the end of the day, it was almost as if she hadn't been there. Life in the castle continued and Paulet – ever the nemesis of his former prisoner – actually wrote to the Queen of England complaining again at the huge expense to him of having to feed Mary's servants, especially now she was gone. At the age of forty-four, Mary Stuart had departed from the world, and under normal circumstances that would herald the end of anyone's story, but Mary lived an extraordinary life and in a way, her death was indeed her beginning as she herself pointed out.

Fotheringhay Castle no longer exists. In fact, there is virtually nothing left on the spot to remind us that such a dramatic event took place there. There are no monuments, no statues, no relics and not even a recent plaque to commemorate the event. Instead there is just an empty space where history took place. It has been said that it was Mary's son James who had the castle demolished after finally learning of the injustice meted out to his mother, but this is, unfortunately, a myth that has sprung up. Although the castle was torn down the truth is that once everyone had departed following the trial and the execution, Fotheringhay fell into ruin as it was effectively abandoned. Gradually its walls started to crumble and locals began to help themselves to the stones and wood for their own homes.

Within fifty years it was a complete ruin and unsalvageable. The great hall was actually removed and placed in the manor of Sir Richard Cotton at Connington as a tribute to Mary (he being of Bruce ancestry), but even that building was demolished in the eighteenth century so there is no trace of it there either. There is now little, if anything at all, remaining apart from a grassy mound on the site of the keep, plus small fragments of one of the walls.

The site itself is a Scheduled Monument, so is protected and open to the public, and from there you can enjoy the view of the meandering River Nene nearby, but it takes an enormous amount of imagination to link this beautiful spot to the final act of Mary's life. I would urge you though to consider visiting, especially if you have been following Mary's trail through this book. It was the place – or for us, the space – where she drew her last breath, and the place where she took her last steps and uttered her last words. For me, it seems almost offensive that that final day should be almost completely lost to the ravages of time and decay.

Visitor Information

This really should be the place that we stand and stare and remember the cruel events that took place there, but there is virtually nothing of the castle remaining. To visit, the postcode is PE8 5JF but make sure you take your imagination with you.

Peterborough Cathedral

Following Mary's execution, there was a huge outcry, not least in her adopted country of France. Due to the fact that communication was slow in the sixteenth century, and also that the French ambassador was forced to wait three weeks before dispatching the news, it was nearly a month before France became aware that their former queen had been executed by a foreign power. The anger was almost palpable. There were concerns of an uprising against England, but this was averted. Even Mary's former enemy, Catherine de Medici, exclaimed to Pomponne de Bellievre, one of her envoys,

> I am most grieved that you have been unable to do more for the poor Queen of Scotland. It has never been the case that one queen should have jurisdiction over another having placed herself into her hands for her safety as she did when she escaped from Scotland ... the cruel death of the poor Queen of Scots.

Catherine then had a full insurrection on her hands as Catholics in France looked to blame the king for Mary's death, something that caused the House of Guise to implement the strictest security in the Parisian capital.

On 12 March a Requiem Mass was heard in Notre Dame, with both Catherine and her son King Henry present, when the priest Renaud de Beaune remembered that it had been thirty years previously that he had watched as a young Marie Stuart had married her childhood sweetheart Francois in that very cathedral.

Many of us saw in the place where we are now assembled to deplore her, this Queen on the day of her bridal, arrayed in her regal trappings, so covered in jewels that the sun himself shone not more brightly, so beautiful, so charming withal as never a woman was. These walls were then hung with cloth of gold and precious tapestry, every space was filled with thrones and seats, crowded with princes and princesses, who came from all parts to share in the rejoicing. The palace was overflowing with magnificence, splendid fetes and masques, the streets with jousts and tourneys. In short it seemed as if our age had succeeded that day in surpassing the pomp of all part centuries combined. A little time has flowed on and it is all vanished like a cloud. Who would have believed that such a change could have befallen her who appeared then so triumphant, and that we should have seen her a prisoner who had restored prisoners to liberty, in poverty who was accustomed to give so liberally to others, treated with contumely by those on whom she had conferred honours, and finally, the axe of a base executioner mangling the form of her who was doubly a Queen, that form which honoured the nuptial bed of a sovereign of France, falling dishonoured on a scaffold, and that beauty which had been one of the wonders of this world, faded in a dreary prison, and at last effaced by a piteous death. This place, where she was surrounded with splendour, is now hung with black for her. Instead of nuptial torches we have funeral tapers, in the place of songs of joy, we have sighs and groans, for clarions and hautboys, the building of the sad and dismal bell. Oh God, what a change! Oh vanity of human greatness, shall we never be convinced of your deceitfulness ... the marble, the bronze, the iron, are decomposed by the air or corroded by rust, but the remembrance of her bright example shall live eternally.

Mary had requested that she be buried in France, but that request was never granted. The people of France expressed their sorrow loudly, with constant demonstrations against the English queen and the Protestant faith, and the future pope, Maffeo Barberini, wrote an elegy to her. Spain too reacted in an angry way, forcing Queen Elizabeth to close all the ports in England fearing an imminent invasion. In Scotland, her people were also reacting, showing their fury that their former queen had been executed by the monarch of the nation they had been at odds with for centuries. The same could not be said for her son James, now on the throne of Scotland. Despite the judgement of his actions and emotions being changed dramatically down the years by historians who made him more compassionate, there was little evidence that he grieved for his mother. At one stage he was heard to exclaim, 'Now I am sole King,' although to be fair to him, there were also reports that he heard the news with sadness and retired to his bed immediately. The next day he ordered the Scottish court into official mourning, but did not plan any act of retribution against his new ally, Elizabeth. The Scottish people did look for revenge though, and armies were raised with the sole idea of razing any town they encountered once entering England.

Newcastle was the first on the list, but the revenge seekers needed the help of James to bolster their numbers before they could attack, something he was unwilling to do. Posters and leaflets were distributed throughout the southern part of Scotland urging an uprising against the English, some with strong and offensive words directed towards Elizabeth, calling her a 'Jezebel' and 'whore'. As an act of appeasement to his people, James cut off diplomatic communications with England, but relented soon afterwards when one of Elizabeth's envoys arrived to explain that the English queen had not actually agreed to the execution, despite signing the document.

While all this was taking place, Mary's corpse was still lying in Fotheringhay Castle, unburied. It lay, poorly embalmed, in an extremely heavy lead coffin, with no decision made as to what to do with her.

Eventually, after nearly six months, she was transported to the nearby Peterborough Cathedral in the dead of night, so as not to arouse any emotions from supporters. There was a funeral cavalcade that consisted of around 100 women dressed in black, paid for by the government, and the whole cortege, lumbering slowly along the dark and uncomfortable roads, arrived at two o' clock in the morning. A Protestant ceremony followed, attended by a representative of Elizabeth, plus the imprisoned servants of Mary, who understandably took no part in the rituals, being staunch Catholics. Then the coffin, weighing some nine hundredweight, was placed in a vault on the south side of the cathedral, where it was to stay for the next twenty-five years.

It seemed an odd resting place for a French and Scottish queen, who had never visited Peterborough at any time in her life. The refusal to return her body to France seems petty and vindictive, but there were serious concerns of another skirmish with the French, and so she was buried far enough away from London so as to run no risk of any more outpourings of emotion.

Peterborough Cathedral is a magnificent building, started in 1118 and consecrated in 1238. It was originally an abbey but after that was closed by Henry VIII in 1539 in his attempt to take complete control of the church, a bishop was appointed and so the building became a cathedral.

As well as Mary's initial burial site, it is still the site of Katherine of Aragon's grave, on the north aisle near the high altar – Mary was on the opposite side. Although our Mary trail could visit the cathedral, there is nothing there to remind us that this was her first burial site. All the same, it is one of the loveliest and most impressive cathedrals in the country. If we had been alive in the immediate aftermath of her death, then we may have seen a plaque that had been put up by one of her ardent supporters, Adam Blackwood, which read:

Mary, Queen of Scots, daughter of a king, widow of the King of France, cousin and next heir to the Queen of England, endowed with royal virtues and a royal mind (the right of Princes being oftentimes in vain implored) by barbarous and tyrannical cruelty, the ornament of our age, and truly Royal light is extinguished. By the same unrighteous judgement both Mary, Queen of Scots with natural death, and all surviving kings (now made common persons) are punished with civil death. A strange and unusual monument this is, wherein the living are included with the dead; for, with the Sacred Ashes of this blessed Mary, know, that the Majesty of all kings and princes, lieth here, violated and prostrate. And because regal secrecy doth enough and more admonish Kings of their duty – traveller, I say no more.

It didn't remain in place for long.

One year after Mary was executed, Spain finally implemented the plan to invade England with King Philip claiming his inheritance of the English throne, now that the Scottish queen was dead and her son had failed to convert to Catholicism. This was the invasion that Mary had secretly wished for to release her from prison, but of course it had come too late. The Armada failed and England stood firm.

Visitor Information
Peterborough Cathedral is one of the greatest English 12th-century buildings. Tours can be arranged if you visit its website. It is a wonderful building but, as I've said, there is little to remind us that Mary Stuart's body rested here for twenty-five years. The postcode is PE1 1XS.

Westminster Abbey

Elizabeth died in 1603 at the age 70. She was succeeded by James VI of Scotland, who was then proclaimed James I of England and Ireland. In the document to announce James as the new King of England, Mary is not mentioned or referred to at all, yet she could look down with the knowledge that she had finally got what she had always wanted, the throne of England, albeit in her son's name. She had also won the battle she fought for all of her life, as every subsequent British ruler has been descended from Mary Stuart right up to the present day. One of James's first acts was to build a tomb for Elizabeth I at Westminster Abbey in the north aisle of the chapel. It was impressive and expensive, and soon pressure was put on him to honour his mother in the same way, so in October 1612, Mary's body was exhumed and reinterred in Westminster. The monument to her was equal to that of the English Queen, costing in the region of £2,000, and it is the closest the two were ever to be.

Mary is represented in white marble, lying full length beneath a canopy with her hands pressed together, as if in prayer. She can be seen to be wearing the headdress that was so part of her attire in her final days, and the long flowing dress that now looks so familiar. At her feet lies the lion of Scotland. Her face has been modelled on a mask from her final years and the features are similar to the famous Sheffield portrait. It appears to be an exact impression of how she was in her middle age. There is a very long Latin epitaph, written by the Earl of Northampton, paying tribute to her as a woman of many virtues, without referring to the many controversies of her life. This is far too long to include here, but there is an English translation available when you visit the tomb.

Mary was at peace at last, or should have been. A rather unsavoury search of her tomb in 1867 by Dean Stanley, looking for the remains of James I, disturbed the serenity of her resting place. Once the remains of the king had been found, Mary's coffin was also spotted. It lay, completely intact, against the north wall of the vault, among many others, including those of young children and infants, plus that of Arbella Stuart, a childhood companion of Mary's. Her coffin wasn't touched and the vault was closed once more, hopefully to remain that way for evermore.

It goes without saying that a visit to Westminster Abbey is a must on the trail of Mary as this is the closest we will ever get to her physical form but, hopfully you will feel her presence at any of the places I have described in this book. The tomb of Mary, Queen of Scots is one of the most popular tourist spots of Westminster Abbey, along with that of Elizabeth I, of course. It is remarkable that these two great women leaders should have lived at the same time and had such an impact on sixteenth-century politics.

Visitor Information
Possibly one of the most recognised buildings in London, England, and indeed the United Kingdom, Westminster Abbey is constantly thronged with tourists, but is a total 'must-see' for the end of our trail. However, it is also a place of worship so as with all such places, please be respectful. The postcode is SW1P 3PA.

IMAGINING THEIR PAST
IN THE FUTURE

Both Mary and Elizabeth's stories, as the years pass, will be dramatised and changed for effect. It sometimes saddens me that artistic licence is taken in re-writing a time and events that need no alteration, particularly in films. Having said that, the famous play by Friedrich Schiller in the eighteenth century dealing with the meeting of Mary and Elizabeth is a complete fantasy, yet it does bring to life both of their stories. Elizabeth brought about Mary's downfall, yet it can be argued that Mary herself was the architect for all of the trials and tribulations that she endured in her life. Whether she willingly agreed to marriage to Bothwell or not, the fact that she entered into matrimony with the man accused of murdering her second husband is bordering on stupidity, yet Mary wasn't a stupid woman. She was just someone who lived by her emotions, which at times overcame any other sense and logic.

What would have happened if Mary had been given the pleasure of meeting her 'sister' as she had so many times requested? Would her life had played out any differently? It's tempting to see her as the scheming woman who would do anything eventually to win the English crown, in addition to those of France and Scotland, but her love of Elizabeth was genuine as this ode to her clearly shows, written in 1568,

> Once thought, that is my torment and delight, Ebbs and flows bittersweet within my heart and between doubt and hope rends me apart, while peace and all tranquillity take flight. Therefore, dear sister, should this letter dwell upon my weighty need of seeing you, It is that grief and pain shall be my due, unless my wait should end both swift and well. I've seen a ship's sails slackened by taut ropes, on the high tide at the harbour bar, and a clear sky suddenly fill with cloud; likewise fear and distress fill all my hopes, not because of you, but for the times there are, when fortune doubly strikes on sail and shroud.

Hopefully Mary will never be forgotten, and it is my wish that books like this will keep her memory alive for some time to come. Children of of very recent years would have had reminder when they sang the familiar nursery rhyme,

> Mary, Mary, quite contrary,
> How does your garden grow?
> With silver bells and cockleshells
> and pretty maids all in a row.

Inevitably, as with most things connected to Mary, this has caused some confusion to historians, but the suggestion was that the garden referred to the ornamental garden at Holyrood Palace that Mary loved so much.

The silver bells are the Sanctus bells used in her private chapel at Mass, the cockleshells are supposed to be the pilgrim badges of Catholics, although this was also interpreted as the bells that Mary and her 'four Maries' used to wear on their shoes as children, and of course the pretty maids are the aforementioned companions.

There is a word of warning though, as many historians suggest the rhyme was about Bloody Mary and the sayings relate to matters far more sinister, and as it wasn't penned until the eighteenth century, then there is no real way of knowing.

Also as the years pass, and as little else is now likely to be discovered from that time in history, these small links are a gentle reminder to a younger generation, even if they have the same impact as the 'artistic licence' of plays and films.

In conclusion, I think it is not an exaggeration to say that Mary was one of the most colourful and controversial characters in the royal history of what we now regard as the United Kingdom. Her desire to see the union of Scotland and England did eventually take place, but many years after her death, yet she was indirectly responsible for it.

She will always be argued about and there will always be those who regard her in a negative way, as an adulteress and murderess who used her feminine wiles and charms to bend each new adversary to her desires, or those (of which I am firmly one) who believe she was a woman born out of time – unable to make a considered decision without the guidance of a strong presence, someone who tried in vain to calm the stormy waters that surrounded the kingdom of Scotland, and someone who was treated in an appalling fashion by the very person she had turned to for help, despite all of the warnings given her.

The fact that she spent around twenty of her forty-four years in a prison of some sort, shows a life that was as dramatic as it was desperate. I still hold on to the belief that I felt her presence at Bolton Castle and that I had a conversation with her (no matter how trivial the subject) and I hope that after reading this book and visiting some of the places I've described, whether you are new to Mary or a lifelong follower, you also have that moment.

To be kind to all, to like many and love a few, to be needed and wanted by those we love, is certainly the nearest we can come to happiness.

Mary, Queen of Scots

ACKNOWLEDGEMENTS

I am so grateful to Amberley Publishing for allowing me to write this book, as Mary (or Marie if you live in France like me) has been a passion of mine since childhood. I wouldn't for one moment pretend to be an expert on her life and I have no shame in saying I have leant heavily on other people's vastly superior knowledge. Over the course of my life I have been an avid collector of books on her life, and so virtually every one of them has helped in the writing of this one, but I must refer to some that stood out more than others.

Mary, Queen of Scots – Her Environment and Tragedy, written in 1905 by T. R. Henderson, was invaluable for contemporary quotes on her life as events were described in rich detail.

The Girlhood of Mary, Queen of Scots, a huge work by Jane T. Stoddart of 1908, gives so much information on her upbringing and what shaped the woman to come.

Acknowledgements

Mary Stuart's Scotland was written by the former Liberal leader Sir David Steel and his wife Judy and gives fascinating insights into many of the buildings I have had the pleasure of visiting in Scotland.

The best and most concise book on Mary has to be the *Mary Queen of Scots* biography written by Lady Antonia Fraser. For me this is the one that can never be surpassed and I can read it over and over again, even though the story will never change. It here that I learnt about the different landscape Scotland had in the sixteenth century, being virtually treeless and amid a mini ice-age. These pearls of wisdom can only come about through meticulous research and I am indebted to her for her powerful writing.

I must also mention the many people I have met travelling through Scotland, England and northern France as part of my research. The friendliness of the guides in Scotland and their knowledge was something that made my time there so much more enjoyable. If you ever find yourself at Dundrennan Abbey, then take some time to talk to Glyn. A more passionate and knowledgeable man on this subject you're unlikely to find. I also have to thank the man at Inchmahome Priory who let me take photos from afar as the water was too choppy to visit on that occasion. Nothing was too much trouble for him.

Finally, and an unusual acknowledgement, but a big thank-you to my elder then-teenage cousin Elaine who, in 1971, took me to the cinema to see the film starring Glenda Jackson and Vanessa Redgrave. I only went because the boy she was due to go with let her down. It was that moment which started this obsession!

BIBLIOGRAPHY

Bell, Robert (ed.), *Bittersweet Within My Heart: The Love Poems of Mary, Queen of Scots* (Chronicle Books, 1993)

Carroll, Stuart, *Martyrs and Murderers: The Guise Family and the Making of Europe* (Oxford University Press, 2011)

Doran, Susan, *Mary, Queen of Scots: An Illustrated Life* (British Library Publishing Division, 2007)

Fraser, Lady Antonia, *Mary Queen of Scots* (W&N, 2009)

Guy, John, *My Heart Is My Own: The Life of Mary Queen of Scots* (Harper Perennial, 2004)

Guy, John, *Queen of Scots: The True Life of Mary Stuart* (Mariner Books, 2005)

Henderson, Thomas, *Mary Queen of Scots: Her Environment and Tragedy* (Scribner, 1905)

Lewis, Jayne Elizabeth, *Mary Queen of Scots: Romance and Nation* (Taylor & Francis Ltd,1998)

Mackay, James A., *In My End is My Beginning: A Life of Mary Queen of Scots* (Mainstream Publishing, new edition, 2000)

MacRobert, A. E., *Mary Queen of Scots and the Casket Letters* (I. B. Tauris, 2002)

Miller, Joyce, *A Wee Guide to Mary, Queen of Scots* (Goblinshead, 1996)

Plowden, Alison, *Two Queens in One Isle: The Deadly Relationship of Elizabeth I and Mary Queen of Scots* (The History Press, 2004)

Porter, Linda, *Crown of Thistles: The Fatal Inheritance of Mary Queen of Scots* (Pan, 2014)

Roberts, Mary, and Samuel Roberts, *The Royal Exile; Or, Poetical Epistles of Mary, Queen of Scots, During Her Captivity in England: With Other Original Poems by a Young Lady* (Nabu Press, 2010)

Steel, David and Judy Steel, *Mary Stuart's Scotland* (Orion, 1995)

Stoddart Jane, *The Girlhood of Mary Queen of Scots* (Hodder & Stoughton, 1908)

Swain, Margaret, *The Needlework of Mary Queen of Scots* (Ruth Bean Publishers, 1986)

Watkins, Susan, and Mark Fiennes, *Mary Queen of Scots* (Thames and Hudson Ltd., 2009)

Weir, Alison, *Mary Queen of Scots: And the Murder of Lord Darnley* (Vintage, 2008)

Wormald, Jenny, *Mary, Queen of Scots: Politics, Passion and a Kingdom Lost* (Tauris Parke Paperbacks, 2001)

DVD

Mary Queen of Scots (Charles Jarrott, 1972)

Novels

George, Margaret, *Mary Queen of Scotland and the Isles: A Novel* (St Martin's Griffin, 1997)

Gregory, Philippa, *The Other Queen* (HarperCollins, 2009)

Plaidy, Jean, *The Royal Road to Fotheringay* (Broadway Books, 2004)

Plaidy, Jean, *The Captive Queen of Scots* (Crown Publishing Group, 2006)

Tannahill, Reay, *Fatal Majesty: A Novel of Mary, Queen of Scots* (SOS Free Stock, 1999)

Yolen, Jane, *Queen's Own Fool* (Speak, 2001)